Welcome to
BUTTERNUT CREEK

A Widows of Butternut Creek Omnibus

Welcome to
BUTTERNUT CREEK

A Widows of Butternut Creek Omnibus

The Welcome Committee of Butternut Creek
The Matchmakers of Butternut Creek

Jane Myers Perrine

THE WELCOME COMMITTEE OF BUTTERNUT CREEK
  Copyright © 2012 by Jane Myers Perrine
  Publication History: FaithWords paperback, April 2012

THE MATCHMAKERS OF BUTTERNUT CREEK
  Copyright © 2012 by Jane Myers Perrine
  Publication History: FaithWords paperback, November 2012

First Doubleday Book Club Printing: November 2012

Published by arrangement with
FaithWords
Hachette Book Group
237 Park Avenue
New York, NY 10017

Visit Doubleday Book Club online at http://www.doubledaybookclub.com

ISBN # 978-1-62090-674-3

Printed in the United States of America.

Contents

The Welcome Committee of
BUTTERNUT CREEK

*This novel is dedicated to Cheyenne Steve,
my dear friend.*

Acknowledgments

My deepest gratitude and love go to my husband, whom I have followed to small-town churches from Dixon, Missouri, to Burnet, Texas. Without him, I wouldn't have had the experience to write this novel or the confidence to keep going.

To all of the kind people in the churches George and I have served, many thanks. You have taught me so much and shared your lives and your stories with me. Mary Alice, no one in this book is based on you.

I appreciate Tim Tutt and Priscilla Holt for sharing several anecdotes and Jessica Scott, a fellow writer, soldier, and friend, for sharing her expertise. Any errors are mine.

Many thanks to my wonderful editor Christina Boys and the terrific people at Faith Words/Hachette Book Group who have faith in Butternut Creek, its inhabitants, and the author.

Finally, I cannot thank my agent, Pam Strickler, enough for her guidance and belief in me. Truly, without her, this novel would not have been written.

Prologue

From the desk of
Adam Joseph Jordan, MDiv.

I'm a sad burden for Birdie MacDowell.

Over the years, she's often told me that.

Miss Birdie has been a member of Butternut Creek Christian Church since—well, as long as anyone can remember. Certainly long before I showed up. I'm not sure at what age one becomes a pillar of the church, but Miss Birdie has been one for at least forty years. I think she probably took over running the church while she was on the cradle roll. For that reason, I often think of her as both Miss Birdie and, in my mind only, the pillar.

The cause of her distress is and always has been my ministry, plagued by what she calls my sad ways and errors as well as what she describes as either disastrous decisions or, less catastrophically, the poor choices on my part. She tells me at least once a day, and several times on Sunday, that her ability to put up with all my failings plus my inclination to use incomplete and run-on sentences have equipped her for sainthood.

Not that Miss Birdie hasn't attempted to change me since the day I arrived ten years ago, to—in her words—help me avoid mistakes, both spiritual and social and, I'm sure she'd add, physical. Probably grammatical as well. She believes, she says, that this is her mission, the reason God placed her in Butternut Creek at this time: to train this imperfect fellow God has left in her care. Miss Birdie takes that responsibility seriously.

Two or three times a week she drops in to see what I'm doing, to give me excellent words of advice, which I promptly either reject or forget. Not that it makes any difference which. If I could remember her advice, I'd reject it, and vice versa because it doesn't meld with my beliefs about what is best for the church and best for the congregation.

That propensity to think for myself is what makes her unhappy, makes her long for the imminent arrival of her crown and halo instead of the eternal martyrdom of having to put up with a young and still—in her opinion—very inexperienced minister.

She often bemoans the fact that the elders didn't heed her exhortation and call a man far more experienced and godly than I. Instead they called me, inexperienced and impulsive as I am, because I was all they could afford. A more experienced minister would be called to a larger church in the city. A married minister would expect to be able to feed his family on his salary.

And so I then became the thorn in Miss Birdie's side, her cross to bear, and her hope for everlasting salvation.

That relationship, in great part, is what this book is about. But it's also about what happened during my first year in Butternut Creek: the people in town, their joys and burdens and everyday dilemmas, death and sorrow and love, the stories my friends and members of the congregation have told me and even the gossip I've heard, as much as I attempt to avoid it.

I dedicate this book to the wonderful people of Butternut Creek with my love and admiration, and in the desperate hope that someday Miss Birdie will forgive me for my many errors.

Chapter One

On a blazing-hot June afternoon in the middle of a clogged US 183 in Austin, Texas, Adam Jordan clenched his hands on the steering wheel of the stalled car and considered the situation. As a newly ordained minister, he probably should pray, but he felt certain the drivers of the vehicles backed up behind him would prefer him to do something less spiritual.

The day before, he'd headed west from Lexington, Kentucky, toward Central Texas, a twenty-hour, thousand-mile trip, in a car held together by his little bit of mechanical skill and a lot of prayer. Sadly, on Tuesday, the Lord looked away for a moment as Adam attempted to navigate the crowded tangle of highways that is Austin. The radiator coughed steam as the old vehicle stopped in the center lane of more traffic than he'd ever seen gathered together in midafternoon. Did rush hour start at three o'clock here? He soon learned that rush hour on US 183 could last all day and much of the night, because the city grew faster than its highway system.

He got out of the car and began pushing what had once been a brilliantly blue Honda across two lanes of barely moving traffic and onto the shoulder amid the honks and the screeches of highway noise and curses of angry drivers. If his defective directional skills hadn't led him on a fifty-mile detour into South Austin, the pitiful old vehicle might have made it to Butternut Creek—but they had and the car hadn't.

As happens to everyone and everything over the years, the Honda had faded and frayed until no one could tell what it once had been. The identifying hood ornament had long since fallen off, and the paint was a crackled and blistered gray. And white. With rust peering through it. But it usually ran.

Adam's first thought was to abandon the heap right there, but he'd heard Texas had laws against that. Instead, he called Howard Crampton, an elder of the church and the chair of the search committee that had called Adam.

"Hey, Howard," he said when the elder picked up the phone. "I'm stuck in Austin on 183."

For a moment, Howard said nothing. Finally he asked, "Who is this?"

So much for believing the church breathlessly awaited his arrival. "Adam Jordan." When silence greeted that, Adam added, "The new minister."

"Hey, Adam. Good to hear from you. Sorry I didn't recognize you at first. I'm in the middle of a bank audit and my brain's filled with numbers. What can I do you for?"

"My car broke down on 183, north of something called the Mopac."

"Know exactly where that is. I'll send a tow truck to pick you up."

"All the way from Butternut Creek?"

"Not too far. Sit tight."

As if he could do anything else.

And that's how Adam entered Butternut Creek: sitting in the cab of the tow truck, chatting with Rex, the driver, about fishing and hunting, neither of which he did back then, with his car rattling on the flatbed behind the two men. Although his disreputable arrival didn't signal a propitious beginning, he fell in love with the town immediately.

They entered on Farm-to-Market—FM—road 1212A, which passed between the Whataburger and the H-E-B. Rex pointed out the football stadium and high school about a hundred yards to the north and up the hill. Then the residential section began, big Victorians shoved jowl-to-jowl with bungalows and ranch houses, split levels alongside columned Colonials, interspersed with apartments and motels. Here and there, large, beautifully manicured lawns stretched out, some decorated with a gazebo or fountain while in a yard next to them appeared an occasional pink flamingo or enormous live oak trees dripping with Spanish moss.

Everyone waved as Rex chugged along Main Street. Adam waved back, instantly charmed by the town, by the people who smiled a greeting, by the sturdy brick buildings with Victorian trim and enormous old trees standing tall and full and casting shade and shadows across the lawns and the streets.

"Town square just over on the other side of the courthouse, that way, Padre." Rex nodded to the right. "I'm fixin' to leave you and your car at the church. I'll help unload it. Don't look like you've got a lot of stuff."

As Rex turned the steering wheel, the truck lumbered into the church parking lot. "You leave your keys in the car and I'll pick it up later."

Adam swiveled to look at the driver. "Leave the keys in my car?"

"Padre, you're in Butternut Creek. No one steals cars here." He glanced back into the rearview mirror. "Especially not that one."

While Rex lowered the car onto the asphalt, the new minister turned to study the parsonage.

His eyes lifted, up and up. He'd seen Victorians but never one quite so big. When the pulpit committee had come to Lexington to interview him, they'd described the house, but he hadn't realized the massive size of the pale yellow edifice: three stories, each six or eight windows across, doors and shutters of a dark green, every inch of surface covered with painted wooden curlicues of a dark purplish color—maroon?—plus newel posts and bric-a-brac and, bringing it all together, gingerbread. What in the world would he do with all that space?

As he studied the turret and the bay windows and everything else on the house, he felt sure the parishioners expected him to multiply and be fruitful, producing enough babies to fill every bedroom and all the children's Sunday school classes. He shook his head. Bad planning not to have brought a wife with him.

Sadly for the hopes of the congregation and all those empty rooms, no prospect for a bride had presented herself over the last few years, not since his fiancée Laurel dumped him after she decided she didn't want to marry a minister. The teas and worship services and good works, she'd said, weren't really her thing.

The church management professor at the seminary had warned the newly minted and still-single ministers not to date a young woman in the congregation. It could cause jealousy. It would cause discomfort if they parted. Gossip could ruin a minister's reputation.

Although warned by the professor, Adam had ignored the problem being a single minister presented several months ago. He'd known a few women interested in marrying a preacher, but they were in Kentucky. Even they wouldn't covet that position enough to follow him to Texas. Besides, he'd always felt a little uncomfortable with the forward women who made their determination to marry a minister clear. Not that he felt comfortable with any young woman. That personality flaw probably doomed the possibility of, like Abraham, his fathering a multitude of nations or even two or three children to fill those rooms.

Maybe the extra space could be used as classrooms for Sunday school? A library? A boardinghouse to bring in a little additional income for the church?

Adam reached forward to try the front door. It opened right up. Getting used to all this trust in small-town Texas was going to be hard. Would he insult someone if he locked the door?

Inside, his footsteps echoed. As he walked, he looked around the great expanse of hardwood floor, the huge and beautifully curved staircase leading up to a second story, the empty parlors on each side of a hallway that led back and back into unknown areas he'd explore later. The silence crushed in on him, and he felt even more alone than he had when his parents left him at boarding school years earlier.

"Grab a box, Padre," Rex shouted from outside, interrupting his reflections.

"Coming." Adam ran back out to the car and flipped the trunk open. Within a few minutes, the two men had unloaded the car and lugged everything inside.

When Rex left, the sound of his work boots thudding across the polished floor, Adam glanced at the tiny heap of his possessions in the middle of what looked like a family room or maybe a dining area, and then began to explore. First he ambled back to the front porch, which looked as if it surrounded the entire house. His neighbors to the right and across the street lived in similarly huge Victorians. Then he turned to the left to study the beautiful brick church just north across the parking lot. Huge live oaks dripping with Spanish moss shaded the green lawn. Strength and love and serenity seemed to flow from the steepled roof and huge white columns. How could he have been so blessed to do the Lord's work here, in this perfect place?

Of course, he hadn't met Miss Birdie yet.

❦

Adam's college days and nights had been spent in a dorm room. During seminary, he occupied the furnished parsonage of his student church up near Maysville, Kentucky, a town founded by Daniel Boone and famous as the birthplace of Rosemary Clooney. Because, as an adult, he'd lived in furnished spaces, he possessed no furniture: not a card table, not a desk chair, not a bed. Oh, he did have a sleeping bag from the youth retreats and church camp, a television that he hoped to hook up to cable soon, and a computer with the sermons he'd preached over the past three years. He'd shipped all his books ahead. All those boxes should be stacked in the minister's study at the church. Other than that, all his earthly possessions were in a couple of boxes and two ancient suitcases.

He studied the pile of his things and shook his head. This little bit to fill a huge parsonage.

Miss Birdie was horrified when she brought him dinner that evening.

"You're Adam Joseph Jordan?" Without identifying herself, she strutted into the barren desolation of the parsonage like a five-star general inspecting her troops. The fact that only one slightly terrified man stood before her didn't lessen her resolve.

"Yes, Miss Birdie." Adam knew who she was. Howard had warned him, told him how to address her and how to act in her presence. In that moment, he realized Howard's words of caution, the admonitions Adam had laughed off, were disturbingly true.

"Well, I swan." She looked way up at Adam. "You are a tall, skinny boy, aren't you?"

At six-four and 160, Adam had been tall and skinny as long as he could remember. Most people didn't comment on it.

She studied his face and height for a few more seconds. "With a name like Adam Joseph Jordan, guess you didn't have much choice but to become a minister." Then she took off across the entry hall. Her tiny feet, shod in tie-up shoes with fat rubber soles, squished across the hardwood floor before she stopped and stood between what Adam had labeled as two large parlors.

She wore her white hair in a no-nonsense, almost military style: short and parted on the right. No curls, no waves. Straight with a hint of bangs brushed to the left. Her chest held as high as a proud robin's, she turned to look at the empty space. Every inch of her body showed disdain as she inspected the area. How could such a tiny, thin woman give off such as air of authority, control, and doom?

How could she intimidate a man more than a foot taller than she? But she did. Adam cringed inside.

Chagrin oozed across her features. "Tut, tut, tut." She made a quick turn in the middle of the room to glare at the new preacher, then closed her eyes and shook her head. When she finally opened her eyes, she glared at him again.

"What kind of minister . . . what kind of person has no furniture at all?"

Adam smiled at her in an effort to ingratiate himself. She didn't smile back. He'd disappointed her, as he figured he would many more times.

Did she expect Adam to be ashamed of his lack of furnishings?

To look mortified? He didn't because he wasn't, but Miss Birdie wouldn't understand. Generations separated them. She'd probably never heard of a futon. When he didn't flinch—at least, not outwardly—or apologize for his shortcomings, she said, "Hmph."

He'd rapidly learn that she expressed some of her most powerful comments with sounds.

With a quick turn, she marched down the short hallway and into the room where his few possessions resided. She glared at the pile of stuff.

"What's this?" She pointed at his pitiful collection of belongings. "You really don't have any furniture? None?"

"I have a television and a computer and a . . . that's about it." Instantly recognizing that his words didn't satisfy her a bit, Adam added, "I'll have to work on that." He again attempted to disarm her with a smile but learned in a moment that Miss Birdie was not disarmable, especially when the truth lay so heavily on her side. "Treasure in heaven, you know," he added.

Ignoring the biblical reference, she said, "Where am I supposed to put this?" She nodded toward the quilted tote that dangled from her arm and emitted a mouthwatering aroma. "Where are you going to eat it?" She tilted her head and squinted at him. "Are you the kind of man who stands at the kitchen counter to eat?"

Yes, Adam was, although he hadn't realized it qualified him as part of a decadent class of humanity. After disappointing her about the furniture, he couldn't confess he was guilty of what she so clearly considered a lack of proper etiquette, of gentility and acceptable rearing. She would have turned, he feared, and taken that dish away. The aroma of what she'd prepared called to him, made his stomach growl after a ten-hour drive without stopping for meals because he'd been afraid the old car would conk out if it got a rest and a chance to think about how much farther it had to go.

"Oh, no. I plan to get some furniture and sit at the table. For the moment, I'll have to stand at the kitchen counter to eat." He nodded his head, then shook it, not sure which action was required to respond to her question. "Only for a few days."

"Don't suppose you have a bed?"

"Sleeping bag."

"Sofa? Chair?"

He shook his head.

She took a step forward and scrutinized him. Adam felt judged and found wanting. No hope of redemption existed. Miss Birdie's expression didn't even hold out the promise of grace. "Do you have a towel? A bar of soap?"

"Soap. Yes, I have soap." Glad to have finally passed one of her tests, he pointed toward a box and a small suitcase. "And probably a couple of towels." He waved at a tattered suitcase held together with a belt. "Somewhere."

With a deep sigh—one that Adam felt came from the very depths of her soul and left no doubt what she thought about this feckless young man who stood to eat and yet had the audacity to undertake the task of becoming her spiritual adviser—she placed the dish on the kitchen counter, turned, and squish-squished out of the house. Without a *Good-bye* or a *Blessings* or a *Welcome to Butternut Creek*, she left.

After she slammed the front door, Adam discovered a spoon and plastic tumbler in one of his boxes and was able to eat some of the delicious chicken spaghetti right out of the dish. Still, he kept checking the entrance hall in case Miss Birdie might fling the front door open and shout *Aha!* when she found out he hadn't even bothered to find a plate because he was a rude and boorish young man, as most twenty-five-year-old bachelors he knew were. The fear of her appearance made locking the door seem like a good idea.

He put the leftovers away in the refrigerator provided by the church. Inside were a carton of milk, another of orange juice, butter, and a dozen eggs, all left by some helpful person. If he could find a frying pan, he could fix breakfast in the morning.

Over the next few hours, more members of the congregation stopped by. They smiled and welcomed Adam and brought cakes and bread and vegetables and fried chicken and a brisket.

Once that slowed down, Adam considered unpacking, but he had no hangers and none had been left in the tiny coat closet. Probably some hung in the huge number of closets upstairs, but he didn't feel the call to explore tonight. All those large empty rooms would probably depress him. He left everything in the suitcases, boxes, and plastic bags. Surely everyone—except Miss Birdie—would understand.

Next he called his parents, who'd retired to London after his father sold his company for gazillions of dollars. It was very early morning there, but his mother was glad to hear he'd arrived safely and promised they'd visit soon. His father expressed amazement that Butternut Creek had telephone service.

Tomorrow he'd email his sister in Kenya. Not that she'd worry. Traveling between refugee camps as she did was a lot more dangerous than the trip through Tennessee and Arkansas he'd just made.

Having completed everything he needed to take care of right away, at nine thirty he rolled out the sleeping bag, plugged in the television, and searched for a baseball game. Unfortunately, only one station came in, a feed from Austin transmitted from Llano. The picture was snowy, and the sound faded in and out. The problem constituted another introduction to the difference between city and rural life, but he didn't mind. He listened to the local news and watched the blurry rerun of a sitcom before deciding to go to bed. Or, to be more exact, to go to sleeping bag.

Filled with gratitude to be here, he said his prayers and dozed off as soon as he finished.

After the long, exhausting trip, he slept well.

❧

The insistent ringing of the doorbell started at nine o'clock. Adam shook his head in a futile effort to clear it, slipped into jeans and pulled on a T-shirt. When he opened the door, two muscular men stood there, carrying a sofa between them. Adam stepped back and watched as they brought it in without a word. They settled it against the wall of the room where he'd slept, then headed back out to a large truck with HILTON FURNITURE painted on the side.

"What are you doing?" he asked as the furniture came inside. "This isn't mine. I didn't order it and I can't pay for this," Adam attempted to explain as they carried in a large dining room table. They didn't stop.

Like a yappy little dog, he ran after them asking where all this had come from.

"You're in the wrong house," he said but the men continued to ignore him. Taciturn and focused, they kept unloading and placing the furniture where they thought it appropriate: a recliner, a coffee table, that dining room table with six hefty chairs, a queen-size bed—well, almost everything a bachelor minister needed to set up housekeeping except, of course, that big bed they'd taken upstairs, which suggested marriage at some time down the road.

During this entire time, the men didn't pay the slightest bit of attention to him. When they had finished, Rodolfo—the name embroidered on his shirt—handed Adam a clipboard and pen. "Please sign, Pastor."

He took the invoice and read it, attempting to find out the source of the furniture and where it should have been delivered. There was nothing on that page except the word widows and his address. Well, not the real address because, as he later learned, no one knew one another's numerical addresses. This house was described as "the parsonage next to the Christian Church."

"I can't pay for this."

"It's taken care of."

"Everything's been paid for?"

"Uh-huh." Rodolfo took the page Adam had signed, then tore off and handed the minister a copy. Followed by his crew, he left.

"Who paid for it?" Adam ran along behind the crew.

"Don't know."

"You're sure you're in the right place?"

"This is the parsonage, right? Next to the Christian Church?" He turned back and pointed at both. At Adam's nod, he and the other men got into the truck.

"Who are the widows?" Adam shouted as they drove away. When the truck disappeared down the highway, he wandered inside to look around the newly furnished rooms.

Where had all this come from?

The only person he could think of who knew he didn't have furniture was Miss Birdie. Well, the other church members who'd dropped by must have noticed the lack, but they hadn't seemed to mind. Perhaps they believed the rest of his stuff would be delivered later. Or they might have realized that young ministers seldom had money and wouldn't have a great number of worldly goods.

But Miss Birdie had cared deeply about the inadequacy. She'd taken it almost like an insult to her personally and to the church that had called him. As he walked through the parsonage on the hardwood floors he bet the ladies had buffed earlier in the week, he remembered her deep disappointment in his lack of possessions and her sharp words.

Now a sofa sat against the north wall of the larger parlor, a great green-plaid beast with soft pillows. He'd have a place to sit and watch television. He sat down. Comfortable and exactly long enough to take a nap during a slow ball game.

Miss Birdie wore comfortable shoes and inexpensive clothing. Surely she didn't have enough money to buy all this. Was Adam wrong about that, too?

Only a few minutes later while he admired the rest of the furnishings, the doorbell sounded again. When he opened it, a white-haired gentleman stood there.

"Jesse Hardin." He grasped Adam's hand in a huge hand. "Got a card table for you." As he dragged the table inside, Jesse said, "My wife and I own a farm outside town. Do you like to ride horses?"

"Well, I'm from Kentucky so I should," Adam began. "But I don't."

"Well, if you want to give it a try, give me a call."

A few minutes after Jesse left, Howard Crampton dropped by with two folding chairs and put them in the breakfast nook with the card table.

"Great cowboy hat," Adam said, noticing the wide-brimmed hat the elder wore.

"Son." Howard's expression was someplace between a smile and a frown. "I'm going to teach you a little something about Texas. Don't ever call this a cowboy hat. You could insult some good ol' boy who might take exception, physically, to your sentiments. This"—he pointed to his head—"is my Stetson. Some men prefer a Resistol, but real Texans wear Stetsons."

Adam nodded. "Thank you, sir." He dropped his gaze. When he did, he noticed Howard wore cowboy boots, too, with intricate tooling on the toe, but Adam sure wasn't going to ask about those. Instead he asked a completely different question, the one that really bothered him. "Howard, who are the widows?"

"Don't worry about that." The elder shook his head. "You'll find out soon enough. Relax today, get settled."

Before he could ask more, Howard sprinted out.

Now Adam really worried.

After Maudie Adams left, a set of towels hung over the bars in both upstairs bathrooms, the bed was made, and more linens were folded in a closet. Later that afternoon, two high school football players lugged in an enormous rustic oak armoire, which they settled against the wall opposite the sofa. Adam's little portable television sat in splendor inside.

He had furniture. An abundance of furniture. More than he'd ever owned or thought he'd possess. The sight of his parlor and the new furniture filled him with a feeling of comfort, security, and joy. Even if they were temporary, even if the furnishings belonged here, stayed in the parsonage for the next minister of Butternut Creek, the sight of this plenty and a self-indulgent pride of ownership filled Adam with such an agreeable warmth that he struggled to force back that unholy and impious sentiment and attempted to refocus on the spiritual.

That not quite accomplished, he wandered onto the front porch and settled on the swing, pushing back with his feet a couple of times until the movement became established. A soft breeze dried the perspiration he'd worked up from watching those fine new belongings being brought in.

He looked out across the wide green yard he'd need to mow soon.

Then his gaze again turned toward the church with the tall pillars in front, two on each side of the massive front door that looked as if it could have been part of the Arc of the Covenant. His eyes climbed the spire to the cross atop the steeple.

On that lovely, gentle evening, he whispered a verse from Psalms: "I give thanks to You, O Lord my God, with my whole heart, and I will glorify Your name forever."

The beautiful town wrapped itself around Adam, enveloped him in peace while the pale blue of the sky relaxed and refreshed him as the last rays of the sun warmed the air. The wonders of creation filled Adam with awe as day became night.

"All is right with Your world, dear Lord."

And it was.

Yes, it was and it still is.

Chapter Two

Birdie's feet hurt.

But pain wasn't the worst of her worries. Neither was the certainty that the new minister was a disaster. No, her biggest concern was money. Actually the lack of it.

She glared at the back of the last customer as he strolled out of the diner. He'd left her a quarter and a dime. Thirty-five cents on a seven-dollar order. She shoved the tip in her pocket and balanced his dirty dishes on her arm.

The lunch crowd was getting stingier and stingier. Due to the uncertainty at the asphalt plant, the town's biggest employer, fewer people ate out and those who did left smaller tips. With two teenage granddaughters to raise on her salary and tips and the payments from her husband's Social Security, eking by was difficult. Sadly, *eking* was the best she could do. She needed new shoes if she continued to spend six hours a day on her feet, but couldn't buy them now, not with school starting in a couple of months, not with the girls' expenses.

She dumped the dishes in the plastic bin and rolled it into the kitchen, then returned to wipe down all the counters and tables. That finished, she pulled out her cell to call Mercedes Rivera, her lifelong friend, who had a break at work now.

"The new minister is a disaster." Birdie spoke into the cell as she settled in one of the booths. "I don't know what to think of the man. He's so darned young." She knew her friend would disagree. That's what she always did, but Mercedes disagreed courteously.

"Now, now, we all have to start someplace. He'll learn through experience."

"I don't want a minister to learn his job by practicing on me. I want a minister with an established connection with God."

"Stop complaining, Bird. I swan, you're getting so grumpy."

Birdie didn't respond. If she said what she wanted to, she'd just prove Mercedes right, again, so she didn't say a word.

"Think of him as a novice," Mercedes said. "Someone who will benefit from your influence."

Birdie snorted. Mercedes had learned years earlier—back in the toddlers' class at church when she'd attempted to use the purple crayon Birdie wanted—not to confront her directly. Now Mercedes attempted to lead Birdie.

"We're not Catholic," Birdie snapped. "We don't deal with novices."

"Then an apprentice. You'll get him in shape. You know you will."

Birdie leaned back against the high back of the booth and sighed. "I've got a lot going on with the girls and work. You know, I'm not a spring chick. I may be too old to train him."

She knew Mercedes struggled not to laugh—or be heard laughing over the phone—at the statement. Her friend was always polite.

After a pause, Mercedes said, "Bird, Bird, Bird, as if you'd allow something as insignificant as being busy or growing old to turn you away from your duty."

The problem with a lifelong friend was that she knew Birdie far too well.

"Rodolfo told me the preacher was really pleased with the new furniture." Mercedes changed the subject as she always did when Birdie was upset. "Nice of you to bull . . . to persuade people to donate."

Birdie harrumphed.

"I know you don't like to be thanked for good works, but it *was* nice of you."

"Hated to see the house bare," Birdie explained. "He didn't have a thing, not a stick of furniture, nothing worthy of that beautiful old parsonage. I couldn't stand it."

"All right. You got the community together to provide furniture only to preserve the architectural integrity of the house." Mercedes didn't contain the laugh this time. "I should know better than to compliment you for doing something nice."

Birdie glanced at the clock. Nearly two thirty. She needed to get home if she wanted to see the girls. "Talk to you later." She folded the phone and stuck it in her pocket.

As usual during the summer, the girls had slept in this morning. Bree, a junior, had volleyball practice until six and Mac, a sophomore, would be marching with the band until five thirty. If she hurried home, she could see them before they took off.

Her daughter had given the girls silly names: MacKenzee and Bre'ana. Whoever heard of putting an apostrophe in the middle of a name or identical vowels at the end? Birdie had given her daughter a sensible name. Martha. Martha Patricia. Had Martha lived up to such an honest, trustworthy name? No, at seventeen and without finishing school, she'd run off with a no-good man who'd deserted her when she got pregnant the second time. Everyone had told her he was all hat and no cattle, but Martha wouldn't listen.

Martha, irresponsible Martha who'd always needed a man to take care of her and couldn't take care of anyone else, spoiled by her father and disciplined by her mother, had come home to have the baby. She'd disappeared only weeks after MacKenzee's birth, as Birdie had suspected she would. Birdie had ended up raising two girls when she was looking to retire, but what else could she do?

The community had shortened the girls' names to Bree and Mac. With that, every trace of Martha disappeared from Butternut Creek except the memories of her miserable mistakes and her terrible grades in the permanent record of the school district.

All that had happened a few months after Elmer's death. The double loss about killed her. Not that she let anyone know, but inside, deep inside, she'd felt as if she didn't have anything left but a future of pain, exhaustion, and sorrow. But the girls, they'd pulled her out of that. They'd brought new meaning to her life, as well as worry and fatigue.

After she finished wiping down the last table, Birdie shouted, "Bye, Roy," to the manager as she left the diner. He waved, then went back to separating the checks and credit card receipts.

After the two-block walk to the bungalow she and Elmer had bought forty years earlier, she entered and shouted, "I'm home, girls."

"Hey, Grandma." Mac came down the stairs to hug her. The child had curly brown hair, matching brown eyes, and the sweetest smile in the world. "Gotta go. Band practice starts in fifteen minutes and I need to get my trumpet out of the music room."

"Did you eat lunch?" Birdie shouted as the girl ran out the door.

Then Bree, always in motion, dashed across the room, her long, straight dark hair swirling behind her. Everything about this older grandchild snapped with energy. She made Birdie tired just watching her. With a quick wave, she passed her grandmother and shouted as the screen door snapped shut behind her, "Love ya. See you to-night."

At least she'd seen them. Birdie grinned for a second. They were good girls, turned out well. If she weren't so worried and weary, she'd admit she loved them more than anything. They'd been the joy and center of her life since she'd first held them, but Birdie'd never tell them. Well, maybe on her deathbed. They'd get swelled heads if she got all sentimental. Besides, she wasn't real good about expressing feelings. They'd all feel uncomfortable, her most of all.

Stepping out of her shoes, she headed toward the laundry room and tossed a load into the washer. Within two hours, she dropped folded towels on a spot she'd cleared on Bree's unmade bed by shoving several stuffed animals on the floor. She hoped the child could find the pile when she needed them.

She rotated her left shoulder. Impingement. That's what the doctor had said a month ago, then sent her to physical therapy. When her shoulder started hurting, Birdie quit picking clothes up and straightening the girls' room. They were old enough to do that. If Bree couldn't find a clean uniform because they were all in her athletic locker or Mac complained the jeans she'd planned to wear that day were dirty, Birdie just shrugged. Amazing how quickly the girls discovered the location of the dirty clothes hamper and learned to use the washing machine.

For a moment she paused, considered her thoughts, and shook her head. She had become a crabby old lady, exactly like Mercedes had told her, politely and as only a friend of long standing could. The realization had surprised her a little, but this was not the time or place for self-examination. She had plenty to do and no time to find a new attitude.

On Bree's side of the bedroom hung posters of men and women with tattoos. She called them tats and wanted a rose on her back. What did she call it? A "tramp stamp"? If that didn't beat all. Birdie'd never allow that. At times, the girl acted a lot like her mother, except that Bree made fair grades and didn't get in trouble, and had the possibility of a college scholarship in either volleyball or basketball.

Birdie smiled. A MacDowell in college. Every member of Mercedes's family had gone to college, most to graduate school, but Bree would be the first MacDowell.

In contrast with her sister's, Mac's side of the room looked spare. Desk with a lamp on it, desk chair, dresser, and bed. One of the posters on her wall showed some scientist from England with numbers floating over his head. Stephen Hawking, Mac had told her. Why would anyone have a poster of a physicist—that's what Mac said he was—on the wall?

The other poster showed Wynton Marsalis playing a trumpet, the instrument Mac played. The portraits of the two men faced each other across the bedroom, precisely hung and as straight as if they'd been lined up with a ruler. Birdie felt as if she should straighten the stack of clean towels to conform to the rigid angles of the room.

Forget it. Little Miss Perfect—Bree's name for her younger sister— could refold them if they didn't please her.

In her own bedroom, Birdie padded barefoot across the scuffed hardwood to put her shoes in the closet and slide into a worn pair of slippers. On the way, Carlos the Cat attacked her ankles before he ran under the bed.

Lord, she was tired. She leaned against the wall. For a moment, she felt dizzy from exhaustion, but she shoved the feeling aside. She couldn't get sick. What would happen to her granddaughters if she did? How would the church survive this new minister without her guidance? She attempted to pray for strength but it took too much effort and never seemed to help much anyway.

Or maybe it did. Maybe she'd be in an even worse state if she didn't pray.

She needed to sit down for a minute, rest. After pausing in the kitchen to pour herself a glass of tea, she went out to the front porch of the small house and settled into one of the Adirondack chairs. Elmer had built them so he and Birdie could sit on the porch and wave to neighbors. He'd died only a year after that and she no longer had the time or the desire to sit there. She hadn't when Elmer had placed them there, but he'd enjoyed that hour together even if it made Birdie want to leap up and start sweeping the steps or pull a few weeds.

Early evening was surprisingly cool for June, although the weather was never really cool in Texas during the summer. Less hot, at maybe eighty-five degrees. The big maple she and Elmer had planted years ago shaded the area. A nice breeze cooled the porch as peace and quiet overcame her. She took a deep breath and leaned back, closing her eyes to breathe in the warm Texas air laden with the scent of gardenias.

The calm lasted five minutes before she got antsy. She hated peace and quiet. Too much to do. She wouldn't relax until they put her in the casket, if then. She pulled the phone out of her pocket to call Pansy about the food pantry. The woman would destroy the entire effort if Birdie didn't step in and set her straight.

❧

When Adam explored the entire house the next morning, the sheer size again overwhelmed him. Downstairs, the tiny basement had a dirt floor. Spiderwebs hung from supports and a twenty-watt light-bulb illuminated a small circle, but a washer and dryer sat in the corner so he didn't mind the primitive surroundings.

The second floor had five bedrooms, each larger than both the bedrooms together in the Kentucky parsonage, and two bathrooms. The space on the third floor stretched across the entire house with storage closets built into the eaves. It seemed like a huge playroom for all those children he didn't have.

He strode up and down staircases and across halls and into bedrooms, his footsteps resonating loudly on the hardwood floors. Last night, his sleeping bag had felt warm and familiar. Tonight he'd haul his things upstairs, and approach the nuptial bed.

Before he could decide which to do—to laugh at or worry about that thought—he checked his watch. It was after nine o'clock, the time he'd decided a *real* minister started the day. He'd dressed like a real minister in a pair of black slacks and a white shirt with one of his two ties: a red one and a ministerial one with black and gold stripes. He also had a Christmas tie his best friend had given him. Red with elves on it that played "Santa Claus Is Coming to Town." He doubted he'd have many chances to wear that one, now he was a real minister.

Because he was already running late, Adam hurried, descending the steps from the second floor two-by-two. Reaching the first floor, he grabbed a file folder and his Bible and headed out the door toward the church.

"Hello, Preacher," a woman called from behind him as he headed north across the lawn.

When he turned, Adam saw a smiling blonde coming down the steps of the even larger Victorian next door, a plate in one hand and a little girl grasping the other.

"I'm Ouida Kowalski." She nodded at the child. "This is Gretchen."

"Weed-a?" he said.

"Yes, that's how it's pronounced. It's spelled O-u-i-d-a. A Southern name and a family name. Most people who aren't from here don't know it." She smiled and held the plate out. "I heard you're young and single so I brought you some sweet rolls for breakfast."

He took the offering and couldn't help but smile back. "Thank you. Are you a member of the church?" he asked, completely ignorant of who was and who wasn't.

"No, not of any church." Her smile didn't diminish. "George, my husband, says we're missing the spiritual gene. I don't know." She shrugged before leaning toward him. "But even if we're heathens, we're good neighbors and are delighted you're here. That parsonage has been empty for too long. I hope you don't mind, but the kids have been playing on the swing set in your yard."

Other than noting the existence of grass, he hadn't studied the back lawn in detail. "No problem. Glad someone can use it."

"Mama." Gretchen tugged on her mother's hand.

"Better go," Ouida said. "Again, welcome."

The sun shone and the birds sang and his neighbors had brought him breakfast. There could be no better place to be in the entire world.

When he entered his office, an immediate problem confronted him: sixteen boxes of books and only two small bookcases, already filled with dusty tomes that he felt sure no one had perused in years. Maybe centuries.

"Excuse me."

He turned to see a plump dark-haired woman.

"I'm the part-time secretary, Maggie Bachelor." She held out a hand and gave him a hearty handshake. "Good to meet you. I just got here, running a little late. I work from nine to eleven four days a week. I answer the phone, type the newsletter, and print the bulletin." She ticked off each duty on her fingers. "I'll need everything written out and on time so I can get the bulletin and the newsletter done." She put a sheet of paper on his desk. "Here are the deadlines."

She reminded him of a hummingbird. She talked fast—not that hummingbirds talk—but she also flitted from place to place.

"Do you have your sermon title, scripture, and hymns?"

Fortunately, he'd realized that his first week would be busy and had worked on the sermon last week. "It's from the tenth chapter of . . ."

She pointed at a pad and pen on the desk. "Write it down."

"Do you have a hymnal handy?" Adam had imprudently neglected to memorize the page numbers of the hymns. Actually, he'd neglected to choose any but wasn't willing to confess that failing.

"On your desk, too." She fluttered her fingers toward him and left.

Following her instructions, Adam jotted down his sermon title and scripture, then hunted through the hymnal. Finished, he stood and walked the information out to Maggie.

She glanced at the hymns he'd chosen then glanced up at him. "Oh, dear, Pastor, the congregation doesn't know the last two."

"Won't it be fun to learn them?" he asked.

Her expression assured him it wouldn't. She picked up a pen. "I'll choose a couple we know."

"I'd like for the congregation to sing the ones I picked. They go with the theme of the morning."

"Well, if that's your choice, but . . ." Her words, expression, and shrug warned of dire consequences. "Well, then, here's your visitation and hospital call list for today." She handed him several note cards.

At eleven thirty, half an hour after Maggie left, Adam heard a knock at the office door. Just outside, he saw a large man wearing enormous paint-stained overalls with an orange-and-yellow Hawaiian shirt underneath.

"Ralph Foxx." The visitor stretched out a meaty hand. "Two x's on the end, like that old baseball player, Jimmie double-x Foxx. Played for the Philadelphia A's."

Adam didn't know about the baseball player and hadn't realized the A's had ever been in Philly, but he still shook his visitor's hand and gestured toward chairs covered with books. "Please sit if you can find a place."

"Don't mind if I do." Pulling a chair in from the office, Ralph settled down and made himself comfortable. Adam later discovered settling down comfortably was one of his greatest talents. Talking was another. Within minutes Adam had learned about Ralph's sciatica, his wife's hysterectomy, and much more. He didn't know how to shut off this font of information, but what else did Adam have to do this morning except pick up his car, which Rex had called to tell him was ready?

Adam discovered within a week that the retired men of the church felt it was their duty to keep the minister company, especially a single young man like him who obviously had nothing else to do and needed to be amused.

"Are you working today?" Adam successfully interrupted after five minutes.

Obviously disappointed the minister had gotten a word in, Ralph shook his head. "I'm a painter. Seasonal work. Not much business today. That's why I'm retired *this* week."

"Then maybe you can help me."

The two men spent the next hour moving the church's books to the library and putting the new minister's on the shelves as Ralph talked on and on. Finally, Ralph said he couldn't work anymore, because of that sciatica. When he left, Adam knew more about the Foxx family and its far-flung branches all over the country than he'd wanted, but he'd also learned a few things about church members. Not a wasted morning.

"Getting old isn't for sissies," Birdie mumbled to herself. Stiff and straight in the chair of the physical therapy waiting room at the hospital, she flipped through a magazine. Old Elgin Crump who lived down on Highway 28 slumped in his wheelchair. Must be at least eighty-five. Next to him sat Susan Pfannenstiel, her walker pulled up next to the chair.

Two younger patients waited alone, reading magazines. One was a cheerleader, a friend of Bree's, who'd fallen from the top of a pyramid during halftime at a basketball game. Those stunts should be outlawed. What had happened to the cheerleaders of her time, back when they wore uniforms that covered their navels and reached to their knees? Back then, they just jumped up and down and shouted. Now they jiggled their bodies and built towers the girls toppled off.

Birdie didn't recognize the young man. Maybe six feet tall but she couldn't tell. He slumped. His dark hair fell almost to his shoulders, rumpled but clean, like a man who cared about hygiene but had no interest in his appearance. She'd noticed when he came in that his jeans and khaki-colored T-shirt hung straight from his broad shoulders like he'd lost weight and hadn't bothered to buy clothes that fit.

Mostly she'd noticed his stumbling gait on the crutches when he entered, the lines of pain etched on his face, and the missing right leg. And yet, with the stubble on his world-weary face, he was handsome in a lost-soul way, in the dangerous and slightly disreputable manner many young women would find intriguing.

Was he Effie Peterson's nephew? Couldn't be too many amputees in the area, but he didn't look a bit like the happy kid who used to visit his aunt—no, his great-aunt—years ago. She'd heard Sam'd come back and was living in Effie's house. No one had been inside since Mercedes and Birdie and her granddaughters had cleaned it after the funeral. Probably covered with dust now and smelled musty.

She should go say hello to the young man, even if he wasn't Sam Peterson. Wouldn't hurt. Might be the only time anyone from the church could get in touch with him, but she hated to step up. No one would ever guess Birdie MacDowell hesitated to do anything. She usually didn't, but speaking to anyone about her church never felt comfortable, not in the least, especially if she had to approach a man who looked so unwelcoming, and do that out here in the middle of a waiting room with people watching.

But doggone it, she had to. God would expect it.

To protect her left shoulder, she pushed herself up with her right hand and briskly walked to his chair.

"Hello." She stretched out her hand. "I'm Birdie MacDowell."

He ignored her hand but made brief contact with eyes that held no emotion.

"Are you Effie Peterson's nephew Sam?"

He dropped his gaze to the magazine.

"I'm a member of the Christian Church on the highway, the one your aunt attended. We'd surely like to see you there sometime."

He didn't say a word, didn't nod or lift his eyes or change expression.

She'd tried, which was all anyone could expect her to do. "We're a friendly church," she said to the top of his head. "Give Pastor Adam a call if you need anything." She took a few steps backward, almost tripped over the footrests on Elgin Crump's wheelchair, then turned and headed for her chair.

As she settled back in her seat, she noticed everyone staring at her before their gazes fell back on what they were reading. She didn't care. She was supposed to welcome people to town, invite them to church. She'd done her duty.

When she considered the problems and pain that plagued the others in the waiting room, she guessed she was pretty lucky to have only this shoulder acting up. Not good at all for a waitress to have a bad shoulder but better than a bad back or a bad knee.

"Mrs. MacDowell," the physical therapy clerk, a flighty teenager named Trixie, called from the doorway.

Inwardly cursing the weakness she hated to display, Birdie again pushed herself up with her right hand and straightened to walk into the therapy area. Curtains covered the treatment area in the back while other clients walked or pushed and tugged on the machines and weights on the main floor. Birdie stepped on a stool to pull herself onto a high table. Across the room, a pretty redheaded woman watched another patient for a few seconds before turning and approaching Birdie.

"I'm Willow Thomas, the new physical therapist." She held out her hand.

Birdie took it, noticing the woman's gentle grip. She figured the dead-fish handshake wasn't a sign of weak character but an effort not to crush anyone's arthritic joints.

"Welcome home, Willow. We're all glad to see you back. I remember you from way back when you sang in the Cherub Choir at church."

She smiled in as friendly a way as she could muster with the darned pain. "Won't ever forget when you and your friends used to come into the diner after football games when you were in high school."

How old was Willow? A little younger than Martha's age, she guessed. Thirty-two or thirty-three. Probably she'd been too old to have met Sam when he visited Effie during the summer, too wide an age difference.

The young woman smiled, a lovely expression that made her features glow. "I didn't know if you'd remember me. It's good to be home."

"You're still one of our kids. Hope to see you in church again Sunday."

"My sons and I plan to be there."

Birdie swelled with a sense of accomplishment. Someone had accepted her invitation, even appeared pleased to get it.

"I'm not going to work with you today because I have a few folks to evaluate," Willow said. "But I wanted to introduce myself. Christine will oversee your exercises."

"As usual," Birdie grumbled to herself. Christine, a PT aide, was sweet but so young she didn't know anything. Birdie had attempted to talk to her about the Beatles and the first Gulf War, but she had to explain history and culture before 1990 to Christine. It was a whole heck of a lot easier to count the exercises out loud than attempt conversation with the child. Christine placed the cane in Birdie's upraised hands and watched Birdie move it slowly forward and back over her head.

In a few minutes, Birdie heard the clerk call Sam Peterson.

"How's the pain been?" the aide asked Birdie.

Obviously Christine hadn't seen Sam yet or the young woman wouldn't be paying attention to her.

"Fine, just fine," Birdie lied. She couldn't let on she was getting too old to carry heavy trays. If she did and lost her job, how would she support her granddaughters? If she didn't tell anyone, if she gritted her teeth, she could push through exactly like she always had.

"Well, that's good. Willow wants me to teach you another exercise to loosen up your shoulder and increase your range of motion."

Then Christine glanced away from Birdie and her eyes grew enormous. Birdie lifted her head to see Sam limp into the therapy room and watched the reaction of the females. It was as entertaining as she'd expected. Trixie could barely take her gaze off him and tripped over Angus's wheelchair while Christine just stood mouth open and outright gawked at the man. The cheerleader, who had been absorbed by her magazine back in the waiting room, followed his unsteady progress with wide eyes.

Sam didn't notice. He barely lifted his gaze as he manipulated around the obstacles. When he did glance up, his eyes landed on Willow, who was talking to the cheerleader and hadn't seen him yet. His reaction stunned Birdie. He stopped still, completely motionless, and gaped at Willow. Birdie bet she was the only one who had a handle on the meaning of his expression because the others were too busy watching other parts of the man, but she recognized it. Right there between the therapy table and the exercise ramp, he fell in love. At least, that was the way Birdie saw it. She was seldom wrong.

For barely a second, his expression was unguarded and vulnerable. Almost immediately, so quickly she might have thought it hadn't happened, his features became sullen again as he looked at his foot and swung himself forward.

Back before his leg was blown off, Sam had appreciated women. He liked how they smelled, flowery and sweet. He liked their soft roundness, which made him feel even tougher and stronger in comparison. As a marine, he loved the way their pink and pale blue and mint-green clothing floated and swirled like pastel butterflies around his drab camo or dress blues.

He appreciated their soft spirits, their generous gestures, their winks and smiles. He never had trouble attracting any of them.

So why did the sight of this woman hit Sam so hard? She didn't look soft and sweet. She wore tailored black slacks and a crisply starched white shirt, buttoned almost to the top. The combination didn't make her look anything like a butterfly. He doubted she'd ever swirl around him.

For whatever reason, his reaction to her hit him hard, like the kickback of a rocket launcher, with a shock that shook his world.

Red hair and, he guessed, green eyes. Since her beautifully rounded backside was all he could see, he didn't know.

When she turned to pick up a file, she glanced at him and smiled absently before returning her attention to the patient.

Yeah, green eyes and dimples and long lashes and a slender, slightly tilted-up nose. Her smile seemed cursory, as if she'd barely noticed him while she concentrated on her other patient. Not a usual female reaction to him.

But even her perfunctory smile made him feel like a man for the first time in months. Probably because the greeting came from rounded lips on the more-than-pretty face that topped her great body. He guessed she thought the severe hairstyle made her look more professional, but it didn't. The sleekness emphasized her cheekbones and eyes and skin, almost everything about her. He bet she dressed like that to look strong and in-charge, but a woman who looked like her could never hide behind a starched shirt.

For a moment he swayed on the crutches as he checked her out. How old was she? Thirty-something? She didn't look like it, but there were a few—he didn't know what to call them. Not wrinkles because they didn't make her look old. Maybe brackets or creases? No, she had a couple of *grooves* around her eyes, and frown marks between her eyebrows that emphasized dark circles under her eyes. A year ago, he would've thought he was just the man to cheer her up, but his confidence had ebbed considerably since the injury. As much as he liked them, his interest in women had lessened, too, until now.

"Excuse me, Mr. Peterson." Trixie stepped in front of him, grinning and fluttering her eyelashes at him.

He hated women's reactions to him now. His looks had been inherited from the general and generations of military men going back centuries. He had nothing to do with his appearance, plus he didn't really want anyone noticing him for any reason. Right now, he didn't feel too good about himself and was hardly a great choice for anything, not even a date. He had more problems than he could handle himself, let alone burden anyone else with.

Unfortunately, the longer he allowed his hair to grow, the scruffier his whiskers, and the deeper his frown, the more women fell at his feet. Most of them didn't mind the fact he was missing a limb and lost his balance more times than he could count, but *he* did. Most of the females wanted to rescue him, to take care of him, to fall in love. He didn't want to be taken care of or rescued. Didn't need to be fixed and refused to fall in love.

He didn't want romance. He didn't want a relationship. Right now, he didn't even want to pick up a woman, not with the stump at the end of his leg guaranteed to scare her off. With that and the pain any kind of movement caused, celibacy seemed pretty much his only choice these days.

But still Trixie stood in front of him, smiling and winking and flipping her hair while he swayed on the crutches.

Willow Thomas sighed. Whenever a good-looking guy arrived in PT, Trixie lost every bit of her nearly invisible veneer of professionalism. More good-looking guys than Willow had thought came here: college kids with broken bones and high school football players with bad knees, all far too young for Willow. But this one looked about Willow's age if she discounted the deep lines of pain and the snarl Trixie's attention brought forth.

Flirting was like breathing for Trixie. Willow had counseled the young woman, attempted to explain, then finally lectured her on the difference between their clients in PT and possible dates for the weekend. Trixie's efforts at professionalism lasted until the next good-looking guy entered the room. Now she was nearly drooling.

Even displaying depression and anger like most of the vets she worked with, the new patient was hot. Willow had to admit that. This patient—she glanced down at the schedule—Captain Samuel Daniel Peterson looked so fine, even Willow felt an instant attraction. Hard for any man to make her feel that way.

But she ignored it. She was a therapist who treated all patients the same: professionally.

"Captain," she said as she approached him. "I'm Willow Thomas, one of the physical therapists here." She reached her hand out. When he glared at it, she drew it back. "I'll be doing an intake at your next appointment. Today Trixie, our PT aide, is going to check your range of movement and degree of strength to get a baseline."

Willow smiled. He didn't.

"Please let me know what I can do to help."

He glanced up at her, making eye contact for a second. He had beautiful blue eyes, but they were red with broken veins. She knew well what that meant, had seen it often before. Seemed sad that this man should let himself go, drink so much it showed.

Then he dropped his gaze again, an admission that he really didn't care where she went or what she did as long as she left him alone. So she did, but not before she glanced at his reflection in the mirror that covered the entire west wall. As she moved away, he'd again lifted his eyes and watched her.

Chapter Three

That evening, Adam looked out the kitchen window while he rinsed the plate off. He had a dishwasher that would take him days to fill, so he washed his one dish and a fork to use at the next meal.

Outside, Ouida watched her girls—Gretchen and the other one whose name he couldn't remember. It was still light although the sun headed rapidly to the west. His evening chore completed, he walked outside to join them.

"How did your day go?" Ouida asked.

"Hospital visits went well. My car made it to Llano and back, which is always a relief."

"Are you unpacked and completely moved in?"

There were still ten unpacked boxes in his study and huge piles of books that overflowed onto the chairs and formed heaps on every surface. "Pretty much," he said.

The AME church a block away had evening services. Over the sounds of crickets and children playing, he could hear the music and harmonies: "Amazing Grace," "Sweet House of Prayer," and several that he couldn't place but lifted his heart and calmed his soul.

Within five minutes, Gretchen had curled up on her mother's lap and Carol—aah, yes, that was her name—yawned, struggling to keep hold on the chain of the swing.

"Okay, girls." Ouida got to her feet and shifted Gretchen to her shoulder. "Let's go home and get ready for bed."

The three left through a gate in the fence, overgrown with the beautiful orange flowers that Ouida had identified as trumpet vines. Once their voices faded, Adam was left alone with the breeze and the succulent scent of a Texas evening floating on the sweet notes of a spiritual.

Sunday morning dawned warm and bright, the normal state for summer mornings in Texas. After a final read-through of his sermon, Adam ate breakfast and showered. While he shaved, he studied himself in the mirror. His hair touched his collar, and, he realized, he did look young, really young. Had he expected a few days in ministry would age him? Well, yes. Unrealistic but he still looked too young to preach, as young as Miss Birdie had proclaimed, eight years younger than his twenty-five years. Would growing a mustache help? Maybe a beard?

He shouldn't start that today. Miss Birdie probably wouldn't approve of facial hair. She wouldn't consider her minister standing in the pulpit with a light stubble to be at all professional. Not a good impression for his first Sunday here. From the nearly bare closet, he pulled a suit—his only suit, a ministerial black that served as both his marrying and burying suit. Once dressed, he headed out. That walk across the parking lot was his last moment of peace for the rest of the day.

"Hear you're not married." Jesse Hardin leaned against the doorjamb of the minister's church office with a mug in his hand, ready for a chat.

What single female relative did Jesse have he'd like to introduce Adam to?

"I've got a niece. Lives in Llano. Nice girl."

"I'm sure she is. Thanks. I'm not looking at the moment."

When Jesse nodded and started toward the chair in front of the desk, Adam said, "I'm going to wander through the building, greet anyone who comes in." Ignoring Jesse's obvious disappointment, Adam left.

With a smile and a firm handshake and feeling very ministerial, Adam greeted everyone as they entered the church. Several children waved and headed toward their Sunday school class.

"In a church this small, Pastor, we don't have many kids," Miss Birdie said. "Most of them come with their grandparents." She gestured toward a hallway. "That used to be the elementary wing, classrooms filled with kids. Now they're all in one class and we take turns leading it." She headed off toward a classroom. "I'm teaching the children today."

If they knew what was good for them, they'd behave.

At eleven, when he heard the playing of the chimes, Adam entered the church through the door between the study and the chancel area. About forty-five people gathered in groups of three to five, scattered through a sanctuary built to hold two hundred. Maggie sat next to an aisle. Some huddled in the back row with the intention, perhaps, of leaving early. Nearly every one of them had white or graying hair and wore glasses except the two girls sitting with Miss Birdie and a few kids with their grandparents. As he had been told but now realized, this was an old and dying church.

As the service began, Adam asked the congregation to stand for the first hymn, stated the page number, and nodded toward the organist. He expected they'd all start singing together. Didn't happen. As Adam began in his wavering and consistently off-key tenor, he noticed everyone stared at him, mouths firmly closed. Behind him, Adam heard the voices of the three women in the choir. It was as if the four were a gospel music group, perhaps Adam and the Eves or the Pastor and the Pips. Somehow Adam, the most pitiful of vocalists, sang lead while the choir acted as backup. Fortunately, the organist played so loudly, no one could hear him anyway.

After communion and the reading of the scripture, Adam stood to preach. Within ten minutes, he noticed a restlessness in the congregation. Men checked their watches and women set their purses on their laps. Was the sermon that bad? He hadn't thought so. He'd worked very hard at polishing up one of the favorites from his student church, but everyone seemed ready to leave. Not only ready, but determined. One child began sobbing until his grandmother handed him a cookie. A timer went off on someone's watch.

Realizing he'd lost the congregation, Adam hurried to finish, dropping the last two points and heading fast and straight for the end. When he'd written it, he'd thought the words were such a clear, uplifting statement of shared convictions it would turn the entire church around, the triumph of faith calling the congregation to action.

Unfortunately, as soon as he said, "And in conclusion," people put the hymnals in the racks, dropped their bulletins on the pews, and sat forward, ready to bolt. Adam stopped midsentence, came down from the chancel, raised his hand, and pronounced the benediction. Even before he said "Amen," people tumbled from the pews and rushed down the aisle and out.

Disappointment filled him. He'd hoped to meet more people, to get feedback on how he'd done, how much he'd inspired them, how they looked forward to a future together. Had his sermon been so terrible they all needed to leave without talking to him? He hurried toward the door at the back of the sanctuary with the hope of greet-ing someone, anyone, but only one person remained.

"You did a good job," Howard said, his voice and expression filled with relief. The elder must feel vindicated that Adam hadn't fallen down the chancel steps or dropped the offering. The fact that the minister he'd called could preach a passable sermon must take a lot of heat off him.

"But I should have warned you about something," the elder con-tinued. "We have to get out of church by eleven fifty or the Method-ists will beat us to the Subway for lunch."

Adam checked his watch. Noon.

Howard nodded. "There's going to be a long line today."

Seminary didn't give students the most practical information. Why hadn't they taught him the importance of getting out of church before the Methodists?

"Cut your sermon a few minutes and don't sing so many verses of each hymn. Should take care of things." Howard grabbed Adam's hand and shook it. "You'll have it down in no time." He hurried off.

Adam had hospital calls to make but decided to pick up a sand-wich at the Subway, to see what the place was like and meet the congregation.

❦

"Pastor Adam?"

He glanced up from the sermon he'd been working on to see Miss Birdie striding through the door.

"Come on in," he said although the invitation didn't seem neces-sary as she was halfway across the office and followed by another woman he recognized from the previous day. He stood.

"Hello, Preacher." She glared at him. "You know me. This is Mer-cedes Rivera." She waved toward the other woman before she said, "They call us the Widows."

They Call Us the Widows. Sounded like a great name for a movie, a Western maybe.

Then he remembered: widows was the word written on the de-livery form from the furniture store. He started to ask about that, but before he could, Miss Birdie spoke.

"Mercedes is the town librarian." She motioned toward the at-tractive Latina again. "You need any information on anything or about anyone in town, she's the one to call."

"Birdie just finished her breakfast shift and I took a break from the library," Mercedes explained. "She wanted to come see you."

"I have a bone to pick with you," Miss Birdie said.

Not a surprise. She'd probably picked a couple of carcass-fuls of bones with quite a few ministers.

"Won't you sit down?" he asked cordially.

Miss Birdie stretched her arm out and waved it around the room, where piles of books still filled every surface and boxes covered much of the floor.

"Sorry about the mess in here. I'm attempting to bring order to my books. Didn't realize I had so many."

"Well, you'd better hurry, because people are going to want to sit in these chairs," Miss Birdie stated firmly.

"Bird means *she* wants to sit down now," Mercedes explained in a whisper, as if Miss Birdie couldn't hear.

With alacrity, Adam picked the stack of books from a chair and looked for a place to put them. Finding none, he placed them on the floor beside the chair, then cleared another for Mercedes. Both women sat. That completed, he hurried to sit—to hide—behind the desk. Didn't actually hide, but he appreciated the separation provided by the broad surface and the tower of books between them.

"Pastor, we dropped in to welcome you on your first official day in the office." Mercedes smiled at Adam, then flicked a nervous glance at her friend.

"Yes, and then I have a bone to pick with you," Miss Birdie repeated.

He didn't doubt that.

"I don't want to coddle you. Mercedes thinks I should give you a little more time . . ."

"Yes, I do—" Mercedes began.

"But you have to know what people are saying."

"Birdie feels it's our duty to tell you what *she* says people are saying, although I believe we should give you a chance to settle in first before we make suggestions."

Miss Birdie glared at the other woman. "Pastor, Mercedes and I've been friends for more than sixty years. Occasionally we don't agree. I say strike while the iron is hot."

For a moment, Adam smiled—inside—at the difference between the women. Mercedes looked a bit uncomfortable, a slight flush on her light brown skin, but attractive with her black hair, beginning to gray at the temples, pulled back into a neat French braid. In contrast, Miss Birdie's short hair meant quick and easy preparation. Wash and comb. No fuss.

Mercedes wore a nice navy dress with matching pumps while

Birdie wore a pink uniform. Aah, yes. Now Adam remembered. She was a waitress.

"In the first place," Miss Birdie continued, "you don't look like a minister at all, not in my opinion."

"Her opinion counts for a lot here," Mercedes said with an apologetic smile.

"You're too tall, too young, your hair's too long. You're almost handsome, if you weren't so skinny and didn't have all that hair." She leaned forward and fixed her eyes on him. "That means some of the younger women and a few of the widows might covet what isn't theirs to claim. After all, you're a man of God."

She kept her eyes on Adam as if he planned to seduce the younger women right here, right now, and right in front of her. He didn't know where to find any gullible young women and wouldn't know how to seduce one if he could find her. Besides, he didn't plan to start doing that, certainly not in front of the Widows.

But he knew Miss Birdie expected an answer.

"Thank you for the information." Then he added, "I'll get a haircut as soon as I can." First, he needed a salary check because he had about twenty dollars in his billfold, which he planned to use for food and gas.

Miss Birdie's glare told Adam he'd better do her bidding and soon.

Before he could explain the cash-flow problem, Mercedes said, "But you have a humble charm." She warned her friend with a glance before facing the minister again. "We can work with you, help you. Bird—that's what I call her—can steer you in the right direction."

Whether Adam wanted to go that way or not.

"What we're here about—"

"What *you* are here about." Mercedes broke in.

"It's those songs you chose for Sunday," Birdie said before Mercedes could interrupt again. "Nobody knows them." She pursed her lips before saying, "Did you notice no one was singing? We want the old favorites back."

"Very nice sermon, Pastor," Mercedes said. "One of the best we've had in years."

Miss Birdie didn't agree or disagree with her friend's compliment. From their short acquaintance, he felt as if the pillar might believe no one should praise a young minister before she had him properly trained.

"All right," Miss Birdie grudgingly conceded. "A nice sermon but terrible hymns. People have been telling me they don't like those new ones."

The church management professor at the seminary had told his class to be careful when the word *people* was used because that usually meant the speaker and a few others he or she'd been able to browbeat into agreeing. He smiled in an effort to look cooperative and appreciative.

"A nice smile," Miss Birdie said. "But I don't care about nice smiles at the moment. I expect results."

"I wanted all parts of the service to fit a theme, the idea of a new beginning for the church. I chose the hymns for that reason."

"A bunch of people mumbling or not singing at all can hardly add to any theme." She fixed him with a glare that let Adam know she expected him to pay attention to her every word. "We like the familiar songs."

"That's a very good point. You know what I believe I'm going to like best about you, Miss Birdie? You always state your opinions so clearly."

Mercedes said, "That's true, but no one has ever complimented Bird on that before."

Miss Birdie glowered at her friend, then turned to study Adam's face. He had no idea what opinion she reached about his sincerity. He attempted to look exceptionally earnest.

"Do you ladies mind if we pray together?" he asked. Without waiting for a response, Adam began, "Loving God, we gather here in Your name, to listen and do Your will. Open us to work together to Your glory, we ask in the name of Your son. Amen."

"*Open us to work together?*" Miss Birdie asked. "Pastor, after sixty-plus years of church attendance, I've learned to interpret ministerial prayers, to translate the words preachers use." She scrutinized Adam. "Sometimes I'm a little wary. What do you want to say with those words?"

"Bird, why do you always question?" Mercedes said. "*All of us together* sounds nice. We should all work together in the church."

Not one to be deterred by a prayer, Miss Birdie repeated. "About those hymns, Pastor Adam."

His lips quivered. He found her determination amusing. If he didn't, she'd probably drive him nuts. Unfortunately, she caught that quick expression before he was able to wipe it away.

"It's not funny, Preacher." She kept her eyes on him as if daring his wayward expression to return. "I brought a list of songs we like to sing." She handed him a sheet of paper. "And the page numbers."

"Very thorough." He glanced at the paper and recognized many of the old hymns popular in the Kentucky churches. "Thank you."

"And you'll use them? During the service?" She continued to study his expression.

Adam could only hope she had a little trouble deciphering it because, as young and inexperienced as he was, he had no idea how to react to her demands. No, to her *suggestions*.

"I promise you at least one a Sunday, and I'll work with the choir on the new hymns."

"Oh, Pastor, you surely noticed our choir isn't very big. Just three sopranos and Ralph, who can't really sing anymore," Mercedes explained. "Good view of the congregation from up there. Ralph likes to sit in the choir so he can see what everyone in the sanctuary is doing during the service."

"But still, they can lead you in learning some new hymns," Adam suggested.

"We like the old ones," Birdie said clearly. "None of us wants to change."

"How are you going to learn new hymns?"

"We don't want to." She bit the words off slowly and precisely. "We are happy with the ones we know."

"Oh, don't be so old-fashioned." Mercedes smiled at Birdie, then at Adam. "I liked some of them. We sing several of the spirit songs at the women's retreats but never have here."

Traitor, Miss Birdie's frown said.

"I'm surprised you're working today," Mercedes observed.

Adam had noticed that Mercedes always attempted to change the subject when Miss Birdie scowled.

"Most of our ministers take Mondays off," the librarian said.

"I don't know what day I'll take off, but I just got here and there's so much to do to get settled. I do have a question for you ladies."

"Pastor Adam, I've learned a smiling minister often means he's fixin' to make an unwanted suggestion," Miss Birdie stated.

"Oh, not at all. This isn't difficult. Wonder if you ladies could tell me about the Widows."

"Oh, that's us." Mercedes grinned and pointed at Miss Birdie then at herself. "We're the Widows. We put together the sympathy dinners and take food to the sick and watch over the fellowship dinners, whatever service is needed here at the church and in town."

"You sound like real treasures." Adam considered carefully how to ask the next question. "I wonder if you know anything about the furniture that Rodolfo from Hilton's delivered to the parsonage."

They glanced at each other. "Pastor, this is a small town,"

Mercedes said. "In a small town, we look after each other. Don't you worry. It's taken care of."

"Would you please thank the group for this gift? I appreciate the generosity."

"You just did." Mercedes pointed at Miss Birdie and herself. "We're the only two Widows left. We ordered the furniture, but lots of people donated. We'll pass that on."

Miss Birdie nodded but obviously didn't want to talk about this subject anymore. He guessed discussing her good deeds made her uncomfortable.

"One more thing, Pastor Adam," Mercedes said. "There's a young vet, an amputee in town. Sam Peterson. His great-aunt Effie died and left her house to him. He's here for rehabilitation at the hospital."

Adam jotted the name on a note card. "I should visit him."

"Yes, you should." Miss Birdie nodded vigorously. "We've tried several times but he won't open the door. He lives in a little green house on Pine Street."

"You'll recognize it because it looks empty and has a dozen old newspapers on the lawn."

Adam nodded and stood, feeling the visit was over. The Widows didn't move, which meant, obviously, it wasn't. He guessed that decision was up to them. He sat back down.

"Tell us a little about yourself, Pastor Adam," Mercedes said. "We know you're from Kentucky." She edged forward in her chair. "How old are you?"

He sat back down. "Twenty-five."

"You don't look twenty-five," Miss Birdie said. "You don't even look eighteen. How can we trust someone as young as you . . . ," the pillar said through pursed lips.

Mercedes shushed her friend, quickly changing the subject. Adam admired how well she could redirect the pillar. "Tell us about your call to become a minister," she said. "I always like to know."

"Grew up in Kentucky where my father had a business. As a kid, I always went to church. After I graduated from the University of Louisville, I taught high school for a year."

"And the call to ministry?" Mercedes prompted.

"I heard the call one day while I was standing in front of a class of thirty-five ninth-grade English students who had no desire to read *Julius Caesar*." That sounded shallow. The reason went much deeper, but that had always been his story because it was short and because the actual Damascus road experience really had taken place right there, in class. It came not only in the voice of God but also in the sullen silence of the students.

With a sweet smile and ignoring a glare from Miss Birdie, who obviously still had a few more bones to pick with him, Mercedes said, "I hear you're single. Have you heard that Birdie and I are matchmakers?"

He felt sure that a look of pure terror washed over his face, because he could feel panic rising inside. Adam pulled himself together and said, "Do a lot of single women live in town?"

Mercedes sighed. "Not as many as we'd like. Most of our young people go off to college and stay in the big cities, so matchmaking's an enormous challenge nowadays."

"But working with what we have, we've been very successful," Miss Birdie added. "We're resourceful and motivated."

Both Widows nodded. The gesture chilled him.

"Yes, we've been very successful." Mercedes tilted her head. "Would you like us to try for you? We've noticed you aren't keeping company with anyone here in Butternut Creek."

"I've only been here a week."

"Perhaps you have a young lady back in Kentucky?"

Adam held up his hand and considered what to say to let them know—politely but firmly—he didn't require their services. "No thank you. I'm a hardened case, ladies. No woman wants to put up with a man married to his vocation." Adam shook his head and added, "I'm not good with women. I'd be too much of a challenge."

He knew immediately he'd made a big mistake. Miss Birdie shared a quick, amused glance with Mercedes.

"We enjoy nothing as much as a challenge," Miss Birdie said.

All hope died within him. As he'd begun to suspect and was borne out over the next years, the Widows loved a dare, rejoiced in achieving the impossible.

Only a few minutes after the Widows left, Adam wondered about Miss Birdie. Mercedes presented herself as she was: friendly and easy to get along with.

But he hadn't met anyone like Miss Birdie before. Oh, every church had a kitchen lady, the woman in charge of nearly everything including meal preparation and service and keeping the congregation in line. Miss Birdie was different, though, stronger than most but also caring and concerned about the flock. How did a person combine her judgmental personality with a heart that had organized the furniture purchase and sent her minister to call on an amputee?

He wished he understood her better. *How can I minister to her if I don't know her?* he reflected.

Of course it could be she didn't care if he ministered to her or not, as long as he did what she expected.

The church administration professor at the seminary had told the class there were members of a congregation, often a clan, who wanted to own the minister, who hoped to be the only family he ate Christmas dinner with, who expected the minister to attend every family gathering including the birth of a nephew or grandchild. Adam didn't think Miss Birdie fell into that category.

The professor had explained there was a second group who wanted to be the only ones the minister listened to, to control the church by controlling the pastor. He'd said ministers should do everything possible to avoid that situation.

The professor had never met Miss Birdie.

Chapter Four

Rockets exploded around Sam Peterson. Amid the screams of the wounded, officers barked directions as mortar shells screamed toward them. Over the rocky landscape hung the acrid smell of ammo and war and the coppery stench of blood. Gunfire rained down on them from the surrounding hills.

He wished the Taliban didn't love hanging out in obscure caves.

"Incoming," Gunny shouted.

"Gunny, we need suppressive fire." Sam pointed west. "Where the hell is the second squad?"

Reacting with the instinct of long training and months in Afghanistan, Sam lifted his M4 to answer the barrage. As the suppressive fire began, he shouted to his radio operator, "We need close air support now and—"

Before he could finish the sentence, a second mortar impacted, driving Sam's face into the dirt. A blast of pain punched him, burning through flesh and bones and nerves.

He reached for his leg. It wasn't there.

His leg had been blown off and he lay alone and bleeding out on the hard surface made slick with his blood. He shouted to his best friend Morty for help, but Morty stretched out next to him, motionless, blood pooling around his head and his eyes staring into the darkness as the battle continued to rage.

"Medic!" Sam yelled, but no one came. Despite pain that nearly knocked him out, he reached for his first-aid kit and grabbed a tourniquet. Fighting against the throbbing and a darkness that threatened to envelop him, he wrapped the nylon strip around his thigh and tightened it with clumsy fingers slick with blood, turning the plastic grip until the flow stopped.

That finished, he clenched his fists and forced himself to breathe, to pull air in and out of gasping lungs. He lay alone in the dark and the throbbing anguish, waiting for death in a foreign country. With the last bit of strength he possessed, he reached out and put his hand on Morty's shoulder.

When the din grew louder, his eyes flew open. For a moment, he floated, caught between the pandemonium of war and the pounding noise of wherever he'd awakened. Above him, Sam saw not a black sky pierced with the flashes and trails of rockets and mortar fire but a ceiling covered with that ugly white popcorn stuff. He took a deep breath. Fresh, clean air. He'd had that nightmare again and hoped Morty didn't die at the end. He always did. It destroyed Sam every time.

He wasn't in Afghanistan. He'd been airlifted out six or seven months earlier. Now he lay in his aunt Effie's bed in Butternut Creek, Texas, in the house he'd inherited from her when she died. Even here, he was alone and in pain and isolated.

Butternut Creek. A stupid place for a marine. He should be in battle at the head of his division, leading his platoons instead of lying in a pale pink room in a cottage. What kind of marine ended up in a place called Butternut Creek?

This one, obviously.

Finally awake, he shook his head to clear it. A mistake. The motion made his head throb.

He shouldn't drink so much. But it had felt so good at the time.

After nearly a minute, he realized the uproar that awakened him came not from a battle in Afghanistan but from the backyard. Sounded like a couple of platoons fighting off insurgents out there. Either that or a bunch of very loud kids. He assumed the latter only because he couldn't figure out how that many marines could fit in his yard or why they'd be there.

He didn't need the noise, not when he'd drunk a fifth of whiskey last night in an attempt to overcome pain and insomnia and memories. He glanced at the clock. Nine thirty on Wednesday, no Tuesday, morning. Maybe Monday.

Who cared? For a moment, Sam considered the pros of getting up. Deciding to try for a few more hours of sleep, he put a pillow over his head. At the same time, a loud crack came from inside the house. As much as he'd like to ignore what sounded like a broken window, he couldn't. Someone could be robbing Aunt Effie's house.

No, it was his house now, his responsibility.

After a few seconds of silence, he heard a knock on the slider. Very polite burglars.

With a struggle, he sat up and slipped on the bottom of a sweat suit but didn't bother to cover the T-shirt he slept in. Then he turned in the bed, put his left foot on the floor and into a slipper, grabbed the crutches, and shoved them under his arms.

The knock came again.

Once the crutches were in position, he struggled to swing what remained of his right leg around, then stood and steadied himself before he hobbled across the thick shag carpet. If he decided to stay in the house for longer than a few more months, the fiend of a rug that grabbed his crutches with every step would be the first thing to go.

Then came still another knock on the slider. "Hold your pants on," he shouted, then cursed. He'd hoped they'd left by now and he could go back to bed.

He avoided the pile of trash on the floor, bottles and old newspapers and boxes from microwave dinners. He should pick those up someday. Noxious fumes made up of the odor of trash and spilled booze, mixed with the smell of an old house left shut up for all the months after his aunt died, filled the room.

When he reached the slider in the dining room, he pulled the lacy curtains back to see a large hole in the middle of the right panel. He tried to open the door, but with the broken glass, it stopped after only a few inches. Two boys stood in front of him with expressions of fear and remorse on their freckled faces.

"We're sorry, sir," said the taller kid. Then he gulped.

Two pairs of round, green, guileless eyes stared at him. He'd heard someone, probably them, fooling around in the backyard for several days, but this was the first time he'd seen the perpetrators. Amazing only two boys made so much racket.

But he didn't fall for those eyes. He knew how easy innocence was to assume, although the apology had sounded fairly sincere. In his youth, he'd had to apologize plenty of times and knew exactly how to seem earnest and repentant. He'd fooled everyone but his father the general.

"Don't know how that happened, sir." The younger boy pointed toward the broken slider. "One moment it was fine and the next, it wasn't."

The older kid scowled at him.

They were cute kids with spiked red hair and burnt orange

University of Texas T-shirts worn with jeans and athletic shoes. They had to be brothers. But at that moment, Sam didn't care if they were good guys or gangbangers. His missing foot had started to throb again, something the VA medical staff called phantom limb pain but felt excruciatingly genuine to him. The raw agony made him want to scream, except he was a marine. Marines didn't scream.

On top of everything, he was here and his troops were . . . how many thousands of miles away? The fact he wasn't with them tore at him so badly he hurt inside almost as much as in the missing limb.

And Morty was dead. He died every night.

Gritting his teeth, Sam turned, balanced himself on the right crutch, and leaned over to pick up a fist-size rock. Shards of glass covered the floor and stuck to the curtain. By the time he'd struggled to stand back up, he saw the boys squeezing through the narrow opening and inside.

"Don't suppose this"—he tossed the rock into the air several times and looked through the broken pane—"had anything to do with the broken window."

The eyes of the shorter boy grew even rounder. "No, sir," he said.

The older brother shushed him and said, "Yes, sir. Sorry, sir."

The kid was either very polite or he knew Sam was military. Probably because of his camo sleeveless T-shirt.

"Names."

"I'm Leo." The older boy straightened his thin shoulders and stood at attention. "He's Nick. Thomas. Our last name is Thomas."

If anything could, the sight of Leo's posture would have made Sam laugh. "How old are you?"

"I'm ten." Leo pointed at himself. "My brother's eight."

"When does school start?" The pain began to move up from the missing foot through his absent shin and settled in his shattered knee. He didn't feel like chatting but couldn't figure out how to get the two to leave. He could shout at them, curse at them, but even he had his limits. He couldn't do that to kids.

"In August," Leo said.

"Where's your mother?"

"She works, sir." Leo pulled his hands out of his pockets and held them straight and flat against his side.

"At the hospital, sir." Nick squared his shoulders, mimicking his brother.

Aha. If he didn't hurt so much, he'd have figured out much earlier that these two redheads must belong to the luscious PT he'd met at the hospital. He grinned, inside.

"And your father?" Might as well collect all the information he could.

He hadn't thought the boys' eyes could look any sadder, but they did.

Leo lowered his gaze. "Back in Chicago."

"With his stupid new wife Tiffany," the younger kid muttered.

Leo gave Nick an elbow to his ribs.

"When my folks split up, we came back here." Leo grimaced. "Is Butternut Creek the stupidest name you've ever heard of for a town, sir? All my friends back home—" He swallowed hard. "All the guys laughed at me when I told them we were moving to Butternut Creek, Texas." His voice dripped with disgust.

"Yeah, mine, too," Nick added.

"Shut up," Leo said. "Your friends didn't even—"

"Yeah, they did. And I have as many friends as you."

"Do not." Leo turned toward his younger brother and glared at him.

"Stop." The sound of squabbling made Sam's head pound harder, in time with the throbbing of his leg. "Let's get back to basics. One of you broke my window, but you both were playing in my yard where you shouldn't be. Stop arguing and man up."

"Wow. He said *man up*." Nick's voice filled with wonder.

"Okay, man up, squirt," Leo said to his brother, then turned to Sam. "Nick broke the window."

"Did not."

"He was pretending to toss a grenade into the guardhouse to save me. He didn't mean to hit the glass, but he did throw the rock."

"It was an accident," Nick whispered. "It sort of slipped out of my hand."

Sam glared at the boys for a few seconds and wondered what he was getting into by talking to them, by allowing them to enter the silence he surrounded himself with. Nothing good. Nothing he wanted to get involved in. "What are you going to do about it?" he demanded because he couldn't think of any other way to respond and he guessed it would kill their self-esteem if he mocked them or sent them away. Not that he had reason to care about their self-esteem.

Why was he acting like such a nice guy when he did not care about people and pain throbbed through his missing leg? The brothers looked at him then at each other. They shrugged.

"Don't know," Leo said.

The tendrils of the headache had started to move down Sam's neck. He had to get the boys outside so he could close the drapes, settle on the sofa, and do his exercises. He needed darkness, not sunshine. For a moment, he tried to gather his thoughts and consider how he could get them out of there. He turned away from the slider and leaned against the table.

"Look," the younger one whispered. "He's got tattoos."

"Tats, idiot," the older brother said. "He's got barbed wire on his right arm."

"And something marine-y on the other," the younger one said. "Look at those muscles." A note of awe filled the whispered comment. Sam would have laughed but that would hurt his head. Instead he glared at them and said, "Have your mom call me."

"Oh, no, sir. Please don't make us tell her." Leo's voice quivered. He cleared his throat. "We'll do anything if you won't tell my mother."

"She gets sad and *really* disappointed in us." Nick's lips trembled.

"Have her call me," Sam said in his command voice. "Seven-one-four-four." In Butternut Creek, everyone shared the same prefix so he didn't bother with it.

"Seven-one-four-four," they repeated simultaneously.

"If you don't tell her, I'll call her. You won't like what happens after that." With those words, he pointed toward the slider. "Now. Go!" As they dashed out, Sam slid the door shut as far as he could and closed the curtain. Then he steadied himself on the crutches as he stumbled toward the sofa in the living room with glass crunching beneath his shoe. Once there, he fell on the cushions and took a bottle of pills from the end table. He popped three in his mouth and swallowed them dry, in too much pain to stand and get water.

He leaned his head against the back of the sofa, closed his eyes to relax, and began to imagine himself going down in an elevator while he read the floors. "Ten," he said. "Nine, eight . . ." The pain lessened with each number.

As the muscles of his neck loosened, the phone rang. The jangle made his shoulders tense up and increased the pounding of his headache. Hadn't thought it could hurt more.

Probably the general or a wrong number. No one else knew where he was. He'd let it ring, because he didn't want to talk to the general. Actually, he didn't want to talk to anyone but most of all, not to the general.

As much as he liked the solitude, Sam hadn't planned to be alone here. The general had meant to be here when Sam arrived in town, but he'd had a mild heart attack. At the time, Sam had felt relief not to have the general close. Not that he could imagine the old warhorse fussing as he took care of his only and deeply disappointing son, but he hadn't wanted him there at all. Ever. His presence would have intruded on Sam's privacy.

The general had improved greatly, but the cardiologist refused to release him from his care for another month. Good old Dad always followed rules and commands, usually at the expense of his family.

Sam knew he should have outgrown that bitterness years ago.

He closed his eyes and started counting down again. "Ten . . . nine . . ."

When he felt better, he'd call the insurance agent about replacing the glass in the slider. The number should be somewhere, maybe in the box of stuff his aunt's lawyer had left.

Then he'd call the liquor store and arrange for another delivery.

"Preacher?"

Adam looked up from his Bible, attempting to bring himself back to the present from the time of David. Maggie stood at the door. "Yes?"

"I need the hymns for Sunday."

He picked a piece of paper from the printer tray, glanced at it, then grabbed the list of Miss Birdie-approved hymns and a pen. With that, he crossed out his choices and changed every hymn to one of Miss Birdie's choosing.

That should make her believe she'd broken him in, which should make his life easier. His plan was, little by little, to slip in some of the newer hymns and drop most of the Fanny Crosby hymns and several of the old favorites she enjoyed. "Jesus Is Tenderly Calling Me Home" had always made him feel as if he were at a funeral. However, allowing Miss Birdie to win the first skirmish seemed like an excellent strategy.

Finished, he handed the list to Maggie and headed out to call on Sam Peterson. Easily finding the right house, Adam picked up all the papers—two weeks' worth—and placed them on the porch next to the front door, then rang the bell.

He didn't hear the sound of the chime inside, so he knocked. And knocked again. No one came, and it seemed as if no one would. If Captain Peterson didn't want visitors, Adam had to respect that.

Besides, even a minister could hardly force himself on the man. Adam backed away from the door and turned to step off the porch.

He'd keep trying. He wanted to meet this man and he knew Miss Birdie wouldn't let him forget his duty.

Chapter Five

Friday evening Adam lay half-on-half-off the sofa, watching some action program he couldn't concentrate on.

The time since his arrival had gone well. Most of the congregation liked his preaching, although the pillar—Miss Birdie—made several suggestions. He'd made a number of much-appreciated hospital and nursing home visits and met the ministers of the Lutheran and Episcopal churches, spent a few hours at the food pantry every week, had coffee with Father Joe, and done a lot of ministerial stuff. But books and boxes still covered the surfaces and floors of the office. Someday he'd get to them.

As busy as he'd been with all those activities and events and meetings and services to fill time, Adam felt on edge. For the past few days, he hadn't been able to sit still. In the parsonage, he'd paced through the parlors and up and down the hall several times, even up the stairs to wander into empty bedrooms and the attic, then back down, over and over. None of that movement brought relief.

Adam stood and moved to stare out the front window.

Somewhere out there lay what he needed. Could he find it tonight? How would he be able to locate his fix in a new town?

Where to start?

He didn't know, but he had to find something to get him through the night, to allow him to sleep, to take the edge off.

He had to find a pickup game of roundball.

After changing into athletic shoes and sweats, he found his basketball and dribbled it down the stairs, across the hall, and outside.

During Daylight Saving Time, sunlight in Central Texas lasted until nine thirty. If he could find a court, he'd have about an hour to shoot hoops.

Some people ran. Others walked or swam. Adam played basketball. He'd always needed the physical demands of the game to release all the pent-up tension and nervous energy his body built up with inactivity. Add to that the stress accumulated over the days without exercise, the jitters of being a new minister, the strain of knowing Miss Birdie watched his every move. His body screamed for a hard game of basketball.

He missed the competition, the moves, the jukes, and the almost chess-like thinking that took place in nearly every game, even pickup games.

Easy to find a game in Kentucky where basketball was pretty much another religion. If no one at the seminary was playing, he'd cross the street to the university or to Prall Town, a nearby neighborhood.

He jogged down streets lined by crepe myrtle. Heavy with flowers, their branches stretched up and up before crashing down in cascades of pink or purple or cottony white. Every now and then, a dog came to the fence and sniffed or growled. Several barked loudly enough to be called back by waving neighbors.

"Good evening, Preacher," a man called from his yard.

Recognizing the voice and face of a church member but not remembering his name, Adam wandered over to the fence.

The member of the congregation glanced at the ball Adam carried. "Looking for a game?" He pointed. "Over yonder. A block south and a couple more east. Goliad Park. Always a game going on."

Adam followed the directions. As he got closer, the noise and the glow of lights blazing through trees drew his attention.

On the court, two teams, players of different sizes and colors, worked hard, sweat dripping down their faces and bodies causing dark skin to glow like ebony. Near the fence stood several more guys and a couple of girls, all watching and cheering. On a court farther south, young women played.

If this had been a party or social hour, Adam would have walked away, uncomfortable because he didn't know anyone. But this was *ball*. He didn't lack confidence here. "I've got next," he yelled. Did the rules and phrases from Kentucky work here?

The games stopped. Everyone—those on both courts and those watching—turned toward him. Adam knew exactly what they saw: a newcomer, a tall, skinny old guy carrying a ball. Most of the players outweighed him by thirty pounds, and Adam had at least five or ten years on them. A few snickered. Others grinned and laughed.

"I've got next," he repeated, undaunted.

They nodded before resuming their games.

While they played, Adam dribbled toward one of the baskets outside the court and tossed up a few shots, then moved farther away and put several more in.

"You shoot like that when you're guarded?"

Slowly and deliberately, Adam took another shot, missed, rebounded, and put it in before glancing at the speaker. The kid outweighed him and was stronger but Adam had more experience, a few inches' advantage in height, and longer arms.

Sweat glistened on the player's dark skin, which meant he must have warmed up and been playing already. Should be good competition.

"Try me." Adam tossed the ball to him.

Expressionless, the kid watched him for a second, then put the ball on the cracked asphalt and dribbled, glancing left, then right, and from Adam's feet to his eyes, watching and judging his movements. With a fake to the left and a drive to the right, the other player broke toward the basket. Like a hustler, Adam gave him that one. An early score made the other guy overconfident and cockier.

The kid turned with a big grin. With swagger and attitude, he tossed Adam the ball. The preacher had the guy exactly where he wanted him. Before he could react, Adam put the ball in the air for a long shot. The ball didn't make a sound as it passed through the metal chain of the basket. All that swagger and attitude disappeared, and the two got down to playing ball.

For the next thirty minutes, they fought. Despite the breeze, sweat poured down them both. They threw elbows, tripped each other, shoved and talked trash. Adam's trash talk consisted of "Oh, yeah?" and "Who's your daddy?" among other tame taunts, but it worked okay for him. The kid used tougher phrases filled with words the preacher hadn't used in years, but they didn't bother him. He didn't really hear them. All he cared about was the game, the competition. When he played ball, Adam wasn't clumsy or uncertain or too young and inexperienced. He was in the zone.

Within a few minutes, a small crowd had gathered, including the guys who'd been playing when he arrived. After a hard-fought game, Adam won thirty to twenty-six.

"Hey, Pops, you play pretty well for a skinny guy," his opponent said.

Adam read the subtext: *pretty good for a skinny white guy*. The nickname showed the kid recognized the preacher as being older, but he didn't care. He'd more than held his own against the youngster. That felt good.

The other guy spun the ball on his finger and studied Adam. "I'm Hector Firestone."

"Hector." Adam nodded but didn't say more for a few seconds. He was so winded he could barely talk, but darned if he'd let Hector know that. "Just call me Pops."

As he walked home that night, dribbling the ball in front of him and making moves toward phantom baskets, Adam cooled off and considered the next day.

Sam Peterson. He had to visit him again. Or try to.

Sam groaned, inside. He didn't want to face intake with a PT who had read his eyes and understood what the redness meant. But here he sat, in her office, waiting for an interview and for the therapist to lay out a program to fix him. He looked out the window between her office and the treatment room.

As if feeling his gaze on her, Willow glanced at him, then away as she chatted with a patient. He grinned as he considered what he'd say to her. He noticed again the brackets between her eyes and understood them better. Moving to Texas, a cheating husband, and two active boys, as well as a new job, could wear a woman out. Maybe a year ago, he'd have sympathized, but compassion no longer made his top twenty list. In fact, compassion came well below "attempt to function" and "could care less."

As she entered the office, Willow Thomas turned a friendly smile at him but still didn't react like other women. Her lack of response probably was good but still odd in a *life-is-pain* sort of way. The only woman he'd seen in months whom he *might* like to attract didn't respond to his charms. Not at all. Not that he wanted to attract her, not now, but a positive response, the usual *my-my-my-aren't-you-hot* reaction, would feel good.

With another surreptitious glance at the redhead, he realized what a bunch of bull his desire *not* to attract her was. He'd like her to find him attractive and not only for the ego boost.

Once in her office, he'd shoved the crutches against the wall and settled into the chair, glad to take the weight off his shoulders. Aware of the warning from his doctor and the PTs in other hospitals not to cross his legs, he did exactly that, right over left, to see if he could get a rise from the professional and gorgeous therapist.

Before her death, his mother would've said he was acting out. He didn't care; he wanted to see the woman's response. Most likely, her dimples and honeyed smile would disappear.

Leaning back, he attempted to use the biofeedback exercise again. His leg hurt, but he found it difficult to relax in this chair with the commotion outside and the proximity of the redhead.

"Hello, Captain Peterson." She stood in front of him. "Make yourself comfortable," she said.

Yeah, fat chance.

"As you know, I'm Willow Thomas, one of the two PTs in the department. I'd like to review the notes Trixie made the other day and conduct an intake interview with you."

As Willow closed the door, he saw her eyeing his crossed leg, but she didn't say a word about it. Choosing her battles, he guessed.

"How are you doing today?"

"Peachy."

She nodded like she believed him, settled at her desk, and brought a file up on her screen. She perused the information for a moment before turning in the chair to look at him. "Why don't you tell me about your injury?" She picked up a clipboard. "You served in Afghanistan? A marine?"

He nodded.

"Your records say you were stabilized in Hawaii then transferred to Walter Reed in DC?" At his nod, she continued, "A transtibial amputation. That's fortunate."

"Oh, yeah, losing your leg is always lucky. All of us amputees celebrate it every glorious day."

She blinked. "I apologize. I can't believe I said that." She bit her lower lip. "I shouldn't have used those words. What I meant is a transtibial amputation is easier to treat, easier to find a prosthesis that fits, one that will be comfortable. The loss of part of your leg certainly is not a lucky event." She attempted a smile but it came off more worn-out than cheerful. "An unfortunate choice of words. I'm sorry."

He nodded again.

She studied the screen. "I see you already have your initial prosthesis." She glanced at the leg, which obviously didn't have one. "Do you have it with you?"

He'd have to use a few more words to explain. "It's at home. It's not comfortable."

She nodded, with sympathy. He hated sympathy and the sweet smiles and pitying glances that came with it. He slid down farther in the chair. He knew he was behaving like a butthead, but he figured if he was drowning, why should he go alone?

"We'll see what we can do to alleviate the pain, maybe add some cushioning. You're going to have to get used to the prosthesis you have before the prosthetist can fit you for a new one."

Like the new one would be better.

She glanced at his records again. "All right, let me check your file. I have copies of your initial intake from Hawaii and another from DC." She looked up with green eyes as clear as a high mountain spring, exactly the same color as her sons'. On them they looked full of spirit and mischief. On her, they promised healing.

He'd rather they promised something else.

She turned away from the screen to face him. "How did you happen to end up in Butternut Creek when you could have rehabbed at Walter Reed or other large facilities?"

He'd have to speak or he'd look like even more of a jerk than he was. "Didn't want to stay in DC so the general—that's my father—pulled a few strings. He was a marine, too. My aunt died a while back and left me a house over on Pine Street."

"On Pine Street?" She smiled at him. "I live close to that, in the new apartments on Eleventh."

"Oh?" He nodded as if the information were new.

"Why don't you tell me about your daily schedule," she asked. "What's your level of activity? What kind of physical activity do you take part in?"

He narrowed his eyes and grinned—inside. "I do a lot of elbow bending, ma'am." He mimed the actions of pouring from a bottle to a glass, then drinking. With a slow, mocking grin, he added, "I do it very well. No pain. No problems."

He had to hand it to her. A complete professional, she allowed not one sign of judgment or disgust to cross her face, to give away her opinion of a man who spent his day filling himself with booze to smooth off the ragged edges of pain and splinters of loss. She must have interviewed a lot of angry, depressed wounded vets.

"But you're a physical therapist," he said to the top of her head as she made notes. "Why are you asking me questions about occupational therapy?" He knew the difference. He'd been interrogated by dozens of people in many different departments since the injury.

"This is an intake session that covers all areas, to make sure you receive optimal care. Also, many of our services overlap."

He nodded and enjoyed the view of her beautiful hair.

"You drink a great deal?" she asked without a trace of emotion. "How much would you say you drink a day?"

"As much as necessary. I drink until I feel better, pass out, or can't feel anything."

She studied him for a moment, her face expressionless. "You do know alcohol can change the effect of or weaken some of the medications you're taking?"

Too stupid a question to answer. Of course he knew. He didn't care. No drinker would, but at least she didn't give him the lecture about how he was ruining his life.

She scribbled a few notes before asking, "Do you live alone?"

He nodded.

"How did you get to the hospital today?"

"The community bus for cripples."

When her gaze flew to his face, he felt a spark of contrary pleasure. He'd gotten to her, but not for long. She looked back to her page, cool as ever.

"Tell me about how you handle the chores of daily living."

"Chores of daily living?" He laughed without one note of humor. "They don't get done."

"We offer in-home services like housekeeping, a medication aide, help with bathing."

"No," he said. When she glanced up he added, "Thank you," but didn't mean it.

"Are you aware of the veterans' support groups in the area? One meets at—"

He snorted.

"I take it you're not interested." When he didn't respond, she said, "When you're ready, if you're ever interested, I can give you some information. One meets at the Christian Church." She jotted more notes. "How well do you sleep?"

"Have trouble nodding off."

"Pain?"

He nodded. "But once I have a couple of nightcaps to blunt the pain and fall asleep, I don't want to wake up. Could probably stay in bed all day." He paused. "If it weren't for the kids."

She glanced up at him quickly, a touch of confusion in her eyes. "Kids?"

"Yeah, sounds like a dozen but I've only seen two boys. About this high, and this high." He used his hand to indicate their heights.

"Two boys? In your neighborhood?" The confusion had changed to concern.

"In my backyard."

She blinked. He was getting to her. Good. She looked nervous.

"Yeah, redheaded little fiends, make more noise than you could imagine. Running around in my backyard."

"Redheaded little fiends?" She closed the file with a slap and leaned forward. "In your yard?" Her voice remained even but her eyes flashed.

He'd pierced her calm facade. Could he tell her she was beautiful when she was angry? No, too clichéd and too forward. Rudeness didn't bother him these days, but he hated clichés. He nodded and hid a grin of triumph.

"They broke my slider yesterday. Threw a rock through it."

She glared—only a bit—but emotion in those eyes was much more interesting than her cool, professional demeanor. Obviously the kids hadn't told her. Of course, it had only happened the day before. Probably hadn't gotten up their courage yet.

"Yes, the little scamps did. Took me forever to clean the glass off the floor. Talk about chores of daily living. Using a broom and dustpan is difficult for a guy with one leg."

She swallowed and attempted to mask her response. Cool on the outside but obviously upset inside. "Has the glass been fixed?"

"I took care of it right away but it cost more than I had in the budget."

The therapist's beautiful green eyes grew large.

"Funny thing." He paused. "I gave them my phone number, to have their mother call me. No one did." He shook his head. "Guess she doesn't care. Guess she can't control them."

She took a deep breath. A determined look covered her face, and her eyes showed a resolute glint. She glared over his head, her lips narrowed to almost nothing. An amazing transformation from compassionate professional to troubled mother.

"As you have probably guessed, those two were my sons. Your expenditure will be taken care of and the nuisance addressed." She stood. "If you will excuse me." She headed toward the door and opened it. "I'm going to ask Mike to work with you on strengthening your leg and core muscles and on improving your balance. We'll complete the intake during your next appointment."

He watched her walk out the door.

He didn't get as much pleasure out of ticking people off as he used to, but, as long as he got a reaction, he wasn't about to stop. What else did he have to do, other than watch the great parts of Willow Thomas as she moved away from him? He figured she'd refuse to add that means of entertainment to his treatment plan.

The occupational therapist would expect him to find a wheel-chair basketball league or learn to whittle, but neither of those interested him nearly as much as Willow Thomas and the way her eyes flashed when she became upset.

Nothing scared him more than the attraction toward this woman. He was a mess and so was his life. He knew what a bargain he was *not*. She had too much on her plate now without taking on a bitter cripple.

Besides, his interest was completely physical. The woman had a great body, and she was nice enough. But he had no interest in an emotional entanglement with a single mother of two rambunctious boys, or any woman for that matter.

Watching her didn't commit him to anything, however, and it gave him more pleasure than anything had in a long time.

Chapter Six

Willow pulled into the parking lot of her apartment complex, parked, and turned off the ignition. Her husband had bought her this very expensive car two years ago, back when he was seeing Tiffany but still felt guilty about it. The insurance payments took a big hunk of her paycheck. Her lawyer should have done a better job on that. Also, the backseat was tiny and the gas mileage was terrible, but it looked great and went very fast on the highway.

As she tapped her fingers against the steering wheel, she knew she was delaying entering the apartment, postponing the discussion with the boys. What was she going to do with them? What should she do about them? They were young boys who'd lost their father, friends, and home to come to a small town hundreds of miles away from Chicago with a completely different culture and climate.

Knowing they'd want to be active, she'd enrolled them in a day camp until school started, but not enough had signed up so the last session was canceled. By that time, it was too late to enroll them in the summer soccer league. She could hardly take them to work, but she thought they'd be safe playing in the park, walking to the library, and wandering over to the box store on the edge of town. After all, they were eight and ten. Never had she thought they'd trespass and break a window.

She shouldn't have allowed the captain's revelation to bother her so much. For heaven's sake, she'd run out on a patient during the intake sessions. How incompetent did that appear? But she'd felt overwhelmed by life, and breaking down in tears in front of the captain wouldn't seem professional to him or to anyone. Certainly not to her.

Exactly what she needed: to have Leo and Nick running wild

and to have a patient think she was a terrible, uncaring mother. That would hardly justify his having confidence in any area.

Would it have mattered if the patient hadn't been Captain Peterson? As much as she tried to ignore it, the question wiggled into her brain. Yes, he was handsome and charismatic. His eyes smoldered. Wasn't that the word they used in romance novels? Didn't the hero always have smoldering eyes that burned into the soul of the heroine? But this wasn't a book and he wasn't the hero and she shouldn't care about the opinion of a patient more than that of anyone else.

Nor was this about her. This was about Leo and Nick and how she could guide them without making them more unhappy about their situation.

But as hard as she attempted to ignore this—she certainly was deep in denial this afternoon—she had to admit she liked how the captain had looked at her, as if he found her an attractive woman, maybe even sexy. Her self-esteem had suffered when she first found out about Tiffany, but the captain seemed to . . .

"Mom?"

She glanced up to see Nick standing at her window.

"Is there something wrong?" He frowned a little as if wondering why she was still in the car in the parking lot. "Are you sick?"

"No." She smiled at him. Plenty of time to talk about that broken slider once she was inside with both boys. "Just thinking. But I do want to talk to you and Leo."

"Oh."

That one syllable, spoken in the high, shaky voice Nick used when he was worried or frightened, tipped her off. He and his brother *had* broken the slider and hadn't told her. Not that she'd doubt the captain, who had no reason to make the story up, but she'd wanted to ask the boys first. Now she knew.

"Let's go inside." She opened the door and handed the sack of hamburgers to him. Probably shouldn't buy their favorite fast food when she was going to have to punish them, but after a long day of work, she couldn't face cooking. "Where's your brother?"

Nick gulped as he took the bag. "Watching television," he said, his voice still wavering.

When she unlocked the apartment and Nick shoved the door open, he said, "Mom wants to talk to us."

If she hadn't already known what had happened, the sight of Leo leaping to his feet and glancing at his brother in silent communication would have tipped her off. She closed the door, walked toward the window, and opened the blinds. That completed, she turned back to face the boys. "Boys, does either of you want to tell me about Captain Peterson?"

"Mom, he's the coolest man," Nick said. "He has tattoos—I mean tats—and he's a marine."

"He was wounded," Leo added, his voice filled with admiration. She could tell by his face that her eldest had just realized a wounded marine might end up at physical therapy. "Have you met him?" he asked.

She nodded.

Nick and Leo exchanged glances again.

"Guess we'd better tell you what happened," Leo said.

"Yes, and after you do that, explain why you didn't tell me about it and what you're going to do to repay the captain." She'd have to be tough because she didn't want anyone—not only the captain—to think she let the boys get away with anything.

But making the boys compensate him for the broken door meant she'd have to see him again. She didn't want to, not outside the secure walls of the hospital, the safe haven of the physical therapy department where she could hide behind her professional demeanor. He and his scrutiny made her feel attractive, like a woman again, as her husband had done for years. But Grant taught her not to trust men, and she'd learned that lesson well. With two sons, she didn't dare make another mistake.

Adam hurried across the parking lot toward the church, carrying the plate of warm muffins Ouida had handed him on his way out of the parsonage.

Surely there could be no better place for a bachelor than living next to a friendly neighbor who baked. He whistled as he entered the church. When he spotted the frown on Maggie's face, the whistling stopped.

"You have a guest." She continued to type the bulletin, but her tone and lack of eye contact suggested he might not be pleased with the identity of the visitor.

Guessing who it was, Adam attempted to recapture his exhilaration. It eluded him. He hadn't seen Miss Birdie's old van outside, but she could have walked. No destination in town was too far to walk.

"Who is it?" he whispered.

Maggie kept her eye on the screen and didn't answer. Surely setting the margin couldn't demand so much attention.

Squaring his shoulders, Adam pushed the door open and walked into the minister's study. He knew he should call this his study, but he worried about acting too possessive, as if claiming this as his might make the extraordinary place disappear. Magical and un-Christian thinking, he knew.

Yes, Miss Birdie stood next to the desk. She hadn't heard him enter and rubbed her shoulder as if . . . Well, for a moment, she looked vulnerable. Like a real person, like a church member whose minister should comfort her instead of wanting to run and hide every time he saw her.

When she heard him come in, the pillar dropped her hands and turned toward him. Her lips curved, an expression he couldn't read but made him suspicious. She looked almost friendly.

He had to quit judging Miss Birdie. She was a member of the congregation, a child of God who deserved to be loved and accepted by her minister. Adam smiled back. "What can I do for you?"

"Well, first you need to do something about these books all over the place."

"I agree, but . . ." He realized as he began to defend the mess that the books weren't the real reason for her visit. Oddly, instead of appearing confident, she looked almost uncertain about her purpose. Adam guessed the hesitation would disappear as soon as the reason for her presence emerged. Miss Birdie wasn't one to hem and haw.

The minister gestured toward the two chairs he'd cleared after her first visit and walked to the desk. Piles of books and tottering stacks of paper littered the surface. As if he'd always meant to do exactly that, Adam opened the large bottom drawer, swept the mess inside, and closed it. "Won't you have a seat?"

"No, I need to get some things done before the lunch crowd comes in." She paused. "Preacher, I'd like you to be my guest for breakfast in the morning."

Now Adam felt incredibly foolish. He'd misjudged Miss Birdie again and should look out for that tendency. He needed to be more accepting. "How nice of you. Thank you. Eight o'clock at the diner?"

"No, no, no. A little earlier. Maybe seven fifteen? Before the crowd gets there."

Why so early? Had she said *before the crowd*? Although Adam hadn't eaten there yet, he thought most people who had to get to work would arrive about seven. And if she wanted to discuss something important, why would the restaurant be a better place to converse than the church office?

There he went again, trying to explain and understand her

invitation instead of accepting it gratefully. "Seven fifteen. Thank you. I'll be there."

She walked to the door before turning and looking a little uncertain. "Oh, and wear a tie, please. Don't suppose you could get a haircut?"

Odd.

"I . . . aah . . . want to show my minister off to all my customers."

"I'll try." But before he could complete those two syllables, she'd disappeared, again without a good-bye.

That night, as Adam walked home after a tough game of three-on-three with Hector and his friends, two questions repeated through his brain. First, considering the aches and pains he suffered from the blocks and shoves, should he play ball with kids ten years younger? Without resolving that concern, because he knew he'd never give the game up as long as he could still dribble, he pondered Miss Birdie's odd invitation to breakfast. Attempting to understand the twists and turns of the pillar's brain baffled Adam, and yet hadn't he promised himself not to always believe she had ulterior motives? Hadn't he decided to trust Miss Birdie? He gave up trying to figure her out as he approached the front steps of the parsonage.

❧

As Adam contemplated himself in the mirror at six forty-five Thursday morning, he knew he had to get a haircut. Most of the first check had paid for repairs on the car. He'd set the rest aside for food because he'd run out of the goodies people had brought those first weeks. Surely he could scrape together enough to get a haircut soon. At least he was wearing a tie, he thought as he straightened it.

Adam left the house at 7:05, plenty of time to walk to the diner. When he entered the restaurant, he looked around. All the booths lining the walls plus the five or six tables in the center of the room and every stool at the counter were occupied, mostly by men drinking coffee and talking. He spotted a few members of the congregation and was headed in the direction of Howard's booth when Miss Birdie intercepted him. Her plastic nametag said only BIRDIE. If he wanted to escape her wrath, he figured he should never call her that.

"Good morning, Pastor Adam. We're busy this morning so you're going to have to share a booth."

Odd. He thought she wanted to share breakfast with him, to talk to him about something personal, a problem or concern, but how did she expect to do that here? The place was packed. People held up cups for refills all over the room. She obviously had to work.

And this was *before the crowd*?

Adam pointed toward the booth where the elders sat. "I'll join them."

"No, no, I have a place set and ready for you." She grabbed his arm with her free hand and gestured toward the corner with the coffeepot she held in the other.

Adam had made it a rule never to oppose a woman armed with a hot carafe. However, when the two got within six feet of the booth, he realized a young woman sat there, her back to them as she read the paper. He stopped.

"Someone's already there," he said although he knew full well why someone was already there. The matchmaker had roped him in, set him up. He'd been dumb enough to believe her sincerity, accept her invitation, and walk into her trap.

When would he learn?

With a quick glance at the woman in the booth—who, fortunately, hadn't noticed that he and his captor stood only a few feet away—then another peek at the door, Adam calculated his chance of escape. Could he run fast enough to get out of the diner before the woman in the booth could lift her eyes from the opinion page of the *Austin American-Statesman*?

Foolishly he hadn't figured Miss Birdie in his calculations. The pillar motioned toward Adam with that pot of hot coffee. Once she ascertained he wouldn't attempt to run, she said to the young woman, "We're full today. Do you mind sharing the booth?"

Miss Birdie continued to wave Adam forward and, unwilling and suspicious but not wanting to insult the young woman, he followed. Besides, he couldn't run without causing a scene and infuriating Miss Birdie. Neither seemed wise, and he was hungry.

"Hello." Adam nodded as the woman glanced up.

A lovely smile, he noted, dimples showing on a round, sweet face. Her dark hair was pulled back with one of those plastic styling things he'd seen advertised on television and wondered both how they worked and if anyone bought and used them. At least this woman had.

"Hi." She gestured at the red upholstered seat across from her. "Please join me."

Adam slid in before glancing at Miss Birdie, whose smile stretched bright and broad and triumphant across her face. What next? A victory dance?

No, she simply turned a cup over and filled it. "Your breakfast will be right out. I ordered for you, Preacher," she said. "Pastor, this is

Reverend Patillo, the minister at the Presbyterian church. Why don't you two get acquainted? As ministers, I imagine you have a lot in common." She dashed off, leaving them alone and looking as proud as if she'd posted a MISSION COMPLETE banner.

Not that Adam felt particularly alone with fifty to sixty people crowded into the café. The eyes of every one of them studied the two in the booth surreptitiously. Was the entire town in on Miss Birdie's matchmaking scheme?

"I'm Mattie. Have we been set up?" She chuckled, a warm, friendly sound but hardly the siren's call of immediate chemistry. "You must be Adam Jordan from the Christian Church. I'd heard a single minister was coming to town and figured it was only a matter of time before someone tried to get us together. How long have you been here?"

"A few weeks."

"I'm surprised this hasn't happened earlier." Mattie took another sip of her coffee. "I want to . . ."

"Sorry to interrupt, but here're your breakfasts." On her right arm, Miss Birdie carried a platter holding two large plates and two small ones. "Toast and half a grapefruit for Reverend Patillo." She placed them in front of Mattie. "The rest for Pastor Adam. Hope you enjoy this, Preacher."

With those words, she set down a platter in front of Adam with a stack of pancakes topped with whipped cream and strawberries and syrup and another with four pieces of bacon, a small steak, three sausage links, a couple of biscuits, an enormous mound of scrambled eggs, grits with oceans of melted butter on top, and hash browns. It took up nearly the entire table. That finished, she folded her hands in front of her and smiled, her glance shifting from minister to minister. "Isn't she just about the prettiest thing you've ever seen?"

He responded, "I can't eat all this."

"Course you can. Wouldn't hurt you to put a little meat on those bones. Take the leftovers home for breakfast tomorrow."

Adam studied the amazing amount of food. Except for the grits, the food would last for a week. Even though he'd lived in Kentucky for years, he'd never learned to like grits. They must be a taste acquired immediately after weaning. To him, grits tasted like ground Styrofoam. It wasn't that he disliked them; he just saw no reason to expend the effort to swallow something so tasteless.

"Now, you two enjoy. Take your time." She patted his arm, friendlier than she'd ever behaved. "No reason for you to hurry. We have plenty of room." With that, she rushed to another booth.

Adam glanced at the packed room and the line out the door. Oh, sure, plenty of room. Within minutes he discovered that even if he were interested in Mattie, it wasn't conducive to romance to have half the town watching while the other half wished they'd stop eating and leave, giving up a booth big enough for four or five of them.

"You don't think she's too obvious, do you?" He attacked the pancakes.

"She's sweet." Mattie picked up a packet of jelly, tore it open, and spread the contents on her toast.

"No, she's not. She's controlling and has to be right."

"And she thinks every minister should be married, even women pastors. I've heard she's not too certain women should be in ministry unless we work with children, but if we are she wants us married." She grinned. "Right?"

He smiled back. "But only because she cares."

"You two are getting along well." Miss Birdie appeared with her ubiquitous coffeepot and topped off their nearly full cups.

Adam noticed she looked very pleased, probably sure her plan to marry off two ministers was going well.

The pillar wandered off but kept her eyes turned toward them. He should tell her that if she wanted to play matchmaker, she shouldn't hover or gawk. Instead, he took a bite of sausage. After a few bites, he studied the plates again. "Mattie, can I interest you in a piece of bacon? Sausage? Steak?"

"No, thanks. I'm fine." After taking a sip of coffee, she asked, "What are you preaching on Sunday?"

"I'm planning to use the lectionary text from the gospel. What about you?"

"Me, too. How are you going to approach it?"

For a few minutes the ministers discussed the meaning of the verses and their structure and historical background as well as examples they could use in a sermon. As they exchanged opinions, Adam noted and ignored Miss Birdie's fluttering around the table. He hadn't thought the pillar could do fluttering. She filled their cups, removed plates, even dropped ice in the overflowing glasses and brought more orange juice. Inside Adam laughed because he knew hearing them talk about the interpretation of biblical texts must make Miss Birdie crazy.

Besides, he was having fun. He liked discussing sermons with another minister, and he felt more comfortable with a woman than he had for years because he didn't think of Mattie as a woman—not that he'd tell her or Miss Birdie that. She seemed like another minister, a colleague but not a possible wife or a woman to impress or date. He felt at ease with her, and the constant surveillance of Miss Birdie amused him.

"I need to tell you something," Mattie said after Miss Birdie had run out of things to bring or empty or pick up or wipe down and had left several huge take-home boxes, which Adam filled with enough food for breakfasts for the next week. Before Mattie said more, she searched until she spotted Miss Birdie waiting on a table on the other side of the diner. "You are the nicest single man I've met in Butternut Creek."

"Oh? Are there many of us?"

"Actually, you're the only one I've met under fifty." She grinned. "Right now, I have no desire for a relationship. I broke my engagement before I came here and am not interested in anything, not for years."

"Pretty bad, huh?"

She nodded.

"Fine with me. I'm not interested in dating now, either. New job, new life." Adam leaned forward and spoke softly. Miss Birdie would probably believe that those heads close together meant something romantic. "How would you like to go to a movie every now and then or go out for lunch? Maybe discuss the lectionary once a week. That should throw the town matchmakers off."

"I'd like to. I could use a friend." She picked up her check. "Give me a call."

❦

At nine, after the preachers and most of the morning crowd had left, Birdie pulled out her cell phone and punched speed dial. She'd always thought they were a stupid expense until the girls became teenagers. Then they'd become necessities.

"A total waste of time. Not a spark between them," she said as soon as Mercedes answered. "They spent most of the time discussing the lectionary. What's the lectionary?"

"Someone divided up the Bible into verses to use in sermons."

"Why would anyone do that? What's wrong with the way the Bible was written, all those books. All together."

"The lectionary covers most of the Bible in a couple of years so you have an idea of the complete Bible instead of just sections."

"Sounds too complicated." Let down and disappointed, she shook her head, as if Mercedes could hear that. "Well, that's what they discussed. For nearly an hour. Hmph. Didn't work at all."

"It could," Mercedes answered. "After all, sometimes it takes a while for the seed to take root. They have something in common. Don't be so impatient."

"Bah, I'm not impatient."

"I'm not going to debate that with you because I have to get back to work. Bye."

After Mercedes disconnected, Birdie stared at the phone and wondered about her minister. Why hadn't he found a wife on his own? He was an attractive young man even though his hair was a lot longer than she felt a Christian young man should wear. Of course, Jesus wore his hair long, but Pastor Adam wasn't Jesus.

"Miss." One of her customers waved his hand and held up his cup. "Coffee."

She shoved the phone in her pocket and hurried toward him.

This matchmaking stuff was a lot harder than she'd remembered. Was there another single woman in town she could fix the man up with? Willow Thomas was her only thought, but she was saving her for Effie's nephew.

Which pretty much left her baffled, not her normal state and very uncomfortable.

Chapter Seven

Noise from outside once again jerked Sam awake far earlier than he wanted to be conscious.

This time the commotion didn't come from the exploding mortars or flashes of rockets that tormented his nightmares. No, someone was knocking on the front door. They did it again, with at least two sets of knuckles. And then again. Someone he didn't want to talk to—which included about everyone in the world—waited outside. The sound made waves of pain bounce against his skull from the inside.

He groaned. Although he didn't hear voices, he had an idea of exactly who stood outside and had changed to even more insistent hammering. He had learned that people in this town didn't leave when he ignored them, but he was still willing to try.

He squashed the pillow over his head so the streak of sunshine didn't hit him right in the eyes and tried to fall back asleep. If changing position didn't hurt so much, he'd turn over and bury his face in the mattress.

"Captain Peterson, it's Willow Thomas, the physical therapist from the hospital."

Exactly what he feared.

He squeezed his eyes shut, turned one ear against the mattress, and put the pillow over the other. Didn't work. He still heard the knocking and the shouting. It wasn't going to stop. The look in the PT's eyes yesterday had revealed a determined woman who didn't act like she'd turn aside from her duty because of a locked door or being ignored by the person inside.

He hated tenacity in a woman.

"I have my sons with me. They want to talk to you."

Oh, sure. He'd wager chatting with a worn-out, crippled shell of a man who'd yelled at them was exactly what those two kids wanted to do.

His head throbbed. With the pounding and shouting, the pain reached a higher level. Why wouldn't she go away? Didn't she have work?

"Captain, the boys have all day free and I'm staying here, with them, until noon. We're not leaving until you come out even if we have to knock on your door for the next three or four hours."

He couldn't escape. After all, the woman worked with amputees all the time. Probably understood them very well, knew their reactions. She probably believed that before they were wounded and became so angry and frustrated and rude, wounded veterans *had* been nice guys. She probably thought he was a nice guy, deep inside. He could easily prove her wrong, only not right now and not from his bedroom. He'd have to get up to show her what a jerk he could be.

He tossed the pillow aside, turned in bed, pushed himself to his foot, and shoved the crutches under his arms. He glanced at himself in the mirror. He looked like he'd come off a five-day binge. Maybe he should quit drinking so much. He considered that for a second before he decided it would be easier to take down the mirror instead.

"Hold on," he shouted. Last night he'd fallen asleep in his camo cutoffs and T-shirt. Wrinkled and scruffy but fairly clean, they covered most of him. Attempting to go around the worst of the trash, he caught a crutch on the carpet and with a loud expletive nearly collapsed in a heap. He regained his balance and shoved away from the wall, then hobbled across the living room to the front door. Once there, he glared at the three members of the Thomas family through the glass panel.

"Yeah?" he mumbled.

"Captain, the boys have something they want to say. Can we come in and talk to you?"

He looked behind him at the squalor of his house.

He hadn't minded the mess when the window man was here the other day—the repairman was a guy—but allowing these three in? Two kids and his PT? Besides, he wasn't sure what else lay under the mess. Probably mice and cockroaches. As far as he knew or cared, there could be wild boars or feral cats under it all.

The stench had begun to bother him yesterday but not enough to do anything about it. Now company waited. Maybe they'd leave as soon as they came in and the miasma nearly asphyxiated them. Of course, he didn't plan to let them in. He could stick his head outside, hear the apologies, and shut the door, coming back in alone.

When she saw the conditions, if she didn't run, Willow Thomas's eyes would be filled with sympathy, which he didn't need, or with disgust, which might be a good thing. Right now, he could see they sparkled with determination, which signaled she was not going away. Why fight the eventual outcome?

He flicked his glance toward the boys. Even with the spiked hair, they looked innocent but frightened. Shame filled him as he realized he couldn't let them see what he was really like.

When they'd been in before, the boys had entered the dining room—which he seldom used and was fairly uncontaminated. If he let them in, they'd see everything. Everything.

No, he didn't want them back inside, in the part of the house he used and trashed. Didn't want them to know what a slob he was or how much he drank or how little he cared about anything and certainly not how little he cared about himself or his future.

"Captain Peterson?" Willow repeated from outside. The determination in her voice convinced him even more she wouldn't be content to stay outside.

In an effort to make an inroad in the mess, he tried to kick bottles out of the way. Hard to do with only one leg. Sam took a few steps away from the door and used a crutch in an effort to shove a few under the sofa. He nearly fell between the cluttered end table and the pink velvet love seat.

Finally, he gave up with a curse, deciding he wouldn't feel ashamed. This chaos stated clearly who he was. He manipulated himself back to the door, opened it at the same time she pushed on it, then moved away so they could enter.

Willow didn't flinch when she and the boys entered. Probably had visited a few wounded vets in her time and knew what to expect, but the boys stood still, just inside the door, and studied the mess with wide eyes.

"Look at all the bottles," Nick said in a voice filled with awe.

"Do you recycle?" Leo asked.

He'd been wrong. The fact that kids had been exposed to his excesses made him feel more ashamed than he thought possible.

"Any pizza left?" Leo scampered toward a box.

"You wouldn't want it if there were," Sam said. "It's really old." He shoved an empty fried-chicken bucket off a chair and onto the floor, then lowered himself onto the sofa between a couple of Chinese delivery sacks and dropped his crutches on the floor before he asked, "To what do I owe this visit?"

"Boys, come here," she said to her sons. The boys' heads turned back and forth as they admired the jumble and heaps of trash. Finally, her words brought them back to reality and, he supposed, the reason they stood in the middle of his living room.

The two moved a few steps to stand next to their mother, reluctance showing in every step. The journey seemed as tortured and protracted as a trek through deep snow in weighted combat boots.

"Leo and Nick have something to tell you." When they didn't say a word, she nudged Leo.

"We're sorry, Captain Peterson," the older brother said. "We shouldn't have been playing in your backyard without your permission."

Nick nodded. "And I shouldn't have been throwing rocks. I'm sorry about your window."

Sam didn't say a word, just watched the trio and waited.

"The boys apologize for causing trouble and that you had to buy a new window. Unfortunately . . ." She paused, took a deep breath, and exhaled through her lips.

Beautiful, sensual lips that promised more than he wanted to consider now. Not that she actually *offered* anything other than the apology, but he wasn't too wounded to fantasize.

"Unfortunately," she repeated, "with our move and my starting a new job, money is a little short right now. The boys will work off their debt." She glanced at the boys, then toward him, uncertain for a moment. "If that would be convenient for you."

He couldn't imagine anything less convenient than having two kids around the house unless it would be the presence of these two kids and their mother.

The two boys nodded, looking as solemn as imps with spiked red hair and freckles could.

"No." Sam waved the offer away. "Not necessary."

"Yes, it is, Captain Peterson." Her chin jutted out a bit, only enough to show her determination. "They need to learn that bad behavior has consequences."

And *he* was the consequence? He grinned a little, inside. Being the consequence not the instigator of bad behavior was a first. It amused him. At the same time, he had no interest in actually being the consequence, and had to get the idea out of her determined, red-headed mind. He sat forward and clasped his hands in front of him. "The boys tell me that your husband ran off with a younger woman."

At his statement, she paled. For a moment, he regretted the words even though he'd meant to hurt her. But his inability to behave in a civilized manner should make her gather her sons and make a dignified, if quick, departure. Actually, he'd prefer an undignified departure—he'd like to see her scramble out.

He'd obviously underestimated the character of Willow Thomas.

She lifted that chin a fraction of an inch more and stared at him. "That does not mean that Leo and Nick can get away with breaking a window and not taking responsibility for the damage. Although it may not appear that way to you now"—she glared at each son—"they were raised to behave better."

She looked so brave and the boys so solemn that he had to steel himself. These were exactly the kind of people he'd have enjoyed before . . . All the more reason to beat her off with words and attitude.

"Ms. Thomas, I'm not going to take care of your sons because you can't control them."

That should do it.

She took another deep breath, but before she could say anything, Leo stepped forward. "Sir, Mom expects us to behave ourselves. We were wrong to play in your yard without your permission and really wrong to break your window. Now we have to man up."

The old Sam, the pre-injury Sam, would've laughed to have his words used against him. This Sam shook his head. "You can't shame me into this."

"Please, Mister . . . um, Captain." Leo took another step toward Sam and swallowed. "Please. We're good kids and we won't bother you, but we can"—he looked at the mess—"we *can* clean this place. We're good at that. We know how to vacuum and dust. Mom's taught us a lot of stuff."

"Please?" The younger brother used every bit of his body to express his contrition: quivering lips, sad eyes, and bowed posture. Sam thought even the spikes in his hair bent in shame.

He thought he'd discarded compassion for others in the strife of the last few months, but the remorse of these two kids was more than he could handle. He recognized it as emotional blackmail. It worked.

"All right." He gave up, amazed at how easily the family had defeated him. "You can police the area."

"Yes, sir," Leo said. "Thank you."

At the same time Nick said, "Wow! We get to police the area."

Willow nodded. "Thank you. How much did the window and the installation cost?"

"Four hundred dollars."

The boys gasped.

"That means each of the boys owes you two hundred dollars' worth of work. At five dollars an hour, that means forty hours of work each. Does that seem fair?"

"Too much."

She glared at him, and he found himself nodding. He could shut himself in his bedroom if he had to and drink himself under the bed.

"Was there any other damage?" She looked at Sam, then at the boys.

"No, that's all," Sam answered. "Forty hours of work from each." Would he survive it?

"When can they start?" She glanced at her watch.

"What day is it?" Didn't really make a difference. Every day seemed the same to him. He only remembered appointments because someone called him the day before to remind him.

"Thursday."

"Next week," he said. Maybe they'd forget by then.

"We can start right now, Captain," Leo said.

Sam shook his head to clear it, but it didn't help. He'd planned to sleep until noon at least, but before he could suggest next week again, Willow spoke.

"I have cleaning supplies in the car. Boys, go get them."

As the two ran out, he glared at her. "Don't you think I have cleaning supplies?"

In fact, he didn't. He'd used up the bits left in his aunt's pantry and hadn't bought more because it was hard enough just to carry food home. Besides, he'd had no desire to clean. Living like this had seemed right, but still, her assumption was insulting.

"Of course you do, but you shouldn't have to pay for them. Not when my sons did the damage."

He nodded.

"I brought some work to do," she said.

Sam noticed the laptop hanging from her shoulder. He hadn't noticed that when she came in. What man would when a woman looked like her?

"I have a lot of paperwork to catch up on." She checked her watch. "I'll stay until noon and fix you all lunch before I leave."

"Ma'am, despite the fact that I'm disabled, I'm perfectly capable of supervising two kids."

"Of course you are."

He could read the implication. Although she'd read his file and knew his background, she was careful with her sons except when they ran around on their own. He admired that.

"You don't want to leave them alone with a stranger, especially one whose house is filled with bottles and trash," he said. "I have a lot of bad habits, but I don't hurt kids."

She didn't agree or argue or deign to answer but turned toward the dining room, picking up bottles as she went. As she moved away, she left a view of that great derriere and a trail of perfume that floated behind her and smelled so sweet it masked the odor of the room for a second or two.

The boys came loudly back into the house, loaded with supplies. To make sure they understood his reluctance, he frowned.

Didn't faze them.

"We'll start by picking up the cans and bottles," Nick said.

"No, leave that for me," Sam said. He didn't want these two picking up beer cans and drained tequila and bourbon bottles.

"I'll take care of the bottles," Willow said.

He nodded. "Okay, you guys shovel up the other trash while I take a shower and get dressed."

"Go ahead." Leo waved him away. "We'll be fine. We know how to do this."

"Yeah, we're good at it." Nick dropped his bucket on the floor. "We clean for Mom all the time."

No matter what they did, it couldn't get any worse. Not even a herd of goats could make this any worse.

"You sure have ugly furniture," Nick said.

"Remember your manners," his mother said.

"Shut up," Leo whispered.

Sam bet the older brother had just given the younger an elbow to the ribs, but he hadn't seen it. He turned toward the bathroom and longed to shut himself inside while these two fought it out and while the luscious Willow Thomas leaned down to pick up trash. Because he hated to miss a single second of her efforts, he delayed the shower for a few minutes, until she finished.

Chapter Eight

Before lunch a few weeks later, Adam wandered over to the square, not a place he frequented. In the middle of a green lawn and big trees sat the courthouse, an ornate brick edifice built in 1865 with a tower and cupolas on each corner. A street wrapped around it with several gift shops, a tearoom, and an antiques mall facing the turreted brick building. Butternut Creek even had a small country music venue across from the courthouse, a site that must have once housed a movie theater.

Benson's Barbershop was between a tanning salon and the library and looked a lot like the shop his father had taken him to as a kid. Adam entered and sat down to wait because the barber stood at a huge chair, cutting the hair of an elderly man. On the counter were a couple of jars filled with combs and a blue liquid, a germicide, Adam guessed. Hunting and fishing magazines covered a table.

"There you go, Roscoe," the barber said finishing up with the elderly man. He opened a bottle of something red that smelled like roses and rubbing alcohol, patted it on Roscoe's neck, then lowered the chair and said, "I'm Joe Bob. What can I do for you, young man?"

When Roscoe departed, Adam climbed into the chair. The barber tied a cape on him and raised the chair. "I like my hair long on the top and shorter than it is around the ears and in the back," he explained. In the mirror, he watched Joe Bob nod.

The barber picked up a clipper, turned it on, and started in. Before Adam could say *That's too short*, the man had nearly skinned him. Adam could feel his head growing larger—at least, that's how it looked in the mirror—as his hair got shorter.

Then Joe Bob put the clippers back on the counter, took a pair of scissors and a comb from the disinfectant, and started trimming. Adam sat mute, because he couldn't think of anything to say. Besides, the damage had been done with the first pruning. After three minutes, the barber dropped the tools onto the counter and opened that bottle of red liquid.

"No, thank you," Adam said quickly. He didn't want to smell like roses on top of having no hair left.

"Eight dollars."

Adam took out his wallet, handed the barber a ten, and glanced at himself in the mirror. He had whitewalls an inch wide over both ears—and, he imagined, in the back, but he refused to use the mirror to check on that. The top measured a quarter inch if stretched. He looked like a new marine recruit. On marines, the shearing looked macho, but Adam looked like a hayseed, like Oliver Hardy. Like . . . he didn't know like what, but not himself.

After five seconds of observing the scalping, he couldn't take it. He turned and ran, leaving the barber a two-dollar tip he couldn't afford because he couldn't watch his reflection long enough for Joe Bob to hand him change. On the other hand, this was a bargain. For ten dollars, he wouldn't need to pay for a haircut for months.

❧

"Pastor Jordan?" Birdie MacDowell tapped gently on the carved door of the pastor's study. Adam knew it was Miss Birdie because Maggie had shouted the information when Miss Birdie's ancient van pulled into the parking lot.

The pillar, not usually so meek, didn't come in. Had a summons directly from her minister filled her with dread?

Adam should have known better. When he got to it, he discovered the door was locked. He opened it and the pillar shoved the door wide to dash inside, followed, of course, by Mercedes.

"Why did you call us? Has someone died?" Miss Birdie glanced around her as if expecting a grieving family in the study. "Was there an accident? I know a tree didn't fall on the church because I didn't see any damage."

Frightened the summons would give her a heart attack, Adam hurried to say, "No, nothing like that." The words didn't calm her.

"A fire in the kitchen?"

"Bird, calm down." Mercedes patted her friend's back, then turned toward Adam. He could tell the exact moment she noticed the haircut. She stopped talking, her eyes grew larger, and her mouth dropped open. Quickly recovering, she said, "Every time Bird's called to the preacher's study, she worries. She's certain something terrible has happened to someone in the church."

"Oh, my Lord." The pillar stopped glaring at the chaos of the minister's study and scrutinized him. Then she stalked toward him, keeping her eyes on his newly visible ears. "You got a haircut." Her voice filled with awe.

"As ordered," he said.

"Look, Mercedes." Miss Birdie pointed at Adam as if her friend couldn't figure this out on her own.

"I noticed, Pastor." Mercedes put her hand over her mouth— probably hiding a smile or perhaps stifling a giggle.

He couldn't blame her.

"You must have gone to Benson's on the square, didn't you?" the pillar asked. "They cater to the old men and the ranchers." She shook her head. "Good thing your ears aren't too big or you'd look like a jug."

Having Miss Birdie notice that his ears didn't stick out didn't make him feel a bit better.

"You might should go to Marble Falls, next time, Preacher," Mercedes suggested. "You know, the best thing about hair is it grows."

The pillar continued to stare, her glance falling to his newly naked neck. "Terrible cut. Your neck's long and bare, like a giraffe's."

Exactly what he wanted to hear.

"No, it's not, Bird. You know giraffes have fur," Mercedes said.

As if that helped.

"But all in all, you do look better," Miss Birdie added.

"Don't worry, Preacher," Mercedes added. "It looks . . ." Adam thought she wanted to say more, but he was learning she had a complete inability to lie. She didn't utter another word.

In an effort to change the subject, Adam waved toward the cleared chairs. He now had much smaller piles of books and papers *beside* each chair. A great improvement in his opinion, but he could tell by her posture Miss Birdie didn't share that view. "Please make yourselves comfortable, ladies."

"Comfortable would be in the kitchen where we have pie and coffee," Miss Birdie grumbled.

"Now, Bird," Mercedes chided. "Preacher, she doesn't always realize how crabby she sounds."

Miss Birdie straightened and turned regally toward her friend. "Yes, Mercedes, I do. I sound the way I want to sound."

Before the two could argue more—an event that probably happened fairly often—Adam said, "But there's no privacy in the kitchen and I need to talk to you about something confidential."

The Widows exchanged a satisfied glance when they heard the word *confidential*.

"After all," he added, reeling them in, "anyone might walk into the kitchen or overhear our conversation from the fellowship hall. If I had important, private, hush-hush information to share with the two of you, I wouldn't want anyone to overhear."

Her attention grabbed, Miss Birdie seated herself and asked, "What is it, Pastor?"

As Mercedes settled in another chair, the pillar studied Adam. As much as Adam had rehearsed what he planned to say, speaking and looking at Miss Birdie at the same time made him more than nervous. She'd pick up on that uncertainty and exploit it.

So he looked at Mercedes instead and took a deep breath in an effort to calm himself. "I'm not sure exactly how to phrase this."

"Should've thought about that before you invited us to your office," Miss Birdie stated.

Adam could feel his lips quiver. Her predictability amused him, but only for a second or two. When she noticed his expression, she glared. Had she thought he was laughing at her? He hoped not. He bet no one laughed at Birdie MacDowell.

He continued solemnly. "You're right as usual, but the matter is a little sticky."

"Has Harvey Wallace finally run off with his receptionist?" Mercedes asked.

"Did the bank turn the church down for the loan for the new air-conditioning unit?" Miss Birdie said at the same time.

"No, no." He gave them a quick update on the lack of action on the air-conditioning before, smiling at both of them, he returned to the subject at hand. "You know how much I appreciate everything the Widows have done for our church."

Miss Birdie nodded. "We're still doing it, Pastor. We aren't done yet." She spoke forcefully, as if warning him of the consequences should he dare to stick his nose in the business of the Widows.

"Of course not. Everyone tells me you're miracle workers. I know that from how you welcomed me—you're practically the welcome committee of Butternut Creek. And you do so much for the congregation and the town. Truly, you are the heart of the church."

Both Widows smiled proudly.

"Yes, we know, but it's pleasant to have it confirmed." Miss Birdie nodded with the grace of royalty.

"Howard tells me there were six of you only two years ago." He pretended to study the list on the desk. "Now there are only two Widows."

"Oh, yes." Mercedes sat forward in her chair. "Effie Bannister died and Blanche Moore went to live in a nursing home in Cedar Park. Emilia Post moved to Atlanta to stay with her daughter."

"And Jenny Dunn married her no-good second cousin and went to live with him in Conway," Miss Birdie finished.

"With only two of you left, I'm concerned." Adam shook his head in an effort to show sympathy and worry. "How can you do all the good works the Widows have always done? Strong and willing and committed as you are, the two of you cannot do *everything*."

"We don't do everything," Mercedes said. "As much as we try. Pansy Martin helps a lot."

"But she's not a widow, you know," Birdie said, watching Adam closely as if she'd picked up on his purpose.

"No, her husband is amazingly healthy for a man his age," Mercedes added. "Will probably live for years."

Before either woman could say more, Adam continued, keeping his voice clear and pastoral. "The Widows are a living treasure. We don't want to wear the two of you out."

Mercedes preened at his words. Miss Birdie looked skeptical.

"Are you setting us up for something?" the pillar asked. Her expression said that whatever it was, she would not like it.

"Mercedes." He leaned toward her and smiled. "You keep the town library working wonderfully and keep up with your big family."

He turned his gaze toward Miss Birdie. "And you're so busy with your job and taking care of your granddaughters. With everything else you do, I don't want to take advantage."

He attempted to color the words with both admiration and concern, but Miss Birdie wasn't buying a word of it.

"My job's just not hard, Pastor, and my granddaughters don't take a lot of care. I can handle it all."

"Never thought you couldn't, but I don't want to take advantage of your good nature."

When Mercedes laughed, Miss Birdie glared at her. He'd probably gone too far with that last remark. Possibly no one in Butternut Creek would describe the pillar as *good-natured*. Adam hurried to distract them.

"Do you mind if we have a word of prayer?" Without waiting for an answer, he bowed his head. "Mighty and most merciful God, we come before You with praise for these women and their service." He glanced up to see Miss Birdie frowning, as if attempting to discover where the prayer was leading. He quickly lowered his gaze. "We ask, most loving God, that You will find others to share their good works and that You strengthen all who serve You. Amen."

Finished and feeling fortified, Adam said, "I have a few pastoral concerns to share with you."

He picked up several index cards from his desk. "Sam Peterson," Adam read, then glanced at the women. "I still haven't been able to get in touch with him."

"Such a sad thing." Mercedes shook her head. "He used to visit Effie during the summer, played baseball with my son. Now he's lost his leg. I hear he lives like a hermit."

With an echoing shake of her head, Miss Birdie added, "We set up a schedule to make sure he has enough to eat. When I call him, he doesn't answer the phone. I saw him at the hospital and invited him to church, but he wouldn't talk to me."

"Guess the best we can do is keep him in our prayers and keep trying." He dropped the card on the desk and looked at the next. "Willow Thomas has come back to town."

"Yes," Mercedes said. "I knew her back when she was Willow Brubaker, kin to the Brubakers down on Lampasas Road." She pointed east. "The Brubakers lived in the big yellow house next to where the post office used to be. Willow went off to school, married a man from Chicago about ten or twelve years ago, here in the sanctuary."

"I saw her at the hospital, too," Miss Birdie added. "She said she'd be coming to church."

"As usual, you ladies already know more than I do."

He picked up another card and gazed at it. "Winnie Jenkins gave me the information on the woman they hired as the new CEO of the asphalt company. She's very new to town."

Mercedes reached for the card. "I'll call her."

Adam handed her the card. "Winnie recommends you give her another week or two to get settled, both in her apartment and the company."

"Oh, Winnie did, did she?" Miss Birdie said, then made a low *grumph* sound. "Who is she to make suggestions? The nerve."

Adam had no idea what to say to diffuse the unexpected.

Fortunately, Mercedes ignored her friend and slid the information into a zippered pocket of her purse. "I'll handle this," she said evenly.

Before continuing, Adam took a deep breath. A mistake. The pillar's expression showed she'd noted the hesitation and didn't think she'd like the next suggestion.

"As I said, I talked to Winnie Jenkins lately."

"Bossiest woman I've ever met," Miss Birdie mumbled.

"Hush, Bird," Mercedes hissed.

Adam kept going, hardly skipping a beat, afraid the pillar would interrupt if he did. Not that anything he said or did would waylay a determined Miss Birdie. "She's at loose ends now. Since she retired from the plant, she doesn't have anything to do."

"I understand. The business was her whole life, Pastor," Mercedes said. "Except for coming to church, I don't think she had another interest but work."

"Difficult to be a woman in a man's business," he added.

Miss Birdie sniffed. "An asphalt company. How in the world did a woman get into the asphalt business?"

"A lot of hard work," Adam said, attempting to sound more like a minister than he felt at the moment. "I know both you ladies understand and respect hard work and dedication." He ran his thumb across the corner of the cards.

"Preacher, you seem nervous," Mercedes said. Then her expression changed, as if she'd suddenly understood his nervousness, the *real* reason he'd asked them to his office. When she glanced at her friend, Adam's eyes followed hers.

"Winnie's not a widow, you know," Miss Birdie said, biting her words off clearly so any idiot—even her young, inexperienced minister—could understand exactly what she meant. "She's never been married."

"Yes, I know. That's why I hesitate to ask."

The pillar's eyes narrowed. "Ask us what, Pastor?"

Adam took another deep breath. "If you could find it in your hearts, I wonder if you could make her an honorary Widow. She's looking for a place to serve."

Miss Birdie raised an eyebrow and said, "An honorary Widow?"

"She's an intelligent, active woman who suddenly doesn't have a thing in the world to do. In my opinion, she'd be a big help with the important jobs you do."

For a moment, Miss Birdie studied her minister as if she couldn't believe he'd asked this seriously.

"I don't believe you know who the Widows are, not completely," Mercedes said with a slight edge to her usually soft voice. "You want us to invite an old . . . umm . . . an unmarried woman to become one of the *Widows*?"

"Preacher, you've started meddling." For a moment, Miss Birdie closed her eyes. "Although it may be I don't know everything."

His mouth almost dropped open.

"Those last few words, Preach, those are Bird trying to sound less grumpy," Mercedes explained.

Miss Birdie turned toward her friend and glared. "You don't have to blurt out everything you think."

That reaction pretty much destroyed the idea of the pillar's being less irritable.

Then, looking like the voice of reason and acceptance, Miss Birdie turned back to Adam and smiled, one of the affable smiles he'd begun to distrust. "But she's an old maid," she clarified. "A spinster as my mother used to say."

"Perhaps a bachelor or a single lady," he suggested.

Miss Birdie nodded. "Possibly, but *we* are called the Widows for a reason. She is not a widow. However," she said magnanimously, "we'll consider it."

Mercedes nodded as well. "We'll get back to you."

Probably the best outcome he could hope for.

❦

"I heard—" Hector's voice was tinged with disbelief and betrayal as he approached Adam. "We've all heard you're a minister." He looked back at the other guys, who shook their heads. They had just finished a game, and Hector and Adam and a team of three of Hector's friends had lost. "Say it isn't true. Are you a preacher, Pops?"

"Is that so terrible?"

"Oh, yeah," Hector said. "Why didn't you tell us?"

"Why should I? When I tell people I'm a minister, they change. They don't feel comfortable. I just want to play ball."

"But how can we . . . cuss and push and all with a minister around?"

"That's what I mean." Adam took the ball, dribbled down the court, and put up a shot like the one that had been blocked. It went in. "I'm just like you but older and with a cleaner vocabulary. Don't worry." He tossed the ball back to Hector.

"But Pops . . ."

"Maybe I'll see you in church some Sunday morning. Christian Church on the highway. Service starts at ten thirty." He smiled. The guys didn't.

As Adam walked away, he could feel eighteen eyes watching his progress. He turned back. "You'd better get used to who I am because I'm coming back."

❦

"Bye, Roy," Birdie called to the manager as she left the diner between her shifts. She'd stop at Busch's Bakery. Always good food there. As she pulled her tips out and counted them, she entered the store.

"I'd like that dobos torte." She gulped as she saw the price. It would take most of her tip money, but she had to buy it. She was on a mission.

Butch Busch—how could a parent give a child such a terrible nickname?—studied her for a second. "I could cut the torte in half. That would be exactly the right size for a small family."

"But no one would want the other half of a torte."

"Sure they will. I do this all the time." He took a knife, sliced the pastry in half, and placed the larger section in a box.

She knew he didn't. Everyone in town knew about everyone else's struggles. With the worry about jobs, she bet not all that many people bought pastry items. Butch's were expensive because he used real butter and pure imported vanilla. Worth every penny, but Butch knew she couldn't afford the entire thing.

After she counted out the coins, he handed her a little box he'd tied with a lovely blue ribbon bow.

"Thanks, Butch."

"You're welcome. It feels good to know someone's going to enjoy that."

She hoped the recipient would. Heading down the street, her steps grew slower the closer she got to Effie Bannister's house. Remembering the conversation at the hospital, she knew she wouldn't be welcome, but maybe this gift from the bakery would help. If he opened the door, she might could slip around him and get inside the house for a short chat. Surely he couldn't push an old lady out.

Surprised, she paused on the sidewalk in front of the house. The old newspapers that had dotted the yard had disappeared. She strolled up the walk, now swept clean, and noticed a lovely red geranium on the porch. The window of the front door sparkled. It looked almost as nice as it had before Effie passed, before it stood empty for months. The porch swing still looked a little rickety but, on the whole, certainly better than it had since Effie's nephew moved in.

What had happened? Maybe he hired a service, but she didn't think so. No use speculating. She climbed the steps to the porch and knocked. No one came.

She knocked again. Over and over, for nearly three minutes until she heard cursing coming from inside. The young man certainly sounded like a marine, but even that experience couldn't have prepared him for how stubborn she could be.

He tossed the door open and leaned against the jamb. "What's wrong with you people?" He glared at her. "Haven't you learned to go away when someone doesn't answer your knock?"

"I'm Birdie MacDowell. We met at the hospital."

He nodded.

"I was a friend of your aunt."

He nodded again.

"May I come in?"

She could tell from his scowl he didn't want her inside so she squeezed between his broad shoulders, the crutch, and the doorjamb. Once inside, she walked to Effie's pink floral sofa before she turned to watch him. He looked flummoxed. People often responded to her like that.

"Thank you," she said. "Are you going to stay in Butternut Creek for a while?" She placed the box on the coffee table and sat on a chair upholstered in floral brocade. Although the decorating had obviously been done by a woman and years earlier, the place looked better than she'd expected for a bachelor's place. Tidy.

He balanced on the crutches and moved toward her, then dropped onto the sofa. "Don't know."

"If you do, you might want to paint." She looked at the wallpaper with roses climbing trellises. "Effie sure did like pink."

He didn't say a word.

"And fix that porch swing. Someone could get hurt."

He didn't look as if he cared.

With a gentle shove, she pushed the bakery box toward him. "I remember how much you used to like dobos tortes when you spent your summers here."

He stared at the box before he lifted his gaze to her. He smiled and almost ten years fell from his face. He looked like the happy, carefree teenager she'd known. Oh, it wasn't a big smile, but it was worth every penny she'd paid for the pastry.

"You remembered?" he said in a soft, disbelieving voice. "You brought me a dobos torte?" He untied the bow and looked inside the box. "Aunt Effie made these every time I visited."

"She said you could eat more than any boy she ever saw."

For a moment he looked at the torte hungrily, as if he wanted to drag a finger through the caramel topping, down through the chocolate buttercream, and lick it clean.

Instead, he looked up at her. "Would you like a piece?" he asked politely.

"Thank you, but there's just enough for you. Now"—she shook her finger at him, then pointed toward the kitchen—"you'll want to refrigerate that."

"Yes, ma'am, but I don't think it's going to last that long." He smiled—a big smile this time—and put the box back on the table. "Thank you."

"We'd like you to come to church someday."

He shrugged but didn't say no.

"I'm glad you're back. We all are." She stood. "I'm sorry about the injury."

His face contracted into the furrows and lines of pain.

"How old are you?" she asked. "I remember you played baseball with Mercedes's nephew Felipe. He's twenty-seven or -eight."

He nodded but didn't say anything, so she kept prodding. "He's married, two kids. Are you married?"

When he didn't answer and she couldn't think of anything to say that didn't sound even ruder than she usually allowed herself to be, she said, "Hope you enjoy that torte. I'll let myself out."

She walked toward the door, but before she could open it he said from the sofa, "Thank you, Miss Birdie." He cleared his throat. "You'll never know how much I appreciate this."

Once she'd closed the door and stood on the porch, she congratulated herself. She'd made an inroad. Now she'd have to tell Mercedes. They'd work on getting inside again and bringing him food, make him feel like part of the town, maybe get him to church. Exactly what the boy needed. Later, they could attempt a little matchmaking. She feared working something romantic out between two people with problems like Willow Thomas and Sam would take a lot of effort, but she knew where his interest lay. Only meant they had to set up opportunities between the two and push Willow a little.

On top of that, they still had to find a woman for the preacher to fall in love with. The Reverend Patillo seemed real nice, but Birdie hadn't seen a single spark between them.

No, Birdie was fresh out of ideas. She'd considered everyone she knew, people at church and at the diner. Granddaughters' friends were all too young. Mercedes might have some suggestions. And yet with everything on Birdie's plate and all Mercedes did with her family and with only two Widows left to carry the load—well, it wore her out.

Maybe they could use some help, like the preacher had suggested.

She had her job and the girls plus all the time she spent to keep the church headed in the right direction. This matchmaking might could take a lot of planning and work. She had no idea how to start. Life and love had changed a lot since she'd married her Elmer—bless his soul—over forty years earlier.

All right, they could use help. Not that the preacher's suggestion would work. Even if he'd suggested different words to describe her situation, Winnie Jenkins was still an old maid. Although Birdie's love life was long behind her, at least she'd had one. What did an old maid know about romance?

On top of that, Winnie Jenkins was the bossiest woman Birdie had ever known.

Chapter Nine

After lunch on Monday, Willow dropped the boys off in front of Captain Peterson's house. Her first impulse, once the boys were out of the car, was to drive away immediately, not even waiting to make sure they got inside okay. She knew why. Oh, yes, she did. The sight of the man filled her with the most unprofessional thoughts: longing and even—doggone it!—desire. She could feel the draw of the man out here, fifty feet away from him, separated by the wall of the house. What an absurd reaction for a woman with two children and very little trust in men.

What a coward she'd become, to refuse to approach the captain. What a terrible mother. She forced herself to wait, to make sure her sons got inside safely, as if there were danger that the boys would be captured or attacked on the short sidewalk between her car and the front door in a residential neighborhood in Butternut Creek.

Forcing herself not to take off as if the Indy 500 had begun and she was the lead car, she waved to the boys when they reached the porch, watched them knock and enter the house. Sam waved back at her, then closed the door.

She had to face facts. The sight of the man gave her a pleasant rush. For a moment she remembered herself as the high school junior who used to drive past Stephen Nielson's house in the hope of catching a glimpse of him. She'd had such a crush on him. One day he'd been in his yard when she drove by. The sight of him had so unnerved her she'd stopped the car with a squeal of tires, thrown it into reverse, and backed down the street at fifty miles an hour so he wouldn't see her. As if everyone in town didn't know her mother's old red convertible. How cool had she been?

Obviously, age plus all her education and marriage and the birth of two sons hadn't elevated her level of coolness. She wanted to catch a glimpse of the captain nearly as much as, paradoxically, she didn't.

She attributed this need to her wounded ego and her low libido, severely damaged by her husband's defection to Barbie-doll Tiffany who had no sags or stretch marks.

Then her cell rang. She grabbed it and flipped it open.

"Willow, where are you?" Trixie said. "You have a patient waiting."

"Be right there." She glanced at her watch. For heaven's sake, she'd sat there for several minutes mooning about the man. How completely unprofessional. How immature.

Before she could consider at length what an idiot she'd become, she put the car in gear and took off, forcing her mind back to the business at hand and away from her foolish yearning.

❦

"Oo-rah," Sam shouted. A trickle of sweat eased down his back. Little shade in his backyard. The only tree had lost its leaves already, which didn't seem right. Not that he knew anything about trees, but it seemed too early for that. Maybe he could get Leo and Nick to research the problem—which would give him a little peace, use up a few of their hours, and maybe save the tree.

The boys threw their thin shoulders back and echoed his words. "Oo-rah."

"Semper fi, men," Sam said.

"Semper fi," the boys repeated. Their lips twitched a little as if they were attempting to hide grins.

"No smiles, Gyrenes." Sam had about reached the end of his marine vocabulary, at least the words he could use in front of kids.

"Sir, no, sir." They stood straight, kept their expressions serious, and watched every move Sam made.

Which presented a problem. Sam had no idea what to do next. On top of that, the prosthesis Willow had cushioned had begun to hurt a little. Oh, it felt a lot better, but still didn't feel like a real leg.

Since noon, the boys had cleared the yard, a patch so small it had taken only an hour to pull weeds and pick up a few pieces of trash. They'd cut the grass using an old push mower Sam showed them how to oil. Not that there was much grass. Aunt Effie hadn't been any better a gardener than he was and probably hadn't watered the lawn when she was so ill. Here and there a few clumps of grass and weeds huddled together, shorter now but dry and close to death.

The brothers watched him with what looked like admiration. A heady experience for him but not an emotion anyone should feel toward him.

Of course, with his eyes slightly clearer—he'd finished off only a few longnecks the previous evening, placed the bottles in the trash, and actually fallen asleep at a normalish hour—he didn't look like quite as much of a wreck as that first day. He'd shaved this morning, nicking himself a couple of times. Even with those wounds, he didn't look completely disreputable.

"Gyrenes, how many hours have you worked today?"

"Six, sir."

They knew they hadn't worked forty hours. His reckoning said they'd worked thirty-one each. He could tell them they were finished, that they'd earned all the money they owed him, but he knew they wouldn't accept his ignoring the remaining hours of work. They didn't want to disappoint their mother. Besides, he enjoyed having them here, though he'd never admit it.

"Sir, I looked in the shed and carport. You don't have a hose," Leo said. "And you don't have a sprinkler."

"I found a spigot on the side of the house," Nick added. "It works. You have water."

"We can go to the hardware store on the highway. It's only two blocks away." Leo pointed vaguely to the south. "Mom lets us walk there by ourselves."

He knew she did because she'd given them money to buy him a dipped cone from the Dairy Queen next to the hardware store. They'd walked from there to here with only a few licks missing, because they'd had to stop the dripping.

Reaching in a pocket, he pulled out his wallet and handed them some bills. "Get what you think we need, but stay within budget, okay?"

They took off running. Sam walked to the small patio, poured himself a glass of water, and waited.

Last week, the junior marines had swept and wiped and vacuumed and cleaned. He'd documented the hours each boy had worked inside. He even counted the time spent eating the lunches their mother had brought or prepared, but he was running out of chores.

Yesterday they'd sprayed and squeegeed windows, cleaned out the kitchen cabinets. They'd packed up some of Aunt Effie's dishes and clothing and possessions like the lacy tablecloth and fluffy mint-green bedspread he'd never use. The boys stacked the bags and boxes on the front steps.

When their mother brought lunch, they'd stuffed several bags in her car. She'd promised to drop them off at the community thrift shop, then left them alone to eat and work. Her attitude had seemed very professional, like he was her patient, but he'd seen her studying him once or twice with what he thought was a spark of interest. Could he fan it into an ember? Maybe a fire? Did he still know how to do that?

Not that he wanted to. Not that he needed anyone now, and he felt certain she didn't, either.

So why did he keep thinking about her and their being together?

Whenever he got the chance, he watched her leave, had even dragged himself to the front door so he could observe her. Today she didn't get out of the car. Disappointing. Just that little bounce in her step and wiggle in her hips made the day worthwhile.

Stupid to feel this way, dumb to want what he couldn't and shouldn't have. What in the world would a woman like her, educated and gorgeous and the mother of two great kids, find attractive about a worn-out loser like him?

With her professional training and experience, Willow Thomas—unlike most women—knew what lay beneath the face that attracted other women, knew about the pit that existed in his soul, was aware it drew in anything positive and hurled it into the dark chaos inside him. And yet, once she'd vetted him, she'd left her children with him. Maybe she didn't think he was as bad as he knew he was. Not that he'd ever hurt the boys, but he was hardly the ideal example for them.

Within twenty minutes, the boys were back with a long hose, a receipt, and his change, plus the biggest, most gimmicky sprinkler he could imagine.

"See, this part goes around in circles," Nick demonstrated, "to get the grass around the sprinkler, and the top part spurts water like a fountain to really soak the ground."

"And there's a button on the bottom so you can change the pattern from a square to a circle." Leo showed him how to do exactly that.

"I think that is one of the most amazing inventions I've seen in years." He bet it wouldn't last a week, but the kids were so proud and excited about it, he didn't say that.

"They had one that you could program to roll across the lawn," Leo said.

"But it cost too much." Nick added.

"This one looks terrific. Good job, Gyrenes."

"Thank you, sir." Nick saluted.

"We'll hook it up now." Leo ran off.

Within five minutes, the sprinkler was pumping out water and spraying and making loud hissing sounds. Might not last, but he had to admire the creativity of the person who'd designed this incredibly complicated and shiny piece of equipment that threw out torrents of water in all directions and sounded as if there were an angry cat inside.

The boys were delighted with themselves and the purchase.

"We have to show that to Mom," Nick said.

Sam doubted she'd be deeply interested in the contraption but knew she'd come to the backyard, *ooh* and *aah*, because her sons purchased and set it up. He really admired how much she cared about the boys.

He grinned. They were great kids. He'd like them around even if they didn't have a gorgeous, intriguing mother. He'd miss them when they finished their hours. Oh, yeah, he wouldn't mind sleeping late or not picking up after himself before they came, struggling to wipe off the kitchen counters, but he'd miss the companionship and the way they seemed to look up to him. A balm to his scarred soul.

What had happened to the man he'd been a few weeks ago?

"What's inside that door inside?" Nick asked. "You know, the one you never open."

Leo elbowed his brother in the ribs and muttered, "Shut up."

After he glared at his brother, Nick continued, "You know, the other door off the living room. One goes to the bathroom. One goes to your bedroom. What's behind the third door?"

"Oh, yeah." Sam dropped onto the sofa. "That's the extra bedroom. For my father."

"Your father?" Nick looked at Sam with huge eyes. "You have a father?"

"Everybody's got a father." Leo scoffed. "Someplace." Then he turned to Sam. "Where's yours? Is he coming to visit?"

"The general's in DC now. He'll be here in a few weeks, maybe."

"We should make sure his bedroom's clean," Leo said.

They were right. When Sam arrived, he'd taken the first bedroom he came to because he'd been exhausted after the trip. His father would sleep in the other bedroom when he arrived. Sam hadn't opened that door because he didn't want to think about that ever happening. Still, he'd have to face his father's presence someday, and now seemed like a good time, with the boys here. "All right, marines, let's police these quarters."

"Sir, yes, sir." The boys ran inside ahead of him and opened the door to the unused bedroom.

"It doesn't smell good, Captain," Nick said.

"Probably need to air it out. Can I open a window, sir?" Leo added.

By the time Sam arrived at the door, Leo had thrown the window open. A breeze blew through and ruffled the feminine white lace curtains. Sam had sneaked out that window as a kid to wander through the neighborhood. Once he'd met up with Annie Morgan in the park for his first make-out session. Probably shouldn't share those memories with the boys.

Nick had pulled the bedspread back. "No sheets."

"Get some from the linen closet in the bathroom."

"We need to check in the closet and dresser, sir, to see if there's anything inside to clear out," Leo said.

Sam nodded. "Take the closet and I'll go through the dresser."

In less than an hour they'd finished. The room smelled better after Nick bombed it with air freshener, which caused a five-minute evacuation. Once back in the room, they made the bed and put together a small bag of stored clothing and knick-knacks for Willow to take to the thrift store. Leo had insisted they hang a framed photo of bluebonnets found in the closet, to brighten the room. It took another ten minutes to decide where to put it, measure, and pound a hanger into the wall.

What next? Sam wondered as he considered the bright room and the punch of color from the bluebonnets. Nothing left to do in here. Maybe if they went outside, he could think of something.

"All right, you jarheads, this afternoon we're—" He had no idea what they were going to do. Fortunately, almost as soon as they'd re-formed in the backyard, a woman's voice drifted over the rickety fence.

"Captain," she shouted.

He turned to look at a tall attractive woman in her sixties, he guessed. White hair swept back, a nice smile.

"I'm Winnie Jenkins." When he didn't recognize the name, she added, "From the church. Glad I found you home. The ladies have prepared some food. I'm parked in front of your house."

He hoped she'd brought a dobos torte.

"I could use help."

"All right, Gyrenes," Sam said, and the boys stood at attention. "Marines always assist women unloading their cars."

"Sir, yes, sir."

"Fall out."

The boys zoomed past him—not difficult—through the house and out the front door before he made it inside. Within seconds, they came back carrying pans covered with aluminum foil and

Tupperware bowls. Plastic cake carriers dangled from both of Nick's wrists.

"Where do you want these, Captain?" Winnie said.

By this time, he'd finally arrived in the kitchen. Fortunately, earlier this morning the boys had cleared off and scoured the small, round breakfast table and the counters. He hadn't had time to mess them up again.

"Anywhere you find room. I'll—we'll put them away later."

"This one"—she held up the pan she had in her hands—"is a very nice brisket Pansy Martin made for you. Over there are two chocolate cakes." She turned toward him. "I didn't realize the duplication. I hope you like chocolate."

"Yes, ma'am," Nick and Leo said in unison. "We do."

She smiled at them. "Are you going to help the captain eat all this?"

Because the boys looked at him with bright, hopeful eyes, Sam had to say, "At least the desserts."

"The ladies made some vegetable casseroles." She turned a serious gaze on him. "We really want you to get healthy, young man. You're far too skinny. That's why we used a lot of cheese and butter in all our dishes."

The *fatten-you-up* result of their concern sat all over the kitchen surfaces and he'd enjoy every bite of it.

"Thank you, Miss Winnie," he said. Yeah, he really had become a wimp who could be bought with lots of cheese, extra butter, and brisket.

"This is my specialty." She patted a covered bowl. "It's my orange gelatin and carrot salad."

His stomach clenched at the memory of gelatin salads at church dinners, but he smiled. "Your salad takes me back to when I was a kid." Which was the truth. He'd hated it then and bet it tasted just as bad as he remembered.

She beamed. "Someone's bringing a ham tomorrow. All this"—she waved her hand—"and the ham should hold you for a week."

"Miss Winnie, this should feed me for the rest of my life. Thank you." He leaned over—almost falling but steadied himself on the table—and kissed her on the cheek. An odd reaction he couldn't really explain but he knew if he tried to say something, emotion would overwhelm him.

"Oh, my, young man." She put her hand to her face and held it there. "How sweet of you." Then she picked up the basket she'd brought in. "When you're through with the dishes, I'll pick them up and take them back to church. Or *you* could bring them back," she added. "We'd love to see you."

Not committing himself, Sam said. "Please thank everyone."

When she left, the boys gazed at him with that hopeful expression that usually got them whatever they wanted. "Okay, guys, but if you tell your mother I let you eat chocolate cake this close to dinner, we're in big trouble. All three of us."

Fortunately, they'd finished the cake, rinsed the plates and forks, and headed for the backyard by the time Willow showed up. Was he happy to see her only because he always liked to see her or because he had no idea what to do with the guys next?

He'd have to think of some odd jobs before they came again. Shampoo the furniture? Paint the house? No, repairing the rickety fence would probably work best. For now, he'd enjoy her presence and consider the chores later.

"Hello, boys." Willow hugged each son before they wiggled away. "I see you're wearing the prosthetic device, Captain. How does it feel?"

He shrugged. "Fine."

"How did the day go?"

"Fine." He nodded. For some reason, he lost the ability to communicate when she stood too close. What an idiot he was, a marine who shot macho weapons in war, who'd faced incredible odds and death, but who couldn't carry on a conversation with a fragile-looking redhead.

"Captain, I didn't drive today. The boys and I are going to walk home. Would you like to go with us?"

Her smile was friendly but not particularly inviting, the expression of a mother asking the boys' little friend to join them.

Nevertheless, he wanted to kiss those gorgeous lips and pull her next to him, to cover himself with her long hair, to touch her and . . . He refused to complete the thought. After all, her sons were only a few feet away.

"No thanks," he said.

"Oh, please, sir," Nick begged.

This time, he didn't give in to their expressions. And Willow Thomas was much more inviting than chocolate cake and one hundred times more delicious.

"Good exercise," Leo said.

"You guys give me more than enough exercise," he said.

She smiled, almost in relief he thought. "Don't forget your next appointments," she said. Then the three left, the boys hopping down the porch steps and along the sidewalk with her.

He longed to join them, be a part of that group. To be carefree as he'd been when he visited Aunt Effie, back when he ran along the sidewalk with his friends looking for a pickup game of basketball or riding bikes to the lake.

Instead, he watched her walk away.

❧

They were getting too close, Sam realized as he got ready for bed that night. He hit the counter in the bathroom with his fist.

It hurt.

He remembered the laughter of the three as they walked away from the house. He smashed his hand against the counter again. Hurt even more.

He could feel the town and the people and the boys and their mother all sneaking inside his carefully constructed barrier. He didn't want them inside. He did *not* want to care about anyone or anything. All he wanted was to be left alone in this mess of a house. He couldn't take *feeling* again, didn't want to, refused to.

Now the house was clean and people walked in and out.

He cursed as he hit the counter again but not as hard because, although depressed, he wasn't stupid.

What should he do if she and her sons and the insufferably friendly people of Butternut Creek persisted in trying to tear his defenses down? These people needed to leave him alone, stop bringing food and tortes and dropping in. He wanted to be dead inside. He wanted to stay that way, had no desire to join the happy throng parading through his house. Why had he let them inside? He should've guessed the cheerful name of the town described exactly the positive attitude of the people who inhabited it.

He cursed Butternut Creek.

For a moment, tears gathered in his eyes, but he refused to let go. He had to be tough, had to remember who he was and what he'd left behind, the parts of himself he'd abandoned in Afghanistan, one visible from the outside, the other losses hidden inside.

He lifted his gaze to the mirror. A useless man looked back at him. If he forgot Afghanistan, he'd forget Morty and the others who'd died there and those who still fought. He'd start agreeing with people who said he was lucky to get out alive, even if he had lost a leg, and he couldn't do that. Morty had died on an isolated mountainside, killed by an enemy they hadn't even seen. Losing his best friend while he still lived didn't feel a bit lucky.

He scrubbed any trace of grief away, then hardened his expression. He was a marine, not a pansy. Not a rainbow of peace and light.

❦

Once the sanctuary emptied on Sunday morning, Adam wandered back down the central aisle, unzipping his robe as he walked. Hot to wear on an August morning with the air-conditioning spitting very little cool air into the sanctuary. Another repair. The crack in the wall from the corner of the baptistery to the ceiling and the peeling paint on the windowsills also needed to be fixed. He and the church members could repair and paint the walls themselves, but the air-conditioning would cost.

The bank had turned down their loan request. Where would the money come from?

Adam hadn't seen Captain Peterson in church. Not that he'd expected to. He'd gone by Sam's house two more times, left notes in the door, and telephoned twice, but no one answered. So he'd written a letter.

"Dear Lord," Adam whispered. "Please help me reach him."

It was the first Sunday of the month, which meant it was time for the fellowship dinner. As in all churches and as he'd learned with dishes people dropped off at the parsonage, the food was great. He hurried to his study, hung up the robe, and studied the jacket that lay across a chair. Too hot. He checked his tie in the mirror and wished he could leave that in the office as well, but a new minister without his suit coat and his tie would probably cause Miss Birdie to hyperventilate. At least his hair was not "too long" anymore. It had grown a little, enough so his scalp didn't show around his ears quite as much. Nearly enough that people didn't stop on the sidewalks and snicker, although Hector and his buddies hadn't let Adam forget.

Once in the fellowship hall, Adam said grace. He'd learned the minister's trick of saying the blessing only a foot away from the serving table. When he said "Amen," he moved quickly into the head of the line and arrived at the counter spread with dishes of so many kinds he hardly knew where to start. He piled on the sauerkraut and sausage, the pickled beets—which he seldom had—the chicken and dumplings, the beans, and more.

"We'll fix you a plate to take home," Pansy said. "You can make a couple more meals out of it."

Adam was beginning to enjoy being spoiled.

After about two months here, he knew almost half of the people gathered by name. Willow Thomas sat with two kids. He waved but steered clear of her. If he sat next to her, tongues would wag. He chose a chair across from two couples—all four with white hair—he barely knew and talked with them for a few minutes.

At least until Ralph approached, dragging a young blond woman behind him. Adam wanted to slip under the table, but people found such behavior by ministers unseemly. Unfortunately. Because she looked nearly as uncomfortable as he felt, Adam smiled and hoped someone would take the chair next to him before she got there.

No one did.

"Hey, Preacher. Want you to meet my niece Nancy from San Saba." Ralph pulled out the chair and shoved the reluctant young woman in it. "She's visiting today."

Nancy glared at Adam, uncomfortable and rebellious, as if her presence were his fault. He smiled but had no idea what to say to a female who obviously wished she were anyplace other than sitting next to him.

❦

"That's not the way to handle it." Birdie watched from the long serving counter between the fellowship hall and the kitchen as the preacher politely attempted to engage Ralph's relative in conversation. "Too obvious."

"Neither of them looks happy," Mercedes observed. "How old is Nancy?"

"Don't know. Hear she has a boyfriend the family doesn't like, but forcing her on the preacher isn't going to work." Birdie could hear a note of satisfaction in her own voice. Why? Shouldn't she rejoice if anyone found a good match for the preacher? Of course, but this woman didn't look like "the one."

"We have to keep looking," Mercedes said.

With a nod, Birdie checked out the crowd in the fellowship hall. About half of the diners had filled their plates and another half stood in line. Of all those people, she couldn't see another single woman in the place younger than sixty. Well, except Willow Thomas, but Birdie had plans for her.

"We have a problem," Winnie whispered, pointing toward a platter on the counter.

"Heavens preserve us," Birdie whispered. They were out of fried chicken. How could such a thing have happened? Distracted by the preacher's love life, she hadn't noticed. How could she have acted so irresponsibly?

"What do we do now?" Mercedes picked up an empty plate while Birdie shoved a casserole of Pansy's delicious chicken spaghetti into the space left on the counter.

"I'll run down to the H-E-B and pick up more," Winnie suggested. She pulled her keys from her purse and studied Birdie, a question so obvious in her eyes even Birdie couldn't ignore it.

Mercedes watched both women and waited.

Birdie knew what Winnie's words and actions meant: a test of Birdie's leadership, a day of reckoning, Armageddon in the kitchen of the Christian Church. If she took Winnie up on her offer, there was no retreat, no going back. Winnie would be a Widow against all the rules of widowdom.

Birdie sensed that everyone in the fellowship hall froze, as if time had stopped. Every eye in the hall lifted to the two women. Those in line stared, their gazes hopping back and forth between Birdie and Winnie as if they were watching a tennis match. Birdie saw that the preacher—poor young man, he should be spared a scene like this—had been attempting to chat with the blond visitor. His efforts at conversation stopped as his glance leaped toward the Widows and the wannabe.

The moment immobilized those at the tables with their forks halfway to their mouths, but their stares glued to Birdie's face.

The time had come.

How should she answer the challenge?

Not a sound came from the room, but it seemed as if Winnie's words and the jingling of her keys still echoed around them.

Then Birdie nodded. "Get two large buckets."

With that, everyone went back to eating or talking or picking up food from the dishes scattered across the counter while Winnie hurried out the side door and into the parking lot.

Mercedes said, "She did a good job in rounding up and delivering the food to Sam Peterson."

Birdie knew exactly what her friend meant. She'd done the right thing to add one more Widow to the group, but she had needed an excuse, like fried chicken.

"Hey, Grandma." Bree stood in front of her, piling her plate with more food than a girl should have been able to put away without gaining at least a pound or two—no matter how tall and thin she was. Bree had her mother's eyes but her height came from her father. Dad gum man.

"Hello, dear." Birdie patted her granddaughter's hand. "Where's your sister?"

"Over there with Willy Marti, Jesse's grandson." Bree rolled her eyes. "Grandma, she's too young to have a boyfriend."

Before Birdie could answer—she agreed but now wasn't the time to discuss the fact—Bree hurried over to the dessert table and grabbed the last piece of Pansy's better-than-sex cake.

"They're good kids." Mercedes picked up a pile of empty dishes and put them in the sink to soak. "You know they are. You worry too much."

"Their mother was into drugs at fifteen. That could happen to them also. No one's immune." Birdie joined her friend to clear the counter as the last few members filled their plates. "Could end up like their mother." She hated to even consider that, but they could, either one. The possibility broke her heart.

"Do you see any signs they're doing drugs?"

No, she hadn't, and she knew what to look for. She'd watched her daughter's slide and been powerless to stop it. Even now, tears clouded her eyes as she thought of that precious child and how she'd destroyed her own life.

When Birdie didn't answer, Mercedes said, "I haven't heard anything bad about them, and you know I hear everything. They're good kids. They make good grades."

"Lots of things to worry about with kids today." Birdie picked up a sponge and wrung it out in the sink. "Pregnancy. You know how many girls don't finish school." She'd spoken to each granddaughter often to warn them of the dangers of unprotected sex, to beg them to abstain until they were old enough to handle the responsibility involved. How likely was it they'd remember that when one of them was out in a car with a pushy teenage boy whose testosterone levels were through the roof—the usual status for a high school boy—and the moon shone romantically and love songs played on the radio?

Just then, Winnie hurried in with the chicken, which started a rush on the counter.

"They're good girls," Mercedes said as she picked up a few serving spoons.

Yes, they were good girls, Mac and Bree, but a lot of unknowns awaited them outside the walls of this church and the little house they shared, temptations that could lead them astray, exactly as they had dear Martha. She had no idea how to keep the girls safe without tying them to the sofa.

And she didn't know any knots that would keep them there.

Chapter Ten

H ey, Captain," Nick shouted. "Did you realize there's a chocolate cake all wrapped up in foil in the freezer?"

Sam eyed the bundle as he spread mustard on three pieces of bread. "How do you know it's chocolate cake?"

"I peeked." Nick paused. "You know, only to make sure it . . . umm . . . wasn't something that might spoil." He fingered the foil. "I think if we unwrap it while it's still frozen, the frosting won't come off." Nick put the lumpy package on the counter and carefully stripped off the covering.

"Looks good." Leo snapped off a small chunk of frozen icing and chewed, his head to the side as if considering the flavor. "And it tastes good. No freezer burn."

Sam picked up the note wrapped inside and read it. "It's from Farley Masterson."

"He doesn't like us," Nick mumbled from a mouth full of frozen cake.

"You know Farley Masterson?" Sam asked.

Sam did. Deputy Masterson had given him a hard time when he visited his aunt. Not that he didn't deserve some of it, but Masterson was a hard man who didn't like boys. The guy must have mellowed a bit. Nice of him to bake Sam a cake.

"Yeah." Leo nodded. "He doesn't like us."

"He said we're loud and have bad manners. He upset Mom." He shook his head. "We hate it when that happens."

"He's the reason we started playing in your yard. We didn't think anyone lived here, not at first. 'Cause you didn't yet, not when we first came around."

"It worked out okay." Sam glanced at both boys, who looked at him with wide, admiring eyes. He was getting deeper into the lives of these kids than he should, liked them more than was wise, but he couldn't ignore them the way that jerk of a father did. "You might want to let it thaw."

Before he finished the sentence, the boys had used a sharp knife and a lot of force to cut the cake into large slices, placed them on napkins, and began to wrap it up in foil again.

"Don't forget your mother, men."

Looking guilty, they cut a small piece for their mother.

"Mom's not a big eater," Leo said. "Always watching her weight."

"Eat your sandwiches first," Sam warned with a grin. He figured these two devoured everything that wasn't locked away before she had a chance.

He picked up the small piece of cake, covered it with foil, and handed it to Nick. "Put this in the refrigerator. Don't eat it."

"Sir, yes, sir."

After they finished lunch, including the still-icy cake, Sam picked up the clipboard and totaled the boys' hours. "That does it," he said. "You guys are finished. You've paid off the four hundred dollars." He glanced up expecting to see smiles. Instead, the boys studied him with the sad, puppy-dog expressions that broke the small section of his heart he allowed the brothers to touch. The part that expanded every day, whether he liked it or not.

"Don't you have more work we can do?" Nick asked.

"You guys are good workers. I can't think of anything more and I don't have the money right now to pay you."

"You don't have to. Maybe . . . maybe we could just hang out with you." Leo stood and came to attention. "For free, sir."

"Hang out?" Sam said.

"You know. Do stuff together." Nick followed his brother's example and stood. "Sir."

"I know what *hang out* means, Nick. You guys want to hang out here?"

The surprise in his voice must have wounded the boys. Did they think he didn't want them around? They nodded, their expressions even more vulnerable. Crap. He couldn't hurt them. "Okay, but doing what?"

"Well," Nick said in an uncertain voice. "Could you . . . could you . . ."

"What?"

"He wants you to take him to the first day of school. He's afraid to go alone," Leo said. "Sir."

Double crap.

"Am not *afraid*." Nick glared at his brother but knew better than to punch him, not in Sam's house. Instead, he thrust his lower lip out as if daring him to disagree. "I'm not afraid." Then he turned to Sam. "Sir, Mom wants to take me, but I'm too *old* for my mother to take me to school."

"Are you enrolled?"

"Sir, yes, sir," Leo said. "I'd like you to go with me, too. We're both at the elementary school, so you'd only have to go one place."

"Won't your mother want to take you and meet your teachers?"

"Sir, yes, sir." Nick made a disgusted face by stretching his lips out and frowning. "But we're not little kids. We don't want the other guys to make fun of us."

"How does your mother feel about this?" Sam guessed she'd be hurt, but what did he know about this woman's feelings?

"She won't care," Nick said.

"It's going to hurt her," Leo corrected. "But we're men now. Gyrenes."

"Gyrenes honor all women and care about their mothers," Sam said. "Gyrenes don't hurt their mothers' feelings. That's not being a man. That's being a grunt. Do you want to be a grunt?"

"Sir! No, sir," they shouted in unison as they stood at attention.

"And I don't have a way to get you to school. Have you noticed that, marines?"

Nick said, "Sir, no, sir," at the same time Leo said, "Sir, yes, sir."

"Sir," said Nick, his thin shoulders held straight and high, his narrow chest thrust forward. "My mother can pick you up. You could go with us."

"Why would I want to do that, marine?"

Neither boy had an answer. Their silence and the solemn entreaty in their eyes made him feel like a heartless, selfish jerk. They were kids, just kids.

"What day?" Sam asked.

"Tuesday after Labor Day, sir," the boys said in unison.

Had they practiced this?

He had several handy and completely believable excuses, good excuses. His leg hurt. Even after having more cushioning and doing exercises in PT with the prosthesis, he couldn't walk for long. He didn't have a car and he didn't like getting into a car because he looked so clumsy and Willow's car was really low. He could tell them he had no interest in their lives. But he couldn't lie. And he couldn't hurt them.

He wasn't their father. He wasn't even related. He had no responsibility here. Still, he knew exactly what was going to happen next.

"Sir, please?" The last word ended with a quaver in Nick's voice that made the kid swallow hard and glance, embarrassed, at his older brother.

Sam could tell them no if real Gyrenes stood in front of him, but not these two. They needed a man in their lives, even a half-used-up man like him.

In his head he cursed. They were opening him up like a trout being gutted. It hurt.

"Then, sir, yes, sir, I will come to school with you next week."

The boys looked at each other and laughed and shouted, then started toward him.

"Do not break formation, marines."

They stopped, completely still, and came to attention. "Sir, no, sir," they said.

"Sir, will you wear your uniform?" Leo asked.

Where had he put his uniform? Had the general taken it back to Ohio with him? It wasn't in his closet. Other than jeans and T-shirts, nothing was. "No, but I will wear my marine T-shirt."

"Cool," they said, still at attention but smiling happily.

He'd never seen such happy marines. No, kids. He couldn't make these guys into fantasy. They were kids. He was a washed up ex-marine with only one leg. In his fantasy, these boys had become his men, his troops. Pitiful.

Even worse, every time they were here, he hoped their mother would drop by, so he could catch an eyeful of her. Even more pathetic.

Okay, if the boys wanted to hang, he had to come up with something for them to do. If they had the material, they could start on that fence, but they didn't. They'd already measured but the lumberyard couldn't deliver until next week. Neither he nor their mother wanted them to just sit around and watch him sleep. He had allowed them to spend a little time watching DVDs of old war movies with him, and that would eat up thirty minutes before they became restless. What could they do the rest of the time?

Maybe he could teach them manners. A couple of weeks earlier, the general had sent him stationery in case he felt like writing anyone. Oh, sure. The box lay in the bottom drawer of his dresser, still sealed in cellophane or whatever that plastic stuff was.

"Marines, time to write a thank-you note to Mr. Masterson for that great cake."

After Leo completed that chore and Sam found a stamp in the package of stationery, the boys ran to the corner and mailed it while Sam watched from the porch.

He was becoming a mother hen, but if anything happened to those kids, their real mother would kill him. Or shout at him. Or give him that disappointed look her sons had described. Sam didn't think he could take that.

"What are you guys doing?"

His attention had been so focused on the boys he hadn't realized Willow had approached the house, even climbed the steps of the porch, and stood only five feet from him. What kind of marine allowed an incursion like that? What kind of *man* didn't notice a woman like Willow standing that close?

"Mom." Nick bounced up the steps. "We saved you a piece of cake."

"Chocolate cake," Leo added.

"Where did it come from? Did you bake it, Captain?"

"I'm not much of a cook, ma'am."

"There was a note from Mr. Masterson with it," Leo said.

"He must have donated it when Miss Pansy brought me food."

"Because we ate so much, Sam made us write a letter to thank him," Nick said, then gulped when Leo glared at him for giving away the fact they'd eaten chocolate cake, not exactly a health food.

"Thank you for helping the boys with their manners." She smiled at Sam. "I've tried. It's not easy."

"Come on inside, Mom. The cake's in the refrigerator." Leo opened the front door for her.

"Do you mind?" She glanced at Sam, oddly uncomfortable; he noticed.

"No, ma'am." He liked calling her "ma'am." It put a little distance between them. Probably why she called him "Captain." "You'd better hurry before your sons eat the whole thing themselves."

Nick took her hand. "Come into the kitchen."

She glanced over her shoulder and caught him watching her. He lifted his eyes to her face. Had she noticed? Probably didn't matter. Most likely she was accustomed to guys checking her out.

"Have a seat." He remembered as he spoke that there were only two chairs at the kitchen table and the stepstool the boys dragged in so the three of them could all sit there. She took one chair and he took the other.

Nick took a fork from the drawer, placed it on the table in front of his mother, then stood at attention next to her while Leo brought her the piece of cake.

"Looks lovely." She looked at the sliver and grinned.

"It's not very big, is it?" Leo said. "We should have cut you more."

"This is exactly the right amount. Thank you."

"We asked the captain to take us to school," Leo said. "Along with you. Is that okay?"

"Oh?" She glanced at Sam, but he couldn't read the expression. Was she hurt that they wanted him along? No, he thought she looked more nervous than displeased.

"Is that all right?" he asked.

"Of course. I'll have the boys give you the information when we know more."

She cut the tip of the cake, placed it on her tongue, and closed her mouth to chew.

Oh, Mama. He could watch her do that all day.

It only took her a few seconds to finish the small piece. Then she glanced at Sam. Obviously he hadn't hidden the emotion that had flooded him as he'd watched her savor the cake.

"Gyrenes, pick up the equipment in the backyard." With a quick movement of his head, Sam signaled for the boys to leave. As they ran out to obey his orders, he put his hand on hers.

She glanced down at their hands, then lifted her eyes to his. "Captain, this is a very bad idea." She stood but he held her hand in place so she couldn't move away. She didn't struggle but she didn't sit, either. "Captain . . ."

"Sam," he said.

"I need to go. It's not a bit professional for me to be here." She nodded toward his hand. "Like this. Alone."

"You're not my only physical therapist. What's-his-name works with me, too."

"Yes, but I do work with you and will supervise the fit of your prosthesis."

He grinned. Although he didn't know why, the expression was usually very successful with women.

"Oh." She blinked.

Obviously the grin worked on her, too, because she sat back down slowly, as if she'd lost the strength in both of her legs and the will to resist. He could only hope.

He was glad she'd settled in the chair next to him because standing, balancing on one good leg and a prosthesis wasn't easy. Even seated, he couldn't keep his feet steady on the floor. Sure that falling out of the chair wouldn't show his macho-ness, Sam kept his right elbow on the table to stabilize himself. Feeling secure enough to make a move, he leaned forward to run his thumb down her cheek. He hadn't flirted with or attempted to seduce a woman in forever. Had he forgotten how to do it?

She blinked again and swallowed, but she didn't say anything. Then she shivered a little. He grinned, inside. He still had it.

Slipping his hand behind her neck, he pulled her forward gently and leaned in enough—keeping himself balanced—to touch her lips with his. Then he pulled her even closer until their mouths met, hard against each other. He nibbled her lower lip. For a moment she relaxed and opened her mouth a little, but when he started to slip his tongue inside, she pulled away and leaped to her feet.

"No fair," he said. "I can't stand up that fast."

"I . . . I . . . have to see how my sons are doing." But she didn't move, just stood still and studied him.

"Coward," he whispered.

"No, I'm not."

"Then what?"

She shook her head. "I don't know. I . . . my husband . . ."

"Must have been a complete idiot."

For a moment she stared at him. Then she grinned. "Yes, he was, but Tiffany's a young and gorgeous creature. One day he's going to realize she has no brain, but right now he doesn't care."

Pushing on the table, he stood. "Don't run away."

"I wasn't." She looked down for a moment before meeting his eyes. "Okay, I was. And I am, but . . ."

"You felt something."

"Oh, my, yes. Only the dead wouldn't have, but I don't think I'm . . . I mean, it was . . . but I'm not ready."

"If you weren't ready, you wouldn't have felt it."

She glared at him. "A fine argument. I bet it works with some women, but I know that sometimes the body acts before the brain can kick in."

"Maybe the brain should stay out of this."

"Oh, like with my husband and Tiffany?"

Not what he meant at all, but he'd stupidly reminded her of the general treachery of men. From the flash in her eyes, he could tell he'd blown any chance he had, at least for a while.

"Sir, we put everything in the shed." Leo clattered through the slider, across the dining room, and into the kitchen with Nick following.

"Are you guys finished?" Willow asked.

"Yes, ma'am," they said together.

"Then we need to go, Captain." Willow grabbed Leo and started toward the front door, holding her son like a shield.

"Just a minute, Mom. I've got to police the kitchen." Nick glanced at Sam as he picked up her plate and fork to take them to the sink. "Sir, you have something pink on your mouth," he said.

Twirling, Willow dropped Leo's hand, took the plate from Nick, and shoved him toward the door, then turned on the hot water and squirted dishwashing liquid. "Go on outside, to the front porch. Now! I'll be right there."

"Did you cut yourself?" Nick asked Sam. "Are you bleeding?"

Leo's thoughtful gaze leaped back and forth between Sam's face and Willow's.

"Shoo." Willow waved her hands at her sons while Sam burst out laughing. "This is not funny, Captain."

But it was. He laughed harder than he could remember laughing for months.

"Go on out to the car, boys," she said and waved them out the door.

When they left, he said, "I'm going to kiss you again." He watched her scrub the plate so hard she might remove the pattern from its surface. "Someday."

"Don't count on that." She twisted the dishcloth as if she wished she could wring his neck. Then she turned and glared at him. "You have a very high opinion of yourself." Before he could answer, she tossed the dishrag on the counter and hustled out after the boys.

He stopped smiling. Okay, so he'd kissed her and he wanted to do it again. But after that, what? Going after a woman with two kids counted as serious business. He didn't want to hurt any of them, but he sure wasn't ready for commitment, exactly like Willow.

What was he doing?

❦

The Thomases walked down the sidewalk and got in the car. In the rearview mirror, Willow could see the boys whispering. She put the keys in the ignition but kept her eyes on her sons.

After several seconds of Leo giving information, Nick said, "You're kidding?" Then he glanced up at her, eyes wide.

She dreaded considering what her sons might be saying. Actually, she had a pretty good idea, and she knew Nick, her lovable but big-mouthed child, would blurt it out as soon as he heard it all.

With the boys settled in the backseat, she put the car in gear and pulled onto the street. As she did, Nick said, "Mom, Leo said you kissed the captain. Did you?"

"Shut up," Leo whispered. "I told you not to say anything."

"Okay, okay," Nick said. After only a few seconds, he added, "Mom, do you like the captain?"

From the muttered "ouch" she heard, she bet Leo pinched his brother. "Of course. He's a very nice man. I really appreciate the amount of time he takes with you guys."

"No . . . ouch, stop it," Nick began before, she guessed, Leo elbowed him. "Do you *really* like him? More than you liked Dad?"

Of course her sons would wonder. They liked Sam. They knew he'd kissed her and wondered about the entire situation. "It's not like that."

"Then what's it like?" Nick persisted.

This time there was no *ouch* from the backseat.

"Yeah, what is it like?" Leo said.

"He's an attractive man, but I'm his physical therapist. It wouldn't be professional for me to like a patient, someone from work."

"That's dumb," Nick muttered. "Dad did."

"It's still not appropriate. Hard to understand, but that's how it is."

She'd pulled into the parking lot behind the apartments, found a place, and shut the car off. Was she safe?

As she opened the car door, Nick said, "But when he's better and you aren't his therapist anymore, then you could like him more, right? Kiss him again?"

"I don't know."

Before she could step out, Leo asked, "How could you not know? He's great, he likes us, and he likes you. Why wouldn't you like him back?"

She stood and watched the boys pile out of the back, then closed the door and hit the lock button. "It's more complicated than that."

"Wasn't complicated for Dad," Nick said. "He and Tiffany . . ."

"Shut up, squirt." Leo gave his brother another jab.

"Don't hurt your brother," she said, leaping on the opportunity to change the subject. "Just because you're the big brother doesn't give you the right to . . ."

"Yeah, just because you're the big brother," Nick said, "you're not the boss of me."

She sighed, deeply grateful for the interruption of the quarrel.

Not that a good mother would encourage bickering, but she preferred that to their curiosity and the uncomfortable questions. Someday, of course, she'd have to face their inquiries honestly and work through her feelings, because whatever might or might not happen with Captain Peterson affected her sons as well.

As she listened to Leo and Nick argue, she knew the reprieve was temporary. Nick never let go of anything until the answers completely satisfied him.

❧

The next day, Willow considered herself in the full-length mirror in the PT department. Everyone had cleared out and she'd grabbed her purse and her laptop to head for the door when her reflection caught her attention.

She wasn't the type of woman men fell in love with immediately. Despite her fragile exterior, inside she was too pushy, too cold, too in-charge and controlling, not a bit girlie and flirty. The traits made her a great physical therapist, but not, as Grant had often said, a great wife.

The jerk. Fortunately, she hadn't listened to him. Much.

For example, her hair, which he'd mentioned more than occasionally. She'd never been able to do anything with it so she pulled the unruly red tresses back and forgot about them except when wisps escaped and refused to be pulled back.

Tiffany had gorgeous blond curls and waves, artfully shaped and colored and pampered by an expensive hairdresser. Willow had considered such spending unnecessary. No, she shook her head. She wasn't a bit girlie.

She turned sideways. She did have a great figure, through no effort of her own. Men liked that. Grant had. Sam did.

White shirt and navy slacks. Comfortable, flat shoes that didn't make her legs look yards long, like Tiffany's. Hers were actually longer than Grant's third and present wife's. She'd just never showed them off. Although very effective for stealing husbands, short skirts and strappy sandals on three-inch heels didn't work in the PT department or as the mother of two active boys.

Why after all these months did she continue to compare herself with that woman? Certainly she was better than that. If not better, at least different. She'd always accepted herself, always had pretty healthy self-esteem until Grant chose the über-feminine Tiffany.

All of which brought her back to the original question: Why did Sam find her attractive? He could have his pick of women, and yet he'd settled on her, at least for now. Maybe because she was handy? Propinquity?

Doggone, there she went again, unable to even think a man could find *her* attractive. Grant had done a job on her, ruined her self-esteem and trust—but she'd allowed that. Why? She had great kids, was terrific at her job, and had started a new life for herself and the boys.

Doggone number two, she sounded exactly like her mother comforting her back when Willow didn't have a date for the prom.

But she couldn't stop wondering. Why, after all this time, did she allow her cheating husband and his third wife to control her life and her thoughts? Habit? Guilt? She bet neither of them ever thought about her. What had she gotten for remembering the hurt? She leaned closer to the mirror and noticed two thin grooves between her eyes. Then she wiggled her jaw, an action that hurt because she clenched her teeth too much. All she'd gotten was wrinkles and painful muscles.

"Mizz Thomas?" The janitor stuck his head inside the door. "Are you still working?"

"No, Ralph, come on in and clean." She glanced at the clock. "Five thirty. I didn't realize I was so late." The boys would be wondering where she was.

As Ralph rolled the cleaning cart inside, Willow turned slowly to study the department. She'd done a great job here in the few months since she arrived. The number of patient hours had increased significantly. Although the hospital hadn't purchased as much new equipment as she wanted, she'd added a lot and requisitioned more.

"Mizz Thomas?"

"I know. You need to get to work." She grabbed her lunch bag and remembered the brownie Nick had placed inside, saved from dinner with Sam the previous evening. Not a complete brownie. There was a corner nibbled off, but he'd given her most of it. Yes, she had great kids who loved her. She didn't need a man to make her feel whole.

On the other hand, why not? Having Sam around added zing to her life. Captain Peterson's interest and her response made her reluctance to become involved with him seem ridiculous. She liked men, especially this man.

She wasn't ready to consider kicking over the traces just yet, but she would be someday. As her grandmother Brubaker used to say, God willing and the creek don't rise, she'd do exactly that. Just not this week.

Wednesday afternoon, Sam headed down the hospital corridor toward the physical therapy department. She'd have to see him today. Willow could run away from his house, but she couldn't run away from the physical therapy department.

Maybe not quite true. His glance flew around the PT room. All the other staff members helped patients, but he couldn't see Willow.

"Come on over, Captain." Mike stood at the parallel bars. "Willow's seeing hospital patients this afternoon. She wanted me to work with you and to tell you the prosthetist will be here in September to fit you."

Sam handed a PT aide his cane and grabbed hold of the bars.

"How is the one you're wearing now?" Mike asked.

"Okay. Slips a little. I'll be glad to get the new one."

"Once you're warmed up, let's practice balance."

After twenty minutes, Mike glanced at the clock. "Thought Willow'd be back by now, but sometimes it takes longer depending on patients' needs. When she gets back, I'll tell her how much progress you've made. Good job."

Willow had gone to see some of the hospital patients. Made sense. All of them shared that duty, but why now? Why at the time of his appointment? Did it mean anything? Was she trying to avoid him?

He didn't know, but next week when they took the boys to school, she couldn't pretend the kiss hadn't happened. She couldn't ignore or avoid him.

Chapter Eleven

Adam stood at the door of Sam Peterson's house and knocked again. Inside, the television blasted. From the gunshots, he guessed it was a cop show. Outside, the breeze blew across the porch. "Captain, I'm Adam Jordan." He spoke clearly and loudly enough to be heard over the sounds from inside, he hoped. "I'd like to visit with you for a minute."

Still no one came to the door.

Pleasant out here, he thought as he turned to study the neighborhood. Small houses but all neat and tidy, well kept.

The sun had begun to head west, huge and orange and brilliant. He'd been up since sunrise to pray with a member of the congregation having surgery and was tired. Surely the captain wouldn't mind if he sat down on the ancient swing at the end of the porch to rest, if he swung for a couple of minutes to cool off. After Sam had ignored Adam several times when he called or came by, the minister felt fairly certain he wouldn't answer the door now. If the marine ran out here and screamed at the preacher for sitting on his swing, Adam would still be ahead. He would have met the elusive man.

Adam settled onto the swing and shoved with his feet to get it moving. After only seconds, the swing supports gave a screeching groan. He quickly and with a good amount of trepidation lifted his eyes to the ceiling of the porch. Well-warranted trepidation, he realized. As if in slow motion, the wood in the ceiling began to splinter around the hooks. Then time sped up. Before he could stand, the swing dropped onto the porch with a deafening crash and a crack that knocked his breath out. It felt like he'd broken every bone in his butt.

The sound of the falling swing and shouts of pain had to drown out the television. Adam would probably get to meet the captain soon.

As he sat groaning and gasping in the wreckage of the swing, his knees bumping against his ears, the front door opened. A man Adam guessed with fair certainty to be Captain Peterson launched himself out faster than the minister thought a guy on a cane could move.

"What the hell?" the marine shouted. A normal response in the situation.

Because the swing had broken into small pieces, Adam had nothing to hold on to that would help him get to his feet. To tell the truth, he didn't want to stand and still could barely breathe. There was no way something like this could be handled with dignity. If he could have, Adam would have rolled off the porch and hidden in the scraggly shrubs surrounding it.

But a minister couldn't do that. A minister had to be made of sterner stuff, aware of his mission and ministry. In an effort to gain an iota of composure, Adam forced his aching legs to straighten and stand, stifled a moan as he realized how much his body hurt, smiled, and reached out his right hand.

"Hello, Captain Peterson," he said on a gasp for air. "I'm Adam Jordan, the minister of the Christian Church."

The captain watched him, his gaze moving from the broken swing to Adam's feet, then slowly up the length of the minister's body, pausing to glance at the outstretched hand, and up to Adam's face before he burst out laughing. He leaned against the wall to stay upright.

Again, a normal response. The preacher looked down to find his feet covered in the bits of the ruined swing. He looked up to see two holes the size of CDs with splintered wood around them. After several seconds and despite the pain, he broke into laughter as well.

"So, you're the minister who's been bugging me," Sam said between guffaws.

Adam nodded.

"Well, come inside before you break something else."

The house looked nearly spotless except for the coffee cups and empty glasses on the end table and the newspaper on the floor.

"I have help," Sam said following his gaze. "That's why it doesn't look like a bachelor lives here. Willow Thomas and her two sons go to your church. The two boys . . . well, it's hard to explain, but they've been cleaning and picking up for me."

"I know them. Nice people."

"The kids broke the glass in my slider. Seems the only way I meet people is when they attempt to destroy my house."

"I'm sorry. I shouldn't have," Adam babbled. "The swing looked so inviting. We'll fix it. I'll get some of the men from church. We'll get you a new one."

Sam waved the offer away as he fell into the sofa and dropped the cane on the floor. "My father's coming in a few weeks. He'll need something to keep him busy."

"Then I'll pay . . ."

"No need. Sit, please." He watched as Adam took the chair across from him, then said, "You look young to be a preacher."

Adam nodded. "You look young to be a war hero."

An expression of utter despair covered Sam's face, wiping away any trace of the laughter that had been there, reaching deep in his eyes. "I'm no kind of hero, Preacher."

"We have a vets' group at church . . ."

"Don't try to fix me."

"I'd never do that. I just . . ." But Adam didn't complete the thought. He probably had been. That's what people like him did. "I won't do that again."

After Sam nodded, the two men sat in silence. Getting inside should make Adam feel good but it didn't. He'd immediately stuck his foot—big as it was—into his mouth.

"So," Adam tried again. "What do you like to do?"

Sam shook his head. "You said you wouldn't try to fix me again."

"Didn't mean to. I was trying to start a conversation."

Sam leaned back and glared at the minister. "Preacher, I'm not fit for company, much less a chat." Brackets around Sam's mouth and between his eyes suggested he was in pain. "Why don't you come back another day?" he said. "If you bring pizza, I promise I'll let you in."

"Why don't I order delivery now?" Once inside, even dirty and hurting all over, Adam refused to let go of this moment of contact. He didn't wait for an answer before pulling his cell, punching it on, and asking, "Pepperoni okay?"

Sam watched Adam for a few seconds, then, finally, smiled. "Okay, Pastor, you win. Anchovies, pineapple, and roasted"—he paused and looked toward the ceiling—"eggplant." He lowered his eyes to scrutinize the minister. "You're going to order that?"

Adam nodded. "I figure this is a test of some kind. You want to let me in on what it is?"

"Are you really going to let the pitiable amputee guilt you into ordering a pizza with roasted eggplant?"

Adam shrugged. "In the first place, I was going to have that stuff put only on your half. In the second, the pizza places in small towns like this don't put roasted eggplant on pizzas. The ingredients at the Pizza Palacio are pretty basic." He punched a button.

"I like you," he said. "I like a man who has a pizza place on speed dial." He laughed, actually laughed. "Don't ask for the pineapple or eggplant. Marines don't eat pineapple on pizzas."

When Adam finished the order, Sam didn't look as if he were in any hurry to begin a conversation so Adam jumped in again. "Your father's coming soon?"

Sam nodded again, the smile gone. This man presented a challenge—not in the same way as Miss Birdie but definitely a test of a minister's pastoral skills. Not that Adam had developed many of those yet.

"How did you happen to come down here by yourself? Why didn't you wait until he came, too?" Adam realized as the words came out that they sounded as if he didn't believe Sam could take care of himself. "I mean . . ."

Before he could make another mistake, Sam said, "Because I wanted to be alone." His glare reminded Adam he wasn't alone, that the man who sat across from him had invaded his isolation.

After another few minutes of silence—little by little Adam was realizing Sam didn't plan to make this easy—he said, "You know, I did call you. Several times."

"People in this town are odd like that. You'd think if a person didn't answer his phone or the door unless pushed to it by someone invading his porch and destroying his property . . ." He stopped and glared at Adam. "Where was I? Oh, yes, you'd think those people would leave you alone."

"If you had an answering machine," the preacher suggested, "you wouldn't have to talk to people but you'd know if there were any important calls."

"I don't have an answering machine," Sam explained as if talking to a slow child with only a tenuous grasp of the English language, "because I want to be left alone."

They spent a few more minutes staring at each other until Sam picked up the remote and turned on the news. Fifteen minutes of silence later, the doorbell rang. Adam leaped to his feet. A stab of pain in his hip reminded him of the earlier accident.

"Get me a beer while you're up," Sam said obviously willing to take advantage of the preacher's service while not wanting much to do with the preacher.

But at least he was inside. A small success but a success. He couldn't wait to tell Miss Birdie. Or maybe he wouldn't. Maybe he'd let her ask him about it.

Birdie hated Fridays. Each waitress had one day she had to come in early and set up: Check the salt, pepper, and sugar, fill them if necessary. Make sure the napkin holders were full and that, overnight, nothing disgusting had entered the diner or plopped itself down on one of the tables. Start the coffee—although she'd always asked Roy, the manager, why they couldn't buy timers for that and why the late-duty waitresses couldn't check the tables. He ignored her first suggestion and told her the waitresses who worked until nine were too tired. If she didn't need to keep her job, she would have pushed, but she did. She'd shut up. That's why, still half-asleep, she stumbled past the tables until she reached the switch to turn on the lights.

Outside the front window, it was still dark. One streetlight glowed half a block away. No one wandered along the street yet. Customers would show up at six, the same time the cook ran into the restaurant and turned on the grill.

But someone stood out there, or something. Birdie couldn't tell what. At the bottom of the window, just above the frame, the top of something white showed against the gloom. Maybe a large dog. Could be a cougar. Someone had said they'd seen one out by the lake the other day, but she doubted they'd come this far in, this close to people.

She blinked. Her sight had become cloudy—probably needed cataract surgery—but when she opened her eyes and focused them, the blob was still there.

Curious, she walked to the window and attempted to make out the form.

Oh, my Lord, it was a child. What was a child doing out there at this hour? And alone? She hurried to the front door, unlocked it, and looked out at the child, then swept the street with a glance, expecting to see an adult nearby. No one out there but this little creature.

Birdie took a step toward the child but it—or he or she—moved away and huddled in a small ball as if trying to disappear, to hide in a tiny, invulnerable package. The sight squeezed Birdie's heart, an organ many thought she didn't possess.

"Are you hungry?" Birdie asked.

The little girl didn't move. If anything, she shrank even smaller. Then her stomach growled.

"Let's go inside and get you something to eat." Birdie held out her hand.

The child studied her, glancing first at her face, then dropping her eyes to study Birdie's uniform before moving back up to her face. A quick peek through the window seemed to convince her that Birdie and this place were safe. She stood and followed Birdie.

Once inside, Birdie locked the door and turned to speak. She stopped as she realized how dirty the child was. She leaned forward to scrutinize her, but when an odor reached Birdie, she leaped back. Soiled lace on the child's socks confirmed that it was in fact a girl— and one who wasn't just grubby but indecently so: snot-nosed, black-fingernailed, sooty-faced, torn-shirt, and muddy-trouser filthy. Far more dirt covered the little one than she could have picked up in a few hours or overnight.

Tears ran down the girl's face, leaving pink trails on grimy cheeks. She lifted her arm to wipe them away and left a trail of mucus across her face as well as the sleeve of her ragged shirt. How old was she? Four or five?

"Let's wash you up before you get breakfast."

The girl nodded.

"I'm Birdie—Miss Birdie. What's your name?"

"Missy," she said in a wavering voice.

"Where's your mother?"

Tears filled Missy's eyes again. "Don't know. Lost." Sobs shook the child's entire body, and she buried her face in her hands.

"Where's your daddy?"

"Gone," the child whispered. Then her stomach started to growl again, not dainty *grrs* but reverberations so loud it sounded as if her insides contained a ravenous lion.

Birdie glanced at the clock. If she worked really fast, she could give the child a quick cleanup and get her breakfast before people started to arrive. If the girl's mother hadn't showed up by the time the crowd thinned, she'd do *something* about it. She had no idea what.

"How old are you, Missy?"

She held up four fingers.

"What's your last name?"

"Last name?" Missy thought for a moment before getting to her feet. "Mommy calls me 'Missy' or sometimes 'sweetheart.' Is sweetheart my last name?"

If the mother didn't show up, Missy'd given little information that would help find her. Birdie tried again.

"One more question, Missy Sweetheart. Where did you sleep last night?"

"Outside," she whispered. Her voice shook.

Birdie shut her mouth. The questions didn't help any and drove the child to tears.

"Okay, let's go." Birdie took the girl's tiny, grubby hand and led her toward the restroom. She tried to wipe away whatever grime she could, including washing Missy's face and hands with paper towels. All the task accomplished was to make the child look a bit less like a hobo and more like a girl. Birdie then took Missy back into the dining area and settled her at a booth facing the front window. Her mother could see Missy through the window if she was looking for her. Why wouldn't she be?

In the light, she could see Missy's freckles across pale skin and her dark eyes filled with sadness. "You look outside and tell me if your mother comes by." Missy nodded.

Birdie set a glass of milk and another of orange juice on the table before she went back to making sure they were ready for the morning crowd. Another waitress and the cashier arrived a few minutes before six. They each asked for an explanation of the waif at the front table as they prepared for their jobs. The cook arrived just as Birdie opened the front door and the early customers crowded in.

When Birdie picked up Missy's breakfast ten minutes later and took it to the booth, both glasses were empty but the child lay on the red plastic seat and slept. Birdie was a sucker for a sleeping child. She watched her for a few seconds before she took off her sweater and placed it over the girl. After that, she took a few steps and placed Missy's breakfast in front of Howard Crampton.

"Not what I ordered," he objected.

"That's okay. You'll like it. It's hot."

By nine, the breakfast bunch had mostly left and Birdie had time to check on Missy again. The child was waking up.

"Hungry?"

When Missy nodded, Birdie put another order in. "More milk?" she asked.

Missy used her fists to wipe the sleep from her eyes and nodded.

What was she going to do with the child now? She didn't want to turn her over to foster care, not when the girl looked so pitiful and small and sad and lonely. Why had Birdie allowed herself to get caught up in the situation when she already had plenty on her plate? She couldn't take on the care of a four-year-old.

Of course, the mother would probably show up soon, probably in a few minutes, explain what had happened, and everything would be fine. No problem. For that reason, Birdie went to the door and looked up and down the street again. All she saw was a normal morning in Butternut Creek: stores opening, people parking and walking toward the courthouse, a few men playing chess under the branches of the live oaks around the square. She recognized almost everyone, and those she didn't know didn't look a bit like a hysterical mom searching for her lost daughter.

So where in the world—or in the state of Texas—was the girl's mother? Why had she left her daughter alone for so long? A mother doesn't just misplace her child. Even the worst mother would certainly realize she was gone by now.

Birdie had a lot of questions about Missy she needed answers to but didn't feel many answers would be forthcoming from Missy. She took out her cell phone, punched a number, and waited for Mercedes to answer. "Meet me at the church ASAP," she said and hung up without waiting for a response. Mercedes would be there.

"Judy, cover for me. I'll be back for lunch," Birdie told the other waitress. "Come on, Missy." She held out her hand.

On the way to the church, Birdie used her key to open the door of the thrift shop run by many of the churches. Not all the churches because there were some groups that refused to cooperate, not even to feed the hungry or to help a pitiful, lost little girl. She pulled out a change of clothes and underwear for the child, taped a note to the cash register—"Please charge $10.58 to the account of the Christian Church"—and headed over to the church office.

❦

Adam looked up from his notes to see Miss Birdie stride into the study holding the hand of a very dirty child.

"Didn't expect you to be here," the pillar said as she stopped and glared at him for being in his own office. He guessed he'd never please her.

"Awfully early for you," she added.

Glancing at the clock, he nodded. "I had some things to finish up. I could leave if it's inconvenient to have me here."

She didn't, of course, get the joke. Instead she said, "You can stay. You might have some ideas." Her voice suggested she doubted that.

He stood and walked around the desk to kneel in front of the little girl. "I'm Adam. Who are you?"

"This is the Reverend Jordan," the pillar explained with a glare toward him. "Sometimes you're too informal, Preacher."

"I'm Missy," the child said. "I lost my mommy."

"When was that?"

She shook her head.

"Losing your mother can't feel good. Where did you put her?"

Missy shrugged. "I don't know." Her voice quivered.

"Do you live in Butternut Creek?"

The girl smiled. "What a funny name."

"Guess not," he said to Miss Birdie. He picked Missy up and sat on one of the cleared chairs with her on his lap. The child patted him on the cheek.

"What do you know about this lovely young lady?" he asked the pillar while bouncing Missy up and down.

"Nothing. She was alone outside the diner when I opened up this morning." The pillar went on to tell the story. "When her mother didn't show up, I brought her over here to give her a shower and talk to Mercedes about what to do now."

"How nice of you," he said. "Most people would have left her there, ignored her, decided she was someone else's problem."

The pillar said nothing, embarrassed to be called a good person.

Adam smiled at Missy again. "Missy, do you know where your daddy is?"

"Away," she said with no particular emotion.

"Your grandmother or grandfather?"

"Grandpa's with Jesus." Missy nodded confidently.

"Someone's taken her to church." He glanced up at Birdie before looking back at Missy.

"And your grandmother?"

"Virginia," she said which didn't help a whole lot. Was that a name or a location?

Before he could seek clarification, the child said, "I want my mommy." Tears clouded her eyes.

"Of course you do, and we're having people look all over for her." Adam reached to the desk and got a tissue to wipe her eyes. "Can you tell me anything you remember?"

"I was cold." She shivered. "And scared." She began to sob.

"Why don't we take a walk and see if you remember anyplace," Adam said.

But a fifteen-minute walk during which Adam carried Missy didn't jog her memory.

Once they got back to the church and his study, Adam joggled Missy on his lap.

Miss Birdie said, "I called DPS—protective services. They're sending a social worker."

Adam felt a great sense of relief. Someone who knew how to handle this would take over.

"Sweetheart, a nice lady will be coming to take you someplace to wait for your mommy."

"Take me someplace?" Fear tinged Missy's voice. "What nice lady?" She looked at the pillar, her eyes wide again. "Are you the nice lady?"

"No, another lady will find a place for you to stay," he said. "A very nice lady. She'll be here soon."

Missy hopped off his lap, ran the short distance to Miss Birdie, and grasped the pillar's hand. "Want to stay with you."

Because she'd taken in her two granddaughters, Adam knew a soft place for abandoned little girls existed in the pillar's heart, as much as she attempted to hide it. From her expression, he could also tell the conflicting emotions that raged inside her: fear and consternation but also duty and compassion. Miss Birdie possessed an easy-to-read face, though usually it showed only frustration with her pastor. The range of her feelings at this moment intrigued him.

"She won't be lost very long," Miss Birdie said as if considering the addition of one more to her family. "The police should find her mother right away. I bet she's looking for Missy as we speak. But she really needs a shower."

"Why don't you take her to the gym and wash her up." Years ago, the church had had an active recreation program with great facilities. Someday, he hoped to start that again, but the entire area needed a lot of work and the church barely had enough money to keep the main building functioning. "I'll wait for Mercedes and children's services and call the police."

When they returned twenty minutes later, he'd finished the calls. Missy's brown hair stood up in wisps from being towel-dried and her freckles showed against clean, pale skin.

"I got her a change of clothes at the thrift shop but put the dirty clothes in this." She held up a plastic sack. "Too dirty and ragged to wear again, but I thought maybe the police could find something on them if it comes to that. Nothing in her pockets, no identification. Of course, I'm sure someone is looking for her."

Adam nodded but added nothing to the conversation Miss Birdie carried on with herself.

"You know, I have two girls I'm already taking care of," she said. "You know my plate is full now."

Yes, he did, but he didn't dare insult her by suggesting she couldn't do everything.

When he didn't say a word, the pillar said to the little girl, "Missy, when the nice lady gets here, she'll find you a place to stay until they find your mother."

"Please," Missy said in a trembling voice and with a beseeching expression only the hardest of hearts could resist, then she climbed on to Miss Birdie's lap and put her arms around the elder's neck.

A sudden rush of tenderness covered Miss Birdie's face before she again donned her no-nonsense, pillar-of-the-church expression. "All right." She nodded. "Bree and Mac will help and she'll be with us for such a short time."

"You can use the Presbyterians' day care," Adam suggested. "The ministerial benevolence fund can cover that."

Seconds later Mercedes walked into the room. "Sorry, I got held up at the library." After listening to how Missy had ended up in the pillar's lap, the Widow made more calls to check on legalities with her various relatives and make sure Miss Birdie would be immediately approved for foster care if necessary.

Twenty minutes later, the police arrived. They found out little from Missy but took her picture, clothes, and fingerprints. They also noticed smudges on the child's shoes they thought might be her mother's fingerprints. Or maybe not, but they'd send them to the lab in Austin. They'd check the hospitals in Austin and the morgue and put out a bulletin about the girl covering a hundred-mile radius. With so little to go on, they couldn't do more.

The two Widows left with a little girl between them.

"I'm sure she won't be with me for long," Miss Birdie said as she closed the door. She'd looked more worried and uncertain than Adam had seen her during their short acquaintance.

He vowed to help her as much as possible, but he wouldn't insult her by letting her know he was looking out for her as much as for Missy.

❦

Sam would never have opened the door if he hadn't looked out the window and seen two horses standing in his front lawn. A man stood with them, a man he recognized. Sam's mind associated the man with horses, but how hard was that connection when the man stood with two horses? Still, Sam thought it was an important link, something from those years he'd visited here.

Oddly, today he was up, showered, and dressed earlier than usual, but after fixing his own breakfast, he had no idea what to do next. Probably the reason he didn't usually get up so early.

"You don't remember me," the man began as Sam stepped out on the porch.

Not true. Sam could remember him, but he couldn't remember how.

"I'm Jesse Hardin from the Christian Church."

Sam took the man's callused hand and shook it before a memory surfaced. "Hey, I do remember you. You're the horse man. Aunt Effie used to take me to your place to ride." Sam grinned. "Those are some of the best memories of my life."

But he still didn't understand why these two horses—the gray with a saddle and the Appaloosa with only a blanket across her back— stood there, munching on the sparse grass of what he and the boys laughingly referred to as the front lawn.

"Thought you might like to take a ride this morning." Jesse jerked his head toward the animals.

"This morning? A ride?" He grinned. "In town? Is it legal?"

"Sure. I called Mercedes the other day. Her sister the judge approved the ride as a medical treatment for a vet, one of our boys."

"Medical treatment?" Sam stepped onto the porch, closed the door behind him, and studied the animals.

"Saw a program on the TV about amputees, vets who've lost their legs. Seems that if they ride a horse, it helps build up muscles and gets them used to a prosthesis better. Cheers 'em up, too."

"Really?" Sam turned to study Jesse. Was the man kidding him?

"Yup. Figure if it's on the TV, it must be true. Want to try it?"

Oh, yeah. Much better than walking between parallel bars.

"Supposed to also help with your balance and build your core, whatever that is." Jesse pointed. "You get the horse with the pad, Captain, because that's supposed to allow you to feel the horse better. That's what the guy on the TV said."

For a few seconds, Sam studied the horse. Tall creatures. "How do I get on?"

Jesse smiled. "Figured that out before I got here. You go to the edge of the porch and put your leg—the right one—over the back of the horse. I'll stand down there and give you a hand if you need it."

Sam had visions of himself rolling over the horse, ending up sprawled on the ground. But marines didn't mind falling on the ground. Marines were tough. He could handle this. "Okay. Let's go."

Jesse ran down the steps, pulled the Appaloosa toward the porch. He angled the horse so she straddled the steps, pushing her a little sideways and closer. The horse obeyed calmly, an action that made Sam feel more confident. This didn't seem like a creature who'd run away with him or buck him off.

"Gracie's a gentle old lady." Jesse stood on the other side of her and held out his hand. "You're perfectly safe."

With a nod, Sam approached the horse, leaned over to put his hand on her neck, and shifted his weight before raising his right leg to mount Gracie. When he settled on her broad back, she shifted a little but stayed still enough for him to relax, regain his balance, and pick up the reins. Jesse stood, unobtrusively, next to Gracie but didn't offer assistance.

When Sam felt secure, Jesse said, "Stay right there," as if Sam planned to gallop off.

The older man took the reins of his horse, got on, then reached for Gracie's reins. "The program showed the horse being led. Don't know why."

"If the program said that, go ahead."

It was fun, sitting on Gracie's back, her gait rocking him. Keeping his balance was harder than he'd thought but truly much more enjoyable than the parallel bars. He could feel strain in the muscles of his leg and other parts he hadn't worked on in PT. He didn't care. He was on a horse, ambling along the street and out to the countryside northwest of town. He felt great.

After fifteen minutes, Jesse turned the horses around. "Don't want to wear you out the first time," he said. "The program said once a week so I'll be back next Friday, if that works for you."

"Thanks, Jesse. That works great for me." He'd clear the entire day, the entire week, if he needed to.

They headed back toward town, through the rolling scenery and the green grass of the Hill Country.

"Next spring the bluebonnets will cover all this." Jesse waved at the fields. "Ever seen the wildflowers?"

Sam shook his head. "I always visited in the summer." Would he be here next spring to see them? He had no idea. Right now, he looked only far enough ahead to riding Gracie again, to ambling along the farm-to-market road toward Llano on her back.

On the way home, his thighs cramped and his back began to hurt from holding his posture. It felt like a good kind of hurt, the kind that came from exercise, not injury. The lethargy that filled him was just plain old exhaustion. He should sleep well tonight.

Odd how he'd begun to care about this community and the nice people. Jesse didn't have to do this, but he rode in front of Sam, perfectly happy to be ambling along the road, spending his time doing something for Sam. And the ladies had brought him so much food, he seldom had to microwave a frozen dinner. Because of them, he'd started to feel positive emotions, to be thankful, to feel alive—almost happy.

And he regretted every one of those feelings.

Chapter Twelve

Birdie stepped out of her shoes and wiggled her toes before she slipped on a pair of soft slippers. She closed her eyes for a moment—only a few seconds because she'd fall asleep if she stopped moving. Lord, she was plum wore out. Seemed she was always tired. And now what had she done on top of everything else? Taken this child in.

The child was sleeping so maybe Birdie'd take a nap. Yes, she would, later, after she put the groceries away and thawed something for dinner and . . . well, a few other things. After she finished all that, she'd take a nap. Of course, by that time, Missy'd probably be awake. She sighed as she rotated her shoulder to relieve the stiffness and headed into the kitchen.

She had to take care of herself. The girls couldn't get along without her and she'd just added one more child. All right, Missy was temporary and didn't really count on Birdie, but others did.

If she did too much and got sick, what would the church do without her? Everyone would leave things to this young minister, who might begin a guitar service, or use PowerPoint to display praise songs on the wall, or introduce all kinds of foolishness without her supervision. Not that he'd showed that inclination yet, but she needed to be here in case the tendency broke out unexpectedly.

No, she couldn't get old. She refused to get sick. Probably she should pray about it, tell God to either give her more strength or chip off a few layers of responsibility, but she didn't have the time or energy to instruct God about how to run the universe, not right now.

The girls would be home soon. They'd figure out how to watch Missy. First they'd . . .

A knock came on the front door. She glanced down at the sofa where Missy slept with Carlos the Cat curled up happily next to her. Don't that beat all? Carlos was usually an attack cat, but there he lay, snuggled against Missy. Then she opened the door as she moved her shoulder to get that final kink out.

❦

Adam watched as Miss Birdie again rotated her shoulder and grimaced. The pillar did have a breaking point, was actually human. He had to remind himself that she was nearing seventy and had the aches and pains of an elderly person—not that he'd ever call her that when she could hear—and the responsibilities of a much younger woman. As her minister, Adam had to remember she was a beloved child of God and treat her as such, even during the times she acted so determined and in charge—and scheming.

"I didn't know if you had a bed for Missy," he said. "I went over to the thrift shop and got a blow-up mattress and a nightgown and some clothing for her." He held out a large box and a small package. "Hope everything fits."

"Thanks, Pastor." She actually smiled at him, as if her minister had done something right, finally, but the smile didn't change the fact that she looked exhausted.

"Do you need anything else? Toys? More clothing?"

She shook her head. "Missy won't be here long. Maybe tonight. Maybe not. Her mother's looking for this little one. She has good manners and has gone to church. Someone has taken good care of Missy, taught her well, and must be worried."

The two both looked at Missy.

"Let me know if I can do anything," Adam said.

"Think I can't handle this?" Before Adam could answer, she plowed on, "Like a bachelor knows anything about children." She snorted.

The truce was over. Of course Miss Birdie would fight anyone who tried to shoulder part of her burden, but he'd do what he could even if he had to conceal his actions.

"My neighbor does. Ouida said she'd watch her in the evening, when you want to do something with your granddaughters. And I can take Missy to day care and bring her back. Besides, I do have a sister. There are things I can do."

Her glance showed she didn't accept that. "How old is your sister?"

Two years older than he, but Adam didn't say that. She'd just point out that he'd been too young to take care of a sister that close in age.

It didn't matter. He could allow her to win this one. Victory always cheered her up, and she deserved that.

❦

Much earlier than Sam wanted to be out of bed, he studied his reflection and thought what an idiot he was.

To look almost civilized, he'd chosen his one dress shirt, white and fairly presentable. Because he had no iron, he'd steamed it in the shower. He tightened the belt on khakis that hung on him. Add to that fairly new athletic shoes he'd found in the box of stuff the general had sent to him. He hadn't opened the carton until late last night after he'd had a couple of drinks. Only a few because he wanted to be able to function at the same time as he buffered himself from any memories rattling around loose inside, any reminders of activities he'd participated in back when he had two legs. Fortunately he'd found nothing but clothes and shoes.

He looked at himself in the mirror again. Over the last few days, he'd changed: better-looking clothes, shaved, and not hungover. What would he do next? Get a haircut? Not likely, but this "presentable" stuff seemed to be creeping up on him.

Who was he trying to kid with the white shirt and new shoes? He wasn't normal, lovable ex-marine amputee Sam Peterson, not inside or out, so why was he attempting to *look* like that? The kids didn't care about his appearance, which left only Willow Thomas to impress and she . . . she . . . Well, he didn't know about her but he did know about himself. He had no business dressing up to . . . what? To attract her? To date her?

To marry her?

Crap. What a load of crap.

He put the comb down, shook his head so the clean hair looked unkempt, and pulled off the shirt. With the prosthesis, changing shoes and trousers was more of a hassle than he wanted to face. He grabbed the cane and hobbled back into the bedroom.

In the corner, Aunt Effie's chair was piled with dirty clothes. On top of the dresser sat a pile of clean clothes he hadn't shoved into a drawer. Folding and putting clean clothing away was a hassle he'd learned not to bother with. A pile on the dresser worked fine and let him know when he needed to do the wash again. No one in this house cared if his T-shirts were wrinkled or not. He grabbed his marine T-shirt, the one the kids wanted him to wear, and tugged it on.

He'd have to wash clothes soon, not one of his favorite chores. Manipulating out to the washer and dryer in the back of the narrow carport with a load of clothing under his arm stretched his ability. After a few attempts, he'd learned to put the laundry in a dirty clothes bag and drag it behind him.

Dumb stuff to be considering. For a treacherous minute, he wanted to check himself in the mirror again, but he didn't. He didn't care how he looked. He was clean and that was all Nick and Leo cared about, if they even cared about that.

Seven o'clock. Ready and waiting. They'd pick him up in fifteen minutes. He grabbed his cane and headed toward the living room. He needed a drink. He functioned better dead to feeling of any kind.

Vodka? Did he have any vodka? No one would smell it on his breath. No one would notice if he were unsteady, not that he could get that drunk in fifteen minutes. A drink or two would take the edge off. He headed toward the kitchen exactly as a knock sounded on the door. Too late. He should've known the boys would keep on their mother until she gave up and headed over here early.

Why had he agreed to this?

"Just a minute." Sam forced himself to close the world out and quiet his thoughts.

"D'ya need some help, sir?" Leo shouted through the door.

"No," he called back. "Be right there."

For a moment, Sam hyperventilated, dragging in huge gulps of air while his heart pounded in his chest and sweat dripped down his face, all signs of an impending panic attack. "I'm doing fine," he said to himself in a low voice, attempting to calm his breathing and slow the heart. He hadn't had a panic attack since shortly after he got here. Why had one hit him now?

"I'm fine," he repeated quietly. As the VA counselor had coached him, Sam pursed his lips and pretended to blow an imaginary candle out to decrease the amount of oxygen he took in. His heart began to slow.

"Captain?" Willow called.

Oh, great, exactly what he needed, an anxious professional like Willow wondering what was happening.

"I'm fine," he said, loudly this time. And he was. His breathing had slowed and his heart no longer thudded as hard in his chest.

"I'll be right out," he shouted as he limped into the kitchen, got a glass of water, and drank it slowly. After that, he splashed cool water on his face and wiped it off, glad he'd caught it in time, before he went into full anxiety mode. He felt a little wobbly, but that would clear up soon.

He shuffled back through the living room and opened the door. "You're a little early," he said.

Willow scrutinized his face. She could probably read the physical signs of distress but didn't mention it, quickly turning her gaze away.

Couldn't she meet his eyes? Did she still feel a little uncomfortable about that kiss?

Or maybe it wasn't that kiss at all. Maybe as a professional she recognized the signs of a recent anxiety attack but didn't want to address it now. He didn't, either.

The boys wore jeans so new and stiff they crunched a little as they walked, with new burnt orange T-shirts and matching athletic shoes. All ready for the first day of school. Their mother wore slacks and a nice shirt, her usual dress, almost like a uniform for work. She'd changed from her professional shoes to some with a thin heel—what were they called? Kitten heels? Why did he know that? Probably from watching that late-night program with Stacy and Clifford when he couldn't get to sleep. Or was he named Clinton? He didn't know and didn't really care, but the shoes looked great on Willow.

"Cool," Nick said. "You're wearing your marine T-shirt. Sir."

"Come on, sir." Leo leaped down the steps and ran to open the car door.

"Mom says you get the front seat because it'll be easier for you to get in." Nick danced next to the car and watched Sam. "She knows stuff like that."

"It's a really low car," Willow apologized.

"We can help if you need us to hold your elbow or anything." Nick held out an arm.

"Get in, goofball." Leo dragged his brother to the driver's side of the car, pushed him into the back, and followed.

With the car door open, Sam sat on the edge of the seat, then turned as he picked up his right leg and placed it inside the car. In a car like this, it was a little awkward but not a difficult task. He grabbed the armrest and closed the door while Willow got in the other side.

"Sorry," Sam said. "I should've opened the door for you." He'd forgotten a lot about how to treat a woman.

"Thank you, Captain, but I'm perfectly capable of getting in the car by myself."

"I know that. That doesn't mean a gentleman should allow you to."

As she turned the key and started the engine, she glanced at him, then quickly away, concentrating carefully on the nonexistent traffic as she pulled onto the street. He grinned. She still couldn't look at him, which suggested . . . well, he didn't know what but *not* indifference.

"It's a short ride, sir," Nick said.

"He knows that. He used to live here," Leo said in an older-brother voice.

"I don't remember much about town." Sam looked over his shoulder at the boys. "I haven't been here for . . ." He paused to consider. ". . . for about fifteen years, and I haven't gone anyplace but to the hospital and the grocery store since I got back. Is the junior high still next to the H-E-B?"

"Did it used to be?" Nick said. "No, it's that way." He pointed vaguely to the east.

The boys attempted to explain where everything else in town was located and how the old IGA had become a department store and where the new post office was, as if he remembered where the old one had been. While they chattered, Willow kept her eyes on the road with so much attention she could've been driving at the Indy. After a few blocks of a carefully navigated route, she pulled into the driveway of the school, found a parking space close to the front door, and let out a deep sigh.

Sam would have laughed at her relief, but that would probably spook her more. To spook or not to spook? The question made him feel somewhat Shakespearean but didn't solve the dilemma that was Willow Thomas.

After their mother stopped the engine, the boys pushed out of the backseat and ran to his door to pull it open.

"Sir, we're here, sir," Nick and Leo said in unison.

As were a lot of other parents, all headed toward the building with their children. People might think they were a family, too. He'd never been a part of this kind of a family, not with the general always away or busy. Not that the four of them were family. Fantasy. When would he learn fantasy was not his friend?

He turned in the car, picked up his leg, and placed it on the ground before pushing himself to his feet and picking up his cane.

"Sir, take my hand." Nick stretched his arm out.

"No, lean on me, sir." Leo shoved his younger brother aside.

"Thanks, guys, I can make it. However, I think your mother is closer in height to me. If she could just give me a hand to get over the curb."

An expression of doom flashed across Willow's face, but, like a professional, she reached out, took his hand, and placed it on her arm. Although she attempted to hide it, she shivered, only a bit. Fortunately, he knew exactly what that meant.

He grinned. She kept her gaze at the ground as if it were filled with craters that presented insurmountable obstacles for an amputee, as if there were an IED buried nearby that she needed to guide him around.

It wouldn't hurt to allow himself this fantasy for an hour or two. Maybe it wouldn't hurt to feel nearly normal, pretend he was like those dads with kids running ahead of them and with a pretty woman by his side, even if only for a short time.

Chapter Thirteen

The fantasy collapsed an hour later, as soon as Sam got home. Once inside, the solitude hit him like the thick humidity of the Texas coast on an August afternoon.

He was alone. No family, no redheaded sons, no wife. Alone.

What irony. For months he'd wanted to be alone. He must be doing better if he'd started wanting people near, but it didn't *feel* better.

He took a step toward the kitchen. If he couldn't find vodka, he'd call the liquor store. They were always happy to deliver. But he stopped himself. He didn't want liquor and numbness. At least, not complete oblivion, not like he used to.

He wanted someone with him. He wanted to hear the boys in the backyard, but that wouldn't happen, not with school starting. And as skittishly as she behaved, their mother didn't seem likely to drop by for a visit just because he was such a nice guy.

He took a few steps toward the phone, picked it up, and hit the quick dial. "Hey," he said when the general picked up. "When will you get here?"

He'd become really desperate if he wanted to talk to his father and actually looked forward to the general's arrival.

❧

Willow breathed a sigh of relief when the captain got out of the car. She hadn't thought he could leverage himself up, not from this low car. He'd refused to allow her to give him a hand up or a shove in the back but struggled to get out on his own. *Men!* she thought, then changed her generalization to *Marines*. Stubborn and independent but admirable and inspirational—and the boys adored him.

Not that she wanted to consider those positive qualities because she didn't want to care about the captain as a person, as the man who'd pretty much adopted her children or, at least, had provided day care. That couldn't be fun for a single man like him.

Then she realized she'd spent the last few minutes watching him move up the walk and take the steps one at a time. She'd noticed again how fine he looked from every direction, front, back, and sides. What an idiot. She put the car in gear, checked behind her, and pulled out. Unfortunately, she had never become accustomed to the power of the engine. It sounded like a race car: *vroom.*

Was he dating? Surely, having grown up here, he knew people, probably families with women his age unless, of course, they'd all moved to the big city. The fact that he wasn't driving yet would cut down on that. The places to take a date in Butternut Creek were limited.

She shouldn't be considering either the captain's love life or his body. With a glance at the clock, she turned her mind back to her schedule for the day. Nearly eight thirty. She'd arrive early for her first appointment. After that, she'd go onto the floors to evaluate several patients.

But no matter how hard she attempted to concentrate on work, a corner of her brain kept bringing her back to that moment in the hallway at school, when Sam had put a hand on the shoulder of each son and smiled down at them. Leo and Nick looked up at him in such awe and, well, yes, love that the air around them seemed to sparkle.

No matter what he said or did, Captain Peterson was a good man, a man who cared about her sons. That scared her a lot, because she could fall for a man who spent time with the boys. Grant seldom did. She could care for a man who—oh, who was she kidding. She was already incredibly attracted to this man for reasons that had nothing to do with his relationship to her sons. She was attracted because, despite his attitude, he was smart and handsome and sexy. She'd begun to think no man could make her catch her breath, make her peek out the window of her office just to see him exercising.

For heaven's sake, she sounded like a lovesick schoolgirl. No, not true. He made her feel like a desirable woman. She hadn't felt that way since she'd found out about Tiffany.

❦

"Reverend Jordan," Maggie shouted from her office. "Phone."

He picked up the receiver. "Adam Jordan."

"This is Detective Somerville calling. Want to fill you in on the investigation about the child's family."

He grabbed a pen and a sheet of paper. "Go ahead."

"We identified her mother through fingerprints as Deanne Smith, lives in San Saba."

"Melissa Smith. So we know her last name. Have they located any relatives? Friends?"

"The local cops went by the house, but no one's home. Looks as if someone lived there until a few days ago. Newspapers in the front yard and mail in the box, but only junk mail. Nothing personal." He paused to clear his throat. "Mrs. Smith teaches third grade at the elementary school. She didn't show up for teacher training last week. The police checked at the school board office, but the emergency contact in Virginia doesn't answer."

"Missy said *Virginia* when we asked about her grandmother," Adam interjected, though the detective knew that from when they spoke earlier.

Somerville continued, "We ran down the references but none of the people listed have talked to her recently. That's about it."

"A dead end, huh?" Disappointed, he sat back in the chair.

"Sir, we'll keep investigating. Hard to believe she could just disappear without a trace."

"What about Missy's father?"

"No information and not a trace of men's possessions in the house. Also not listed on Mrs. Smith's job or rent applications." He paused. "The police have Mrs. Smith's fingerprints from her background investigation, which is how they were able to match the ones the lab found on the child's shoes. They'll put the prints in the system to see if anything shows up."

"You mean like a body?"

"Yes, but also could be a Jane Doe in a hospital. I'll let you know if I hear anything."

❧

Bree'd be home in an hour from volleyball practice and Mac was studying upstairs. As she cuddled the child who'd fallen asleep in her lap, Birdie enjoyed the soft, sweetly scented warmth of a little girl. At the same time, she realized her shoulder ached and she was simply too old for this.

The preacher had called her earlier about Missy but had no helpful information. "Dear Lord," she whispered, "You need to have Missy's mother turn up soon. I'm worn out."

Too tired to carry the child upstairs to the blow-up mattress they'd put in Birdie's bedroom, Birdie carefully placed her on the sofa and made sure the blanket covered her. Then she headed into the kitchen to see what she could thaw and heat up for dinner.

The previous night, Missy'd fallen asleep at ten thirty after Mac had spent nearly an hour rocking and calming the child. Birdie'd been asleep for only a few minutes when Missy's sobs awakened her. She stumbled across her bedroom to the corner where Missy slept and picked the girl up.

"Mommy. I want my mommy."

"I know, sweetheart, I know." She sat on the edge of her bed and rocked Missy until she quieted.

When she got back in bed, Birdie pulled the sheet over her shoulders and attempted to fall back to sleep but two questions haunted her:

When was Missy's mother going to show up?

And why had she, an old lady feeling older each day, taken the child in?

❦

Sam had gone off the wagon last night. Not that he'd been securely on it. At least, not completely, but the pain and the isolation and the longing . . .

What kind of a wimp had he become? Why had he turned to alcohol again when he knew it didn't help? He knew the emptiness and the ache would still be there long after the fleeting surcease of tequila . . . well . . . ceased.

He was supposed to be at the hospital in an hour. The van would be here in forty-five minutes. He pushed himself up to a sitting position, knowing no amount of counting backward would make him feel better. Even the idea of walking up and down between the railings in PT intensified the pain.

And he'd have to see her again. Willow Thomas, who'd been avoiding him for nearly a week. The boys had come over after school a couple of afternoons. Like he wanted that or needed them.

Yeah, he did. He might try but couldn't lie to himself how much he enjoyed the kids. With the start of school, Willow had given them permission to visit him but they had to leave here at five, walk home for dinner, and do their homework. Because he'd taught them discipline, expected them to honor women, they didn't dare leave a second late.

He thought karma meant if he did good, he'd get good back. In his case, karma should mean if he followed the rules and got the boys ready to go home on time, he'd see Willow once in a while. Obviously it didn't work that way for him. Sometimes life came back to bite you. No good deed goes unpunished.

What other clichés could he think of to put off getting up?

He now had thirty-five minutes to get dressed and eat and be ready for the van.

The short period of preparation explained—mostly—why he looked scruffy. Not enough time to shave made his beard show dark. With only a few minutes to take a shower and no time to blow-dry his hair, it still dripped when he ambled into the therapy room on his cane. Clean, of course. Dirty wasn't an option. Sadly, arriving hungover with a pounding headache and queasy stomach seemed to be.

While several clients pulled on bands attached to hooks or lay on treatment beds lifting canes over their heads, he stood alone by the parallel bars.

"You don't look well, Captain."

Willow had appeared in front of him looking bright, smiling in her best professional manner. Her perkiness made his head hurt even more.

"Tough night?" she asked.

He'd shake his head if the movement didn't cause pain to shoot up his neck and scramble his brain. "I'm fine."

"I need to observe you today." She picked up a clipboard. "After that, I have to make some notes and do a few measurements for the prosthetist. I'll send him a report today because he's coming here to see you next week."

Sam pulled himself between the rails and attempted to walk as well as possible. Dumb. Not as if he needed to impress her with how little he limped.

"Captain," she said. "You're slouching." She placed her hand on the small of his back and pressed. "Straighten here." Keeping the pressure on, she watched him take several steps. "Does that feel better?"

It did. Took some strain off his leg, but he wondered how long he could maintain that position. He'd been surprised how much strength and muscle he'd lost over the months before he started rehab.

She watched him, evaluating every movement. "Try not to swing your right leg so much. That's hard on your hip. Use your muscles, not that rocking motion."

"Easy for you to say," he mumbled.

"Probably so, but if you over-rotate any part of your body, you'll have trouble later." She smiled, again professionally, as if he were a pitiful wretch she had to rehabilitate—which he was, of course.

Women were seldom attracted to a pathetic shell of a man.

After a few repetitions of the exercises, she said, "Captain, please come with me so I can take a few measurements." She turned precisely and strode toward her office. Her posture cried, *I'm a professional and not the least bit interested in you.*

If she wasn't attracted, why the statement? Why the attitude?

The tension in his neck decreased as he followed her, gorgeous even under the lab coat. He grinned and his headache lessened a little.

"Please sit down, Captain." She gestured to a chair as she settled behind her desk.

With his cane, he pushed the door shut. Then he shoved the chair closer to her. She pushed it back and moved hers in the opposite direction. Unexpected. He'd never had a woman react like that.

"Captain," she said in an unruffled voice.

One more thing he'd lost: his touch with women. The always successful Sam Peterson charm didn't affect this woman, at least not now, not in *her* department. He knew it had a couple of times, but today Willow looked cheery and chipper, spunky and totally, obnoxiously in charge.

She watched him coolly. "I need to make some measurements, but you'll need to remove your prosthesis."

Another problem: Sam didn't feel toward her as he should with a professional.

"That means I'm going to have to take off my jeans," he said stupidly. Obviously he'd have to unless she'd developed X-ray vision, a superpower he hadn't noticed she possessed.

As for taking off his jeans, he didn't think that was a good idea. Although she didn't seem to think of him as a man, he couldn't forget she was a woman. Panic spread through him. "Why don't you have Mike measure?"

"Because, Captain, this is my job."

Her voice firm, she glared at him. Though he didn't think it was possible, her posture became straighter and even more professional. He didn't know how she did that because she'd sounded like a real medical badass only seconds earlier.

"I'm the PT who works with the prosthetist, Captain. That's my job, my specialty."

Great. He'd insulted Willow. Her words made him feel like a complete jerk. No, as the man who'd tried to be his counselor at the VA had told him a million times, he'd decided to act like a jerk. She'd just caught him at it.

Why did *this* woman attract him? His usual choice in women was pretty and petite and adoring, cute and compliant. Those women didn't glare at him, and they didn't act like *any* kind of badass.

No matter how educated and trained and competent she was, he wasn't feeling patient-like enough toward her to drop his pants.

She stood, opened a cabinet, and pulled out a gown. "Put this on." She placed it on her desk only inches from him. "Take off your trousers. Now. I'll be back to measure."

He hesitated.

"Suck it up, Captain." She glared at him. "If you want to get rid of the clunky old prosthesis, the one you hate, the one that rubs and doesn't fit well, do this. I have to send Leland the information." Then she raised one eyebrow. "I'm a trained professional."

He'd had measurements taken and been examined, prodded, and photographed by nurses and doctors and PTs in Hawaii and DC. It never bothered him before, but this . . .

"Next time, wear shorts so you don't have to change." She swirled and stalked out of the office, closing the door behind her.

He picked up the gown and studied it. A marine wouldn't wear something like this. But he couldn't have worn shorts, either. Everyone would see he was missing a leg. Everyone could see the prosthesis, if he wore shorts.

Was he ashamed? No, but it was unsightly. He'd have to expose that ugliness and loss to the world, at least to the part of the world that lived in Butternut Creek.

Why? Why should he feel that way? He'd lost that part of his leg when fighting for his country. It should be a badge of honor.

It *was* a badge of honor, of service, not a disability to hide.

That decided, he reached toward a pencil holder on Willow's desk and pulled out a pair of scissors. With his thumb, he measured a few inches above his knee before he began to cut the leg of his jeans off.

Finished, he examined his new semi-shorts. The right leg of the trousers hit mid-thigh. A little uneven but, all in all, it worked. He tossed the gown back on the desk, removed the prosthesis, and leaned back in the chair.

Willow tapped on the door. "Ready?"

"Come in."

She opened the door and stopped, looking not at his missing leg but at the new semi-shorts. "Very clever," she said with a smile.

He felt pretty proud.

The measurements completed, she said, "Leland will be coming next week with a new prosthesis. You're going to be surprised by how comfortable this one will be, how much you can do with it after you get used to it."

"Like playing basketball? Running?"

"Don't see why not."

"Dancing?"

"Of course."

"Good, because I never could dance before."

She smiled. Nice of her because he bet she'd heard that joke a thousand times. Her expression encouraged him to add, "I'm no prize, an amputee who drinks too much. I don't have the slightest idea what I'm going to do when PT is over and I'm completely rehabilitated, at least physically."

"Perhaps—" She turned toward him with an expression of . . . well, interest. Not interest in him as a man but as her patient. "Perhaps I should set you up for vocational counseling."

"What I mean is that I find you very attractive but I don't have much to offer."

"You sell yourself short, Captain. I'm sure many people find you personable." She made a few more notes on his chart, added something on the computer, and kept busy for a few minutes.

While she did, he watched her and mulled over the statement. Personable. Exactly what he'd been looking for. What did that word mean, really? Almost any other adjective, perhaps *charming* or *handsome* or *sexy*, would've made him happy. But *personable*?

"Do you?" he asked. "Find me personable?"

"Of course. What woman wouldn't?" She turned toward him. In that softer voice, she added, "Captain, please remember, I am a professional, at least trying to be. For a moment I forgot that. I should never have kissed you." She shook her head. "Never. As your therapist, I can't let that happen again." Her expression softened and she looked a little bit regretful.

With that small amount of encouragement, he attempted to take her hand.

Did he never learn?

"Don't you listen to anything I say?" She scooted away from him.

From her determined expression—eyes narrowed and chin forward—he knew she wanted him to leave. She was on the job so she didn't feel open to a bit of flirting. He had to remind himself she was like no other woman he'd dated, pursued, flirted with, or lusted after.

He had to learn to back off, to give her room. He had no experience doing that. Until his leg was blown off, he'd always gone straight forward, regardless of the torpedoes.

Now he had to adjust to too many things in his life, and changing in any way had become harder than he'd ever thought. Nevertheless, with Willow he had to rein himself in. He forced himself to change the subject.

"Tomorrow night the boys are staying for dinner. Pizza. Join them?"

"Oh, that's right. They did mention that. I'd forgotten."

"Would you like to join us?" he repeated courteously, in a friendly way, not a bit pushy.

"Captain, I can't."

With tremendous effort not to crowd her, he didn't say a word, but he worried. She wouldn't take the boys away from him and his evil influence, would she? Stupid thought. The boys weren't his but he had to know. "Can Leo and Nick still come?" He pushed himself to his feet as he waited for her answer.

"Of course. They'd be really disappointed if they couldn't." She smiled—slightly—at him. "They look up to you. I'd never interfere with that. I'll pick them up at seven. They have some chores to do at home."

As he opened the door, she added, "You'll be sober."

He turned to face her. "Of course I will. I'd never hurt them." No, he wouldn't—except, of course, wanting to have a couple of shots of vodka before he took the kids to school, but she didn't know about that and he hadn't done it.

"Wait, we—" she began at exactly the same time the phone rang.

Christine knocked on the door and shouted, "Willow, we need you."

He opened the door and pushed past the aide.

"Captain, we need to talk," Willow said as Christine entered.

He left the department, walked down the corridor and outside, where he settled on the bench to wait for his ride home.

As he sat there, he worried. The *you'll-be-sober* question hurt, but the *we-need-to-talk* statement scared the crap out of him.

Chapter Fourteen

Nervous didn't even begin to describe how Sam felt that Saturday night. He'd enjoyed the ladies but had never found one he couldn't easily replace with another.

Until now. That scared him.

He'd thought Willow felt the chemistry, too, but if she had she was ignoring it. Oh, sure, she'd agreed to let the boys come for dinner. She'd pick them up in a few minutes. He might not even see her. She might honk and the two would run out.

He checked the kitchen clock. A few minutes before seven. While they waited for their mother, Nick and Leo had run out to the backyard to look at the rickety fence that was their next project together. The dirty forks and glasses sat in the sink, and the boys had torn up the pizza box and put it in the recycle bin. He looked at his watch, then remembered he didn't wear it anymore because Morty had given it to him. It hurt too much to wear it.

Besides, he bet the time hadn't changed since he'd looked at the clock only seconds earlier.

To waste a few minutes, he went into the bathroom, moving smoothly and without a cane. He still had one but seldom used it. The PT had helped incredibly; the Thomas family, even more.

Once there, he picked up a comb and pulled it through his hair. It was getting too long. Too much bother to wash and dry, but he had to keep it, at least until the general arrived. The man hated long hair. A lot.

Wasn't he too old to enjoy tweaking the general? He considered the subject. No, he wasn't. It was still fun.

When the doorbell rang, he turned and hurried down the hall. Opening the door, he saw Willow holding a pitcher.

"I brought you something." She smiled.

A smile and a gift—that was good, right?

"The boys are in the backyard." He walked toward the slider and pulled it open. "Nick, Leo, your mother's here."

"Mom, we saved you dessert," Nick said. He ran in and, after a glance at Sam, took the pitcher from his mother.

"The pizza came with brownies," Leo chimed in. "We know how you like them."

As the boys raced into the kitchen, Willow glanced at him.

"Your sons tell me you love chocolate." He held his hands up in front of him and shook his head. "This was all their idea, not mine. You are my PT and a professional who isn't interested in kissing me ever again. I'd never attempt to bribe a professional with chocolate. *They* insisted on saving the brownies until you got here."

She looked perplexed, as if she had no idea how to answer.

"Mom, come on," Leo shouted.

"Sir, what would you like to drink?" Nick asked as the adults entered the kitchen. "Mom makes the best peach tea in the world." He paused to consider that statement. "You know, if tea was really important to us men."

"Tea sounds great," he said. "You guys know where the ice is. I hide it in the freezer."

Sam lifted his gaze to Willow but she seemed busy, intent on taking glasses from the cupboard. He leaned against the doorjamb and, with pleasure, watched her move through the small area with such purpose.

Maybe they'd leave after they finished. He hoped so because the thought of the little talk Willow had mentioned terrified him more than facing a dozen rocket launchers aimed straight at him.

Willow studied the table but not the captain. No, she kept her gaze away from him, as if she didn't notice him sitting there. She attempted not to act really obvious in her effort to pretend he didn't exist.

With the glasses filled, napkins on the table, and the tiny box of brownies set in the middle, they all settled in. The boys chattered and asked questions about the marines, which Sam answered. Other than "Do you need more tea?" Willow said nothing.

When Sam glanced at her, she thought he looked perfectly friendly but, perhaps, a little worried. Why had she mentioned she wanted to talk to him? Guilt, of course.

When they were finished, Willow had the boys clear and wipe down the table while she started to wash the dishes. Considering they'd used three forks for dinner and a total of seven glasses, it wouldn't take long.

"I can do that later." Sam stood before he added in a casual voice, "Did you want to talk about something?"

She turned toward him, but her eyes shifted, not making contact with his because she really didn't want to talk to him. Why had she said she needed to? "I'm afraid we can't, Captain. We have to leave. We're going to church in the morning."

"It's not even eight o'clock yet. Do you think thirteen hours is enough time to get ready for church?" he said, his voice dripping with sarcasm. He grinned because now he was enjoying her obvious discomfort. "Or have you lost your nerve? About our chat?"

Well, she wasn't going to let him get by with that implication.

"Boys," she said, "I need to talk to the captain. Go in the living room and watch television for a few minutes."

Aware of the no-nonsense tone of her voice, the boys ran from the kitchen.

"Guys, I have a new war movie on the DVR," Sam called after them. "Go ahead and watch it."

"Thank you, sir," they said in unison.

"What's up?" He leaned against the counter only a few feet from the sink.

"I sometimes overthink things, Sam . . . Captain." Was that ever an understatement, she thought as she put the last glass in the drainer.

Sam waited for her to go on.

"Yesterday, as you were leaving my office, I realized I had to clarify that terrible question I asked." She glanced up, her voice sincere and urgent. "I took additional training in prosthetics. That's why I was hired here. I'm the person, the best person, in the department to help you with your rehabilitation."

"Okay." He shrugged. "I'm good with that. In fact, I'm grateful that you have that training and expertise. I understood that before I left."

"I know. I probably don't need to reiterate that."

"You can iterate and reiterate all you want, but I did catch your meaning."

"I know." She paused and cleared her throat. "I also need to apologize for my rudeness, for telling you not to drink. That's none of my business. I was flustered and confused." She grimaced. "You do that to me. I wish you didn't because I hate to feel uncertain and fluttery."

He grinned.

Darn, he was nearly irresistible when he grinned. Of course, listing the times that he *wasn't* nearly irresistible would take up very little time or space.

"I want you to know how much I appreciate all you've done with my sons. I know you wouldn't do anything to harm or endanger them."

"Okay." He nodded.

"I should never have implied . . ."

"You didn't imply. You stated."

She nodded. "I should never have said that. I'm sorry."

"Okay."

She should stop. Certainly she'd expressed enough regret for tonight, but she couldn't. "One more thing."

"You're in a real orgy of apologies, aren't you? Bet you'd prefer not to talk about orgies with me."

She glared at him before saying, "Just one more. I messed up by kissing you. I'm sorry about that, too."

"That's what you've said, but I wouldn't say you messed it up. It was a very nice kiss. You do that well. I enjoyed it and thought you did, too. I wouldn't mind doing it again." Before she could interrupt, he held his hand up. "But I'm going to leave that up to you. If you want to kiss me"—he pointed toward his mouth—"you know exactly where to find my lips."

She tossed the dishcloth in the water, hard enough that it splashed up into her face. "That's not what I had in mind when I started this apology."

"Okay, but kissing's mostly what I have in mind when I'm with you."

"Forget that." She glared. "The kiss."

"You really mean what you're saying? Forget that kiss?"

She nodded.

He shook his head. "I'd prefer to *remember* that kiss and try a few more, just as an experiment, to see if we really like them."

"We both liked that one. That isn't the problem."

"Seems to be with you."

He grinned as she felt herself becoming angrier—but at herself, not him. She yearned to say something clever and sophisticated, a few biting words to shut him up, but she couldn't think of words of any kind. Besides, she'd probably sputter if she tried.

"Okay, okay," he said. "As hard as it is for me, I'll behave. And just so we'll both be more comfortable, I'll wear shorts to the hospital. Then you won't have to tell me to drop my jeans."

"Mom?" Leo asked, his voice high and puzzled.

They turned to find the boys staring at them from the dining room.

"Why do you want Sam to drop his pants?" Nick asked.

She blinked several times as her cheeks reddened. Then she picked up the dishcloth and wiped the counter with quick, nervous strokes, ignoring the question.

"Nothing," Sam said. "She's giving me instructions on measuring for my new leg."

"You're getting a new leg?" Nick's eyes dropped to Sam's knee. "Cool. Can we see it?"

"Sure. Your mom's going to make sure it fits right."

"Awesome, Mom." Leo smiled at her, but his gaze fell to Sam's knee, too.

"When?" Nick asked.

"Soon," Willow said as she emptied the sink and rinsed it. "Let's go. You have to clean your bedrooms." When both sons groaned, she tilted her head and gave them *the look*. "You have to take care of your own home, not just the captain's."

"Yes, ma'am," they said in unison, obviously not daring to give her lip both because of her expression and because Sam watched them carefully.

"A marine respects women," Nick and Leo said together.

"Bye, Sam," Leo said. "Thanks for the pizza."

Willow left with a wave. "And the brownie."

As she drove away, she wondered where this thing, whatever it was, with Sam—with the captain—was going.

With a shake of her head she pulled her thoughts back to reality. There was no "thing" with Sam. Her husband had left her barely a year earlier. In no way did she feel strong enough, trusting enough, to enter any relationship with a man, especially a man who had no idea what he wanted or where he was going, a man who'd even called himself a bad bargain.

❦

Sam watched the three head toward the car. He didn't hold the boys' sudden departure against them. The look their mother had given them had scared him, too.

So, other than being terrified by her glower, what was going on between him and Willow? The feelings bouncing back and forth between them seemed both better and worse.

Wait. Did he want things to get better or to get worse between them? Kissing was good, but *better* scared him; *worse* depressed him.

He watched as the car drove off, the two boys waving back at him. With an answering wave, he turned the porch light off. At that moment, the idiocy of the situation hit him. He was deeply attracted to a woman who thought he was personable. Personable. The facts: She smiled at him, seemed to enjoy his company although she didn't fall all over herself to be with him—all of that very low level of attraction showed how desperate he was for her attention. These were not the signals given off by a woman who wanted him. Right now, he didn't mind the barely noticeable signs because the entire situation was ambiguous.

For him, ambiguous was a good first step. It was certainly a lot more positive than hating everyone and drinking himself into an anger-fueled stupor.

He should accept all this, the ambiguity and uncertainty, sit back and see where it led them, not bug her too much.

Oh, sure. Relaxing and allowing life to flow by sounded a lot like Sam Peterson.

As she greeted members of the congregation and handed out bulletins, Birdie felt a glow of pride in the interior of the sanctuary. She'd worked hard to remodel the area a few years earlier. Colonial architecture with white columns on each side of the platform—what was the correct word for the platform? Wine-colored carpet covered the three steps. A lectern jutted out on one side of the chancel—that was the word! *chancel*—with a pulpit on the other. The covers of a few of the pew cushions showed wear, but the rest looked good. She had no idea why some were worn; not that many people sat there.

Not that she could enjoy the view as much as usual. On the back pew, Missy ran back and forth, occasionally stopping to clap her hands and dance. Her behavior completely baffled Bree, who sat on the bench next to the child.

"New dress," Missy said to Susan Pfannenstiel, who'd just started down the center aisle. "And new socks. With flowers."

"Very pretty," Susan said.

As the child showed off her new clothing, the organist played softly. Supposed to be a time for meditation but never was. People chatted and greeted one another instead of praying. That was a fight she'd given up on. Guessed fellowship was important. Besides, contemplating the Almighty didn't mesh well with entertaining a four-year-old.

"How's she doing?" Susan whispered.

"She's had a tough time," Birdie said. "She cries a lot, doesn't understand why her mother isn't here. I have no answer."

Behind the communion table was an old-fashioned baptistery. It consisted of an opening the size of a large window with burgundy velvet curtains on each side and a painting of the Jordan River on the wall. Beautiful, one of the best parts of the church in Birdie's opinion.

When she saw it, Missy straightened, obviously intrigued. After studying the scene for nearly a minute, the child stood up on the pew and pointed. "Look," she crowed, "a puppet show." Missy clapped her hands, obviously expecting an imminent theatrical performance.

The congregation burst into laughter.

"That's not for a puppet show," Bree explained in a low voice. "That's the baptistery."

Missy frowned. "What's a baptry?" she whispered back.

Birdie took a few steps toward her and whispered to the child, "That's where people become members of the church."

"Aah." Missy nodded. "Do they get to play with the puppets?"

Fortunately at that moment, Jesse Hardin headed down the aisle. "Horse man!" Missy shouted.

Jesse grinned at her and reached in his pocket. He pulled out a peppermint candy and handed it to the child, which distracted her nicely.

Then the organist began to play more loudly while the minister and the tiny choir processed down the aisle singing the opening hymn. The congregation rose and joined in, mumbling the words in rhythm with the organ.

Pastor Adam looked nice in his robe, mature and almost spiritual. His hair had grown so his scalp didn't shine through as much. His sermons were pretty good. She'd keep working with him, send him a few emails every now and then about how he could improve. Obviously he'd taken her advice because he showed great progress under her guidance.

Ten minutes into the service, she sat next to Bree and Missy. She'd forgotten how distracting a child could be. Oh, she'd prepared. On the pew between them were a doll with several outfits and accessories, four or five coloring books and a box of crayons, and a few little books. Missy wanted each of them at the same time. A few minutes later, none of them interested her.

Obviously the child had attended church regularly. Missy knew about prayers, closing her eyes and folding her hands piously—for all of ten seconds until she was ready to do something else.

When in the world would Mrs. Smith ever show up? Birdie needed her nearly as much as Missy did.

❦

"Why don't we have a children's sermon?" Adam asked Maggie.

The part-time secretary had just pulled her chair up to the desk and picked up her cup of coffee. She blinked. "I don't know, Pastor. We haven't had kids for so long, I guess it looked foolish for one or two children to sit up in the front with the preacher. Or no one, most mornings."

"How are we going to appeal to families if we don't have something for their kids? Do we have children's church or a nursery?"

"We haven't needed them since the last minister left. He had five kids."

"But the two Thomas boys were in church, and so was Missy."

Perhaps he could borrow Carol and Gretchen for Sunday morning if only for children's sermon, to swell the crowd. Oh, not only for his evangelistic purposes, but exposure to religion and the kids at church wouldn't hurt them much.

"How many of them are going to stay in town? As soon as they find a relative for Missy, she'll be gone."

A fact he knew well. Adam had called the police a couple of times, but they hadn't found out more. The emergency phone still didn't answer. Although obviously well cared for, Missy had not been reported as missing. The child seemed to be alone in the world, but both he and Miss Birdie knew she had, or at least used to have, a mother who loved her and who'd taken her to church and hugged her and bought her new clothes.

Where could she be?

At least she probably hadn't died. The police had sent the fingerprints all over the country; they didn't match those of any Jane Does they had in the morgue.

After nearly an hour of sermon preparation, the phone rang. Adam answered, again forgetting he had a secretary for two hours a morning. Would he ever get used to that? "This is Adam Jordan."

"Good morning, Reverend Jordan. This is Detective Somerville from the police department."

"Glad to hear from you. I've been thinking a lot about Missy. I hope you have good news."

"We found Missy's mother."

"Terrific."

"St. Michael's Hospital in Austin called. Fingerprints match a Deanne Smith who's been in a coma since August nineteenth. Airlifted from Butternut Creek. Hit by a car a few blocks from where the little girl was found."

"Great." Adam jumped to his feet, happy for the match although sorry for the injuries to the mother. "Sounds as if you found her. What took so long?"

"Snafu on that end. They identified her through a purse found near her but didn't send the prints until yesterday."

"How is she? What do we do next?"

"As I said, she's in a coma. You have all the information we know. Maybe you could visit her, see if you can find out anything."

"Glad to." After he hung up and jotted down the information, he wondered what to do next. Should he take Missy to see her mother? Probably not, at least not today. He should investigate a little, find out if this Deanne really was her mother and see if her condition might frighten the child.

"Maggie." He hurried through the reception area. "I have to go to Austin. Be back in a couple of hours."

The old car made it to Austin with no trouble. Rex had performed mechanical miracles with the ancient vehicle. When he got to St. Michael's Hospital, Adam checked in at the ICU and went to Mrs. Smith's bed.

Yes, this was Missy's mother. She had the same fly-away hair and freckles but her skin was pale, nearly gray. Her chest lifted rhythmically. The tubes and machines hooked up to her might scare Missy, as would her mother's stillness. He explained the situation to a nurse checking Mrs. Smith's vitals and asked her advice.

"Sometimes it's difficult for a very young child to see her mother like this, so quiet and on all the equipment," she said. "Maybe you could take a picture and talk to her about it before she came."

"But you do think I should bring her."

The nurse glanced at Mrs. Smith, then at him. "You'll have to decide, but often it's better for her to see that her mother is alive, even with all the machines. Otherwise, she might worry more."

"Will she be okay?"

"I really can't discuss the injuries without a family member. However there's a reasonable chance she will recover. It may be a slow process."

"Thank you."

With the nurse still hovering and taking care of Mrs. Smith, Adam pulled out his cell to snap a picture and attempted to find the best position that showed the fewest machines. Before he left, Adam stood next to the bed and picked up Mrs. Smith's hand. "Your daughter Missy is fine," he said. "She's being taken care of in Butternut Creek." He repeated the sentence several times, then gave a short prayer for healing before he lay her hand back on the bed.

The seminary's professor of pastoral care believed that people in a coma were able to hear. Adam hoped his words brought peace to Missy's mother.

When he got back to Butternut Creek, Adam headed for the diner where he knew Miss Birdie would be cleaning after departure of the lunch crowd.

"They found Missy's mother," he said as he approached the pillar.

"Praise the Lord!" She lifted her arms toward the sky. "Preacher, I love that little girl and I'm really happy for her and her mother. But"—she sighed and dropped into a chair—"I'm even happier for me. I'm pretty sure raising another child would be the death of me. Now." She pointed at the chair across from her. "You sit there. I'll get you a cup of cup of coffee, then you can tell me all about it."

"No, Miss Birdie, you sit down and I'll get coffee for both of us."

She didn't argue.

❦

On Thursday afternoon, Birdie settled in a chair with a clear view of the PT room. She felt a tiny bit of shame because she'd had to shove Susan Pfannenstiel and her walker out of the way with her hip. Not hard, but she had to get to that chair first. She needed to see what was happening inside.

In the center of the room, Sam swung his way across the parallel bars. A man—some kind of expert from Austin, she guessed—stood at the other end of the bars and watched.

Where was Willow? She couldn't see her anyplace. Just Sam and the man and that nitwitted, man-hungry Trixie.

When Sam reached the end of the bars, the man nodded. He reached down and patted Sam's thigh and knee. The captain had a new fake leg, Birdie guessed. Okay, the correct term was *prosthesis*. She hadn't seen the other one because Sam always wore trousers, but he had shorts on today. The artificial limb—that sounded like a good term—was shiny metal with all sorts of belts and hinges.

Then Willow wandered over. That's exactly what she did: wandered. She didn't rush to see Sam, like she was really interested in him. Of course, Willow had never displayed the slightest bit of interest in Sam—a terrible failure for the Widows not to have worked on that, a loose end they should have tied up.

Birdie MacDowell, you are a foolish old lady, a dreamer, she lectured herself. Although she tried to hide it, she was a romantic, had been until Martha had run off with that no-good man. With that experience, Birdie felt ashamed to admit she still believed in true love and the dreams a mother has for her daughter's future.

Because she'd failed with Martha, perhaps she'd build up some treasure in heaven by bringing other people together, people who would be loving and faithful and responsible—and happy. Yes, she was a silly old woman, but how could matchmaking between two lonely people hurt anyone?

At least, that's what she thought until Sam looked up at Willow.

His expression was grim and his eyes bleak. Could it be pain from the new prosthesis? Birdie didn't think so, because almost immediately he smiled at Willow. Pleasantly. Yes, he wore a *pleasant* smile, not that amazed, love-shocked expression she'd seen that first day they met. He and Willow looked like patient and therapist. Where had the passion she'd seen in Sam's eyes gone? What had happened to the love-at-first-sight look that had burst across his face?

Bah. She'd let her matchmaking slide and look what had happened. Nothing. Actually, they'd moved backward. Not a bit of attraction showed between these two beautiful young people who were absolutely meant for each other. Not just because they seemed to fit but also because they were about the only single young people in town except for the preachers.

Pastor Adam and the Reverend Mattie had spent hours at the diner, drinking coffee. Often they were joined by ministers from the other churches and spent the time discussing sermons or planning upcoming church events. *Hrmp.* Hardly a romance blooming there despite the fact she'd heard the two single ministers went to Marble Falls to see a movie every now and then.

Perhaps she could salvage something from the rubble of her effort with Sam and Willow. If Willow was no longer interested in Sam, she and Pastor Adam could be a good match.

But what about Sam?

No, Sam and Willow were the couple they had to bring together now. Sam was obviously still in love with Willow. After the Widows completed that task—which had turned out to be much more difficult than she'd expected—they'd undertake finding a wife for the preacher again.

For now, she needed to meet with Mercedes and Winnie. They'd lost every bit of momentum and better get busy PDQ. She'd be jiggered if she couldn't make at least one match.

Chapter Fifteen

At nine o'clock, Maggie stuck her head into Adam's office. "Do you have your tickets, Preacher?"

His sermon for Sunday was in terrible shape and needed a significant amount of spiritual intervention to rescue it. Alas, that hadn't happened yet. For that reason, he welcomed Maggie's intrusion. He glanced up at her and asked, "Tickets for what?"

The question staggered her. She froze in shock, incredulity obvious in her expression. She held her hands over her heart as if she wasn't sure it was still beating. "For the football game." Her voice held the distress of a woman hearing her minister hadn't prepared for the second coming.

"Is that tonight?" he asked.

Obviously the wrong question. She gaped at him.

"It's the first home game of the season," she enunciated clearly so he could understand.

Texas football. Nothing like it, everyone told Adam—over and over and over. He'd thought the huge high school arenas where Kentuckians flocked for basketball were something, but high school football was even bigger in this state. In Texas, football was the number one sport and there wasn't a number two. Maybe way down the list at number five, basketball or baseball or volleyball would show up, but only as an afterthought.

He turned to look outside. "But it's hot, supposed to be ninety today."

She tilted her head. "So?"

"Who plays football when it's this hot?"

"Are you kidding, Preacher? This is Texas." She waved her hands around her, pointing at, he guessed, the entire state. "It's always hot here at the beginning of football season. The temperature drops a little after the sun goes down, and by October it's downright chilly."

Maggie wore a bright gold T-shirt with BCHS LIONS embroidered on it in black. The abbreviation made sense. BUTTERNUT CREEK HIGH SCHOOL would be hard to fit across anyone's chest. As a mascot, a lion sounded okay. The animal was, obviously, the color of butternuts.

He should've noticed Maggie's apparel when she'd entered the office. Blame that oversight on his surprise at her words. He'd been brought up to go to football games when the leaves changed and temperatures fell. By late October, Midwesterners didn't think they were having fun until snow covered them and they shivered in nearly zero weather, bundled up in blankets and heavy coats, knit caps, and electric socks. In fact, that was one of the reasons why Kentuckians all looked forward to basketball, a game played inside by people in shorts.

"Don't the players get sick in the heat?"

"Hydration," she explained as if he were a little slow or, maybe, some kind of an alien, which he believed anyone from outside the state was during the fall ritual called football season. This reaction showed that as much as people wanted to believe they were alike, deep down an enormous chasm existed between football people and basketball fans.

He'd have to adapt.

He'd also have to buy tickets. And a T-shirt. Probably a sweatshirt for those chilly October evenings.

Maggie left after giving him exhaustive instructions about how to accomplish all this, where to go and who to talk to and that the school board office where tickets were sold closed for an hour at noon. She drew a map and made him write everything down, clearly certain an outsider couldn't figure out how to undertake the mission by himself.

Not that the instructions were helpful. She said things like, "Next to where the post office used to be," and "Down the block from where Eddie and Susan Parker—you know, from the Methodist Church—lived before her mother died."

Shortly after Maggie left and before he could get back to performing CPR on that sermon, Miss Birdie called.

"Do you have your ticket for tonight?" she asked before he could even say *hello*.

"I'm fixin' to," Adam said, delighted he'd worked that Southern expression into the conversation.

"Because," she continued without waiting for a response, "my granddaughter Mac is going to lead the middle school band."

"That's terrific. I didn't realize she was a . . ." What did they call them? ". . . drum major."

"She's not. You know she plays in the high school band."

As if Miss Birdie hadn't told him several dozen times. "Yes, and you've also mentioned she's great on the trumpet."

"First chair." Adam could hear the pride in her voice. "Well," the pillar continued, more excited than he'd ever heard her, "one of the senior drum majors was going to lead the middle school but she got sick and the other one sprained his ankle so he's staying on the platform this evening, not marching." She took a breath. The torrent of words must have left her winded. "The director asked Mac to lead the middle school. He has a great deal of confidence in her."

"She must be really excited."

"Scared to death. She's never done this, but the director believes she can." Miss Birdie paused. "You'll be there." Not a question. A command.

"I'll be there."

"At halftime, after the high school band plays, the middle schoolers will march to the middle of the field and play the national anthem with the older kids. You'll be able to recognize Mac because she'll be out in front. And the band'll be wearing their summer uniforms—no hats—so you can see her face."

After he hung up, Adam realized how much he'd begun to feel like part of Butternut Creek. During halftime at the first home game of the long-awaited season, one of the church's kids would be leading the middle school band.

At one thirty, Adam grabbed Maggie's map—as if one could get lost in Butternut Creek—and made his way to the school board office to purchase season tickets. After that, he stopped by the sporting goods store to get a shirt. At six thirty, dressed like a proud BCHS Lions fan, he left home. Plenty of time to get to the stadium before the game started at seven thirty. Plenty of time to pick up a hamburger and fries at the band booster club's tent and find a seat.

By seven twenty-five, the stands were packed. After greeting more church members than usually attended the service on Sunday morning, Hector and some of the basketball players, and other ministers who attended the game, he started looking for a place to sit in general admission. Fortunately, the Kowalskis were there and called for him to sit with them about halfway up the twenty or thirty rows of bleachers.

Excitement and anticipation radiated from the crowd. Most fans wore gold or black and many waved pompoms or noisemakers or large foam-rubber hands. From the end of the stands, the high school band played "Wabash Cannonball" and the cheerleaders jumped and danced. Their long blond hair—yes, six of the eight had blond hair—swayed with the tempo as they ran toward a huge hoop in the middle of the field with HENSON TIRES ROLL WITH THE LIONS painted on the paper covering it.

Then thunderous shouts erupted from the crowd. The band began to play something peppy—the fight song, Adam guessed—when the team burst from the locker room. The players stopped for a moment to jump up and down together. He had no idea why they did that but everyone in the stadium greatly appreciated the action and shouted even more loudly. After all that exercise, the team broke through the paper on the hoop and ran down the field to nearly deafening cheering, the tooting of air horns, and the sound of feet stomping against the metal bleachers.

Aah, Texas football. A dizzying and deafening experience.

By halftime, the sun had set and the temperature dropped to seventy-five but the enthusiasm built every time the team scored. After the first half, the Lions led twenty to sixteen.

But nothing that had gone before prepared Adam for half-time. First, the band of the opposing team came onto the field and very nicely performed country music tunes. The band played and marched, the flag team waved their banners, and the drill team strutted out and performed.

Once the visitors marched off, the Lion band took the field to the roar of the crowd. Here and there, Adam could make out a football player, without pads and jerseys, marching with the band.

Of course, in their cowgirl outfits and the hats they used as part of their dance, the BCHS drill team was definitely superior to the other one. And the banners of the flag team floated higher than those of the visitors had. Adam wasn't sure what banners had to do with football, but the BCHS young women twirled them remarkably well. Noisy applause and cheering swirled around the field and ascended into the darkening sky.

But he hadn't seen anything yet.

Marching in place as if waiting for a signal, the middle school band had assembled behind the goalpost at the north end of the field, to his right. In front of them, hands raised, stood Mac. When she turned toward the field, she blew three quick toots on her whistle and started marching, followed by about a dozen rows of musicians. Moving together, silently in step, they marched through the end zone and across the goal line. Everyone watched as they passed the ten-yard line, then crossed the twenty-, thirty-, forty-, and the fifty-yard lines. When they crossed midfield, Mac glanced over her shoulder for a second but kept moving.

Wasn't it about time to stop their progress? The band filled the area between the two forty-yard-line markers. But Mac didn't stop them. She tooted three times on her whistle, the same signal she'd given to start the band. The toots didn't change anything. The musicians all kept marching along in perfect rhythm behind her.

Mac turned toward the stands. He could read her expression: panic, pure terror, covered her face. When she reached the thirty-five-yard line, Mac stopped.

Unfortunately, the band didn't.

A large boy with a tuba bumped into her, almost knocking her down. The first two rows of musicians silently surged around and past her. Mac regained her balanced and ran down the field to get ahead of the band. Once there and marching briskly and smartly, the musicians followed her over the twenty-five-yard line and the twenty. As well as the confusion covering the faces of the junior high students marching along in silence with their instruments at their sides, he could see the increasing terror on Mac's.

A hush filled the stadium. Would they ever stop and lift their instruments to play? If they didn't stop soon, they'd push Mac against the chain-link fence at the end of the field, moving in perfect rhythm behind her, on and on until all were smashed against the fence, instruments crushed among them, still lifting their feet in perfect rhythm but going nowhere.

The crowd remained mute, watching the band march noiselessly down the field, keeping exact distance in front of them, marching in unison.

In one last effort, Mac stopped, turned toward the band, and shouted, "Stop!" The first two rows nearly mowed her down. The boy with the tuba ran into her again, but this time she kept her balance. Nimbly, she returned to the front, leading the group toward the edge of the field. Like lemmings, they followed her.

Just before Mac stepped onto the track, the sound of a whistle split the air: One long and three short came from the platform where the injured drum major stood. The band members stopped. The whistle sounded again, two short tweets. The students lifted their instruments. Mac turned, stepped onto the curb on the edge of the field, raised her arms and dropped them. On the downbeat, the band—still at the edge of the field and facing the scoreboard—started playing the national anthem. The high school band joined them. Silently, the crowd stood. Some placed their hands over their hearts, others removed their hats, but all faced the flag. A few sang, their voices wavering above the stands.

As the last notes faded, Mac ran from the front to the back of the middle school band and blew the whistle again in a pattern that must have meant, "Turn around," because the band did. After her three toots, they marched toward the opposing goalposts with Mac leading to the wild applause of the crowd.

They had succeeded. They'd marched, they'd played, they'd departed.

Adam didn't hear one laugh or snicker, only pride bursting from the people for their kids. Sadly, he wasn't as respectful and had to struggle not to smile, but he, too, succeeded. After all, Mac was one of the church's kids, and all of the musicians belonged to the community. He clapped and shouted wildly with the rest of the Lion faithful.

An occasion the town would remember forever. Probably one Mac wanted to forget.

❧

After the game, Mattie and Adam and the most of the other ministers met up for something called the Fifth Quarter, an effort to keep the young people off the highway and sober after a game.

This was the biggest gathering place in town that didn't charge a fee. Besides, the Presbyterians didn't mind dancing as long as it was in good taste. The Christian Church, fearing a fight and a split, refused to discuss the situation, and the Baptists condemned the sinful practice.

For that reason, they'd ended up in the fellowship hall of the Presbyterian Church, a separate building so dancing—that wicked and corrupting behavior—didn't actually take place *in* the church. Besides, with adult volunteers outnumbering the students two to one, any depraved acts would be quickly halted.

Miss Birdie stationed herself next to the punch bowl, daring any teenagers to attempt to spike the beverage. For a few minutes, Adam wandered through the room and greeted people. Hector introduced him to a couple of his friends. Looking a little shaken, Mac sat in the corner with a few girlfriends. She gave him a wavering smile. Bree danced with a young man he recognized from the band.

Before Adam could move any farther, Miss Birdie grabbed his arm and pulled him toward the refreshment table. The grabbing and pulling actions were clues that she wanted to talk to him.

"Do you know why we do this?" Before he could say a word, she hurried on, as usual. "You know, there's not much to do here in Butternut Creek. McDonald's closes at nine."

He nodded, then shook his head. As usual, he had no idea which response she wanted.

"The movie theater's way over in Marble Falls. Twenty-mile drive on a dark, winding road. There are volleyball and football games and school-sponsored events, but not every night. So they"—she nodded at the group of about one hundred teens—"are in danger. We have these parties to give them a better choice, to keep them safe and sober and off the road."

"Keg parties all over, nearly every night." Mattie placed a plate of cake slices on the table. "Not just beer but hard liquor, too. You'd be amazed how many kids get drunk four or five nights a week—then drive. They think they are immortal, but I know better. I performed the funeral for Randall Sacks in May."

"Had a basketball scholarship to Texas–El Paso." Miss Birdie sighed and shook her head. "Coming home from a party last spring, driving eighty miles an hour on a country road, his car hit a tree. Killed him instantly."

At that moment, they were diverted by the arrival of the football team. The crush of hungry players ate every bit of food in sight.

"I have a bone to pick with you," Miss Birdie said as the crowd thinned, turning away from the refreshment tables and toward their friends. She paused for a moment. The short silence struck fear into his very core. He never had any idea which of his weaknesses she'd attack next.

"Have you visited Sam Peterson?" She glared at Adam, certain he'd failed her again.

His spirit lifted. "Several times," he said. "I bring pizza, we watch sports and talk."

"Ummh," she grunted, as if in grudging appreciation that he'd finally, finally done something right. "Did he say anything about . . . anyone in town?"

"Like who?"

She fluttered her hands, an action that seemed completely out of character. "Oh, any woman in town."

"We don't talk about women."

"Pssh." She emitted a sound Adam hadn't heard from her before.

"His father's coming," he said, glad to have a morsel of information to impart. "Should be here by Wednesday."

She glanced at Adam, eyes wide. "Wednesday? Oh, my! We have to get cracking."

A wave of relief washed over him. Sounded as if the matchmakers were on the move for Sam and whoever the chosen woman was. Also sounded as if he was safe for the time being. Adam hated to throw Sam to the Widows, but, because nothing he could say would stop them, he rejoiced at the reprieve.

"He says you brought him a dobos torte." Adam kept his eyes on her expression to see how she'd respond to the fact that he knew about her act of kindness. "He really appreciated that."

"Hrmph." She turned away, an action that signaled the end of the conversation on her part and also meant the end of the conversation on *anyone's* part.

Adam picked up a cup of punch, filled a plate with cookies, and wandered away, feeling liberated until her voice echoed through the area.

"Pastor Adam, why don't you dance with someone," the pillar shouted in a voice so loud and demanding that everyone froze and turned toward her, then followed her eyes to study Adam. She pointed at the Presbyterian minister, then nodded. "Ask the Reverend Patillo to dance."

Miss Birdie hadn't given up. Why had he thought she would? He'd never be safe.

Chapter Sixteen

Birdie stood over Mac's bed and searched for words of comfort. She couldn't find any.

Missy was spending Saturday at Ouida's, thank goodness. One worry taken care of. But Birdie had worried about her granddaughter ever since halftime at the football game and had come home to check on her after the breakfast crowd left. Once she talked to her younger granddaughter, she had to return to the diner to serve the lunch crowd. After that, she'd called a meeting with the other Widows. Lord, what a day. "Give me strength," she whispered. "And I'd really appreciate it if You'd make this shoulder stop hurting."

Mac slept, her face innocent and lovely, so much like Martha's. She had to stop worrying Mac would turn out like her mother.

"Mac," Birdie called. The girl didn't wake up, and she hated to disturb her. In a heap on the floor beside the bed were the clothes Mac had worn the night before. If the child's sloppiness didn't shout *trouble*, nothing did.

She didn't want to have this conversation. She wasn't the best person to console anyone, much less this child she loved so much.

"You're a coward, Birdie MacDowell," she muttered, having decided to let the girl sleep. She turned and attempted to tiptoe out. Unfortunately, tiptoeing across linoleum plus rubber soles didn't equal silence. As she squeaked across the floor, Mac woke up.

"Good morning, Grandma." She stretched and yawned.

"How are you?" Birdie turned and walked back toward her granddaughter's bed. "About last night, at the game?" Birdie settled on the side of the bed.

Before Birdie realized what her granddaughter had in mind, Mac sat up and put her arms around her.

"It's okay, Grandma." She squeezed Birdie. "Thanks for asking," she mumbled against Birdie's shoulder.

Birdie had no idea what to do, how to react to a sign of affection since they were very seldom shared. For a moment, tears stung her eyes, but she blinked them back before she patted her granddaughter on the back and whispered, "There, there." As if that helped.

Letting go of her grandmother, Mac said. "Hey, it really is okay. I was mortified, but I talked to Pastor Adam for a while last night at the Fifth Quarter. He helped me a lot."

"He did?"

"Why are you surprised?" Mac tilted her head. "He is our minister."

Birdie hadn't meant to sound amazed although the fact *had* astonished her. Why? He'd visited Sam Peterson and helped with Missy. She hadn't seen him chat with Mac, but that could've been when she'd gone to the kitchen to make more punch. Maybe she'd have to admit he did have some good material in that tall, skinny body. After all, he'd gotten a haircut like she'd told him.

"He said we all have to accept the fact we aren't perfect, that we all make mistakes. He said I'll be famous for years to come, that people will say, 'Do you remember the night Mac MacDowell marched the junior high band all the way down the field?'"

"That's good?" Birdie attempted to figure this out.

"We decided it's good. We'll all laugh together and I'll be a legend. He told me he'd once scored a basket for the other team in seventh grade. When he goes back, everyone still kids him about it."

Birdie nodded. "It's okay."

If Mac felt okay, her grandmother was fine. "I need to get off to work." She stood.

"Thanks, Grandma. I'm going to get up in a while." Within seconds she was asleep.

So, Birdie guessed, Mac's jeans on the floor didn't reveal a meltdown, only a tired teenager. She picked up the clothes and tossed them into the hamper because, as much as she didn't mind clearing up a little bit for an exhausted child, darned if she'd do her wash.

She had something more important ahead. If this wasn't a time to call a meeting of the new and expanded Widows, Birdie didn't know when would be. The information the minister had given her about the arrival of Sam's father constituted an emergency. The entire matchmaking enterprise faced complete failure.

Oh, the preacher was a lost cause, she mused as she headed over to the diner. No need to even discuss him. Maybe later they'd try to get him married. If the preacher didn't approve of their machinations—sadly stalled at the moment—he could get busy finding a wife on his own.

For now, they'd have to write Pastor Adam off unless a new, single woman turned up, which seldom happened in a town this size, out here fifty miles from Austin. In fact, the appearance of two single women within a few months of each other constituted a minor miracle.

They could count on no help from the Methodist Church. It was too late for a female minister to show up there this year. They'd had that little musical-chairs dance the Methodists did when all their ministers changed churches a few months ago. Now the Methodists were stuck with a man with a solid marriage and three darling children.

They had to marshal their forces on only one front. The captain and Willow Thomas—*that* was the relationship they needed to work on. If she weren't so tired, Birdie'd come up with a really good scheme. Although she hated to admit defeat, she had to admit her usually top-notch matchmaking skills had stopped functioning. She hoped Winnie or Mercedes would have an idea.

❦

Winnie sat so straight, it looked as if she'd had recent back surgery. She also beamed, obviously delighted to be sitting with the Widows in public although only the three of them remained in the diner. Guess it had been a good idea to include her. New blood, fresh ideas, and she seemed proud to be part of the group, as she should be.

"I believe the preacher is a lost cause," Birdie said. The other Widows nodded. "I've tried, goodness knows, we've all tried. He's not interested. But"—she paused to emphasize her disappointment—"that Sam Peterson." She shook her head. "He seemed to be smitten with Willow Thomas. Don't know what changed. What do we do about him?"

"You're sure there was something between Willow and the captain?" Winnie asked.

For a moment, Birdie bristled. How dare anyone question her?

Mercedes put her hand on Birdie's arm. "Winnie wasn't here when we discussed this before, Bird," Mercedes interjected. "She's asking for confirmation and information. That's all."

"All right." Birdie nodded. "Oh, yes, I saw it. He fell in love with her right away, at first sight."

"Although Bird doesn't look very sensitive," Mercedes explained to Winnie, "she's very good about recognizing all sorts of emotions."

"I haven't seen that look in weeks," Birdie moaned.

"Then we have to bring them together somehow." Winnie nodded, as if she were the boss of the Widows.

If Winnie's only contribution was to state the obvious, what good was she? They needed ideas.

"Perhaps we could invite them someplace, then leave them alone," Winnie suggested.

Hmmm, that idea had possibilities.

"Where?" Mercedes asked. "You mean like a meeting?"

"Don't think we could get Sam to attend a meeting or even drag him out of his house," Birdie said. "He's a real hermit."

"Not even the church?" Mercedes asked.

"Don't think so. He hasn't been to church since he got here," Winnie said.

"Then they'll have to meet at Sam's house," Birdie stated with a decisive nod. All of her nods were decisive, but she put greater resolve into this one.

"We'll have to set something up there. How do we get the two of them together, alone, at Sam's house? Any thoughts?" Winnie asked.

Maybe Winnie would work out, but she had to stop acting like she was in charge.

Winnie opened her purse and pulled out a small notebook and a pen. "We have logistics to work out." She uncapped the pen, ready to write.

"We'll have to do that before his father arrives on Wednesday," Birdie said, proud to know something the others didn't.

"His father's coming Wednesday?" Mercedes asked. At Birdie's nod, she added, "We don't have much time."

"We'll have to get rid of the two boys somehow." Winnie noted that on her page.

"I'll ask my granddaughters to take care of them," Birdie volunteered. "But Bree has a volleyball game Monday night so it will have to be Sunday or Tuesday."

"Tomorrow's too soon to get everything together," Mercedes added.

"All right, Tuesday evening." Winnie wrote "Tuesday" on her pad. "What are we going to do?"

By the time they'd finished planning, they'd decided to invite Willow and the boys to dinner at Sam's house. They'd tell Sam they were bringing dinner for him, then—after the guests he didn't know about arrived—have Bree and Mac whisk the boys and Missy away. Once everyone else left, the Widows would serve the food, then take off, leaving Willow and Sam alone.

"I don't know what more we can do," Birdie said. "If that doesn't work, I'll wash my hands of those two." But she knew she wouldn't.

She glanced at the clock. "Now I need to pick up Missy. We've got a good plan. Should work. Let's meet in front of the captain's house at seven fifteen."

❦

No matter how carefully events were planned they didn't always succeed, Birdie reflected on Tuesday evening.

Winnie had scrupulously charted out the entire time. She'd brought a boom box and romantic CDs by Barry White. Mercedes had chosen a lovely wine and made her delicious gazpacho while Birdie had brought a dobos torte and great vegetable dish. Winnie also contributed two lovely steaks, seasoned and ready to grill, and baked potatoes.

But when they rang the doorbell, a tall man with white hair opened the front door.

The three women nearly dropped their bundles.

"Hello, ladies. I'm Sam's father, Mitchell." He spoke in a voice filled with authority.

As if she couldn't have guessed that. The man looked exactly like Captain Peterson with twenty years added, the posture of a general, and an air of command.

"What are you doing here?" Birdie blurted sounding ruder than usual. Probably should have welcomed him but the words had jumped from her mouth because, doggone it, the man really upset their plans. "We weren't expecting you until tomorrow."

"Come in, ladies." He stepped back and gestured them inside. "I got here about an hour ago. The drive took less time than I anticipated. Sam tells me you're bringing dinner. Hope you don't mind an extra."

He smiled, a nice, friendly expression. Didn't look much like a general except for his straight back.

"My son says you're the best cooks in the state."

He included all the women in the compliment but seemed to pick Winnie out for special attention. Winnie must have noticed that, too. At the age of sixty-something, the woman's cheeks turned pink. Didn't that beat all?

When the three women bustled inside followed by Bree and Mac and little Missy, they caught sight of Sam and Willow in the living room with the two boys sitting on the floor.

"Look, we have more guests," Mitchell Peterson said, waving toward the Thomases.

It was that stupid corn pudding. It wouldn't set and had slowed them down. And finding Missy's bear. The child had refused to leave the house without it. Otherwise, they would have been here before the Thomas family arrived. What a fiasco—well, maybe not. Everyone was settled. If they could get rid of the general . . .

Willow stood and smiled at each Widow. "I must have made a mistake. Sam"—she gestured toward the captain—"seemed surprised when the boys and I showed up."

Sam gazed at Birdie. She hoped that was laughter in his eyes but didn't know. Surely he didn't mind seeing Willow, did he?

"Wish you'd have mentioned the Thomases would be here," he said. "I'd have been less confused and more welcoming."

Birdie turned toward Winnie and Mercedes. "Didn't you tell the captain what we had planned?"

"Oh, dear," Winnie mumbled as she attempted to cover. "I thought I had."

"But we weren't supposed to do that," Mercedes said. "You told me . . ."

Poor dear, she always told the truth, as inconvenient as it often was.

"I thought we'd told you," Birdie spoke over Mercedes's attempt to explain.

"I didn't realize there'd be eleven of us," Willow said. "Hope you have plenty of food."

Birdie hadn't realized that, either. Unless they planned to act out the miracle of the fishes and the loaves, they hadn't brought nearly enough food. Of course, they had plenty considering that five—the boys, Missy, and her granddaughters—would be leaving and the Widows weren't eating. The food would stretch to include the general, but they didn't want him here. How could they get rid of him?

"Hi, Mrs. Thomas," Bree said. "We thought the boys might not want to eat with the old folks."

Birdie glared at her granddaughter.

"With the adults," Bree corrected herself. "We thought we'd grab a hamburger, then go to the carnival at the middle school."

"Carnval," Missy added with a big smile.

"How nice," Willow said.

The boys looked disappointed, glancing at Sam with adoration.

Then their eyes turned toward Sam's father and the three Widows and glazed over as if they realized what the evening with all these adults might be like.

"Okay," the older one said as the other nodded.

"Is that all right with you?" Bree asked Willow.

"Of course. I'm sure they'll enjoy that. Thank you." Willow waved at the boys as they ran out the door.

"Bye-bye." Missy followed the others outside.

As the door slammed shut, Birdie looked at the six still left. What in the world would they do with Sam's father?

"Dad, I want you to meet these nice ladies from the church." Sam introduced each. "Ladies, this is my father, General Mitchell Peterson."

"We met at the door," Birdie said. "And I remember you. Everyone called you Petey back then, when you were a kid."

"Back when you visited Effie, years ago," Mercedes added. "Before you were a marine."

"Of course, ladies. Good to see you again." His gaze returned to Winnie, who didn't say a word.

"We call ourselves the Widows. We like to serve people in the church, and"—she raised her voice to speak loudly and clearly—"none of us is married." She glanced at the general, then moved her gaze to Winnie. "No, we're all single ladies, all three of us."

"Ladies, let's go to the kitchen and put this meal together." With that, her chest held as high and proud as a woman as thin as she could manage, Birdie led the Widows through the swinging door and into the kitchen.

"What are we going to do with him?" Winnie whispered.

"It's what *you* are going to do, Winnie," Birdie said. "Not us."

Winnie frowned as she placed her dishes on the counter. "I don't understand."

"You're going to take the general off our hands," Mercedes said.

Winnie whirled around. "What do you mean?"

"You're going to have to lure him away," Birdie attempted to clarify.

With a gasp, Winnie said, "I can't . . . what do you mean? I don't have any experience in luring."

"Did you see how Sam's father watched you?" Birdie took a step closer when Winnie shook her head vigorously. "Did you?"

"You're going to have to flirt with him," Mercedes said.

"I'm a single woman, an old maid. I don't know how to flirt," Winnie protested. "I never learned."

"You're going to have to do it," Birdie commanded. "For the cause."

"You're going to get him to take you out to dinner so Sam and Willow can be alone." Mercedes spoke very slowly and clearly to get her point across.

Still Winnie shook her head.

"Okay, listen." Birdie pulled a chair out from the table and guided Winnie toward it. Once she shoved Winnie into the seat, she sat across from her and glared. "Do you remember the plan? *Your* plan? We get rid of the children, we serve Sam and Willow, then we leave them alone. Right?"

Winnie gulped, then nodded.

"What should we do with the general?" Mercedes asked.

"I don't know." Winnie shrugged.

Birdie stood and leaned over the newest Widow, who didn't look a bit happy to be part of the group at this precise moment. "The general's interested in you."

"He can't be. Men have never been interested in me."

"Well, the general is," Mercedes stated.

"As I said, I don't know how to flirt. I haven't tried since I was twenty and was not notably successful back then." Winnie glared at the others. "You may have noticed I'm not married. I'm not good or comfortable with single men." She paused. "Is he single?"

"Yes, his wife died years ago."

"Why doesn't one of you do it?"

"Because Mercedes is keeping company with Bill Jones down at the bank."

"Okay, but what about you?" Winnie glared at Birdie.

"I'm an old skinny woman who looks like a strip of beef jerky. He didn't even notice me, but you're pretty and feminine."

Winnie opened her mouth to object.

"And he likes you," Birdie added before the other woman could say a word. "He thinks you're attractive."

With a frown, Winnie considered this. "He does?" She looked from Mercedes to Birdie. "Do you really think he finds me attractive?"

"Why wouldn't he?" Birdie tugged the reluctant seductress to her feet and pulled her toward the swinging door between the kitchen and the dining room. "Go get him." She shoved Winnie out.

For a moment, Winnie froze as the other Widows stared through the little glass slit on the door a few inches below eye level. When the general looked up and smiled, Winnie started forward, walking in a bent-leg style, her hips swinging.

"She was right." Mercedes groaned. "She has no idea how to se-duce a man."

"She's going to break something," Birdie whispered. "Her hip or her ankle."

When the three in the living room saw Winnie's posture, three mouths dropped open and six eyes opened wide.

"She's going to ruin our plan," Birdie whispered.

Fortunately, the general stood, approached Winnie, and gallantly held out his arm. She placed her hand on it. Actually, she grabbed it as if she were drowning and his arm were a life preserver swiftly floating past. He didn't seem to mind.

As Winnie turned coyly away from the general, Mercedes and Birdie could see her working very hard to flirt. Birdie wished she couldn't. It was too painful. Winnie batted her eyelashes as if they were butterflies preparing for flight, screwed up her mouth into an imitation of a Renée Zellweger pout—attractive on neither woman—and tilted her head as if her neck were broken. The final effort was a breathless, "Hello there," accompanied by a Groucho Marx twitch-ing of her eyebrows.

All of which seemed to delight the general. Thank goodness.

"Why don't we leave these young folks alone and go out for a bite," he said. "Just the two of us."

Winnie looked terrified. Her eyes sought out the kitchen door. With the hand the general hadn't captured, she gave a wavering thumbs-up.

"We'll see you later," the general said. "You two have a good time." With that, he turned toward the front door with Winnie on his arm and hustled her outside.

"That was easy." Mercedes straightened. "And you don't look a bit like beef jerky." She grinned. "Well, only a little bit," she added with that infernal honesty. "You're attractive in sort of a dried-up way."

"Oh, just stop talking and fix the food," Birdie said.

❦

Once the Widows served dinner, Sam stared at Willow across the ta-ble. He couldn't think of anything to say. He refused to talk about the weather or his prosthesis or the boys, which left little else.

"You know, we've never talked about Butternut Creek." Good topic. "I used to visit during the summer and you grew up here. Maybe we have mutual friends."

But after a few minutes, they discovered they didn't. Oh, she knew Mitzi Harris, whose younger brother had played baseball with Sam. She'd dated Matthew Morgan, older brother of Annie, Sam's make-out buddy, not that he mentioned *how* he knew Annie.

"Do you think we ever met back then?" Willow asked.

Neither could remember. After all, the last summer he'd spent here, he'd been a skinny fifteen-year-old and she'd been a sophisticated college student. They hardly ran in the same circles.

"Probably not," she said. "You visited in the summer and I spent most of my summers working at camp or picking up extra hours at college."

After exhausting that subject, they still didn't have anything to talk about, at least not as long as the Widows wandered in and out to clear the table and pour coffee.

"As much as I like it, I didn't have a thing to do with this," he murmured as the women disappeared into the kitchen. "With our being alone."

Willow smiled at him. Good. That was a start.

"I didn't think you did. You looked as if you didn't know we'd been invited."

"Miss Birdie is a devious and determined woman," Sam said as he noticed a pair of eyes peeking through the narrow slit in the kitchen door.

"She certainly is. And you looked as startled as I felt when Miss Jenkins hunted your father down."

"She did, didn't she." He grinned at the memory. "Sort of stalked him."

"I don't think he minded," she added.

"Guess their plan to get us alone hadn't taken the general's early arrival into consideration." The entire situation struck him as so funny, he started laughing. She joined but, when she stopped, he glanced at her. Her gaze wandered across his face, almost in surprise but also with interest and attraction.

She blinked—a little dazed, maybe? "I haven't seen you laugh before."

He bet she hadn't. Her reaction seemed like a good sign except she sat at the table on a chair and he sat across from her on another chair.

And that nice sofa stood empty in the living room.

Who was still in the house? He glanced at the slit again to see two pairs of eyes staring back. Not the time to make a move. He preferred to do his courting—if that was a viable option in this situation—without an audience.

Before he could say a word, the eyes disappeared. The sound of hushing and movement came from the kitchen followed by a loud "Good-bye," spoken in unison. The door from the kitchen to the carport slammed loudly.

With all the stuff they were carrying, he hoped the remaining Widows could get out that way. The general had brought Sam's car down, the classic Mustang. Before his injury, when he was home on leave he'd spent every free hour rebuilding it. With the Mustang there, the narrow carport was a tight fit. Still, the Widows either managed it or were going to spend the night there, because they didn't come back in.

Now he and Willow were alone. To make sure, he stood, walked to the swinging door, and pushed it open. "Miss Birdie?" he said. No one answered, but on the counter was a CD player with several discs. Who had left that?

"They're gone." He allowed the door to swing back.

Willow leaped to her feet. "Then I'd better go, too."

"What about your sons?" He walked toward her. "When Nick and Leo come back and you're not here, they'll worry."

"Nice try, Captain. You can tell them I went home."

"How will they get home? Do you want them walking in the dark, alone?"

"You make it sound as if danger lurks around every corner." She paused to consider that for a few seconds.

He wondered if she was trying to think of an excuse to leave and a time when she should come back for the boys. He waited.

"You're right," she said after a deep sigh. "I don't."

He took her hand. "Why don't we sit and talk? Get to know each other?" He attempted to make his voice sound casual and nonchalant, as if they were friends who wanted to chat and enjoy each other's company.

Didn't work. She tugged away and took a few steps to sit in one of the chairs, her hands folded primly on her lap.

But Willow Thomas could never look prim. Oh, she'd tried, pulling her hair back, but the soft brilliance of her red curls made him want to wrap a strand around his finger and . . . actually, everything about her made him want to touch her.

Sadly, she didn't look as if she felt the same way. But she might. He wouldn't know if he didn't try. "I thought maybe on the sofa?"

"I thought maybe facing each other." She pointed from her toward the sofa. "So we can see each other as we . . . um . . . chat."

Her eyes showed a note of panic. He grinned, inside.

"Do you think I'm going to attack you?" He colored his voice with a note of wounded sincerity.

Her eyes flew open and she glanced up at him, worried she'd hurt his feelings, he guessed. She was a very nice woman.

"Of course not."

Before she could figure out what he had in mind, he took her hand and pulled her to her feet, using the end table for balance and leverage. Ignoring her protest, he dropped her into the middle of the sofa and sat down next to her, his arm across her shoulders in case she tried to escape.

That didn't work, either. She slid away from his arm and to the other end of the sofa. "I went to the University of Texas," she said. "Finished my degree and got a master's in physical therapy. Married. Moved to Chicago where the boys were born," she concluded. "And you?"

"All over Europe and Asia with my parents. A&M, so I guess we're rivals. Marines," he said, matching her staccato delivery. "Iraq, then Afghanistan. Walter Reed. Here." He wanted to slide closer but he didn't have the smooth moves he used to. Lack of balance and lack of practice. Instead, he reached out to pick up her hand and used his thumb to rub circles on her soft palm.

At least he did until she pulled her hand away, stood, and sprinted to the other side of the room. Once there, she crossed her arms and glowered at him.

He'd blown it again. How many times did he have to remind himself that Willow didn't react like the women he'd flirted with before?

"Captain, what do you think you're doing?" she demanded.

Her voice sounded neither frightened nor wary but as if she'd pretty well tagged who he was and what he had planned.

"Why don't you tell me more about living in Chicago?" he asked in an even and—he hoped—fascinated voice.

"Because I don't believe learning all about the scintillating life of Willow Thomas is your ultimate objective."

"What do you believe that objective to be?"

"Oh, come on, Sam."

Why was he so fumblingly obvious with this woman?

"I *have* known a few men before you. I know your objective." She took a few steps back.

He had no idea where she planned to go. Outside? To the chair? Home? No, she began to tap her foot and continued to glare at him. Not a bit promising, but better than her leaving.

For only seconds, he considered playing the sympathy card, but he knew it wouldn't work, not with her. Besides, he didn't want to use it with her. He went for humor. "Maybe you could think of kissing me as therapy."

As he'd known it would, the suggestion fell flat. He groaned—inside. He'd always been much cooler with women, had seldom needed to make an effort. Willow was tough. With her, he sounded like a lecherous idiot.

She studied him. "Great line, Captain, does that ever work?"

Crap. She'd called him "Captain." "I liked it better when you called me 'Sam.'"

She didn't answer.

"And no, that never works because I've never used it." He shrugged. Might as well be honest. "I've never used a line before."

"Aah, women just usually fall at your feet."

Could this get much worse?

Surprisingly, the situation improved. She sat down again. Sadly, she'd chosen the chair. "However, we could try a different kind of therapy."

He couldn't believe she'd agreed with him.

"You know, maybe more conversation."

Great. At least she hadn't suggested going home.

"Why don't you tell me about your father?" She relaxed back against the chair.

"My favorite topic."

She smiled. "You don't sound enthusiastic."

He didn't bother to answer.

"He's a handsome man, very military. I notice you call him 'General' instead of 'Dad.'"

"Doesn't take much insight to notice that." He spoke with withering condescension in his voice, but the tone didn't seem to bother her. She raised an eyebrow.

"That's basically who and what he is—a general, not a father." Not what he wanted to discuss so he said, "And your husband left you?"

Instead of the verbal slap he deserved, she said, "Aah, so we're getting into the *who-can-hit-whose-hot-buttons* section of the conversation. My, we've come a long way and quickly. I believe, Captain, you're hiding behind these attacks."

He should have remembered she was a professional, trained in counseling jerks like him as well as how to work with damaged muscles and frozen joints.

"My ex-husband is a doctor, ten years older than me, separated but not divorced from his first wife when we met. We were married for ten years, had two great children. He met Tiffany at the hospital two years ago. She's a drug rep. Imagine my surprise when I realized that, to feel manly and boost his ego, he needs a new, younger wife every ten years."

"Idiot."

"I agree." She shrugged. "It hurt me, but the boys . . ." She glanced at him, serious. "I hated how much the split hurt them. A few months after that, I got this great job offer. We moved because Butternut Creek's a great place for children to grow up." She took a deep breath before she said, "It has been, thanks to you, Captain. You've been wonderful for them. They need a man in their lives."

Great. She saw him as a good guy, a surrogate father, the man in the lives of her boys.

"But I don't. Need a man in my life, I mean."

He studied her. If she didn't need a man in her life, why was she so uncomfortable with him? "But you liked that kiss."

"Captain . . ."

She kept calling him that.

"I'm grateful to you . . . ," she said.

Not what he'd hoped for. Grateful, personable—the words she chose made him feel pitiable.

"I went through a rough breakup, devastating because I didn't know it was coming. We've moved, I started a new job. I feel as if I'm juggling so much that if I add more, I'll drop everything."

"It's not like I'm looking for a relationship," he said before he realized what a mistake those words were. Willow was a relationship woman if he'd ever met one.

She glared at him. "Oh, a quick hookup?"

"No, not that." Sam shrugged. "I didn't mean to insult you. It's me. I'm no prize. I have no idea what my future's going to be."

"You've said that before, but I don't agree. You have a degree from A&M . . ."

"In military science, hardly useful now, but that's not the issue. I'm not interested in a relationship because I need to get some things straight before . . . before I can do anything with my life. I have to figure out what's in my future, if I have one."

As the words left his mouth, he knew he was lying. Yes, he needed to get his life back in order, but the rebuilding was happening, sort of on its own. It had started with the move here. He owed a lot to the friendliness of the Widows and the church, to Jesse and the weekly horseback rides, to Nick and Leo and Willow plus the staff in the PT department. He didn't know what was ahead but he suddenly recognized he looked forward to it, a little. He'd thought about teaching, maybe math or science to kids Nick's age. The idea had been nagging at him for weeks.

Not that he was ready to share any of that, certainly not with a woman who showed such a cold, aloof expression.

"Me, too," she said with that determined lifting of her chin. "Then do we understand each other completely?"

No, they didn't. Not at all, but he felt pretty sure they should leave it alone.

"Captain, I find you a very attractive man."

A better word than *personable*. However, he knew there was a "but" coming.

"But . . ."

Yeah, there it was.

"I'm not ready. If I were . . ." She shrugged. "If I were and I weren't your physical therapist, a relationship might be possible."

"I find *you* attractive." Hot, too, but this was *not* the time to mention that. Probably should stop now, but he'd never been good about recognizing that. "And you're grateful to me for being friends with the boys?"

She glared and leaped from the chair. "Not *that* grateful."

"Not what I meant." He pushed himself to his feet because he felt at a disadvantage sitting while she stood. Like a pitiful cripple.

She really was gorgeous. He wanted her, but he had no idea what to say next to communicate his feelings when she looked so unreceptive. He repeated, his voice steady and as sincere as he could make it, "That was not what I meant."

He'd really screwed this up.

❧

Willow glowered at Sam for a few seconds until she felt her expression slowly softening. Could she trust him? He hadn't made a move toward her. And yet, six feet away, she could feel his interest in her. No, more than that. He wanted her. His eyes blazed with desire that he did nothing to hide. The intensity of his need vibrated between them. Surprisingly for a woman who hadn't allowed herself to feel for two years, she responded to that need.

"That wasn't what I meant. Do you believe me?" he whispered, studying her as if searching for a hint of her feelings.

She nodded. "I believe you," she murmured into the simmering connection that stretched between them.

"Why do you keep pushing me away?" Sam said. "I can read your eyes. I know what that look means."

"Confusion, that's what you see." She had to gather herself together. She didn't want this, not at all.

She was, of course, lying to herself. "I have no idea where this . . . this *whatever* is going or even if it is going anyplace. I don't believe we can call what we share a relationship. Maybe lust or interest or two lonely people searching for companionship."

He gave a bark of a laugh. "Companionship?"

"I'm not ready for anything now. Nothing."

"Not what I'd hoped to hear, not how I feel or want, but . . ."

"But?" She pushed him to continue.

"But if I say anything more, I'll tick you off."

He took a step forward. From his grimace and his whispered curse, she could tell he realized the action had been a mistake.

"I'm pushing again." He stopped and shook his head in chagrin. "I can't seem to stop myself."

She took a step back, aware of how dangerous his proximity was to her peace of mind.

"I shouldn't have moved." He stood very still but still watched her.

With another step back, she ran into the wall. Unable to get farther away, she swallowed, lifted her gaze to his, and held her hand in front of her like a crossing guard.

Unfortunately—or perhaps fortunately because who knew what she might have said or done next—and before the silence lasted too long, the front door opened and the kids spilled into the house, Missy asleep in Mac's arms. Sam took a step backward to drop onto the sofa and Willow turned toward the children. The movement broke the contact with Sam, easily done because the connection had been tenuous at best. Relieved, she hugged her boys and thanked the girls.

The seven of them—well, five of them, because Sam didn't join in and Missy slept—chattered for a few minutes before the girls left. Willow hurried out with the boys before they could do much but wave toward the captain. The quick departure seemed unfair to the boys. Leo and Nick wanted to talk to Sam for a while, but Willow couldn't stay in that small living room any longer, not with Sam there filling the air with, oh, the *Samness* that had become so toxic for her peace of mind.

Hours later, with the boys bathed and sleeping, Willow turned over in bed again and punched her pillow while thoughts tumbled through her brain. Had she made a mistake? Should she have accepted Sam as he was? Didn't she deserve happiness?

That was, of course, pretty much the center of the problem. Could Sam bring anyone happiness in the shape he was in now? Could she accept it, as confused and broken as she felt? He wasn't the only one dragging baggage with him.

Another huge part of the equation was Willow herself and what she'd refused to face in months. She tossed the sheet aside, turned the reading lamp on, and opened the drawer on the night table. Inside, under a couple of books, a pair of scissors, and a package of emery boards, lay a professionally taken photo of her family, all four of them, taken over a year ago. In the photo, Willow sat on a bench with one boy on each side. Grant stood behind her, his hand on the shoulders of the boys. He looked distinguished—which he was; wealthy—his tailored suit and perfect haircut witness to that; and like a good father and loving father, protecting his sons and sheltering his wife. At some time, he'd meant to be all that, probably, but even at the time the portrait had been made, he'd been in the midst of his affair with Tiffany. Not a smudge of remorse or shame for the deception showed on his face.

How could she still allow the man who had so easily shoved her aside to reach into her brain and control her life after all this time?

Carefully, she pulled the picture out of the frame, then picked up the scissors and snipped Grant out of the photo. The disembodied hands on the boys' shoulders looked odd, but she felt better. Since she found out about Tiffany, she'd felt angry, both at herself for being so naive and at her ex for being who he was. With that action of removing Grant from the family circle, she realized anger no longer burned inside her and she no longer felt like a failure.

She had to admit she hadn't accomplished that reconciliation by herself. Thanks to Sam, she felt like a woman again. What in the world could she do about the sensations he'd awakened? The awareness that zinged back and forth between them?

After placing the butchered picture back into the frame and tossing Grant's head in the wastebasket, she stood and went to the dresser to pull her cell phone from the charger. She flicked through the pictures until she found the one she'd taken of Sam and the boys working in his yard. All three smiled. Nick and Leo looked up at Sam with admiration. Like Grant, he had a hand on each boy's shoulder. His smile showed how deeply he cared about her sons. She knew he'd never hurt them.

And, good Lord, he was so handsome, so good with her sons it made her ache.

Did she love him? She was incredibly attracted to him, but did she feel more? Did she even know the man, the real Sam Peterson?

Why all the questions? When had she become such a dithering idiot?

She'd become a dithering idiot when she realized how close she was to making a decision based on little more than chemistry, exactly as she had with Grant.

❦

An hour after everyone left, Sam put down his book and finished his beer, the only one he'd drunk that evening. The general still hadn't come home. Should he wait up for him? It was after ten. Pretty sure the general could take care of himself and that Winnie Jenkins wouldn't lead him astray, Sam headed back to his bedroom.

After washing up and getting in bed, he stared at the ceiling. For one of the few times in months, his thoughts didn't focus on war and bombs and Morty. No, instead he thought about his future. Did he want to teach? Did he really want to go back to school to pick up the necessary hours?

And why in the world did this bug him at *this* moment? Why should he consider change, any change, now? Wasn't getting used to the loss of his leg and the addition of the prosthesis and putting up with the general and being shot down by Willow enough stress for now? He picked up his book and immersed himself in a fantasy world of science fiction until he turned off the light at nearly midnight.

And the general still wasn't home.

Chapter Seventeen

Rockets exploded around Sam Peterson. The screams of the wounded reverberated through the narrow ravine. Gunfire rained down on them from the surrounding hills. He lifted his M4 to answer the barrage but a second mortar impacted, driving his face into the dirt. A blast of pain punched his leg, burning through flesh and bones and nerve. He reached for his foot. It wasn't there.

Sam knew this wasn't real, but he couldn't wake up. He lay in bed, covered with sweat, his missing leg hurting more than it had when the mortar fire tore it away. If he didn't wake up soon, he'd have to relive touching Morty's body. He hated that part, hated this endlessly repeating horror.

Even as he lay there, putting off the moment he dreaded, he sensed he wasn't alone. He fought his way through the fog of terror and sleep to open his eyes a slit.

"Son, wake up." The general sat on a chair next to the bed. His hand hovered over Sam's left shoulder.

Sam slowly regained consciousness. Probably had the nightmare because of the general's arrival. Change always brought it. He'd hoped he'd never have to experience it again.

In the glow of a night-light, he could see the general's face, drawn and white.

"You've had this dream before," the general stated.

Were there tears in the general's eyes? Of course not. If he'd taught Sam one thing, it was that men didn't cry. Of course, he'd also learned from the general that men didn't show emotion, men followed orders, men were always strong. Men were men, and marines were *real* men.

For a few more minutes, the general sat of the edge of the bed.

Once he reached out to touch Sam on the shoulder but pulled his hand back. With that, Sam remembered another rule: Men didn't show sympathy.

Most of his life, Sam had believed that.

He struggled to think of something to say to the man who didn't look like the general, but they'd never talked. Why start now?

"Go to sleep. I'll stay," the general said. He pulled the chair from the corner and settled into it. "I'll be right here."

Sam quit struggling for words. Within seconds, peace enveloped him, almost as if the general's presence protected him. At least for now, Sam didn't have to worry about reliving that nightmare. The general was there. He'd wake Sam up again if it came back.

Then he remembered no more.

When he woke up, Sam felt better than he had in months. Rested. Sunlight filtered through the blinds and shone in his eyes. The aroma of bacon coming from the kitchen had wakened him.

He hadn't had bacon for months, not since he left the hospital where it had been slimy and limp. He didn't even bother with the prosthesis, just grabbed his robe and crutches and hobbled toward the scent.

The general stood in front of the stove in a camo T-shirt and matching shorts. Around his waist, he'd tied a towel, an incongruously pink one Aunt Effie had left behind. "Hungry? Sit down, son." He waved toward the table. "Breakfast's almost ready. Do you still like your eggs sunny-side up and runny?"

"Yes, sir."

When silence fell, broken only by the sounds of cooking, Sam said, "Where'd you get the bacon?" He hated the heavy stillness that pressed down and nearly suffocated him around the general and had to punch holes in it with words, even if just a stupid question. "I don't think I have any."

"Son, all you had was a couple of six-packs of some Texas beer, half a loaf of moldy bread, peanut butter, and the leftovers from last night." He dumped the eggs on a plate and added the bacon. "Winnie—Miss Jenkins—and I went to Marble Falls last night after I was chased out."

Sam noticed a grin, barely perceptible to anyone but him. He'd trained himself to read the general's few facial clues.

"Don't think we chased you out. Looked like you didn't mind all that much. Where'd you go?"

"Went to a movie, then decided to give you and Willow a little more time together and went to the H-E-B to stock up on food." He placed the plate on the table, poured two cups of coffee, put one in front of Sam, and sat down. "Eat."

Sam leaned against the table and swung into the chair. "Did you have fun on your date?"

The general drank from his cup, then smiled—really smiled, not just a barely detectable curve of the lips. "Yes. And you?"

"It wasn't really a date."

"Winnie tells me she and the Widows want to get you and Willow together. How do you feel about that?" the general asked.

Sam took a bite of toast, not about ready to have a heart-to-heart about his feelings with the man.

"She seems like a lovely woman, but she's got those two boys." The general shook his head as if in regret.

Even knowing the man was playing him to get a reaction, Sam had to respond. "Great kids, sir."

"So you like them?"

"Great kids." He dug into his breakfast, aware that the general kept an eye on him. "Sir."

After nearly a minute of playing who'll-break-the-silence-first, the general said, "Wonder if you'd try calling me something other than 'sir' or 'General.'"

Sam's gaze jumped to the general's face. "Like what?"

"Like 'Dad'?"

Why would he ask that after all these years?

"I don't know if I could do that, sir."

"I really messed up, didn't I, son?" The general shook his head, but his expression wasn't the stony, disappointed one he usually turned on Sam. He looked sad and watched his son with such desperate longing and sorrow that Sam had no idea what to say or do.

Because he didn't want to respond, Sam took a bite of the crispy bacon and chewed. He wasn't ready to call the man "Dad," but it sure seemed like he'd hurt the old man's feelings. He'd never believed he could do that.

Was the old man getting soft?

❦

Sometimes together, sometimes separately, Adam or Miss Birdie carried Missy to see her mother every day. Several of those days, Mrs. Smith had awakened when she heard Missy's voice but then fell back asleep without saying a word. The doctor said she was out of the coma but slept deeply as her body struggled to regain and build strength. The nurse said her vital signs always improved after the visits from her daughter.

As they drove to Austin, Adam glanced back to see Missy asleep in her car seat, then he looked at Miss Birdie.

"You look tired," he said before he considered the consequences of pointing that out. She must have been really exhausted because she didn't turn the killer glare on him.

"I am, Pastor." She sighed. "I love that little girl, but I didn't think Missy'd be here this long. Three weeks." She sighed again, which made him realize the toll this had taken on her.

"I didn't, either. I'm sorry so much has fallen on you." He turned off the highway and headed south on the Mopac.

"No, no, it was my idea. And everyone has helped. Jesse and Barb had Missy spend the weekend with them. She rode a pony and fed the ducks, had a great time. She likes to play with Ouida's girls. Even Willow and her sons have entertained Missy several Sunday afternoons."

"Good. I'm glad they've pitched in."

"She still cries at night."

"Which means you don't get much sleep."

Miss Birdie rushed on, ignoring his effort to sympathize. "She asks about her mother over and over. Pastor, it's heartbreaking. I try to answer her questions and comfort her, but I'm not the most comforting person in the world."

"Miss Birdie, you took her in when she had no place to go. You have been wonderful. You gave her a home, you hold her and care for her." He pulled onto the ramp leading to the hospital. "You allowed her to stay in one place, safe."

"You've helped, too. Thank you for picking her up from day care."

Feeling good after those unexpected words of appreciation, Adam pulled into a parking space and turned off the engine. Missy awoke, and he carried her into the hospital.

When they arrived in Mrs. Smith's hospital room, she was sitting up in bed. Most of the tubes and wires were gone and a tray with bowls of Jell-O and broth sat in front of her.

"Mama," Missy shouted as she ran toward her mother.

"Be careful," Miss Birdie said. "She's still not well. Just hold her hand."

"Hello, darling," Mrs. Smith croaked. She cleared her throat and looked up at Miss Birdie and Adam.

He introduced himself and the pillar and told her they'd been taking care of Missy.

"I remember your voices," she said. "Thank you."

"Your husband, Missy's father. Can you tell me where he is?" Adam asked.

"We've been divorced for years. I have no idea where he is." She patted Missy's hand. "We're pretty much alone here. I have family in Virginia. My mother has gone to Richmond to take care of my sister and her new baby."

Explained why no one could locate her.

"Do you want us to notify them?"

"No, thank you. I called my sister an hour ago. My mother's coming as soon as she can book a flight. But I worry about her. Mom has heart and health problems of her own. I can't dump mine on her."

"Can you remember what happened?" Adam asked. "How you and Missy got separated?"

"I'm not exactly sure. Missy and I took the bus to Butternut Creek for the craft show. That's all I remember. They tell me I was struck by a car—hit-and-run. I guess no one realized I had a child with me."

"They couldn't tell us your injuries," Adam said. "Privacy issues."

"Broken ribs, which punctured my lungs, broken leg plus a concussion. They're keeping an eye on my heart, but I don't know why or how long I'll be here." She waved toward Adam and Miss Birdie. "Thank you for taking care of Missy."

She smiled as she listened to her daughter chatter about day care and Miss Birdie and the cat and life in Butternut Creek, but after a few minutes she looked so tired Adam knew it was time to go.

"Here's my card." The minister placed it on the bedside table. "Call me for any reason. Would you like a prayer?"

Mrs. Smith nodded but was asleep before he said "Amen."

"Mommy's better now," Missy said on the drive back.

"Yes, she is, but she's not well enough to come home yet," Miss Birdie said. "Maybe in a few days."

Home to where? The house in San Saba without anyone to help? The care of Missy and an injured woman could wear Mrs. Smith's mother out. Maybe home health care could send a nurse out, but how long would it take to set up additional help? Could she get physical therapy there?

Maybe a nursing facility in the interim. There were several good ones in the area, but, again, what about Missy? If necessary, Miss

Birdie would volunteer to continue caring for the child, but she looked worn out. Where else could Missy stay, and where could her mother recuperate without draining her own mother?

He'd think about that. A sketchy plan had formed, which he'd have to explore.

Friday afternoon in the PT department of the hospital, Sam was acutely aware of the interest with which the general watched him go through his exercises with Mike, lifting weights to build up muscles lost during the long recovery.

For several repetitions, he pretended to jerk, to have trouble with the weights. Stupid, he knew, because this was easy stuff, but he had a lot he still needed to punish the general for, years of resentment.

That anger seemed weaker and more juvenile now than it had when it had kept him alive after the amputation. Back then, he wanted to wave the handicap in front of the general, flaunt it, make him suffer for all the man had done to Sam, the screwed-up thinking that had ended in his nearly bleeding out next to his best friend. His dead best friend who wanted to do whatever Sam did—and Sam had wanted to be exactly like the general.

They'd entered the marines together, he and Morty, to serve and honor. Morty hadn't come back and he'd come back without a leg. He needed revenge for those losses, but it didn't feel as good as he'd believed, as he'd hoped.

Not that he'd allow second thoughts to stop him. Could be the longer he made the general feel bad, the sooner Sam would feel better.

But he couldn't forget the tears on the general's face the other night and his words the next morning. They might not have been tears. Could have been a reflection. And the words? The general had to know how he'd warped his only son's beliefs and sent him off to war. How could he possibly expect Sam to call him "Dad"?

Now that he had something to fight the general with, he wasn't about to let go of it until the man suffered. One night of the general's regret did not make up for an entire childhood of neglect. Besides, people didn't change, not at his father's age. He'd go back to normal after the novelty of seeing his son with just one leg wore off, and Sam wasn't about to be made a fool of when he did. With that, he added more weight and struggled to lift it.

"Hey, that's enough, big guy," Willow said.

He turned to see her leaning against the wall only a few feet from him.

"What are you trying to prove?" she asked.

Couldn't tell her. His plan was neither sane nor admirable, but it kept him going.

The sight of her—so patient, so gorgeous, so tenacious—calmed him.

"Showing off?" she asked. "Save that for someone who'll appreciate it, Captain."

Those words were an ego buster.

"Not, of course, that all the women in the department don't enjoy the sight of your terrific shoulders and abs, but we're attempting to hold ourselves back."

The general laughed. Sam felt like an idiot.

"We want you to work on building up the muscles in your thighs, too, but first"—she nodded Christine, the PT assistant, away—"I need to talk to you."

When she settled on the bench only two feet from him, he could smell that vaguely citrus fragrance he thought of as Willow's. He took a deep breath. As Aunt Effie would've said, he was smitten.

Then he remembered the general and glanced at him. The general looked back and forth between his son and Willow and nearly grinned. He appeared pleased, at least as much as the general indulged in such shallow emotions.

"General Peterson, why don't you come over here? Next to us?" Willow hesitated before she looked at Sam. "Do you mind if your father listens in?"

What could he say without sounding petty? Oh, he didn't mind *acting* petty, but preferred to behave like a better man around Willow.

"Whatever you think is best."

The general stood—straight and tall, the only way the man knew how to stand—and marched over to them.

She lifted Sam's leg, rested it on the bench, and gently turned it. "The prosthesis fits well. No bruising, no rubbing." She placed his foot on the floor. "How does it feel?"

"Fine."

The general patted Sam on the back, sort of like he was saying, *Good boy.*

Sam felt like a puppy.

Then Willow proceeded to study his thigh, pushing and prodding with a cool, professional demeanor. Finally satisfied, she said, "I'm releasing you from three-times-a-week physical therapy, Captain."

Stunned, Sam sat silently, mouth open. Would he see her again?

He didn't believe they'd built enough together to cause her to stop by his house on her own. Maybe if he kidnapped her sons, she'd come over to ransom them.

Before he could say anything, she added, "But that doesn't mean you're free of this place." She lifted her arm and waved it inclusively around the area. "I have several new patients arriving next week for initial evaluation, so I'm turning you over to Mike and Christine and reducing your appointments to one every two weeks. We still need to keep an eye on your progress and add a few exercises as you build your strength." She glared at him. "I expect you to keep up the regimen at home."

"Oh, he will," the general stated.

Sam attempted a grin because he knew this should sound like good news. It probably would have been if he hadn't hoped to, somehow, make Willow fall in love with him right here, next to the physical therapy table.

The general patted him again.

"I've printed out your exercises." She held out a folder. "We'll send some weights home with you. All the instructions are in there."

"Great," he muttered.

"Mike and Christine'll take great care of you."

"Oh, sure." He drummed his fingers on the surface of the bench. "But what about you and me?" Sam asked, then slammed his lips shut as he remembered where they were and who was watching. "I mean, you're no longer my therapist," he added with a pathetic wink, as if he expected that to convey his meaning and interest in the new relationship. Yes, really pitiful.

"That's correct." She stood.

"Thank you." The general took her hand and shook it. "I appreciate all you've done for my son. Maybe you'd like to join us for dinner."

"Sir, I can ask her out on my own."

"Of course you can." He glanced at his son before turning the charm on Willow. "What I'm planning is a celebration of a milestone in Sam's recovery. You and your boys," the general continued. "And Sam and a lady friend of mine, Winnie Jenkins."

"Thank you for asking, but . . . ," she began.

"Your boys love Sam. Maybe we could go to a movie they'd enjoy." The general took her hand again and poured on the charm. "We'll have a great time together."

"Dad," Sam muttered, surprised that, because he'd slipped into his teenage years, he'd also slipped back into using that word.

When the general turned toward him with a grin—when had the

man started grinning all the time?—Sam added, "Stop interfering." Then he turned to Willow, knowing what her response would be but hoping not. "Would you join us?"

"I can't, Captain." She grimaced. "You know why. I'm not ready. You're not ready."

"How ready do you have to be to go to a movie with my family?" the general argued.

"Dad." There, Sam said it again. Let that distract the old man. "She said no. Respect that."

"It's very nice of you, General." Willow held her hand out to shake his. "Thank you for the invitation, but no."

"Pick you up at six?" The general held on to her hand.

"No, but thank you again," Willow said.

"I'm not giving up." The general winked. Sam felt sure his father's wink was one of the signs of the apocalypse. On top of that, Willow must think they were the winkingest family in the state.

Then the thought hit him. As the general held Willow's hand and smiled at her and invited her to dinner with the family, Sam knew why. He realized what had happened.

The general had become one of the Widows.

Sam was doomed.

He sneaked a glance at Willow as she walked away and realized being doomed didn't sound bad at all. If he couldn't pull this off on his own—and he hadn't been notably successful—he shouldn't turn down help from anyone.

Chapter Eighteen

Hector tossed Adam the basketball. With a fake to the right, Adam drove toward the basket, leaped, and slammed the ball down for the last play in a close victory.

"Hey, Pops," shouted one of his teammates. "You've got hop."

Adam grinned. He had hop. What a great compliment.

"Pretty good for an old guy," Hector said.

Pops shook his head. He'd gone from a baller with hop to an old guy.

As the players began to pack up their belongings, Adam grabbed the ball and shrugged into his sweatshirt. The temperature in September fell once the sun disappeared.

"Hey, Pops." Hector ambled toward him. "Can we talk?"

"Sure. What's happening?"

The two never talked much, other than basketball. Adam knew Hector had a younger sister and life wasn't easy for them. He'd kept the door closed tightly on his life off the court, and Adam hadn't pried.

"It's about my sister . . . I wonder if . . ." He searched for words. "I wouldn't ask if I could handle the situation myself, but I can't." He swallowed. "I've tried."

"Go ahead."

"Umm . . . my mother died five years ago and my dad . . . he isn't much of a father. He aims to be, but . . ." Hector shrugged.

Adam didn't say anything, afraid he'd cut off the words.

"He's an addict. Lost his job about a year ago. Got arrested two weeks ago. Possession with intent. Can't make bail."

Adam had read that in the "Arrests" column of the weekly newspaper. He hadn't been sure that Harold Firestone was Hector's father. He should have asked. His excuse? That hadn't been their relationship. Wrong decision for a minister—and yet it was because he was a minister that Adam had been careful not to push Hector away by intruding in his life.

"We don't have money to pay the rent next month. Do you know anyplace we could get assistance with some bills or a place we could live? Not for me." He pointed his thumb toward himself. "I can get along on my own, but I need a safe place for my sister."

Adam studied the kid who attempted to look cool and manly, to show no emotion, but he could see how tightly he clenched his jaw and looked away.

"You don't have money to pay the rent for October? Why didn't you talk to me about this?" Why hadn't Adam approached him? "Why didn't you ask earlier?"

Hector shrugged. "Not your problem, Pops."

"I'm a minister. I'm supposed to help people."

He bristled. "Don't need charity, Pops. Not for myself." He glared. "But I need help for Janey."

"Where are you living now?"

"We still have the apartment for a while."

Adam didn't push about how much longer they could live there, especially without an adult. The whole situation seemed hard enough for Hector to bring up. The last thing Adam wanted was for him to pull away.

"How old is your sister?"

"She's eight." He glared at Adam. "I can take care of her in a lot of ways, just not this one." He shook his head. "She needs a place to sleep until I get things back together."

"You can't quit school."

Adam hadn't thought Hector could look more menacing, but his expression hardened.

"Don't lecture me, Pops."

"What about family? Can they pitch in?"

"After Mom died, we lost touch with her side. My father's family—I don't want Janey near any of them."

"Teachers or coaches?"

Hector stood. "If you don't want to help . . ."

Adam held up his hand. "I need to know the facts, Hector. That's it. Sit down and talk to me."

Slowly, he did.

"Why did you come to me?"

Hector took a deep breath and looked straight ahead. "It's not

easy for me to talk about problems, but I need to, for my little sister."
He turned to study Adam. "I trust you, Pops. You've always been
straight, never cheated in basketball, and I like that. Yeah, I trust you
and you've got that church with lots of people that might could help."

Adam nodded. "Okay, I'll check, see what I can find for Janey,
but you stay in school, for now. All right? Until we—you and I—work
this out. Then we can decide."

"Then *I'll* decide."

Adam watched as Hector turned and loped away. What in the
world would he come up with? Not one seminary class had either
covered the problem Hector faced or suggested a solution.

But that idea about the parsonage kept niggling at the back of his
mind, a solution to two problems. That big old house with all those
rooms and one man banging around in it, and those two bedrooms on
the second floor with a bathroom between them and the double parlors
on the first floor that stood empty except for the dining room furniture.

Adam's concern wasn't only Janey. He had to get Hector a place
to stay as well, to make sure he got to school and had what he needed.

But what did that entail? Were there permits? Insurance? Should
Adam look into being licensed as a foster parent? No doubt about it,
he needed help.

❦

Saturday morning during football season wasn't a good time to meet,
and this morning was worse than most. The football game Friday
night had gone into triple overtime and the Lions had lost. Still, he
had to call the Widows together for an emergency session.

He gazed around the circle: the pillar, Mercedes, and Winnie.
"You may wonder why I've asked you to come," he began. Bad opening. Those stilted words showed a pretentiousness he disliked. Also,
he could see that Miss Birdie's feathers had been ruffled, so to speak,
by his tone or hint of condescension. "I have a problem. I'm asking
you ladies to help with . . ." He stopped and considered his words.
"To come up with a solution."

Feathers nicely arranged and unruffled after his retreat, the pillar
nodded. Taking their cue from her, the other two Widows agreed.

First, he talked about Missy and her mother; then he explained
Hector's situation. "If Mrs. Smith goes back to San Saba, she might
not get the care she needs. I don't know about that for certain, but I
do know taking care of Missy and Deanne would be hard on Deanne's
mother, who's in poor health herself."

"I do worry about that," Miss Birdie said.

"With Hector and Janey," Adam continued, "there's no one, no family to watch over them."

All three women nodded in sympathy. Then he laid out the plan to have them all move into the parsonage. Looks of horror crossed the faces of the two original members of the group, but the provisional member smiled.

"How many people is that, Preacher?" Mercedes asked in a steady but unenthusiastic voice.

"Five." He counted them on his fingers. "Missy, her mother and grandmother, Hector, and Janey."

"I think that's a wonderful idea." Winnie looked toward the others and interpreted their glares. "Why not?" she asked, her voice filled with conviction.

"The parsonage is a home." The pillar nodded, only once but with so much emphasis Adam feared for the muscles of her neck. "For the preacher."

"And for his family," Mercedes added with a matching nod with even more conviction.

"Not," said Miss Birdie, emphasizing each word with a waggle of her index finger. "*Not* a boardinghouse."

"*Not* a bed-and-breakfast," Mercedes agreed.

With that, the two original Widows sat back, folded their arms, and glared at Adam.

"I like the idea," Winnie said. The other two turned toward her and glowered. Bless her, Winnie didn't back down. She looked back at them and nodded, then turned toward the minister. "I like the idea," she repeated. "It's what Christians do, provide for others in need."

Adam studied all three Widows for a few seconds, remembering the points he'd considered last night and this morning. At that time, he'd had them firmly in mind, but he should've written them on index cards. At the time, he'd forgotten how a glare from Miss Birdie could paralyze his thought process.

"The parsonage is for the minister and his family," the pillar stated.

"I'm not married," he said. "No family. You know that."

"Of course we do, Pastor." Mercedes's voice dripped with compassion. "We're doing our best to take care of that situation."

"Although you've done nothing to help us," the pillar added.

Inside Adam smiled. Yes, bless their hearts, they were. Despite the embarrassment it caused everyone involved, they wanted to find him a soul mate in a town not blessed with a surfeit of single women.

If they couldn't find a soul mate for him, they'd settle for a woman he could live with in harmony, if not with passion, for fifty years; together, they'd raise a big family.

"Although I do appreciate your efforts"—Adam chose his words carefully—"I am *still* a bachelor. Even if I were somehow to stumble upon a charming young woman . . ."

Their expressions showed such obvious doubt this would happen that he forgot where his line of reasoning was heading.

Finally, nearly ten seconds into the silence, Winnie prompted, "Even if you did find a young woman yourself . . ."

"Even if I found a young woman to marry, it would take me a few months to court her . . ."

"Not if you got busy," Miss Birdie stated.

He ignored the words and pressed on. "It would take me a few months to court her . . ."

The three nodded, as if encouraging him—whether to finish his sentence or start courting, he didn't know.

"Then let's say an engagement period of six months or a year," he said.

"Six months," the pillar said as if this had been a multiple-choice quiz. "Plenty of time. You need to get the process moving. No namby-pambying."

"I don't think that's the word you want," Mercedes interrupted. "*Dilly-dallying* is what you're looking for."

"Or *shilly-shallying*," Winnie suggested.

"I don't care." The pillar glared at the two other Widows, then turned back to the minister.

"After the wedding," Adam said before any of the Widows could take a breath. "We'd need some time to get used to marriage . . ."

"Three months," Winnie recommended.

"You're not getting any younger," Mercedes said gently.

"I wouldn't even be close to thirty by that time," Adam objected. They didn't notice.

"As I add all those numbers up, there won't be a baby in the nursery until—best-case scenario—two years from now," Winnie said. "Only one baby, and that's only if the preacher moves fast. And at that rate"—Winnie showed the math abilities she'd used to run the asphalt company—"it would be four or five more years before that parsonage would be filled with children, assuming they popped out every year or two."

The prospect of his imaginary wife popping out children at that rate rendered Adam speechless. Even more stunning was their discussion of their imaginary sex life. Solely for the purpose of procreation, of course. He felt an incredible constriction in his chest as these three discussed the begetting process as calmly as they figured the proceeds from the spring bazaar.

"All of which means there's no reason to keep those rooms unused now," Winnie concluded. "It will be years before a family fills them. Even"—she turned to face Adam—"if you get busy this year. Right?"

Mercedes and the pillar watched the new Widow, their expressions softening little by little until they turned toward the minister.

He was so dumbfounded by what they might be thinking or what they might say next, his throat closed up.

"Guess she's right," the pillar mumbled.

"This would be a Christian way to use the space," Mercedes said.

Winnie asked, "How well do you know this Hector? Is he an honest young man? Does he attend church?"

"We play basketball together."

"Oh, yes. Basketball," the pillar said. "Odd activity for a minister."

"I've always heard Hector's a nice young man. Honest and hard-working," Mercedes said.

"Mercedes knows everyone," Miss Birdie told Winnie before she said to Adam, "From what my contacts in San Saba say, Mrs. Smith is a good, honest woman."

"Would they pay rent?" Mercedes tilted her head to consider that.

"I wouldn't think so," Winnie stated. "That would probably change our tax-free status."

"And we do want to help a young man and his sister in trouble," Mercedes added firmly. "Perhaps we could hire him to do some jobs, so he'd have some spending money."

Stepping back into the discussion, Adam asked, "What do we have to do to make this happen?"

Winnie pulled out her notepad and flipped it open. Pen in hand, she said, "I'll check about the insurance."

The Widows took over. Within fifteen minutes, they had considered all the tasks and assigned who would be in charge. Within a week, they'd have beds and curtains and other furnishings donated and the necessary paperwork taken care of. His only job was to call the plumber to check the leak he'd noted in that Jack-and-Jill bathroom.

That evening, when Miss Birdie and Adam took Missy to see her mother, Mrs. Smith was again sitting up. Her face had lost the gray cast and her eyes held a hint of sparkle. Next to her sat an older but frailer version of Deanne.

"Grandma," Missy shouted and ran to the woman.

"This is my mother, Eleanor Peppers," Deanne said. "If you couldn't guess that."

He watched Mrs. Peppers cuddle Missy, then glanced over at Miss Birdie, who smiled broadly.

"We weren't expecting you for a few days," Adam said.

"My other daughter and the baby are doing fine, and I was so worried about Deanne and Missy that I jumped on an earlier plane." She turned to smile at her daughter. "She's doing well."

Yes, she was, but even with as much improvement as she showed, Deanne had a lot of recuperating ahead.

"I've been walking in the hallway to build up strength, but I'm still weak," Deanne said. "They say I may be able to go home soon, after a little more PT."

"Perhaps to a nursing facility," Mrs. Peppers said. "We don't know what's available in San Saba or what her insurance will cover."

"Where are you staying, Mrs. Peppers? Do you have a car?"

"I flew in this morning and grabbed a cab here. I'll be staying at the hotel next door." She glanced at her granddaughter. "I'll keep Missy with me at least overnight." Eleanor rubbed her granddaughter's back. "We'll go shopping this afternoon and to the park. We have a conference with Deanne's doctor tomorrow to work out a time line."

"If you need us to pitch in," Miss Birdie said, "let us know."

Deanne held out her hand and took Miss Birdie's. "Thank you so much. I'll never be able to repay you for your kindness."

After a few more minutes, Miss Birdie and Adam walked out. Odd to have only the two of them.

"I'm going to miss her," the pillar said. "But I'm so glad she has family." She sighed. "I'm even happier that I can get a good night's sleep."

After they got in the car, Miss Birdie said, "I was thinking about that parlor next to the front door. Maybe if we put a couple of beds there for Eleanor and her family. They can use the guest bathroom down there. You know, that's what a church does."

Then she fell asleep, her head against the headrest, soft snores escaping her mouth. Adam wouldn't mention that to her later, of course. He didn't dare. He'd never tease a snoring pillar.

❧

Wednesday morning, Adam checked his calendar. Winnie, the church treasurer, wanted to meet about the stewardship drive, and Howard had left a message about the next board meeting.

As he considered those appointments, the phone rang. He fought the urge to answer, because Maggie worked until eleven. As she'd often reminded him, *she* answered the phone when she was in the office.

After a few seconds, she knocked on the study door and came in.

A problem with her answering the phone was that the church had no intercom. Maggie had to come into the study to give him messages or tell him to pick up. Sometimes she just shouted. However, that was the way she wanted to do this, so Adam accepted.

"That was Rita Mae Parsons. She said Charley hasn't returned her calls."

Charley was the town handyman, a plumber and a good one. When business was slow, he did about anything anyone needed done.

"I let him in the parsonage about eight thirty and showed him the leak in that upstairs bathroom."

"Well, you know how Rita Mae worries," Maggie said.

She should. Charley was a good Presbyterian and the father of three small children. An enormous, woolly mammoth of a man, he stood six-three and weighed well over three hundred pounds. Everyone in town loved him and feared he'd have a heart attack before he was forty.

"His truck's in front of your house."

"Still? He got there two hours ago."

"Yes and Rita Mae wonders if you'd go over and check on him."

"Sure." Adam stood and headed off toward the parsonage.

Once inside the front door, he wandered through the first story, searching for a body. None there. He couldn't have missed Charley's body lying on the floor.

He called, "Charley?" No answer but he thought he heard a soft pounding from above. Adam moved toward the stairs, still looking around as if Charley could hide under the few furnishings gracing the house. As he climbed the steps, the pounding grew louder.

"Charley?" he shouted.

The sound increased and Adam heard a muffled "Help." He ran into the guest bedroom, through it, and to the bathroom. Charley's enormous denim-covered butt stuck out of the cabinet under the sink.

"I'm stuck," he said.

That much was obvious. Less clear was how to get him out. Adam started to ask, "How did this happen?" but that, too, seemed obvious. The cabinet had a sink on the top and, beneath that, two doors separated by a vertical strip of wood. Charley must have reached in the right side to check the leaking pipe, pulled himself too far in, and now, as far as the preacher could tell, couldn't get out.

"You're not laughing, are you?" Charley shouted, his voice slightly muffled.

"No, Charley." Although it was hard not to, Charley was such a nice guy that he couldn't. "Push," Adam suggested.

"I have been pushing." He gave a deep sigh, which made the cabinet vibrate.

"Okay." Adam studied the situation. "You push and I'll pull." The minister reached for the tool loops on Charley's overalls and attempted to tug him straight back. The plumber didn't move.

"Let's try again," Adam said. "On the count of three." He took a firmer hold of the loops, braced his feet, and counted, "One, two, three." Unfortunately, when he jerked back, the stitching didn't hold. The loops ripped off in his fingers and he stumbled backward. After a clumsy attempt to catch himself, Adam landed in the bathtub, his legs straight up. His head had narrowly missed hitting the hard enamel. Wouldn't that be great to have someone find them up there like this? Adam unconscious in the tub and Charley stuck?

By the time he figured out what had happened and got out of the tub, Adam realized Charley was laughing.

"You okay, Preacher?" he shouted between guffaws. The entire cabinet shook with his laughter.

Adam scrutinized Charley's position and that enormous rear end again. "Have you tried pushing against the back of the cabinet to work yourself out?" he asked.

"No, I'm enjoying the peace and quiet so much I decided to stay here the rest of the day and meditate," he said with a sarcasm Adam hadn't heard from him before. Of course, the preacher had never seen him in this . . . um . . . position before.

"Yes, Preacher, I've tried pushing myself out twenty different ways," Charley added long-sufferingly. "I'm scratched up and bruised but nothing's worked."

The idea of slathering the plumber with soap to pop him out didn't seem pleasant and probably wouldn't work because Adam couldn't reach the stuck areas. He bet Charley wouldn't cotton to the idea, either.

"Don't try to lather me up with butter," the plumber warned like a veteran of situations like this.

Adam didn't ask for details.

"What do you suggest?" They both paused to think. "Let's try that again, my pulling again and you pushing." This time Adam reached for the utility belt the plumber wore, which was firmly stuck between his body and the sides of the cabinet. It had the advantage that it wouldn't rip off. Probably.

"Okay."

"I'll count to three, then you push." Adam grabbed the belt and said, "One . . . two . . . three."

The minister could hear Charley straining inside the cabinet, using his knees—which were on the tile floor—to push against the wood surround as Adam pulled hard. For a moment, he thought they'd done it, that the plumber was free.

Instead, the shaking of the cabinet caused the toilet-paper holder on the side of the cabinet to pop off. It also made the pretty bowl of soaps the ladies had left next to the sink leap into the air. The yellow rose-shaped soaps scattered all over the room as the dish crashed to the floor and broke.

And when Adam's hands slipped off the utility belt, he flew back into the tub, banged his right arm against the spigot, and turned the shower on. For a moment, Adam sat there, a little dazed, attempting to figure out what had happened as cold water rained down on him. By the time he turned off the faucet, he was soaked.

"Pastor, you okay?"

Dripping, he struggled from the tub and surveyed the wreckage. "Fine. A little wet." Carefully Adam picked up the pieces of china on the floor because, the way this was going, he figured one of them would cut off an appendage if he didn't.

"I can't think of anything else to do." The minister studied the situation and shook his head. "Maybe I should call someone."

"No, Pastor, please don't," Charley begged. "I know I need to lose weight, but everyone will laugh if they know I got stuck here. Please keep this quiet."

"Okay," Adam agreed, guessing how mortified the plumber must feel. "But I can't think of anything unless I cut you out of there."

"Yeah, that's what it's going to take."

Adam could tell from the shaking of the vanity that Charley had sighed.

"I've got a saw in my tool kit and I've got a chain saw in the truck," he said.

"Charley, you don't want me using a chain saw anywhere near your body. I'd probably disembowel you or cut off some really important equipment." Adam pulled a small trimming saw from the plumber's toolbox. "Where should I start?" He studied the situation. "I'm not very good with tools."

"Start at the top."

From the empty left side of the cabinet, Adam glanced inside and discovered a good amount of room in there. He probably wouldn't take off Charley's ears. Kneeling, he started sawing. Fortunately, the piece was narrow. Unfortunately, it was made of some kind of wood harder than steel.

"Probably white oak," Charley mused as Adam sawed. "Used a lot in these older houses. You don't see it today on bathroom fixtures. Usually just laminate or veneer surfaces. This piece was made to last forever. Good craftsmanship."

Great. He was ripping up good craftsmanship with this saw. Of course if he didn't, Charley'd be stuck in this guest bathroom until he lost enough weight to extract himself. It reminded Adam of a story from Winnie-the-Pooh, one of his childhood favorites.

When at last Adam cut through the wood, he put the saw down, pulled on the work gloves he'd found in the toolbox, grabbed the lathe of wood, and pulled. It didn't break, but slowly the piece bent back against the nails that held it in place and came loose in his hands.

With that, Adam moved out of the way and Charley pushed himself from the opening. Once on his feet, the plumber took a deep breath and punched his body, looking for wounds. "I'll probably have a few good bruises," he said before scrutinizing the mangled cabinet. "I'll fix this. I'll use one big door so anyone can easily get in here to make repairs."

"Sounds good," Adam agreed.

Charley leaned down to study the plumbing inside. "The pipe's an easy fix. I need to replace this fitting here." He pointed. "See where that leak's coming from?" Then he looked at Adam. "You're not going to tell anyone, right?" Perspiration and supplication covered his round face.

"This is between a pastor and one of the flock," Adam responded.

"You're not going to tell Reverend Patillo, are you?"

"No, Charley—between you and me. No one else."

"Thanks. I'll call my wife then get right back to this. She worries." He pulled out his cell. "I'm going to tell her it was a bigger job than I thought." He looked at Adam, his eyes and voice filled with sincerity. "And I'll go on a diet tonight, I promise."

Chapter Nineteen

We're making cookies, Captain," Leo said.

"For Mr. Masterson," Nick added.

Sam gazed around the kitchen. He hadn't been gone for an hour, only enough time for a short walk and a visit to the library to pick up a couple of paperbacks. What did he find when he got home? The general sitting at the table while Winnie and Leo added ingredients to a bowl and Nick greased a cookie sheet.

Not being much of a cook, Sam knew he didn't have a single cookie sheet in the house. He didn't have a bowl or measuring cups or flour. He possessed nothing to use in baking because he and the boys had packed it up and Willow had taken it to the thrift shop. What he *did* have was a mess in his kitchen and two interfering busybodies—the general and Miss Winnie—who didn't know the difference between meddling and helping.

But he also had Leo and Nick there. That was good. That felt right. "Hey, guys, how are you?" Then he realized what Nick and Leo had said. "Cookies? For Mr. Masterson?"

"Yes, sir." Nick waved a napkin covered with shortening. "Your father, the general—" His voice filled with awe. "The general," he repeated and seemed to savor the words, "said a marine helps others."

"He said since Mr. Masterson baked that cake for you, we should return the favor," Leo said.

"Gosh, General." Sam infused every syllable with sarcasm. "What a nice thing to do. How are you helping in the effort?"

"I'm sampling."

"He's telling us what to do," Winnie said, but her words contained a spark of humor.

"He's good at that," Sam said. "He can command and *I'll* sample." Sam sat and placed his books on the table. "What kind are you making?"

"Snickerdoodles. Already in the oven." Nick nodded in that direction.

Aah, yes, the aroma of cinnamon filled the kitchen.

"And chocolate chip because the general likes those best." Leo attempted a surreptitious swipe of dough but Winnie spanked his hand.

"They'll be done soon," she warned.

"Then what?" Sam glanced back and forth among the four, certain something else was going on. He bet two of them had planned this and two of them were innocent pawns in the duplicitous scheme. But if so—he glanced around the kitchen—where was Willow?

"Mom's picking us up at five," Leo said.

Aha, the pieces were falling into place.

Leo glanced at the clock.

"The general says we're all—you, the four of us cooks, and Mom—going over to Mr. Masterson's house to give him the cookies."

"*Most* of the cookies, 'cause we want to eat a few, too," Nick said.

Sam glared at the general. "You've got to stop butting in."

The man smiled. Not an answer Sam trusted. Actually, not a response he'd ever seen before except way back when he'd been a little kid, before the general had become *the general*.

"Might as well give up on that," Winnie said. "I think that's how he got to be a general: butting in and ordering people around."

At five fifteen, before Willow even reached the porch, the boys had waylaid her and explained the plan. As they did, she glanced up as if looking for him. Then the boys came back inside for the wrapped cookies and hurried outside as the general grabbed Sam and hustled him out. Not that Sam really minded or protested too much.

"This isn't my idea," Sam said. Somehow—although Sam knew it had been part of the general's plan—he and Willow had ended up together several yards behind the others.

"You're moving well." Willow studied him professionally. "How's the pain?"

"Can't we just talk? I mean about something other than my leg or the pain?"

"Sure." She glanced up at him. "I left the hospital only a few minutes ago. I'm still in physical therapist mode. Let me switch that off." She blinked then smiled up at him. "There, I'm in person mode. What would you like to talk about?"

He had no idea because he'd been so distracted by that smile he'd barely heard what she said. He only knew what he didn't want to discuss: his leg and going to a movie with Winnie and the general and Willow and the boys, just the six of them. Instead he asked, "Would you go to a movie? With me?"

She stopped. "And your father and the boys in Winnie's car?"

He quit walking and stood next to her. "No, only the two of us." He wasn't exactly sure how he'd handle that. He would be able to drive his car, but he hadn't tried yet and he bet a Mustang wouldn't be the best vehicle for him now. Great car for a single man to show off his machismo. Horrible car for an amputee to try to get in and out of.

"I don't think that's a good idea, Captain."

He held up his hand. "Please call me Sam. You're in person mode now."

"Okay, Sam, but I told you I'm not interested in a relationship and you said you weren't, so why?"

"I don't believe I said exactly that. I think I said I don't know where I'm going or what I'm doing with my life so probably I'm not in a place where I could pursue a relationship."

She shook her head. "No, that's not what you said. I would have remembered that."

He hunched his shoulders and stuck his hands in his pockets. "What's wrong with going to a movie? I don't know if you've noticed, but Winnie and the others are trying to get us together. It's not going to stop. If you think 'making cookies to repay Mr. Masterson's kindness' is the real reason for this outing, you're wrong. We've been set up."

She tilted her head and scrutinized him. "Are you saying we should give in without a fight?"

"I don't know what I'm saying. I want to take you to a movie. Why's that such a big thing? I haven't asked you to marry me or to sleep with me or to have a relationship *of any kind*. It's only a stupid movie."

She blinked but didn't say anything, only stared at him, her mouth slightly open.

Because she hadn't objected yet, he kept going. "I'm tired of staying home with the general. He's not a great deal of fun. And, yes, you attract me. And, yes, I want to kiss you again, but it's only a movie, not a commitment for eternity." He stopped when he realized he'd shouted the last few words. He took a deep breath before glancing ahead. The others had stopped in the middle of the sidewalk about twenty feet ahead of him to watch his tantrum with great interest.

"Oh," she said calmly. "Well, if it's only a stupid movie, fine. I'll get a sitter for tomorrow night. I'll pick you up at six thirty."

"I can . . ." Well, no, he couldn't drive but he hated that she assumed that.

"Don't get all macho on me." She glared at him. "I have your records. I know you haven't driven yet. Forgive my self-interest, but I prefer to get there and home alive. If we go out again, after you've practiced, you can drive."

He nodded and stayed on the sidewalk as she walked toward her sons. He watched her, thinking that that had gone a lot easier than he'd expected. On top of that, she'd said he could drive the next time they went out. Maybe not exactly those words, but that's how he interpreted them. They would go out again.

Of course, he still had no idea what to expect or what he wanted in the future, but one thing was sure. He felt good being with Willow. Cheerful. Even optimistic, a little, as much as he allowed himself to be.

The shouting had felt good, too. It had opened something inside he'd kept closed up. It had loosened his frustration. Maybe he should yell more often.

He watched Willow and her sons as the whole crowd went up the steps, rang the bell, and handed the box to Mr. Masterson. After a minute of chatting, the do-gooders turned and started back.

"Mr. Masterson really appreciated that." Nick hopped toward Sam. "He said we could come over and make a pie with him sometime."

"He said thank you and didn't even mention the time we were in his backyard," Leo said.

"Yeah, I know how he felt. I remember the time I found two short, redheaded, very noisy marines in *my* backyard."

"Captain." Nick ducked his head and laughed.

"But you like having us around and you *were* glad to see us," Leo said. "Once you got used to us and stopped drinking."

These were great kids. He hated that they knew, that they'd witnessed his worst traits. Maybe if he behaved really well, they'd forget that drinking-too-much part.

Maybe they could even accept him and their mother being together. He bet they'd like that. In fact, he knew they'd be on Sam's side.

Could he get them to influence her? He didn't think that would work. She didn't look ready for more, and she wouldn't like him using her sons to further a romance.

But at least he and Willow were going to that stupid movie together.

❦

"I need you to do two things for me." Sam hated to ask the general for help. Wouldn't have a few years ago.

The general stood by the stove, turning the bacon. With that idiotic pink towel hanging from his belt, he didn't look as imposing and inaccessible as Sam remembered him.

"What do you need, son?"

He'd never called him that, "son," when he'd wanted to hear it. Not in high school when he'd won letters in football, track, and baseball and had gone to state in the hundred-meter. Not even when he'd gone to A&M on a football scholarship. The general hadn't paid him much notice at all until Sam had gotten his leg blown off, the biggest foul-up of his life.

"I need to practice driving my car. Would you help me?" The request hadn't hurt at all. "I'd thought about getting hand controls," Sam explained as if the general had asked that. "But they told me at Walter Reed I should be able to drive once I got used to this new prosthesis."

"Fine. When?"

"In an hour?"

The general nodded as he put a plate in front of Sam, and the few words of conversation ceased.

As he was shaving after breakfast, Sam considered his reflection. He looked a lot healthier. His face had filled out some, possibly due to the good cooking of the Widows and the big breakfasts the general served.

But his hair took more time to wash and dry than he wanted to spend. It took hours to groom the mess and a fortune on what they called "product" to tame it, but if his long hair didn't bug the general, what fun was that? It looked as if the general had won this fight without even fielding a platoon.

❦

When they arrived at the high school parking lot, the general took out some books he'd stowed in the trunk and placed them on end to mark a course for Sam to maneuver through.

"You're doing fine, son," the general called out as Sam knocked down six books in a row. "Be patient. Give yourself time."

It wasn't that Sam couldn't steer; that was easy. It was controlling the speed that caused him problems. Alternating between the brake and accelerator felt as if he had to pull his foot from thick mud. He didn't have the motion down well, which meant he didn't slow as quickly as he'd like.

"You're getting better." Although he had paled when his son nearly mowed down a post near the entrance, he didn't cringe when Sam barely missed the chain-link fence surrounding the area. Of course the man had faced bombs, mortar, and grenades in battle.

The two near wrecks had taken place only moments after Sam had taken control of the car—or *not* taken control, because the vehicle had taken off on its own. After fifteen minutes of intense effort, Sam seldom headed toward total destruction of the Mustang or the fence or the general, who occasionally had to leap out of the way. Yes, his driving had improved but the pressure on his knee and the stress of attempting to drive perfectly had worn him out. Not that he'd tell his fa . . . Not that he'd tell the general. He stopped the car, got out, and walked around to settle into the passenger seat.

"We'll come back tomorrow," the general said as he strapped himself in the driver's side.

Sam nodded. "I want to get my hair cut."

Did he detect a grin on the general's face? A quick shimmer of gloating in his eyes? But all the man said was, "Okay, let's get to the barbershop."

"*Not* the barbershop. Aunt Effie used to take me there when I was a kid. They shaved me. Head for the strip mall on the highway east of town. I saw a place there."

They found themselves in a shop with neon pink chairs and curtains that he hadn't thought the general would enter. Now the man sat in the reception area on one of those feminine chairs and leafed through a book on hairstyles as if he planned to dye his hair blue or get a Mohawk.

When the stylist had completed the cut, Sam studied himself in the mirror.

"How do you like it?" the young woman asked, razor in hand.

He nodded. It looked better. He looked better. Nearly human again. Would Willow like it?

Crap. He hadn't done this for her. Maybe for the boys, so they wouldn't get the idea that long hair was masculine. For himself because it was easier, but not for Willow or the general or anyone else.

But the questions remained: Would she like it?

"Nice cut." Willow admired the new Sam after he settled in the passenger seat. He'd been great looking before, but now he looked gorgeous and tough. She could barely drag her eyes away from him to watch the road.

Sam had pulled himself in and settled in the car without, of course, a smidgeon of help from her, thank you. As she pulled away from the curb, she asked, "What's the occasion? The long hair didn't bug your father enough?"

He laughed. "How'd you know?"

"Hey, I have two sons and I've worked with military men for years." She flipped on the blinker to turn onto the highway and toward Marble Falls. "I know 'tude and machismo."

From Sam's relaxed position, she guessed he didn't feel a bit emasculated with her driving. At least, he didn't hold on to the edge of the seat and point out oncoming cars. They talked comfortably about her life with two sons and his with a military father.

Later, during the movie, he did the stretch-and-drop maneuver to drape his arm over her shoulders. She hadn't had a man do that since she was a teenager, but it still worked and he had the maneuver down pat. She even put her head on his shoulder and he nuzzled her a little.

When they left the theater, she had no idea what to do next. She hadn't been the driver on a date before, if this was a date. She decided not to take him to a make-out place, although she remembered a few from her youth. They could go to his house, but the general was probably there with Winnie, which cut down on privacy. The boys would be at her apartment with a sitter, and she wanted to spend more time with Sam. Alone. Talking. Maybe more.

❦

As Mattie and Adam left the theater, he recognized the couple a few yards ahead of them and called, "Hey, Sam, Willow."

Adam was a little—okay, very—surprised to see the two of them. An odd pair, but they looked good together. When the couple stopped walking and waited for them, Adam asked Sam, "You get a haircut? I can tell you didn't go to my barber."

"I learned from your experience." Sam smiled.

"This is Mattie Patillo, minister at the Presbyterian Church." Adam nodded at her. "Mattie, I'd like you to meet Willow Thomas, a member of the Christian Church, and my friend Sam Peterson."

"Pleased to meet you." Mattie grinned.

"So how'd you like to get something to eat? There's a coffee shop just down the highway." Adam pointed. "Easy walk."

After he said that, Adam glanced at Sam. Could he walk that far? His gait looked good and comfortable now, but would it last?

"What do you think?" Willow asked Sam.

"I'm game," he said.

Then Sam took Willow's hand and gazed at her with an emotion Adam hadn't seen in his eyes before. Of course, the two men had only shared a few pizzas and watched some preseason football so he'd have been unlikely to see tenderness in the soldier's expression. Thank goodness.

"Sam's been so good with my sons." Willow turned toward Adam. "You know Leo and Nick are active kids."

The minister nodded, still keeping his eyes on Sam.

"I'm very grateful for all he's done."

To Adam, the words almost sounded as if the trip to Marble Falls were a debt she was repaying with her presence. Evidently Sam read it that way, too, because he kept his eyes on her face and all the tenderness the minister had glimpsed there seconds before drained away, replaced by a blank stare. When Sam looked away for only a second, Willow's expression held longing.

What was going on between these two? Would they be good for each other? Maybe. A current flowed between them even as they attempted to ignore it. What could he do to help?

Oh, good Lord. He sounded like Miss Birdie. Immediately he said, "Come on. Let's go. This place has great pie."

❧

Willow felt more and more nervous the closer the car got to Butternut Creek. Once or twice she glanced at Sam, then back toward the road.

Now that he was no longer her patient, she really wanted to kiss him again, but she had no idea how to put a move on a guy in the car. Her date had always done that. Was Sam as confused as she was? Probably he'd never put a move on the driver, but she didn't doubt he'd figure out how.

Maybe she should pull into a dark area, turn toward him, and let him take over, but that sounded passive and unlike her.

"Please don't let me out under the streetlight in front of my house, because I want to kiss you," he said, his voice seductive as well as holding a note of amusement.

She glanced at him, then quickly turned her head and kept her eyes on the road. Could she tell him she felt the same without the words catching in her throat?

"I want to kiss you, too." Yes, she could say that.

He grinned. "Could you find some place to pull over before we get to my house so my father and the neighbors aren't watching us?"

Life didn't get much better than that. Well, it would when she stopped but for now, that comment and his smile were enough.

"Especially not Mrs. Gohannon who lives across from you. Biggest gossip in town." She kept her eyes on the road and drove along the curving highway toward Butternut Creek. In fact, they were nearly to his house before she pulled off into a neighborhood park, turned off the lights and engine, and turned toward him. As he slid across the seat, she held up her hand.

"Not so fast. I have a question for you."

He groaned. "You overthink everything."

"That's probably true, but I need to know this. Why are you interested in me? I'm not like the other women I imagine you've dated. I don't flirt. I'm not a bit girlie."

"You're right. You're nothing like the women I'm usually attracted to. Obviously I've been interested in the wrong kind of women."

Why did he have to be so darned charming? She steeled herself to say, "I'm divorced and have two kids and work long hours."

"Exactly the kind of woman I've been looking for."

"What? Why?"

He took her hand. That felt really good. How could only a touch fill her with so much pleasure?

"I have no idea," he said. "I knew you were the one when I first saw you. After I got acquainted with you, I was even more certain."

She considered that for a few seconds. "You're not saying it was love at first sight."

"Probably not. Maybe attraction at first sight or chemistry or a lightning strike, but you are the woman for me. I'm not going away until we can figure this out." He shrugged. "Maybe we can't. Maybe we have too many complications, but I want to try."

He drew his index finger down her cheek and gave her the smile she'd attempted to ignore. As if any woman could.

"You have no idea how beautiful you are, do you?"

How could she resist him?

"Okay." She nodded. "I need to point out that this is a local make-out place so just one kiss. I don't want the cops to check on us. That would be embarrassing."

He placed his hand on her shoulder and moved it slowly to her neck.

She took off her seat belt and moved closer to him. "Only a kiss for now."

"But . . ."

"Hey." She held up her hand. "That's the deal. Take it or leave it." Oh, sure, as if she'd drive off now. "I want us to get to know each other better."

"Kissing is a great way . . ."

"For now I prefer the old-fashioned way. Conversation."

"You drive a hard bargain."

She grinned and nodded. Then Sam increased the pressure on her shoulder and she slid into his arms, at least as close as she could with the console between them. Since this was to be the only kiss tonight, she hoped it would be good and memorable.

And it was. Oh, Lord, it was.

❦

A few days later, the Widows met at the diner after the lunch rush to discuss the church and duties and who was sick and who needed help.

But they didn't mention Sam and Willow because they'd done everything they could and weren't prepared to admit failure or congratulate themselves for possible success. They'd just allow that relationship to simmer.

"What about the preacher?" Winnie asked. "Who else can we find for him?"

"How 'bout that new CEO at the asphalt company?" Mercedes suggested.

"Her husband died not too long ago. She's not ready."

"I'm fixin' to give up on him," Birdie said. "And you know how much I hate to concede defeat."

"I had hopes for Howard's niece," Mercedes said. "Too bad she was only visiting for a week."

Birdie shook her head. "Left before we could even introduce them."

"Not a spark between Pastor Adam and Reverend Patillo?" Winnie asked.

"None at all. Lost cause." Birdie shook her head. "All right," she stated. "Let's get down to business. Winnie, take notes." Birdie didn't think of Winnie as the third Widow, not like Mercedes did. In Birdie's mind, Winnie was a provisional Widow. Maybe a Widow-in-waiting but not a full-fledged Widow, not yet. But she did take good notes.

When Winnie nodded, Mercedes, chair of the church elders, said, "Don't forget, there's an elders' meeting Wednesday evening. Will you both be there?"

The other two nodded.

"And we need to call a meeting of all the women of the church about the spring festival," Birdie said.

Before they could really get started—because Butch did make those nice apple coffee cakes for the diner and each had a healthy slice—Birdie's cell rang. After a short conversation, she turned it off and stood, fixing the other women with an unwavering gaze. "Ladies, we are needed."

Mercedes and Winnie leaped to their feet, gathered their purses and totes, and followed Birdie.

The Widows had accepted the mission.

❧

"Heaven help me," Adam murmured as he turned off the phone. In fact, heaven help all of them because the Widows were on the way.

Oh, he knew good and well the women were the best people to get the job done. They'd get the rooms in the parsonage fixed up in no time and do it right. But the whirlwind of the three of them—because Winnie had become an even greater force when triangulated with the other two—could rock the foundation of the house.

This was why Adam had started over to the church as soon as he called them, to get away. After a few steps, he paused beneath the huge oak tree that stood on the edge of the parking lot, midway between the parsonage and the church. He couldn't—could not—abandon the Smiths. Deanne had been discharged and would be arriving within the next hour. He'd called Howard to collect her, her mother, and Missy, and drive them here. No matter what the preacher might tell himself about all the work that awaited him at the church, he couldn't allow the family to walk unsuspectingly into a house filled with Widows.

Adam turned, slowly, and ambled back to the parsonage just as a pickup pulled into the parking lot and Jesse stepped out.

"Got a load of furniture from the thrift shop for you, Pastor." Jesse went to the back of the truck and opened the tailgate. "Give me a hand?"

Within minutes, they had beds set up in the previously unused parlor on the first floor. As they finished, the Widows bustled in with armloads of linens. Within a few more minutes, the parlor had been turned into a bedroom for Missy and her mother and grandmother. After another load arrived from the thrift shop, they put a bed in each of the two empty bedrooms on the second floor. The women made all the beds, tossing a colorful quilt on each.

Finished, Jesse, the Widows and the preacher stood in the hallway and looked into the larger parlor, admiring their work. Wall-to-wall beds, but the family didn't want to be separated.

"We fixed up the upstairs bedrooms," Mercedes said. "Just in case Hector and his sister do need a place to stay. And who knows? Maybe others will need a temporary shelter."

"It's truly a service to the community, Pastor," Winnie added.

Then Miss Birdie made a noise Adam hadn't heard before and couldn't describe. It suggested possible agreement and maybe a bit of pleasure in the thought.

The pillar looked around the parlor and nodded. "Nicely done." She straightened the quilt a bit. She might have meant the remark as a compliment for her minister, but Adam wasn't sure. It could have meant she admired the pattern of the cover.

"I'll be back in a little bit, Pastor," Winnie said as she hustled out. "Have a few more errands to run."

"I have to get back to work." Miss Birdie took off after Winnie, and Jesse followed.

The departures left Adam alone with Mercedes, with whom he always felt comfortable.

"Preacher," she said. "I talked to my grandniece—she's a social worker for the state—about Hector. She made three suggestions. First, he could petition to be an emancipated minor and he'd be Janey's guardian. Second, she could be placed in foster care with you—or, third, both Firestones could be in foster care with you. If you plan to board youngsters here, you should be licensed as a provider, just to make sure it's all legal." She handed him some papers. "Fill these out and I'll take care of that."

Adam nodded. "Thanks for doing all this."

"You know, Deanne couldn't have taken care of herself in San Saba," Mercedes said. "Even with her mother there, she wouldn't have received the physical therapy and nursing care she needs. Taking care of both of them would have exhausted Mrs. Peppers. We've done a good thing, Preacher. I'm glad you and Winnie talked us into this."

Once she left, Adam put the laptop on the dining room table and started to work. He finished the bulletin and sent it to Maggie, filling the service with Miss Birdie's favorite hymns. She deserved a reward.

By noon, Winnie had returned with Sam's father and a dozen grocery sacks. The two stocked the cabinets and refrigerator with enough food to last if nuclear war broke out.

After they left, Howard pulled into the parking lot and helped Deanne inside. Missy and Eleanor followed her. Pale and tired,

Deanne fell asleep as soon as she hit the bed. Missy curled up on the toddler-size bed and slept. Adam tugged the quilt over her as Howard brought in several plastic sacks of what Deanne had accumulated in the hospital.

"I have the key to my daughter's house," Eleanor said. "Howard's going to drive me to San Saba. I'll pick up some clothing and Deanne's car. Be back in a few hours." She glanced at the two sleepers.

"I'll stay here. Don't wear yourself out." As he watched them move down the sidewalk, Adam allowed pleasure to flood him and remembered his favorite verse from Micah: ". . . what does the Lord require of you but to do justice, and to love kindness and to walk humbly with your God?"

The church was doing the Lord's work, reaching out in kindness. He was blessed to reap the bonus of having company in the huge and previously echoingly lonely parsonage.

Sam glanced at the clock. Seven thirty. In the morning.

How was he supposed to sleep with the general whistling—yes, whistling!—in the kitchen? The man had never whistled, at least not in the span of Sam's memory. Of course, for a lot of that time, the general hadn't been at home. He'd been overseas or transferred so Sam didn't know that the general *never* whistled, but whistling suggested happiness. The general had seldom showed any emotion, much less happiness.

Wondering why in the world he was considering this when all he wanted to do was fall back to sleep, Sam pulled the pillow over his head. He hadn't noticed this before, but whistling has a particular pitch that is not at all moderated by the placement of a pillow over one's ear.

"What are you doing out there?" he shouted toward the kitchen. "Somebody's trying to sleep in here."

The whistling stopped abruptly, a realization that bothered Sam. The general had finally showed a positive emotion and Sam had told him to shut up. Amazingly, he had. Now Sam felt guilty.

He rolled to the edge of the bed, attached the prosthesis, and pushed himself up. By the time he reached the kitchen and could see the general standing at the stove with that stupid pink towel protecting his camo shorts, Sam regretted his outburst. He'd acted like a grunt.

"Sorry I woke you up, son."

"Sorry, Dad." The word and the apology slipped from his mouth without passing through the censor he usually kept on his statements to the general. Sam hoped maybe he wouldn't notice.

He noticed. His smile reached his eyes. "Oo-rah," he said.

Who says "Oo-rah" at seven thirty in the morning while preparing breakfast?

The general put the eggs and bacon on a plate and set it on the table. "Sit down, son. Have some breakfast."

"You didn't know I'd be up now." Sam scrutinized him. The general was smart, always prepared, but, "This is your breakfast, right?"

"Hey." He held his hand up. "I can always fix more. Why don't you sit down and enjoy?"

Rude to refuse. Besides, the stubborn man wouldn't eat the food after he'd offered it to Sam. It'd be stupid to turn it down. If he did, no one would eat it. Sam sat, pulled the plate and fork in front of him, and dug in while the general put bread in the toaster and tossed a couple more slices of bacon in the pan.

"Winnie says I should cut down on bacon." The general looked into the skillet longingly before picking up the slices with a spatula and wrapping them back in the package, uncooked.

How serious was this relationship? The general had known her for only a few weeks and was giving up his beloved bacon? Sounded very serious.

"So," Sam said casually. "Are you going out with Miss Jenkins again?"

The general grabbed the toast when it popped up, smeared margarine and jelly on it, and brought it to the table. He placed one slice on Sam's plate, then sat down and tore the other piece in half. After he'd taken several bites, he swallowed and looked at Sam.

"You know how much I loved your mother."

"That's not what I mean."

"I know, I know. Maureen was very special. After she died, I never found another woman I liked to be with, one who was interesting and attractive. I enjoy being with Winnie."

Sam had always suspected the general had mourned his wife's death as much as Sam had grieved for his mother, but he'd never showed it. He'd stood stiff and emotionless at the cemetery during the interment. Sam had done exactly the same, a perfect little image of his father but feeling like a scared little boy inside. Not that he'd ever told the general that.

In fact, much of the problem was that neither of them knew how to share his feelings. He'd believed they still didn't, but the general sure seemed bent on trying.

"I didn't date much, even years after Maureen died. After all, I was trying to bring up a young son . . ."

"I was ten," Sam corrected.

"Yes, but that seemed really young to me. I had no experience with any kids but recruits." He shook his head. "Son, I apologize for my failures. I had no idea what to do with you."

So you sent me to stay with relatives or to boarding school during the academic year and to Texas or Ohio in the summer, Sam wanted to say, but he held the words back. For years he and the general had argued about the man's lack of interest and what Sam considered to be abandonment, but they'd never discussed emotion. Maybe Sam had grown and changed a little, because he didn't want to cover the same ground again.

Or maybe his tours of duty had made him realize how hard it would be for an officer to raise a child by himself.

"You and my career were my only priorities for years. You don't have any idea how much I regret not getting to see you grow up."

"You never told me." Sam attempted to control his reaction and not sound judgmental.

The general shook his head again. "Really messed up with you, son. Don't ever think I'll forgive myself for that but . . ." He caught Sam's eyes. "But I'd like to make up for it. I tried to be a good father but had no idea what to do. I treated you like a recruit because I didn't know how else to relate to a kid. It's what my father did."

"Hereditary?" Sam couldn't resist getting that dig in.

"Hope not. Hope you'll treat your sons differently. You've done well with Willow's boys. They respect and love you. Wish I'd done that well."

Hadn't he treated Nick and Leo like marines? Maybe it was a congenital problem. Not that they were his sons.

Sam shrugged. "I don't know. After all, I don't see them every day . . ." The general hadn't seen him every day, either, but Sam had to let go of that offense for now. "I'm not the one who has to take care of them or build their character. Being their friend is a lot easier."

"Maybe, but, son . . ." The general paused and seemed to search for words. "Son, please give me another chance. You're my only child. I miss you. I know your mother would've wanted us to get along, to be family."

"Hard for me to guess what a woman who's been dead nearly twenty years wants."

The old man's face hardened as if he were hurt that his son had rejected him. But what was Sam supposed to say? Or do? A lifetime of disappointment and anger, and the walls he'd built to contain it, would not evaporate because the general called him "son" and said "please." Even if Sam wanted to just let it all go, he still felt it, all of it. And he didn't know if he could survive without that core of fury.

"Yeah, sure," he said, pretty sure the general would pick up on the sarcasm. "Maybe we could go fishing sometime. Isn't that what fathers and sons do?"

"I'm not giving up," the general said.

Sam knew he wouldn't. The man never did. Unfortunately the general sounded wistful, an emotion much harder to ignore than his command voice.

"Changing the subject a little." The general stood and poured himself and Sam each a cup of hot coffee. "About Winnie. I think she's an attractive and intelligent woman. I enjoy being with her and see no reason to be alone the rest of my life."

Sam almost spilled his coffee on his lap. "Are you getting married?"

"Don't know."

Sam stared at the general. "You're serious?"

"Sure am."

"But you haven't known her for very long."

"You fell in love with Willow pretty quickly, didn't you?"

"We're not talking about me, sir."

"No, but there are times a man has to take action." The general smiled. "Of course, you have a lot of years ahead of you. I'm sixty-two and had a health scare. It hit me that I'm not going to live forever, and I have to take fast action to get what I want. You never know what's going to happen."

Sam could have died with Morty in Afghanistan. The sentence hung in the air between them as if the general had actually uttered the words.

Sam considered the general's statement as he finished breakfast. Did he want to spend the rest of his life alone because he didn't take action or plan or make decisions? But he didn't want to consider that now. Too intense. Too threatening.

"Were you serious about going fishing?" the general asked.

Stupid for Sam to have said that. He knew the general well enough to know that if he was determined to go fishing, they'd end up in a boat on the lake this afternoon.

When he scrutinized the general, though, Sam realized he'd spoken hesitantly, as if he were afraid of Sam's reaction. He didn't want his father, a respected officer and a proud, courageous man, to fear the reaction of his own son. What could Sam say to convey that?

"You know, there's a vets' group that meets at one of the churches on Wednesday evenings. I'm planning to go next week. Want to join me?" the general asked.

The suggestion shattered the tenuous communication. "Don't try to fix me, sir."

"I'm not, son." The general stopped and blinked. "But maybe when you're ready, we could go together." He glanced at the coffee cup then back up. "I attended a veterans' support group weekly in Ohio. Started . . ." He stopped and swallowed before continuing. "Started when you got hurt. I couldn't handle it."

Sam couldn't think of a sentence more unlikely to come from the general's mouth. "There's one at the Christian Church. Would you come with me?" he asked again as if Sam hadn't just shot down the request. *Dogged*, that word described the general perfectly.

"Why?" He'd never asked the general "Why" about anything. A strict do-as-I-say man, the general had never allowed it.

"Because I need it. Because I think you might, too."

"I'm not a wimp. I can handle this."

"I know you're not a wimp," the general stated. "But I've learned I can't handle what happens in battle alone. I found out I do a lot better in life when I can talk about what happened with vets who've been through the same thing." He scrutinized Sam's features. "I don't sound like the man you grew up with, do I? When you were wounded in Afghanistan, I felt so guilty I could barely function. Going to the group saved me. I discovered I can't do everything on my own."

Those words dropped inside Sam and burned. He had no idea what to say and, so filled with emotion, wasn't sure he could speak. The idea his father had been devastated by Sam's injury, that the amputation had changed the general's life, was something he'd never guessed and couldn't digest now.

He fell back to his default emotion: anger. "I thought you'd come down here to bully me into rehabbing."

"To bully you," the general repeated. "I'm sorry you expected that."

Who was this man who looked so much like the general but spoke like a concerned and loving father? Sam never could have imagined the words or the soft voice.

"Go ahead and get dressed." The general stood. "I'll clean up. If you want to, we can talk later."

With those words and the ones his father had spoken in the last few minutes, guilt began to eat at Sam. The realization surprised him. Had his feelings defrosted enough for him to regret his actions? To accept the general's concern? Must be all the warm bacon fat melting the cockles—whatever cockles were—of his heart.

There he went with his normal habit of defusing an emotion by making fun of it. Sometimes Sam was full of it. He just didn't know what to do about it. Change? Maybe. But how?

Chapter Twenty

Failure was not an option for Miss Birdie. She never fell short in anything if she could help it. And yet the minister stood there behind the pulpit and preached, looking almost handsome and much more confident than he had before she'd taken him in hand. Preached a pretty fair sermon now. Did good work, the evidence on display right there in the congregation.

Eleanor and Missy sat next to Bree. Mrs. Smith improved every day what with Mike, the PT from the hospital, dropping by every few days for exercises, the visiting nurse helping with medication, and the aide who came by to give Mrs. Smith baths.

Winnie and the general had arrived together and settled in a front pew, an unexpected and serendipitous success for the Widows that she and Mercedes didn't mind crowing about.

But the preacher stood up there alone. He deserved a woman, a wife, a soul mate. If they didn't find him someone, he'd probably go along happily playing basketball three or four times a week, welcoming people who needed a place to stay into the parsonage, going to football games, but never finding love.

Birdie studied the sanctuary. Attendance had grown some. A new couple—white-haired like the rest of the adults—sat on the side aisle. The Kowalski girls came with the preacher and went to children's church. But other than Willow, no single woman sat in the congregation, waiting for Birdie to introduce her to the preacher, waiting to fall in love with him and marry him.

Birdie closed her eyes and prayed for the Lord to get involved because she thought only through holy intervention would a mate be found for the preacher.

"Pops?"

Adam looked up from the bench next to the basketball court where he sat to tie his shoes. Bobby Franklin, one of Hector's teammates on the high school team, stood next to him, silhouetted against the lights.

"What is it, Bobby? Sit down."

"You know about the problems Hector's having with the rent and all?"

Adam nodded.

"Him and his sister are sleeping in the park now."

"What?" He looked up at Hector, dribbling and shooting, then looked around the thick trees surrounding the court. "He and his sister are sleeping here? For how long?"

"She's waiting for him over there." He nodded toward a thin girl in pink overalls huddled on the bench next to the court. "Two nights. This will be the third."

"Why didn't he tell me? I'd have done something."

"He's ashamed. He figures he should be able to take care of the family. He's a man."

"Even men need help sometimes." Adam stood. "Thanks, Bobby. I'll talk to him." When the young man started to say more, the minister said, "Don't worry. I won't mention you told me anything."

Adam picked up a ball and dribbled toward the basket where Hector practiced. "How's your sister? You guys still okay?"

Hector didn't turn toward him, just kept shooting.

"You want to play horse?" Adam asked. "Loser has to answer a question from the winner." Not subtle but he felt certain Hector wouldn't fill Adam in on his life without cover.

Hector glared at the minister, then nodded.

After a hard-fought game, which Adam won—actually, it was possible Hector threw it—the minister took the ball and held it. "How are you and your sister?" he repeated. "Where are you sleeping?"

"That's two questions."

"Okay, where are you sleeping?"

Hector didn't make eye contact, just jerked his head toward the trees.

"You're sleeping here? Out in the open? Is that good for you? Safe for your sister?"

The kid studied his feet. Finally, he looked at Adam and said, "I don't know what to do. We got evicted even though I had a week left on the lease."

Unbelievable anyone could do that to a couple of kids. "What now?" Adam asked. "What are your plans?"

Hector shrugged.

That was enough. "Go get your stuff. You're coming with me now. I have plenty of room at the parsonage."

He scowled. "We don't need charity."

"It's not charity. We have room. You may not think you need help, but Janey needs a safe place to live."

"Janey can go with you. I'll make my way."

"Buddy, your sister needs you."

"I'll visit her. I'll walk her to school."

When it became obvious that argument wasn't going to work, Adam came up with another one. "I don't know anything about taking care of a little girl." Adam pointed toward Janey. "All those cute little braids and barrettes in your sister's hair? I don't know how to do those."

"Yeah, that takes practice," Hector agreed.

"There are two empty bedrooms on the second floor. Right now, we have another family living in the parsonage, on the ground floor. She's just out of the hospital. I think . . ."

"You have other people living in that big, ugly house?" Hector interrupted.

The minister nodded.

"Oh." Hector considered that. "Then it would be okay. It wouldn't be like we were charity cases, right? Other people stay there, too."

"That's what churches are for."

"Not always, Pops. Not always." He glanced toward his sister. "I talked to the counselor at school. I want to be a legally emancipated minor and take care of Janey myself."

"Fine."

He examined Adam's expression for a few seconds, as if searching for clues about his feelings, as if Adam might have deeper motives for moving him and his sister into the parsonage. How sad he had to be suspicious, but Adam respected his caution.

"Okay, we'll come. Let me go get our stuff." He turned and took a step.

"I have a couple of rules," Adam said before Hector could move away.

He turned back and glared. "Yeah?" The kid's body stiffened, and his voice held a note of suspicion.

"First, you have to stay in school."

Hector nodded. "Plan to."

"And you have to be home by eleven on school nights. No drinking."

"No problem."

"And I'd like you to come to church on Sunday morning."

Hector's lips tightened.

"I'm not going to force you, don't plan to convert you, but I'd like you there. The parsonage belongs to the church. This would be giving back, thanking the congregation."

Hector nodded. "Okay, sure." He waved toward his sister. "Janey, come here. We're going to have beds tonight."

Adam watched them walk toward their campsite before realizing he should give them a hand. He ran behind the two. When he reached the clearing, Adam heard a low growling and something—a bear? a lion?—rushed toward him and leaped into the air. Before he could move, it landed on Adam's chest and knocked him to the ground. He looked into the face of a creature of some kind. It was enormous with a head the size of a pumpkin. A tongue lolled from its mouth, which made Adam believe the creature was friendly—just very drooly. His face got wetter with each passing second. The rhythmic pounding of the creature's tail against the ground implied the monster liked the minister.

"Chewy, come here," Janey said in a soft, high voice. The animal, who really did look like a Wookiee, pushed himself up and romped toward the girl, wagging its tail.

Adam stood slowly.

"That's Janey's dog Chewy," Hector said. "I didn't tell you about him, afraid you'd change your mind. Janey loves him."

Once on his feet, Adam could see exactly how massive the canine was. With the tawny coat, it resembled a lion, but the plumy tail and the darker patches on the side revealed that this dog had a long and varied ancestry. Afghan hound? Sheepdog of some sort? Perhaps even a little elephant in its genetic makeup?

"I have a fenced-in yard. He'll be fine."

"He won't like being out there all the time. He sleeps with her," Hector said. "She says he makes her feel safe."

This was not the time to debate Chewy's living conditions. Adam had to get these kids to the parsonage and security. "We'll work it out," he said to Janey, whom he could barely see over the huge dog. "Don't worry. But first, let's get you to bed, in a real bed."

Adam picked up a couple of sleeping bags and headed to the parsonage. Behind him, he could hear the dog crashing down the path. He sped up.

Adam dreamed he was with Shadrach, Meshach, and Abed'nego in the fiery furnace. When he woke up, sweat poured down his body. He lay there wondering if the Hill Country had been hit by a heat wave overnight or if someone had, for some reason, turned up the parsonage furnace to one hundred.

As his brain slowly cleared, he realized a huge lump—a hot, breathing lump—lay next to him. Adam sat up. Chewy lifted his head and grinned. He hadn't known a dog could smile, but this one did, pleased to be here in bed next to Adam. Not that the bed belonged to the minister anymore, other than the narrow sliver he occupied. Chewy owned the rest. His tail hit the mattress as if he were a canine Ringo Starr.

How did he get in here? Adam took a few tissues from the box on the night table to wipe his face as he rolled off the bed and stood. The bedroom door was open. He knew he'd closed it; either Chewy could open doors or the catch hadn't held. He guessed the latter. Chewy didn't seem all that smart.

"Pops, breakfast," Hector shouted up the stairs.

Breakfast? Hector had prepared breakfast?

Knowing he'd have to shower later but also mindful that he now lived with five other people, Adam pulled on jeans and a T-shirt before heading quietly down the back stairs to the kitchen. Chewy bounced down behind him, occasionally nudging the back of his legs to hurry him along.

Although the signs of cooking lay all over the counter, no one was in the kitchen. He let Chewy out before searching.

"Pops, we're in here," Hector shouted from the dining room.

Adam had never used the dining room. Actually, with the furniture repositioned to accommodate the downstairs visitors, the table had ended up shoved in the smallest parlor, the one he used as an at-home office.

"Good morning." Deanne still wore her robe, but seeing her up and at the table pleased the minister. Hector sat at the end of the table, looking like the father of the family. Missy sat on a chair atop multiple pillows next to Eleanor.

In a bright pink shirt and overalls, her hair arranged in thirty or forty braids, Janey walked across the cramped space as carefully as if she were on a tightrope, balancing a cup of coffee for Adam.

Besides the necessities—plates, napkins, sugar, and milk—on the table were bowls of oatmeal, glasses of orange juice, and one plate piled high with toast. Hector grinned at Adam's surprise.

"Breakfast is my specialty."

"Great! Good morning." He settled in one of the heavy, formal chairs.

"Morning," Missy said through a mouthful of toast.

Hector pointed at an empty chair. "Sit down, sis, and eat fast. We need to get going."

"Thanks for the coffee, Janey."

She looked at Adam with eyes so big and dark and filled with uncertainty, it almost broke his heart. No child should look that lonely and scared.

"Thanks for breakfast, Hector," Deanne said. "It tastes really good. I love being up for breakfast."

"How are you two going to get to school? Do I need to drive you?" Adam hadn't thought about that before. Hadn't thought of a lot of stuff before he brought the kids home, but they could figure things out as they went.

"I can walk. Janey's school's on the way. I'll take her," Hector said.

"What about lunch?" Deanne asked. "Should I fix sack lunches for you?"

"It's okay." Hector swallowed hard as if he didn't want to say more.

Adam bet they had free lunch and he didn't want to admit it. The minister was glad they did, glad that during the tough times they'd had at least one good meal a day.

"What time do you eat dinner?" Adam shoved the bowl away and took half a piece of toast.

"Practice is over at six thirty, but I'm always ready to eat," Hector said. "Janey'll get home about four and likes a snack."

He turned to the child. "Janey, can you walk home all right?"

She nodded.

"It's only a few blocks," Hector said. "She can probably see the steeple from her school."

"The door's always open," Adam told her. "If I'm not here, come over to the church."

"I'll be here all day," Deanne said.

"I'll get home . . ." Hector stopped and grinned when he said the word *home.* "I'll be back about seven." He picked up his bowl and began to clear the table.

"Don't worry about that," Deanne said. "I'll take care of cleanup."

Before he left the dining room, Hector said, "You need to get a hoop, Pops. Right on the edge of the parking lot would work."

Hector and Janey grabbed their books and headed off to school. Eleanor washed and dressed Missy to take her to day care while Deanne cleaned up. Shortly after that, Chewy let Adam know he wanted inside, his deep, loud barks echoing through the neighborhood. As Adam let the dog in and started upstairs for a shower, he wondered: What in the world was he doing? He wasn't that much older than Hector, and certainly no wiser, and he had absolutely no experience with kids.

There hadn't seemed to be much of a choice. He'd do his best, try his hardest. Surely he'd do better than a drug-addicted criminal, right?

That afternoon Adam hadn't left himself enough time—not unusual—to visit the nursing homes and still get home to welcome Janey at four. While Deanne slept and her mother read in his television room, Janey sat at the kitchen table, copying words from a book. Still so serious for a child her age, she looked up and nodded before returning to her work.

The next night, Adam carefully closed his door, then tugged on the knob to make sure it was completely shut, that Chewy wouldn't be able to visit him. Satisfied, he turned off the light and got into bed. Before he could pull the sheet over him, he heard the *click*, *click*, *click* of dog paws. The sound stopped by his door. Then began what he guessed was the sound of a dog's muzzle hitting the door.

He smiled. Tonight he'd get a good night's sleep.

Of course, he didn't know Chewy well. After several thuds on the door, Adam heard the thud of Chewy's bottom against the floor. Before Adam could close his eyes, the sound of shrill howling filled the air.

Hound. There had to be hound somewhere in Chewy's genetic background, because the baying filled the parsonage.

"Shut up, Chewy," Hector yelled.

Didn't do a bit of good.

If he wanted to sleep, if he wanted the children to sleep, if he hoped Ouida and her family slept, Adam had to do something. He got up, walked to the door, and opened it. A thoroughly delighted Chewy pranced into the room and leaped onto the bed.

By the time Adam got back, Chewy had shoved the quilt into a gigantic lump and settled on it, smiling.

Adam studied the situation. Putting Chewy outside wasn't a solution, but he could prepare a pallet on the floor for the dog. Except he had a pretty good idea who'd end up sleeping there.

❦

A few days later, the phone rang in Adam's study. Maggie had left, so he picked up.

"Pastor Adam," Mercedes said when he answered. "I wonder if you could drop by the diner after lunch, about three thirty. I have a problem I'd like to discuss."

"At the diner?" he asked. "Wouldn't you rather meet at the church?"

"No, n-no," Mercedes stammered.

Why not? As usual with the Widows, he suspected something, something he didn't look forward to. The suspicion scared him. In fact, the tone of Mercedes's voice frightened him. But he couldn't turn her down; the Widows were, after all, members of the church.

"I'd like to meet there because . . . um . . . I like their . . . um . . . chocolate pie. And raspberry tea. Delicious." She sounded pleased to have come up with not just one but two reasons.

After Adam agreed and hung up, he considered what had just happened. He didn't trust the invitation but couldn't figure out how to get out of it or why it had been tendered. He only knew the reason was much deeper and more devious than chocolate pie and raspberry tea.

Ten minutes later, the phone rang again. "Adam Jordan," he said as he picked up.

"Reverend Jordan, this is Pattie Malone calling from the high school. We have a faculty meeting so I won't be able to meet you this afternoon."

Won't be able to meet? Adam considered the words. Aha. Now he knew why Mercedes had called.

"Ms. Malone, I'm going to ask you some odd questions."

"Oh?" Her voice held a note of confusion and an entire concerto of apprehension.

"I'm assuming Mrs. MacDowell set this meeting up?"

"Yes. I'm Bree's volleyball coach. Her grandmother said you wanted to meet about Bree's going to a church-related school like Texas Christian, maybe getting a scholarship for athletics because she belongs to a Christian church."

"Great idea," Adam said. "Are you married?"

"What?"

He could tell from her voice she thought he was nuts or scary. Didn't blame her. He did sound crazy, but Ms. Malone would understand if she really knew Miss Birdie. "Coach, I'm a bachelor . . . ," Adam began.

"I can assure you . . . ," she sputtered.

"Let me finish. Mrs. MacDowell wants to introduce me to unmarried women. She believes a minister should be married. I'm sorry she . . ."

But he couldn't finish because the coach started laughing. When she was done, she said, "My divorce was final only a few days ago. Almost no one knows that. How did she?"

Adam groaned. This was not the time to tell the coach about the Widows and their grapevine, which infiltrated every corner of Butternut Creek. Instead he said, "I'd be happy to meet with you about Bree. Maybe at the high school whenever it's convenient for you. And don't worry about being set up anymore. I'll take care of Mrs. MacDowell."

A promise he wasn't all that sure he could keep, but he'd try. Maybe having a wingman would help.

He called Sam.

"Do you know about the Widows and their reputation as matchmakers?" Adam asked.

"Do I! They've been trying to get Willow and me together since I got into town. Why?"

"I'm meeting them at three thirty at the diner. I don't want to face them alone. Want to join me? I'll pick you up a few minutes before then."

"I'm not convinced I want them to stop working on Willow," Sam said. "But I'll cover your back."

❧

When the two men strode—Sam had much improved his striding technique—into the diner at exactly three thirty, Miss Birdie looked up from the table she was clearing. Her eyes opened wide when she saw both of them, then she searched behind them. Looking for the coach?

For a moment he and Sam stood at the door, hands at their sides, and stared at her. Adam felt like Gary Cooper in *High Noon* but wasn't sure if he was the good guy or the bad. He almost expected Miss Birdie to say, *Draw, you dirty varmints.*

Of course, she didn't.

Instead she demanded, "Sam Peterson, what are you doing here?"

Both men took a few steps inside. In his head, Adam could hear the click of boots across a rough wood floor. In reality, his athletic shoes made almost no sound on the vinyl tile.

"Coach Malone isn't coming," he drawled.

She blinked. "Oh," she said in a voice filled with studied surprise. "Was she coming? Here? Today?"

Had he caught her off guard? If so, not for long.

"I asked you a question, Preacher." She put her hands on her hips and glared. Miss Birdie didn't need a gun. She could disarm dirty varmints by glowering at them.

"The preacher wants to talk to you about something," Sam said as he took a couple of steps backward.

"Lily-livered coward," Adam whispered to his friend, then turned to stare at the Matchmaker, a name that struck terror in his heart.

"Miss Birdie." He stood his ground and cleared his throat. Refusing to give in to fear, he said more loudly, "Miss Birdie, you have to stop pushing me together with women."

"It's for your own good, Pastor Adam. You're not doing anything to find yourself a wife." She nodded decisively. "Someone's got to step in."

"You don't. And Mercedes and Winnie don't. When"—he paused to underline the word—"when I'm ready to get married, I'll take care of finding the bride myself."

"But . . . ," she started.

His imaginary spurs jingling, Adam took a step forward and looked deeply into her eyes. She stopped talking.

"I appreciate your interest and efforts, but you need to leave me alone." There, he'd said it.

Of course, Miss Birdie didn't accept the ultimatum.

"And when is that going to be?" She took a step toward the minister, keeping her eyes on his, matching him glower for glower.

But he didn't retreat. With another step toward her, Adam lowered his head, glaring at her from under the rim of his nonexistent Stetson. "When I'm ready."

He didn't break eye contact. The Preacher and the Matchmaker stared at each other for what seemed like hours until Sam stepped between them. A dangerous tactic.

"Now, Miss Birdie," Sam said in a soothing tone, as if he spoke to a spooked horse. "All the preacher's asking for is time."

She considered his words for probably fifteen seconds before she nodded. "All right, Preacher, I'll give you time, but you'd better get the lead out."

As good as it was going to get. Adam stepped back and nodded. "Sam has something he'd like to say as well."

"You want me to leave you and Willow alone?" She squinted. "We've done a good job with the two of you."

"Yes, you have. But I can take over now."

She looked Sam up and down, then nodded.

Sam and Adam turned to leave, striding with pride.

They left the door swinging behind them.

Sam had lived all over the world but had visited his aunt only during the summer, so he had never been to a high school football game in Texas. Adam had told him to prepare himself, but he didn't think anything could have equipped him for the crowd and the noise and the excitement. Even when he'd played college football in the packed Kyle Field with the fans and the corps shouting, he hadn't felt the energy that buzzed through this stadium.

The best part was sitting with Willow on his right and Leo and Nick on his left. Until nearly the end of the first quarter, the boys stayed with them, happy to attend the game with him. A few minutes into the second quarter, with the Lions ahead fourteen to three, Leo spotted some friends passing a football next to the bleachers and the boys ran off to join them, leaving Sam alone with their mother. Too bad, he'd just have to make the best of it.

Sam reached for Willow's hand and held it between them on the bleacher. She smiled at him, then leaned against him for quick second.

Could there be a better way to spend an evening?

Once they arrived back at Willow's apartment after the game and finally got the wound-up Leo and Nick settled in bed, Willow preceded him into the living room. For a moment Sam stood in the archway, feeling happy and comfortable. At peace, he realized. Life was good. Even when he started toward the sofa and a second of imbalance reminded him of the loss of his leg, he felt better than he had in months, possibly years.

Then he settled on the sofa next to Willow, put his arm around her, and kissed her.

The pleasant interval lasted for quite a while, until Sam pushed it. He should have—did—know better, but had given in to his baser urges.

Willow removed his hand and shoved him away. "That's enough. Don't forget I have two sons only a few feet away." She pointed down the hall.

"Let's go into your bedroom and shut the door." He reached out for her, but she scooted to the end of the sofa. The other end.

"Sam, not here." She shook her head but a smile softened her words.

"We could go to my house, but my father's there." He shook his head. "*That* would be uncomfortable." He thought for a moment. "We could find a motel."

"Sam." Her voice became very serious. "I'm not going to sleep with you." She held her hand up. "You may have gotten the idea I'd be willing."

He nodded.

"But I can't." She pointed down the hall again. "I have two little boys who lost their father and love you very much."

Sam swallowed. Did they really love him?

"For that reason, I have to protect them. Before I make any . . . umm . . ."

However she finished that sentence, he knew he wouldn't like it.

"Before I make a decision about you and me, Leo and Nick need to know they can count on you. They need to know that you're not going to run out on them if you find something better to do or another woman you like better."

"I'd never . . ."

"I need something, too. I refuse to fall in love with a man who can't make a commitment to me and to the boys."

"That's your problem. I didn't ask you to fall in love with me," he said, although he felt pretty sure he'd acted like he wanted exactly that. "Or to marry me, just, you know . . ."

"But I don't become intimate with a man unless I love him, unless there's a commitment between us."

"Commitment." He knew his voice reflected the absolute terror the word awakened. "I can't commit to anyone. I don't even know who I am and what I'm going to do with myself." He could feel sweat dripping down his neck.

"Then," she said in a soft, sad voice, "it might be time to figure that out."

The words burst from him. "Stop trying to fix me."

"For heaven's sake," she snapped. "I'm not trying to fix you. I'm trying *not* to fall in love with you."

He scrutinized her face. She looked sincere. She sounded angry. "How could you ever fall in love with me? I mean, possibly? I'm a mess. My life is a mess."

"You sell yourself short. You're handsome. Women fall at your feet."

"Not all of them," he said. Her, for example.

"There's more." She ticked off each point on her fingers. "I admire your courage and how you fight to get better and stronger. I appreciate how much you care about Leo and Nick. I like the way you make me feel. I thought for a while I'd never again feel this way with a man."

"That's good," he whispered as he attempted to close the small space between them.

She stood. "But I refuse to fall in love with you unless I trust you completely and until you can commit to us, at least try to. I will not have my sons hurt again. I will not make the mistake of loving a man who only wants my body. Not again."

"Hey, I want more than just your body, but that's a good place to start."

She made her feelings about his flip remark obvious with a glare. "One more thing," she started.

"One more thing? Don't you think you've dumped enough on me?"

"One more thing," she continued. "I will *not* commit to you until you can share all that anger and pain you keep inside you with me or with a therapist or your father. I don't care which, but if you don't get it out and talk to someone about it . . . well, you have to or you'll explode and the collateral damage from that could hurt me and the boys badly."

"Thank you for your opinion as a professional."

"Sam, it's for all of us. You *have* to work through what happened in Afghanistan."

There it was, all laid out for him, logically and honestly. At this moment, he hated honesty and logic because he wasn't nearly ready to face his feelings, his future, or, actually, anything.

Her words and expression summarized the whole predicament. His problems affected not just him, but Willow and her sons. He respected her for that, but did he want her enough to give in to those demands to communicate, to commit, to care?

Even more important, could he? His life would be less complicated if he'd been attracted to an accommodating woman.

"Does that mean Nick and Leo can't come over anymore?" Losing the boys would about tear him apart.

"Of course they can. They need a male friend." The expression in her eyes softened. "They admire you very much. You're good for them. What they don't need is the unrealistic hope that someday you'll be their father."

Crap. Not that he hadn't considered the possibility of having those kids for his sons, but he'd knocked it down every time it popped up, like a game of Whac-A-Mole.

Would having kids be so bad?

❧

Years earlier, when she was still a little naive and believed in true love, Willow had allowed herself to be taken in by a handsome charming man. How could she have been so gullible and trusting?

Despite all his good qualities, Willow knew one thing through her experience with wounded vets: A man who held in all that pain and anger would explode at some time. He could start drinking again or find relief with other women or just walk away. That would devastate Willow and her sons.

Not seeing him again outside the hospital, not having him look at her with longing while she both hoped and feared he'd kiss her, all of that she'd miss. The feel of his warmth next to her, of his touch and smile.

Oh, bother! She'd already fallen in love with Sam and would really miss him. She'd have to accept that and hope Sam figured things out, opened up, and included her in his life.

❧

"I want my old life back," Sam shouted. He wanted all the good stuff he'd lost. He wanted to be with his men in combat. He wanted his leg back. Most of all, he wanted to fight and to joke with Morty again.

None of that was going to happen, but that didn't mean he didn't want it.

He pulled the bottle from the dresser, a fifth of the best Kentucky bourbon. He needed it. He deserved it. His life sucked. He'd screwed up with Willow because he couldn't give her what she needed and deserved. He'd screwed up because that was what Sam Peterson did best. Right now, he wished the general would leave—go home, move in with Winnie. He didn't care but he wanted to be alone to wallow.

He broke the seal and opened the bottle. No need for manners or a glass in the solitude of his room. He put the bottle to his lips, leaned his head back, and drank deeply. It tasted good. How long had it been since he'd had a drink of real liquor? Weeks, at least.

As the gulp went down, it warmed him inside. An artificial heat, not to be confused with any emotion. He knew that. Didn't mind. At this moment, he needed to feel something other than pain.

He sat on the edge of the bed and removed the prosthesis. He should wash it. He'd do that in the morning. Of course it wouldn't dry by the time he needed to wear it. So what? But he couldn't break the habit of checking his leg for redness and irritation. Everything looked fine. Willow and her prosthetist had done a good job on the fit.

He cursed. Everything, even the stupid leg, reminded him of Willow.

Settling the device against the head of the bed, he took another deep drink. The glow spread through him, down to his fingers and even the toes on his missing foot.

But the sensation filling his body didn't feel as good as he remembered. It deadened his brain and made him dizzy. He took another swig but still didn't feel any better. He couldn't even count on whiskey.

For a moment, he stared at the bottle before screwing the cap back it and shoving it under the bed to hide it. Last thing he needed was a lecture from the general about his drinking.

With that, he turned off the lamp on the bedside table, lifted his thigh to put it on the bed, and lay back on the pillow.

Rockets exploded around Sam Peterson. The acrid smell of ammo and war and the coppery stench of blood hung over the rocky hill.

Then his leg exploded with pain. He reached for it, felt nothing but blood and jagged bone.

"Morty!" he shouted and sat straight up.

In bed, he realized. In Aunt Effie's house. With tears running down his face he gasped for air.

"You're fine, son."

He swung his head to see the general, sitting in a chair only inches from the bed. Just like the last time. "I'm here."

Without even thinking—because if he had thought about it, Sam wouldn't have done it—he reached out for his father and pulled him to sit on the side of the bed next to him. Folded in his father's arms, he sobbed. His father patted him on the back. Neither said a word but for a moment, peace and acceptance filled him as his father wept with him.

"Son, I'm so sorry," his father kept repeating. "I'm so sorry."

After a few minutes, Sam struggled for control and pulled away. "Why?" He wiped his cheeks. "Why are *you* sorry?" He didn't think he'd ever heard the man say that word. No, that was wrong. He'd used it a while back, the first time Sam could remember hearing that word escaping from the general's usually tight lips.

But they weren't taut now. His face looked . . . droopy. Sad. And his lips, his whole expression looked soft as if he were begging, as if this moment were very important for him.

"Why?" Sam asked again.

The general returned to his chair. "I wasn't much of a father. I wasn't much of a husband, either." He shook his head. "Military families put up with a lot. I had the admirable excuse that I had to serve my country. I used it every chance I had."

"You did serve the country."

"Other parents in the military spent time with their families. Morty's dad—he went to every football game he could, every talent show."

"Morty's dad retired as a captain."

The general shrugged. "What's wrong with that?"

"You wanted to be a general. Morty's dad didn't."

"Morty's dad had better priorities than I did."

"Dad, I was a lot like you. I pushed and pushed and pretty soon I outranked Morty. That's what a Peterson does. It's what your father did, and his father."

"Generations of Petersons who taught their sons how to go off to war but never how to stay home and be a real parent." He shook his head. "I should have cared more about being your father than being a general."

Sam's thoughts flashed back to his grandfather, a three-star general who looked exactly like this general, who'd hit only two stars. Had he been a disappointment to *his* father as well? Sam hated to admit it, but perhaps he should or could be a little more understanding and less self-centered. The realization made him feel like a jerk.

"You weren't responsible for Morty's death," the general said after a long silence.

He could feel his body straighten and stiffen. "I don't want to talk about that."

"Morty didn't become a marine because of you." The general looked in Sam's eyes. "You know that, don't you? He was always crazy about the military, wanted to be a marine like his father, like me."

Sam couldn't form the words to answer. The general was right. Morty had been as crazy about being a marine as Sam had. Deep down, Sam knew that, but in his grief and guilt he'd denied it. Because he had lived, had come home. Morty hadn't.

"His death was a tragedy." The general shook his head and looked down at his folded hands. "But it was his choice to be in Afghanistan on that hillside. You never pushed him."

Sam closed his eyes to consider the general's words. The burden of sorrow lifted a little more.

As Sam reflected, the general stood. With that motion, he kicked the bottle Sam had shoved under the bed. He leaned down to pick it up. "Yours?"

Sam shook his head. "Take it back to the kitchen or pour it down the drain. I don't need it."

The general looked skeptical. "Not sure it'll be that easy, son."

"I know." He wished it were. "But it's a beginning, and I'm determined. I'll start meetings as soon as I find one."

The general looked almost victorious.

"I mean AA. I still won't go to the vets' group at the church," Sam said. "Not yet."

Once the general left, not quite closing the door behind him, Sam lay back against the headboard. He thought back twenty years, nearly twenty-five, to a memory of him and Morty shouting "Semper fi" and storming Guadalcanal or planting the flag on Iwo Jima. Even though they didn't know what the words meant, they'd sing, "From the halls of Montezuma to the shores to Tripoli," at the top of their lungs.

They'd been exactly like Leo and Nick, he realized. For the first time in over a year, he thought about Morty and smiled. Oh, not for long because it still hurt, but he felt hope. He closed his eyes as a tremendous burden began to fall from him. Maybe he'd started to heal.

Chapter Twenty-One

Saturday afternoon, Adam signed for the FedEx delivery and turned to carry the heavy box inside.

"Whatcha got, Pops?" Hector sat on the sofa and watched cartoons. The two males were alone. Five minutes earlier, Janey had run off to play with Carol in the Kowalski backyard and the Smiths had taken a trip to San Saba to get ready to move back home.

"A package from my mother." He shook it as he walked to the kitchen. It sounded full. "She sends me stuff, mostly food, every now and then, to make up for the fact she and Dad live so far away." He dropped the carton on the table, picked up a knife, and began cutting through the tape, then opened the box and dumped the contents.

Hector watched as a shower of candy bars and packages labeled shortcake and biscuits and crisps cascaded out. "Man, she must feel real guilty."

"Can't get these in the United States." Adam held up one of the chocolate bars. "These are one of my favorites." He handed Hector a package of Turkish delight. "You're going to love these. Try one."

Settling at the table, Hector opened the package and scrutinized the square candy. He grinned and said, "Where do these come from?" before he popped the rest of the piece in his mouth.

"British Isles. My folks live in London."

"London?" He sat forward and took a box of cream crackers. "You mean, like, London in England?"

Adam nodded. Chewy sat next to them, his chin on the table.

"Don't give any of this to the dog." Adam reached to the counter for a box of doggy treats and tossed one into the other room.

"Why are your parents in England?"

"My dad sold his business a few years ago and they moved there."

He shook his head. "You must be really rich."

"My father is. I'm not."

"Bet you don't understand what it's like to grow up poor." He opened the box and took out a handful of crackers.

"No, I can't imagine, but I care."

"Yeah, Pops, I know you do." He tossed a handful of crackers in his mouth, chewed, and swallowed. "Why aren't you in London with them?"

"They like it. They travel a lot, go to Paris or Italy for a week or two. Mom likes the shopping. My father likes the theater." He shrugged. "I don't. I like Texas and the church and roundball."

"Man," Hector said through a mouthful of crackers, then chewed for a minute and swallowed. "Man, they're rich and you aren't? They live in London and you live here? You're really nuts, you know."

Adam grinned and sort of agreed. "But I'm happy."

"They ever coming to visit you?"

"Christmas, maybe."

"They're coming from London to Butternut Creek, Texas? How are they going to feel about that?"

They'd hate it. Adam knew that but wasn't about to tell Hector, who'd lived here all his life. Instead, he began to separate the goodies by category at the same time Hector attempted to sample one of everything.

"Hey, Pops, want to shoot some hoops?" Hector asked around a mouthful of shortbread.

"You're getting so good, I can't compete."

The kid grinned. Adam could still play him fairly even but not for much longer. By next year, when he was a senior, he'd beat Adam nine out of ten times. But there was still that tenth time to look forward to. When he got to college, Adam would be no match. Surely he'd have pity on an old man.

"We have a game Tuesday at Dripping Spring. You coming?" he asked.

"Where else would I be? If I didn't take your sister to watch you play, she'd hitch a ride." The change in Janey when she attended Hector's games amazed Adam. She shouted and cheered and jumped up and down for the entire time. When the final buzzer sounded, she again became the sweet but melancholy child.

But she seemed more comfortable with Adam, smiled at him a few times a week, allowed him to help her with her homework, and demanded to attend her brother's games.

"I know that's right," Hector mumbled as he savored a bite of candy. "Save a couple of these bars for her. Janey loves chocolate."

❦

Monday morning, Adam finished his morning meditation seated under the big oak with Chewy curled up at his side, his huge head on Adam's leg. The minister looked toward the parsonage. The lights in Hector's and Janey's rooms on the second floor glowed through the shades as the two got ready for school.

On the first floor, lights from the kitchen and the front hall reflected on the trees on the south side of the house and shone from the parlor where Deanne, Eleanor, and Missy had spent the last two and a half weeks.

That morning they had an event to celebrate. The three were going home.

As Adam walked toward the parsonage with Chewy prancing at his side, he watched Jesse make a trip between the parsonage and his truck, packing all they'd accumulated. Adam dropped Chewy's leash—the dog wouldn't run off—and hurried over to the porch to pick up a box filled with Missy's toys and clothing.

Deanne and Eleanor stood at the window, both smiling, but Deanne's lips quivered. Adam put the box down, went inside, and asked, "Are you okay?"

She nodded. "We're happy to be going home, to get back to our little house in our little town. I'll be able to start teaching in a week or two."

"That means you're happy?"

"Yes, but we'll miss you. You've been so good for us, so wonderful to care for Missy. If it hadn't been for your taking me in, I don't think I would have healed nearly as quickly. And I couldn't have cared for Missy, as sick as I was. The burden of the two of us—well, I know that would have worn my mother out. Thank you."

"Ready to go," Jesse shouted.

Adam picked up the box and took it to the truck. With that, the Smiths got into their car and took off while Jesse backed out. Adam waved until they turned onto the highway and disappeared.

When he could see them no longer, Adam heard the sound of someone running down the sidewalk. Turned out to be Miss Birdie.

"She's gone?" she asked.

"They just pulled out."

"Doggone, I thought I'd have enough time but we had a big

crowd this morning and I couldn't leave." She reached into the pocket of her apron and took out a tissue to surreptitiously wipe her eyes.

He pretended not to notice. "How 'bout a cup of coffee?"

He and the pillar sat at the table and drank coffee in silence for a few minutes before she said, "Taking care of Missy was a nice experience for me. Sweet little girl, but I'm old to watch a little one." She reached in another pocket and pulled out a box. "I brought her a little present, seeing she's been brought up in the church. It's a cross, one my mother gave me when I was her age. I'd like her to have it."

"You could mail it. Or you could take it there."

She nodded. "Of course I could." Then she stopped absolutely still, as if something clicked in her head. "Mrs. Smith." She stopped to think about her words. "She's not married, is she?"

"You never give up, do you?" Adam shook his head. "You lost your chance. If you wanted to play matchmaker, you should have done that during the weeks Deanne was staying here."

"I can't believe I blew that opportunity." She looked at her cup then glanced up. "I'm losing my edge."

"Miss Birdie, a woman recovering from a terrible accident, who's in pain and worried about the future, is hardly the best candidate for a matchmaker." She looked so deflated, Adam added, "Besides, you'll never lose your edge. You'll remain sharp until you whip me into shape. I have faith you can do that."

For a moment, she grinned before becoming the pillar again. "Have to get back to work. No use diddle-daddling here." She stood. "Don't you have work to do?"

❧

Adam had just finished putting the last touches on the bulletin for Sunday when the phone rang. Because Maggie had left an hour earlier, he answered.

"Christian Church."

"Reverend Jordan, please."

"This is Reverend Jordan." A wave of pride washed over Adam every time he said that. Perhaps someday, answering the phone in the church he served would feel commonplace or even a bother. But not yet, not after only five months.

"This is Gussie Milton from the church in Roundville. I don't believe we've met. I coordinate youth events in the district."

Before he could answer, she continued in a voice filled with so much enthusiasm, he couldn't help but be drawn in. "In February, the district high school kids have a winter retreat at the campground in Gonzales. Nice lodge, lots of fun. Great spiritual growth."

He remembered winter retreats from his youth—about ten years ago. They'd probably influenced his later decision to be a minister greatly, plus they'd been a lot of fun. "I . . ."

She kept on as if he hadn't spoken. He hadn't really, just one syllable, so he listened. "We have about fifty to seventy-five kids from all over Central Texas. Mac and Bree usually come, but we haven't received any registrations from Butternut Creek."

He glanced at the pile in his IN box. It neared a foot high and teetered. If he searched through the papers on the bottom, the entire structure would fall onto the floor, knocking over several other stacks.

Filing was his downfall. Maybe Maggie or Winnie would help. For a moment, he regretted not heeding Miss Birdie's advice about cleaning up the mess.

However, vowing to correct the deficiencies didn't help at this moment. "I don't know . . ."

"If you don't have them handy, I can email more," she said.

Aha! Not in a pile on the desk or the floor. In a very long list of unread email.

"Just a minute. Let me look—"

"My email is gussie@gussieM.org." She chattered on as Adam opened his email queue. "We have such a great time . . ."

"You sent it September fifteenth," he said once he'd located the folder. "I'm sorry I haven't gotten back to you."

"That's okay." She sounded as if his ignoring her email for seven weeks and her having to call him were not an inconvenience. "Hope you'll be able to bring some of the kids."

"I'll check with them."

"Great. Now, what will you volunteer to do here? We need leaders for small groups, song leaders, and a recreation chair."

Talking to Gussie Milton reminded Adam of being caught up in a tsunami. She made every opportunity sound exciting, like exactly what he wanted to join in on.

"Why don't we get together and discuss this? Meet me in Marble Falls for coffee?" she said. "It's halfway between Roundville and Butternut Creek. I'd like to meet you and discuss some ideas and get you signed up to help."

❧

"Son, I'm going to the vets' group meeting at church tonight." Wednesday evening, the general paused at the door and eyed Sam, who sat on the sofa with the remote in his hand. "Want to come with me?"

The general kept asking and Sam kept refusing, usually by telling the general he didn't need to be fixed.

But he did. Oh, maybe not like an outside force vacuuming out the old crap and forcing new crap on him, tightening the bolts, and whatever else *fixed* consisted of. But since he'd last seen Willow, his brokenness had become more and more obvious to him. He missed her. Not having her around was nearly as painful and incapacitating as not having his leg.

No, that was a bunch of bull. It wasn't nearly as bad, but she made him feel the loss less.

The boys came by once or twice a week. He liked that. But they'd looked so hopeful back when he and Willow had gone out, when they'd thought he and their mother would be together. Guess it was a good thing they hadn't raised the boys' hopes. Now they knew he'd never become their new father.

The realization of the lonely life ahead of him without those three would've about broken his heart if he weren't a marine. Marines didn't suffer from broken hearts and marines didn't give in to emotions.

Still, over the last few weeks the certainty had grown that he needed Leo and Nick and Willow in his life. Yet he had absolutely no idea what to do next.

"Son?" the general repeated.

How long had he been waiting for an answer while Sam's brain had wandered off?

"Not tonight," Sam said.

When his father left without another word, Sam flicked the set off, tossed the remote on the sofa, and glared at the dark screen.

Communication, that's what Willow had said. Get rid of the anger inside. Bring it into the open and face it, share it, stop allowing it to run and ruin his life.

He pushed himself to his feet, walked into the dining room, picked up a pen and several sheets of paper from the computer area his father had created in the corner, and sat down. For a few minutes, he just stared at the paper and drummed the pen on the table. Then he started to write.

Within minutes, the floor was covered with balls of wadded-up paper. On the table he'd amassed a pile of napkins he'd used to wipe his cheeks because every effort to write what had happened hurt so much tears ran down his face.

But he didn't stop. When he had one page pretty much the way he wanted it, he started on the next. It took fewer attempts to get this right because once he got going, the story flowed from him with the tears.

An hour later, the four-page letter completed, he wiped his face one last time. He'd discovered there were times a marine needed to expose all the anger and pain, reaching down deep to haul it to the surface and expose it. Doing that wasn't a bit wimpy, especially the page about Morty. Unlike Morty, Sam had lived through the battle, had survived to relive and write about every bloody moment of it.

Finished, he folded the pages and stuck them in an envelope, not sure what he'd do with them. Probably should share everything with the general. Now that he'd started reliving the past, he probably should go to the meeting with him, maybe next week. If his father had made an effort to change, Sam could, too. He pushed up from the table and wandered into the living room with the envelope in his hand.

But he hadn't written the letter for the general, although he would give it to him to read later. It wasn't for the other vets, even though he knew he needed to attend a session or two, maybe more, as well as the AA meetings. No, he'd written the account of his experiences in Afghanistan for Willow, but he didn't know if he had the guts to share it with her. In fact, at this moment, he knew he didn't. He couldn't. Writing about the event had about killed him.

He tossed himself on the sofa and leaned back. If he didn't share with her, he'd lose her. He couldn't take that. He had to admit: He was in love with the woman, had been from the first time he saw her.

He loved her.

Holding the envelope in front of him, he studied it. Did he love her enough? Opening up to her would hurt both of them. He didn't know if he could bear to watch her read his words, but he did know he couldn't mail something like this to the woman he loved, couldn't expect her to read it alone.

"Preacher, it's four o'clock Friday afternoon. What are you still doing here?"

Without looking up from the surface of his desk, Adam knew who had entered, and not just from her voice. If he glanced up, he'd see the pillar standing at the door, tapping her foot.

He looked up. She was.

"Working on my sermon," he explained, knowing it would make no difference what he said. When Miss Birdie made the trip to the church and had fire in her eyes, Adam knew she owned him for the next hour.

"You can do that later." She attempted to stomp into the office, impossible to do in her rubber-soled shoes but she made a pretty good attempt.

"It's four o'clock," she said. Then, more loudly, she repeated, "Four o'clock on Friday."

What was she talking about?

"The parade." Her tone suggested he had the brain of a gnat.

When he heard the words, Adam realized he did have the brain of a gnat.

"The parade," he said as he jumped to his feet, grabbed a jacket, and struggled to stick his arms in the sleeves while running after the pillar. She moved faster than he'd thought she could, across the highway, down the block, and onto the square.

The square and Adam had a transitory relationship. Because he wasn't a tearoom-and-antiques sort of guy, his visits had been limited to renewing his driver's license at the courthouse annex and occasionally joining Mattie for lunch at Tea Time, a restaurant that served the quiche and sweet persimmon tea she loved, or grabbing a meal at the diner.

Now he was running through a mob of crazy football fans. Like there was another kind. As he joggled through them to the other side of the square, Adam greeted people he recognized from church and from games. He spied Mercedes about fifty feet away. Finally, Miss Birdie stopped on the edge of the curb next to her friend and motioned Adam to a place behind them.

"I saved your places," Mercedes said.

"This is the best side to view the parade from. That's the reviewing stand." The pillar pointed to a table only a few feet to the right. "The kids really strut their stuff as they pass here."

"Every high school class and some of the classes from the middle schools build a float." Mercedes stood on her toes to look across the square. "Should start any minute."

"The bands march and the teams and clubs ride on the back of trucks."

That riding in the bed of a pickup seemed dangerous to Adam but appeared to be an old Texas custom. Not that they'd be speeding through; the students should be safe.

Across the street, he spotted Willow and Nick and waved. Where was Leo? Maybe in the parade. Sam stood at the corner maybe twenty feet from Willow, keeping his eyes off her so carefully Adam guessed the romance wasn't going well. He needed to drop by with pizza soon because he knew Sam wouldn't call him.

"Can you hear them?" the pillar asked. "Look, you can see them."

Adam followed her pointing finger toward the first float of the parade and heard the bands as the trucks moved forward. Leo marched with a group of kids behind a banner that proclaimed, YOUTH FOOTBALL. As the group went by, Nick kept up a relay, running to Sam then back to his mother at least five times since Adam had been watching, as well as jumping up and down and pointing toward his brother.

Sam waved at Leo, then looked past Nick to stare at Willow. His eyes showed so much longing Adam felt sorry for him but wanted to kick him at the same time. He guessed Sam was the problem in the relationship—but if he was so unhappy, why didn't he do something?

Nick did. He grabbed Sam's hand and tugged, not enough to make Sam lose his balance but enough to get him moving. The boy kept hold of Sam's hand and moved slowly but—as the cliché went—inexorably toward his mother. Expressions of panic and hope alternated across Sam's face, but he didn't stop. He didn't pull his hand from Nick's.

When the two reached Willow's side, she turned to look at Sam with a polite nod before she looked back to watch the parade.

Sam watched her profile for nearly a minute, yearning raw on his face. At least, that's what Adam thought it was. As with most facial expressions and body language, he wasn't always sure what they expressed, but even an illiterate like him could read Sam.

Fortunately, Miss Birdie had a master's degree. "Those two look miserable," the pillar said.

Sadly, they did agree on this one basic fact.

"Bird, we can't do anything more." Mercedes glanced across the street. "We've done everything we can to bring them together. The rest is up to them."

"Hrmph." Miss Birdie shook her head. "I know, I know, but someone ought to . . ." She stopped speaking as the notes of the "Lion Fight Song" filled the air. "That's Mac." Miss Birdie pointed toward the band, waved at her granddaughter, and began to sing along, "Go, Lions, win this game . . ."

Adam wouldn't have recognized Mac in her band uniform; the visor on the huge hat covered every recognizable feature. The chin straps made the faces of all the members look alike: chinless wonders with huge fuzzy heads and no other identifiable features.

Even though he didn't really know which one was Mac, Adam

waved and shouted as well, then joined the fight song the second time through. "She's doing great," he said with relief.

Miss Birdie glared at him. "She's not going to lead the band into the fence, you know. They're just marching around the square."

After the band passed, a truck with Bree holding a sign that read VARSITY VOLLEYBALL drove by the reviewing stand.

"You have great girls," Adam said.

Without answering, the pillar elbowed him in the side.

"What was that for?" he asked, a little confused. He thought he'd been behaving well.

"Look over there." She moved her head in the direction of the northwest corner of the square. "Who's that man with Reverend Patillo?"

"I don't know." Tall and good-looking, but Adam didn't see evidence of an attraction between the two of them. Not like the chemistry Willow and Sam attempted to deny. "Do you want me to go ask?"

"Oh, for heaven's sake, Pastor Adam." She didn't have to change expressions. The glare she'd used earlier still fit this occasion. "You might take some interest in your future. If you aren't going to allow the Widows to help—"

"Meddle," he corrected.

She ignored him, as he'd expected. "—then you're going to have to do some of this getting-married-and-raising-a-family business yourself." She shoved him. "Go over and introduce yourself to the competition."

With growing confidence in his ability to withstand the pillar's demands, Adam ignored her and watched the parade.

❦

The day of his meeting with Gussie Milton, Adam arrived at the coffee shop in Marble Falls early and grabbed a table facing the door. How would he recognize her? He had no idea what she looked like. There was a woman in her fifties he thought might be her. She was a little plump and wore a camp shirt and athletic shoes. But she seemed to be there with her husband. Just as Adam was about to approach the couple, the bell on the door jingled.

For nearly a minute, Adam watched a woman of about thirty, pretty and slender in a charcoal-gray suit and high heels. She had dark curly hair tamed by a clasp at the nape of her neck. She stood at the door of the coffee shop and looked around. Then she spotted Adam and a brilliant smile broke out.

The smile said *Gussie*. The rest of her—the polish, the fashion sense—didn't. He feared his mouth had dropped open, but when he checked, it was closed.

"Hi." She reached out to grab his hand in a strong grip. "I'm Gussie. It's great to meet you."

Yes, it was Gussie. He recognized her voice.

"Let me get something to drink." She dropped a large canvas tote on the floor beside the table and walked away.

A few minutes later, she returned with two foaming cups, placing one in front of Adam while she sat. With an elegant motion, she dropped her big yellow purse on the floor and at the same time grabbed and placed the tote on the table. Then she pulled out a folder and flipped it open. Every movement done with the speed of a runner and the grace of a dancer.

"Where do you want to start?" she asked, smiling at Adam with an expression of pure delight.

He blinked. This woman was so full of energy and joie de vivre that she left him nearly breathless.

"Sometimes I move too fast. Sorry." She laughed, the sound he recognized from their phone conversations. Yes, this was Gussie. Whoever would name a girl Gussie?

"My father's favorite uncle, Augustus," she said as if she knew what he'd been thinking. "That's who I'm named for, but I'm only Gussie, not even Augusta or anything elegant or even normal." She smiled. "Everyone wonders so I always answer before they have to ask. And"—she shuffled through a few papers—"I'm a photographer and graphic designer."

"In Roundville?"

"Oh, no. In Austin. But my parents live in Roundville and I want to be close to them." For a moment, she lost the smile. "They're getting older. And I love the church there. I grew up in it. It's a short commute to town and worth it so I can live at home with my folks. I'm an only child."

Adam felt her warmth and happiness flow over him from across the table. He took it in until he realized she was watching him, a little perplexed, as if she'd said something and he hadn't responded.

"I'm sorry. What did you say?"

"That's okay. I often see that blank stare when I talk. Sometimes people can't take in everything I say at once, but that's how my brain works." She laughed. "Where do you come from?"

He gave her some quick background before he asked her to tell him about herself, adding, "And your family. You mentioned your parents. What about your husband and children?" Adam knew he'd never be subtle and suave, but she didn't seem to notice his stumbling curiosity.

"No husband. No children. No time." She shook her head. "My job and the church and my parents are all I can commit to now."

How had the Widows missed her? Had they thought she lived too far away? He couldn't imagine a small thing like a distance of fifty miles slowing Miss Birdie down.

By the time Gussie leaped to her feet—he was quickly discovering she never did anything slowly or quietly—ten minutes later, he'd studied the schedule she'd worked up for the retreat weekend. He wrote his name in a few slots while she brought a pot of coffee over and poured them each another cup.

"Those servers are always too slow," she explained as she sat down.

They chatted for a few more minutes. Once they concluded the business of the retreat, she grabbed her papers, stuffed them into the tote, waved, and dashed out the door. Her exit left Adam feeling as if a thoroughly enchanting hurricane had just passed through.

Feeling enchanted wasn't his goal. First, it would be stupid to be attracted to a woman who worked in South Austin, who lived an hour's drive away, a woman who cared for her parents and supervised the youth of her church in her bit of extra time. Second, if he didn't want an entanglement, he shouldn't be enchanted.

But Gussie was hard to resist.

A few days later, Sam called Adam. He said he was on the way over to the church. Adam was terrified. Was Sam coming for counseling? He had known a day like this would come but hadn't expected it so soon.

Adam had taken courses about counseling in seminary, had even worked at a counseling center and as a hospital chaplain, but he'd never been on his own and certainly never with someone he knew. In all those sessions with strangers, there had always been someone—a faculty member or a psychologist or a supervising chaplain—looking over his shoulder, suggesting, helping, and telling him later both how to handle the situation and what to do as well as what not to do.

Today he'd be on his own.

What if he messed up?

What if he said the wrong thing and hurt the situation? Who in the world was he to help anyone else with their problems?

"Dear Lord, please help me." After a few seconds, he added,

"Give me wisdom and compassion and a lot of help. And toss in whatever else You think I may need."

A knock interrupted the anxious prayer.

"Amen." He leaped to his feet and shouted, "Come in."

Leaning on his cane, Sam walked in.

"Bad day?" Adam asked, then kicked himself. Had that been the wrong response to the cane?

He nodded. "Sometimes I overdo, but I'm fine." He came over to the desk without closing the door and lowered himself into the chair, leaning heavily on his left hand.

Should Adam close the door? Inside, he shook his head. He worried too much.

"How can I help you?" Were those the wrong words? "What can I do for you?" Again, had Adam insulted the marine and the handicap? This time his prayer consisted of, *Dear Lord, give me the right words and tell me when to shut up.* Then he moved a chair next to Sam's and sat.

"I was wondering what I could do for the church."

"What?"

"The church has been so good to me." Sam smiled and shook his head. "I really can't believe how good. The women have brought food. Howard Crampton came by the other day to fix the porch swing. You know, the one you broke."

Adam nodded.

"Did you know Jesse brings a horse by and takes me riding once a week?" Sam asked.

"He told me that. He really enjoys it."

"I appreciate all this. I'd like to do something in return, something that doesn't require actually attending worship."

"Sort of service in absentia?"

Sam nodded.

"Okay, what do you have in mind?"

"I'm not a handyman so carpentry and plumbing are beyond me, but I'm open to about anything else."

"A few of our people volunteer at the library, teaching English as a second language and literacy. They always need help." Adam thought for a few seconds. "They can always use extra hands at the food pantry on Tuesday and Thursday mornings."

"Teaching, huh?" He considered that. "I'll go to the library and ask about it."

Adam wrote a phone number on a piece of paper. "Call Ruth Cook. She's in charge of scheduling."

"Thanks, Adam."

The minister silently breathed a sigh of relief. That had been easy. But why had Sam come by the church? To the study? He could have asked that on the phone.

"Guess I'll head out." Sam stood, but turned at the door, scrutinized Adam for a moment, then shut the door without leaving. "There's something else I need to talk about." He took a few steps toward the desk. "I don't need a minister and I don't need some easy religious words or simplistic clichés to pacify me. Right now, I need to talk to a friend. You're the one I've chosen." He put his hand on the back of the chair. "Actually, you're my only friend in town other than two kids and the general, and he's the problem." He shrugged. "Are you willing?"

"Of course." The feeling of inadequacy melted away, as if God answered his prayer. Why in the world did he find it so difficult to accept the fact that God endowed him with certain gifts as well as the ability to use them? Why did he find it hard to believe that God had already answered his prayers by blessing him with talents to serve? "What can I do for you?" Adam asked pastorally as Sam dropped into the chair again.

He leaned his head on the high back of the chair and closed his eyes. "Do you get along with your father?"

"You mean other than his telling me going into the ministry was the waste of a good mind and an expensive education?"

Sam leaned forward and smiled. "Yeah, like that."

"My sister's a doctor who goes from refugee camp to refugee camp in Africa. We're both great disappointments to our father. Mom's pretty much okay with us. Don't know what he expected. We were raised in the church."

As the men discussed how to get along with a stifling parent, Sam and Adam became better friends. They tossed out ideas, joked and shared, even discovered that, at different times in their lives, when business or the military had called their fathers away, both had been sent to boarding schools.

But Sam didn't say a word about Willow.

"Thank for listening," Sam said after thirty minutes. "I don't think the general is a problem that can be solved."

"Maybe if you didn't call him 'the general,'" Adam suggested. "Have you thought about calling him 'Dad'?"

"Hey." He glared at the minister. "Don't try to . . ."

"I'm not trying to fix you."

"All right." Sam grinned and relaxed. "I've tried calling him

'Dad'—both to his face once or twice and in here." He tapped his head. "It doesn't feel right. At least, not yet."

"Maybe with practice."

"The really weird thing is the man never spent time with me when I was a kid. Now I wake up and find him sitting next to my bed. Crying." He shook his head. "Man, how am I supposed to deal with that?"

❧

"Pastor, we need to get to the bottom of this," the pillar said as she marched into the minister's study a few days after the meeting with Sam. She stopped in front of the desk and put her hands on her hips.

Adam quaked at the ominous words. Miss Birdie was in full *the-minister-has-done-something-so-foolish-I-cannot-believe-it* mode. "The community center is holding its craft fair the same Saturday as our spring bazaar." She bit the words off.

He relaxed. Not angry at her minister, at least not this time.

"Bird doesn't like anyone competing with the Widows for good deeds," Mercedes stated as she followed the pillar into the office.

"That's not the reason at all, Mercedes." She lifted her glare toward her friend. "You know that. It's just that . . ." She sat and leaned toward Adam. "It's just that we've always had our bazaar on that weekend. Everyone knows that. Competition won't be good for either group."

"Bird doesn't like to be left out," Mercedes stated. "She likes to know everything that's going on."

"No," Miss Birdie protested. "It's just that . . ." She sighed. "All right. That's true." She smiled ruefully. "I don't like to be left out. I do like to know who's doing what. I hate to be blind-sided."

Adam nodded solemnly. "I understand, but sometimes things happen."

"I know that very well, Preacher," Miss Birdie snapped. "Pushiness and impatience may not be attractive traits, but that's who I am and what I do best. I'm not fixin' to change at this time in my life."

"Bird's very proud of that," Mercedes stated.

"No, I'm not." The pillar shook her head. "Well, maybe a little, but I also know there are times I should step back and leave things in the Lord's hands." She sighed. "I'm not good at that, Pastor."

"Bird's not patient."

"Patience is a hard lesson to learn," Adam agreed.

"Especially if you don't want to." After receiving a glare from the pillar, Mercedes added, "Like me. Hard lesson for me as well."

"For all of us," Adam agreed again.

Having exhausted that area of accord, the three glanced at one another, each waiting for someone else to begin a new topic. Adam hesitated because he had no idea why the women had come. They should have gone over to the community center to discuss the conflict.

But he'd learned it was never a good idea to make a suggestion to the pillar. If she liked it, she'd expect him to take care of it. If she didn't, she'd tut-tut and tsk-tsk and hrmph, generally making him feel like an idiot.

However, Adam felt that there was something else going on now. Although she was angry about the usurping of the date of the spring bazaar, the conflict didn't seem uppermost on the pillar's mind.

She knew she could wear Adam down with her glare. He held out for nearly a minute of scrutiny before he blurted out, "Anything else?"

"It's about the youth retreat," Mercedes said. "Bird's upset because you haven't done a thing about it."

"I can tell him—" the pillar began.

Before she could finish, Adam spoke quickly. The youth retreat seemed like a safe topic. "Yes, I have been late doing that. I have the forms. Gussie Milton called last week. I met her in Marble Falls to discuss scheduling."

When he mentioned Gussie's name, the two Widows glanced at each other, then—in unison—toward Adam and said, also in unison, "You met Gussie Milton?"

They beamed. Miss Birdie tilted her head up to look at the picture of Jesus knocking on a door, a gift from someone to a former minister that hung right behind the desk. "Dear Lord," she said to the figure on the canvas. "You do answer prayer. Thank You."

Adam recognized his error immediately. He should never have spoken Gussie's name. It was like tossing M&M's to a chocoholic. Forgetting anything else they might have wanted to say, both slid to the edges of their chairs, folded their hands in their laps, and watched Adam like cats watching a cricket, just waiting for it to move.

"What do you think of her?" Miss Birdie asked happily, as if she foresaw the restoration of her reputation as a matchmaker. Not that she'd introduced Adam to Gussie, but he bet she'd take credit for it.

"Very nice," he said hastily and pulled open a drawer to snatch up the registration forms Maggie had copied. He tossed them across the desk to the Widows in the hope of forestalling any more questions or considerations. "Here are the forms for Mac and Bree. Does anyone else need them?"

He'd also hoped Miss Birdie would pick up a couple of forms and they'd leave. Stupid of him.

Neither woman moved or said a word. Just grinned. He'd made them very happy.

The intensity of their reaction scared him to death.

Chapter Twenty-Two

Y ou can't park here."

Birdie turned to glare at Winnie, the bossiest woman she knew.

"It's reserved for tenants and guests only." Winnie pointed toward the sign.

She'd be so glad when Winnie married the general and they could kick her out of the Widows. "The lot's nearly empty. No one within thirty feet of us and it's convenient. After all, we're doing the Lord's work."

"That doesn't mean we can flout the rules. If we parked on the street . . ." Winnie stopped talking when Birdie turned off the engine, pressed the button that opened the back doors, and got out of the van.

Mercedes was supposed to have come, but she had an ailing uncle and that family was so close you couldn't separate them with WD-40. That meant today Birdie was alone with Winnie to deliver Thanksgiving baskets to shut-ins. The two of them occasionally didn't see eye-to-eye. The provisional Widow didn't respect seniority and was darned inflexible and pushy.

"Susan Pfannenstiel lives in the blue house . . ."

"Oh, for heaven's sake, Bird, don't you think I know where she lives? She's been in my Bunco group for years."

Had Winnie called her "Bird"? She only allowed Mercedes to do that. She'd need to take that up with Winnie sometime, set boundaries, but for now they had a mission that didn't include arguing in public.

"All right, let's visit her first, then we'll pick up the basket for . . ." Just as she started to wave toward the home of another shut-in, Birdie saw Sam slinking along behind several azalea bushes. Was he trying to hide from them?

"Isn't that Sam Peterson?" Winnie asked. "What's he doing?"

"Skulking," Birdie said. Then she grinned. "Right across from Willow Thomas's apartment. Don't that beat all?" But did he have the courage to go in? "I'm going to talk to him, make sure he's going inside to talk to her."

"That's not a good idea."

"She must be home because her car's right there." Stupid kind of car for a mother of two to have, but that wasn't the topic now.

"You can't do that," Winnie stated. "You have to let him alone, allow him to do what he needs to do."

"Haven't you learned?" Birdie turned back toward Winnie. "You can never be sure other people are going to do what they should do, not without some strong suggestions."

Winnie shook her head resolutely. "Leave Sam alone to make his decisions. That's what Mitchell said."

As if Birdie cared what Mitchell said. Well, she did, actually. He was Sam's father and might have more history and broader insight on his side than she did, but she remembered that look on Sam's face at the parade, the longing. "I want to do something. I can't just stand here . . ." When her voice broke, she cleared her throat before continuing. "I can't allow a person to ruin his own life, not without trying to point him in the right direction."

"Bird, we can't control everyone and everything. Sometimes you have to let go and trust people to take care of themselves."

"Hrmpp." She turned to glare at Winnie. What did the woman know? Where would the world be if everyone stepped back and didn't try, at least *try*, to set people on the right track? "There are times when people need direction." Darn, her voice broke again.

"Besides, what's your plan? Capture a marine and force him inside to talk to Willow?"

Yes, that had been her plan. Not a good one for a woman with a bad shoulder and an unwilling co-conspirator.

She turned to look toward the bushes that had barely covered Sam, but he was gone. "All right," she sighed. "I guess we'd better get on with delivering the baskets." She reached into the backseat, pulled out a basket, and handed it to Winnie to carry. The woman could do something more useful than issuing orders and disagreeing.

❧

He'd become a total idiot.

When Sam first saw the Widows in the parking lot, he dropped, totally by instinct, onto the ground behind a hedge as if hiding from enemy snipers instead of two elderly women.

But he knew how dangerous they could be.

Fortunately, the prosthetic joint held up well. It had folded easily and evenly at the same rate as the left leg. When he slid forward to peek through the branches, he realized Miss Birdie could see him and Miss Winnie had pointed at him.

Now he was stuck. He could hardly leap to his feet and pretend he hadn't been hiding—but he couldn't stay here, either, huddled like an idiot behind these shrubs. What was wrong with him? He'd fought in war, led his troops into combat, but now he hid from the Widows? They weren't even in full force and they scared him.

How could he ever explain this to his father?

Escape was the only answer. When he saw Miss Birdie turn to talk to the other Widow, he stood and ran faster than he'd thought he could toward the apartment building.

This was not the way he'd envisioned the morning. It had started out as a walk. As he strolled through the tree-lined streets, he'd reached into the pocket of his jeans to feel the crinkling of the envelope beneath his fingers. It had been on the dresser for several days. This morning he'd put it in his pocket, thinking if he saw Willow, by accident, he'd have it handy if the opportunity arose to share it with her. He didn't have the courage yet to share it on his own, directly. Only by accident.

How he'd do that he didn't know. See her at the H-E-B, shove the envelope at her, say, *Here. I thought you'd want to read about the horror that's been my life for the past year*, then smile and walk away? So far, that was the best plan he'd come up with.

But somehow as he walked he'd found himself across the street from Willow's—and the boys'—apartment building. He hadn't planned that, but his feet had brought him here. The place pulled at him like a huge electromagnet, and he possessed the resistance of a poached egg. Stupid analogy. Eggs aren't attracted to magnets, but the rest fit pretty well. He had no willpower when it came to the Thomas family.

What were the Widows doing in that parking lot? Were they setting something up between him and Willow? Not that he'd mind, but they couldn't have known he'd be coming this way.

Why were they in the parking lot of Willow's building?

Could be they weren't waiting for him, not matchmaking for him. Maybe they planned to fix Willow up with someone else.

Who?

He didn't know if there were more single men in town. Perhaps they'd decided to match Adam and Willow. The preacher was a good guy. They'd get along well. The minister would make a great father for the boys.

But not if Sam had anything to say about it. He made a decision without a second of thought: He had to reach Willow before the Widows did, before they found another man for her. Using the reconnaissance skills he'd learned as a marine, he started south, surreptitiously glancing toward the parking lot on his right every few seconds.

Nothing had changed. The women still chatted. Their presence had to be about Willow. Why else would they be here? Of course, fifty other people inhabited these apartments. Many more lived in the houses surrounding the complex. They could be sticking their noses into someone else's life. Maybe their appearance had nothing to do with him or Willow.

But if it did . . . He couldn't lose Willow and the boys.

He lost sight of the women as he dashed across the street. A few seconds later, he approached the building. Through a breezeway, he could see the Widows. As he watched, they broke formation and quick stepped across the asphalt, a movement that filled him with panic. Had he left things like telling Willow he loved her and sharing and communication until too late? Were the Widows marching in to correct that? Winnie held a basket, no doubt the pretense they'd use to get in the door. Willow would invite them to stay, and before she knew it she'd be matched up with some eligible Butternut Creek bachelor.

Not on his watch.

Boldly he entered the building and headed toward the Thomases' apartment at the end of the wing. He knocked. Then, afraid the Widows would stride into the building while he still stood out here, he knocked again, harder.

❧

Willow looked out the window to see if the boys were coming home from practice. The apartment had a lovely view of the flat black asphalt parking lot and a few weary bushes. She waved when she recognized Miss Birdie and Winnie out there, but they couldn't see her. She watched as they walked off toward a house facing the parking lot, probably doing good deeds.

Then she saw Sam crossing the street.

What in the world was he doing out there?

She stepped back from the window, out of sight. Was he coming here? What would she do if he did? How would she handle it? She'd missed him, really, really missed him. When her sons talked about what they'd done with Sam, she'd actually been a little jealous of them.

Of course, he could be visiting someone else. But she didn't think so.

Before she could gather her thoughts, a knock sounded on the door and reverberated through the apartment. Or was that the rapid beat of her heart and the fear clenching at her throat?

Of course, maybe it wasn't Sam. Maybe he'd gone somewhere else. Could be a neighbor or a delivery person or the Widows. Who knew?

But she knew. Sam stood outside her door. He knocked again, actually hammering as if he didn't plan to go away. Slowly she turned and opened the last physical barrier between them. "Hello, Sam. This is a surprise." She flinched. What a cliché. Couldn't she come up with something clever?

"A pleasant one, I hope." He grimaced at his words and looked as uncomfortable as she felt.

She'd add another cliché to this soup of old chestnuts they both seemed to be swimming in, but her brain couldn't come up with a thought of any kind, trite or not. Still standing in the open doorway, she said, "The boys aren't home. They have flag-football practice this morning. They'd love for you to come to a game sometime."

"Sure." He nodded. "I didn't come to see them."

She tilted her head warily. "Oh?"

"Are you expecting anyone?"

Who? Like the Widows or all those eligible bachelors in Butternut Creek? "No."

"Can . . . may I come in?"

She studied him for a few seconds. "Okay."

"Would you like a cup of coffee?" she offered. That would slow things down, give her time to gain control of herself and find a few brain cells that Sam's sudden appearance hadn't fried.

"No, thanks." He walked around her and inside.

As she stepped back and closed the door, she glanced in the mirror. She wore tattered jeans and a burnt orange University of Texas T-shirt with matching socks but no shoes. She hadn't combed her hair so it stood out like a giant Brillo pad. No makeup. She looked terrible.

"You look great," Sam said. He watched her, thinking she didn't look any more comfortable than he felt. Maybe he should accept the coffee. When they settled in the kitchen, he could tell her about how he'd started tutoring English as a second language at the library three mornings a week. He really enjoyed it, felt good to . . .

Good try, Peterson. Postpone whatever's hard to face; delay the difficult. He knew darned good and well why he wanted to chat about trivia. He didn't want to hand the letter to Willow, but putting this off was cowardly.

"I have something I want you to read." He handed her the envelope.

She glanced at it before she lifted her eyes toward him and frowned. "What's this? You want me to read it?"

"Yes."

"Now?" She took it from him.

"That would be good. If you don't mind." He leaned on the arm of the sofa to lower himself in the seat.

"Okay." She sat across from him on a rocking chair and opened the envelope. She lifted her gaze toward him, then began to read.

After a paragraph, she stopped and looked at him again. "Are you sure?"

He nodded, afraid to speak but also too choked up to say a word.

As she read, she began to cry. Reaching for tissues from the box on the end table next to her, she cried into them. As she read through the pages, she sobbed. "Oh, Sam," she said once. On the section about Morty, he thought.

By the time she finished the letter, he'd reached in the pocket of his jacket and pulled out a handful of tissues and wiped his own face.

For a moment, she stared at the end of the letter, then up at him before she stood, walked to the sofa, and sat on his lap. She put her head on his chest, pulling him close to sob against him. "Oh, Sam," she whispered. "I'm sorry. I'm so sorry."

He put his arms around her and enjoyed the moment, keeping her close and soft against him, feeling her concern and tenderness seep in and begin to warm those cold places inside, to heal the bleeding holes. After a minute or so, she turned and pulled his lips toward hers for a kiss that lasted for a more than satisfactory time, filled with much more than satisfactory emotion.

Then she scooted off his lap to sit next to him and took his hand. He'd prefer to have her in his arms, but this was okay.

"What does this mean, Sam? Is this a commitment?"

"I still want to sleep with you," he said. That wasn't what he'd meant to say.

She stilled for a moment, looking at him apprehensively. "I thought we'd . . ."

"But that's not all." He cleared his throat. "I also want to wake up with you every morning. I want to eat breakfast with you and Nick and Leo, to take the boys to school and to play football with them when they get home. I want to watch them grow up and visit them in college and hold their children, our grandchildren. But most of all—" Sam took his hand from her grasp and tilted her chin up so she had to look into his eyes. "Most of all, I want to sleep with you every night for the rest of our lives."

"Oh, Sam." She wiped her eyes again, then gave him a kiss that erased any doubt about how much the prospect of that future pleased her.

They'd just gotten to a really good part when she heard a key in the lock.

"Oh, dear." She attempted to arrange her hair while he smoothed her shirt.

The boys shoved into the apartment, laughing and pushing each other. When they saw Sam with his arm around their mother, they both stopped, stood completely still, and gawked at them. Then they shouted, "Sam!" and ran to him.

Juggling the boys, one on each arm, Sam grinned. How had life become so good?

But before he completed the thought, Leo stepped back, grabbing his brother's arm to pull him away as well.

"What are you doing with my mother?" Leo asked. Concern laced his voice as if he needed to protect her.

Sam grinned. "We were kissing." He glanced from Nick and Leo's scrutiny toward Willow, who looked as if she wanted to throw herself over the back of the sofa and hide from the questions she read in Leo's eyes.

Her older son glowered at Sam and put his thumbs in his belt. "What does this"—he pointed at his mother and Sam—"mean?"

Nick mimicked his brother's stance and facial expression although his glare came nowhere near the antagonism in Leo's.

"Nothing, boys," Willow said. "Sam and I were just talking about . . . oh, things."

He could read their expressions. Nick accepted her words. Leo didn't.

"My intentions are . . ."

Sam stumbled on the last word. He couldn't say *pure* because his intentions were hardly that. Still, he couldn't laugh, he had to complete the sentence, because Leo looked so serious.

"You hurt my mother," Leo said. "I hear her crying at night."

Sam closed his eyes and thought *Crap*, then turned toward Willow. "I'm sorry. I . . . I guess I knew, but I had to work this through, put my life in order."

She put her hand on his. "I know."

Both boys watched the two grown-ups. "Leo," she said to her very solemn son. "Don't worry. We're okay, Sam and I."

Sam nodded and stood to take a step toward what he hoped, if all went well, were his sons-to-be, the greatest kids in the world.

"Are you going to be our father?" Nick asked, cutting through the adult obfuscation.

Sam grinned and said, "Yes," before Willow could answer. "If we can convince your mother."

"Mom?" Nick's voice rose. "Mom, can we keep him? Please?"

"You make him sound like a puppy." Willow stood and grinned at all of them. "Give us a little time, guys. Okay? This is pretty new."

With that, Leo and Nick launched themselves toward Sam again. Careful not to knock him down, they stood one on each side and threw their arms around him. He reached out to Willow, put his arm on her shoulders to pull her into the group hug as the boys peppered them with questions.

"When are you getting married?" Leo tossed out.

"We haven't . . . ," Willow began as Sam said, "As soon as we can talk her into it."

But the boys didn't hear either because Nick spoke over the words. "Are you going to have more kids?"

"Hope so," Sam said at the same time Willow said, "We have to discuss that."

"We probably should get married first," Sam added.

"Where are we going to live?" Nick jumped up and down as he threw the questions. "Are you going to paint the house in marine colors? Can we have a dog?"

For a moment, Sam felt as if he stood a few feet away from the group. From that distance, he could see himself with one arm around Willow and the other hand resting on Nick's shoulder and smiling like a fool.

But he wasn't a few feet away. He was inside the circle, part of the family. He could smell the apple scent of Willow's hair and the sweaty odor of the boys and feel the damp perspiration on Nick's neck.

And joy exploded around Sam Peterson.

❦

At twelve thirty, the fellowship hall of the Presbyterian Church looked full, wall-to-wall tables filled with the good citizens, and probably a liberal sprinkling of the sinners, of Butternut Creek. The churches had joined together for the community Thanksgiving dinner, free to everyone.

Behind Adam, the women of several churches prepared vegetables and mashed and sweet potatoes while men pulled turkeys from the ovens, set them on the woodblock counters, and carved them into huge slabs.

With the help of Ouida, his sweet next-door neighbor, Adam had contributed one. She'd prepared the dressing, stuffed the cavity, basted the bird, then put it in the oven of the parsonage. All he'd had to do was watch it and baste it and warm up gravy from a jar. In her solemn way, Janey had been a great help keeping him on schedule. The bird had turned out great. Amazing how his cooking skills had improved with Ouida living next door.

Adam stood third in the serving line, dropping globs of potatoes on a plate before handing it to Hector to pour gravy on everything. In the South, hard-boiled eggs were put in the gravy, an addition Adam neither understood nor enjoyed. Last Sunday at the church Thanksgiving dinner, he'd attempted to pick the pieces from the otherwise delicious dish. The pillar saw it and gave him her death glare, which always shriveled the recipient. Today he'd have to hide someplace in the back of the kitchen, maybe in a pantry, to pluck the rubbery egg whites out.

But that would come later, after they'd served everyone who dropped in for the meal. Across the counter, Mattie cleared and wiped tables. Janey, with her hair decorated in orange barrettes, stood by the desserts and smiled every now and then.

"She's a lot happier. Thanks, Preacher," Hector whispered. "She's feeling safe."

The high school basketball season had begun nearly six weeks earlier. Hector had a great start, leading the team in rebounds. A few scouts from small colleges had come to look over the senior center and had been impressed by Hector, only a junior. What would they do with Janey while he was in college? She could stay at the parsonage. Both she and Hector could call that home.

But Adam didn't need to consider that now. People were waiting for mashed potatoes.

"Pick up that nearly empty pan so I can exchange it." Mac shoved him aside. Sweat rolled down her forehead. The temperature today had reached eighty by noon and seemed about one hundred with the heat from the ovens. Finally, at two, the line closed and the servers fixed themselves plates.

After the volunteers cleaned up, Hector and Janey headed to the basketball coach's house for a get-together, so Adam was on his own. He wandered through town reflecting on how thankful he felt, how blessed he'd been to end up here. For a moment, Adam considered heading to Sam's house, but he was spending the day at Winnie's with his father and Willow and the boys. Nice for all of them.

After a few more blocks, he realized he was only a football field away from the pillar's house. She'd done so much today. With the bad shoulder she attempted to hide from everyone, Adam wondered how she felt. As her minister, he should check and thank her for her service. Adam wouldn't tell her he was concerned about her. She'd hate that.

Once in front of her neat little cottage, he took the steps to the porch with a leap and knocked at the front door.

"Have you swept off that porch?" Miss Birdie shouted from inside.

He looked around. A broom leaned against the wall next to the front door with a dustpan hooked onto it.

"I . . ." Adam attempted to speak, to identify himself and explain why he was on her porch.

"Don't backtalk me," she said firmly. "Get your south-forty in motion and sweep that porch."

What was a south-forty?

"And don't even try to get inside," the pillar continued, "until you complete that chore or I'll tan your hide."

Mystified but obedient, the minister picked up the broom and walked to the end of the porch. Maybe her shoulder was acting up and she felt grumpy and she couldn't do the task herself. More likely, she didn't realize it was him.

How carefully did this need to be done? Should Adam sweep between the rail supports? Knowing Miss Birdie, she'd expect that. If he didn't do it right, and she did know it was him, he bet she wouldn't really tan his hide—but he also knew how her words could take off a few inches of skin. Besides, he had nothing better to do.

Fortunately, the porch was small, maybe six by eight. He went over it once, grinning as he imagined her reaction. He swept the leaves and trash into the dustpan and scrutinized the area. A plastic bag was tied to the rail. He pulled it off and dumped the contents of the dustpan inside. After checking the porch again, Adam concluded that if he wanted to get inside the house, he'd better give it another sweep.

Finally satisfied, he tied the plastic sack, shook the broom over the railing to get rid of the dust, and turned toward the door.

"I'm finished," he shouted.

No response came from the house for nearly a minute. Absolute silence. Then the curtain across the window in the door was pushed aside. Miss Birdie stared out. She blinked and stood as if transfixed, her eyes still on Adam's face.

Suddenly the curtains dropped and the door opened.

"Oh, Preacher." Bright red suffused her face and covered her neck. "Oh, Preacher, I'm so sorry."

He glanced around the porch. "Did I miss a spot?"

"Come in, come in." She waved her hands toward the living room. "Please sit. Let me have that broom and the bag and the dustpan." As Adam entered, she pulled the items away and stood there, holding them, silent, in the middle of the room, her mouth a perfect O.

He hadn't thought a woman as commanding as the pillar could look mortified.

Adam smiled amicably, as if sweeping her porch was the exact thing he'd hoped to do that day. "I was in the area and stopped by to see if you've recovered from the dinner."

"Oh." She tossed the broom and other stuff in a corner. "Oh, Preacher, I'm so sorry. I thought you were Bree."

He didn't answer but felt sure confusion showed on his face as well as the desire for an explanation.

"She was supposed to help at the community dinner but didn't show up. For punishment, I planned to make her sweep the porch." She dropped in a chair. "I thought she'd knocked instead of coming right inside because she knew I'd be angry." Then she leaped to her feet. "Let me get you a slice of pie and some coffee." With a twirl, she left the room.

Having filled up on more pie at the dinner than one person should, he really didn't want more. His caffeine intake had reached a new high, so more would probably result in jitters. But he could not turn this down. He'd embarrassed the pillar and doubted her deep humiliation and sincere expressions of regret would be offered again.

If she wanted to apologize, ply him with sweets and coffee, why should he refuse? Seemed the least a preacher could do. For her spiritual growth, of course.

They were both good. The pumpkin pie tasted spicy and delicious, but he enjoyed the humble pie even more.

❧

Traditionally, the church celebrated the Hanging of the Greens on the Sunday evening after Thanksgiving. With the service over, Adam looked around at the sanctuary beautifully prepared for Advent. Garlands framed the baptistery; wreaths hung on the fronts of the pulpit and lectern while a red bow marked each pew. A huge Christmas tree stood in the narthex—what the congregation called the lobby— its white ornaments glowing on the dark tree. The decorating finished, everyone had adjourned next door for more decorating and refreshments.

Adam strolled back toward the parsonage, again stopping under the big tree to contemplate the house and the church and the town and life in general. He zipped his jacket, pulled his hat from a pocket, and put it on, because November evenings in Texas did get chilly. After taking a deep breath of the crisp air, he blew it out, forming a cloud of moisture in front of his mouth, and listened to the hymn "Come, Oh Come, Emmanuel" ringing in the church steeple.

Through the big windows of the parsonage, he could see the activity inside. The ladies of the church—and a few gentlemen with carpentry skills who didn't mind being bossed around—bedecked the house. After all, who could expect a single male minister to decorate the way a minister's wife would?

On the porch railings and inside, up the staircase, they'd attached evergreen branches and bright red bows. In each front window, electric candles glowed. The parsonage looked beautiful and, he bet, smelled wonderful. He'd never be able to concentrate there.

As Adam blissfully watched, Miss Birdie strode out of the house with Chewy following at her heels. After attempting to shoo the dog away several times, unsuccessfully, the pillar ignored the creature and headed straight toward her minister, pointing toward the steeple from which the music emerged.

Her expression and stride warned him he was in trouble.

"What is that song?" she demanded when she was close enough for him to hear.

"It's an Advent hymn, Miss Birdie, because we're in Advent. In churches, the Christmas season doesn't start for four more weeks."

He'd explained this over and over, but the information never sank in. Everyone wanted Christmas carols. "That's why we're playing 'Come, Oh Come, Emmanuel' instead of 'Silent Night.'"

She put her hand on her hips. "All of us"—she waved her arm toward those inside the parsonage and generally around town and the state and perhaps throughout the universe—"want Christmas music. You ministers can say anything you want, but for us, it's not Advent. It's almost Christmas. It's time for Christmas songs."

Adam glanced over her head toward the parsonage. The flickering glow of the candles and the light coming from Janey's and Hector's rooms on the second floor warmed him. In a few days, his parents would arrive to spend the holidays in Texas. They'd hate it, but they'd be here.

Thinking about the Firestones and the memory of the Smiths as well as wondering who might move in next, Adam was filled with joy. Add to that the bustle of church members inside and out, the scent of pine, and the sound of chattering and laughter, and the Victorian house was no longer the vacant building he'd moved into in June, no longer the echoingly empty residence of a single man.

He smiled. The choice of music—Advent hymns or Christmas carols—didn't seem important. "All right," he said, giving in.

Much to her surprise, Adam took the pillar's hand. "Deck the halls with boughs of holly . . . ," he sang as the two of them strolled toward the parsonage. She joined in after a few notes. "'Tis the season to be jolly . . . ," they sang together.

Taking care not to hurt her shoulder, Adam escorted the pillar up the front steps and onto the porch before he pulled her into a quick dance step as they sang, "Fa-la-la-la-la-la-la-la-la."

Wonder of all wonders, Miss Birdie laughed as they twirled inside.

The aroma of pine boughs mingled with the spicy scent of hot apple cider and surrounded them. In the hall, those church members who had gathered there joined in—"Don we now our gay apparel"—as Janey and Hector clattered down the stairs of the old Victorian house.

Adam was home.

The Matchmakers of
BUTTERNUT CREEK

This book is dedicated to all who love without prejudice, who serve without judgment, and who open the circle to include all God's children. It is dedicated to those who answer the question from Micah, "What does the LORD require of you but to do justice, and to love kindness, and to walk humbly with your God?" with their lives.

Acknowledgments

This book could not have been written without the love of church members who have supported and taught me since I was a child. Thank you.

Nor could it have been written without the joy my husband, George, has brought in all our years of marriage. I give you my eternal love and appreciation.

Many thanks to my writing friends, too numerous to mention, who have generously guided and critiqued and taught me everything I know and without whom I would never have published, and to Ellen Watkins, my pal.

To my agent, Pam Strickler, and editor, Christina Boys, great gratitude. You have believed in me and made my books better. Everyone in Butternut Creek thanks you as well. To all the nice people at Hachette, your expertise and kindness have made the way so much easier.

Prologue

From the desk of
Adam Joseph Jordan, MDiv.

I continue to be a sad burden for Birdie MacDowell. Since I arrived at the church in Butternut Creek seven months ago, I've attempted to lift that weight from her shoulders and to correct the many errors she expects me to atone for.

If she were to comment on the first paragraph of this letter, Miss Birdie would point out that I wrote a run-on sentence and ended it with a preposition. Despite my earnest efforts, I have failed her again, at least grammatically.

When I first arrived here in Butternut Creek, called to serve the Christian Church, she saw me as too young and too inexperienced for almost everything. She was correct. She believes she always is. Personally, I'd hoped the passage of time would take care of both my flaws, but Miss Birdie is not one to wait around and hope for change.

Although she's never expressed this, an odd omission for a woman who prides herself on her speaking out fearlessly, she knows that a man of my age (too young) and with a sad lack of piety could never act as her spiritual guide.

She's probably correct. I am woefully incompetent to lead another person to faith when I struggle daily with my own flaws. Thank goodness for grace from the Lord if not from Miss Birdie.

But I have discovered a few things in the months I've been here. First, I fell in love with this small town in the beautiful Hill Country of Texas the moment I arrived: the friendly people, the Victorian houses, the live oaks shadowing the streets, the downtown square surrounded by coffee

*shops and gift stores and antiques malls with a few businesses—the bar-
bershop and the diner where Miss Birdie works—sprinkled in.*

*Second, I found out I do possess some skills. I preach a good sermon,
teach an interesting adult Sunday school class, have an active youth
group, and make much-appreciated hospital calls and evangelistic visits
regularly. I've also improved my basketball game.*

*But there was one area in which Miss Birdie still found me lacking:
finding a wife and producing children to populate the children's Sunday
school classes.*

Yes, she wanted me to find a bride. Wanted *is an inadequate word
here. Even* determined *doesn't approach the level of her resolve. Add to
that adjective* single-minded *and* unwavering *and the total comes close
to her desperate need to marry me off. Do not add* choosy *to that list because she'd marry me off to any single woman still in her childbearing
years who lives within a fifty-mile radius of Butternut Creek. Her task is
made nearly impossible by the dearth of single women in small Central
Texas towns.*

*Could be she expects God to create a mate from my rib, but that hasn't
happened yet. Nor do I expect to wake up, as Boaz did, to find a bride lying
at my feet. Of course, if a woman should appear in my bed, whether at the
foot or cozily snuggled next to me, her presence in the parsonage would
create a scandal from which neither the church nor I would recover.*

*Because Miss Birdie has renounced these biblical approaches to find-
ing me a wife, I shudder to imagine what she has in her fertile and scheming mind. All for my own good, of course.*

*For the protection and edification of all involved, I decided to document
every one of the efforts she and her cohorts, the other three Widows, have
made in their attempts to find me a mate. In addition, this book will cover
my next year as minister in Butternut Creek, my search for experience and a
wife, as well as the joy of living here with the wonderful people who inhabit
this paradise.*

*I send it off with my love and my blessing and in the desperate hope that
someday Miss Birdie will smile upon me and say,* Well done, Pastor.

Chapter One

Adam Jordan stood in the upstairs hall of the huge Victorian parsonage. A wide hallway stretched to his right with three bedrooms on each side. At the end of the hallway, a stairway led up to a finished attic. He turned in the other direction and started down the curving stairs, his shoes clicking across the hardwood floors. The sound echoed through the three-story house, an enormous space for one man.

"Hey, Pops, Janey and I are leaving for school," Hector shouted.

But he no longer lived here alone. Six months ago, Hector Firestone and his younger sister, Janey, had joined him when they were left homeless.

"Bye, guys. Have a good day." Adam watched them head off before he left the parsonage, Chewy panting by his side.

For a moment he paused on the porch to look around. To the north stood the stately church he served. From here he could see only the parking lot and the back entrances, but on the front and facing the highway, tall white pillars stood out against the red brick. On the other side of the parsonage sat the house of his neighbors, Ouida and George Kowalski and their two young daughters.

As he breathed in the clean, warm air, he noticed a partially masticated backpack under the swing on the porch. He glared down at Chewy, the enormous, ugly, and affectionate creature who had arrived with Janey. Chewy smiled back at him.

"Bad boy," Adam said.

Chewy's tail went into overdrive. Adam often wondered why the dog didn't ascend and hover like a helicopter with all that spin.

"Bad dog," he repeated, which caused Chewy to perform pirouettes on his back legs.

Adam didn't have time right now to investigate or return the item to its owner. Since the habit had started a month earlier, Chewy brought home backpacks and sweaters and hoodies and water bottles, anything he found. Adam tried to keep the dog inside, but Chewy was an escape artist who zoomed through the front door whenever someone didn't watch carefully. He'd return home hours later, exhausted and happy and smelling of whatever disgusting substance he'd found to roll in. In expiation for that behavior, the dog delivered these offerings of his deep affection.

Reminding himself to get Hector to return the backpack, Adam glanced toward the Kowalski house. He hoped to see his neighbor Ouida, a Southern name that, oddly, was pronounced *Weed-a*. Many mornings she greeted him with a daughter hanging off one hand and a plate of muffins in the other. If not, he'd walk across the lawn between the parsonage and the church he happily served.

At six this morning, when he'd had to get up and let Chewy out, Adam had glimpsed Ouida's husband, George, heading toward the garage in back. In contrast with Adam's shabby robe, George wore a dark suit, tailored and conservative. Once Adam had seen George dressed casually when Ouida had forced him to help her plant a garden. Even then he looked successful and well dressed if unenthusiastic in spotless khaki slacks, expensive athletic shoes that never got dirty, and a shirt that fit him perfectly. Occasionally, Adam saw George pushing his daughters Carol and Gretchen on the swing, still immaculately dressed, still unenthusiastic.

He and George had waved. As Adam and Chewy started back to the house, George backed his spotless black Lexus out and headed toward his accounting business in Austin.

Now, three hours later, Adam waited, but Ouida didn't appear. Disappointed and muffinless, he headed toward the church, Chewy frolicking behind him.

❧

Running late as usual, Ouida set Gretchen on a kitchen chair and tied the little girl's shoes. George always told her if she planned better, she wouldn't always run five or ten minutes behind. She agreed in principle, but Carol and Gretchen, their young daughters, never stuck to a schedule—possibly because they couldn't tell time—all of which left Ouida attempting to catch up all day long.

This morning Carol couldn't find her favorite socks, which turned up, inexplicably, in the bathtub. George would've told Carol to choose another pair of socks. He didn't understand that forcing Carol to choose another pair would upset her and make her even slower.

Then, after Ouida and Gretchen had walked Carol to preschool, Gretchen . . .

Well, it seemed to be one thing after another. When she finished tying the shoes, Ouida picked up the plate of apple-cinnamon scones. "Let's see if we can find Pastor Adam."

With that, Gretchen ran to open the front door and hurry out to the porch. "There, Mama." She pointed toward Adam's back.

"Wait, Adam," Ouida called.

He turned and smiled. She hurried toward him as quickly as a short, round woman—she was all too aware of her plumpness—carrying a plate and holding the hand of a toddler could.

Living next to the parsonage had advantages, the best being that ministers and their families were nice people. However, preachers also nagged non-members about their faith and invited them, over and over, to come to church. She and George didn't want to, they were perfectly happy as they were. Adam didn't hound them, which made her like him even more. After she'd explained, he simply accepted the fact that the Kowalskis lacked the spiritual gene. "Do you like scones?"

"I like anything you bake." They chatted a few seconds before Gretchen tugged on her mother's hand in an attempt to pull her mother back toward their house.

"Thanks," he said with a wave and headed to church carrying the plate of goodies.

Ouida watched him walk away, then turned toward her home, thinking perhaps someday she and Adam could enjoy a real conversation without a child distracting her. They should have him over for dinner, should have done so months ago, but she just didn't get everything done.

Once inside, Ouida settled Gretchen in the kitchen with her toys and tackled the pile of wash in the laundry room where she could keep an eye on her daughter. After she had a load of sheets churning, she pulled the plastic bag of George's clean shirts and shorts from the freezer, opened the bag, and allowed them to warm up before she sprinkled and ironed them. George had heard that putting clean laundry in the freezer killed bugs. She allowed him to think she did but, honestly, if she put all the sheets they used in the freezer, there wouldn't be room for food. Besides, they didn't have a bug problem. But seeing that plastic bag of his things kept him happy.

By the time she'd ironed a couple of shirts, dumped the wet towels

and sheets in a basket, and started another load, she'd already taken
Gretchen to the bathroom several times.

"Let's go outside." Ouida helped her daughter into a sweater,
picked up the basket, and followed Gretchen through the back door.
The breeze would dry the sheets in no time. She loved how they
smelled when she made the bed, like spring. For a moment, she
leaned back, closed her eyes, and drew in the warmth of the sun.
Usually, the lovely day would warm her inside and out, but not today.
No, within she felt a niggling that was connected somehow to the
laundry in the freezer and sticking to a schedule. Something didn't
feel right, but she had no idea why she felt like that.

Aah, Texas! Mid-March and Adam wore a light jacket. The lack of
snow in the winter and the warmth of early spring were the trade-offs
for the horrendously hot summers here.

His poor old Honda sat in the church parking lot. After nearly a
year of sitting in the sun, it looked worse than it had when he'd arrived. Paint flaked off by the handfuls and huge patches of rust showed
through. It looked as if an especially virulent paint-eating bacteria
had attacked it. Not apparent from the outside, a spring poked through
the upholstery on the passenger side, which meant that any rider who
didn't have a cast-iron butt opted to sit in the backseat. Still, it usually ran, and often the radio worked.

The other car in the parking lot belonged to the part-time secretary, Maggie Bachelor. The lack of vehicles could mean no one awaited
him inside, or it could mean that whoever did wait for him hadn't
driven. Few places in town couldn't be reached on foot.

When he entered the church office, the look on Maggie's face
warned him all was not well. She jerked her head toward the open
door of his office in a manner that tipped him off. Miss Birdie and
maybe another Widow or two waited in his study and, he felt sure,
not patiently.

The Widows came with the church—a group of women whose
husbands had died (obviously) and who did good works. Without
them, there would be no community thrift store or food pantry, no
Thanksgiving community dinner or outreach to the homeless.

"Mary Baker went to the hospital this morning with chest pains,"
Maggie said, scratching Chewy's head and sneaking him a bite of her
breakfast burrito. "Jesse says his wife's feeling poorly, is going to the
doctor and wants your prayers, and . . ." Maggie paused before she

said in a slow, calm voice, "And Gussie Milton called about ten minutes ago." She glanced at Adam and winked. "Here's her message." She handed it to him with another wink.

Like everyone in town, Maggie showed great interest in his love life. Although it was non-existent at the moment, they all had high hopes for his eventual marriage and fatherhood. In fact, they hoped he'd be a modern Abraham, the father of a multitude. He had no expectations of such a prospect despite the Widows' shoving every woman in town at him until they finally settled on Gussie being the perfect mate. For that reason, he attempted to keep his expression neutral. Impossible. Only hearing the name *Gussie* made him want to laugh and sing and celebrate. If they heard one of those sounds, the Widows would start planning a wedding.

So he nodded and took a deep breath before heading toward his office, preparing himself for whatever was coming.

"Hear you haven't found a wife yet," Birdie said.

Miss Birdie sat in what she considered *her* chair: in front of Adam's desk but slightly turned so she could see the door as well, in case someone interesting stopped by.

Winnie Jenkins sat next to her and smiled at Adam. "Good morning, Preacher." She wore her white hair swept back and had a nice smile. An engagement ring sparkled on her left hand.

Miss Birdie wore her aggrieved look-what-I-have-to-put-up-with face, her usual expression with the young, inexperienced man who'd foolishly assumed he'd minister to her.

Short, no-nonsense hair and thick-soled shoes completed the picture of the pillar of the church. Because she barely topped five feet and had that snowy white hair, Miss Birdie resembled one of Santa's kindly and jolly but skinny elves. Ha! Amazing how quickly those lips became a straight line, her expression hardened, and disapproving words gushed from her mouth in time with her waving index finger.

But she had a good heart.

Yes, he repeated to himself, she had a good heart and was a beloved child of God.

"Sit down, sit down." With her right hand, the pillar waved graciously toward the chair behind his desk as if this were her office.

He could tell from the way she cradled her left arm that her shoulder hurt. Tough injury for a waitress.

After he placed the plate on the desk, he sat and tossed the message from Gussie next to it.

The pillar's eyes pounced on that piece of paper. He could read her thoughts, knew she was considering reaching over, picking the message up, and reading it. After an internal struggle that showed in her changing expressions, she must have decided that this would be ruder than even she dared to behave.

"It's a lovely morning, isn't it?" Winnie glanced at the plate.

With no reason to keep Ouida's goodies for himself, he took from his drawer the stack of napkins that he kept just in case something delicious showed up.

Each took a scone and savored it. He hoped it would distract the pillar from her purpose. Once in a while, he succeeded in slowing her down, but like a blue heeler, a favorite breed of dog among Texas hunters, she returned to the scent every time. "Mercedes will be here soon," Winnie said. "She had a meeting."

That explained the absence of the third member.

"I saw in the *Butternut Creek Chronicle* that Mac was initiated into the honor society," Adam said in what would be a failed effort to head the pillar off. Still, he tried. She expected it. He enjoyed it.

"Yes, she was, and Bree was named to the district third team in both volleyball and basketball. Don't try to distract me by mentioning my granddaughter, Preacher." She leaned forward to capture his eyes. "You know how proud I am of those girls, but that's not why I'm here." Once she knew he was paying attention, she settled back and smiled.

Now in charge, she was in no hurry. In every conversation, Miss Birdie considered him either the bait or the victim. Didn't much matter which. Neither came to a good end.

"What time are you leaving for the youth retreat tomorrow?" the pillar asked.

"I'm going to pick the kids up from school at three."

"Who's going?"

She knew this, but if it kept her from confronting him with whatever was on her mind, answering didn't bother him. "Your granddaughters, Hector, and his friend Bobby."

"What are you going to do there?" Winnie asked, sounding interested. "At the retreat?"

"I'm leading a small group and preaching at worship Sunday."

"What are you driving?" The pillar continued her interrogation with a glare at Winnie to leave the questions to her. "Not your car, I hope."

"Howard loaned me his van."

"About that sermon." She leaned toward him. "Don't make it long and boring. Young people like short."

"Right." His agreement always made her happy.

For a moment, the pillar studied him while Winnie grinned at the engagement ring the general, father of Adam's best friend, had placed on her finger only weeks ago.

"Will Gussie Milton be there? At the retreat?" Miss Birdie spoke casually, almost tossing off the comment.

Exactly what Adam had expected was the reason for her visit. He tensed, almost feeling the trap vibrate milliseconds before it snapped shut. *Dear Lord, please grant me patience and wisdom*, he prayed silently. *Patience and wisdom. Amen.*

"Yes," he said aloud.

"She's a nice young woman. Unmarried, as I remember."

As if she didn't know that. "Yes," he said.

Then, in a quick attempt to change the subject, Adam turned toward the other Widow and said casually, "Winnie, now that you're going to marry Sam's father . . ."

"Don't know if she will," Birdie grumbled. "They may live in sin for tax purposes."

"Birdie." Winnie put her hands on cheeks that were turning pink. "How could you say that? Mitchell and I . . ."

"But don't try to sidetrack me, Preacher. *You're* not married yet, not engaged yet. That's our biggest worry and failure," she said with a sorrowful sigh that told of the unimaginable depths of her disappointment.

"All in good time," he temporized. "All in good time."

Miss Birdie wasn't finished. "What I'm saying is that if Gussie Milton's going to the retreat, you'd better put those days to good use."

He heard the wagging of a finger in her voice and shuddered to contemplate what Miss Birdie had in mind. She probably expected him to marry Gussie on Friday evening and have her heavy with child by Sunday.

"About Winnie's wedding," he said, restating his topic.

"About Gussie Milton," Miss Birdie countered.

"We hear she left a message this morning," Winnie said.

"I haven't read it yet." He gestured toward the pink slip.

Both Widows leaned far forward in an effort to read that square of paper tantalizingly close to them in the center of the desk. He picked it up, folded the note, and stuck it into the pocket of his shirt.

Then, thankfully, because he didn't put it past Miss Birdie to pluck the message from his pocket, Mercedes Rivera stuck her head in the door. "Sorry I'm late. Long meeting." She hurried in and settled in a chair on the other side of Miss Birdie.

"Welcome, Mercedes," he said.

In contrast with the other Widows, Mercedes, the town librarian, had dark hair, liberally streaked with white and pulled back into a French braid. With a fuller body than Miss Birdie, she also displayed a sweet smile, one that Adam almost always trusted. She was polite and, most important, seldom harassed him.

Adam took the few seconds her arrival gave him to return to his topic. "When Winnie marries Sam's father—"

"If she does," Miss Birdie said.

"We are going to—" Winnie started to say.

"—the number of Widows is going to decrease again," Adam finished.

"We're not going to kick Winnie out," Mercedes said. "We'll still have three Widows."

"Miss Birdie," he said with deep concern in his voice. "With work and raising your granddaughters and all you do for the church, I fear you might become . . ." He paused to think of a word that wouldn't insult her. There were none. Miss Birdie was easily affronted.

"Weary in my efforts?" She glared at him for suggesting she might possess limits of any kind.

He couldn't mention her health problems, especially that bad shoulder. If he did, she'd—as they said on the basketball court— open a can of whoop-ass on him.

"You're a very busy woman. All your good works are far more important than getting me married off." He turned to Winnie. "And with your engagement . . ."

❦

Birdie glanced toward the other Widows, then back at the preacher as he trailed off. In that instant, Birdie noted a fleeting expression of satisfaction flit across his face and realized she and Winnie and Mercedes had walked right into *his* trap.

"Well, Mercedes, you missed our entire discussion," she said in an effort to circumvent whatever the preacher was fixin' to bring up. "We're finished. Time to get a move on." Birdie struggled to stand, but when she lifted herself an inch off the chair, that blasted shoulder collapsed and dropped her back down. Doggone it! Betrayed by her own body, but she'd be darned if she'd let anyone know about it. She pretended she'd only changed position.

"Not quite," the preacher said. "We were about to discuss the Widows with Winnie's change in status."

Mercedes whispered to Birdie, "I didn't think that's what you wanted to talk about."

Always truthful, that Mercedes. How in the world had Birdie ended up with a friend like her?

"Let's talk about the Widows," Adam repeated insistently. He stood, walked around the desk, and settled in a chair closer to them. "You'll be shorthanded with Winnie getting married."

"If she does," the pillar grumbled.

Winnie frowned at her but remained silent. Winnie was well aware that arguing with her never accomplished a thing.

"Oh, no, Preacher. With Pansy and Winnie to help us . . . ," Mercedes began.

"Pansy is a wonderful help to the congregation, and a great cook. But she isn't a Widow and she's married."

Birdie leaned to the right, still attempting to find a comfortable position. "Pastor, you're the one who convinced me to break with tradition and make Winnie Jenkins a Widow when she'd never married. Not that I'm saying we should make Pansy a Widow, mind you." Fact was, Pansy had turned them down before. With her mother's poor health, she said she just didn't have time. Besides, if they started letting just anyone join, they wouldn't be the Widows would they?

"I have another suggestion," the preacher said.

Birdie didn't like suggestions, not from anyone, but he just kept right on suggesting.

"Blossom Brown," he said.

"Blossom Brown?" Birdie snorted. "Silly name for an elderly . . ." She paused for a second, realizing she and Blossom were about the same age. "Silly name for an adult."

"Besides, Preacher," Winnie said, "she's not a real widow. She's a grass widow."

"Her husband left her for some young trophy wife," Mercedes said. "Not that the whole situation isn't sad, but her husband didn't die. She's . . . she's . . ." Mercedes paused before she whispered, "divorced."

"Yes." He gave her a ministerial nod. "She went through a difficult divorce."

"Sad, so very sad." Birdie infused her words with sympathy before she snapped, "But she's not a real widow."

"Ladies, whether he died or ran out on her, Blossom is alone in that big house by the lake, and she wants to serve someplace."

Mercedes nodded. "I know this has been hard for her, but Blossom"—she raised her hand in front of her—"well, I don't want to sound judgmental or unkind, but she's not like us, not a bit." She dropped her hand and said, "She's rich and has a cook and a house-keeper."

"Why would she have the slightest interest in doing the work the Widows do?" Winnie asked.

"Guess you'll know that only if you give her a try." He paused. "She's alone. No children."

"Pastor." Birdie took charge of the discussion. "She's what we call 'high maintenance.' That champagne-colored hair doesn't come cheap. And those nails? I'll bet she gets them done weekly in Austin. How could she scrub a floor?" Birdie shook her head. "Why would she want to?"

"And, well, she's not from here," Winnie said. "She doesn't know how to do things."

"Not the way we do them," Mercedes agreed.

"I believe," Adam said, "she was born in Louisiana, and she seems to be a true Southern lady."

"Well, I can't understand a word she says with that accent. Besides." Birdie leaned forward. "I can't see her as a Widow." She nodded, a motion that they all knew signaled the end of discussion. Not that the preacher ever acknowledged it.

"You couldn't see Winnie as a Widow but she worked out."

"Not completely. I've had to train her."

"What?" Winnie sat up straight and blinked. "Train me?"

"All right. Winnie worked out fine. Then she decided to get married." Birdie sniffed pointedly. Winnie's choice still rankled. "As for Blossom Brown, she's not really a member of the church. Doesn't she still belong to that la-di-da church in Austin? She and her husband seldom attended services here. Maybe once a month, if that often."

"And she wears *hats*, Preacher," Mercedes said. "No one wears hats anymore, except Blossom. Bird, do you remember that yellow one she wore last Easter? Prettiest thing I've ever seen and must have cost more than you make in tips in a couple of weeks."

"Which again makes me wonder *why* she'd want to be a Widow," Birdie said. "We're plain folks, Mercedes, Winnie, and I. We don't wear beautiful tailored clothing and fancy hats."

"Because she's lonely. She needs the church now. Whether she's come every Sunday, she's attended more often than some of our members. Ladies, she needs to be part of the church. She needs to be a Widow." He paused and seemed to search for words before he continued. "When I visited her last week, she told me she'd gotten the house in the divorce settlement and would be living out here permanently. She has nothing to do with her life now that she no longer entertains for her husband or travels with him."

"Beautiful house," Mercedes said. "Out on the lake."

"I hear she has a wonderful view," Winnie added. "I'd love to see the inside."

For almost a minute, Birdie exchanged looks with the other Widows, silently weighing the pros and cons. In the end, that beautiful lake house tipped the scales. But nothing had been decided, and Birdie didn't want the preacher to think otherwise.

"We will discuss this." She stood, pushing herself to her feet with her good arm. "I'm not promising anything."

"Pastor, don't forget the spring bazaar and chicken spaghetti dinner coming up next month," Winnie said as they gathered their possessions to leave.

"Make sure you get some signs out and get a few articles in the newspaper. And remember your responsibility at that retreat, finding a wife." Birdie turned toward the door and strode out, the other two following.

Once they stood in the parking lot, Birdie said, "I think we made ourselves very clear."

"Yes, you did," Mercedes agreed.

"But, you know, he doesn't always do what we tell him to," Winnie said.

A grievous disappointment to them all.

Adam knew exactly how the Widows felt. Unfortunately, courting a woman was one area he had no idea how to approach. Tell him to preach a better sermon and he'd work on that. Give him a list of shut-ins and he'd visit. Mention that a kid needed a place to spend the night and he'd make up a bed in a spare room of the parsonage.

But find a wife in a town with no single women except for Sister Mary Timothy down at the Catholic Church and his friend Reverend Mattie Patillo? He had no idea how to manage that.

He reached in his pocket and pulled out the note Maggie had left him about Gussie's call. "She'll see you Friday at the retreat," he read. "Call her cell if you have questions."

He smiled. Not a particularly personal note. He'd prefer a protestation of undying love.

Then a terrible idea hit him. Certainly the Widows wouldn't track him down at the youth retreat in the thickly wooded campground south of Gonzalez. Surely they'd stop short of stalking him there, of appearing and coercing Gussie to accept his clumsy courting.

Of course they wouldn't do that.

But he wasn't about to place a bet on their ability to resist temptation.

Chapter Two

Gussie Milton wasn't a pink person. She preferred vibrant colors, hence her yellow car, the red accent wall in her bedroom, and the pile of orange and bright green and purple T-shirts that lay next to the duffel bag on her bed.

Her mother loved to tell about the time a three-year-old Gussie refused to go to church in a frilly pink dress, how she'd removed that ultra-feminine garment and put on jeans and a UT shirt. Gussie always wondered why a mother who named her daughter for a favorite uncle could expect that daughter to wear a pink dress.

"Gus," her father called from downstairs, interrupting her inspection of the jumble of colors on her bed. "Want to watch television with us? One of those singing shows is on."

"No thanks, Dad. I have a lot left to do."

She picked up the date book on her desk and turned to toss it into a tote. Three bags were lined up by the door: the red one for work, the orange one for the district youth, the one covered in sunflowers for church. Her entire life, organized in totes. She sighed. Someday she'd like to add a purple tote labeled MY LIFE, because she didn't have one now.

Always active in youth group and retreats and summer camp, she'd fallen into that again when she graduated from college and came back home. Her friend Clare Montoya had suggested the reason she worked with teenagers was because she didn't have children of her own. A possible explanation. However, even if she didn't work with the church kids, she still wouldn't have children of her own.

Little by little, she'd taken more responsibility, from working with the high school youth here and growing the group from three to fifteen regulars, to taking "her kids" to camp, to being in charge of the district youth. She loved it because working with young people gave her life meaning. Their joyful faith inspired her and pulled her out of herself.

After she put the book in the orange bag, her cell rang. She glanced at the caller ID. Jimmy Flock, a minister from San Antonio. Did she want to talk to him? Yes, despite having more preparation to do than she had time for, she'd answer. He always supported the district youth programs. "Hey," she said. "You're not calling to cancel for the retreat, are you?"

"Would I do that? No, just checking to see if you need me to do anything."

"Bless you. I can't think of anything."

Then he said exactly what he always did. "How's your love life?"

Didn't he realize what a pushy and intrusive question that was? No one asked a woman of thirty-one about her love life because chances were good she didn't have one. Maybe it had been witty banter fifty years ago, but now it was just plain embarrassing. As usual, she answered with a joke: "Oh, Jimmy, we don't have time for me to tell you the details."

"Still not married, huh?"

"I'll let you know when that happens."

"Okay."

"Anything else?" she asked.

After discussing a few details of the youth retreat, he said, "I looked over the information you sent in the mail. I see that new minister in Butternut Creek—what's his name? Adam something?—is preaching Sunday morning. What's he like? Have you met him yet?"

"Yes, for coffee a few times to discuss the retreat. Seems like a nice kid. He'll be fine." She looked at the piles of clothing and her full totes. "Hey, I've got a bunch of stuff to do, but I'll have time to talk more when I see you tomorrow."

Why, she pondered after she hung up, why did people believe her marital status was any of their business? Particularly people who didn't know her well.

Because she was a compulsive list maker, she settled in front of her laptop to check the one about what she needed to take with her. She had it all ready. As long as she was there, she sent a quick email to Clare, her friend since the church nursery and one of the few people who knew what had happened to Gussie thirteen years earlier. Gussie's other friends had moved away after graduation. They kept up by email and with occasional visits, but Clare—dear Clare—

was always around. Though now that Clare had three children and lived an hour outside of Austin, they didn't get together nearly as often as they would have liked.

That finished, Gussie turned back toward the heap of clothing, picked up a TCU T-shirt, folded it, and lobbed it toward her duffel bag. As she reached for a pair of jeans, she grinned in anticipation of the upcoming retreat. She loved teenagers and always enjoyed working with the other adults. Maybe she'd get to know that young minister from Butternut Creek better, too. Seemed like a nice guy.

After filling the bag, she zipped it and slung it over her shoulder as she headed down the stairs toward the living room.

"About ready, dear?" Her mother picked up the remote and muted the television as Gussie dropped the bag by the front door.

"I have a few more things to pack. Tomorrow morning, I'll grab everything and take off." She sat next to her mother on the sofa. "You'll be okay?"

"We old folks will make it through the weekend, especially with all the help you've rounded up and the freezer full of meals." She patted Gussie's hand. "You worry too much."

She knew she did, but this was her mother who'd loved and cared for and supported her during the most terrible months of Gussie's life. Without her parents, she'd never have made it through. She owed them everything.

"How's your blood sugar?" Gussie asked. "Can I get you a cookie or a glass of milk?"

"Stop hovering, dear. I'm fine."

"Hey, Gus, looks like you're ready to abandon us." Her father came from the kitchen with a glass of tea.

"Henry, don't say that. You know how much she hates to leave us."

Maybe she shouldn't go to the retreat. If anything happened to them while she was gone . . .

"Gus, don't worry. We've been taking care of ourselves for decades."

"Find yourself a nice young man while you're there," her mother said. "You know, we'd like grandchildren while we're still young enough to play with them."

Must be a symptom of growing older, the desire to match everyone up, like Noah taking the animals onto the Ark two-by-two. Or it could be biblical, that Be-fruitful-and-multiply section of Genesis. Maybe it was a biological instinct, preservation of the species. But for her parents, maybe it was as her mother said: They'd like to see a grandchild before they died.

"Yes, Mother, of course. That's exactly why I go to these retreats with lots of high school kids and married ministers. To find a husband."

"Leave her alone, Yvonne. She'll get married when she finds the right man."

Her mother sighed. "But how will she do that, Henry? She never meets any single men."

"Leave the girl alone."

"Yes, leave the girl alone." Gussie laughed and headed toward the door. "I have to run in to work for a few hours, finish up some stuff." The daily drive to Austin to her photography studio was an accepted trade-off for her choice to care for her parents in Roundville.

Everything would be fine. She knew that, but her mind kept running, making sure. A compulsive fixer, she knew all the checking, planning, thinking, and analyzing she did was in an effort to control a life that had spun out of control. Think everything over and over, make lists, foresee every possible risk, and make absolutely sure nothing, not the tiniest thing, could ever go wrong. At times she felt as if she were juggling armadillos.

"Okay, God," she whispered. "Be my strength. You and I can handle everything together."

❦

"We have to do something about the choir." Birdie leaned closer to Mercedes. The Widows—this afternoon only the two of them because for some odd reason Mercedes had insisted they not include Winnie—had met at their usual place, the diner where Birdie waited tables. Both had a cup of coffee. Between them sat a few slices of banana bread from Butch's bakery left over from breakfast.

"What?" Mercedes groaned. "You and I can't sing. Not that we'd be any worse than Ralph and the three women who mumble the hymns."

"They're pitiful. It would be nice to have them sing something, like a prayer response, instead of having them sit up there in the choir loft and watch the congregation."

"I swear, last Sunday Ethel Peavey was doing a crossword puzzle inside her music folder." Mercedes broke off the corner of the last slice of bread and nibbled on it. "And Ralph Foxx fell asleep. Terrible to have an elder sitting behind the minister and snoring through the sermon."

"You know I occasionally disagree with the preacher." Birdie fixed Mercedes with a glare that dared her to comment on the statement. "But he does deliver a good sermon. We don't have a choir up there, only four people who don't even stand for the hymns."

"And what will we do about a fill-in organist? With Jenny on maternity leave, who's going to play?"

"I don't know who's available in town, but we have to have someone. The choir can't lead congregational singing, and you know how terrible the preacher's voice is."

Her friend glanced down at her coffee, studying it as if she could read fortunes in the grounds, not that she'd find any in a pot Birdie brewed. She recognized her friend's slight hesitation and knew it to mean nothing good. Before she could jump in to forestall Mercedes's words, the other Widow lifted her eyes toward Birdie and asked, "What do you think about Farley Masterson?"

"What should I think about him?" Birdie shook her head. "He's a grumpy old Methodist . . ."

"He's our age, Bird. Maybe a few years older."

"Okay, he's a man our age who's a Methodist and grumpy."

"He's nice looking for a man of his age, and you two have a lot in common." Mercedes blinked twice.

Oh, she knew that expression, too. She'd first seen it when Mercedes had grabbed Birdie's Betsy-Wetsy doll back in the church nursery. It meant nothing good.

If there was one thing Birdie didn't want to talk about, it was what she and Farley had in common. They'd both lost daughters to drugs. Oh, the two girls—women now—were still alive as far as Birdie knew, but their addictions had ruined them, made them leave their homes and families and go to some big city where getting drugs and finding a way to pay for them was easier.

But Birdie's daughter, Martha Patricia, had left behind her two daughters for their grandmother to raise. Sometimes the stress of rearing teenage girls made her feel more than her nearly seventy years of age.

A friend for most of those years, Mercedes could read Birdie's face easily. "You know you love those girls. You'd've shriveled up and died after Elmer passed if you hadn't had those girls around."

"Mercedes Olivia Suárez de Rivera, I have never, ever, in my whole life contemplated curling up and dying."

"But you do dote on those girls."

"I swan!" The woman was so persistent Birdie wondered why she'd put up with her for all these years. "Where is this conversation going?"

"I'm only saying that you and Farley Masterson have that in common."

"He's not raising his grandchildren."

"No, but . . ."

"Mercedes." Birdie raised her right eyebrow. "Why are you talking about Farley Masterson? I haven't seen the old coot"—she stopped and changed that description—"I haven't spoken to the man in years."

"You know he used to keep company with that widow over in San Saba."

Birdie scrutinized her friend's face. "Are you interested in Farley? Do you want my permission to keep company with him?"

"Oh, for heaven's sake, no." Mercedes shook her head. "You know I've been seeing Bill Jones down at the bank for years. We're comfortable together."

"So why did you mention Farley?"

Mercedes blinked again. Birdie knew her friend wasn't trying to sneak away with her favorite doll, but the expression did mean she had something devious in mind.

"You aren't suggesting that I—that *I* should keep company with Farley Masterson, are you?"

"Would that be too horrible? When you are alone—and you will be, Bird, when the girls both go off to school—wouldn't you like to have a man in your life?"

"I'm gobsmacked," she said.

"I'm not sure that's the word you want," Mercedes said. "That's fairly new British slang."

"What does it mean?" Mercedes always thought she knew everything. Drove Birdie crazy.

"Astounded, bewildered . . ." Mercedes began counting the words off on her fingers.

"Then it is *exactly* the word I'm looking for." She paused for maximum effect. "I'm absolutely gobsmacked. In the first place, I know Farley from back when he was sheriff. He picked up my daughter about every week, brought her home. We spent quite a bit of time together. Our relationship was not particularly friendly back then and hasn't improved."

"And in the second place?" Mercedes encouraged.

"In the second place, have you forgotten that the challenge for the Widows is to find mates for other people, for our minister, not for ourselves? I'm happy with my life as it is, extremely happy." She snorted, which *should* have suggested the topic was closed.

"I . . . ," Mercedes began.

"Don't have time for anything more in my life, much less a man. Now let's talk about what the Widows can do for others."

Her friend closed her mouth, but Birdie could tell the subject wasn't finished. Mercedes was as stubborn as she was. Probably the only reason they'd remained friends all these years.

"Is this the reason you didn't want Winnie here? Because you wanted to talk about the old . . ." Birdie paused. "You wanted to talk about me and Farley"—she rolled her eyes—"in private?"

"Well, not only that. I miss you and me, the two of us being alone to chat."

Birdie didn't believe that excuse for a moment, but before she could respond, Mercedes asked, "What do you think about inviting Blossom Brown to be a Widow?"

"*If* we were to invite her, what would she do? What skills does she have?" Birdie asked, then answered herself. "She couldn't plan a sympathy dinner. She's always had a cook."

"Don't need her to plan meals. Pansy has that well in hand. She's always done that. Pansy's a good worker even though she's not a Widow."

"Blossom's always had servants. She wouldn't like to clean the thrift shop."

"We don't know that. We could give her a chance," Mercedes said in the pleasant voice that fooled so many people into thinking she was so very sweet and so completely unlike Birdie. "Make it sort of like a test. If she can't do it, we could train her, you and I. You're a great trainer."

"Pfutt."

"We could make her a provisional member, like we did with Winnie. It wouldn't hurt. With the bazaar and dinner coming up, she could help. More hands would lighten the load." Mercedes glanced at her old friend. "Not that we *need* the load lightened."

Birdie pondered Mercedes's words for nearly a minute. "All right. We should probably do this. It'll make the preacher happy."

"If he's happy, he'll be less suspicious of our efforts to get him married." Mercedes broke off another piece of banana bread. "Why don't we invite Blossom to go with us next time we visit the preacher or ask her to join us for coffee some afternoon. Get to know her a little better."

Good idea. As much as she'd like to punish Mercedes a little bit for suggesting she allow Farley Masterson to court her, not even at her most difficult—which could be pretty darned difficult—could Birdie turn down a sensible proposal. She nodded. "You ask her. She's more likely to come if you call. I scare her. Winnie probably does, too."

Chapter Three

Adam ran his finger around the collar of his shirt, attempting to loosen it. He wore one of his three dress shirts to the office every day but seldom buttoned it or wore a tie. He'd noticed last Sunday that the shirt collar seemed tight around the neck. He'd solved that by using the neck expander—a button and an elastic loop—he'd found in his desk, left, he guessed, by a previous minister with a similar problem.

Because he'd planned to preach at the retreat Sunday morning in a shirt and tie, he tried on another. Also tight, and not only around his neck but in the shoulders. The next one felt snug as well.

Could he have put on a little weight? Maybe some muscle? He couldn't weigh himself because he didn't have a scale. The total always depressed him because as much as he ate, he never gained a pound.

Maybe he had. Could be all those meals Miss Birdie forced on him, the food the congregation dropped off, and Ouida's treats had begun to work. He studied himself in the bathroom mirror. He looked less skinny. He'd either have to buy new shirts or invest in a few more neck expanders. Fortunately, the knit shirts still fit. He'd preach in one of those. He tossed a few in his duffel bag and left it open to finish packing in the morning.

The next day, on the drive to the retreat, Mac sat next to Adam in the front seat of the borrowed van. Bree lay on the bench seat at the far back because Hector and Bobby had taken the comfortable swiveling seats in the middle. "Long legs," the guys had explained.

As they pulled into the campground, the sun was heading toward the horizon. They got out of the van and stretched. Adam noticed the sound of crickets at the same time the smell of wood smoke from the lodge greeted them.

The setting didn't impress the guys.

"This is really . . ." Hector paused to think of a word.

"Rustic?" Adam suggested as he popped the back of the vehicle.

"No, primitive."

"Yeah." Bobby nodded. "Do they have running water?"

"Haven't you been to camp before?" Mac pulled two small bags from the vehicle.

"Basketball camp, but that's in dorms on a college campus. I have to check this out." Bobby swaggered toward the recreation hall. Nice kid, Adam knew, but Bobby loved to show a little 'tude.

"Not luxury," Adam said. "But . . ."

He didn't finish because Gussie exploded out of the building in typical Gussie fashion, waved, and shouted, "Welcome."

"That's Gussie," Bree said to Hector. "She directs the retreats and camps every year. She's great."

Wearing jeans and a bright green T-shirt with WALK IN FAITH printed on it and her dark hair curling around her smiling face, she looked very different from the professional woman he'd met before. The kids with him grinned because no one could *not* smile when she did. Adam both smiled and blinked. Fortunately, his mouth hadn't flopped open. He glanced at the kids, hoping none had noticed his response.

Mac had. She wore a sly smile that looked exactly like Miss Birdie's at her most dangerous.

"It's okay," she whispered. "I won't tell Grandma you like Gussie. I know what she's like."

He had to believe she'd keep her word. No other acceptable choice.

"Come on in. Time to get your packets. Don't forget to pick up a T-shirt and sign up for chores."

"Sign up for chores?" Bobby grumbled. "Hector, what did I let you talk me into? I could've stayed home. My mother has a whole list of chores for me."

After Bree and Mac gave Gussie a quick hug, they led the grumbling Bobby and Hector into the enormous and echoing all-purpose room. Several adults and about thirty kids wandered around and greeted one another.

"Pick up your stuff, then take your bags upstairs and find a bunk," Gussie said. "Girls on the south; boys on the north. Meet us down here in a few minutes at the basketball court."

"You gonna play?" Hector asked Bree.

"Sure. I play on the team at school. Varsity." She glared, looking tough. "You know that."

"Yeah, but . . . don't want you to get hurt," Bobby said.

"Let's wait and see who gets hurt," Bree challenged.

Later in the day during a quick pickup game, Adam watched as both Bree and Hector went up for a rebound. Although Hector had five inches in height and fifty pounds on Bree, she had sharper elbows and more determination. She came down with the ball.

"Hey," he said as he rubbed his side after the game. "You don't play like a girl."

"Told you."

"We were taking it easy on you," Bobby said.

"Next time, don't." With that, Bree dribbled toward the dining hall. She reached the edge of the court, turned, and shot. As the ball swished in, Adam cheered.

Before Bobby could grab the ball, Gussie came out with a bag. "Looks like a terrific game, guys." She smiled at everyone and motioned for them to gather around her. "Tonight the youth group from Roundville is setting the tables." She grinned at the groans from her youth. "Hey, don't complain. You get to do this because you're special." She clapped to quiet them. "Dinner in twenty minutes. We have just enough time for Slinky races on the steps down to the pool." She started flinging the toys around. "Winner doesn't do chores tonight." With that, everyone took off toward the pool.

❦

After dinner, Gussie stood and waved at the group. "Welcome!" she said and the kids all clapped and stamped their feet and shouted, "Gussie! Gussie—"

She quieted the group, made announcements, then asked, "Anyone want to sing?"

Campers shouted song suggestions.

"Okay, let's start with this one. Everyone join in. 'If you're happy . . .'"

Gussie had a wonderful voice, strong and clear. She walked around the tables as she led the group, encouraging and bringing the voices together. When they began "Silver Spade," she coaxed harmony from the group with a movement of her hand.

Was there anything Gussie couldn't do?

After several songs and a glance at her watch, she said, "Cleanup crew, get started. Adults, meet at the center tables. Vespers at seven."

As Hector stood to start his chores, he said, "Gussie's got a great voice. We need her in our choir."

"She'd sure liven up the service," Bobby added. "You know, it's pretty boring."

Bree laughed. "She'd sing a solo every Sunday and probably keep Mr. Foxx awake."

Then Mac grinned at Adam. If he'd thought she hadn't noticed how much Gussie had entranced him during the singing, he was wrong.

❧

At the counselors' meeting after dinner, the adults listened while Gussie handed out schedules and took questions. Then she introduced Adam as "the new kid on the block." She smiled at him in exactly the same way she'd smiled at Jimmy Flock, the gray-haired minister. Pleasant, happy to see both of them. Darn. The attraction obviously didn't go both ways.

"We're going to need a patrol outside from midnight to two o'clock," Gussie said. "After that, those most determined to escape should be asleep and we can get some rest. I'll take it tonight but need another volunteer and two for tomorrow night."

"I'll join you tonight," Adam said before anyone else could speak.

"Terrific. We can get to know each other," Gussie said. "Who'll sign up for tomorrow?"

The schedule of vespers, games, refreshments, and corralling campers attempting to escape the building kept him busy after the meeting. By midnight, the youth were simulating sleep while the adults had dozed off as soon as their heads hit the pillows.

The time had come to meet Gussie in the dining hall and start on their rounds.

And it was time for Adam to consider how to behave with Gussie. Oh, he wouldn't back her against a tree and kiss her passionately until she begged for more. Not that he'd turn that down if the opportunity appeared, but it didn't seem realistic. Nor would he attempt to gaze longingly into her eyes. In the dark, she wouldn't notice anyway.

As he opened the screen door to enter the dining hall, he still had no plan. He saw Gussie at one of the tables waiting for him, her face pensive. She was lovely in repose. Usually, all that joie de vivre lit up her face. The vibrancy was what everyone noticed. Now, in this moment of calm, he realized she radiated beauty as well.

"Hey," she greeted him with a smile. "Let's get going. You're the muscle and I'm the mouth. If we find anyone, you grab them and I'll lecture."

She handed him a flashlight, and they stepped outside into the glare of the halogen lights that surrounded the dining hall. Moving beyond that, they headed toward the lake.

"The lake's man-made, of course," Gussie said.

Man-made lakes. Exactly the best choice of subjects for a romantic rendezvous between a man and a woman alone beneath the glow of a full moon and surrounded by the soft darkness and a sweetly scented breeze.

"Of course?" he asked. Pitiful effort, but that was the best reply he could come up with to begin his wooing.

"Caddo's the only natural lake in Texas. The rest are manmade."

"Interesting." He sounded like an idiot. He wished he could come up with a dazzling and witty comment about manmade lakes, but no flirtatious responses leaped to mind. "Where's Caddo?"

"Over on the border with Louisiana. Pretty place. You should go there someday."

"I should."

Those words pretty much stopped the tête-à-tête. As they moved down an uneven path, he thought about reaching out to help Gussie over a log but knew she wasn't the kind of woman who wanted or expected a gentleman to take care of her and make sure she—a delicate flower—didn't trip.

"How are things in Butternut Creek?" she asked after they'd walked nearly the length of a football field—Adam had adjusted to this normal measure of distance in Texas.

"Are you asking about the state of the church or how Miss Birdie and I get along?"

She laughed. "Yes, that's really what I wanted to ask. How are the two of you doing? I'd imagine a young, single minister wasn't what she had in mind."

"You know her well."

"Not really. I've met her, but my parents have known her forever. She's a legend in the churches of Central Texas."

"She's working hard to train me. If I'd only do everything she wants exactly as she wants it, she's sure I'd be much happier and more successful."

"Perceptive of you."

They arrived at a picnic table halfway around the lake with a clear view of the dorms above the dining hall. A halogen light stood twenty yards away and lent a hazy glow to the area.

"Why don't we sit here and keep an eye out?" he asked.

Silence fell between them again as the two looked across the lake. A comfortable silence. A *friendly* silence.

"Why the need for a patrol?" he asked. "Do kids often sneak out of the dorms?"

"Usually not. These are good kids. They'll stay up and talk and fool around, but most of the time, the adults keep them in line." She paused.

He read into that an unvoiced concern. "But?" he prompted.

"It doesn't hurt to have the campers know we're out here, just in case. We've had a few incidents, but only one that amounted to anything, one best forgotten." Her voice lost the usual animation. "One that really upset me."

He couldn't read her expression because the tree branches trapped and diffused the dim light, but he could read her slumping shoulders.

Before he could ask another question, Gussie jumped to her feet.

"Well, enough of that." Her voice sounded happy, and her stance looked filled with confidence.

Which was the real Gussie Milton? Oh, he knew people had good moments and bad, but the change in her had come so suddenly that it took him a few more seconds to realize what had happened. That quick flash from a melancholy Gussie to a high-spirited Gussie confused him.

"Let's get going." She headed toward the other end of the lake. "While we're sitting here, someone could be climbing out a rear window."

"Aren't there enough adults inside to make sure that doesn't happen?" He took several long steps to catch up with her. "Aren't adults sleeping by all the doors and windows?"

"Yes, but after a long drive and a couple of hours rounding up kids, the adults sleep deeply. Kids can crawl over them and right out the windows."

"But the dorms are on the second floor."

"That makes it more of a challenge." She laughed. "Besides, there's a flat roof over the kitchen with a big tree next to it."

"Sounds like you've had experience."

"Hey, kid, I wasn't always an elderly stick-to-the-rules counselor. That's why I know how to handle the campers."

"Hey, lady," he said. "You're not that much older than me."

She laughed, a sound that expressed complete lack of agreement.

❧

Saturday, the second day of the retreat, started warm. By one thirty, it had increased to just plain hot. After the morning group meetings, lunch, and the usually ignored hour of rest, Gussie settled on one of the benches surrounding the basketball court where Adam and four players from Butternut Creek battled against a team from Kingsland in a playoff game of the annual challenge. Didn't seem quite fair because Butternut Creek had three high school starters—Hector, Bobby, and Bree—but Adam seemed to be the force the other teams couldn't match up against, and Mac held her own.

As everyone watched, Adam drove and hustled and focused, pointed out the defense, distributed the ball, shouted instructions to the others, and had a great time doing it all. This was an Adam Gussie hadn't seen before, didn't realize existed. This was a man who took charge with confidence.

"Dish the rock," he shouted at Bobby, who liked to hog the ball. Then Adam said, "Good job," after Mac successfully battled for a board. A few seconds later, he set a screen for Hector for a shot from downtown.

Halfway through the game, the players were soaked with sweat.

Oh, my. Adam not only played ball well, he looked great. Gussie blinked several times but couldn't ignore him. No longer *Pastor Adam*, in her mind he'd assumed a completely different identity: *Basketball Adam*. Sweaty and hunky *Basketball Adam*. His T-shirt clung to broad shoulders she hadn't realized he had, and to a nicely muscled body. Skinny but, she hated to admit, very appealing. Since when had she found "sweaty" attractive?

The realization threw her off balance and made her feel as if a weird and wonderful force had taken over her being and filled her with lustful thoughts and desires she hadn't experienced for years. *Good heavens, Adam is a hottie.*

She felt slightly blasphemous having such thoughts about a minister.

❧

After their second win, Adam passed bottles of water to the other players, then picked up one himself and poured most of it over him before he took a deep drink.

"Great game, guys," Adam said.

"Thanks, Pops!" Hector high-fived him, then Hector and Bobby did a complicated handshake that included fist bumps.

"Hector, box out better on the rebounds," Adam coached. "Mac, great hustle."

When they'd cooled off, Mac said, "Let's sit down and study the competition."

"Hey, girl," Bobby answered. "We're good. We don't need to watch them."

After Hector glared at him, Bobby headed to the side of the court to study the competition.

"Sometimes he has a problem with attitude," Hector explained before he joined Bobby.

"You coming?" Mac said. "Good view of Gussie from where Hector and Bobby are," she whispered.

Adam attempted to give her the same glare Hector had used. Didn't work. She just grinned at him.

"Mac?" he threatened.

"Okay, Pops. I'll shut up." She joined the others, and he followed.

Although determined to watch the other two teams fight it out, Adam's eyes slid toward Gussie, who concentrated on the competition and cheered for both sides. He did have a good view of her.

"Great play!" Gussie's shout echoed around the court as she smiled. He really liked Gussie's smile.

Adam felt an elbow in his side, then Mac whispered, "If you're going to fool anyone, you have to stop looking dopey."

So he watched the game and forcefully kept his eyes on the players until the team from Llano won.

※

In the break before the final game, Gussie went back into the cool of the main building to splash water from the drinking fountain on her face. Fortifying herself, she glugged down several gulps of water.

"You okay, Gussie?" From one of the tables, Jimmy Flock watched her with concern.

"Fine, just really hot out there." Water trickled down her chin as she fanned herself.

"Okay. Be careful." He dropped his eyes to his book.

Odd that the minister who always questioned her about her love life hadn't recognized the fact that lust had just broad-sided her.

She forced herself back outside to watch the final game. She had to face and accept the fact that she'd felt again, that attraction had filled her, had sizzled inside her. It still did. Yearning had escaped from the core of her being, and she could ignore neither her attraction to Adam nor the despair it caused. She preferred to think of all men as being gender-neutral but couldn't manage to believe that about Adam anymore.

For a moment, she longed to go back in time thirteen or fourteen or twenty years, to be the young Gussie Milton who'd believed in love and goodness, who trusted others. But that person had died nearly half a lifetime ago.

She watched the game, her gaze following Adam all around the court.

"Go, teams," she cheered as the team from Llano was able to get the ball over midcourt for the first time in a couple of plays.

How old was he? Twenty-five, she guessed. Twenty-six? Had that been on the application and the background check they'd had to run? Probably. Six years younger. The age difference made her feel like a dirty old lady, sitting here, ogling him.

After the game, she'd put all thoughts of his manly features back in the lockbox in her brain that she bolted securely. For now, she'd allow herself to watch and enjoy. She stood and clapped after Bobby made a spectacular jumping, twisting dunk and joined in the cheers when Adam stole the inbounds pass.

"Cut," Adam yelled, and Bree worked her way under the basket for an easy layup.

"Pops," Hector shouted after he'd stolen the ball. With a perfect bounce pass, he fed Adam, who made a long shot.

Then Bobby dribbled inside for a dunk and Mac made a pair of free throws. The game was over, and Butternut Creek had won. Gussie stood and clapped. "Great game," she shouted.

Then she very firmly locked up her feelings again.

❧

"Time for vespers, guys." Adam tossed the last of the crumpled-up napkins in the recycle bin.

"You religious people sure spend a lot of time praying," Bobby said. "Not that I mind 'cause I know this is a church thing, but wouldn't one prayer a day pretty much say what you need to? Why not make it a little longer so you get everything in? Or maybe bless all the meals at the same time."

"Yeah," Hector agreed. "I mean you say them at every meal and in the morning and a couple of times at night. I bet you people pray before you take a shower."

"Or play basketball," Bobby added.

"No, never before a game of basketball." Adam turned toward

the guys. "I don't pray then because I want the other team to pray while we run all over them."

"Pops, that was weak." Hector finished wiping the tables. When he tossed the dishcloth toward the dish basin with sudsy water, Adam swatted toward it and missed. "See, you can't even block my shots."

❦

Adam watched Gussie during the group skits later after vespers. What in the world had happened? Her smiles and laughter seemed forced and artificial. When his group had parodied a gospel group singing rap, she looked distracted while everyone else laughed.

After they'd finished the skits, he caught up to her as she stopped to check her message box. "Hey," Adam said. "This is a great retreat. Thanks for all the work you do."

She glanced at one of the notes in her hand before she looked up at him. "It's fun, isn't it?"

"Something like this can change lives. I hope it has for Hector."

"Me, too."

"I first considered going into the ministry at summer church camp," he said at the same time Gussie scanned another message. "Anyway, you look busy. Thanks again and good night."

She nodded. "Night."

❦

Gussie could kick herself. It wasn't Adam's fault that his presence scared and befuddled her, but she couldn't allow him or anyone else to see how much he attracted her. For heaven's sake, she was Gussie Milton, old maid, and she had a yearning for this . . . this *kid*. Not that she planned to jump his bones—where had that phrase come from?—although the idea didn't horrify her as much as she'd thought it might.

But the attraction didn't mean she should behave rudely, even if she had no idea how to act. She called after him, "Loved your group's skit."

He turned, waved, and walked away.

❦

After the closing prayer Sunday morning, Adam picked up his bag to stow it in the van. As he turned back toward the dispersing youth, he noticed that Hector had picked up Bree's duffel bag.

Well, well, well. A romance? Not that he'd kid either Hector or Bree. He figured Bobby and Mac would take care of embarrassing them.

Once everyone had settled in, he checked on the seating. Bree and Hector shared the back bench. Bobby and Mac took the chairs, and Adam drove alone. Just as well. The kids would fall asleep anyway and be useless in keeping him awake.

As he started the van he glanced at the crowd, searching for Gussie. Stupid because she had no interest in him, but he kept looking. Finally, as he drove out of the campground, he saw her in the rearview mirror watching their vehicle pull out.

❦

At eight forty-five Monday morning, Adam heard the door into the reception area from the parking lot open and knew trouble had arrived. Couldn't be Maggie. She didn't show up until later. He guessed it was at least one Widow, maybe more. Right now, he didn't feel like facing any of them. Could he sneak out a window?

Stupid response. He couldn't hide from the Widows. He'd known they'd descend on him as soon as the pillar had debriefed her granddaughters and they could gather. Oh, maybe he could dodge them for an hour or two, even a day, but they'd catch up to him eventually, hunting him down like a pack of Miss Marples.

At least he'd arrived early to prepare himself. In front of him, he had a cup of coffee and a Bible. He'd spent a few minutes in meditation, but they hadn't given him enough time. He wished he had another thirty minutes to brace himself, but he didn't. He folded his hands and awaited the inevitable.

"Pastor, are you here?" Mercedes called.

Before she'd finished the sentence, the pillar stomped into his study, folded her arms, and stared at him while she stood at the door like a rock in the middle of a creek. The three other Widows—Blossom had joined them—flowed around her and headed toward the chairs in front of the desk.

He stood and reached toward Blossom. "Welcome. Good to see you."

She smiled as she shook his hand. Then all the Widows, including the newest, sat.

Except for Miss Birdie. When she finally strode toward the desk, she stood behind the chair Blossom had snatched and glared. "We came to discuss the retreat," Winnie said.

Before he could say anything, Blossom looked over her shoulder at Miss Birdie. She must have felt the intensity of her expression. "Why aren't you sitting down?" she whispered.

"Because you are sitting in my chair," Miss Birdie whispered back. The pillar had the loudest whisper of anyone Adam had ever heard. When she whispered, people obeyed.

Including Blossom. She leaped to her feet, scuttled to another chair, and sat down. With a smile, Miss Birdie lowered herself into her place.

"You'll notice, Preacher, Blossom has joined us *this morning*." Miss Birdie's voice underlined the temporary nature of Blossom as a Widow—it was the pillar, after all, who had the final say.

"Good to see all of you," Adam said.

"We came to discuss the retreat," Winnie repeated.

"Went very well. I believe the young people had a great time." He smiled at Miss Birdie. "What did Bree and Mac tell you?"

The pillar leaned forward. "They told me *nothing* happened between you and Gussie." She sat back and shook her head in disgust.

"Oh, dear," Blossom said. "Is that good or bad?"

Birdie ignored her and plowed ahead. "That's what my granddaughters say. Nothing happened."

"I don't know why we bother to send you off on these weekend excursions," Winnie said, "if you aren't going to take advantage of them."

Adam could explain that his finding a wife had not been the purpose of the retreat but he'd said it so often and the explanation did so little good, he didn't.

"Bree did say that you and Gussie patrolled the grounds Friday night," the pillar said.

"Alone," Mercedes added. "Only the two of you."

"Did anything happen?" Winnie asked. "Did you make a move?"

"Yes," Adam said.

Three of the women scooted forward in their chairs and watched him like a boggle of weasels eyeing a terrified rabbit. Blossom moved forward a few beats later, which made him think the newest and possibly temporary Widow didn't realize exactly what was going on.

"I . . ." But he couldn't say any more, because he'd started laughing so hard at their hopeful expressions. Three of them looked at him as if his response had exceeded the bounds of decorum. Blossom still looked confused and uncertain. Their expressions made him laugh harder.

When he could finally speak, he said, "Do you really believe that *if* anything happened between me and any woman, I'd tell you about it?"

When the comment made them look both confused and

exasperated, he added, "Not that anything has happened between me and a woman recently, but I *do* have a private life. You may deny that, but I do deserve a little space of my own."

"I guess you do," Winnie said grudgingly. She turned toward Miss Birdie and said, "He does have that right. He doesn't have to tell us everything."

The pillar narrowed her eyes and said, "We still expect you to do something about . . ."

"Yes, yes, I know." He grinned. "Thank you, ladies, for your concern. It's good to see you. Now, tell me about plans for the spring bazaar and chicken spaghetti dinner."

"We're meeting every afternoon, the ladies of the church, to start on crafts," Mercedes said. "Blossom's a real hand with colors and painting."

Miss Birdie counted on her fingers as she said, "Pansy's getting the food organized, Winnie's getting donations from the businesses, I'm working with the community center on the setup, and Mercedes is in charge of publicity."

"Sounds as if everything is well in hand." Not that Adam doubted that. He hurried to introduce another topic before they were tempted to return to their own. "I've heard Jesse's brother still needs care. Can you tell me anything about him?"

Sunday evening, Ouida stood on the porch and drew in the beauty of Butternut Creek. She loved the town at this time, as the day wound down. The sun had set and the sky had paled to gray. The girls were in bed, sweet smelling from their baths, and she had a moment of quiet.

"Ouida, would you get me a newspaper?" George called. As she went back inside and crossed the living room, she picked up the newspaper and headed toward the kitchen.

When George placed his shoe-shine box on the kitchen table, she handed him a section. He placed his shoes on top of it. His best pair. Oh, he had other pairs, but this was his favorite: Italian and expensive but, he always said, very comfortable. They were gorgeous. A little flashy for George, Ouida had always thought, with the narrow silhouette and the midnight-gray trim a little lighter—only a tiny bit—than the glossy black leather.

He sat down and, using a special rag, began his favorite Sunday chore by gently cleaning any dust or dirt that dared to settle on the glossy leather surface.

For a moment, she wondered if George loved those shoes. He

took such good care of them. Cleaned and shined them every week, never wore them on a rainy day, never two days in a row. The consideration made her blurt out an unexpected question.

"George, do you love me?"

He stopped wiping the shoes for a second before he said, "Of course." Then he put the rag down, opened the box, and took out the brush and polish he used only on these shoes.

"Why?" she asked.

"Why wouldn't I?" Keeping his eyes on his work, he carefully and evenly spread the polish and rubbed it in. After inspecting the right one to make sure he'd covered every millimeter of surface with polish, he set it down and picked up the left to repeat the process.

As if realizing that Ouida's minute of silence meant he hadn't answered correctly, he said, "You're my wife."

"And?" she prompted.

"And you take good care of me?" His statement became a question, as if they were on some kind of marital *Jeopardy!*

She didn't answer. Darned if she'd help him out on this. She really needed to know how George felt, not how she hoped he felt, but he didn't speak, either. Finally she said, "How?"

He shrugged, still focused on the shoes. "You always have dinner for me when I come home and you iron my clothes."

"So you could hire a cook and a laundress and I'd be *de trop*?"

After he finished precisely covering the left shoe with polish, he put it down, looked up at her, and blinked as if he couldn't understand why she'd brought this up. This conversation did not appear on his schedule.

Poor man, he had no idea what to say, but she had to know. Did he keep her around to take care of this huge house because she cost less than a maid? Had she accepted being banished to this small town with their two little girls—a town she loved and girls whom, heavens knew, she adored—anyway, had she done this for a man who'd pretty much abandoned his family for his office in Austin?

With another blink, George shook his head. "You take care of the children, too."

"So add a nanny to the staff."

"And . . ." George's cheeks actually turned pink before he looked down at his shoes. He took a few seconds to test how dry the polish was before he mumbled, "And I like you in bed."

"Aha! So you could hire a . . ."

"Ouida, don't say that." This time he spoke sharply and looked her in the eyes. "You know what we have is special."

"How?" She took a step toward him. For once in her life, she felt powerful, intimidating. Hard for a round woman with lots of freckles to do, but she did. George watched her looking, well, intimidated.

"Because . . . it's you and me. We've always been together."

"But you're never home, George. I'd like to see you sometimes. The girls would like to get to know you."

He stood as if that change of position would place him in control of the situation. "I've just started a business."

"Years ago. But if it were new, would that make up for nearly abandoning us?"

"I haven't abandoned you. I make a good living for this family. As the owner of a business, I hire people who depend on the company to support their families. That's important."

She closed her eyes and shook her head. She hadn't reached him. She still couldn't make him understand. She sighed. "And your family isn't," she whispered.

"Of course you are. You . . ." He fumbled for words. "Ouida, my shoes are dry. I have to finish up." He sat back down and picked up a brush.

She stopped trying. She knew George's priorities. Work first, family, distant second. Now she had to figure out what was best for Carol and Gretchen and for her. The girls needed a father, she knew that, but they didn't have one now and she didn't have a husband except for those treasured moments at night. That wasn't enough any longer.

In their usual places at the diner at two o'clock Monday afternoon, the Widows awaited the appearance of Blossom Brown. Winnie Jenkins, still bursting with pride at being a real Widow for six months, stirred sweetener into her tea. Mercedes had arrived from the library mere seconds earlier and settled in a chair while Birdie placed cups of coffee in front of the other Widows, then put another on the table in front of Blossom's empty chair.

"When are you getting married?" Birdie asked Winnie.

Winnie blushed. Silly for a woman their age to blush, but she did. Birdie couldn't criticize. Well, she could, but that would sound spiteful.

"Oh, we don't know. Mitchell wanted to wait until Sam got married. He says his son's wedding should have first priority."

"That was weeks ago," Birdie said. "When are you getting married?"

Winnie smiled. "I don't mind the wait. After all, I've been waiting my whole life for the right man."

Sentimental dribble, Birdie thought, but she wouldn't call Winnie out for those emotions. After all, Birdie had had her dear Elmer for nearly thirty years. Winnie deserved a good man, too.

Okay, Birdie accepted that, but she didn't need to hear about all that sweetness and light.

"Did you see Sam and Willow in church the other Sunday? With the boys?" As usual, Mercedes changed the subject when she saw conflict ahead.

"They looked happy. A great success for the Widows." Birdie smiled for a second, only until Blossom hurried in, her short hair perfectly coiffed and a pink jacket covering a matching pink sweater. She held a quilted basket, which she set on the table.

"You're late," Birdie said. "One of the tenets of the Widows is that we don't keep other people waiting."

"Oh." Blossom's round face flushed. "I'm sorry."

She had such a soft sweet voice. Birdie didn't like soft, sweet voices, not a bit.

"I didn't realize there were rules," Blossom explained. "I thought the Widows only went around doing good."

"Well, of course that's our main principle," Mercedes said gently. "But we have to plan our good deeds," she continued. "And we don't keep the others waiting."

"Of course. I'm sorry." Blossom settled into the fourth chair. "I'm a little late because my cook just finished making this." She opened the basket, pulled out a plastic container, and opened it to show a coffee cake. "Doesn't that look delicious? It's still warm."

Mercedes had a look on her face that said, *Don't you know you don't bring food to a restaurant?* But she'd never express that thought aloud.

"Don't you know you don't bring food to a restaurant?" Birdie said.

"They sell food here," Winnie added.

"We all take turns paying for our treat," Mercedes said.

Blossom's little pink mouth formed an O. "I . . . I didn't think. I wanted to bring you all something special, to show how much I appreciate your inviting me to be a Widow."

"You haven't been accepted as a Widow yet, not completely," Birdie said. "There are steps."

"I haven't?" Blossom blinked. "There are?"

"I had to go through a provisional period before I became a real Widow," Winnie added.

"I didn't understand." Blossom reached for the pastry. "I'll put this away."

"No, no," Birdie protested. "As long as it's here, we might as well enjoy it." She reached out to break off a piece, took a small bite and chewed. "It is really good." She cut herself a large piece and pushed the plate toward the others. "Try a little."

Winnie frowned. "Shouldn't we be getting down to business instead of eating?" She pulled out a notebook and pen.

Bossiest woman Birdie had ever met, but she also noticed that Winnie served herself nearly a quarter of the coffee cake.

"We need to discuss the preacher . . . ," Birdie said.

"I think we need to leave him alone for a while." Mercedes daintily wiped her mouth with a napkin.

With the addition of Blossom, Birdie became more aware that nearly everything her friend did was dainty and lady-like. She could only hope the two would not join forces and attempt to change Birdie, to make her softer and nicer. That dog wouldn't hunt.

"Why do you think we need to leave the preacher alone?" Birdie demanded. "One of our missions is to get the man married."

"I know, but maybe we've pushed too hard, Bird."

"Pushed too hard? We've left him alone for days."

"Yes, and we need to leave him alone for a while longer."

"Can't believe you'd say that, Mercedes. Can't believe you believe it. The man is not making the slightest effort to find himself a wife. If we don't try to find him a woman to marry . . ."

"Well, that's the problem, isn't it?" Mercedes said. "There aren't many women around. Who's left to fix him up with? Pretty soon, any unmarried woman is going to run if she sees us." She sighed. "And the preacher is beginning to ignore our efforts. Was he the least bit thankful when we mentioned Gussie Milton? No."

"Oh, tell me." Blossom clapped. "Are we trying to find a wife for Reverend Jordan?"

That woman didn't understand a thing about being a Widow. How could she become one if she didn't comprehend who they were and what they did?

"Didn't you figure that out when we were in his office Monday?" Birdie asked.

"Oh." Blossom blinked. "That's what we were doing. I thought we were discussing the youth retreat."

"Dear," Mercedes explained patiently. "As well as doing good, we attempt to match people up, to get them married."

"Back when we had more young, unmarried people in town, we were extremely successful." Mercedes sighed. "With websites and singles bars in Austin and all the young people leaving town after they graduate, matchmaking has become quite a challenge."

"We matched Sam and Willow, and, if you look at the faculty in the schools, you'll see a number of our successes," Birdie said. "The track coach and that third-grade teacher have been married for ten years. And the assistant principal and the school nurse are expecting their second child. But it is much harder now."

"The process has become more difficult since all my children married," Mercedes added. "We found mates for two of them."

"I don't know many young people, but I'll help in any way I can." Blossom paused and thought for a few seconds. "Maybe we could invite all the singles in Butternut Creek to my house for a party."

The woman did have a lovely house.

"Problem is, that would be Pastor Adam and the minister from the Presbyterian Church," Winnie said. "We've already tried to get them together."

"I talked to a couple of divorced teachers at the middle school but they weren't at all receptive to our efforts," Birdie said. "Very rude, in fact."

"But that's a good idea, Blossom." Winnie wrote that down. "Maybe we'll try that later, after a few more divorces."

The four women considered the suggestion for nearly a minute while they each took another piece of the coffee cake.

"Well, enough of that," Winnie said. "What else do we need to discuss?"

Bossiest woman Birdie had ever met, but she did have a point. Unless more had happened between Gussie and Adam at the retreat than her granddaughters had told her, the matchmaking had hit a dead end.

"Cleanup at the thrift shop Friday, nine o'clock," Birdie said. "Bring brooms and cleaning material and hangers. With the big sale on Saturday, we have to sort everything, get it ready to set up in the parking lot."

Chapter Four

"Hello, Mrs. Boucher. I'm Adam Jordan, the minister of the Christian Church," Adam said as a smiling brunette opened her front door.

When she heard those words, her smile disappeared and she stepped back to close the door. "Thank you. Not interested."

"No, I'm not here for that. I have Aaron's backpack." He held it up.

"Oh." She shoved the screen door open and took it. "Thank you. He leaves everything he owns all over the neighborhood."

"Maybe it's not Aaron's fault." He gestured toward Chewy. "My dog has a bad habit of running off with stuff." Then he showed her a hoodie. "Is this Aaron's?"

She shook her head. "Try across the street. That may belong to April Higgins."

Mrs. Higgins was delighted to get the hoodie back. As he left, Adam said, "If you don't have a church home, we'd love for you to visit."

Had Chewy become their best tool for membership growth?

❦

When he got to the office, Adam wondered where the Widows were. Not that he missed them, but it was over a week since their last visit and they hadn't descended on him again. The lack of a second visit made him realize Mac hadn't squealed. He felt safe.

He'd worked for nearly fifteen minutes when Chewy leaped to his feet, woofed, and danced.

Ouida stood in his door, a plate in one hand and Gretchen dangling from the other, as usual.

"Exactly what I need," Adam said. "I don't know how I'd get along without you."

"You'd probably starve to death." She shook her head. "It's my mission to fatten you up."

She scrutinized his chest and shoulders, which made Adam more than a little uncomfortable. "You've gained weight." She nodded decisively. "Makes you seem older, better looking." She nodded again. "Not that you weren't a good-lookin' guy before, for a minister." She snapped her mouth closed. "I'd better stop before I insult you any more. I came to talk to you."

In the same way she'd studied him, Adam scrutinized Ouida—but only her face—for a hint of a hidden motive. Surely she wasn't in cahoots with the Widows, was she? Was *fatten you up* code for "get you married"?

As Gretchen broke loose and ran to pet Chewy, Ouida glanced toward her daughter before she looked at Adam. "It's about George. My husband."

"Yes, I know who George is." He shouldn't have said that. If his professors in counseling had told him anything, it was *not* to stop communication with a smart answer. "I'm sorry. What about George?"

His reply had put Ouida off. She hesitated and studied him without saying a word.

"I really am sorry, Ouida. Sometimes I say the wrong thing."

"We all do." She took a deep breath. "We've been married for ten years." She seemed to consider her words. "He wasn't always like he is now, so very sober and driven and focused on work. I wouldn't have married him if he had been."

He remained silent but in a pastoral manner. His counseling professor had called it watchful empathy.

"George drives me nuts. At dinner, he eats one bite of chicken first, then one of potatoes, finishing with a forkful of green beans, then repeats that."

"But didn't you know that before you got married?" He stood and walked around the desk to sit next to his neighbor.

"Oh, yes, but back then I didn't know about the other things. His closet is perfect, colors together. He hates disorder. He hates . . . well, he hates everything that is family life and children."

"What? He has a wonderful family."

"Yes, he does." She shook her head. "He changed right after he began his own business seven years ago, right before Carol was born. Probably not good timing with the stress of a new business and a baby."

"Tell me more about George when you first met him. Why did you fall in love with him?" There, that sounded ministerial but not overly so.

"Oh, he's always been a little staid and controlling, but I did see *moments* of spontaneity, of exploration and joy." She caught his eye as if attempting to sell him on her words. "We complemented each other, I thought. My messy life and emotions balanced his purposeful actions and solemnity. And . . . and I felt safe with him." She sighed and glanced at Gretchen, who seemed too occupied with the dog to be listening. Nevertheless, Ouida leaned toward Adam and lowered her voice. "He was raised by his grandmother. His parents died when he was seven. She was strict and unemotional, which probably has a great deal to do with his being quiet and introspective. I loved him because I knew who he was inside, how much he needed me and how hard it was for him to show it." She shook her head again. "I never should've allowed this isolation, his closing down, to happen to him, to the girls. They don't know he loves them."

"How can I help?"

"Adam, I don't know." She sighed again. "He's getting worse, much more distant. I don't know how to reach him anymore, especially since he's not around."

"Have you talked to him about that?"

"I tried. Didn't get anyplace."

"You know I'm always available to talk to. What can I do?"

"Thanks." She smiled. "Listening's probably all you can do now. I'm sorry I dropped all this on you, but it's been building." She tapped her chest. "Inside."

When she stood, Adam got to his feet.

"I'll talk to him again. Sunday, when the girls nap, I will." She reached her hand out to her daughter. "Come on. Let's go. Adam has work to do."

Gretchen gave Chewy a final pat and ran over to Adam for a hug. Then the two exited, leaving Adam to wonder what in the world he could do. There were things in ministry he was inexperienced in and unprepared for. Counseling scared him. What did he have to say that would help anyone?

He hated to use the Kowalskis' marriage as a learning experience. He should probably study up, read a little. He moved toward the bookcase and perused his books until he finally found one on marital counseling in a stack behind the desk. His sermon could wait.

❦

Adam encouraged his ancient car toward the thrift shop. Although it threatened to die on him at the only major intersection in town, he did get there. The vehicle putted and jumped as he pulled into a parking space. He'd need to call Rex.

No better mechanic in the state than Rex. Only one who had been able to keep the old car going consistently, and he charged Adam only for parts. As a good Catholic, Rex felt God expected him to help the preacher and that old car was part of his witness, his true mission. Adam kept his number on speed dial.

Turning the engine off—although it still chugged and sputtered for a few more seconds with the key out of the ignition—he got out of the car, flipped open the trunk to pick up the few boxes remaining from his move, and walked inside the shop.

The thrift shop was always closed on the Friday before the quarterly Saturday sale. He expected Miss Birdie to be there. He never knew what days she took off from the diner and probably never would. Once when he'd asked her about her schedule, she'd let him know that although she was a poor workingwoman, she didn't waitress 24/7. He never asked again, simply accepted that if there was work to be done, the pillar appeared.

"When you find a shirt that is too worn for anyone to wear, chunk it in the trash." Mercedes pointed toward a barrel as he got to work.

"*Chunk*?" Adam asked. "Do you mean *chuck*?"

"She said what she meant, Preacher." Miss Birdie glanced up from her sorting. "Chunk, you know, throw it."

Another word for his Texas vocabulary. "Okay, what do I do after I *chunk* the worn shirts?"

"Put the nice ones back on the shelf and the in-betweens in a box for the sale," Winnie said.

After fifteen minutes of packing and chunking and chatting, they heard the sound of a car pulling up outside.

"Is that Blossom? I told her to be here at nine." The pillar glared at Adam as if the late arrival were his fault.

"Looks like her big car," Mercedes said.

"Expensive and probably eats up the gasoline," Birdie complained.

"Probably pretty fuel-efficient," Mercedes said. "The new cars are."

"Hrmph." Miss Birdie glared at her friend. "You don't always have to correct everyone."

"I told Blossom to bring cleaning supplies." Winnie leaped in to

stop the disagreement. "Hope she brought a mop because the floor
in that back room really needs a good scrubbing."

The front door opened and a pudgy, middle-aged woman entered
toting a bucket and mop. "Where should I put these?" she asked. Not
waiting for an answer, she dropped the stuff, moved back a few steps,
and held the door open.

"We're always happy to have a new volunteer." Adam hurried to
welcome her. "I'm Adam Jordan, minister at the Christian Church and
these are . . ."

"I know who you are and I'm not a volunteer. I'm Miss Blossom's
housekeeper. She made me come. What should I do?"

The four blinked.

"She made you come? Blossom *made* you come?" Adam struggled to understand the comment.

"Where is she now?" Miss Birdie sounded oddly mystified, an
emotion he rarely saw from her.

"She's in the car, getting the food out." The woman held the door
open.

"The food?" Winnie echoed.

"Hello, hello!" Blossom sang as she entered the door holding a
huge basket. "Coffee and pastry for all." Not even noticing the expressions on the faces of the Widows, which ranged from amazement
to horror, she put the basket on the table where Winnie had been
working, right on top of the nicest T-shirts.

Winnie blinked, Mercedes shook her head, and Miss Birdie—
well, Miss Birdie continued to look stunned. Adam had never seen her
taken aback. He'd never believed the pillar could be at a loss for words.

Both Winnie and Mercedes looked at Miss Birdie, expecting her
to take over. When she didn't, Mercedes said sweetly, "Hello, Blossom. You brought your housekeeper?"

"Oh, yes." Blossom motioned in the direction of the woman.
"That's Evelyn, my housekeeper."

"Why isn't she at home?" Winnie said. "Keeping *your* house?"

"You said we were cleaning. I don't clean well." She fluttered her
beautifully manicured hands toward the confusion of the room.

Finally, Miss Birdie found several dozen words. "The *Widows* are
cleaning the thrift shop and sorting clothing," she said in a voice so
cold it could freeze the coffee Blossom had started to pour. "Not our
housekeeper or our maids, but the Widows. This is a community service that *we*, the Widows, do."

This time Blossom blinked. "But I'm not at all good with this sort of thing. I'm not dressed for it." They all examined her lovely pale blue silk shirt and slacks with matching high-heeled sandals.

Because Adam feared Miss Birdie would have a stroke, he stepped forward. "Blossom, the Widows *themselves* do community service. It is their way of being servants, of helping others unselfishly."

"But I brought coffee, and my cook baked us another of those coffee cakes you all enjoyed so much." She smiled at them all.

"Not again," the pillar grumbled.

"Dear," Mercedes said. "Thank you, but as much as we enjoyed that pastry, we aren't an *eating* group. We're a doing-things-for-others group. We thought you understood that when we invited you to join."

"At the suggestion of the preacher," the pillar stated. Her tone said, *Don't blame me for this mess.*

"You don't want the coffee?" She glanced down at the three cups she'd poured.

"Evelyn, thank you for coming," Adam said. "Do you live close by? Can you walk home from here or do you need a ride?"

The housekeeper pointed east. "I'll walk." She scurried out.

"Thank you for coming," Mercedes shouted after her.

"Blossom, why don't you and I go to the table in the back of the store and chat?" Adam picked up one of the filled cups. "Over our coffee?"

"I'm coming, too, Preacher, and I'm not feeling a bit chatty," Miss Birdie said.

"Oh, my." Blossom's ivory skin became paler, and her eyes grew enormous. "Am I in trouble?"

"No, no, only a misunderstanding," Adam assured her as he pushed her toward the back. Once there, he held out a chair for her. Skittishly, she perched on the edge of the seat.

"I don't believe you understand the mission of the Widows," he began.

"We take care of other people, ourselves," the pillar interrupted from where she stood next to the table. "We do the work. We don't have our servants do the work."

Because Blossom looked as if she was on the verge of tears, Adam took Miss Birdie's elbow and escorted her, forcefully, toward the front of the store. "I'll handle this," he said with a confidence he didn't feel. Taking a stand against the pillar had never been one of his favorite actions.

"*We* are the servants," Miss Birdie said loudly as he headed toward the table again and she stomped back to the work area.

He took a chair across from Blossom and took a gulp of coffee. "Great coffee."

Blossom brightened a little.

"I have a favorite Bible verse, from the book of Micah. I'd like to share it with you," Adam said. "'. . . what does the LORD require of you but to do justice, and to love kindness, and to walk humbly with your God?'"

"Very pretty," she said. "But," she leaned forward and whispered, "that Birdie MacDowell isn't a bit humble. Not a bit."

Because he couldn't refute her observation, he hurried on. "Those words from Micah are how the Widows feel. They serve others. When I arrived a few months ago, they got donations to furnish the parsonage. Because of that, we could open it up to an injured woman and her family. Now two homeless kids live there. The Widows furnished the bedroom, provided all the linens. The Widows take food to shut-ins and volunteer within the community."

"Maybe this was a mistake." Again she fluttered her fingers toward the Widows. "I really don't feel that way, you know, humble and kind, and how could I do anything about justice? I probably wouldn't fit in. In fact"—she folded her hands—"I don't, not a bit."

Adam allowed her words to hover between them before he asked, "What will you be doing with your time?"

"I could play bridge." She sighed. "But I'm tired of that. A lot of gossip, and I know too many rumors were going around about Jason and me to enjoy it anymore." She paused. "I could become a docent at the art gallery, but that's in Austin."

"A long drive, and you wouldn't be making new friends here in Butternut Creek."

She bit her lips, then shook her head. "I don't know." Tears appeared in her eyes. "I'm really not good at anything except taking care of Jason and being his hostess."

Adam handed her a couple of tissues.

She swallowed and dabbed at her eyes. "Pastor, I have no skills. I've had hired help all my life, even as a child. They've always done everything."

"Aren't you in charge of the help? Didn't you plan the receptions and dinners and parties for your husband? I imagine you're a good organizer."

"Well, yes, I am that, but there's no need in this group for an organizer with Birdie and Winnie around."

"Maybe you'll find another way to fit in. Please, give it another try. I truly believe you'll be a great addition."

She nodded, wiped her eyes once more, then placed the tissues in her purse.

Had the message gotten through? Adam could only hope it had. Blossom needed the Widows. He only hoped the Widows saw accepting her as an act of kindness.

❦

"Good morning, Adam."

A glorious morning was always made brighter when he saw Ouida with a plate covered by a napkin.

"I'll carry this to the church," she said as if he couldn't quite manage that.

Following her, Adam couldn't help but notice that the short overalls Ouida wore made her backside look as wide as a football lineman's—not that he made a habit of watching women's derrieres. She wore a yellow striped T-shirt, sunny and happy like Ouida, but today she seemed determined about something and her usual stroll had become almost a march. Because Chewy slept in, only Adam followed.

"Where's Gretchen?"

"She's spending this week with my sister up in Plano."

By the time they'd entered the church, waved at Maggie, and entered the minister's study, she'd slowed down a little. She placed the plate in the middle of Adam's desk and turned to look at him.

"Umm, do you do marriage counseling?"

"I can and I do," Adam said although he didn't feel nearly as confident as his answer sounded. "What do you need?"

"Oh, not for me and George." She shook her head. "But I have some friends . . . All right, it's about George and me." She dropped into a chair in front of his desk. "You know that from what I said before."

When she sat, he did, too.

He waited. She didn't speak. He templed his fingers and watched her. He'd learned long ago—actually, last year in seminary—that listening brought more information than asking questions, usually. If it didn't, he could ask questions.

"You won't try to convert me, will you? You know we aren't religious people."

"Yes, I know. You've told me that."

"That's right." Apparently convinced he wouldn't force faith on her, she said, "You probably think we're an odd couple, George and I. I told you that before, but it's the way I need to lead into what I'm going to say." She stopped. "And to get my courage up to share. I told you I loved his logic and his thoughtfulness, his ability to deliberate while I leaped into things."

Adam nodded this time.

She sighed and sat back in her chair. "But he doesn't help me with logic and I can't make him less serious because I never see him."

"Never?" Adam repeated.

"You know he's always working. He works weekends. The girls barely know who he is."

"He's runs a business, Ouida."

"Don't take his side," she warned.

Adam sat back to listen, only listen.

"Besides, he was like that before he started his company. He's away so much I sometimes wonder how the girls were conceived."

Adam didn't comment on that, only hoped she'd move to another topic.

And she did.

"*Kowalski*. Preacher, do you know the origin of that name?"

"It's Polish, isn't it?"

"Yes." Ouida picked up a muffin and broke off a piece. Once she finished that, she placed the partially eaten muffin back on the plate and said, "It's the housekeeping I have problems with. George—his middle name is Miloslaw. If you spell it in Polish, it has lines through both *l*'s."

"Interesting. I didn't realize the Polish alphabet—"

But it seemed Ouida was really wound up. Her words poured from her over his. "George is third generation of the family born here. His great-grandparents immigrated nearly a hundred years ago. Everyone in the next generation was Polish. His mother came from that background, and you should see her kitchen. Do you know how often she mops her kitchen every day?"

"Once?" he asked, although that seemed excessive to him. Before the arrival of the Firestones, he only mopped when the floor got so sticky his shoes made sucking noises when he walked across it. Since then, Hector and Janey shared that chore on a weekly basis.

"Five. Five times a day, after every meal and again if anyone has a snack."

"Really?"

"Polish people are very neat, clean people. That's fine but I'm not Polish and I'm not Susie Homemaker." She nodded decisively. "Oh, not that there's anything wrong with being Susie Homemaker if a woman wants to be that. Or a man, although he'd probably be Stanley Homemaker." She forced her lips together as if trying to keep the words from tumbling out. "What I mean," she said slowly and clearly, "is that we're all different. George's mother and grandmother may have been really tidy people, but does that mean I have to do what they did?"

"Of course not."

"Of course not," she agreed and leaned back in her chair.

This certainly wasn't a marriage counseling session. For one thing, the husband wasn't here. For another, it had taken off without him. This seemed more like the crumbling of a dam during the spring thaw with all the flotsam and jetsam of Ouida's life gushing through the gap.

"Ouida, I'm not sure . . . ," he began in an attempt to harness the flood and sift through the detritus.

"George expects me to be the same kind of housekeeper, but I'm not."

She sniffed. Adam handed her a Kleenex.

"You have two little girls."

"His mother had five children, but she kept the house spotless." She blew her nose. "My mother was neat but she wasn't irrational. We didn't mind a little dust or an unmade bed or a footprint on the kitchen floor. Do you?"

"No, I—"

"George's mother took those embroidered linen runners off the top of the dresser every week, every single week. She'd wash, starch, and iron them before she put them back on." She sat back in the chair. "Starched and ironed those dresser scarves every single week."

"What's a dresser scarf?"

"It's a piece of linen about this size." She measured length and width with her hands. "It goes on the dresser for . . . I don't know why. Maybe decoration. Could be to protect the dresser but they don't. They aren't waterproof. A spill would go right through." She shrugged. "But his mother gave me a pair that she'd embroidered at a wedding shower. I should have known they meant trouble. I should have realized I was not the kind of woman who'd take good care of those dresser scarves, not like Magda did. But it's the boxer shorts I hate most, ironing them." She sighed.

"You starch and iron George's—" Adam stopped, pretty certain he didn't want to discuss this and wondering why he'd asked for clarification.

"No starch. Just iron." She nodded. "That's how he likes them. That's what his mother did for her husband and all the wives in the family back through the centuries of Polish women who married Kowalskis. And his shirts. Those I do starch."

"Why not take the shirts to the laundry?"

"George has a chart. It shows how much better and cheaper it is for me to do his shirts, less wear and tear on the fabric so the shirts last longer. Besides, he says I use the right amount of starch and the ones done at the laundry irritate his neck."

"Have you ever heard of permanent press, wash and wear, no-iron?"

"They don't look as crisp as George likes. He wants the front—" She placed a hand on her chest. "He wants it crisp and without wrinkles. But, you know, I think it's the boxers I mind most. Who sees them?" She stood, looking resolute. "That's where I'm going to start, with those boxers," she said with a vigorous nod. "I'm going to tell him I'm not going to iron them anymore." She held a hand in front of her, palm forward. "Don't try to talk me out of this. If he doesn't like that, he can take care of them himself." With that, she placed the remaining muffins on a napkin on Adam's desk, picked up the plate, and stomped off.

❦

Why hadn't she thought about this long ago?

Ouida nearly skipped across the parking lot and the lawn of the parsonage.

She'd been a limp rag for too long. When she'd started to date George, she'd been overwhelmed that he was interested in her, amazed this tall, handsome, intelligent man had fallen in love with plain old her. In exchange for his love, she'd done whatever he'd asked: given up her dream of being an artist, quit school to work so he could finish his MBA, and moved to Butternut Creek because he thought that would be a great place to raise a family.

She'd give him the last point. She loved the little town and she loved her children and, truly, she loved George. But she was overwhelmed suddenly by her complete loss of who she was, her individuality—which she'd been pretty certain she'd had when she'd entered UT.

Now she wanted more—or, perhaps, less. She wanted to find out more about herself, like why had she given up painting? And why had she allowed herself to change so much?

She entered the house and looked around. Much like their lives, everything was neat as if it had been lined up with a yardstick. George had charted out the financial burden of children, and had showed on that chart—expenses of college, et cetera—that they should have another child in two years, then stop. On his chart, the last child would be a boy.

She didn't want that. Oh, not that she didn't want another child, but the scheduling of their entire lives on an actuarial table no longer sat well with her. He'd probably also plotted out the date of conception. She used to think George's compulsiveness added structure to her life, but no longer. Now it drove her nuts.

She would take charge of their lives now, in little ways like those boxers, and move ahead bit by bit. Perhaps she'd find time to paint again.

Slowly she turned to study the room. It was spotless, and George wouldn't be home for hours. Why did she struggle to keep it perfect when George was sixty miles away? She and the girls could live here like normal people, then quickly pick up toys and sweep and make it immaculate right before George got home. No more mopping the kitchen five times a day. George might have to get used to a footprint here and a dirty fork there.

She looked out the window toward the church. Poor Adam. She'd gone to him and asked for counseling and she'd hit him with all her woes. She must have overwhelmed him, but after all, wasn't counseling mostly listening?

Thanks to him, she'd come to a big conclusion: She had no desire to leave, only to change. She wanted to set up a studio on the third floor, taking up a little of the space where the girls played, and paint the beauty of the Hill Country. All she needed was time and maybe a skylight.

Yes, George did run a business, but he could darned well wear freshly washed boxers with a few wrinkles and no one really *needed* dresser scarves.

Maybe after that, she'd stop ironing the pillowcases.

❦

After Ouida left, Adam had looked out the office window and watched her cross the parsonage lawn toward her house, walking with a determination he seldom saw her use.

How had the session gone? Not at all like the case studies they'd discussed at the seminary or he'd read in those marriage counseling books. Ouida had taken off and left him far behind. He hadn't helped her discover her feelings. She'd pretty much done that herself.

He remembered a line John Milton wrote: "They also serve who only stand and wait." Maybe he'd served by sitting and listening. He didn't seem to have screwed anything up. Probably should let go of his worry that he'd been inadequate in the situation because, yes, he had been, but he couldn't go back and change what had happened.

How could he have acted differently? Short of putting his hand over Ouida's mouth, he couldn't have asked questions or offered much advice. She hadn't needed to be led. Could be she only needed to allow the words to flow out and know he'd listened.

Instead of worrying, he wrote a few comments in the file folder he'd labeled COUNSELING, put it back in a drawer, and turned to his computer.

Adam checked his email, always hoping to see a note from Gussie. He hadn't heard from her since the retreat except for the evaluation she'd sent out to all adults. When he'd sent it back to her, he'd added a note, which she hadn't answered.

What did he expect? She thought of him as a kid, a minister, a camp counselor. She kept busy with her job, her parents, her church. Why had he thought they'd become email buddies, which might lead to more?

But after he'd answered a few messages and written a quick note to his sister, he checked the inbox one more time. Only spam.

❦

It was her last appointment Friday afternoon, almost five o'clock. Gussie was tired; Timmy and Tammy Scheltzbaum, the six-year-old twins who sat stiffly on the stools she'd placed in front of the blue backdrop, were also tired; and their mother sitting in the corner drooped.

"Can you smile?" She always asked that of children who didn't display an iota of personality in the hope they would sparkle and laugh without her having to resort to funny faces and dancing around.

Either they couldn't or they didn't.

She glanced toward the corner where their mother sat.

"Smile, sweeties," Mrs. Scheltzbaum said.

When the children's lips curled a little but no joy filled their eyes, Gussie sighed. She'd snapped a few good portraits of serious siblings but knew their mother expected sparkling as well. Good thing Gussie had curly, floppy hair, which usually amused children. She bobbed her head back and forth, up and down, to allow her curls to bounce. Tammy grinned a little and almost laughed, but Timmy frowned, already too grownup and macho to smile. She bet he was also too old to find the hand puppet amusing.

So she went with funny voices. Not imitations, but voices that ranged from thin and high to growling with odd accents.

"Hey, Timmy," she said with her voice sliding up and down the scale. "Gimme a smile?" As she kept up the schtick, the children relaxed and Tammy gave her an almost-smile.

Through the years, she'd discovered what worked. Impersonating a witch scared children, of course. Pretending to be a dog embarrassed even her and she was nearly impervious to humiliation. Not everyone liked clowns. She'd tried roller skates but discovered the difficulty of taking a picture as she flew by.

The final option? "The Lord said to Noah," she sang. By the time she finished the chorus, the twins were clapping and laughing and she got a great bunch of pictures.

That evening, Gussie sat at her computer while her parents watched television downstairs. She read and reread the note Adam had sent with his evaluation. "Hey," he'd written. "Had a great time at the retreat. Meet for coffee?"

Pleasant but no matter how many times she read it, she could not find a great deal of passionate interest in those eleven words. Actually, she could detect only *friendly* interest, perhaps rote politeness for the old lady from Roundville.

All for the best, of course. She had no interest in romance, certainly not. But companionship would be nice. Talking to a man who sparked excitement within her could be very pleasant.

But maybe not.

Had she felt lust for Lennie? Probably so. He'd been tall and handsome and flashy, but she couldn't remember. Didn't want to remember.

Chapter Five

Adam headed home from the Butternut Creek skilled nursing facility. He'd walked over to see the father of a church member while his car kept Rex company. He breathed in a lungful of fragrant Central Texas air. It was a great day, the kind of spring day everyone waited for. Warm and sunny and the exercise felt great.

Out on the highway west of town, reports of the arrival of bluebonnets had been coming in for nearly a week. When he got the car back, he'd take the kids for a ride to see them. Watching the bluebonnets and Indian paintbrush and what Lady Bird had called "those damn little yellow flowers" was a Hill Country tradition he aimed to join soon.

He missed the spring flowers of Kentucky: a purple crocus poking through still-cold ground followed by lawns covered with sunny daffodils. Add to that forsythia that bloomed bright yellow and redbuds and dogwood trees. Oh, he'd seen those trees in Texas, but in Kentucky their appearance signaled a transition from winter to spring. The seasons had little separation here.

Mercedes had told him to look forward to the sweet-smelling mountain laurels and the glorious magnolia trees, which couldn't survive winters farther north. And tulips, Ouida had told him. She had a plot in her garden, but he always thought of them at Churchill Downs for the Derby. Add the fragile azaleas and hearty crepe myrtle and spring displayed itself in colorful splendor here, too.

As he walked, he thought about Hector's visit with his father in prison last Saturday, a trip he made by bus every month or two. Each time, he returned solemn and remained quiet for a few days, withdrawn and worried.

He never took his sister, and Janey never asked to go. She'd had a rough life with her mother dying when she was a toddler and her father's addiction. Hector said his father had never laid a hand on Janey because he knew Hector would hurt him if he did. Nevertheless, Janey was afraid of the man, afraid of the kind of people who'd come to the house, of the shouting and the fights and the occasional gunfire.

Adam couldn't blame her. He'd be traumatized, too. He'd attempted to get her into counseling but she'd curled up in the corner of the office and refused to talk to the psychologist he'd found who worked with kids. She found her safe place with Hector. She seemed fine in the parsonage and did okay at school. Neither Adam nor Hector could figure out why, as much time as she spent studying, she didn't make better grades. Due to trauma as well? Until he could find someone she'd talk to, they wouldn't know.

Adam strolled down the highway, then turned on Church Street. As he headed toward the church, he could see six or seven cars in the parking lot. The women getting ready for the bazaar, he guessed. On the front porch of the parsonage, he saw two people on the swing with their heads together. After a few more steps, he realized the two were Hector and Bree. Janey sat in the rattan chair and read.

Well, well.

"Hey, guys," Adam said. "What's going on?"

"Just hangin' out." Hector's glare warned Adam not to tease him about Bree's presence. "Knew you wouldn't like us inside without you around."

When Janey glanced up at Adam, a smile flickered across her face. Her smile gave him hope that, little by little, she was healing.

"Pops, we need, we really need, a goal on the parking lot." Hector pointed toward the exact place he envisioned it. "We could have been playing ball while we waited for you."

"And, Pops, we"—Bree indicated herself and Hector—"emailed Gussie Milton and invited her to speak to the youth group the Sunday after Easter."

Adam blinked. Gussie? Here?

"She didn't want to come at first," Hector said.

"Something about her parents," Bree said. "And work and the church and other stuff."

"She has a busy life." Adam sat on the wicker chair.

"But when Bree told her we needed her to talk about summer camp so we can bring more kids, she agreed," Hector said.

Bree must have learned that from her grandmother, using guilt as the ultimate motivator.

"Where'd you get this idea?" Adam asked.

"Mac suggested it," Bree said.

Aah, Mac. Matchmaker-in-training, taking after her grandmother. At least she hadn't told the pillar about his attraction to Gussie, and she'd behaved far more subtly than any of the Widows.

"We're all going to ask friends who don't go to church to come, try to get them interested in church camp this summer," Hector said. "We should have that basketball goal up by then, Pops. That'll bring the guys out."

"Not enough time. First, I have to take that up with the property committee and the board."

Hector shook his head. "Churches. The hoops you have to go through just to get a hoop."

He and Bree laughed at that, but Adam was still trying to get his mind around the idea of Gussie's visit here in a couple of weeks.

"The Widows are going to serve refreshments," Bree said. "Food always attracts people, especially high school people."

"What time?" Adam attempted to mentally picture his calendar, but Gussie's smiling face popped up in the little squares.

"She's going to leave Roundville after church and get here about one thirty. We'll start at two," Bree said. "Grandma said after the meeting the Widows will put together a light supper for you at the parsonage so Gussie doesn't have to drive home hungry."

Oh, yeah, that driving while starving, always hazardous, but not nearly as terrifying as a matchmaking Widow.

But why worry? Spending a few hours with Gussie was great, even if she hadn't wanted to come. The idea of spending a few hours with Gussie under the eye of the Widows didn't count as a positive, but he didn't care. She'd be here.

Of course, they wouldn't be alone, so he couldn't put a move on Gussie. Actually, he'd never put a move on Gussie at any time, surrounded by people or not. The realization would have depressed him greatly if he allowed himself to dwell on the fact. Instead, he grinned in anticipation of Gussie's imminent appearance.

"Why're you smiling, Pops?" Hector asked.

"Sounds like fun," Adam answered.

"Yeah, a lot of kids will be here and Gussie's great," Bree said.

"You two should get together," Hector said. "You and Gussie. She'd make you laugh more."

"That's right. You two would be great together," Bree agreed. "Why don't you ask her out?"

Exactly what he needed. Dating advice from teenagers.

❦

Gussie stared at the screen of her computer, perusing the email she'd sent to Bree. What had she done? She'd agreed to visit the church in Butternut Creek, to talk to kids about camp and the youth program. The event didn't present a problem; she did that all the time.

The problem was, she hadn't done it before with Adam Jordan around.

Too late to back out. Not that she could. This was her ministry, what she did, how she served. She'd remember who she was—an old maid who'd substituted the young people for her children—and who he was—the minister of Butternut Creek. With those identities firmly in mind, she'd be able to be professional and not see Basketball Adam when she looked at Reverend Adam, at least not when she was close to him.

Oh, sure. Someday she'd have to stop lying to herself.

❦

Adam had finally found a donkey for Palm Sunday. With a sigh of relief, he sat back in the desk chair in his office, folded his arms behind his head, and grinned. Victory! He felt like singing loud hosannas but he knew he couldn't carry it off; he would only upset Maggie and it would serve no real purpose.

Jesse Hardin had actually found it. Thank goodness for Jesse. Last year, he'd given Sam Peterson horseback rides to build up the muscles in Sam's thigh as part of his physical therapy. And now he'd tracked down a donkey for Hector to ride on Palm Sunday. Jesse would go to the ranch early Sunday morning, load Maisie into his horse trailer, and bring her to church. The Methodists planned to use the donkey fifteen minutes later and the Catholics after that.

When he'd finished savoring that victory, Adam scrutinized the outline on his computer. As usual, when he had no ideas and the sermon had no oomph, he stared into space, searching for inspiration. None came. He stood and looked out the window. Still nothing.

The silence was broken by a bloodcurdling shriek from the reception office. He turned, ran to the door, and threw it open to see Maggie, his secretary, leaping from chair to chair, moving faster and jumping higher than he'd ever thought she could. Finally, she clambered onto the corner file cabinet, pulled her legs up beneath her, and continued to scream.

Standing by her desk were two redheaded boys: Leo and Nick Thomas. When the paperwork was done, they'd be Leo and Nick Peterson. Their mother Willow had married Sam Peterson in February.

As Adam moved farther into the office, Maggie kept screaming. The kids looked at him, eyes wide, their faces covered with shame, surprise, and a thin overlay of machismo.

After a few more steps, Adam saw the open box on the floor with a stiff, dead animal inside.

"In there, Preacher." Maggie pointed at the container. "The dirty, filthy creature's in there."

"What is it, boys?" Adam asked.

"It's a squirrel, sir," Leo said.

"It's dead, sir," Nick added. "I don't know why it would scare her. It can't attack."

"Women are like that," Adam said. "They don't like dead things." He turned and pointed toward his office. "You two need to explain this to me."

"No," Maggie shouted. "Preacher, you are not leaving me alone with that . . . that thing." She pointed toward the box with a shaking finger.

"Guys, you know this could be dangerous," Adam said.

"But it's dead," Leo said before he added, "sir."

"Rabies, other diseases." Adam pulled a ragged jacket from the lost-and-found, wrapped the box up, and stuffed it into a plastic bag. "I'm going to take this outside, put it in the trash, and call animal control. You boys, go to the restroom and wash up carefully. Maggie, go on home and try to forget this happened."

She slid off the cabinet onto a chair, leaped from that, grabbed her purse, and ran.

By the time Adam had washed his hands in the tiny private bathroom off his study and explained the situation to animal control, the boys stood in the front office. "I'm going to call your parents," he told them.

"Oh, no, sir. Please don't." Leo cleared his throat. "We'll do anything if you won't tell them."

"Mom gets sad and *really* disappointed in us." Nick's lips trembled. "And Sam, he expects better of us."

"You know Sam's my friend. I can't keep this from him. Is he home?"

They nodded.

Adam suddenly realized it was a weekday. "Why aren't you in school?"

"Teacher in-service day," Leo said. "Sam was supposed to watch us, but he's studying. You know he's taking a lot of math classes from Tech so he can get certified as a teacher."

"He was real busy studying and didn't notice when we left," Nick said. "He thinks we're in the backyard, but Leo remembered he saw a dead animal over in that lot next to the church Sunday. He made me come with him."

"Did not," Leo said. "You wanted to come."

"Did not," Nick contradicted. "Your idea."

"Listen, shorty, you—"

"Okay, guys." Sam held his hand up. "So you both sneaked out of your backyard . . ."

"It wasn't really sneaking," Leo said.

"We've never completely fixed the fence at Sam's house." Nick smiled. "At *our* house. He says we'll get around to that someday."

"Okay, I'm going to call Sam." He picked up the phone and punched the number in.

"Please don't."

"When he gets here, you're going to explain how that creature ended up on the floor of Maggie's office and scared her to death." He frowned at them. "You know Sam expects you to respect women."

Both nodded. Their eyes spoke of coming doom, but that didn't deter Adam. Great kids, but they were also very active and imaginative.

Only a few minutes later, Adam stood at the window in the reception office and watched Sam's yellow Mustang pull into the lot. The captain got out. An amputee from Afghanistan, Sam still limped a little, but today he strode with confidence.

Once they were all seated in Adam's office, Sam said, "Okay, guys, explain."

"I saw a dead animal in the back after church last Sunday so we came back to look at it," Leo said.

"You told me you were going to stay in the backyard. I trusted you and you lied to me," Sam said in a tone that reminded Adam that the captain had commanded marines.

"We didn't," Nick began.

"Man up, son," Sam said.

Both boys nodded and said, "Yes, sir," in unison. Probably, Adam thought, the entire conversation would be more suitable if they both stood at attention while Sam interrogated them.

"We lied to you and sneaked out to get the animal," Leo said. "Sir."

"But we didn't plan to pick up the squirrel." Nick added, "Sir."

"Then why did you bring a box with you, Gyrenes?" Sam asked.

Both boys looked so crestfallen that Adam almost felt sorry for them—until he remembered Maggie's terror.

"We wanted to bring it in here and show the preacher. We thought he'd want to see it," Leo said.

" 'Cause he's a guy," Nick added.

"Yes," Adam spoke solemnly. "Dead squirrels count as a particular favorite of mine."

Sam's lips quivered for only a moment before he became serious again.

"After that, we were going to come home and show you, Dad," Nick finished.

"How did that box get on the floor and the secretary end up on top of the file cabinet?" Adam asked.

"Nick dropped it."

"Did not. You pushed me."

"Did not . . ."

Sam held his hand up. "Enough. I don't care how it happened or who pushed who. You both handled a dead animal, which could have made you very sick. You both brought it in here and scared the secretary. You both knew she'd be frightened by a dead animal. Your actions may also have contaminated the offices."

"We didn't mean to," Nick said, his eyes wide and round.

"Doesn't matter," Leo said. "Actions have consequences." He sounded exactly like Sam.

"Yes, actions have consequences," Sam said. "We'll work those out when your mother gets home tonight."

"Do you have to tell her?" Nick asked.

All Sam had to do was raise his eyebrow. Both boys nodded.

"Of course you do," Nick said.

"She's our mother and she loves us and she has to know," Leo said. Words they must have heard from Sam several times.

"I don't keep secrets from my wife." Sam grinned when he said the word *wife*. "I don't lie to my wife and you don't lie to your mother."

"Sir, no, sir," the boys said.

"Thanks, Adam." Sam stood. "We'll handle this at home. Can you think of a service these two could perform at the church?"

"They could write an apology to Maggie."

"They will," Sam said. "What else? We don't have a lot left to do at the house."

"We could finish that fence, sir," Nick suggested as the three left the office.

Adam smiled. Yes, great kids, but he was glad he hadn't inherited them.

"Oh, hey, guys," Sam said. "Wait for me by my car. I need to talk to the preacher."

"Is it about us?" Nick asked.

Sam raised his brow again and the boys shouted, "Sir, yes, sir," and ran out.

"Don't find another dead animal or break a window or anything else while you're out there," Sam shouted at their backs, then he turned toward Adam and grinned. "They might kill me yet."

"You love them. You're happy."

"Never thought I would be again, Preacher, but I am." He paused and glanced at the wall over Adam's head before he said, "Umm . . . I hear Gussie Milton's coming to town in a couple of weeks."

Adam nodded. He didn't bother to ask how Sam knew that. He'd either heard it from Winnie Jenkins, the Widow who was engaged to his father, or he'd heard it the small-town way: Everyone knew everyone's business and everyone talked with everyone else about it, over and over, with embellishments. Actually, didn't much matter which.

"Yes," Adam said in a neutral voice. "She's going to talk to some of the kids about camp this summer. Bree invited her."

"So," Sam said in an equally neutral voice, keeping his gaze on the wall. "How do you feel about that?"

"Pretty angry that everyone in this town is determined to find me a wife."

"What's wrong with that?" Sam made eye contact with Adam. "The Widows hooked me up with Willow and that turned out great."

"I'm glad you're happy, but you would've worked things out with her by yourself."

"Maybe, but if the Widows are determined to match you up with someone, you've got about as much chance of escaping as a gnat in a hailstorm."

"Is that why you're here? The Widows told you to talk to me?"

Sam shook his head. "Willow did. I can't refuse anything she asks."

Adam laughed. "Big, tough marine."

As he finished the sentence, they heard a crash from the parking lot.

"Better go." Sam ran out of the office.

No telling what the boys were up to. Great kids, and he owed them for distracting their father.

❧

At dinner that evening, when Adam shared the news of the donkey with Hector and asked him to ride Maisie, Hector shook his head.

"Can't do that," he said.

"Why not? Afraid of donkeys?"

"Don't know, Pops. Never seen a donkey up close. But I think . . ." He paused and studied Adam seriously. "But I don't think people want a half-black, half-Mexican kid on that animal. They'll want someone more . . . well, more like Jesus. Same color."

"Don't agree with you. The church people like you. But, if they do complain, tough. I don't care."

"You don't care?"

"Besides, you're probably closer to the color of Jesus's skin than anyone else in town. He was born in the Middle East, in Bethlehem, not Dallas."

"You know what I like about you?" Hector said. "You don't go through all that junk about all being God's children, even though we are. You give it to me straight. Thanks."

"You're going to be Jesus?" Janey asked.

"Yeah." Hector smiled at his sister. "Who'd've thought I'd be Jesus in a church procession?"

❧

Birdie balanced a couple of plates on her arm. It was Friday, always a busy day at the diner. But this Friday was different. She could feel Farley's gaze on her as she delivered the order to the corner booth.

Why did the man keep watching her?

Did he hope she'd drop the dishes so he'd get a good laugh? Not out of the question because when she carried so many, her left shoulder complained, and more loudly every day. No doubt about it, if she wanted to last here until Mac got through college, she'd have to start carrying fewer plates. But that meant she'd have to make more trips, and her feet had started to ache.

When she finished placing the order on the table, she turned. The old coot—no, the a-few-years-older-than-she-was coot—still kept an eye on her. A stalker? No, not in Butternut Creek, and not Farley

Masterson. He'd been the police chief for years. No history of lawlessness in his background. Besides, he was probably too old and too slow to be a stalker. Maybe he could be a shuffler or a limper, but being a stalker seemed beyond his physical capabilities at his age.

Five years older than Birdie.

For a man his age, he looked pretty good. For a man his age, he stood straight and had only a small belly that protruded over his belt buckle. Good hair, thick and white. Not bad looking. Not that she felt a speck of interest in the man.

"Okay," she demanded as she strode toward his table after she'd picked up her favorite weapon, the coffeepot. "What do you want?"

"A hot cup of joe would be nice." He pushed the mug toward her.

"I mean, why are you here?"

"Breakfast?" He sounded confused. "I mean, isn't that what everyone else is here for?" Then he smiled.

And she knew. With those words and that expression, she knew he was fooling with her and was pleased he'd upset her, gotten her attention.

"Why else would I be here, Birdie?" He winked.

She turned and stalked off.

Old coot.

Pshaah. What foolishness. She did not have to act so polite. The man was a coot. A seventy-plus coot counted as an old coot. No use trying to wrap Farley Masterson up in pretty words to hide his age.

After tossing her shoulders back in pride, she grunted in pain, then started one more round with coffee. She ignored Farley's wave but knew she'd have to fill up his coffee and bus the table. The vibration of her cell gave her an excuse not to. She wasn't supposed to check it when she was working, but she'd told her boss that if one of the girls called, she'd answer even if she had to drop a tray in the middle of the diner. There was a text message from Bree. "Coach from Hwrd Col calld. Vball."

Bree and Mac used few abbreviations in their texts because, doggone, it took so long for their grandmother to translate them. This one was easy. A coach from Howard College had called about volleyball. It was a two-year school, but a good start not too far away and might offer a good financial package. Heaven knew, Birdie couldn't afford much. The high school counselor had told her it was a good thing Birdie's income was so low because that would help with scholarships and aid. Who knew eking out a living could be a blessing? Well, other than in the Beatitudes.

She snapped the phone shut and attempted to ignore the

realization that her granddaughters were growing up, that they'd both leave for college someday and she'd be alone, exactly as Mercedes had said.

She should rejoice, be happy to have the house back to herself, to order her life around her needs not the schedules of teenagers. But she knew the quiet of the empty house would be oppressive with only the meows of Carlos the Cat to break the silence. She'd miss the clattering of the girls' feet up and down the steps and the slamming of the front door, those things she always nagged them about.

"Coffee," shouted Farley.

She glanced at him. Not even when the girls were gone and she was lonely would she have the least interest in the man.

❧

As Adam listened to the music coming from the AME Church on the street behind the parsonage, he heard Hector come out the back door. Easy to recognize Hector's arrival because doors slammed behind him and he took huge strides that thumped across the dry yard. On the basketball court, he moved like a ballerina—not that Adam would ever tell him that—but he clumped along like a buffalo in real life.

"Hey, Pops." He sat next to Adam. "I'd . . ." Hector glanced at Adam, uncertain. "Pops, that's the church music I grew up with, when I was a kid, when our mother took us to church. I miss it." He shook his head. "I like your church, but it isn't my church, not yet."

For a moment, Adam felt incredibly guilty. "I'm sorry. I shouldn't have forced you to attend the Christian Church."

"Hey, no, Pops. I like being there. I like the people and I owe them a lot, but . . . but I'd like to go there"—he gestured to the source of the music—"now and then."

"Want to go tonight?" Adam glanced at his watch. "The service started a couple of minutes ago. We could run over there."

"You'd come, too?"

"Why not? I'll enjoy it. Get Janey."

Within five minutes, they'd hurried across the backyard of the parsonage, through the gate, and crossed the street to stand at the door of the AME Church.

"Welcome." After a start at seeing Adam, a smile creased the face of the greeter. "Find yourself a place to sit." He gestured to a nearly filled sanctuary.

After they found a pew all three of them could squeeze onto, Adam stood with the congregation and listened. Hard to believe, but the music was better inside the building.

He marveled at the skill of the pianist who seemed to use every key, added notes and trills and beats that he'd never heard, and still pounded out the melody. Adam couldn't help but clap with the congregation and move with the rhythm.

For a few minutes, he drank it in, then turned to look at the kids. Hector swayed with the beat and Janey listened intently, her body moving side to side.

When the pianist started "Oh, Happy Day," Adam joined in. Not that he could sing well, but he knew the words and could feel the spirit moving through him. It took him a few seconds to realize the congregation split into parts, one side singing the line and the other echoing it. "Oh, happy day," his side sang. The other section sang, "Oh, happy day . . ."

He understood why Hector needed this, why he thought the service at the Christian Church was boring. Joy, this service was filled with joy.

When the pianist segued into "There Is a Balm in Gilead," Adam heard a lovely, pure voice coming from beside him. Everyone looked around but Adam looked down. Janey, her eyes closed and head lifted, allowed music to flow from her. The notes filled and swirled around the church. She sang for nearly a minute before she noticed the others had stopped. At the realization, Janey opened her eyes, closed her mouth, and dropped onto the pew, her head down. Immediately the other worshippers picked up the tune and sang on. Hector and Adam sat down, one on each side of her and each took one of her hands. He felt he'd witnessed a miracle.

As the congregation sat at the end of that hymn, the minister asked, "Do we have any visitors with us tonight?"

Adam looked around. The only white person in the sanctuary, he stuck out like a daisy in a bed of pansies. Certainly it was obvious he was a visitor, and so was the little girl with the golden voice. But the minister waited politely, his eyes moving across the congregation until falling—as if surprised—on Adam.

"Yes, brother, we're glad to have you here. Would you introduce yourself?"

Adam stood. "I'm Adam Jordan, minister of the Christian Church." He pointed in that direction. "And your neighbor. Hector and Janey," he gestured toward the kids, "heard the music and came over to join in."

"We're glad you did."

With those words, the entire congregation stood, made a line around the sanctuary, and came by the pew to shake his hand and Hector's while Janey sat with her head still down.

After a rousing sermon during which Adam had been moved to say a loud, "Amen," the minister pronounced the benediction and they all rose to leave.

"You're right. This is more fun," Adam said.

"I can't see Miss Birdie joining in," Hector said. "Or any of the rest of the congregation. But they are good folks, the people at the Christian Church."

"Janey," Adam said as they walked back to the parsonage. "I didn't know you could sing. Thank you."

She glanced at him and gave that tiny smile again. "I like to sing."

"She hasn't sung in years," Hector said. "It felt good to hear her."

Maybe it was a sign of progress.

That night, as he perused a Bible commentary, Chewy, curled up by Adam's feet, lifted his head and cocked an ear. Above them, Janey sang "Wade in the Water." After a few measures, Chewy began to howl along with her. For a moment, only silence came from upstairs, then Adam heard Janey rushing down the stairs. She looked at the dog, put her arms around his neck, and laughed with genuine delight.

Adam had never seen Janey like this, had never known the solemn child could sing or show such happiness. He savored the moment. Inviting the Firestone children to live here had been the right thing to do. Now he was reaping the reward. He was the one truly blessed.

"I love to hear you sing," he said.

She froze when she heard his voice, then lifted her eyes toward him. All the happiness had gone, vanished.

In a second Adam was overcome by a wave of anger deeper than he realized he possessed. As a peaceful man, the emotion frightened him because, more than anything, he wanted to beat up the person who'd put that fear in her eyes. He forced the rage away and took a deep breath before he said gently, "You have a lovely voice."

"Thank you," Janey said with that tiny grin.

"Janey, you don't have to be afraid of me. I promise, I will never do anything to hurt you."

She said nothing but looked a little more relaxed.

"I'd love to hear another song."

After a short pause, she shook her head.

He didn't want to push. "Miss Blossom left some cookies, those big lemon cookies her cook makes. Do you want one?"

She nodded.

"Let's get a few. Then we could watch something on television. What do you think?"

After they were both settled, each with a glass of milk and the plate of goodies on the coffee table between them, Adam watched Janey as she nibbled and watched the program, some reality show with singing. She had lovely dark skin. Her hair was in those intricate braids, today with yellow barrettes on the ends, a skill he knew he'd never master.

"Would you like to sing at church sometime?"

"No." She didn't look up from the television.

Okay. "Thanks for keeping me company," he said.

After a few minutes, she said, "But I'll sing for you sometime, if you'd like me to. And for Chewy."

"I really would. Thank you," he said.

And she smiled.

At nine on the morning of Palm Sunday, Hector pointed from the porch of the parsonage toward the church parking lot. "Look, she's here. A real donkey."

Adam and Janey followed him toward the horse trailer as Jesse led the small animal out.

Hector stroked Maisie's soft muzzle. "I've never touched one."

Maisie lifted her head to glance at Hector as he petted her dark gray and slightly curled coat.

"She's pretty," Janey said looking up at the donkey.

"And she's a stubborn creature," Jesse said. "Hector, you're going to have to keep a tight hold of her and don't put up with any prancing around."

"Yes, sir. Bobby'll be here in a few minutes to help me with her," Hector said. "We'll keep her in line."

"Sure you will, son," Jesse said. "I'm going to tie her to the back of the trailer and stay with her until you're ready for her."

When Adam entered the church, he saw Bree and Mac counting out palm branches on the receptionist's desk.

"We've got this under control," Bree said. "We'll go to the Sunday school classrooms and explain it all."

By the time Adam went back outside at ten thirty, a crowd had begun to gather. The children, each carrying a palm branch, hopped out of the Sunday school wing and stood around Maisie as she snacked on the grass at the edge of the lot. Hector and Bobby wore robes and sandals and stood on either side of Maisie, both holding her reins.

Leo and Nick stood a few feet from them, fascinated. A few yards behind the boys, Willow in a pale pink suit with matching flowered hat and high-heeled shoes leaned on Sam and grinned at her boys.

"Doesn't she look great?" Sam asked. "I have the most beautiful wife in the world."

Winnie and Sam's father stood a few feet away chatting with Blossom. Mercedes and Miss Birdie came out of the building, probably just finished putting the final touches on the cookies for the special coffee hour after the service, while Janey, Bree, and Mac finished handing out palms to the adults.

Ouida stood between her daughters as they swished their branches through the air. "They said I had to come see the donkey," she explained to Adam. "They're very excited about the whole deal."

On the edge of the lot, the bluish purple of bluebonnets shimmered. A beautiful morning, a calm, peaceful moment as the people Adam loved joined together under the light filtering through the live oaks.

Adam took pictures of the crowd, starting with one of Hector holding Maisie's reins while he grinned at his little sister. He snapped another of Bobby and Bree, laughing. A perfect day.

Then through the lens, Adam made out the head of someone with red hair climbing on Maisie's back. Before he could put the camera down and react, chaos broke out.

The donkey brayed and pulled the reins from Bobby's and Hector's hands.

"Help," Nick shouted from the back of the animal at the same moment Adam realized the red hair belonged to Sam and Willow's youngest son.

With a mighty and joyful hee-haw, the donkey took off, bucking and jumping. Maisie headed across the lawn, around the building, and toward the highway with Nick clinging to her back and Hector and Bobby chasing after them.

For a moment, everyone else watched, too startled to move. Leo stood close to where the donkey had been, his eyes wide. Then Willow started running in the direction the donkey had fled; Sam and Adam were behind her, followed by nearly everyone in the church. With a quick look behind him, Adam could see Miss Birdie sprinting toward the front of the pack with Bree and Mac only a few feet ahead of her. The general, Sam's father and Nick's grandfather, was closing in on the leading peloton. Jesse attempted to keep up but fell behind, huffing and puffing. And all of them carried their palms.

Adam glanced ahead. Nick was holding on for dear life, his arms around the donkey's neck, his bottom flopping up and down, his legs flying up beside him. How did the kid avoid being thrown off?

The pursuers hadn't gained a yard on the bucking burro. Then Adam saw Hector trip over his sandals, not the greatest shoes for running. When he stumbled, Bobby tripped over him. Both ended up lying flat on the street, watching the animal take off as they attempted to untangle their long limbs.

Willow had tossed the pretty hat to the side and kicked her shoes off. Pulling her skirt up, she leaped over Hector's legs and continued to race after her son. Although he fell behind, Sam didn't slow down.

"Go rest, son," the general shouted at Sam. "I'll get him."

The man should have known Sam wouldn't leave the chase. Although he fell back, he still followed the creature escaping with Nick on her back.

Clearly Maisie felt the thrill of independence as she ran on. When she turned her head to look back, Adam thought he saw her smile at the group before she picked up the pace. She brayed ecstatically, a sound he translated as, "Born free."

"Help!" Nick yelled again.

"We're coming," Adam shouted. He saw a sign of hope. Maisie seemed to be slowing down, winded after more exercise than she might have been used to, all while carrying a load.

Then a flash passed them: Bobby, running fast and smoothly. Maisie turned to check behind her again, saw Bobby, but couldn't find another gear. Inexorably, Bobby closed in.

Only a few steps behind him flew Hector, shoeless. "You get the kid," he shouted. "I'll stop the donkey."

That's exactly what happened. Bobby pulled up and ran in stride with Maisie, then reached for Nick—who threw his arms around the young man's neck and was dragged to safety while Hector grabbed a rein and pulled the panting animal to a stop.

Shouts and the toots of car horns came from both sides of the highway. Adam hadn't noticed the crowd until the rescue was completed. Had they stopped to watch the show or because they decided it would be better not to hit a runaway donkey with a kid on its back?

When Willow reached the four—Nick, Bobby, Hector, and Maisie—she grabbed her son and held him in a strong hug before she placed him on the street. "Wait till I get you home," she threatened but kept squeezing Nick's hand.

Nick looked shaky, his face pale and legs trembling. He attempted to look tough, chin out and lips firm, but he did not let go of his mother's hand.

"That was so cool."

Adam looked down to see Leo standing next to him, "Preacher, wasn't that cool?" Leo asked. "But I'd hate to be in his shoes. Nick's going to be in so much trouble."

"Think we'll skip church this morning," Sam said as he reached Adam's side and put his hand on Leo's shoulder. "We need to take care of this at home. Sorry we messed up your service."

"Not your fault," Adam said. "You do what you need to do." He looked behind him to see that the congregation had gathered on the sidewalk gasping for air. They watched the Peterson family head around the church and back to the car while Hector led a now docile Maisie by the rope.

"Hector, take the donkey back to the garden," Adam said. "When you take her to the other churches, stay with her and tell everyone she doesn't like riders." He took a step toward the church and began to sing the processional hymn, his thin, wavering voice leading the way. "Hosanna, loud hosanna," he sang, and the congregation followed him back to the church waving their palms. Janey glanced up at him. Obviously feeling sorry for his pitiable efforts, she joined in. Once there, the disheveled congregation went inside and threw themselves on the pews, fanning flushed faces with the palms and breathing deeply.

That morning would long be remembered in the lore of Butternut Creek.

Chapter Six

Gussie hurried home from church after the Easter service. Her parents refused to skip that Sunday. "I haven't missed an Easter service in over sixty years," her father had said. "Not going to let a little allergy problem stop me now."

Gussie had learned years earlier not to challenge any pronouncement by her father that had a number of years in it. *I've been doing this for [fill in this blank with a number] years* always meant she'd better give in and give up.

But was that cough merely the symptom of allergies?

Oh, she worried too much.

"You've become a mother hen," her mother often said. "Silly for a daughter to turn into a mother hen." Then her mother would laugh.

However, the daughter didn't find it amusing. Her parents were in their seventies, which meant both that she had every right to cluck over them and worry *and* that she probably had no reason to believe they would change in the least because they had arrived at this age on their own and were as stubborn as . . . as . . . well, as Gussie was.

Gussie pulled into the drive at exactly the same time her father went into a paroxysm of coughs. She glanced in the rearview mirror and asked, "Are you all right?" She wanted to take him to the hospital right now, but he waved at her and nodded because he couldn't speak.

Mom turned. "Henry?"

"I'm fine," he said between coughs. "I'll get a peppermint to suck on."

Of course, once they got inside, her father didn't stop coughing but took a Benadryl, flipped on the television, and settled into the recliner to watch sports and nap.

"I breathe better sitting up," he explained. Within minutes, he was asleep and the coughing had calmed.

Looked as if he was right. It had been allergies.

❧

Adam's first Easter in Butternut Creek. The men pulled out the huge wooden cross they'd made years ago to put in front of the sanctuary. Everyone brought flowers and put them in the holes drilled in the cross. Really pretty.

The service began with a processional to bring in the cross and candlesticks they'd removed from the altar for Maundy Thursday. Miss Birdie thought that seemed high church, but that didn't deter Adam.

He looked around the sanctuary at a good crowd gathered to celebrate. Maybe one hundred, which still left empty pews in the big sanctuary. To begin the service, Mac played an introit on her trumpet, the clear notes sounding around them and calling them to celebrate.

The joy of Easter, the thought of Christians all over the world celebrating this triumphant day, overwhelmed him. Surrounded by flowers and faith and the family of believers, they came together as God's people and rejoiced.

"Hallelujah," he proclaimed to begin the service.

❧

"George," Ouida called from her dressing table in the master bedroom.

"Yes?" George's slightly muffled voice came from his walk-in closet.

In the mirror, Ouida watched herself brushing her hair. "What would you think if I grew my hair longer?" she asked. "Do you think I'd look glamorous?"

She could hear his firm tread cross the carpet until she saw his reflection behind her, studying her. "No, I wouldn't like it long. Keep it like this. I don't want you to be glamorous."

That firmly put her in her place as dowdy hausfrau. Oh, he didn't mean it as an insult. George just didn't like change.

She could see from his reflection that he held a pair of boxers in his hand. She'd have preferred to discuss those boxers another day, any other day, or perhaps never. She'd hoped he wouldn't realize she hadn't ironed them.

"I've noticed something." He held that blasted undergarment

up. "Yesterday, I felt very uncomfortable in my . . . you know, the part of the body where I wear my boxers."

Poor George didn't like to discuss anatomy, his or anyone else's.

"Oh?" Ouida stopped rubbing cream onto her nose. Why she did that, she didn't know. The freckles would never go away. Probably magical thinking, that if she stopped, more would pop out. Maybe she could add rubbing cream on her nose to the list of things she didn't need to do. After all, George didn't want her to be glamorous. She wiped her fingers off, then turned on the bench to study her husband.

"You didn't iron my underwear." He held up the slightly wrinkled but clean undergarment, one of the dozen she'd washed, smoothed out, and folded before placing them in his drawer yesterday.

"And the dresser scarves?" He reached out to place his hand on the exposed surface of the chest of drawers. "The pretty set my mother made for you. Where are they?"

"I decided we didn't really need them. Who needs a newly washed, ironed, and starched runner nowadays?"

"I didn't say we needed them, but they are pretty and my mother made them. I'd like them back." He used the calm voice that expressed his need for her to do exactly what he wanted, as if explaining to someone with little understanding. He always seemed certain that if he expressed his wish logically and in everyday words, she'd comprehend the situation and change.

She hated it. She hadn't realized until that moment how much she hated that tone.

For a moment, she considered her options. George stood before her, tall and handsome and urbane even holding up a pair of his shorts. The man of her dreams, the man she'd loved for so long, but also the man who expected her to do exactly what he wanted.

When had she become a drudge with so little backbone? Ouida took a deep breath.

"George, with the girls and this big house, I had to cut back some. I can't do everything."

He raised an eyebrow, which made him more good-looking but twice as condescending.

She steeled herself. "I can't do everything," she repeated slowly in the same tone he used with her. "I've decided not to mop the kitchen floor every time someone enters, and not to iron your undershorts. I believe we can also get by without the dresser scarves."

He took a few steps toward her, sat next to her on the bench, and took her hand. "Ouida, I work long hours."

She nodded.

"We have a service to take care of the lawn. I work to pay all the bills. All I ask is for you to do your job inside the house. How much trouble can it be to take care of two little girls and to iron my boxers?" He handed her the garment, stood, and walked toward the bed.

She stifled a scream.

Adam woke up and glanced at the clock. Five fifteen. Still dark outside.

What had awakened him? He listened but heard nothing. He shoved the sheet over Chewy, who took up most of the bed, and got up to check on the kids. After he looked in on both and assured himself they were safe and still asleep, he went back to his bedroom and sat on the edge of the bed. Within seconds, he realized what had interfered with his sleep. Actually, who.

The Widows.

Yes, the Widows had appeared in a dream. No, in a nightmare. They'd all worn black Stetsons and toted .45s. Their appearance was probably an outlet for his anxiety about the looming crisis of Gussie's coming to town and what the Widows had in mind for that afternoon.

For weeks he'd attempted to convince himself the Widows would limit themselves to serving refreshments at the youth meeting. He'd hoped they'd ignore their calling as matchmakers but he knew they wouldn't. Matchmaking was in their blood, was their prime directive.

He'd call Sam tomorrow because if he'd ever needed a marine on his side, it would be this Sunday. He hadn't seen much of Sam recently. His friend had married, become a father to two active sons, and was going to school. Not much time for more than watching a few basketball games together or meeting for pie, but *now* Sam needed to step up to the plate. Adam refused to face the Widows alone, and Sam owed him.

Gussie kept her eyes on the road. It was the Sunday after Easter and there weren't huge numbers of cars roaring along. There were also no runaway trucks coming up behind to crash into her. No danger lurked behind the hills and fences that, if not studiously watched and carefully avoided, might leap ahead of her and wreak destruction.

No, it wasn't the traffic or lack of it or the possible perils on the road that forced her to focus on her driving.

It was what awaited her in Butternut Creek. Not really a *what* but a *who*. A perfectly nice man, a minister who cared for his congregation. He'd built a youth program, taken in Hector and his sister, and seemed to be getting along with Miss Birdie. From what she'd heard, that was a feat few other ministers had managed.

Yes, a nice, tall, skinny minister awaited her arrival with, from what he had emailed, the four young people she knew from the church and ten or twelve of their friends who didn't go to church regularly. Those kids were important. Involvement in church camp and retreats could change their lives.

Right now she didn't care about a single one of those young people. Right now she wanted to turn around, go back home, and hide in her room.

But she'd been hiding for years and it hadn't solved a single problem. Oh, yes, at first it had helped. She'd healed in solitude with her parents around to feed her and care for her, to soothe and love her. But after a few weeks, they'd forced her out of that cocoon. The right thing to do, of course, but she'd felt safer back then. Today she felt vulnerable and just plain scared.

Oh, she knew perfectly well she and Adam would be surrounded by fifteen youths, which would cut down on any frightening experiences. But the Widows would be there also. From what everyone said, they could make life incredibly embarrassing.

Thank goodness the Widows didn't know about the flash of attraction she'd felt for Adam. Gussie usually succeeded very well in hiding from her emotions since . . . since back then, over a decade ago. She had a terrible feeling that if she accepted the fact she was attracted to Adam, all those other feelings that hovered barely below the surface of her mind would flood back, engulfing and destroying her.

At one forty-five, she pulled into the church parking lot. Two or three cars were parked by the entrance to the fellowship hall. Could be there were so few because she was early. Could be some of the young people hadn't driven.

Could be she was stalling and didn't want to go inside.

Most merciful God . . . But she didn't finish. She refused to pray that Adam had a slight fever that would go away as soon as the meeting was over. He'd have to miss the gathering so he wouldn't infect the kids and she wouldn't have to face him.

No, praying for the illness of others to make her life more comfortable did not constitute an acceptable petition, certainly not one made to a merciful and loving God. In fact, the only option was a quick *Dear God, grant me wisdom and courage.* With that, she opened the door, grabbed her purse and tote, and got out of the car.

"Hi!" Bree came running out of the church and waved. "We're so glad to see you. Let me help you." She grabbed Gussie's tote.

The loss of that bag pretty much cut off Gussie's plan to escape. The tote held her brain: all the information she needed about youth work in Central Texas, her calendars and schedules. Yes, her brain. It held records of all those things she did to make up for not having a real life. With no other option, she followed Bree and her brain into the fellowship hall.

A dozen kids milled around inside. No sign of Adam. She hoped he really wasn't sick. Maybe an emergency had come up. But, no, she couldn't wish a disaster, not even a small one of short duration, on others for her own well-being.

On the other side of the kitchen counter were Miss Birdie, Mercedes, and two women she hadn't met before, both with nicely coiffed hair. All four women smiled at her. She was used to a friendly Mercedes, but the curve that might pass as a smile on Miss Birdie's thin lips frightened her. Why, she couldn't explain, but it contained enough glee that Gussie wanted to run back to her car.

"Hello, Gussie!"

She turned to see Adam. He looked friendly and glad to see her but nothing more.

Was that reaction good news or bad news? If he didn't feel anything for her, she should rejoice. She didn't want a relationship. They could become messy. On the other hand, what kind of social incompetent did it make her that she was attracted to him and he liked her only as a person, as a friend, as a colleague?

Ugh. She refused to consider either of those choices, not now. She had a meeting to lead.

Unfortunately, she glanced into the kitchen and saw the intense scrutiny of the four women there. A chill invaded every cell of her body. She resolved not to show fear but she knew she wouldn't get out of here unscathed.

"Hey, Gussie," Hector said. He and Bobby walked over, each clutching the arm of a friend. "Want you to meet a couple of my friends." He nodded toward them. "This is Junior Rodriguez, and Bobby's friend is Mark Scroggins."

She shook their hands, then asked, "Do you play basketball, too?" After a few minutes of chatting about sports, the visitors looked a lot more relaxed. They probably thought because they were inside a church, she'd force them to confess their sins and repent publicly. The conversation ended when Bree called out, "Let's come together. It's nearly two o'clock."

Gussie spoke for ten minutes, then the four who'd been to the retreat gave a quick talk about their experiences. Bobby's comments were short and precise: "It was fun but we had to take out trash and wipe down tables."

At two thirty, they broke for refreshments and the fun began. Or, the mortification. The description pretty much depended on which side one favored.

"Gussie, I want you to meet our two newest Widows." Mercedes approached and introduced Winnie and Blossom.

"Aren't you the prettiest thing," Blossom said in a soft voice.

Gussie knew she wasn't all that pretty but didn't mind the compliment. Then the platinum-blond Widow took Gussie's right hand in what seemed at first a gentle clasp but turned into an iron grip with which she led Gussie toward the sofa where—not surprisingly—Miss Birdie had shoved Adam down on the cushions and now sat next to him.

When Gussie attempted to pull away, the other Widow—Winnie? Was that her name?—took her left hand and dragged Gussie toward the preacher. She could not break away without causing a scene and possible injury. Not that they had any scruples about capturing her, but theirs had been a covert action and hers would be outright combat.

Besides they were at least twice her age. She couldn't fight them without looking like a bully.

Adam glanced up from his conversation with Miss Birdie. An I-should-have-guessed expression covered his face. He had the nerve to laugh. Did he have no idea what lay ahead?

Of course he did, but he could see the humor in the machinations of the Widows while she experienced only mind-numbing terror.

When she approached, Adam attempted to stand. With Miss Birdie holding one hand, the action was futile. He stood halfway up before she pulled him down. The landing caused the sofa to shiver and the cushion to fly up on the end as he made a resounding thud and an "Ooof."

Which of course alerted the young people who had been talking and gathered along the counter for refreshments. They all turned to watch.

Oh, terrific. Gussie didn't wonder what would happen next. She knew. With a final shove to Adam, Miss Birdie sprang to her feet.

"Why don't you sit down here." She waved to the place next to the preacher, the seat she'd just abandoned.

"I think—" Gussie could say no more before her effort to sit in a chair and her path to that chair were cut off by the two women, who were much stronger than anyone their age should be. Quickly and firmly, she'd been shoved forward, spun, and seated. The cushions were so soft, it felt as if she'd dropped into mud. She'd never get out without help. She'd been captured and imprisoned with no choice but to remain until assistance or a crane showed up.

"There you go," the blonde said in a soft Southern accent, most confusing since the woman's determination was made of iron. Before Gussie could say a word or move an inch, Blossom sat between her and the arm of the love seat so the three were packed together, shoulder-to-shoulder and hip-to-hip.

"Isn't this cozy?" Blossom cooed.

It wasn't.

"Now, you two stay there . . . ," Miss Birdie began.

As if they could move.

". . . and I'll get you some cookies." The senior Widow bustled away.

However, her departure did not signal a reprieve. Winnie and Mercedes stood in front of the love seat as if they were playing "Red Rover" and were poised to capture anyone who attempted to "come over."

Gussie whispered to Adam, "Get me out of this."

"Relax," he whispered back. "You can't get away from the Widows. Submission is the only option. It makes the humiliation shorter and less painful."

"Great," Gussie moaned. "Thanks for the encouragement."

Miss Birdie placed a plate of cookies in her lap and handed another to Adam, then brought each a cup of punch, which she put on the end tables. Not, of course, that Gussie could pick up her punch, because Blossom sat between her and the cup. Good thing she didn't really want a drink during this odd little interlude. She attempted to shift position, but the lovely, smiling Widow held her arm securely, another reason she couldn't sip the punch.

"Now," Blossom said as Gussie bit into a lemon bar. "Why don't we chat. Gussie, why don't you tell Adam an interesting fact he doesn't know about you?"

Could this get any worse? Well, yes, Gussie figured it could.

From the refreshment counter, thirty eyes, more or less, focused on the scene, taking in every nuance, every movement, every word.

Then there were six more eyes.

"Hey." A handsome man with a slight limp entered from the parking lot with two redheaded boys. "Sorry I'm late . . ." He stopped speaking and moving when he saw Gussie and Adam shoved together on the love seat with Blossom. "I . . . um . . ." He swallowed, perhaps attempting not to laugh. "Willow's on call this weekend and had to go to the hospital. I brought the boys with me. Guys," he said to the two, "go get yourself some refreshments and bring me a glass of punch." He sat at a table that faced the love seat. "I'm going to sit right here and enjoy the show." He grinned.

"That's my former friend, Sam Peterson." Adam glared at the man. "Thanks, Sam," he said with an edge to his voice that Gussie hadn't heard before. In an instant her brain flashed back on the image she'd stored and attempted—unsuccessfully—to ignore of Adam playing basketball with sweat gluing his shirt onto his wiry but muscular body and macho determination on his face.

With that ill-timed image firmly seared into her mind, it took every ounce of her strength to focus on the visitor and wave. "I'm Gussie Milton," she said.

"I know." Sam waved at her, then toward the treat-covered counter. "Those are my sons, Leo and Nick."

The two boys grinned at her with chocolate-covered lips.

Then everyone, every single person in the room, went back to watching the two on the love seat. Gussie ignored Blossom's request to share information about herself. Instead she chewed on a bite of cookie that had long ago lost any flavor or structural integrity but kept her mouth occupied.

"Aren't they the cutest couple in the world?" Winnie asked.

The young people looked at each other and shrugged.

"What's going on, Pops?" Hector asked.

Adam didn't answer. Probably no way to explain.

"Gussie." Miss Birdie spoke as if she and the two captives were engaged in a private little chat. "Tell Adam something about you that he doesn't know."

Other than being rude, which the Widows didn't mind doing although in such a pleasant way, Gussie couldn't think of anything else to do but answer. She refused to behave poorly in front of her kids or that man facing them from the table—Sam?—who was laughing so hard he nearly fell off his chair.

"I used to play the clarinet," Gussie said after she swallowed and before she took another bite of lemon bar.

"Were you in the band?" Adam asked, his voice filled with interest, as if that were the most scintillating bit of information he'd ever heard.

Exactly the right way to play this, Gussie realized. "Oh, yes," she said with great enthusiasm. "I was in the marching band."

"Isn't that interesting," Adam replied. "Miss Birdie's granddaughter Mac is in the marching band." He beckoned Mac over with two fingers. "Did you know Gussie played the clarinet in the marching band?"

With a grin, Mac approached them. "Isn't that interesting?" she said. "Has Adam told you about the time I led the middle school band?"

After ten more minutes, the Widows gave up. By that time, Hector and Gussie had discussed being tall; she and Bobby had discussed being an only child; and she and Bree had discussed playing volleyball. Gussie had started to relax and enjoy herself.

Miss Birdie cut into the chats. "Well, I guess that's finished." She shoved Hector and Bree toward the door, saying, "Shoo, shoo." The rest of the youths followed.

"Hey, Preacher," Bobby said before he could be pushed outside. "You need a hoop out here so we can play ball."

Miss Birdie closed the door before Adam could answer.

And they were alone, Adam and Gussie, with four Widows bent on . . . oh, she didn't know what exactly. Something evil. She heard Sam and his boys in the kitchen, probably finishing up the cookies, but she could hardly expect help from them. Sam enjoyed their predicament too much to do anything but laugh, and the boys seemed devoted to chocolate. They wouldn't notice her appeals as they stuffed down brownies.

"Preacher, why don't you take Gussie for a tour around the town?" Winnie said.

"What a lovely suggestion, but I've visited Butternut Creek often. I had an aunt who lived here."

"Oh, yes, Grace Carson, your father's sister," Mercedes said.

"Well, then, you two think of something to do for an hour or two. Together." Although devious, Miss Birdie had never been able to hide her plans well. "Then come back and we'll have a nice little supper for the two of you."

"You won't want to drive all the way to Roundville hungry," Blossom said.

"You might have one of those dreaded hunger-related accidents," Adam agreed sincerely.

"Thank you so much, ladies," Gussie said. "I didn't realize that you had this planned. I need to get home. I hate to leave my parents alone . . ."

"Such a good daughter," Mercedes said. "But sometime you're going to have to think about yourself." She paused dramatically. "And your future."

"Your parents aren't going to live forever," the pillar said, a remark greeted by shoves and "shh" from the other Widows. "Not, of course, that I'm hoping they will die soon, but we all will. Someday."

Not sure whether to laugh or scream or stare in amazement, Gussie decided to do none. Instead she said, "It's not that long a drive." She used every muscle she had to force herself up from the engulfing cushion. "If I get weak, I'll grab something on the road."

Gussie wished she had a camera to always remember the expressions on the Widows' faces. Disappointment warred with disbelief that their plan had been scuttled.

"Didn't Mac invite you?" Miss Birdie said. "For dinner?"

Gussie pulled her calendar from the tote and flipped it open. "Oh, yes, she did." She couldn't get Mac in trouble, but she had to get out of this place and away from Adam. "I . . . I'm really sorry. I forgot. Didn't check the book."

Adam shoved himself up from the deep cushions and watched Gussie for a second. She looked frantic. The Widows could do that to a person. "Don't worry. Hector will eat your portion and more. If you need to get on the road, allow me to walk you to your car."

He couldn't believe he'd uttered that stupid phrase: "Allow me to walk you to your car." Sounded as if he were from Victorian England, but having Gussie here and the Widows looking on scrambled his brain. Amazing he could still utter a sentence that actually made sense, even archaic nonsense.

To make matters worse, he held out his arm, crooked at the elbow, as if he were escorting a debutante. Gussie ignored it, maybe hadn't seen it, but the Widows had and they smiled, possibly hoping he'd lure her into a compromising position over the ten yards across the parking lot to her car.

"Don't worry, Preacher," Miss Birdie said in what she considered a whisper but could be heard by everyone within twenty yards. "I won't let them out"—she used her head to point out the other Widows—"until you've finished your courting." Then she nearly shoved them from the building.

Once outside, Gussie said, "Oh, that was horrific." She started laughing so hard she leaned on his arm for support. "Horrific but absolutely hilarious." She took a deep breath and attempted to control her mirth.

He loved to hear her laugh. Sometimes it sounded like bells, going up an octave then back down. Other times it was a hoot or just a burst of happiness, but she never held back. When Gussie laughed, everyone knew she meant it and joined in.

"Adam, I'm so sorry to bail on dinner, but I've never been so mortified and so terrified and so entertained in my entire life." She pulled in a deep gulp of air and attempted to regain control. "I hardly know how to react except to laugh but I can't take any more of this. I can't stay for dinner. It's too funny and too humiliating, and way too . . . oh I don't know. Too everything." She stopped once they reached her car and beeped the doors open. "They are so very careful about every detail of their scheme and so certain they are right that I couldn't laugh in their faces, sweet ladies."

"You might believe they're sweet but they're calculating and devious and darned near impossible to ignore." He grinned to soften his words. "You don't know that because you don't have them bustling around, taking charge of your life and conniving every day to get you married."

"How do you handle it? I couldn't have kept from laughing if I'd stayed for a minute longer."

They both turned toward the church when they heard the kitchen door open. Blossom rushed out with a large box. Gussie closed her mouth tightly, biting her bottom lip.

"Some cookies for you," Blossom said. "In case you get hungry on the way home."

The Widow stood right next to Gussie's car with a broad smile on her face while Gussie nodded and struggled not to laugh. She managed a hurried, muffled "Thank you."

Then Miss Birdie stuck her head out the door and shouted, "How did you get past me, Blossom Brown? You come inside and leave the lovebirds alone." With a start, Blossom hurried away and into the church.

Gussie whooped and tears flowed down her cheeks. "Don't they drive you crazy?"

"I've learned to laugh inside." He sighed as he handed Gussie a Kleenex from his pocket. "You met Sam. The Widows are sure it was their matchmaking that got him married. They feel flush with victory and refuse to give up on me, not while they're on a hot streak. I'm sorry they embarrassed you."

"They delighted me, too." With that, Gussie tossed the tote into the car, placed the cookies on the passenger seat, and got behind the wheel.

"Thanks, Adam. This was wonderful. I'll never forget this afternoon."

He closed the door as she started the car. With a wave, she drove away.

They'd both survived. They hadn't had their britches embarrassed off them; only, maybe, their socks. When the car disappeared down the highway, he stood there, uncertain if he should feel victorious because the Widows had failed or defeated because Gussie had fled and left him more befuddled than ever.

With so little display of interest on Gussie's part—lots of embarrassment, a great deal of laughter, but little attraction—he probably should leave things alone. He'd email her, thank her for coming. He didn't really need to stop with one email. Friends, they could be friends, and that could develop into something more. If he stopped pursuing her, even in his meandering and obviously ineffective way, nothing would happen between them. Ever.

When he'd been in seminary, his professor of church management told the story about a man watching a kid fish. Before he tossed his line into the water, the boy reached in his mouth, pulled something out, and placed it on the hook. Every time, he'd pull in a large fish and repeat the operation. The man, who'd caught nothing, approached the boy and asked how he'd been so successful. The kid spit a bunch of worms into his hand and said, "You've got to keep the worms warm."

"That's what church growth is all about," the professor explained. "Call on your visitors, invite others to come, whatever it takes to keep the worms warm."

And that pretty much described what Adam planned to do about Gussie. With every email, he could stay in touch while he worked up the courage to be more active and to figure out what to do next. He could never tell her that, of course, because he felt pretty sure she wouldn't appreciate being compared to a mouthful of worms.

As hysterical as the afternoon had been, Gussie realized one important fact: The Widows would cause great havoc if they continued to play matchmakers. She had little doubt that they'd keep trying. Adam had said the Widows felt flush with victory. Perhaps that explained it. Their success with Sam and his wife primed them for more efforts toward getting their minister married. After all, they had much more invested in getting Adam married than they had in finding Sam a wife.

Although the afternoon had amused her, she felt mortified that she and Adam had been placed in this situation. If he were at all interested in her, he'd have made a move, called her, asked her out. The fact that he hadn't but Miss Birdie and her co-conspirators had forced them together embarrassed her deeply. It showed so obviously that the chemistry was one-sided.

Had anyone noticed how much Adam attracted her?

And yet, if not, why had the Widows chosen her for Adam? Had they seen her longing? No, impossible. They'd never seen her and Adam together. They were operating on hope, nothing more. Her usual good humor kicked in and she laughed so hard she nearly drove off the highway.

❦

That evening as Adam watched Janey do her homework in the kitchen, Hector threw himself onto a chair.

"I don't have enough money to take anyone to prom."

Mentally, Adam replaced the word *anyone* with *Bree*.

"A girl expects all sorts of stuff like flowers," Hector complained. "Some of the guys are going together, pooling their money for a limo. With my friends, fifty of us would have to pool our money."

Guess he'd better start giving Hector an allowance. With basketball and school on top of taking care of Janey and the work he did around the church, which didn't pay much, Hector didn't have time to get another job and keep his grades up, too.

"Wish I could help more."

"Hey Pops, I understand."

The kid needed some spending money, some—what had his friends called it?—walking-around money. For a few seconds, Adam considered the trust fund money his own father had put aside for him. He'd decided against living on it, but couldn't he share a little with Hector? No, he couldn't. It went against Adam's principles. He didn't mind tapping a parent for a worthy project here and there, but not that trust fund money. He'd never wanted to be a person who lived on someone else's wealth. If he started to accept a little here and a couple of hundred there, he might end up buying more stuff, like a new car that didn't have things falling off it and couldn't make the trip to Austin without constant prayer and Rex's laying on of hands. No, he aimed to support himself on his own money.

"Bobby thought he'd get the family car, but his father has to go in for a late shift."

Bobby's father worked as an aide at the hospital and always tried to take on extra shifts.

"We thought about walking to the civic center but that's not cool." He grinned. "Of course, driving your car to the prom isn't too cool, either, but if we park it down the street, no one will see it."

"You going to meet up with anyone there?" Adam asked casually.

"Maybe. I asked Bree to save me a couple of dances." Hector grinned. "Pops, how're you going to get to the prom. You're a chaperone again, right?"

Adam nodded. "The Episcopal priest's picking me up. Ministers are very popular chaperones. We seem to exude morality and serve as examples of honor and virtue." *And*, he added to himself, *celibacy*.

❦

Friday before prom, Adam dropped by the diner, sat at the counter, and ordered a cup of coffee. "Prom tomorrow," he said to Miss Birdie.

"None of the girls are in school today," she said as she filled a cup and placed it in front of him. "The juniors spent the morning decorating the civic center. This afternoon the girls get their hair done."

"They skip school to get ready for a dance?"

"Preacher, this is the *prom* we're talking about." She leaned forward to scrutinize him as if he were an alien being. "Tradition. Elmer took me. Our first date. It's a special evening. Missing one day of school won't hurt."

Adam nodded. Probably not something a man could understand, especially an outlander like him.

"Bree's so excited. She got a new dress and sparkly shoes. Problem is, the heels are so tall and thin that she walks like she's got a basketball between her knees. I'm afraid she's going to fall on her face. Tonight she's going to practice dancing and moving in them." She shook her head and smiled. "She tried everything on yesterday. Looked real pretty when she wasn't walking."

"She have a date?"

"No, she's going with a bunch of friends. They do that." She picked up a fresh pot of coffee and topped off his cup before she headed toward her other patrons. Going table-to-table, she freshened everyone's coffee until she arrived at one where Farley Masterson sat. Adam had met the man a few weeks ago when Farley visited the Christian Church. Adam didn't know why he'd showed up; he usually attended the Methodist Church.

Just as she had when she'd spotted Farley in church, the pillar carefully headed away, pretending not to see the man. If she hadn't been so obvious, she could have carried it off. But she had and she didn't.

Farley grinned and shouted, "I'm gettin' to you, aren't I, Bird?"

Miss Birdie mumbled something and kept her eyes away from him while she served another table.

Did the pillar have an admirer? Looked to Adam as if Farley fancied Miss Birdie.

Well, don't that beat all, he thought. He almost patted himself on the back as he noticed how much he'd improved his use of Texas phrases. He understood Texan a lot better, too. Now, if only he could use *fixin'* without thinking about it, he'd sound like a true citizen of the Hill Country.

While Adam was congratulating himself, Farley looked up at the ceiling and said, "That fan pulls right smart through here, don't it?"

Adam had no idea what the man had said. Obviously his vocabulary hadn't grown as much as he'd hoped.

Along with most of the ministers in town and dozens of parents, Adam chaperoned the prom. The adults circling the walls, at the refreshments table, and guarding every door made sure that, at least until midnight arrived and the kids adjourned to post-prom activities, no one had the slightest opportunity to misbehave. If they did, punishment would follow immediately, administered by a throng of the righteous.

When he first entered, Adam glanced toward the photographer, hoping to see Gussie. Silly because she'd have let him know if she were coming, but still he hoped. No, a man set up the equipment in front of a large sketch of the Eiffel Tower under an EVENING IN PARIS banner.

The kids were having a great time. Hector and Bree danced in a distant corner, as far away from Adam as they could find. None of the kids knew how to slow-dance. They embraced and moved around the floor like Siamese twins joined at the shoulders. They performed the fast dances with jerky and repetitive movements. He shouldn't laugh because, all long arms and legs, he bet he'd looked goofier at his prom.

"Hey, you're looking good." His friend Mattie, the minister of the Presbyterian Church, stood next to him and put her arm through his.

Had he changed in any way? Yes, he had to admit he had, a little. He'd bought some new shirts at Bealls to replace the old ones that were so tight around the neck. Tonight he'd worn a daring light blue one instead of the usual white. With it, he had on one of the ties Blossom had given him when she cleaned out her husband's closet, black with light blue swirls. Far more exciting than the three ties he already possessed.

Mattie looked nice in a dressy dress that showed more leg and décolletage than he'd ever seen a minister display. Not that she looked cheap or showed too much, but she didn't look much like a lady preacher tonight.

He knew well enough not to tell her she looked *nice*. "Great dress," he said. "I like your hair." She'd piled it on top of her head with little curls dangling down. "You look different tonight." At her frown, he added, "In a good way."

She studied him for a moment, "You know, you are getting better looking. Not as scrawny as you were when I first met you. Maybe you've finally stopped growing and reached the age you can put on a little muscle."

Had she really said something nice about him, in which case he should thank her? Or had she merely moved him up the scale one step, from scrawny to just plain skinny. That didn't feel at all like a compliment.

Then she smiled and squeezed his arm. For a moment, he panicked. She'd looked at him as if he were a man instead of the eunuch who served the Christian Church.

Fortunately, one of the junior girls pulled Mattie's arm. "I need you to help me. My dress ripped a little."

Mattie hurried off and Adam, perfectly content not to wonder about Mattie's message, watched the dancers with less of an eagle eye than the pillar expected him to use.

"Hey, Preacher," Gabe Borden said. He'd been a hotshot guard five or six years earlier at UT, where he'd been nicknamed "Flash." Adam had heard of Flash and followed his career. After a couple of years in the NBA, Gabe retired. No known injuries, simply stopped playing and went back to school for a master's degree and worked as an assistant at UT. He'd landed the job of head basketball coach at Butternut Creek High School nearly a year earlier.

"How're you doing, Coach?"

"Okay. Having fun?" Gabe looked across the crowd of students.

Adam sometimes questioned the evenhandedness of whoever dispensed physical gifts. Gabe had everything. He looked like . . . well, like a former NBA player. Handsome, confident, and charismatic. From what Adam heard, the man had invested well, had piles of money, and sponsored several charities. However, Adam had two inches on him, which evened things out a bit.

Here in Butternut Creek, Gabe attempted to look like a normal guy but he wasn't. He could wear jeans from Walmart, cheap T-shirts, and knockoff athletic shoes and still look like an ad for men's cologne. But Adam couldn't help but like him. That charisma.

"How did you get dragged in?" Adam asked.

"I'm a junior class sponsor, one of the joys of teaching here. We spent most of the day setting up. Fortunately, I like being around high school kids. I'm not as fond of wrapping flowers around poles or covering the ceiling with dark blue crepe paper."

"Lovely. Looks just like Paris."

Gabe raised an eyebrow. "Have you ever been to Paris?"

"Yes, but this is still pretty good for a makeover of the community center." Then Adam tossed out the words, "Coach, do you have a church home?"

Gabe didn't respond. Instead he seemed busy ignoring a willowy blond chaperone who had her eye on him.

"English teacher, recent divorcée," Gabe explained. "She's aggressive, but not quite as pushy as a minister who asks if you have a church home when he's chaperoning the prom. No, not nearly as pushy, but close."

After a few seconds of silence during which Adam felt warned not to ask again but pleased that he had made an effort to reach out, the coach said, "I want to talk to you about Hector." Gabe's eyes searched the crowd for the young man.

"Is there a problem?" Adam hoped not. Next to Janey, basketball was Hector's life.

"Not really. I wanted to pick your brain, get your opinion. I'm thinking about changing his position from a three to a two, from small forward to shooting guard or maybe what they call a point forward, a combination."

"You know I'm not his guardian, right? That he's an emancipated minor. He lives with me, but I don't tell him what to do. Much."

"I don't expect you to, but you know something about basketball so I thought I'd talk this over with you." He paused. "You know, Hector's too thin and too short to play forward in college. He's not a wide body, which is what everyone looks for."

Adam nodded.

"He's a smart kid and a great shooter, good passer. To play guard, he has to improve his ball-handling skills. With my background, I can work with him, coach him to be a guard."

Oh, yeah, Flash would be a great teacher for Hector. "Makes sense. You think more schools would be interested in him as a guard?"

"I think he'll add more to the team and attract more attention as a guard than a forward. What is he? Six-three? Six-four? But he needs to bulk up a lot to play as a wide body."

"Do you know how much that kid eats? If I didn't have the same problem putting on weight, I'd wonder where all that food goes."

"Yeah, he works out in the weight room for hours but can't build muscle. Too young."

For a minute or so, the two men watched the young people dance and listened to the music.

"I'd like to have him dribble the ball everywhere he goes to make him more comfortable with it. Are you on board with this?"

"Sure," Adam started but before he could say more, a student looking very sophisticated in a long red dress took Gabe's arm and pulled him into the crowd to dance.

Adam laughed at Gabe's discomfort until another young woman grabbed him.

Chapter Seven

May whirled past. After prom, Adam attended the spring sports award ceremony, the choir concert at the high school and one at Janey's elementary school, track meets, and everything else that crowded the last days of the school year. In no time, summer church camp loomed ahead. He'd see Gussie for almost a week.

Here was his chance: the promise of six days together, nearly a week to pursue . . . no, to court . . . no, to woo . . . Oh, forget what verb he should use. He wanted to get to know her better and to find out if she felt anything for him. He'd accept the tiniest spark in the hope he could fan it into a great passion; he'd even settle for a warm ember of interest.

He and Gussie had kept up their emails for six weeks, most of them professional about the coming events and also sent to the other adults who'd attend.

But every now and then, he thought of something that happened at church or a particularly Miss Birdie moment he wanted to share with her or news about the youth group. From time to time, she'd answer. They fell into a comfortable and, sadly, friendly rhythm.

Senior high camp started June 8. In addition to the five who'd gone to the retreat, three more kids from the high school were joining them. For that reason, the elders had rented them a larger but utilitarian van.

So much went on the first day and evening, Adam had no chance to put his plan to woo Gussie into action. Crowds of people surrounded

Gussie at every moment, asking questions, seeking direction, or just plain talking to her because she was so much fun to talk to.

Adam waved and smiled at her, and she returned a harried grin. He couldn't get close to her.

He glanced down at the sheaf of papers she'd shoved at him in passing. She'd prepared the list of patrols, and they were not together. He'd ended up with Mrs. Hayes, who taught high school French in Liberty Hill. Gussie had paired herself with the minister from San Antonio. Maybe he could switch with Jimmy. No, that would call too much attention to his interest.

Monday morning, he got a call that Jesse's brother had died and he needed to get back for funeral arrangements.

"I hate to leave," he told Gussie.

"I understand." She didn't look unhappy about his departure.

Had he hoped she'd cry? Throw herself at his feet and beg him to stay because she couldn't stand to spend the week without him? Or, maybe more realistically, look a tiny bit disappointed? Would've been nice.

"You'll be short a male counselor," he said.

She shrugged. "Nothing we can do about that. Your church member needs you." She placed her hand on his arm, then pulled it away quickly.

What was that about?

"I'll be back after the funeral."

But when he got back to Butternut Creek, every emergency possible hit. The mother of a member had gone into hospice and the family asked for his visits. The niece of a friend of Mercedes needed to get married. Maggie scheduled the wedding for Thursday evening as well as sessions with the bride and groom Tuesday and Wednesday.

On Wednesday, he called Gussie to tell her he wouldn't be back and that he'd pick up the youth on Friday at noon.

So much for wooing or courting or even speaking to Gussie.

Adam said a quick word to Gussie when he picked up the kids but nothing more. The place was chaos, and after driving to the hospice in Lubbock twice to spend time with ailing members and their families, he'd worn himself out.

The kids squeezed into the van, stowing the luggage under their seats and in the aisle. Most fell asleep almost as soon as Adam turned on the ignition.

As he drove out, Adam saw Gussie in the middle of a group of kids, laughing and attempting to point them toward the waiting cars.

"Sorry you had to miss camp, Pops," Hector said from the passenger seat.

Adam pulled out on the highway and sped up. He enjoyed a vehicle with acceleration.

"Yeah, wish I could have been there." Adam looked in the rearview mirror to see Bree sleeping in a seat next to her sister. "Why aren't you sitting with Bree?"

"Haven't seen you for a while. Wanted to catch up. Too bad you weren't able to see more of Gussie."

"What do you mean by that?"

Hector grinned. "Don't make me spell it out. You gotta know Mac can't keep a secret for long."

Adam groaned.

"We're gonna keep it quiet. Don't worry." He slid his hat over his eyes. "But, you know, I'm beginning to think God doesn't want you and Gussie together." Then he pretended to fall asleep.

At least, Adam believed the sleep to be feigned. He bet Hector had been warned by junior matchmaker Mac not to push.

Hector did bring up a good point. Why did he have such bad luck around Gussie? Before the week of camp, he'd had such high hopes. Seemed like he was snakebit. Nothing worked out as planned.

Maybe the kid was right. God didn't want him and Gussie together. Maybe God was doing everything a deity could do to keep them apart because He had different plans for them.

Of all the stupid ideas. Like God would kill Jesse's brother or have a teenager get pregnant and ask for a quick wedding—all just so Adam didn't have a chance to court Gussie.

Adam always thought God was busy enough with the universe that He didn't mess in people's lives or favor certain football teams despite the fact that in Texas, a majority believed He was a rabid fan of the Cowboys. Adam preferred to think God was more concerned with opening hearts so the hungry could be fed and the naked clothed and wars stopped.

The sort of thinking that made people believe God was the mighty micromanager who did petty things to mess people up or solve the small problems they could take care of themselves always astounded him. Reminded him of his aunt Hazel who believed God had nearly killed her in a car wreck and put her in a coma to get her to stop smoking. Surely, Adam had always thought, the creator of the heavens and the earth, omniscient and omnipotent, could have come up with a better plan than almost killing the woman now to save her from dying of lung cancer later.

If a Gussie-and-Adam combination truly didn't suit God's plans, then God could make this far easier by putting a lovely single young woman in Butternut Creek to distract him from Gussie. However, he truly didn't—couldn't—believe God worked that way, like a great matchmaker in the sky.

For a moment, Adam considered the idea that God had franchised that arm of the business to the Widows. If they had a divine covenant for their efforts, he might as well give in, accept the inevitable, and marry whoever they found.

Gussie watched the packed van drive off and bemoaned the fact she hadn't seen much of Adam.

"He's a hottie, isn't he?"

Oh, my Lord. Had she said those words out loud?

Gussie looked to her left to see Marcy Swenson, one of the college students who had come to camp as an assistant counselor.

"Who?" Gussie glanced at the girl.

"Reverend Jordan," Marcy said.

"Adam?"

"Haven't you noticed?" Marcy whistled. "How could you not see that?"

"He's a very nice young man. The young people from his church really like him."

Marcy's mouth dropped open. "You haven't noticed?" She jabbed Gussie in the side with her elbow. "Why don't you ask him out? You're about the same age. You're both single. He's hot and you're hot, for your age."

With those depressing words, Marcy took off to help her campers load their cars.

Hot for her age? Gussie had no idea how to respond to that statement. Probably better to dismiss it and concentrate on getting camp cleared.

Adam hated middle-of-the-night phone calls. He always hoped they were wrong numbers or drunks who couldn't dial, but most often they came from a church member in trouble. Last month it had been a heart attack and a quick trip to Austin.

By the third ring, he was sufficiently awake to grab the phone. "Adam Jordan," he said.

"Ouida fell. She wants you to come over."

"I'll be right there," Adam said before he realized George had already hung up.

It took only minutes to dress, comb his hair, and push his feet into Nikes before he ran out of the house to the Kowalskis' front door.

Before he could knock, George opened the door and pulled Adam inside. "She's right there."

He pointed with a shaking finger as if Adam couldn't see Ouida lying motionless at the bottom of the steps, a small pool of blood growing where her hand lay close to a few shards of glass.

For a moment Adam could only stare. Was she dead? "Did you call nine-one-one? What happened?"

George nodded. "Called them right before I called you." For a moment, he struggled to speak. "She fell."

Ouida moaned. Adam strode toward her and knelt.

"Hey, Preacher," she whispered.

At least she was coherent and awake. Good. But she didn't move, her leg bent at an odd angle, and she was so pale she was the same color as her light blue nightgown now liberally spotted with red.

Shock. He tried to remember the first-aid course he'd had years ago. Treatment for shock: Cover the patient, keep her warm, and raise her head. Or maybe raise her feet. He couldn't remember which but that didn't matter because he wasn't going to touch her. EMS would do that.

"Cold," she whispered.

"Get some blankets," Adam said. "Or coats. Something to cover her."

When George didn't move, Adam stood and, in two steps, reached the front closet. He opened it and pulled the winter coats out. None felt very heavy—in Texas, no one had thick, warm coats—until he found a tan topcoat, which he lay across Ouida.

"That's my best coat," George protested. When Adam glared at him, he added, "But, of course, that's fine."

With Ouida covered, Adam carefully picked the largest shards of glass off the floor before anyone could get cut. He stood to toss them in a decorative thingy in the entrance hall, then turned to study George. How was he doing? As he'd have guessed, George wore silk pajamas and nice leather slippers. Other than the man's pallor, George looked like his usual, well-turned-out self: great haircut with minimal bed head, immaculately clothed for the occasion, and in charge. Except, of course, George's bewildered expression showed he wasn't in charge and had no idea what to do next except to pace at a safe distance from the puddle of blood.

With a glance around the hallway and upstairs—no sign of Carol or Gretchen yet—Adam pulled out his cell and hit speed dial. After a few rings, Bree answered. Or maybe it was Mac.

"Hey, I need you at the Kowalskis'. Ouida fell. Can you two and your grandmother come over? ASAP?"

"Who is this?" the young woman mumbled.

"Adam Jordan."

"Oh, yeah, Preacher." She yawned. "This is Bree."

"Bring your grandmother, too. Okay?" When Bree didn't say anything—had she fallen back to sleep?—Adam said, "We need you now, for Carol and Gretchen."

"Of course," she said, immediately awake. "Be right there."

As sirens sounded from a few blocks away, Adam knelt next to Ouida. Still pale. Still cold.

He glanced up the stairs to see a floppy slipper on the sixth step up. Didn't take a genius to see what happened: Ouida had slipped, fallen, and landed here, probably broken her leg. Cut her hand on something. Those were the obvious injuries.

George had stopped pacing and hovered about five feet away. "Should we get her on the sofa?" George asked. "Make her comfortable?"

"No, the paramedics need to decide that."

"I fell," she whispered. "Hurts." Then she started to gag.

"George," Adam motioned toward him. "Why don't you come hold Ouida's hand."

"He doesn't like blood or vomit," she whispered.

Who did? Neither was among Adam's favorite fluids.

"Thirsty."

"I'll get water." George grabbed the reason to escape and ran toward the kitchen, leaving bloody footprints behind him.

They wouldn't give Ouida anything to drink, that was a decision for the paramedics, but the errand got George out of the way and doing something purposeful. Maybe that would either calm him down or rouse him. Adam had no idea which George needed.

Ouida attempted to move, then stopped and groaned.

Thrashing and anxiety, those meant something but darned if he could remember what. He'd take another first-aid course as soon as possible.

When the sirens stopped outside the house, Adam jumped to his feet to open the door. The paramedics ran up the walk and into the house, then took in the scene.

"I'm Shelley," the lead paramedic said. "That's Aaron." Within seconds both she and the stocky EMT knelt next to Ouida, threw the overcoat on the floor, and examined her.

"Mommy."

Adam glanced up the stairs to see Carol and Gretchen sobbing and holding hands.

"Mommy," Carol shouted over and over. And all this time, George stood to the side of the action holding the tumbler of water.

"George." Adam pointed toward the girls. "Take care of them."

George didn't move. If his color hadn't looked fairly normal, Adam might have guessed he suffered from shock.

He did. Of course he did. Finding his wife at the bottom of the steps bleeding must have frightened him deeply, but his daughters needed him now.

"How long ago did this happen?" Shelley asked.

George shook his head.

"George called me about ten minutes ago," Adam said. A stupid comment because they probably had the time of the 911 call, but George didn't seem able to give more information.

Ouida was getting great care from the paramedics, but they needed information and the girls needed to be comforted.

In the movies, the hero slapped the hysterical heroine, which always seemed to work. Adam had always wondered why that wasn't considered abusive. He couldn't imagine that slapping George would have the desired effect—and the man might slap him back. Instead he shouted sharply, "George."

The word woke him up. George chugged the water, placed the glass on the table, and said, "I don't know. I woke up about twenty minutes ago and she wasn't in bed. When I came down, she was there."

While George spoke, Adam headed toward the back stairs to avoid the huddle of health care workers in the hall. Once upstairs, he sat on the top step to the side of the girls, pulled Carol and Gretchen into his arms, and carefully turned their eyes away from the sight of their mother. "Your mother fell," he said as he rubbed their backs gently. "But she's going to be okay."

The girls looked up at him.

"These people will take care of your mommy, patch her up, then take her to the hospital."

"I want Mommy." Carol attempted to turn back and watch her mother.

Had his explanation made them think they'd be left alone? What could he do to comfort and distract them from the scene below as Shelley prepared an IV?

"You're going to be fine, I promise. You won't be alone."

The girls lifted their eyes.

"Are you going to take her to the hospital?" George asked from below.

Shelley nodded. "We'll take her to Burnet and life-flight her to Austin. We don't have the facilities in Burnet to do more than basic care."

"Mommy?" Carol sobbed.

"She'll go to the hospital so very good doctors can take care of her." Adam lifted the girls in his arms. "While your mommy is in the hospital, friends will be here with you."

Mercifully, as the crescendo of crying increased and Shelley repeated another question to George, Miss Birdie strode in followed by her granddaughters. The cavalry had arrived. *Thank you, God.*

He'd known the pillar would come and not due *only* to curiosity. As much as she attempted to hide it, Miss Birdie had a heart of gold beneath that crusty exterior.

She took charge immediately. "Upstairs," the pillar told Bree and Mac.

"You," she told George. "You come here and hold your wife's hand and give the information they need to these EMS people. Preacher." She looked up at Adam. "The girls and I'll take care of Carol and Gretchen. You come down here and support George." She infused those last words with scorn that a man, a husband, would act like George.

Fortunately, George didn't notice. George seemed nearly catatonic.

Within seconds, Bree had led the little girls away from the top of the steps and their view of their mother. When he arrived in the foyer, Adam gave George a slight shove toward his wife.

At the top of the stairs stood Miss Birdie, studying the scene below her, legs apart and arms folded in front of her. She looked like a bulldog—although a skinny one—but Adam knew the frown showed concern and the crossed arms were the way she'd learned to cope with shoulder pain, supporting one arm with the other.

George didn't know that. He glanced up at her and took a step toward his wife, then another. While George read judgment in the pillar's scrutiny, Adam saw her assess what she needed to do. He bet cleaning up the front hall after the crowd dispersed would be her first priority.

"Sir, we're going to need some information. Full name, last name first," said a young man who held a small computer.

George recited the elementary material.

"Date of birth?"

After he entered that information, the young man asked, "Do you know her Texas driver's license number?"

George rattled it off.

"Social Security number?"

George knew that, too.

"What health insurance do you have?"

"It's with Greater Good. Group number is 546C3. Identification number 1212HH1344."

The man did know numbers.

After the EMTs had stopped the bleeding and hooked up an IV, they covered Ouida with several blankets, put a collar around her neck, and carefully strapped her on a board, then a gurney. Believing everything was well under control, Adam headed toward the back stairs to check on the girls and to talk to Miss Birdie.

In one bedroom, Bree rocked Gretchen, who was sleeping soundly. In the other, Mac read to Carol. Both glanced up at Adam when he peeked in.

"You're mother's going to be fine," Adam said. "We're taking her to the hospital."

When tears started down Carol's cheeks, Adam entered the room and stooped in front of the child. "I promise I'll come back as soon as I can. Miss Birdie and her granddaughters will stay with you."

Once downstairs, he pulled out the cell again and called Hector.

"Hey, I need you at the Kowalskis'. Ouida fell. Can you come over and talk to me? ASAP."

"Who is this?" Hector mumbled.

"Adam Jordan."

"Oh, yeah, Pops." Hector yawned. "Be right there."

After he closed the phone, Adam joined George. "I'll drive you into Austin."

When George nodded, Adam noticed a cowlick sticking up in the back of his head. He'd never seen his neighbor with a hair out of place. The fact that it was said a lot about the man's condition. That he'd accepted the ride so willingly said even more.

"Hey, Pops." Hector entered the foyer with his usual high-energy gait but stopped as soon as Ouida was whisked past him.

"Didn't expect all this." Hector waved toward the crowd: George, the paramedics disappearing with Ouida on the gurney, Miss Birdie still at the top of the steps. Before Adam could say a word, Hector said, "Hey, Miss Birdie, you don't want to be standing. Let me get you a chair." With that, he took off into the kitchen. The next time Adam saw him, he was upstairs helping the pillar sit on one of the kitchen chairs.

"Isn't that better?" Hector asked.

"Yes, thank you." Wonder of wonders, Miss Birdie actually smiled at the kid, nearly cooed.

"Be right down, Pops." He disappeared again, showing up almost immediately in the foyer.

"That was nice of you," Adam said.

"Well, she's not exactly a spring chicken, and she shouldn't be standing," Hector explained in a low voice. "But don't tell her I said that. Annoys her." As if Adam didn't know that. "What'd you want?"

Realizing he was pretty tired as well, Adam leaned against the wall. "I'm going to drive George's car to the hospital in Austin after the ambulance leaves. I'll leave mine here. You'll have to pick me up."

"In your car?" Hector asked. "Pops, you've got to be kidding. That old blue thing won't make it. I'll be broken down by the side of the road." He grinned. "Why don't you let me drive that fine Lexus George has and you pick *me* up?"

Ignoring the words, true as they were, Adam said, "I'll call you when I'm ready. It may be this afternoon."

Immediately after they arrived at the hospital, nurses hurried George off to another area of the hospital to be with Ouida. While he waited, Adam drank so much coffee he could actually feel caffeine pumping through his body. It stimulated every nerve and woke up a brain that hadn't had enough sleep, but it made his hands shake as well.

On the muted television, an anchor silently mouthed the news as pictures of earthquake damage flitted past. In the corner of the waiting room, a couple slept on short love seats. Otherwise, the area was abandoned. He could hear the pings and buzzes and an occasional voice from the nurses' station far down the hall. But here, only the snores and grunts from the sleepers interrupted the solitude.

After a while, George entered the waiting room and threw himself into a chair with sagging cushions and wobbly arms. Before they'd left Butternut Creek, George had changed from his pajamas to immaculately tailored jeans with carefully ironed creases; a soft Carolina-blue shirt with a logo Adam didn't recognize, probably because George hadn't bought it at Adam's favorite discount mall; and a pair of running shoes so expensive that Adam had once tried a pair on for fun. If George hadn't dropped his face into his hands, Adam would've assumed his neighbor felt as calm and in control as his clothing suggested.

Nevertheless Adam asked, "How's it going?" to check on his neighbor's mental condition.

George looked up. Terror and anguish alternated across his face and reinforced Adam's earlier concern: George didn't handle this type of stress well. Whenever he'd talked to George—which wasn't all that often—his neighbor seemed cool and logical. Not tonight.

"She's—" George began in a quivering voice. He stopped to clear his throat and continue, "She's in surgery, has been since a few minutes after we arrived. I had to sign some paperwork. That's all I know."

A few minutes later, a woman wearing a lab coat over scrubs approached them. "I'm Dr. Ramirez." She reached out to shake Adam's hand. "Are you Mr. Kowalski?"

"No, I'm her minister." The words fell from his lips because that's what he always said in this situation. He opened his mouth to continue, *Not really. I'm her next-door-neighbor but I'm acting sort of like her minister because she doesn't go to church but I need to be here with George this morning.*

Instead he said, "That's Mr. Kowalski," and pointed to George.

"Mr. Kowalski, I'm the doctor who cared for your wife in the emergency room." She sat in a chair across from the men. "Sorry I didn't get to see you earlier. We've had a blitz in the ER tonight. To catch you up, we got the bleeding on Mrs. Kowalski's hand stopped." With a glance at her notes, she added, "Her shoulder is dislocated and that right leg is broken. Spiral break. As you know, she's in surgery now."

"What are they doing, Doctor?" Adam asked. George looked stunned and long past the point of putting two or three intelligent words together.

"They'll put that shoulder back into the socket—that won't take long—stitch the hand up because those cuts are very deep, and set the leg. They may have to put a rod in her leg."

"The break is that bad?" Adam asked.

She nodded. "She may have to be in traction for six to eight weeks, to heal. You'll know more when the surgeon gets in there with more information."

"Six to eight weeks?" George said as if that were like the wait for the second coming, which he probably didn't believe in.

"Yes, at least. Mr. Kowalski, we're going to have someone from

social services talk to you later this morning when we have more information about her condition."

"Social services?" George asked.

"Her shoulder will be immobilized for ten days or so, and that
leg—" She shook her head. "Mr. Kowalski, your wife's going to need
a lot of care. I suggest a skilled nursing facility. We have many good
ones here in Austin."

George lay back in the chair and closed his eyes. Adam feared
the man had passed out until he said, "She's going to need care for
weeks? In a nursing facility?" in a desolate voice.

When no more words or questions emerged from George, Adam
asked, "How 'bout one located in Butternut Creek?"

"You'll need to check with social services. As I said, one of the
clerks will be up with information and some papers for you to sign,
Mr. Kowalski." The doctor stood. "Please check at the nurses' station
if you have any questions. She'll be in surgery for several hours, but a
room should be assigned by ten. You can wait there."

When George nodded, she walked away.

"I've told her a dozen times not to carry a glass." George sat up
and opened his eyes. "Especially not at night, in the dark. You don't
know what you might trip on." He shook his head and looked be-
seechingly at Adam as if expecting agreement or at least understanding of that edict.

"Dangerous," Adam said. "That's what happened? Ouida fell
holding a glass?" He pretty much figured it was. After all, he'd seen
the shards of glass and the blood. But he imagined his neighbor
needed to talk.

George glanced down at his hands as if seeing blood flowing from
his palm. "I don't know what happened or why Ouida went downstairs. Guess Gretchen asked for water, but I didn't hear her. I don't
usually hear them. Ouida takes care of that."

Adam nodded while George shook his head.

"And I don't know why she had those slippers on. I've told her
not to wear those big floppy things. Too easy to step on, to trip over."
His voice sharpened. "She doesn't listen to me."

Adam had no answer, so they watched the silent television and
pictures of destruction someplace in Asia for two or three minutes.

"Bad tsunami," George murmured as he looked at the screen.

"Lots of people hurt." Adam agreed. "*Tsunami*, an odd word," he
added, having no idea what else to talk about.

George mused a few minutes. "Japanese," he said. "Literally
means 'harbor wave.' What we used to call a tidal wave. Silent *t*."

"Interesting," Adam said.

"You don't have to stay," George said after another long pause.

"I know. I want to stay. I'm your neighbor. Besides, Miss Birdie said I had to call her as soon as we knew more about Ouida."

George nodded. "Wouldn't want to cross her." A note of respect and fear colored his voice. "Not Miss Birdie."

Twenty minutes later, George said, "You know I care about Ouida."

"I know."

"She's the one who takes care of all this." He waved around the waiting room as if she were the hospital's chief of staff. "I mean, she takes the kids to the doctor. She . . . well, she does all the home stuff. The only time I've been in a hospital was when the kids were born."

He leaned forward and fixed Adam with the stare that probably said *trust me* to his clients but only said *I'm out of my element here* to Adam.

"I'm a good accountant," George said. "But—and Ouida knows this—not exactly high on the taking-care-of-others scale. I handle the money. She handles the children and the emergencies at home."

Adam knew that from his conversations with Ouida. She'd also told him George always acted calm and in charge, but not this morning.

"What am I going to do about work?" he asked. "Someone's going to have to take care of the children." George glanced up at Adam. "You probably wonder how I can wonder about work when Ouida's undergoing surgery, but this is how I support my family and I have a dozen employees. If I don't keep the business running, they don't have jobs and we don't have money to live on." His shoulders drooped. "Six to eight weeks?"

"We'll work things out together," Adam said. "Once you know more about the prognosis, we'll work it out."

"What about that mess at home?" George sat up suddenly. "The blood all over?"

"Miss Birdie will take care of that. Don't worry about the house now." He spoke calmly and clearly. "George, the doctors know what they are doing, and their training guided their hands. You and Ouida have friends and family who love you and will be with you. We all hope Ouida will soon be home healthy and whole, in the best possible health." His words were actually those he used in prayers before surgery, but without what George would consider the spiritual stuff.

"Yeah. Okay. Thank you." George nodded and settled back again, but he didn't look as miserable as he had before that stealth prayer.

Two hours later, the surgeon approached to talk with them, pretty much repeating what the ER doctor had said. After that, George spoke with the clerk from social services, who said Ouida would be in the hospital for a few days, then taken to a skilled nursing facility. Adam requested she look into a place close to Butternut Creek.

Later, they went to the room assigned to Ouida. When the bed was wheeled in, she had her hand wound in bandages, her arm bound to her side, and her leg in a cast and hanging in traction. Looking pale and groggy, she waved weakly with her good arm. Immediately a nurse threw the men out so he could hook Ouida up to some machines.

As they waited, Adam's cell vibrated. He clicked on a text message and read it.

"Hector's here with my car," he said. "With Ouida back and probably sleeping, I'm going to take off. Will you be okay to drive your car home?"

George nodded. "I think I'll go to the office and get some work done."

"No," Adam stated. "You need to stay here with Ouida, then you have to go home. You have two little girls who need to know their mother is okay and have their father at home with them. They need that security."

George sighed. "I'm not very good with this father stuff, but, you're right. I'll stay with Ouida for a couple of hours, then go home."

"I'll come back again tomorrow." Adam shook George's hand, then headed for the elevator.

"How's she doing, Pops?" Hector waited in the cafeteria, his calculus book open on a table in front of him.

Adam shrugged. "Okay. She'll be here for a while."

"Oh, man." Hector closed his book and stood. "You can't drive that wreck into Austin every day to see her. That's dangerous."

"Too far to walk," Adam said. "Come on. Let's go. I want to stop and get some breakfast or lunch. Where's Janey?"

"The Olivers down the block are taking care of Carol and Gretchen. She's helping."

As tired as he was, Adam let Hector drive. When they pulled up at the speaker at Sonic, Hector lowered the window. When he finished with the order he mashed the button to put the window up, but it didn't move. The sound of grinding came from inside the door. Never a good sign.

"Great. One more problem with the car. Can't close the window on this side." Hector turned to frown at Adam.

"I had this happen in another car. Grab that edge of the window, the glass you can still see, and pull it up."

"You had this happen on another car?" Hector shook his head. "Have you even had a car that had all its parts and ran well?" As the waitress skated to the car, he handed her a bill, took the change, and handed it to Adam before taking the food. "And isn't your father rich? Can't he buy you a car."

"I like to make it on my own."

"Man, you're crazy. And if you keep driving this car, you're goin' to be dead."

When they'd finished, Hector backed the car out, opened the door, got out, and tugged on the window to close it.

"Remind me not to open it again," he said when he got inside.

❧

When Adam entered Ouida's hospital room the next evening, she was alone and snoring. On the windowsill sat a vase of tulips and baby's breath. A potted plant stood on a shelf.

He didn't want to wake her up. He reached in his pocket to pull out a card and a pen to write a note.

"Adam?" Ouida mumbled as she opened her eyes.

"Hey." He took her hand. "I came by to let you know everyone at church is . . . thinking of you."

"You can say they're praying. I don't mind." She squeezed his fingers and smiled. "I sent George back home. He's not comfortable in a hospital."

George didn't feel comfortable anyplace away from work, Adam guessed, but he didn't say that.

"He won't feel more comfortable at home, either," she said.

"The girls will be glad to have him around." He settled in a chair. "How are you feeling?"

"I hurt. Guess that's expected. They are managing the pain. Even started physical therapy already, moving my fingers around and lifting my arm a little." She shifted in the bed. "Could you get me a glass of water? Help me drink it?"

That action reminded him how incapacitated she was. Couldn't even pour or drink water with only one arm. She faced a long rehabilitation. How would George handle that?

"What's next?" he asked after she'd taken a few sips.

But she fell back to sleep before he'd finished the question.

On the drive home, Adam had to slow down for four or five vultures to fly away from the corpse of a deer in the middle of the highway. Texas offered up a variety of roadkill. Lots of deer, armadillos, and the occasional rabbit, possum, or raccoon.

He gave a sigh of relief and a silent prayer when his old car made it back to the parsonage. He needed a car to drive into Austin without asking Rex to lay healing hands on it before every trip.

Maybe it was time to buy a new car or a less used one, but he had no money. What he had left over from his salary after utilities and food—which had increased about one hundred dollars a month since Hector arrived—went into the little extras for Janey and clothes for Hector, who seemed to grow several inches a week. Adam could see his legs getting longer if he watched for a few minutes.

He'd allowed Hector to drive Old Blue around town, but, for the kid, this was a strictly inside-the-city-limits vehicle. Yes, Adam needed to put aside a little bit, save fifty dollars per paycheck. But fifty dollars a month added up to only six hundred dollars in a year. What kind of car could he buy with that?

That Sunday after the service, Adam stood in front of the church and watched the cars pass on the highway. Janey had gone back to the parsonage while Hector had sprinted out with Bobby to change and hit the basketball court.

Those kids had a lot more energy than Adam. Driving back and forth to visit an improving but frustrated Ouida, working with the Widows to make sure the girls were okay, and attempting to do the other church work and come up with the passable sermon had worn him out. He wanted nothing more than a good nap.

Well, one thing more. He also wanted to avoid Sam. Sounding more and more like a matchmaker, Sam had asked him about Gussie as he left church. When Adam saw Sam's car still in the parking lot, he started to run toward the parsonage.

"Hey, Preacher."

The voice didn't surprise him. He'd heard Sam's uneven footsteps behind him as well as the sibilant sounds of the boys shushing each other, but it did foil his escape.

"I thought if I ignored you, you'd go away," Adam said, still keeping his back to Sam. Sort of like magical thinking. Didn't work.

"Let's talk about Gussie."

Adam took a few steps away.

"Okay, now I understand why you didn't take advantage of that week of camp. You weren't there, but buddy, what are you doing now?" Sam moved to stand in front of Adam and studied him as a marine captain would scrutinize a raw recruit.

Adam should've known Sam was unignorable. As an ex-marine, he homed in on his objective and kept up his attack until the target had been won.

"Tell me something, Adam. Have you ever dated a woman?"

"Of course I have. I was even engaged." He deked and took a step toward the parsonage, but Sam's voice and his smoothly executed military turn cut off that route.

"Tell me about them. How many, when?"

"Ummm." Adam thought back over the past ten years. "Not that many. A couple of girls in high school, a few in college, then I asked Laurel to marry me when we graduated."

"What happened with this Laurel?"

"She didn't want to marry a minister. Said she wasn't into teas and good works."

"And the others? Did you have to pursue them?"

"No, we were friends first, then began to date."

"So, you're telling me you don't know a thing about courting a woman?"

"No, they always just threw themselves at me."

Sam's glare told Adam both that he didn't believe those words and that humor did not fit here.

"All right," Adam confirmed. "I know nothing about this. I dated women I already knew and was attracted to and comfortable with."

"Then we're starting with the basics." Sam straightened. Not that Adam had seen his posture sag in the least, but he'd pulled himself up so he looked even taller and tougher. "Welcome to boot camp for the romantically challenged."

No escape. The parking lot had emptied out. Willow waited in the car, reading. Even Leo and Nick had headed toward the grass behind the parking lot. Looking for dead animals, maybe. Not that any of that family'd be of assistance in any way. Adam bet they didn't interfere or interrupt when Sam addressed the troops.

"Phase one: If you don't have a plan," Sam lectured, "you cannot execute it. Phase two: If you want Gussie, you can't be some passive grunt who lets life go past him. Take action. Man up."

"Man up," Nick shouted from the lawn. Sam glanced at his sons, pointed, and watched the kids move several yards farther away before he turned his iron gaze back at Adam.

"Yes, sir," Adam said, but he refused to stand at attention, even though that's what Sam's voice and posture demanded.

"I don't care what you do or what your plan is, but you have to get started. Take charge. Boot camp is over." With that, Sam turned, motioned toward the kids, and all three marched toward the yellow Mustang. Adam almost saluted.

After they drove off, Adam was left alone in the parking lot. He knew Sam was right. He walked back toward the parsonage contemplating the situation. What to do? How to approach this relationship problem?

Maybe he should pick up a copy of a men's magazine and read a few articles, but he thought of at least two arguments against that. To preserve anonymity, he'd have to drive all the way into Austin. Butternut Creek's only bookstore consisted of a rack at the H-E-B. At the bookstore in Marble Falls, those kind of magazines were kept behind the counter and had to be requested. If he went there, he was sure to run into someone who knew him and would spread news of his purchase all over the county. Ministers didn't and shouldn't read racy magazines was the consensus of parishioners.

Second, many—okay, all—of those magazines were way too steamy for him, past his depth. He wasn't looking for pointers on how to . . . well, those activities covered in risqué magazines were written for people with far more experience than him.

Maybe he'd look for help online.

That evening, he searched for "What do women want?" The experience both amazed him and opened his eyes to another world. He discovered women wanted many things he'd never thought they'd openly discuss.

Then he Googled "How to get the woman you want." The first topic he explored listed ways to get a woman into bed within fourteen minutes of meeting her. Not what he was looking for. Finally he found a couple of very helpful lists and made notes. He pondered the pages, reread them, underlined a few ideas, and put stars in the margin on others. Oh, Sam might tell him to man up, and he was fixin' to, once he decided exactly how to do that.

But first he had to drive to Austin.

❦

Wednesday morning, Adam and Blossom and her housekeeper, Evelyn, knocked at the Kowalskis' front door. When George opened it, his hair stood straight up, almost as if he were a punk accountant—if such people even existed—who'd used too much gel.

"Good morning." He opened the door and waved them inside.

"Did you get much sleep?" Adam asked.

"Oh, a few hours. After Carol finally fell asleep about midnight, I slept until Gretchen got in my bed at, oh, maybe four thirty."

"She probably wanted some attention," Adam said. "Having her mother away from home is frightening for a child."

"No, she wanted breakfast. I convinced her to wait and she fell asleep." He paused. "I'm not certain, but I may have promised her a puppy to get her to let me sleep. The kids have wanted a puppy forever."

"Puppies can be messy," Blossom said.

George sighed. When he did, Adam wanted to shout, *Man up*. He didn't, of course. Wouldn't be neighborly or Christian, and he couldn't carry it off like Sam, but George needed to take control of the situation.

A judgment easily made by a man with no children.

With a glance at Adam as if she'd read his mind, Blossom said in a voice as soothing as a pat on the hand, "George, let's go into the kitchen. I'll get you a nice cup of coffee."

"I don't know where it is," George mumbled. "There is no order to the way Ouida stores things. If I'd planned the kitchen, I'd put it over the coffeemaker, but . . ."

"I have some, a lovely blend from Costa Rica." She pulled a thermos from her purse and headed to the kitchen with George following like a puppy.

But the man wasn't a puppy and he needed to . . . okay, maybe for now, for a few minutes, he needed to be treated like a puppy because finding his wife in a heap had been a shock. He'd been taking care of the children and the house for only two days.

Still, he should have adapted by now. Shouldn't he? But, no, as Miss Birdie had said, they'd all coddled George. That was why Blossom had come. She excelled at coddling, and George had begged Adam never to set Miss Birdie loose on him again.

However, with Ouida being released soon from the hospital to the nursing facility a few blocks away, George would have to perform the tasks ahead of him. Even when she came home, she'd be laid up for eight weeks. Blossom couldn't pamper him forever.

"I brought some of the wonderful coffee cake my cook makes. I know you'll love that," Adam heard Blossom say from the kitchen.

He glanced at Evelyn, who'd begun to straighten up the living room. He hadn't wanted Blossom to bring her, but the other Widows scared George. How could a man be afraid of a bunch of women?

Adam grinned. The Widows had frightened him when he arrived here. Still did every once in a while, especially Miss Birdie, although

Winnie could bark out orders nearly as well. Not that he'd ever let them know they intimidated him.

As Evelyn cleaned, Adam picked up toys and put them in baskets.

They couldn't keep sending in women to do the housework. Evelyn was here really as a favor for Ouida, a mere stopgap measure so she wouldn't worry about her family living in chaos. George had to step it up, either hire someone or do more himself.

Chapter Eight

As Mercedes insisted—my, how Birdie hated it when she got all pushy like that—the Widows had left the preacher alone for over a week. Those few days felt like forever in the life of a matchmaker.

Not that they had anything to discuss, really. Bree and Mac had told her that during the one night the preacher spent at church camp, no sparks had flown between him and Gussie; they'd spent no moments alone cuddling or even chatting with each other, from what the girls had said. Drat the man. She needed to get him moving.

She hadn't pushed him or nagged about the opportunity gone awry because he *had* been called away to take care of the congregation and he'd been busy with his neighbors since Ouida's terrible fall. Poor Ouida was suffering so much, and that husband of hers was nearly useless. Oh, Birdie knew that. She'd dropped in several times to bring food or to help with the girls. George nodded when she spoke and hurried to do whatever she asked but looked like he wanted to hide from her. Helpless and worthless.

However, Birdie had given the preacher enough time. If he believed he'd gotten away easy, ignoring his courting when the Widows had worked so hard to get him going and when they were all distracted by the plight of the Kowalski family, he had another think coming. Birdie knew she was exactly the person to set him straight.

She'd have to be cunning, Birdie reflected as she finished wiping the last table at the diner. Sneaky. Not let him know that she knew that he knew what she had in mind. She'd had a chat with the other Widows, which now included Blossom. She'd accepted the grass widow, realized that despite all her high maintenance, her expensive hair and clothing, she did have some good qualities, wasn't all fancy hats and no cattle. But, poor dear, she wasn't too bright.

Birdie had come up with a new plan of attack. She had an idea of exactly how to handle him.

Poor man. She laughed as she thought about what lay ahead.

Ten minutes later, she arrived at the church and opened the door. Maggie glanced up at her and froze.

"I'll tell Reverend Jordan you're here," she said.

Before Birdie could say she'd announce herself, Maggie shouted, "Pastor, Birdie MacDowell is here."

"Good morning, Preacher." As she entered the office, Birdie turned her friendliest smile toward him.

Adam stood. "How can I help you?" he said with a smile that didn't change the wary expression in his eyes or relax the tension in his shoulders. His face mirrored the same expression every minister who served the church wore when she arrived unexpectedly.

"Please sit down." Adam gestured toward a chair.

Birdie did. As the preacher returned to his chair, she took a moment to sit back and relax, to rotate that darned shoulder. It would bother her the rest of her life unless she finally gave up and had surgery, which she refused to do because how would her family eat if she did that? Who would . . . Well, enough of that. She cleared her throat—the sound caused the preacher to jump nervously—and said, "Didn't the young people have a wonderful time at camp?"

He nodded. "I heard they did."

"Yes, yes they did." She paused, attempting to act as if nothing were on her mind, but *subtle* was not one of her gifts. He watched her, clearly thought he knew where she was heading.

"As always, Gussie was wonderful." Birdie paused for a moment because she really did enjoy watching him become more wary. Baiting the preacher, not a benevolent act but entertaining. "However, that's not what I came to talk to you about."

His relief was audible and visible. He released his breath and his shoulders relaxed. But he still had that uneasy flicker in his eyes. In an effort to calm him, she smiled again because she did have an important item to discuss. Didn't work. He flinched.

"The other day, the Widows were talking about the Kowalskis." Not what he'd thought she'd say, she knew. That counted as a plus. He wouldn't suspect her real purpose.

He nodded, still wary.

"How's Ouida doing?"

"I stopped by for a minute yesterday at the nursing home. She said she felt better and looked forward to coming home in a week or two."

Birdie nodded. "That's good." She sighed, infusing worry and anxiety and concern and caring into that release of breath. "It's George I'm worried about." She leaned forward and allowed her most sympathetic look to cross her face.

"I can't talk about that, Miss Birdie."

"I know, I know. Privacy issues and all that, but I can." She leaned back. "It seems that the man is not pulling his weight, that he's not up to the task."

"He has a wife recovering from surgery, two little girls to care for, and a business to run."

"Exactly what I mean. George is like a one-legged man in a butt-kickin' contest." The baffled expression on the preacher's face told Birdie he had no idea what she meant. "That's Texan for he's not equipped for the job."

"He has a lot on his plate."

Birdie admired professional behavior in a minister. He'd said only what everyone in town knew, nothing more. She'd have to spell it out. "Yes, yes, we all know that, but he should do more. The girls aren't home that much with school and day care and church. He should be able to handle his business with Ouida in the nursing home and the girls taken care of all day. We take him food, we drive the girls around."

"I don't know that he's . . ."

Birdie kept speaking. "When she comes home, home health will come in to take care of Ouida. The Widows have scheduled neighbors and church members to sit with her. But, even with all those people pitching in, he acts overwhelmed."

"It's a big change for him."

"But—" She sat forward again, a movement she knew always caught the attention of any preacher. "But the man is so passive." She paused to make sure he picked up the adjective she used, then repeated it. "He's so doggone passive."

"It's all new to him."

"Oh, Preacher, I know that, but when I grew up, my daddy always taught me that if a man wants something, he should take action."

She fixed her eyes on him and spoke very slowly. "A man shouldn't sit around, passive, waiting for life to happen. If a man wants something, he should go after it." She settled back in the chair and continued to watch him.

It took a few seconds before his expression showed comprehension, the realization that Birdie was no longer talking about George, that Adam had become the topic of her conversation. He blinked once.

"Interesting observation." He nodded. "That's what your daddy used to say?"

He couldn't be teasing her, could he? Well, she didn't know. Sometimes the young man baffled her. He didn't behave like the ministers she'd trained in the past.

❦

It hadn't taken long for Adam to realize that Miss Birdie had left the topic of George Kowalski's problems and faults behind several remarks earlier. His poor neighbor's dilemma had been only a bridge, a jumping-off point, perhaps even a metaphor for the pillar's favorite theme: getting her minister married in spite of his poor efforts at romance. He could—also metaphorically—all but feel her behind him, both hands on his back and shoving him toward Gussie.

Once she recognized that he understood exactly what she had *not* said but implied, she sat back, so pleased with herself that a genuine smile covered her face.

Lord, Adam loved the woman. Always consistent: scheming and underhanded and never afraid to try or say the most outrageous things, but she did everything because she cared. She knew that everyone would be much better off if they gave in and did things her way.

"You're meddling," he stated.

"I don't believe expressing concern about the Kowalskis could possibly be considered meddling."

Her smile became even broader, because there was no way he could tell her he knew good and well what she'd really been talking about. If he did, he opened himself up for advice about how to date Gussie.

His best course of action was to get her to leave. He needed a few moments of privacy to mull her words over. He stood, walked around the desk, and took her right hand, the one at the end of her good arm. "Thank you for dropping by." He helped her to her feet—surreptitiously, of course—and shepherded her through the door. She couldn't refuse to leave without crossing the line between aggressively helpful and what even she would consider downright rude.

With the pillar gone, Adam settled back in his chair and considered what she'd said, the hidden meaning in her words. As much as he hated to admit it, Miss Birdie was right. He had to become more assertive and less passive when it came to Gussie. When Sam and the pillar agreed, he should listen and act. He'd do that, as soon as he figured out what to do and how to do it. Although the Widows seemed unaware of the difficulty involved, Adam knew it too well. Gussie hadn't displayed even an iota of interest in him.

But he'd hidden his attraction to her. Perhaps she'd done the same. Could it be that deep within, she harbored a fiery passion for him, an unbridled lust she hid behind her quick smile and let's-be-friends exterior?

Oh, sure.

And even if she did, he saw obstacles he had no idea how to overcome. The most immediate: how to take action, to show interest in Gussie in case she felt anything toward him?

Should he call Sam? No, Sam had already given him the man-up lecture and expected Adam to act. His other friend was Mattie, but he'd never felt comfortable going to a woman for romantic advice.

He had to dive in and hope he could float. Better to know if Gussie felt the slightest bit of interest in him even if it meant facing rejection.

He pulled up his list of how to get the woman you want on the computer and studied it.

❦

Unable to put the deed off any longer because he feared if he didn't get a move on, Miss Birdie and Sam would visit him again with a stronger message, Adam ended up navigating the highways in South Austin the next day. A bouquet of roses lay on the passenger seat.

He'd picked up two ideas on the net: one, be spontaneous. Women adored spur-of-the-moment-ness. He'd decided to drop in, unexpectedly, to seem impulsive. Or, could be he was too cowardly to call.

Second, women loved flowers, but not red roses. Too clichéd, too obvious, too passé. Roses, yes. Red, no. So he'd headed toward the floral department at the H-E-B and chosen a mixture of yellow and melon and deep orange roses, four of each, because the bright colors reminded him of Gussie.

Because he had a tendency to get lost, he'd looked up the location of Gussie's photography studio and printed off a map. Only a couple of blocks south of Highway 71. He'd chosen to arrive a few minutes before ten in the hope that she'd be between appointments or could find time to see him later, perhaps for lunch. Finding the address, he pulled into a lot, turned off the ignition, picked up the flowers, and got out of the car, which still sputtered behind him, a problem Rex hadn't been able to diagnose and fix yet.

To his surprise, he found himself whistling. He hadn't whistled in a long time. Probably had known instinctively that whereas Miss Birdie could handle a minister who played basketball, she would not approve of a basketball-playing minister who whistled.

Why had he allowed her to run his life? Probably because his life was a great deal easier if he gave in to her on the little things.

He stopped in front of the door to Gussie's studio and gave a long whistle. Wow! She was really successful. Several pictures of Austin celebrities stared out of the front windows of a sleek, modern building: one of a guitar player with a ponytail; another of a well-muscled actor famous for taking his shirt off. He opened the door to a reception area with luxurious chairs, a thick carpet, and a gorgeous blonde at the desk.

"May I help you?" the receptionist asked with a broad smile.

"I'm here to see Gussie?" he asked although he hadn't meant it as a question.

"Was she expecting you?" Her smile became even more friendly, showing soft dimples as if she'd finally realized he was a man.

"No." He glanced around. He was alone in the waiting area. "I thought I'd drop by. Hope to catch her."

Justine—at least that was the name on her desk plate—grimaced. "Oh, dear. That's not a good idea. Miss Milton never takes walk-ins. She's too busy."

Well, that was good for her business.

"Right now, she's at a church down the highway." Justine gestured behind her with her head. "Taking pictures for their directory."

That was the problem with being spontaneous. People didn't expect you and weren't around to take note of the grand gesture.

"Do you know when she'll be back?"

"Let's see." The blonde pulled up something on her monitor and studied it. "She has appointments until four, shooting all day. She'll stay to finish the paperwork and clean up. After that, she'll go straight home."

He'd chosen to go to her office instead of to Roundville because, with her parents around, he didn't feel a tryst could be either romantic or impetuous. Now driving into Austin in a failing car and not finding the object of his journey seemed foolish.

"Oh," he said.

"Can I take a message?" She glanced at the roses. "I could put them in water so they'll be pretty when she comes in tomorrow."

"No, thank you." What explanation could he possibly give for showing up with flowers? He obviously wasn't a delivery boy. "I . . ." He stopped when he realized there really wasn't one.

"You must really like flowers," the receptionist tilted her head a little and winked.

"Oh, sure," he agreed as if he carried them around all the time. "Yes, I do." She winked again, which, he feared, showed an interest in him. Could this get any worse?

Of course.

He'd turned to leave when he heard a door in the back of the studio open.

"Justine?" Gussie called from another room. "One of the ring lights broke and I didn't take an extra. I've got to grab a couple and take off again."

"You have . . . ," Justine began.

Trapped. He was trapped. Maybe he could escape before Gussie knew he'd dropped in. Adam shook his head at Justine in an ineffective and ultimately unsuccessful effort to quiet her. He even held a finger to his lips. It didn't work and he looked like even more of an idiot.

"You have a visitor," Justine finished. "A man."

"What?"

Could he hide? As he looked around him, Adam realized that action would look stupid and be useless. Oh, he'd never been cool around women, but he couldn't remember ever feeling this inept, not even when he and April Gonzalez had locked braces during a seventh-grade party.

"Hi," Adam said when Gussie pulled a curtain aside and glanced into the reception area.

The glow of her smile nearly blinded him. That moment made the entire mortifying experience nearly worth it. Then the brilliance faded and she looked confused.

"Adam? Was I expecting you?" She shook her head. "Did you have an appointment? If you did . . ."

"No, no. I thought I'd drop by. I was in Austin to . . ." He couldn't think of a reason. "And I thought I'd drop by."

"With flowers?"

He nodded and straightened his arm to thrust the roses toward her.

"How nice of you." She smiled as she accepted them. "They're lovely."

They stood looking at each other for a few awkward seconds before she said, "Well, I've got to get back to work. There are people waiting for me to take their pictures."

"I didn't realize you took church pictures," he said in an effort to dazzle her with his scintillating conversation skills.

"Oh, yes, as well as weddings, yearbook photos, quince-añeras, bar and bat mitzvahs, school pictures. All of those pay the bills to keep this place profitable."

"Well, then I'll be going." He waved and nearly ran out.

What a complete idiot he was.

❧

"Cute guy." Justine grinned at Gussie.

"Put these in water." Gussie handed the flowers to Justine. "Please. I have to get back to the church."

She headed toward the back running nearly as quickly as Adam had, hoping to get out before Justine could ask anything. Not that her quick exit would make any difference; she'd have to return to her studio tomorrow and Justine would be here, still curious, still commenting and digging and asking questions.

"I think he has a crush on you," Justine shouted.

Gussie reached the back door before she realized Adam's appearance had flustered her so much that she hadn't picked up the lights. She opened a cabinet, grabbed a couple, and took off.

Once in her car and headed back toward the church, she allowed herself to ponder her ill-at-ease reaction to Adam's appearance and his rapid departure.

Why had Adam been there?

Oh, she knew. She didn't want to face the reason, but she knew. A man didn't stop by with roses unless he had a deep interest in a woman. The realization made her want to smile and scream in frustration. She didn't want him to care about her. She didn't want to care about him.

But those last two internal comments were a load of baloney because yes, she did, and yes, she already did. She couldn't force herself to believe she had no interest in Adam. She had to stop lying to herself.

After what Lennie had done to her in college, she'd never trusted a man again. But Adam . . . Adam seemed different. What she hated was she'd treated him rudely, as if she didn't appreciate his interest or the flowers. She did but had trouble, lots of trouble, reacting to a man normally.

Once she arrived at the church, she shoved the thoughts back and attempted to concentrate on taking photos. But she couldn't get rid of images of Adam holding the flowers and looking embarrassed and how guilty it made her feel.

In fact, as soon as she left the church, started her car, and pulled out of the parking lot, they came back in full force. What should she do? First, as usual, she refused to think about the unpleasantness and her failure to act like a normal person. Instead, she picked up her cell and called her mother to tell her she'd left Austin. But then, she found herself back at her office. It was after six so Justine had left long ago. She wouldn't have to try to explain to her about Adam, not today, at least.

She unlocked the door, turned on a light, and found the vase of flowers on the reception desk. She took the flowers from the vase and wrapped them in paper towels. After that, she carried them back to the car, headed west, and allowed herself to think about Adam. A sweet man. A kind man who took homeless children in. A minister. A safe man.

Oh, crap. Certainly she didn't find him attractive because he was non-threatening, did she? If so, those years of counseling had been a waste of effort and money. Besides, the exact moment the attraction had hit her, he'd been sweaty and intense and so masculine that the awareness of the chemistry had rocked her. The unexpected reaction had felt almost threatening but good, really good. Exciting. As if she were ready, finally, to trust a guy, to care for him as a woman cared about a man.

For a moment, she took her eyes off the road that she traveled so often she could probably turn the driving over to her little yellow Focus and take a nap. She glanced at the roses in the passenger seat. Yellow and orange and—how to describe that third color? Orange sherbet? Lovely, exactly the colors she would have chosen. Turning her eyes back to the highway, she rubbed her fingers across the soft, velvety surface of the petals, then picked up the bouquet to bury her nose in the blooms. The softness against her nose tickled.

How would she explain the flowers to her parents? If she told them they came from a man, her father would worry and her mother would be filled with hope. She didn't want to raise their hopes or expectations or encourage them to dream, but she refused to hide the flowers. Let them decide how to feel. She couldn't protect her parents from hope or trauma forever.

Had she been protecting them as well as herself? The thought had never—well, she'd never considered that before. Obviously, she needed to think this through because she was contemplating a thaw in her relationship with the male half of the world, or, at least, one man in the Texas Hill Country.

She sat in her car in the driveway for a minute after she pulled off the road. As usual, her father's truck sat in front of the house. As long as she could remember, her father had a truck. Even though getting into it posed problems with his bad hips and knee, he refused to give it up. As long as she could remember, he'd never used the back of the truck to carry anything, so why had he always bought this type of vehicle? Because in Texas, a man drove a truck, and usually in the passing lane on the interstate.

Aware that her contemplation of her father's reasoning only put off the inevitable—a skill Gussie had perfected—she picked up the roses and her purse, got out, closed the car door, beeped it locked, and headed toward the house.

"Hello, darling." Her mother greeted her from the sofa where she was watching *Jeopardy!* and knitting. As many sweaters and scarves as she'd made for her daughter, they should have lived in the Arctic. Fortunately, now she'd started knitting tiny blankets for newborns at Seeton Hospital.

Her mother had always looked fragile. Now, with blue-white hair and ivory skin covered with a net of wrinkles, she looked deceptively sweet and frail but she had a will as strong . . . well, as strong as Gussie's.

"Hi, Mom." Gussie kissed her cheek.

"Hello, Gus," her father said as he entered the room. Gussie still struggled to accept the difference between the buff and hearty father of her childhood memories and this thin, stooped man.

"What do you have there? Where'd you get the flowers?" he asked.

Gussie could tell them that a client had given them to her, but she couldn't lie.

"A man gave them to me," she said. "Aren't they lovely?" She held the bouquet up.

"Oh." Her mother's eyes opened wide and her lips trembled. "A man?"

Her father dropped in a chair, so surprised, Gussie thought, that he couldn't stand up any longer, although it was probably that his bad hips bothered him. "A man?" His voice echoed the shock of someone who'd given up on his daughter's ever receiving flowers again from a man.

"Yes, a man."

"One of those elderly men who come up with their society wives to get their portraits taken?" her mother guessed. "They do adore you."

"Mother, those men are flirts but harmless. They'd never give me flowers. They're afraid of their wives."

"Could be that man who owns the office next door. You've always been nice to him," her father suggested. "Watched his store when he went out of town."

She knew what they were doing, her dear parents. To protect her, they were in as deep a state of denial as she was, and she'd allowed it for years. Time to stop.

"The flowers came from Adam Jordan, the minister of the church in Butternut Creek."

"Oh," her mother said. "A thank-you for all your work with the young people."

Gussie hadn't thought of that. Had she allowed her attraction to Adam to color her opinion here? Had the flowers been a mere gift of appreciation? No, probably not. After all, he'd delivered them himself when he could have ordered them from a florist in Austin. Also, he'd looked nervous, and the dozen roses in her favorite colors must have cost more than a young minister could really afford. A note would have said thank you.

"No, the flowers mean more than that."

Her parents turned in unison to study each other. Although they said nothing, they didn't have to. Their ability to communicate silently had always amazed her. In fact, she put that trait high on the mental list she'd labeled *What I'm Looking for in a Husband* back when she'd expected to find one.

Knowing the futility of interrupting the transfer of information between her parents, Gussie waited.

Finally, her mother, with visions of grandchildren dancing in her eyes, said, "Tell us more."

Her father, who looked far less pleased and much more protective of his daughter, said nothing.

"Not much to tell." Gussie struggled to think of words to explain. She'd tried to come up with something on the drive home but hadn't, and inspiration didn't strike now.

After a long pause, her father said, "What do they mean?" He glared at the flowers as if they were a solicitation for something he preferred not to consider.

"What do flowers usually mean, Henry?"

"Back when I was courting you, they meant the young man had an interest in the young woman."

"That's still what it means," Gussie said.

"How interested is he?" her father asked.

Gussie shrugged because she had no idea. More than she'd realized, obviously.

"Now, dear, let them work this out. Although"—she turned back toward Gussie, her face glowing—"I would love to have grand-children."

For a moment, Gussie was almost angry with Adam. He'd made her mother look toward the future. She wished she could reach out and caress the lines of worry from her father's face and lower the level of hope that gleamed in her mother's eyes.

But wasn't hope good?

"I'm thirty-one, probably too old to conceive a baby. I read the other day . . ."

"I had you when I was thirty-eight. What a surprise you were to everyone."

Her father had been forty-two. Now they were seventy and seventy-four, so dear but not elderly, truly. The age she considered *elderly* had been pushed back every year as they grew older.

"Are you considering having children with this man?" her father demanded.

"But first, you'll get married, won't you?" her mother asked. "Now-adays, that doesn't seem to be the norm, but I hope you'd . . ."

What had she started? How had the discussion gotten away from her so quickly and irrevocably?

"Adam brought me flowers. I accepted them." She shook them a little to make a point. Not a good idea. A few petals flew into the air. "Right now, I'm not considering commitment for life, neither of us is." Both parents watched her and she had no idea what to do or say. How could she ease their fears when hers played havoc with her usual logic?

"Let me get a vase for these." Gussie started toward the kitchen. "I'll put them on the coffee table where we can all enjoy them."

"Wait a minute, missy."

When her father used that tone, she had no choice but to stop, turn, and listen. Well, she did have a choice, but ignoring him would hurt his feelings, make him feel like an old man with no purpose in his life.

Also, she needed to figure this out—her feelings, Adam's motive, the entire situation. Maybe if she talked about it, if she attempted to explain, she'd figure out how she felt. For years she'd hidden her emo-tions deep inside, tamped them down firmly and ignored them. Per-haps it was time to feel again.

She sat down, primly and meekly, to answer their questions and, maybe, a few of her own.

"Adam brought me the flowers today at the studio," she said. "He came into town and dropped them off. I'm not sure exactly what they mean." Oh, that was weak.

"Gussie, are you saying that he traveled all the way from Butternut Creek to South Austin to bring you flowers?" her mother asked.

"He probably was making hospital visits."

"Do you think he picked these up from a member of his congregation recovering from surgery?" her father asked as sarcastically as he allowed himself to be.

"No, of course not." She closed her eyes and attempted to sort out her feelings again. How to explain what confused her? Finally she opened her eyes and said, "I met Adam in Marble Falls a few months ago, to discuss the retreat."

"You often do that, with several of the youth workers." Her mother cocked her head. "You mentioned Reverend Jordan. I didn't think this Adam was anything different or special."

"I didn't, either." Oh, she should not lie but couldn't explain this now, not when she felt so uncertain.

"But?" Her father prompted. "I take it he's unmarried."

"Of course."

She glanced at her parents. They watched her, not saying a word but waiting. "Then, when we were at the retreat, I felt a hint of . . ." Oh, she really didn't want to share her chemical reaction to Adam with her parents. "I felt a slight . . . um . . . attraction."

"Aah," her mother said.

Her father leaned forward but said nothing.

"You know I went to Butternut Creek for that meeting in—what? April?"

"Were you at camp together?" her father asked. The man never let anything get by him. "Did you find him attractive then?"

"We didn't have any time together. I . . ."

"Did you avoid him?" he asked.

"No, Dad. He had to leave for a funeral. We really didn't spend time together. We did not have a chance to swear undying love." She shut her mouth quickly. Her frustration had made her mouth off.

"Missy," her father warned.

"I'm sorry."

He nodded, so she continued. "Then, today, he walked into the studio with flowers. I don't know what this means or how he feels or how I feel."

Her parents glanced at each other and smiled.

"What did he say?" her father asked. "When he brought the flowers?"

"Not much. I had appointments and couldn't talk to him."

"So," he said, "this minister shoved the flowers toward you and ran off without a word of explanation?"

"Not exactly *shoved*, but, yes, he did run off before I could think of a thing to say."

"Have you called to thank him for the flowers?" Mother asked, always the one to reinforce rules of etiquette. "At least emailed him? Although I think a personal note is so much more courteous."

Her mother would see that sin of omission as a nearly unforgivable breech on Gussie's part.

"I haven't had a chance. I just got home, but you're right. I'll write." Her last words were said with determination, to make sure her parents understood this was the end of the grilling, that she'd shared as much information as she could at this moment.

They didn't catch on. "Tell us more about this Adam," her mother said.

"I don't know much more. He's a minister, not from Texas. He took in two homeless children."

"He did?" her mother said. "What a fine young man. He likes children?"

Knowing exactly where her mother's thoughts headed, Gussie stifled a groan and stood. "I'm going to put these in a vase before I prick my finger on a thorn."

The roses had been de-thorned, but her parents didn't need to know that. She had to get away. She'd shared a great deal with them but refused to confess to the tumble of emotion inside, the sudden yearning the flowers had brought, the feeling that both delighted and terrified her.

She wanted love more than anything in the world.

And less than anything.

❧

"Pops, what's that closed building in the back of the church? Bree says it's a gym. Why can't we play ball there?" Hector asked. Now that it was mid-June, the days had gotten much hotter. Adam couldn't blame Hector for wanting an indoor court.

"I've only been inside once," Adam said. "When I first got here. You want to check it out?" At Hector's nod, he added, "Grab a flashlight. We don't have any utilities on back there."

After he searched his junk drawer for the keys and Hector found a flashlight, they headed across the lawn of the parsonage and the church parking lot. He hadn't heard from Gussie for days. The tour would fill time and take his mind off that lack of communication.

"Jesse tells me they locked the place up because it had deteriorated to the point it wasn't safe and the church couldn't afford to fix it up." He turned the key in the padlock to remove the chain, then inserted another in the lock, turned it, and tugged at the door. It opened with a loud shriek.

The air inside rushed at them, thick and dank and dust-filled.

"Stinks in here."

"Mold and age," Adam agreed.

Light filtered through windows high on the walls of the building, enough to allow them to see the rough wood of the court.

"This is bad, Pops." Hector stood at the edge of the court and looked around. "But has possibilities." He pointed. "A scoreboard, bleachers."

"Do you know how much a new floor would cost?"

"How much?"

"I don't know, but a lot more than we can afford." They wandered around the court and toward the dressing rooms. "Jesse told me they applied for grants but those went to organizations in big cities with more of a crime problem. They also tried to get the community involved, but the initial investment was too much."

Hector shook his head. "This could be terrific. Everyone in town could use it. We could have events and stuff and charge to keep it up. Rent it out."

"I agree." They walked into the dressing rooms. Lockers stood open, the doors sagging. Rust stains showed in the drains of the showers and basins. "It's the initial cost. Not only the floor but new wiring and plumbing. It's a huge project."

"Yeah." Hector nodded. "But it would be cool to have a hoop we could use closer than the park and in the rain."

❧

That evening, Adam checked email, then sent a message to his parents and to his sister, a medical doctor who wandered through Africa caring for refugees.

When the you-have-a-message tone sounded, he clicked and checked the name of the sender. Gussie. Quickly, he opened and read the email. "Thank you for the flowers. They are lovely." Nothing more. A curt but polite thank-you note that didn't show a bit of encouragement. Hard to convince himself—no, impossible!—that the note was written by a woman who adored him or felt even an iota of attraction and wanted to see him again.

Well, he'd tried. He'd been active and acted spontaneously but her reaction showed she thought of him as a friend who, oddly, brought her flowers. A nice, geeky guy who dropped into her studio without an appointment only to say hi. With roses.

What had he expected from her? A proposal? A declaration of eternal love? Perhaps even a Scarlett O'Hara, "Oh, fiddle-dee-dee, Reverend Jordan" flirtatiousness?

That sounded stupid even in his own brain.

She probably didn't understand why he'd brought her flowers any more than he did. It had seemed like a good idea before he arrived in Austin, but when he remembered her expression of amazement, he still cringed.

But first she'd smiled.

He probably would have sat and stared at the email for a few more minutes and thought of dozens of depressing reasons she'd never be interested in him.

Fortunately, Hector and Bobby clattered in. Their arrival effectively interrupted his moment of wallowing in the depths of unrequited love.

"How 'bout some hoops, Pops?"

As he'd always done, Adam'd figure out life after a hard game of roundball cleared his mind and exhausted his body.

Chapter Nine

Ouida lay in the hospital bed in the middle of the living room and savored the quiet. When she'd arrived a couple of days ago, she carefully supervised the position of the bed. From there, she could look straight ahead, through the clear square in the stained-glass window of the front door and out to the porch and a slice of the street. If she turned to her left, she viewed the side yard toward the parsonage.

Nearly three weeks after her fall, she'd recovered a little. The pain had lessened and her hand had healed well. She did exercises with a ball over and over to strengthen it. Her shoulder sling would come off in a few weeks. PT helped with pain and range of motion. As she gained a little use of that arm, she no longer felt quite as much like a turtle on its back, but she still couldn't put much weight on it. Fortunately, the broken leg turned out to be less restrictive than the doctors had first thought. It had healed enough that she'd be able to get rid of the cast shortly. Still, a long road to recovery lay ahead.

Today the girls had gone to day care. George had gone into Austin for a few hours. She sighed. The poor man was so uncomfortable, it was a good thing for him to get away from here and back to his beloved numbers. He'd left her with the remote, a phone, several books, and a tall glass of ice water. She hoped she didn't need to go to the bathroom until the nurse showed up in an hour.

Peace. It had been so long since she'd had peace. George wasn't wandering around the house looking confused and asking her every five minutes if she was okay and if she needed anything and did she know where his blue shirt or the ketchup was and did she need anything? The girls weren't laughing or running up and down the staircase or making noise of any kind.

Peace.

It bored her silly.

Scattered around the living room were a few of the girls' toys. She loved to have them playing in here. Last night they'd left sticky ice cream bowls on the coffee table. Wonder of all wonders, George had picked them up, carried them to the kitchen, and placed them in the dishwasher without complaint. She'd had to point them out to him, but he did the rest on his own.

"Hey, neighbor," Adam shouted from the front door. "Decent?"

Not that she had any modesty left after her stay in the hospital and her dependency on everyone around. But, for Adam, she felt around to make sure the sheet was tucked in. "Door's open. Come on in." As if anyone locked their doors in Butternut Creek.

"Can I get you anything?" He wandered in.

Adam was the nicest person. Although she'd never been inside the Christian Church except for the Christmas pageant in which the girls had dressed as angels, he took good care of the Kowalski family. If she had even an iota of the spirituality gene, she'd join the church in no time, but she didn't and the whole thing seemed a waste of time. Oh, the girls loved Sunday school and went every week. They brought home crafts she displayed on the bookcase and pages colored in odd shades that showed Abraham as purple or Mary as yellow because, Carol said, most of the crayons were broken or missing. She'd have to donate several boxes, once she could get to the dollar store.

"I'm fine. Sit down and keep me company. Good to see you."

Adam tossed a stuffed animal off the sofa before he settled in. "How's it going?"

"I hate being laid up. I never get sick and I'm not used to people taking care of me. It's driving me crazy."

"How's George handling everything?"

"Okay." She shrugged. "It's not easy for him. He's trying so hard to help. He's doing the laundry and uses so much detergent that the sheets crackle when I turn over, but I'm not going to tell him that. I'm just glad he does the wash."

She really didn't want to tell him about the problems George was having in adjusting, so before he could ask more she said, "Carol and Gretchen love playing in your yard. Thanks for letting them use your swing set."

"I'm not using it much myself," he answered. "Janey loves playing with your girls."

"I've heard . . ." She stopped to consider her words but decided to go ahead. What could he do to a woman in traction? And she wanted to know. "I hear you have a girlfriend."

If there had been any doubt in her mind about the gossip, his reaction changed that. He straightened, blinked, and gulped before attempting to lounge back comfortably.

"Girlfriend?"

She didn't say anything.

"They may be talking about Gussie Milton. She's from Roundville. We know each other through the youth groups."

"Adam, I promise I won't tell the Widows. I know how they are. I've heard stories about their tactics. Poor Sam was hounded until he and Willow got together." She lifted her free hand and pretended to zip her lips. "You can tell me anything. My lips are sealed."

He grinned. "Nothing to report. I tried to date her."

"Tried? You gave up?"

He shrugged.

"I was hoping for a wedding in the future," Ouida said.

"Oh, sure."

"Is she skittish or are you?" She struggled to sit up a little straighter and kept her eyes on his face.

He raised an eyebrow. "Do I have a sign on my forehead that says, MISERABLE AND ALONE. PLEASE HELP THIS POOR LOSER?"

"Guess that means none of my business? Okay, I'll change the subject because I have a favor to ask."

He looked wary.

"Don't worry. It's easy. Please take George for an evening. He's driving me crazy and I'm driving him nuts. He needs some man time. He also probably needs to talk to you about what's happening, about this change in our lives."

"I could do that. When?"

"What night might be convenient? The sooner the better." She attempted to get comfortable but that darned cast and the traction didn't allow it. "Tonight?"

"I'll be home."

"And one more favor."

Again Adam looked worried, so she quickly explained. "Would you pull me up on the bed? I keep slipping down."

❧

That evening Adam wasn't surprised to see George when he opened the front door of the parsonage. "Come on in," he said and led his neighbor back to the television/living/dining-on-TV-trays room.

With his well-tailored khakis, George wore flip-flops and a UT T-shirt. Adam hadn't thought his neighbor possessed flip-flops or a T-shirt. Even dressed in what passed as casual for George, his neighbor didn't look a bit comfortable. Warily he studied the hall and the room. Looking for religious symbols or holy relics?

"Ouida make you come?" Adam asked.

"Not exactly," George said. "She did suggest it. Strongly." He glanced at his bare toes. "She also told me to wear these shoes. She said when guys get together to watch a game, they don't wear wing tips." She wasn't wrong. Sam and the boys came over pretty regularly to watch sports, and he'd never seen them wear wing tips. George shook his head. "I don't know *how* she knows what guys wear to get together to watch sports, but this is what she told me they wear."

Because Adam didn't know if he should laugh or not, if George was joking or only repeating Ouida's advice, he said, "Probably from a beer commercial on television." He waved toward a chair. "Grab a comfortable place to sit. Would you like something to drink? A Coke or tea?"

"No, no." George took the recliner but sat straight up in it.

Adam settled on the sofa. He should give his neighbor time to relax and to start the conversation on his own but didn't feel optimistic that would happen. The only conversations they'd shared had been the night at the hospital when Ouida fell and a few chats while George indulged in his one leisure-time activity Adam was aware of: helping Ouida garden.

"So, how're things going?" Adam asked.

George glanced at Adam. "Terrific," he said with a hint of sarcasm in his voice. The tone made him feel his neighbor did have a sense of humor.

Then George leaned back and sighed. "I'm so out of my depth with this whole thing, I don't know what to do. Ouida's the one who makes sure everything at home runs precisely. I can't juggle things like work and family and cooking. Thank goodness the church ladies bring food."

"You do know that's going to stop in a few days."

George looked at him, panic in his eyes. "What?"

"The meals are to tide you over during the roughest of times."

"Oh." George considered that. "I can't cook."

"Can you use a microwave? They make great frozen foods nowadays."

They watched the pre-game show on television for a minute or two before George said, "You know I don't like to share, right? I'm not a touchy-feely kind of man."

Adam nodded.

"But this worries me. The doctors have said they don't know how well the leg will heal, if she'll have problems or a disability. None of them can guarantee she'll walk without a cane or a walker."

Adam considered saying that there were no guarantees in life but bet George wouldn't be comforted by a cliché. "No, they can't, but she's getting great care, from home health and from you."

George scrutinized him with cold eyes. Obviously, Adam had failed as a man, a minister, and a neighbor.

"I don't know what I can say, George. No one knows at this moment, and it seems to me you're a man who likes certainty." He searched for words. "But all of us are here to help—your neighbors, the church, all of us. And Ouida, she's a fighter. You know that. She's strong."

George clenched his fists and swallowed quickly. Adam bet that was a deep show of emotion for his neighbor. If there was anything Adam knew at this moment, it was that he couldn't allow George to break down. Oh, it would be cathartic and George probably needed to share, but he'd be embarrassed if Adam had witnessed that, might even cut off all contact.

"Do you like baseball?" Adam said in a hearty, booming, manly voice.

"Yes." George nodded and blinked. "I graduated from UT. I'm a big Texas fan, any sport. With work, I don't have a chance to watch it much."

Adam decided his guest needed a break and a little privacy. "Let me get drinks and chips. Do you want pop?"

"You have red?"

"Sure." He tossed George the remote.

By the time Adam returned, put the chips and pop on the coffee table, the Rangers game had started. After a few minutes, George said, "I don't know how to take care of children."

Adam started to say, *What worries you about that?* before quickly pulling the words back. Sounded too much like a preacher, like a counseling session. "Why's that?"

"Ouida does that." George took a handful of chips and munched. "I'm not good with kids." He glanced at Adam. "I work with numbers. I'm uncomfortable and ineffectual around illogical people."

"Illogical pretty much defines children. Especially young ones, like Gretchen."

George nodded. "They're at day care during the day."

"They need you around."

"Sure."

A few minutes later, George said, "I'll have to work at home more."

"Probably."

"I like things neat."

Adam glanced at the precise cut of George's hair, the way even his T-shirt looked as if it had been freshly starched and ironed, and the neat crease of his slacks. "Kids aren't neat."

"I can handle that." He watched a double play end the third inning before adding, "Maybe."

A little less confidence than Adam had hoped for. He took a handful of chips and waited.

"I'm not good with injured or sick people, either," George said as the color commentator babbled on about the first baseman. "That's the hardest part." He shook his head.

"That's tough."

After the fourth inning, George stood. "Guess I'll go home. Thanks for the food."

Adam wasn't sure if what he'd said or left unsaid was right or wrong or the least bit helpful but felt communication was open. Maybe they'd even had a few moments of male bonding, but George was hard to read.

❦

When George came home the next day, the girls had settled on the bed with Ouida. "Come on in," she said. "The girls wanted me to tell them a story."

"Be careful with your mother's leg," he warned.

"Yes, Daddy," the girls said, scooting back a fraction of an inch.

"They're fine. The girls were very careful." Ouida looked down at the girls with a smile. It felt so good to be home with them cuddled around her.

"Mommy, tell us the story about your dog. You know, the deaf one," Carol said.

"Mommy, did you have a deaf dog?" Gretchen's eyes got round with wonder as if she hadn't heard the story dozens of times.

"Yes, sweetheart. Her name was Daffy. Short for Daffodil. She was a blond cocker spaniel with big floppy ears."

"Like this?" Carol put her hands up to her ears.

"Yes, big floppy ears, but she got an infection inside her ears."

"An 'fection?" Gretchen asked. "Did it hurt?"

"Very much. Daffy loved her people but she hurt so much when they petted her that she stayed away."

"Oooh," the girls said together.

She glanced at George and smiled. He leaned against the wall and continued to watch.

"Sweetheart," she said. "Why don't you sit on the chair next to the bed."

He shook his head. "I'm fine here."

She gave up and returned to the story. "Daffy's doctor had to clean out all the bad stuff in her ears as well as the parts of the ear she heard with. When the doctor took off Daffy's bandages, she couldn't hear."

"Oooh," the girls repeated.

"Poor puppy," Gretchen said.

"But Daffy didn't mind. She still danced and helped me load the dishwasher if I dropped a few leftovers for her. She came for dinner and played with the other dogs." She paused to allow her daughters to react.

"And then what?" Carol said.

She could see George smile. He'd heard this story and knew what would come next. He knew the girls did, too, but he seemed to be enjoying this family time.

"One day, I had to go to the bathroom really bad," Ouida said.

The girls covered their mouths with their hands and giggled.

"I went in the bathroom and . . . um . . . sat down but didn't turn on the light because I was in such a hurry."

Gretchen laughed. "Then what, Mommy?"

"I heard tapping on the wood floor in the hall. Daffy was running back and forth, looking for me. She was my dog, you know. She became very worried when she couldn't find me."

"What did she do?" Carol pushed herself closer to her mother.

Using her fingers, Ouida explained. "She ran up and down the hall, frantic. I shouted, 'I'm in here,' but she couldn't hear me."

" 'Cause she was deaf," Carol said.

" 'Cause of the 'fection," Gretchen added.

"I yelled again, but she kept running back and forth. I could hear her searching because her nails tapped on the hardwood floor. Finally, when she passed the bathroom door, I picked up a roll of toilet paper and threw it at her. Not hard. I didn't want to hurt her, just to get her attention so she could find me. The roll missed her by a few inches but she stopped in the hall and looked all around her." Ouida acted that action out and the girls joined her. "And looked confused. I know she was thinking, *Why is someone throwing things at me?*"

"Did she find you?" Carol asked, knowing well the end of the story.

"No, I finished my business and went out to the hall. She was so happy to see me, she danced." She hugged the girls. "After that, I always turned on the bathroom light so she could find me."

George shoved away from the wall and took a few steps toward them.

"Doesn't Mommy tell wonderful stories?" Carol said.

The girls leaped from the bed and put their arms around his legs and squeezed.

"Mama tells wonderful stories," he said as he knelt to hold both girls.

❦

The flowers had finally died. When she first received them, Gussie'd carefully removed any petals that had turned dark and tugged off wilted leaves.

Now the few remaining leaves and petals were crispy. Holding on to them seemed maudlin. She should toss them. Instead she wrapped them in a towel to prevent further disintegration and put them on the shelf in the closet behind her hiking boots.

She'd behaved like a jerk. Because Adam's unexpected visit and the roses had startled her so much and she'd had to explain the flowers to her parents—well, all in all, she'd behaved rudely. As usual, she'd closed herself off. Probably acted almost catatonic when he'd handed her the bouquet, then she'd rushed out as if he had threatened her, which, of course, his very presence did. On top of that, she'd sent that abrupt email and pretended it took care of everything.

Aah, yes, her nemesis, that closing herself off, not responding, hoping that whatever intruded into her safe place would go away if she ignored it. Her normal operating procedure. In times of stress, she isolated herself, abandoned logic, and navigated on hysteria.

Well, she'd ignored Adam to shield herself from the situation for two weeks and still hadn't forgotten. She hadn't heard from Adam since her terse, "Thank you." Why would she? She'd hardly encouraged him to keep in touch.

Bet he wouldn't bring her flowers again anytime soon.

It would only be polite for her to write him a nice thankyou. He'd made an effort to visit her and how had she reacted?

Yes, she'd write him another, more cordial thank-you note. Not that she'd encourage him to answer because she wasn't looking for anything from him.

When had she become such a terrible liar—and to herself?

She turned toward her laptop and composed another short note, a pleasant one. An apology as well as a much nicer thankyou. After reading and editing it several times, she decided it would serve her purpose: Be polite, show interest, don't push. She paused before hitting SEND. Should she tell him she'd like to hear from him? Ask him how things were in Butternut Creek?

"Gussie." Her mother tapped on her open door. "Your father and I are going to bed now."

"Good night," Gussie replied as she hit SEND.

"Are you going to stay up much longer? You need your sleep."

"Only a few minutes," Gussie said.

Was this any life for a thirty-one-year-old woman? Being told by her mother that she should go to bed? As a kid, Gussie turned off her light when her mother told her to, then hid beneath the covers, read with a flashlight. But now . . .

She sighed. She still lived in her parents' home and habits were hard to break. Not that she regretted her decision to stay. She loved her parents and had chosen this life.

No reason not to get ready for bed. She had to get up by six, only eight hours away, and she liked to read for an hour before turning out the light. As she slipped into bed, Gussie took one more look toward the closet where she'd hidden—no, saved—the flowers. Not that she could see them from here.

It seemed like a metaphor for her life: hidden in a closet, nice and safe and isolated at the very time she yearned for romance, for another person in her life, just more, more of life.

Could she change? Live another way? Accept?

Could she allow herself to find another life, a different one?

Could she stop hiding?

❧

Independence Day was a huge celebration that would take place around the courthouse square, a true small-town commemoration. The high school band would play in the pavilion and, because the fire ban had been lifted, a brilliant ten-minute display of fireworks would follow.

Toting lawn chairs, Hector, Bree, Janey, and Adam stopped by the Kowalskis' at eight to take the girls to the show.

"They slept all afternoon so they should be fine staying up so late," George said after he hugged his daughters. "This is Gretchen's first fireworks display. She was too young to take last year."

"Just a minute," Ouida said before they could leave. "The mosquitoes and the no-see-ums will be all over tonight, so give me your arm." She sprayed an oily but fragrant substance on Adam's arms. "Now rub that on your face and spray it on your legs."

"What is that?" Adam rubbed his arms, which covered his hands in the same substance.

"Skin lotion, but also the best thing ever for keeping the bugs away."

Must be a Southern thing, Adam decided.

Once Ouida had sprayed everyone's arms and George had covered their legs, the group oozed from the house on the protective oiliness covering their visible skin.

"Sure hope this stuff works," Hector said, batting his hands at the clouds of biting flying creatures ahead of them.

It seemed to. By the time they arrived at the park and found a place for their chairs, the bugs left them alone. However, the stuff also made the kids so slippery that when Bree and Adam attempted to hold their hands to cross the street, they slid away.

As the sun dropped, the temperature fell to a comfortable ninety degrees.

The mayor welcomed the crowd, the band played patriotic songs, and everyone joined in singing. Janey played with Carol and Gretchen to keep them entertained.

Then the fireworks started. Brilliant flashes filled the sky and explosions went off. Carol looked up at the sky, enthralled, but Gretchen leaped into the air at the sounds. In only seconds she'd forced her body under Bree's chair, sobbing. "They're shooting at us," Gretchen shouted. "They're shooting at me."

They left immediately and watched the display as they walked home, backward, Hector carrying Gretchen. In the safety of Hector's arms, she settled down the farther they got from the noise.

When they'd returned the girls to their home and Bree had helped George wash them off and put them to bed, Bree and Hector sat on the porch swing while Adam sat inside to work on his very sketchy sermon.

Saturday, they went to a church picnic at Jesse's farm. Late that night, after finishing what might be, with the help of the Holy Spirit, an acceptable sermon, Adam checked his email. Because he hadn't checked for a few days, he had dozens of new messages.

He scrolled through, deleted spam, and read a short note from his sister before he saw a message from Gussie.

Why had she written?

Didn't she realize he had gotten her message: *Not interested*? Or did she believe he needed to read it again, over and over because he was so thickheaded? The subject line said, "Hello." Great. That helped a lot, told him exactly what the message contained. Did she plan to stomp on his ego again?

He didn't want to open it. Really did not. He'd thought he'd recovered from the rejection over the past few weeks and from the embarrassment of taking flowers to a woman obviously astounded by his appearance and not interested in him. Guess not. But it could be about the area youth program. He couldn't ignore that. He placed the cursor on the message.

Women really messed with a guy's brain. Did they attend classes for that or did they learn it at their mother's knee? Secrets passed down through matriarchs?

And yet, here he sat, gazing at the list of emails and not opening any more of them, especially not the one with the cheery "Hello." Realizing the stupidity of doing nothing, he clicked on it.

"Sorry about the quick thank-you email I sent earlier. I really did like the flowers. They were on my desk for a week. You surprised me and I didn't react well. I'm sorry. Again, thank you."

What in the world did that mean? Did she want to hear from him?

Answering wouldn't hurt. He typed a short, friendly response that ended with, "I'd love to hear from you." No, that sounded desperate and needy and too emotional. He deleted the words, wrote, "Hope to hear from you soon," and sent it.

❦

Another middle-of-the-night call. Drat.

Adam fumbled for the phone but before he could say a word, a woman said, "Meet me at the diner for breakfast."

He rubbed his eyes and attempted to focus on the alarm clock but they kept closing on him. Only a sliver of light filtered through the blinds. Guess it was what Texans called "dark thirty."

"Who is this?" he mumbled.

"It's Mattie."

"Oh." He paused in an effort to wrap his sleepy brain around the information. "What time is it?"

"Five fifteen."

"Why in the world are you calling this early?" he muttered around a yawn. For a moment he fell back to sleep, but he woke up when Mattie nearly shouted through the receiver.

"I need to talk to you."

"Now? Why?" Fully awake, he sat up in bed. "What happened? Did the church burn down?" Must have been some terrible emergency, a disaster, to warrant such an early call.

"No, I want to talk to you. Meet me at the diner at six."

"Are you dying?" he asked stupidly, but no other explanation had leaped into his groggy brain.

"Of course not. Meet me. I'll explain."

"Can't," he said. "I've got to get the kids going." Not true. Hector could handle that, had done it often before, but Adam liked to give the kids a heads-up, drink a cup of coffee while Hector fixed breakfast. Of course, in the summer, that didn't happen until nine thirty, but that excuse worked. He did not want to get up now. "How 'bout eight?"

"If you want everyone in town to listen in, fine."

"Everyone in town will be listening in or will hear it from a friend at whatever time we meet."

She sighed. "I know."

"Do you want to wear a disguise? Have a secret password?"

"You're really weird this early in the morning."

"My social skills aren't at their best before the sun rises."

She laughed. "Okay. See you at eight."

Coffeepot in hand, Birdie gave the breakfast crowd a quick once-over. Looked fine. Everyone was eating or chatting or sipping coffee.

"Here you go, Charley." She poured a cup for Charley Parsons, the nice town plumber who was a hundred or more pounds overweight. When he sat at her table, she made him eat those fake eggs and didn't allow him to use butter on his pancakes. Actually, she never brought him pancakes, just whole-grain toast with margarine. That's why he always chose to sit at Dolores's table, but Birdie filled his cup anyway. She also picked up the sugar shaker and moved it to another table.

She looked around. No one held up an empty cup.

Except for Farley Masterson. Birdie wanted to completely ignore him but he was a customer and her boss would throw a conniption if she didn't serve every customer with a smile. Besides, he was at one of her tables and she needed the tips, both from Farley and from the person who took his place. If filling his cup would hurry old Farley along, she'd do it.

"Hey, good lookin'." He winked and held his cup up.

Old fool. Did he think she didn't know she looked like a—what had Mercedes called her?—a dried-up piece of beef jerky?

"How are you this morning?" Birdie asked in her brightest, most welcoming voice.

Obviously, Farley didn't recognize how pleasant she was behaving, because he said, "Sounds like you've had a tough morning."

She smiled.

"Dentures hurt?" he asked.

Old coot. He didn't have the slightest idea how to court a woman. "I have all my own teeth, thank you."

He tilted his head, puzzled. "I was being friendly."

"If you have to explain you're trying to be friendly, you might should work on that more."

He winked.

Birdie was stunned. "Are you flirting?"

If he weren't a customer, she'd pour the entire pot of coffee over him. It wasn't hot enough to burn him, not badly.

Fortunately, he stopped talking and looked behind her. "Isn't that your minister by the door?"

She turned to see Adam standing right next to Reverend Patillo. Didn't that beat all? Had they come together? How long had they been standing there?

What was wrong with her? She hadn't noticed their entrance and they had to have been waiting in line for a few minutes. Been too wrapped up in Farley Masterson and his antics and insults.

Of course, the arrival of the two ministers wasn't all that big a thing. They were friends. Often stopped by for breakfast or coffee and a piece of pie, sometimes lunch. As much as she and Mercedes had attempted to match the two up when Adam first arrived in Butternut Creek, it had never taken. So what was he doing here with the Presbyterian minister? Trying to destroy their latest schemes?

They'd come up with a great backup plan for the preacher and now these two showed up together? Birdie wanted to tell Reverend Patillo, *You had your chance. We have someone else in mind for him.* She didn't of course. Childish. And if Gussie didn't work out, the woman minister might go back on the short list, the very short list with only one name on it.

"Birdie?" Farley said. "Coffee."

Where was her brain? She'd never served him. She carefully poured a cup and walked away, without a smile because the man couldn't recognize good, friendly service if she slapped him in the face with it.

She couldn't take her eyes off the two preachers. Actually, the two of them showing up counted as neither a good thing nor a bad thing. The entire matchmaking venture had gotten out of hand. Twenty years ago, maybe even fifteen, she'd have had the preacher married months ago. Now, with her granddaughters and that shoulder and having to train her young minister and work, she'd given up on the endeavor almost entirely.

But if, after all they'd attempted with the preacher, she did stop matchmaking, Mercedes would get after her, would make Birdie feel like a quitter. If the preacher took up with Reverend Patillo, maybe they'd get married and have children to fill up the parsonage and the Sunday school classes.

But if they *did* get married, they might fill up the Presbyterian manse instead of the parsonage, which would destroy any gain except possibly in the preacher's happiness. Not to downplay the importance of the preacher's happiness, but those children were really important to the Christian Church. The Widows were counting on at least four or five kids. The preacher owed them children to fill the parsonage and the nursery, to expand the Sunday school classes, to take part in the Christmas pageant and, when they grew up, lead the youth group.

Of course, as a compromise, the two ministers might split their children between churches, the girls becoming Presbyterians whereas the boys attended the Christian Church. But what if all those children became Calvinists and went to their mother's church to swell that church's nursery, classrooms, and youth group?

Maybe she and the other matchmakers hadn't completely thought out that first plan, the one with Reverend Patillo.

"Miss Birdie?" Adam said as they reached the front of the line.

Birdie smiled at him. She knew she had a nice smile. She knew it didn't look like her dentures bothered her, for heaven's sake, despite what Farley Masterson had said. The old coot was dumber than a red brick.

And yet he seemed interested in her. Mind boggling.

"Follow me," she said, as if the preacher dared not to. When they settled in the corner booth, she said, "I'm not going to give you menus. Reverend Patillo, I know what you want." She studied Adam for a second or two. "Looks like you've put on some weight but not nearly enough. I'll bring you a nice breakfast."

"Only scrambled eggs and biscuits," he said. "No grits."

As usual, she paid no attention to his words. She turned over the cups and poured them coffee before she headed toward the kitchen to place the orders.

As tables cleared, she cleaned them and watched the two ministers. Oh, Reverend Patillo was nice. Her congregation liked her, but Birdie preferred Gussie Milton. Birdie could imagine Gussie's personality filling the parsonage and the church, her enthusiasm lifting the congregation, and her voice leading the choir. Maybe she should sabotage this rendezvous. But how could she without jeopardizing her job and tips?

The longer she watched, the less necessary sabotage seemed. Not all was well with the ministers. Reverend Patillo leaned forward. As she spoke, she glowered and poked the table with her index finger, over and over. Then Adam gave Reverend Patillo the look Birdie thought he reserved only for her, the one that said, *I'm fed up with this but I'm too polite to insult you.*

With Birdie, Adam would then change the subject or look grim and refuse to be forced in the direction he didn't want to go. She respected him for that. Not that she'd ever tell him. Not that she'd allow herself to be drawn off the topic, either, but she admired his efforts.

As the preacher stood, Birdie thought the discussion was over. But no. Reverend Patillo started to cry. Before Birdie could figure out the problem, another customer called for coffee. Doggone customers. Always interrupting.

❧

As much as he enjoyed the sausages and bacon and eggs and hash browns and the omelet and biscuit and all the food he'd eat now and the rest that he'd carry home with him, Adam still had no idea why Mattie had ordered him to show up.

She'd let him know when she felt the time was right, but, for now, she focused all her attention on digging out every section of her grapefruit.

He studied the grits Miss Birdie had delivered and wondered how in the world anyone liked them. Though he'd grown up in Kentucky, where grits formed the core of breakfast, to him they tasted like ground-up Styrofoam. Even covered in butter or margarine, the way Southerners preferred, they were inedible. In Texas, people used hot sauce on everything, but it didn't change the texture. Mixing them with cheese felt like a sad waste of a good dairy product. Nothing could disguise the gritty dish, so he shoved it aside and hoped they wouldn't show up in the carry-home boxes Miss Birdie would put together for him.

When Mattie finished her grapefruit, she took a couple of gulps of coffee.

"So . . ." She paused and lifted her eyes to his face. "How are things going?"

"Fine." Inside he smiled. He knew she wanted him to ask her why they were here, wanted him to force her to explain. Why make it easy for her? She'd awakened him early this morning. He refused to give her an easy out. Besides, as nervous as she was, he guessed he wouldn't want to do whatever she had in mind.

For that reason, he picked up a slice of bacon and began to eat it, nibbling off a piece and savoring the crisp texture and the deliciousness. "This is really good," he said before taking another bite.

"I need your help." Mattie slapped his hand as he reached for a second piece.

"Oh? And you think hitting me will influence me in your favor?"

"I need a date."

He raised an eyebrow.

"For a wedding. You're it."

She sounded desperate, but he didn't want to go to a wedding and he wasn't going to agree, not before she'd explained everything and begged. Maybe not even then.

"A friend of mine's getting married, to a friend of Ron's, my ex." She tapped her fingers against the coffee cup. "I have to go. Ron's best man. He'll probably bring a date. I don't want to go alone and look pitiful."

He nodded. He understood what she was saying but refused to give in so soon. Besides, the potatoes really tasted great, too. He picked up another forkful.

"Adam, I need you to go with me."

He chewed and swallowed and considered. "I don't want to go. I don't like weddings and would never go to one if I didn't have to perform them."

"Please."

"I repeat: I don't want to go. Besides, I have enough problems with the Widows. If you and I actually go out . . ."

"It's not a date, not really."

"You said it was. They'll think it is." With a slight nod, he attempted to gesture surreptitiously toward Miss Birdie. "They'll never leave us alone."

"I don't care. I'm frantic. I've asked every other man I know but none can go. You're it."

"I'm not your first choice? That hurts, even if I don't want to go."

"You weren't even my sixth choice because I knew how hard you'd make this."

He put his fork down. "You thought I'd make this hard?" The statement stung. "I thought I was a cooperative person, easy to get along with."

"But you *are* making this difficult."

Yes, he was. He didn't want to go. He didn't want to make the effort of putting on his only suit—coincidentally called his marrying-and-burying suit—and picking out one of his few good church ties. He bet Mattie'd expect him to get a haircut and he'd have to shine his good shoes. On top of that, he knew, and she did, too, they'd face repercussions here in town because there was no way they could sneak out unless they met in an isolated field and got in Mattie's car like spies.

"My car won't drive that far. I don't trust it."

"We'll take mine." She glared, ready to shoot down every excuse.

"See, that's the problem. Everyone will know. They'll recognize me in your car."

"You are such a wimp." She picked up her toast and nibbled an edge.

"Probably not the best plan, to insult the man you're asking a favor of. Besides, I have no idea how to act like a devoted boyfriend. I'm not a good actor."

"I don't care," she nearly shouted.

"Shh. Whisper."

"Why?" she whispered back. "Have you looked around? I bet everyone in town has squeezed into the place."

He studied the crowd. "Cell phones must be ringing all over Butternut Creek." What the heck, the other diners had heard most of the argument so keeping their voices down now, when the argument had pretty much finished in his opinion, didn't make a great deal of sense.

Obviously, Mattie thought it did matter. She glared and poked the table with her index finger in time with her whispered words. "I need a date for a wedding and you are it."

"Do I have a sign on my forehead that says, TAKE ADVANTAGE OF MY GOOD NATURE?" he asked. "Because you sound exactly like Miss Birdie now. I don't respond well to demands." He slid across the seat and stood.

"I'm sorry." Tears gathered in her eyes.

Oh, crap. He sat down.

"I'm really desperate. I need you to be a friend." She swallowed hard and picked up a napkin to wipe her eyes. "We can do hospital visits while we're in town. I'll buy you dinner, whatever you want, but I absolutely cannot go to the wedding alone."

"Don't go."

"Not an option. If I don't show, Ron will know I don't have a date. Besides, the bride asked me to serve at the reception."

He glanced down at the last of the hash browns, but he'd lost his appetite. All this stress. "Okay," he said. "I'll go. When is it?"

She held out her arms, for a hug, he feared. Adam held up both hands, palms forward. "Stop. All the gossips in town are here. Imagine the talk if you and I were to touch in public."

She sat back. "But thank you. It's a week from Saturday. I appreciate this and I owe you."

He nodded. "I'll collect someday, but you have to promise not to tell anyone," he warned. "The Widows will figure out we're going into Austin together soon enough, but I refuse to give up the information too soon. Make them work for it."

Then the horrible thought hit him. Gussie photographed weddings. Certainly a loving God wouldn't allow her to be taking pictures at a wedding he attended with Mattie on what was really not a date.

❦

"You had a date with Reverend Patillo?" Miss Birdie asked him.

Adam had known this would happen. Hadn't he warned Mattie? No one could hide anything in a small town. What had surprised him was that the Widows hadn't descended on him en masse hours earlier.

The wedding the previous afternoon had been uneventful. Mattie'd navigated the crowd well, avoiding her former boyfriend while, at the same time, somehow flaunting the fact she had an escort and had not withered away from loneliness, thank you, a talent Adam could only recognize and admire. After the ceremony she greeted the happy couple, served a few cups of punch and several slices of cake. Before Adam had a chance to pick up a plate for himself, she dragged him out of the church.

They made a couple of hospital calls, grabbed dinner at a family restaurant, then headed back to Butternut Creek.

The picking-up and letting-off part hadn't gone as well. Mercedes had been watering flowers in front of the church when Mattie picked him up and had stood to watch the entire event, from Mattie's beep on the horn to his running down the steps in what he knew Mercedes would recognize as his only suit. When he got into the car and Mattie took off, Adam had turned to watch Mercedes, who studied them.

Miss Birdie heard immediately. No question. Everyone else in town knew within the hour, but everyone else in town didn't worry him. The pillar did.

"It wasn't a date," Adam explained.

He'd retreated to his office, after church, intending to check messages and call the shut-ins about taking them communion. Frowning Widows had intercepted him. Even Blossom, a woman he hadn't realized knew how to frown, scowled at him.

"Not a date? Then what would you call it?" Winnie demanded.

"A tryst? A rendezvous?" Mercedes asked. "An assignation?"

"Oh, don't show off your vocabulary," Miss Birdie said.

"We're not talking about me, Bird." She turned her glower toward her friend. "This is about the preacher stepping out on Gussie Milton."

"We worked so hard to get the two of you together." The pillar focused on Adam again, mournfully.

No, actually, they hadn't done much more than embarrass the two of them deeply, but this was not the moment to bring that up, not when all four seemed so upset by his defection, by his treachery.

"We-e-ell?" Blossom asked, injecting a note of wounded dismay.

"Reverend Patillo asked me to escort her to a wedding of friends, a favor for a fellow member of the clergy. That's all."

He made a move toward the door to the parking lot but couldn't get closer than a few feet because Miss Birdie stood between him and freedom. For a moment he envied the donkey Maisie for her joyful escape, but he knew it was not a good idea to run over the pillar.

"A friend? Is that all?" Winnie demanded again.

"Ladies," he said. "I am not married . . ."

"Not our fault," the pillar stated.

"We've tried," Mercedes said. "Goodness knows, we've tried to find you a wife."

"It's been a challenge," Winnie chimed in. "But we have done everything we could, and you ruin it by running off to spend the afternoon with Reverend Patillo?"

"Ran off and ruined it all," Blossom said.

The tone of every voice suggested activities of vice and perversion that he could never have taken part in—and certainly not in the short time he and Mattie had been together.

"Ladies," he began again. "I am not married. I have not been keeping company with Gussie Milton although I would like to spend more time with her. You—" He glanced at each woman. "None of you are in charge of whom I see and when and how." He stopped to attempt to think of more words and added, "Or why." Then he waited for a reaction.

"He's right," Mercedes said as the other Widows contemplated his words. "I'm sorry, Preacher. You're right. It's none of our business." She took Miss Birdie's arm. "We need to leave him alone."

"She's right," Blossom added. "I'm sorry, Preacher."

Miss Birdie hrrmphed but allowed herself to be guided away.

And Adam breathed a deep sigh of relief. He had met the Widows and he had won.

Not that he considered this a final victory.

❧

They'd been emailing back and forth for three weeks, Gussie and Adam. Oh, there had been distractions, like when her father had been hospitalized for pneumonia a week earlier. She'd known that coughing had meant something, but had she been able to force him to see a doctor? No, and he'd only decided to when he could no longer breathe.

He'd spent four days in the hospital, then come home so weak he could barely stand. Her mother was beside herself with worry and not really strong enough to care for him. Her blood sugar had gone up due to the stress.

Gussie'd hired a nurse to come in during the day, but when she was home, the entire weight of care fell on Gussie. Not that it bothered her, not that she'd complain, but she did worry about her parents as well as about her ability to care for them as they aged.

She'd told Adam this in emails. He'd supported her and let her unload her worry on him, had probably saved her from more worry than she could have handled alone.

They'd missed church this morning because her father was still so weak. She couldn't leave him at home alone, and her mother still dithered about him. As she finished cleaning the lunch dishes, Gussie heard the doorbell.

"Don't move, Mom. I'll get it."

Worn out and disheveled, Gussie opened the door to see—oh, please, no!—Adam standing there.

"Well." She forced a smile on lips that hadn't seen lipstick for nearly forty-eight hours. Nevertheless, although she felt exhausted and knew she looked terrible, she was happy to see him. "How nice to see you."

It was. He looked great in jeans and a knit shirt. Nice plus good looking and throw in the sudden rush of pure joy and a spark of desire she wished she could ignore—all that equaled perfect man. If she were looking for one.

Oh, shut up, she told herself. Whether she'd been looking or not, an attractive man of exactly the kind she'd have chosen for herself stood in front of her.

"Who is it, Gussie?" her father shouted.

"Come on in." She stepped back to allow him to enter. "My parents are in the living room. Everything's a mess. Sorry. The maid didn't drop by today. Not that we have a maid. I'm it. Or her. Maybe she." Why couldn't she stop babbling?

She led him into a room with the Sunday newspaper spread over the furniture and covering bits of the floor. Her mother sat on the sofa reading with a glass of lemonade on the table beside her while her father, still wearing pajamas, reclined.

"Mom, Dad, this is Adam Jordan, the minister at the church in Butternut Creek. You've heard me talk about him."

Her mother's gaze leaped toward Adam, then moved back and forth between Gussie and Adam. Her father kept his eyes on Adam, searching for clues. Was this man good enough for his daughter? To Gussie's chagrin, his scrutiny shouted that question.

Embarrassed by her father's inspection and aware of how terrible she looked, Gussie still grinned because Adam was here.

"These are my parents, Yvonne and Henry Milton," she said, waving toward them.

Adam, much more comfortable and at ease than she, approached her parents and shook their hands. "I wanted to bring you something, but flowers aren't good for someone recovering from pneumonia and candy isn't good for a diabetic. Instead, I bring best wishes for a speedy recovery from the congregation in Butternut Creek. You still have a lot of friends there."

"Oh, that's why you're here." Her father continued his examination of the man who'd dropped in. "Bringing best wishes from the church in Butternut Creek?" he said, disbelief obvious in his voice.

"How very sweet of you," her mother said. "So thoughtful. Thank you."

For nearly a minute, they all looked at one another and smiled and nodded their heads. Little by little, Adam looked more and more uncomfortable until Gussie drew herself together and said, "Sit down. Let me bring you a glass of lemonade."

She dashed toward the kitchen, then through it, out the hall door, and to the bathroom. As she ran, she could hear her father peppering Adam with questions. She fluffed powder on her shiny nose, smeared on lip gloss, and combed her hair. The best she could do for now.

By the time she got back to the living room with the lemonade, she hoped her father hadn't asked anything embarrassing, like *What are your intentions toward my daughter?*

Surely he wouldn't. But she hadn't brought a young man to meet them in years, not since high school. Not that she'd brought Adam home, but . . .

Oh, sit down and stop overthinking.

She gave Adam his glass and settled on the chair next to him.

He smiled at her and her heart fluttered. Oh, dear. Had she regressed, again becoming a girl whose pulse beat faster when a good-looking man smiled at her?

Well, yes, she guessed she had. It felt good.

After nearly fifteen minutes of her father's questions and Gussie's efforts to silence him, Adam stood. "I don't want to wear you out and need to get to Austin for hospital visits," he said. "Good to meet you, Mr. and Mrs. Milton."

"Don't be so formal. I'm Yvonne and my husband's Henry."

Her husband didn't look happy that this upstart who showed an interest in his daughter should call him anything but *sir*, but he didn't oppose the suggestion.

"Why don't you walk Adam outside, make sure he knows how to get to Austin," Mother suggested.

As if anyone could get lost between Roundville and Austin, but Gussie did as directed. She'd have gone anyway.

"Thank you for coming," Gussie said as they headed down the front walk. "We all really appreciated it."

"Gussie," he said when they reached his car. "I'd like to see you again."

"With my father's illness, I don't know when . . ."

"I understand, but I want to see you."

"I'll email you." She grinned. "I have to apologize for my father's behavior."

"Hey, he's a father. You're his daughter. He cares."

They gazed at each other, Adam with questions in his eyes that she didn't want to hear or respond to. Finally, he said, "Okay," and got into the car, turned on the engine, which responded with a mighty growl, and drove off with a wave. She watched him and wished she didn't have to go inside. She knew a grilling lay ahead.

Fortunately her father had left the living room. Probably worn out already. Although his weakness usually worried her, right now she could only be glad she'd escaped his interrogation for the time being.

Not that her mother's questions would be any easier, only not quite so much like the Inquisition.

"He's a very nice young man, dear," her mother said. "How lovely of him to visit us."

"He was on the way to Austin to make a hospital call."

"Do you really believe that?" Her mother shook her head. "Don't fool yourself. He came to see you. Oh"—she held her hand up—"I know he said he came to see us, but you know very well he wouldn't have dropped in on two elderly folks if we weren't your parents."

Because Gussie didn't know how to respond to Adam's visit or her mother's observation, she said, "I'm going to my room," and escaped. She had some thinking to do.

That evening, she opened her saved emails and read all of them from Adam. Every one confirmed what she already knew. Adam was a nice man. That part didn't scare her. It was the being-close-to-him-and-feeling-his-masculinity part she feared. She knew if she didn't respond to his visit, he'd give up on her. She most assuredly didn't want that. Time to make up her mind and take action.

"Meet me in Marble Falls for coffee a week from tomorrow? Dad goes to the doctor Friday. Surely he'll be strong enough for me to leave him with Mom for a few extra hours by then."

Chapter Ten

Ouida glanced at herself in the mirror of the half bath to check her hair and makeup. George had called twenty minutes ago to tell her he'd passed through Marble Falls. He should arrive home any minute, and she liked to look her best for him. She must be getting better if her appearance had become important.

She'd never realized the joy of going to the bathroom alone before she'd needed help for that most private of activities. The cane and a walking cast made getting into the small half bath difficult but she could do it. If she stuck her foot far to the right, balanced on the sink—she hoped she wouldn't pull it off the wall—and the doorknob, she could fall gently onto the toilet. Her greatest joy came from not having to ask someone to pull her panties down. In the restricted space, it wasn't easy, but she had conquered that.

Independence. After weeks of casts and slings and the hospital and nursing home, she now measured independence in tasks she could do, and she treasured every one. She'd no longer complain about anything, not ironing boxers or mopping the kitchen. If she could go back to the week before her fall, if she could trade off somehow, have a do-over, she'd iron whatever George wanted her to but, "Please, Lord," she whispered, "I don't want to fall down the steps to learn this lesson, not again. I understand."

Then she'd realized she'd prayed. Oh, not a good prayer. More like a mixture of magic and blackmail with a sprinkle of faith, but she'd addressed the words to God. The preacher had influenced her far more than she'd realized. Did that count as good or bad? And did she really want to pray to a God who'd allowed her to fall down the steps so she'd learn a lesson? She didn't think so, but she'd talk to Adam about that.

As she considered her odd moment of faith, the front door opened. George was home.

"Ouida," he called from the living room.

"I'm back here," she shouted.

He didn't hear her, of course. Her voice didn't make it through the closed door, across the kitchen, through the dining room, and around the corner into the living room. His did.

"Ouida?" His voice held a note of panic. He dragged out her name so it sounded like, "Weeeeeeeeeeee-da!"

Not that she'd ever compare George to her cocker spaniel Daffy, but she felt as ineffective and helpless now as she had back then. She could hear his footsteps going up the stairs and echoing above her as he ran through the second story. She heard his steps sounding softly on the stairs to the third floor, then nothing. Had he gone up to the attic playroom? How did he think she'd climb those steps? She'd hobbled up to the second floor only once. She'd come back to the first floor by bumping down on her bottom most of the way.

She still slept in the living room, although no longer on a hospital bed. They'd moved the queen-size bed downstairs, and she got to sleep with George next to her. And he thought she'd climbed two flights to the attic?

George must have come down because she now heard him above her on the second floor. If she still had her crutches, she'd bang on the ceiling, but she didn't and the cane didn't reach that far. Nonetheless, she had to try something. Using the wall and the sink, she leveraged herself to her feet, then leaned to pick up the cane. As she did, she felt herself overbalance. Before she could catch herself, she toppled against the door. It popped open and deposited her on the kitchen floor.

She lay there for a moment and did a quick inventory of her body, fearing she'd hurt herself again. Despite an ache in her good shoulder, which she'd fallen on, and her hip, she felt okay but she'd never be able to get to her feet. No, not alone, and George was too busy running around upstairs searching for her to give her a hand.

"George," she shouted, but she didn't hear movement toward her.

She looked around her. If she could get to the kitchen counter, she could probably pull herself to her feet, maybe. That irritating boot cut down on her mobility and balance so much that she needed something to hold on to, but her shoulder still hadn't gained enough strength that she trusted it.

"George."

Crab-like, she moved along on her stomach, impelling her body with both hands and her left foot. When she'd almost arrived, she heard George descending the stairs.

"George!"

"Ouida?" he called.

"In here," she shouted.

She heard him run through the living room and dining room. When he arrived at the arch between the kitchen and the dining room, he stopped for a second before he said, "Ouida," and rushed to her. "What happened?"

When he knelt beside her, she turned her head and gazed up at him. His eyes were huge; his face, white.

"I'm fine. Just help me up." She reached her hand out, but he leaped to his feet.

"No, no, you stay there. Don't want to make your injuries worse. I'll call nine-one-one and get the preacher over here." He turned and took two long strides to reach the phone.

"George," she said, her hand still held out. "I really am fine. I fell, but I didn't hurt anything. Help me, please. I can't stand up on my own."

He came back to her, slowly, and scrutinized her. "Are you sure?" When she nodded, he took her hand and put his other arm around her to guide and support her until she stood.

"See, I'm fine," she said at the exact time a wave of dizziness hit her. She leaned on George's arm to steady herself.

"No, you're not." George nearly dragged her across the kitchen and lowered her onto a chair in the breakfast nook. "I'm going to call . . ."

"George, I'm really fine. I got up too fast. I'm a little lightheaded."

"Food," he suggested. "Do you need something to eat? I'll get you a glass of milk. That should . . . or maybe a piece of cheese?"

"George, please sit down." Once he did—all the time inspecting her face, searching for signs of terminal illness or fatal injury, she guessed—she took his hand. "I'm fine."

"Don't scare me like that." He took several deep breaths. "Are you sure you're fine?"

"Yes, dear."

They sat like that, gazing at each other and holding hands, until George said, "I've been thinking." He squeezed her hand and leaned toward her. "I never realized how hard it is to take care of this big house and the girls until I had to do that. I don't know how you do it."

She smiled. Nice to be validated. "I love it."

"I can't believe I nagged you about being punctual and keeping a schedule. I'm never where I planned to be doing what I think I should. It's about killed me. I decided to get you maid service, twice a week. Will that help?"

When she didn't answer because his statement had surprised her—no, stunned and amazed her—he continued. "I'm sorry. I never should've said that you have life easy. Trying to do for a few days a week what you do every day of the year wore me out. You need help."

"Oh, George." She caressed his hand and smiled at him. For a moment, she kept her eyes on him and treasured his concern. "Thank you, but I don't need maid service. I love what I do, but I would like to stop ironing so much."

She paused. "And I'd like to start painting again, when I can use my arm."

"Anything," he said. "Whatever you want."

Maybe she shouldn't refuse his generosity. She could accept a day or two of maid service a week, if he really wanted that.

❧

Adam glanced around the sanctuary. Attendance usually fell during the summer, but today it had picked up with school starting in a couple of weeks. Probably close to sixty in attendance. The average had swelled to almost seventy, most of the additional number coming from the high school kids Hector and Bree had roped in. The Mexican and African American kids and a few of their parents added texture to the congregation. Not that sixty or seventy people filled the sanctuary, but it didn't look quite as empty as it had a year earlier.

Sam and his family sat on the side aisle, a consistent four. Actually, add the general and Winnie and that row was nearly filled every Sunday.

Behind Adam in the chancel, the choir still consisted of three women and Ralph. All sat quietly now as they did through the entire service. He wished he could get them to practice, to prepare even a choral *Amen* after the prayer, but that success had eluded him.

The guest organist played a soft prelude but everyone was so busy chatting, they couldn't hear it.

Mrs. Jurenka, the musician, had confessed before the service that she didn't hear as well as she once had. She'd showed him some signals he could use to communicate. The idea of motioning to her after the prayer seemed odd, but with their usual organist on maternity leave, they had to hire whoever they could find. Mrs. Jurenka was it this morning.

She'd played the first hymn well although had stopped before the last verse, which left the congregation sputtering to a halt when they realized that the music had come to an end. However, since almost no one sang except Janey, the young people, and a few visitors, the quick finish didn't much matter.

Later in service, Adam rose to start the prayer. As was his usual practice, he paused several times during the prayer to give the congregation time to meditate.

Not a good idea that morning.

At the first pause, Mrs. Jurenka must have thought he'd finished. Although he had not given her the agreed-upon signal, a chopping gesture, she began to play, "Hear Our Prayer, O Lord," before he could start the prayer again. He waited but she played on. He gave her the agreed-upon signal, then once more. And again. He felt as if he were splitting logs up there, but she didn't stop. In desperation, he hissed at her. Oh, he knew she couldn't hear him, but he felt the need to do something. Throwing a hymnal seemed out of the question. She continued playing. He'd never realized how long that response was, especially when she kept repeating it. Was there some sign he'd missed? Obviously the chopping and the hissing hadn't worked.

Hoping if she could hear him pray, Mrs. Jurenka would stop playing, Adam raised his voice. "And so we thank you for all the blessings of this day . . ." But she didn't stop. "For the beauty of the Hill Country," he said in an even louder and definitely less prayerful voice. Finally, he screamed, "And for the love of the people around us, for the peace and quiet of this place . . ."

By this time, the members of the congregation had lost any semblance of prayerful contemplation and were laughing so hard he feared Hector and Bobby would fall out of the pew. Although Willow attempted to remain worshipful and hush her men, Sam and the boys had long since given up an appearance of reverence. Why did Adam have a best friend who laughed at him during the most trying moments of his life?

As his gaze moved around the congregation, he spotted Gussie on the back row of the sanctuary. Why had she visited *today*? Today of all the Sundays in the world when he'd lost complete control of the service?

She was, of course, as amused as everyone else. Although he

couldn't tell from this distance, she seemed to be laughing so hard she was crying, dabbing at her eyes with a tissue. He loved Gussie's laugh, but not now.

Adam had no idea what to do next because he couldn't shout any more loudly. Then he heard Ralph stand behind him, the chair creaking as he pulled his arthritic bulk up. Adam gave up completely on the prayer and turned to watch Ralph's slow progress from the choir chairs toward the organ.

What was the man going to do?

The eyes of the congregation followed Ralph's movements as well. For a moment, Ralph stopped behind Mrs. Jurenka, who had her eyes closed, obviously feeling spiritual as she began the response another time. After a few seconds, Ralph put a hand on each of the organist's arms, pulled her hands away from the keys, and shouted, "Stop."

The poor woman leaped off the organ bench. Ralph let go of her arms as she shrieked a piercing high note that reverberated around the sanctuary. "What are you doing?"

"The preacher's still praying," Ralph shouted and pointed.

"Oh." She glanced at Adam and nodded before turning and sitting again, her hands in her lap. Ralph tramped back toward the choir, dropped into his chair with a satisfied, "There," and folded his hands across his round stomach.

For nearly a minute, Adam waited in the hope he could somehow redeem the situation, but the laughter continued. Finally, he said "Amen" and sat down. He'd never get the congregation back.

After a few minutes, he stood to deliver a shortened sermon. The service ended in plenty of time for everyone to get to Subway long before the Methodists.

As he greeted people at the entrance, Bobby filed by. Unable to say a word because he was laughing so hard, the young man gave Adam a punch in the shoulder.

"Pops, that service wasn't boring at all," Hector said and he shook Adam's hand.

At the same time Hector left the narthex, Adam realized he was alone with Gussie. Except he knew they weren't alone, not really. Even though he couldn't see them, he knew the Widows lurked nearby. Smiling, probably, gloating, and, he knew, listening. Gussie approached him and held out her hand.

"Hello," he said with an effort to sound detached so the Widows couldn't pick up on how happy her presence made him. He failed. "How nice to see you in church today." He sounded like an idiot. He could hear himself nearly chirping with pleasure. "How nice to see you," he repeated in the deep, professional voice he used for prayers. Now he sounded like a minister welcoming a guest. All he had to do was shake her hand and invite her back. So he took her hand, shook it, and said heartily, "Good to see you this morning. Please come back to worship with us another time."

She smiled up at him and he didn't worry about how stupid he sounded. Her expression assured him that whatever reason she had for visiting the Christian Church during one of the most embarrassing moments of his life was positive. She was here. Maybe this morning's service would be counted as a good. Maybe even something they could laugh about together for years to come, he hoped.

Super-cool as always, he demanded, "What are you doing here?" Chirpy, ministerial, demanding—why couldn't he figure out how to talk to Gussie like a normal person, like a man who found her attractive?

"I wanted to see you." Her voice wasn't what he considered her usual *Gussie* voice. No, it sounded a little tentative. Gussie Milton uncertain?

Maybe that was good, too.

Then she let go of his hand and took a step back. What did that mean?

"Aren't we meeting for coffee tomorrow? I mean, not that I'm not glad to see you, but . . ."

"I wanted to see you *today*."

How much better could life get?

"Preacher."

A voice cut its way through the warm cloud of bliss surrounding him and Gussie. Adam rearranged his muddled thoughts and turned to focus on the speaker.

"How can I help you, Howard?"

"Hot enough for you?"

Adam nodded. He never knew how to answer that question.

Then the elder looked back and forth between the two and grinned. "Nothing, Preacher." He took several steps back. "I'll leave a note in your office."

He hurried away. When Howard reached the door from the front of the sanctuary to the back hallway, Adam could hear soft whispering. The Widows had captured Howard and were now grilling him. Poor man.

"Why don't we go to my office?" Adam asked. "We can talk with a little more privacy."

"Can we escape the Widows?" She used her head to point in the directions of the women.

"I have a secret route. They'll never know we've left."

Feeling like a spy in a bad movie, he led Gussie around the church, surreptitiously checking for Widows, then through the office entrance and into his study without seeing anyone. Once there, he unzipped his robe, hung it on the coatrack, and reached for his jacket.

"Hello, Gussie." Miss Birdie's voice came from the doorway.

"Miss Birdie." Gussie nodded and smiled at the pillar. "So nice to see you."

"What are you doing way up here? So far from Roundville?"

"I was in the area and thought I'd drop by. It's so good to see you."

Signs of struggle crossed Miss Birdie's face. She bit her lips and blinked several times. Adam had learned to read her expressions. This one meant goading Gussie for more information crossed a line between civility and rudeness that even Miss Birdie couldn't force herself to step over. And yet she knew no one merely "dropped by" Butternut Creek.

"How nice," the pillar finally said. Then, fists on her hips, she turned to glare at Adam. "Don't forget where you are and who you are. You are a minister and an example to our young folks. Don't close this door when you're alone with a woman." She gave an emphatic nod.

Adam felt as if he were in eighth grade when his mother found him in the closet with Susie Page. He glanced at the door just to make sure he hadn't closed it. Still wide open.

Then, with a charming smile, the pillar said, "Gussie, I know you've had a long drive and have another going back home. The Widows have prepared a nice snack for you in the garden. Don't worry about Hector and Janey, Preacher. Bree's taking them out for a hamburger." Her voice sweet still, she added, "Don't tarry." She strode out.

Once they could no longer hear her footfalls in the reception office, Gussie fell into a chair and laughed. "Don't you love Miss Birdie?" she asked.

He had to think about that. "Sometimes," he said. "Not always."

"Preacher?" Blossom called from the front office. "Lunch is ready."

The garden was a euphemism for the five-by-five grass squares on the back and sides of the church where every other inch of ground was covered with asphalt. On this side, the west, they were screened from the highway by the gym wing of the building so they could enjoy a modicum of privacy.

"Hector keeps the garden up," Adam explained to Gussie as they neared it. "He earns a little spending money taking care of the lawn in front of the church and the parsonage." He held a chair for Gussie.

Once she was seated, he settled in the chair across from her, slightly aware of the scent of mosquito repellent, ubiquitous in the summer. The Widows must have sprayed out here to make sure not even an insect intruded.

"There you are," Mercedes said with enthusiastic delight, as if they'd wandered off in the wilderness and had finally returned. From her tray, she took forks and crisp, white napkins and placed them in front of each followed by glasses of iced tea, then stood back and beamed at them.

Blossom followed with another plate, which filled up the rest of the space on the table. "Here are a few cucumber sandwiches," she said. "From an old family recipe."

"They look delicious." Gussie smiled at Blossom. "Exactly right for a warm afternoon."

Miss Birdie arrived with a bowl of fruit salad and looked around for a place to set it. Seeing none, she took the spoon from the bowl and scooped a serving onto each plate.

He should never underestimate the wonders the Widows could perform in no time at all. They possessed abilities and powers he could only marvel at.

"You young people go right ahead and eat," Mercedes said. "We'll be here in case you need something."

Three Widows watched him, looking like buzzards, keeping an eye on a particularly flavorful deer carcass.

Adam guessed Winnie was with her fiancé, which was a relief. Although he had encouraged Mercedes and the pillar to increase the number of Widows, he realized he was paying for that at this moment. Three Widows watching them closely, listening to every word, studying each movement frightened him. All four women together would have rendered him incoherent and, possibly, androgynous.

Adam remembered a story his friend had told him, that the Widows had set up a date for Sam and Willow and then sneaked away to leave them alone. And yet, here they stood, as if protecting his honor and Gussie's.

"Thank you," he said. "I think we're fine." He attempted to fill his voice with a nuance that said, *Leave us alone.*

Didn't work.

He repeated, "We're fine," and winked.

When that met with silence, he said, "I don't know if the three of you remember, but this kind of thing usually isn't done with an audience."

"Yes, Pastor, but we're not so sure you know anything about court-ing," the pillar said.

Could this get any more embarrassing? Of course it could.

"You know, he's right," Mercedes stated. "We should leave them alone."

Blossom nodded. "He's going to have to take over at some time. How can he make his move with us watching?"

Gussie picked up her napkin to hide her smile but Adam wanted to sink through the garden.

"Oh, all right." Miss Birdie took a few steps back and wagged her finger at Adam. "Don't leave a mess. Take the plates in the kitchen and wash them. Detergent's under the sink. Leave them to dry in the drainer."

"Thank you, ladies." He didn't mention he'd been doing dishes himself for years and cleaned up the church kitchen after meetings. No need to pick a fight now. Besides, the sooner he agreed, the sooner they'd leave him and Gussie in peace.

Why didn't the Widows consider it wrong for the two to be alone in the kitchen? Did they believe the presence of a detergent and dish drainer would keep him on the straight and narrow, remind him of his position in the community, and stop him from seducing Gussie? It was satisfying that the Widows believed it could happen, if not for the presence of the plates to be washed and placed in the drainer.

Of course, the agony wasn't over yet. The pillar turned to Gussie. "He's a good young man but he's not much of a ladies' man."

Such positive words. Why didn't they just come right out with it, say, *The man's a hopeless idiot with women*, and leave it at that?

"You may have to help him along," Mercedes added helpfully.

Gussie straightened and placed the napkin back in her lap. "Thank you, ladies," she said seriously, although Adam thought he detected a quiver in her lips.

Exactly what he needed, for Gussie to find him and his plight amusing.

"And, Preacher—" Miss Birdie paused for emphasis but he'd heard that waving-finger tone in her voice. "—don't make a move on Miss Milton inside the church."

Aah, yes, that good-example stuff again.

For a moment, Gussie and Adam listened to the galloping clatter of the Widows as they headed around the building and toward the parking lot. A minute later, after what Adam imagined was a short powwow, he heard cars start and drive off.

He had survived, not even seriously wounded.

"Oh, my!" Gussie grinned. "Aren't they wonderful?" Checking Adam's expression, she said, "Well, maybe not. I'd guess having them around all the time and pestering you isn't as much fun as *watching* them nag you."

"Fortunately, Howard warned me about the Widows before I arrived. They do so much for the church and community, I can't stay mad or frustrated for long. Miss Birdie is priceless, but there are times when they treat me like their youngest grandson who isn't very bright and can't figure anything out on his own. Then I don't find them amusing."

He took a sandwich and offered her another.

"No thanks," she said. "I'm really not a great fan of cucumber sandwiches. But the fruit is wonderful."

Gussie watched Adam eat. She enjoyed merely being here, sitting close to him. In the warmth of the sunshine and the whisper of the breeze, she was glad she'd come. Her action had been completely out of character. She'd driven here on a whim, at odds with her usually logical behavior.

Why? Why had she set herself and Adam up for this kind of attention? She should have realized her appearance would send the Widows into a matchmaking frenzy.

She'd stewed about the meeting in Marble Falls all day Saturday, one reason for coming to Butternut Creek. This morning, she'd gotten up, dressed, told her parents good-bye, and hopped in the car. *Impulsive* didn't describe her, but today it felt right.

While she studied him, he glanced up, not saying a word. Probably wondered why she was here, expected a fuller explanation than she'd given him right after the service.

"I'm sorry I've acted like an idiot every time you show up." She paused to think of words. "Both times, you startled me. I'm afraid I was rude."

"Not rude," he said. "You didn't have any warning. Besides, you already apologized." Then he smiled and leaned forward, reached his hand toward her, and touched her fingers.

She nearly leaped from the chair. Then she settled down and froze.

Oh, no. She'd hoped she'd gotten over that reaction. She'd thought the attraction to Adam, the years of therapy, and the love and support from her parents had healed her. Would she ever, ever be okay? Would she ever recover? How could she allow those terrible minutes from years ago to influence—no, to destroy—her life even now? Wasn't she better and stronger and more faithful than that?

Seemed not.

She gave a shaky laugh. "I'm sorry. You startled me."

"I could tell. Ministers are good at reading body language." He kept his eyes on her face. "When a woman leaps into the air at the touch of a hand, it's a sign of something. Usually not something good."

Obviously he didn't accept her reaction as being startled. No, he recognized it as another kind of response. She could only hope he couldn't read the truth in her eyes.

"I'm fine, just overly vigilant." She waved a hand around and attempted to change the subject. "Isn't this a lovely place?"

❧

What was that? Adam dropped his hand back on the table and studied Gussie. Her eyes were wide, her face was nearly white, and she gasped to catch her breath. She'd jerked back, not in surprise. He'd frightened her, a response he hadn't expected. One she hadn't expected, either, he bet.

He remembered a teenager in his student church who'd been abused by her father. She'd reacted in nearly the same way when he'd lightly touched her shoulder to get past her. That poor girl had performed a long jump that could have qualified her for the Olympics. After that, she nearly fainted and he'd kept his distance.

Slowly color returned to Gussie's face, and she attempted to smile pleasantly and normally at him. He didn't buy it. He didn't believe her explanation for a second, but out here wasn't the place to discuss her problems. This didn't feel like a good time, either.

He acted as if he didn't see her struggle for control as he sat back in his chair to leave her plenty of space. "I'm not fond of cucumber sandwiches myself. Not very filling. Let's look in the fridge and see if there's anything there."

Standing, he picked up his plate and glass and other stuff. Usually, he'd have picked up hers as well, but extending an arm in her direction and invading her space didn't feel like a good idea.

Gussie gave him a smile that began with a quiver before, slowly, becoming the one he recognized as hers. "I'm sorry . . . ," she began, then seemed to realize where they were and that neighbors could be watching from the houses that backed onto the parking lot and grassy area. With a sweeping motion that looked a lot more like the Gussie he knew, she grabbed her place setting and headed toward the kitchen door.

"I'm sorry." Her voice sounded calm and strong as they entered. She placed the plate in the sink and turned on the hot water.

"Gussie, you don't need to apologize."

Adam placed his dishes next to the sink and watched her carefully wash off the plates, then scrub each with a scouring pad until he feared she'd scour off the floral pattern. She finished the few utensils and placed everything in the drainer. Then she wiped off her hands and—he guessed—couldn't think of anything more to do, so she turned to him and shook her head. "Will I ever get over that?" she whispered as she kept her gaze on the floor.

He stayed still and silent and waited. Finally, when she didn't speak, he asked, "Gussie, why did you come here?"

"To see you." She sighed and looked up at him. "I really wanted to see you. I believed I was okay, but you've noticed I'm not. I have a problem I can't seem to get past." She took a few steps and dropped onto a folding chair.

He sat in a chair a few feet from her. She looked pale and anxious and just plain terrible. She had trouble meeting his gaze, studying her hands as often as she glanced at him. No, she didn't want closeness now.

Again, he realized he needed to prompt her to respond. "Do you want to tell me about it?"

"I do, but I can't, not right now. I'm really sorry for bringing you into this." This time she did keep her eyes on his face. "I find you very attractive, really . . . um . . . desirable, but . . ."

He'd known a *but* would follow the positive feedback.

"I'd like to have a relationship with you but . . ." She closed her eyes and bit her lip. "Oh, darn. I sound like a character in a soap opera, don't I? I'm sorry I'm so incoherent."

"Gussie, don't keep apologizing. Talk to me."

"Okay." She appeared to struggle for words before she opened her eyes and spoke to him. "I have a problem. I thought . . . I hoped I'd healed because of the way I feel about you, but obviously I haven't. And I feel it's too soon to open up about everything. I'm not ready to tell you what happened and you're probably not prepared to hear it. We don't know each other very well."

He nodded, not at all sure how to react.

"But, if you're willing, I would like to explore what I feel about you. The fact that you attract me amazes me."

"All right," he said because he had absolutely no idea what else to say.

"You are attractive. I am attracted to you," she said. "You're not the problem. I am. As I said, what amazes me is that I can admit the chemistry. I haven't felt like that about a man for a long time."

"Okay." He wished he could come up with words of healing and compassion, but he didn't know her well or what the problem was, although he could guess. He stuck to the tried and true, sounding like an idiot.

"But I'm more broken than I thought. I shouldn't have come here today, but I really wanted to see you." She gave him a grin, a little forced, but encouraging. "I'd thought about our get-together in Marble Falls and decided not to put it off. Probably a good thing because if I'd fallen apart like this at the coffee shop, how embarrassing would that be?"

"When I reached to take your hand, it scared you. I frightened you."

"Oh, yes, frightened, panicked, terrified, completely lost and *bamboozled*—all of those describe how I felt."

Great. Of all the emotions he could raise in a woman, the best he could do was panicked and bamboozled?

But this wasn't about him. "Can you explain?"

"Not really. Not without a whole bunch of stuff pouring out." She looked into his eyes, almost pleading. "I trust you, but I've got a big problem. I'm good with kids and work and church and my parents, but . . . but . . ."

He realized as she spoke those words that the barrier was right there, right after the *but*. He guessed it had to do with men or with a man. He hated to have to clean up the mess another guy had made. Right now, he couldn't force her to complete the statement. He waited.

"Would you take on a project as difficult as me?" she asked. "I really want this, I want to accept how I feel, explore that, build on it, but I'm not sure I should ask that of you." Instead of the fear he'd glimpsed earlier, an earnest plea filled her eyes. "I can't promise anything."

"Yeah." He nodded. "I'd take that on."

"Really?" She shook her head. "Why?"

"Gussie, you are one of the most loving people I know. You take care of your parents, you work with the youth in your church and in the district. You are a person of deep faith. You're beautiful in every way I can imagine."

"Really?" She scrutinized him closely, as if she couldn't believe his words.

"Really."

She scooted her chair closer to him and leaned forward to place her hand against his lips. He didn't move closer to her, only allowed her to touch him. Amazingly, after a few seconds, she put her hand on his neck and pulled him nearer, only a few inches, and placed her cheek against his.

When at last she sat back, she smiled at him. He would have leaned toward her, touched her. More than anything, he wanted to kiss her but he had to respect the physical barrier of the hand she still held in front of her.

"Thank you for not pushing," she said.

Although she insisted she was broken, he felt blessed that she'd come to him, that she'd reached out to him, that she cared about him enough to ask for his patience.

They'd figure out everything else later.

Chapter Eleven

Preacher, good news and bad news," Maggie said. "Which do you want first?"

Adam glanced from the Bible commentary displayed on his computer screen to his secretary standing in the door. "Neither."

"Actually—" Maggie thought for a moment. "Actually, they're both bad news."

Great. "Go ahead."

"Miss Birdie's here."

He nodded. She'd want an update on what happened after the Widows had left the church.

"And she's in the kitchen."

Sounded like good news to him. The pillar wasn't *here*, grilling him. "How's that bad news?"

"That's right. You don't know about Miss Birdie and the kitchen." Maggie came into the office and sat in a chair in front of his desk. "When Miss Birdie is upset, she cleans."

Hearing that Miss Birdie was upset did count as bad news. "How's cleaning bad news?"

"Once she finishes cleaning her house and the diner, she comes here."

"By that time, she must have blown off some steam."

Maggie shook her head. "Oh, no. If she gets here, that means she hasn't calmed down at the other places and is really wound up, has built a lot of momentum. By the time she comes here, she's like a train off the tracks. You need to head her off, Preacher."

"Why? Isn't it good that she's straightening things up?" He turned off the computer to lean forward and pay complete attention to Maggie.

"When she's in this mood, she's ruthless. A few years ago, she took all the books out of the classrooms and cataloged them and put them in the library."

"What's so bad about that?"

"A lot of those books belonged to the teachers, references and coloring books and pictures they'd bought, stuff they brought in to use with the children. Back when Effie Peterson taught the third-through-fifth-grade class, she was infuriated to find her Bible stamped as property of the Christian Church with a little pocket pasted in the back." Her eyes grew large. "You've never seen such a set-to." She shook her head as she remembered.

Adam glanced over his shoulder at the bookcase where the library had been when he arrived. He'd tossed the old, torn books out and donated the rest to the public library. He wondered if any of those had belonged to people who hadn't claimed them yet. Fortunately, no one had made a big fuss.

"And last time she cleaned out the shed, she threw away a bunch of stuff, good stuff."

Knowing the kind of things churches kept—old Sunday school material that would never be used again, broken furniture no one ever got around to fixing, ancient hymnals with brown, brittle pages filled with songs no one remembered—Adam didn't think tossing all that counted as a bad thing.

"When she starts in the kitchen, she changes everything all around. You'll go in expecting the coffee can to be right above the coffeemaker, but it won't be. Miss Birdie will put it where she wants it, although some of us believe she puts it where no one can find it so we'll have to ask her. For weeks after she straightens things up, we can't find sugar bowls or the paper cups." She sighed. "It's not a good thing. It's chaos and havoc until everyone gets used to the new locations." Then, she shook her finger at Adam. "You have to stop her. She's on a toot."

He stood.

"I'll pray for you," Maggie said.

He didn't think she was joking.

As Adam headed toward the kitchen, he felt pretty sorry for himself, too, but a man's gotta do . . .

Before he could finish the cliché, he'd arrived in the fellowship hall. From there, he could see a mound of plates and packages of napkins and saltshakers and nearly everything that had been in the kitchen cupboards piled on the counter. He guessed the pillar was behind the stack someplace.

"Hello, Miss Birdie," he called.

"Preacher, is that you?"

"You sound surprised." He headed toward the kitchen. As he got closer, he could see where Miss Birdie knelt on the floor. "Surely you knew Maggie would send me back."

"Give me a hand up." She reached out her right hand. Once on her feet, she said, "I'm organizing the cabinets."

"Oh, is that what this is called?" He gestured toward the mounds. "Looks like my office when I first arrived."

"Yes, Preacher." She glared at him. "But I'm going to put it all back where it should have been in the first place and I'm going to finish that today. A lot of your stuff is still sitting on the office floor."

A mistake to bring that up. "Do you have to take everything out at once? Can't you go bit by bit?"

"Winnie Jenkins rearranged things a few months back, and no one can find anything. I'm only putting it all back where it should be."

"Can I help?"

She studied him. "I always knew your tall skinniness would be good for something. Put those big packages of napkins up on the top shelf."

After nearly two hours of following the pillar's orders, they'd brought order to the kitchen, but Miss Birdie still hadn't said anything about why she was there. She only grumbled and grunted and emitted a few new sounds Adam couldn't translate. The only words she used were contained in commands for his tall skinniness.

"I've heard you come here and clean the kitchen when there's something bothering you," Adam said as he placed the last forks in what had been the knife drawer. Miss Birdie had relabeled it.

She spun around to look at him. "What?" She huffed. "Who told you that?"

He didn't say.

"Well, I guess that's right," she concurred.

"Do you want to tell me what you're upset about?"

"Don't you know what I'm upset about?"

Oh, he could think of several topics, but her concern about his single state hadn't driven her into the kitchen before. He also guessed he wouldn't get out of this without a stern lecture on his bachelorhood and his lack of appreciation for her efforts to find him a mate before she confessed to her real motivation. He waited.

"You know, we've tried very hard to find you a wife." She glowered at him. He listened to a diatribe about the lack of appreciation he showed her and her efforts. She finished by attempting to make him feel guilty for ignoring all her hard work.

He didn't accept the blame, but he allowed her to vent. When she finished, he said, "Miss Birdie, what's really bothering you? I know you'd like to get me married off, but your matchmaking is more like a hobby. There's something else." He leaned against the countertop.

She didn't answer, not immediately. After nearly a minute of wiping off the already clean counter, she carefully draped the dish-cloth over the sink divider and turned toward him.

"It's Bree." She folded her hands in front of her.

❧

When Birdie glanced back at the preacher, she knew her vacillation showed weakness, but she couldn't help that. He responded with a look of caring, of concern. She hated that.

Birdie really disliked sharing her problems with other people, but she might as well continue because there was no way she'd convince Adam she was fine, just fine. How much should she say? After all, Hector lived in the parsonage. Would the preacher think she was putting him down?

Birdie cleared her throat. The darned man didn't say a word, didn't help her get this out. Only watched her closely. Probably because he knew what a private person she was and didn't want to intrude. Wouldn't you know the one time she wanted him to ask, he didn't encourage her to open up?

People saw her as being gruff and tougher than flint. Although she enjoyed that reputation, the preacher and a few others—well, probably the entire town—knew there was one topic she wasn't tough about. Her granddaughters. She cleared her throat again. The preacher still didn't say anything, only waited for her to come to the point.

"It's Bree," she repeated. "Bree and Hector. Mac tells me they got friendly at the retreat. I know they danced together at the prom, but everyone dances with everyone else. At the reception with Gussie I saw they held hands once. And they're always emailing or texting each other, sometimes even talk on the phone. They probably spent a lot of time together at camp."

"How do you feel about that?" he asked. "About Bree and Hector?"

How dare this inexperienced preacher—still wet behind the ears—how dare he attempt to minister to her? Did he think she needed counseling from someone young enough to be her grandson?

When she didn't say anything, just glared at him, Adam said, "Is Hector and Bree's interest in each other a problem for you?"

What was he suggesting? "Do you mean the race thing? I don't care that Hector is Mexican or African American or black or even purple. What I care about is . . ." Then she couldn't talk. Her throat had closed up and tears clouded her vision. Doggone!

Immediately the preacher straightened, picked up a handful of napkins—the good ones, the ones they used for teas and formal events—and held them toward her. She took one napkin from him, only one because they were too expensive to blow her nose in but, right now, she needed to do exactly that.

Thank goodness, the man knew her well enough not to pat her on the back or make comforting *there, there* noises. Instead he stayed a few feet from her and kept silent. She hated herself for showing this weakness and struggling for control.

"Hector is a fine young man," he said after nearly a minute. "With his mother's death and his father's drug use and jail time, he's been through more than anyone his age should have to go through."

She nodded and wiped her eyes, then blew her nose again.

"He's taken care of Janey for years and still keeps his grades up and plays basketball. I admire him."

"I do, too." She dabbed with the napkin. She closed her eyes for only a second before she glanced at him. "I'm not worried about Hector. I know how much he's taken on and I do respect that. And Bree's a good girl, but . . ." She gulped, a hideously loud noise that embarrassed her both for the rudeness and because, with that terrible sound, she'd exposed feelings she tried to hide. "You know about my daughter Martha Patricia. I worry," she whispered. "I worry so much."

"Of course you do. You love the girls, but Bree is a good kid, a really good kid."

"Mercedes says I'm overprotective, Preacher, and I am, but I love those girls more than . . ." The words wouldn't come. What was happening? She couldn't even speak anymore. When had she become such an emotional softy? Well, since the first time Martha Patricia had handed her baby Bree.

But she sure didn't need to blubber in front of the preacher. She pulled herself straight, wadded the soggy napkin, and tossed it in the trash. "I need to get back to the diner," she stated. "Thanks for the help."

"You know, I am your minister, Miss Birdie. There's nothing wrong or weak about worrying about people you love."

"Hrmph." She turned and headed toward the parking lot. When she'd almost reached the door, she turned around. "What can you tell me about Bree and Hector?" She tilted her head.

"Not much. I saw them together at the retreat and the prom. She and Hector sit on the parsonage porch from time to time. I imagine they were together at the church summer camp, but I wasn't there."

"You didn't think to tell me?"

"Miss Birdie, if I thought there was a problem, I'd have mentioned it to you. But, you know, I also have to respect Hector and Bree's privacy."

"Of course you do." She nodded. As she did, she realized he looked different. She studied him, searching for what had caught her eye. A new shirt? "You look nice today, Preacher. Any particular reason?"

He tried to look casual but he couldn't fool her. He didn't speak for several seconds, a sure sign of duplicity. He blinked several times, which she'd learned was his tell when he considered lying. Then he smiled at her, sweetly, which tipped her off to his intent to fib.

"Are you meeting Gussie later?" she asked. Better let him know she was on to him instead of tempting him to bear false witness. Then she held her hand in front of her. "No, no. Don't tell me. You deserve privacy in your life. I'm not going to pry."

When his mouth dropped open at her words, Birdie gloated inside. Always a good thing to keep *him* guessing, wondering, a little off balance.

With that, she left the building. After a few steps, she paused. What had she heard? What was the sound coming from the kitchen? Sounded like laughter, but why? What had she said that anyone could find amusing? Probably her imagination.

❦

Adam had to tell Gussie the entire thing. Not about Miss Birdie's fears for her granddaughter but about both her cleaning the kitchen and her newfound, and probably of short duration, respect for his privacy.

He laughed again as he drove down Highway 1431 to Marble Falls. A few miles south of Fuzzy's Corner, he heard a loud clunk. Wondering if he'd run into something, he pulled onto the shoulder, put the car in park, and got out.

Behind him and in the middle of the road lay a bumper. Had he hit it or did it belong to him? He didn't want to check, because if his bumper was missing, that would be one more sign that his car was literally falling apart. Gathering his courage, he walked to the back of the car and studied the place where a bumper used to be. Then he turned to look down the road at the bumper twenty yards behind him.

Did a car really need a bumper?

Most likely the state thought it did, so he'd better think of some way to replace it. He opened the trunk, walked back, picked the thing up, and attempted to shove it in the trunk. Didn't fit. He dragged it around, opened the door to the backseat, and shoved it in there. It fit. He and Hector would try to get it back on because he feared Rex would have to charge him more for the part than he could afford.

Finished, he glanced down at his hands. Covered with dirt. Smudges dotted the pale blue knit shirt he'd bought to wear today. He kept those little moist towelettes in his glove compartment. Actually Laurel, his former fiancée, had put some there years ago. Would they still work?

First, he went back to the trunk and pulled out a blanket he'd kept there for years, in case of emergencies. Probably didn't need a blanket in Texas. He wiped his hands on it to get as much of the gunk off as possible, then tossed it in the backseat so he'd remember to take it in and wash it. The bundle looked as if he were transporting either a body or a cache of something illegal.

After he closed the trunk, he opened the door on the passenger side, reached in the glove box, and found four small square packages from KFC. He tore one open. Dry, as were the second, third, and fourth. Perhaps if he spit on them, he'd find they still had some soap, but he didn't think he had nearly enough saliva. He grabbed his bottle of water and squeezed a little on one parched square. When a few bubbles appeared, he scrubbed his hands with that and checked his face in the rearview mirror. His body looked okay, but the shirt . . . well, he'd have to stop by Cheap-Mart on the way into town and buy another.

Thirty minutes later, Adam had settled in a booth across from Gussie. His new shirt wasn't as nice as his other but it didn't have the dark, greasy smudges, either. She, of course, looked wonderful. Happy, full of life, and beautiful, enjoying the rhubarb cream pie in front of her.

"I like buttermilk pie best, but this is a close second." She took a bite and chewed. "You should try my mother's buttermilk pie. It'll spoil you for anything else."

"Okay." He put his hand near hers, so his thumb rested against hers. "I'd love to try your mother's buttermilk pie. She seems like a really nice person. A good cook?"

"She used to be, still is, but with her diabetes, she seldom bakes." She reached for a napkin, which moved her hand away subtly but effectively. "You've met my parents, but I know nothing about yours. Tell me about them."

"They live in London."

"London, Texas?"

"No, and not London, Kentucky, either. London, England." By the time he explained that, Gussie had finished her pie. Then he told her about Miss Birdie in the kitchen. After laughing through that tale, Gussie glanced at the clock. "I need to go." She wiped her mouth and took a drink of water. "I've got a drive ahead of me, but—" She placed her hand on his for a quick touch before she grabbed the check and slipped from the booth. "—but it's been wonderful to see you."

He stood, moving in front of her before she could get away. Yes, that's exactly what it looked like, as if she were attempting to escape. "Can I see you again?"

"Yes." She paused and seemed to consider if she did want to see him again. "Of course I want to see you again. I haven't dated much recently. I sometimes forget how to act."

"Dinner? I could meet you in Austin or Roundville, somewhere closer than Marble Falls."

"Let's discuss that on email, okay?"

As he watched her pay the bill and leave, Adam wondered what *recently* meant. Gussie Milton attracted attention. He noticed that as she walked out. Men kept their eyes on her and grinned. Even the men who were with women scoped her out. No lack of masculine interest in her, so she'd chosen not to date. He could ask her about it but, when he asked her anything personal, she often acted like a doe surrounded by wolves. She'd warned him, but he'd hoped they'd made a little headway. She'd come to see him. She hadn't flinched at his touch.

For heaven's sake, if Gussie's not flinching at his touch showed progress, they had farther to go than he'd thought.

Dear Lord, give me patience, and I could really use it right now.

❧

Rex and Adam scrutinized the back of the car and the bumper that lay on the driveway. Hector had tried to reattach it with duct tape and wire. Not surprisingly, neither worked, so Adam had called the mechanic.

"Rusted out, Padre. Don't know if anything I do can keep it on for long, but putting a new bumper on that car . . ." Rex shook his head. "Seems like a waste of money. Maybe I could find one at the junkyard." He leaned down to inspect the body of the car. "But the car's rusty, too. To get one to hold for a while, it's going to be a little off center. I've got to attach it where I can find some good metal."

"I don't mind off center. That's not going to be the first thing people notice when they see my car. How long will that last?"

"Well, it should last as long as the car does." Rex rubbed his chin. "Of course, I didn't think your car would last this long."

"Thanks for taking care of it."

"I consider it both a work of charity and an experiment. How long can I keep this pile of . . ." He stopped, glanced at Adam. His look suggested he'd realized he was speaking to a minister. "How long can I keep this pile of rust going? We'll have to see, you, me, and the Lord."

❦

Adam hated those late phone calls. Every time the phone rang, he knew it was bad news. Who called with good news at—he blinked to look at the clock—one forty-five? He fumbled for the phone next to the chair and, when he finally corralled it, mumbled, "Hello."

"Pops, can you come get me?"

"What is it, Hector?" He sat up, suddenly alert. "Where are you? Are you okay?"

He and Hector had worked out a curfew. Ten on school nights but only with a good reason. One on weekends. First week of school and he was forty-five minutes late, not a lot.

"I just need you to . . . to come get me."

Adam noted a swishing sound on the *s* in *just*. "Have you been drinking?"

"Pops, please."

Yes, definite slurring. "Where are you?"

"At Hansen's Park, on Highway 29."

"I'll be there in ten minutes." Adam jumped from the chair, pulled his shoes on, then realized he couldn't leave Janey alone in the house. He didn't want to announce Hector's call, to explain the reason.

He picked up the phone and called the Kowalskis. "I've been called out," he said to George. "Can I bring Janey over?"

After George agreed, Adam bundled Janey in her blanket, lifted her, and headed out.

"What's happening?" Janey asked as he started down the stairs.

"I'm taking you next door. I got called out."

" 'Kay," she mumbled and fell back to sleep.

Thank goodness. No need to explain further.

Nor did George ask any questions. He opened the door and let them into the living room.

"Put Janey on the sofa," Ouida said from the bed. "She'll be fine there."

Once he settled the child, Adam said, "Sorry to bother you."

"No bother," George said. "Ouida couldn't sleep so I was keeping her company."

"Thanks." Adam pulled out his keys and started toward the door before he realized Hector had his car. "Umm, one more thing. Could I borrow a car?"

"Sure." George pulled a set from a bowl on the hall table. "Take my car. Leave the keys under the front seat when you get back. We'll bring Janey home in the morning."

"Thanks." With a wave at both of them, he left.

Fifteen minutes later, Adam pulled off the highway and into the park, a well-known site for keg parties. He had to guess that was why Hector was there. He had few delusions about the actions of high school jocks. He'd been one.

Hector stood inside the gates under a halogen light, leaning heavily against an old car with his head bowed. Bobby stood behind him. Adam stopped the car and stepped out.

"What's going on, guys?" Adam asked. "Did my car break down?"

Hector shook his head but still kept it down, not looking at Adam. "Pops, I drank too much. Don't think I should drive."

Adam waited for Hector to continue, the old allowing-the-guilty-to-fill-the-silence-with-excuses-and-explanations ploy.

"I'm sorry." He paused and forced back a belch. "I don't usually drink—oh, I've had a couple of beers before but not much."

"Okay." Adam gestured toward George's car. "Get in and we'll talk about it when we get home." Then he turned to Bobby. "How are you?"

"I'm okay. I don't drink. My mom would kill me if I did. But I came with Hector and none of the other guys were sober enough for me to want to ride with. Thought about driving Hector home in your car, but I don't trust it. We could make it a few feet and it'd die again and we'd be stuck in the middle of the highway."

"I understand, but I'd appreciate if you'd drive it home. It should make it that far without falling apart," Adam said.

Bobby looked over his shoulder at the old car. "Will you follow me?"

"Sure."

Bobby caught the keys Adam tossed him but didn't look pleased.

"I appreciate that, Bobby. Don't know how we'd get my car home otherwise. I'd let you drive this one"—he pointed to George's car and Bobby's face brightened—"but I borrowed it. Go ahead. I'll follow you, just in case."

The short caravan took off toward Butternut Creek going about thirty miles an hour. Adam focused on the off-center bumper in front of them to keep himself from lecturing Hector. That would come later. There were two approaches to driving his car: drive really fast so you got to the destination before the car fell apart, or drive very slowly so that if the car *did* fall apart, you wouldn't be gravely injured. Bobby obviously belonged to the second school. All this meant it was nearly three by the time they pulled into the Kowalskis' drive.

Seeing the lights off inside the Kowalski house, Adam parked in front, shoved the keys under the front seat, and got out of the Lexus.

"Bobby, let me drive you home," Adam said.

"Hey, I'm fine. I live two blocks north and no one in this town's going to jump me." He loped off.

As Adam headed toward the parsonage, Hector shoved himself out of the car and headed after him. He walked fairly well until he stumbled over a clump of grass and struggled to keep his balance.

"Coffee?" Adam asked when they entered. Not waiting for an answer, he headed into the kitchen and flipped on the coffeepot he'd set for six AM.

Why coffee? Because that's what everyone on television and in movies did, although he'd heard it only changed a drunk into a wider-awake drunk.

"I'm going to . . ." Before he finished the sentence, Hector sprinted toward the half bath.

By the time one cup of coffee had chugged out into the pot, Hector had returned to the kitchen looking terrible. Only fair, Adam thought. Actions had consequences, and if throwing up all night taught the kid a lesson, good.

"I'm going to take a shower and clean up." Hector looked at Adam. "Is that all right, sir?"

Hector never called him *sir*. The kid must be worried. Good.

Adam nodded and sat at the table, drinking coffee and rereading that morning's *American-Statesman*. He heard the water go on, then off a few minutes later.

When Hector came downstairs in clean jeans and a T-shirt but barefoot, Adam handed him a cup of coffee, sat down across from him at the kitchen table, and watched the kid. After another cup of coffee and one more visit to the bathroom, Hector still looked terrible but seemed fairly sober. Probably not the best time to discuss what had happened, not with a kid who had vomited and looked sick as a dog. But he figured Hector would sleep soundly for the rest of the night whereas Adam wouldn't sleep at all. No, he'd lie awake all night rehearsing what he needed to say over and over.

Taking care of the situation and getting a few hours' rest seemed like the best choice for him and he didn't care much right now about Hector's preference.

"Talk," Adam said. "Tell me about it."

"I'm not a drinker." Hector took a sip of the third cup of coffee, then blew on it to cool it. Finally, he lifted his eyes. "I should know better. This is how my father started. Look what happened to him."

Adam said nothing.

"Okay." Hector put the coffee down, leaned back in the chair, and closed his eyes. "A bunch of us were going to meet in the park, friends from the high school, other athletes, guys I hang with. I knew there'd be a keg there and some guys would bring the hard stuff, but I didn't plan to drink much. A little beer, that's all. But I started to feel sorry for myself." Hector sat up and made eye contact with Adam. "I wanted to feel better. Right now, my life is crap, and I wanted to feel good." He shook his head. "I should've known better. Getting drunk doesn't solve anything."

"Why did you feel sorry for yourself?"

"It's not you, Pops. You've been great for Janey and me. It's . . . it's . . . what about the future? You don't want me here for the rest of my life."

"Sure I do."

Hector's eyes narrowed. "You do?"

"As long as you need it, you have a home with me. I thought you knew that."

"I didn't know, wasn't sure." He drank more coffee. "But my education? Janey? What am I going to do with my life?"

"We can't solve those tonight, but we'll talk another time, maybe in a few days, when you're doing better. We'll figure them out together, you and I."

Hector nodded but didn't speak until he finally mumbled, "And then there's another problem." He took a long gulp of coffee. "Bree."

"Why's she a problem?"

"I really like her, but I don't have anything to offer her."

"Are you planning on getting married soon?"

Hector's eyes popped open. He considered Adam's words for a second before he laughed. "No, we aren't," he said once he stopped laughing. "Not even considering going steady, but I'd like to take her out. Like to invite her to homecoming but I don't have money for the tickets or a suit and flowers, just like for the prom. I can't swing all that."

"When's homecoming?"

He shook his head. "I don't know. Sometime in September."

"Have you asked her? Does she have a date?"

"I can't, but I don't think so. She expects me to ask her so it's been a little uncomfortable talking to her and avoiding that."

"Okay, we'll talk about that tomorrow, work things out. But right now we need to talk about tonight, what you did."

Hector nodded.

"Underage drinking is illegal."

"I know."

"While you are living in the parsonage, I expect you to follow the law. That means no drinking." He paused. "No drinking at all. Non-negotiable."

"Okay."

"How does the coach feel about drinking?"

"He doesn't allow it. If he knew we were out there, Coach would suspend us for a game or two, maybe even kick us off the team."

"Second, and here's the lecture. Drinking doesn't solve problems. If you're depressed, talk to me, talk to Coach, talk to someone."

Hector glanced at Adam. "And it's my father." He shook his head. "I'm supposed to go see him tomorrow." He glanced at the clock. "I mean, today. I hate going to that prison to see him."

"Don't go."

"He's my father."

Adam nodded. No need to remind Hector his father hadn't taken that responsibility seriously. He knew that. "How 'bout this? Cancel for tomorrow. Next Saturday, I'll go with you and wait for you so you won't be on your own."

"You'd do that for me?"

"Of course I would."

"Thanks." Hector sipped the coffee before he added, "This is going to sound crazy, but it sure would help if we had a hoop out there." He jerked his thumb toward the parking lot. "Working out makes life better, cuts back on stress. I don't worry as much when I'm playing ball."

For a moment, Adam wondered if putting up a hoop would seem like a reward for bad behavior, but he quickly tossed that theory. Hector needed this. He was seventeen, jam-packed with testosterone, recovering from years with an abusive father, and even now bringing up his sister, an obligation he was far too young for. He'd never had a role model to show him how to handle problems. Physical activity probably would help him stay more level. It always helped Adam.

He'd order it set up and worry about how to pay for it later.

Sounded like the kind of project his mother could get behind: Put up a hoop and save a small-town kid.

"I knew I couldn't drive home," Hector said. "That was the hardest part, having to call you, but I figured it would be worse if I had an accident and totaled your car and, maybe, hurt someone."

"Thanks for calling. That showed maturity. I'd hate for you to have hurt yourself or another person. You have to know I care about you more than I care about my car." Adam reached out and placed his hand on Hector's arm. "Even though you have a father and you're not even ten years younger than I am, I think of you as my son. I'm here for you. Always."

Tears rolled down Hector's cheeks. His eyes looked huge in his dark face. "Thanks, Pops."

Adam shoved a box of Kleenex toward Hector. "Take a couple of aspirin and drink a lot of water. Then go to bed. We'll talk more tomorrow."

As Hector filled a glass with ice and water, Adam added, "You are going to homecoming so you should ask Bree right away, before she decides to go with someone else."

"I'll call her tomorrow morning. I'm goin' up to bed."

As he watched Hector start upstairs, a wave of guilt hit him. He hadn't done enough. If he was going to do the father thing, not merely the kid-lives-in-my-home thing that he'd been perfectly content with, he needed to do more than give quick forgiveness and easy grace. No, Hector needed to understand consequences. "Not so fast," Adam said.

"What?" Hector stopped.

"Tomorrow you're going to dig a big hole for me."

Hector blinked. "A big hole?" Then he burped. "Sorry."

"Yes." Adam attempted to sound tough, but he could seldom carry that off. "A huge hole." After a pause, he added, "One more thing. You're nothing like your father."

"Thanks." Halfway up the steps, he stopped and said, "Pops, I'm sorry. I really am."

"Go on. We'll talk more in the morning." Adam watched him disappear.

Attendance at homecoming should be easy to fix. Hector didn't need a tux or a limo. He had the dark slacks from the prom. They'd find him a great shirt and tie. Could he ask Sam to loan him his treasured yellow Mustang? Probably not, but maybe Willow would let him use her car. He knew Hector wouldn't want to drive the car with a bumper that threatened to fall off, a window he couldn't put up, and the risk—actually the promise—of more disasters. Not for the homecoming dance.

The school kept the price of the tickets low so all the kids could afford to attend. As far as he could figure, the flowers would be the most expensive part. He bet the florist would work out something in exchange for a few hours of work from Hector.

Yeah, they'd talk about that tomorrow, after the kid finished digging the hole.

❧

Adam sat on the front porch, working on his sermon while the morning breeze cooled him off. Janey sat at the small table coloring.

In a spot next to the parking lot, Hector didn't look nearly as cool. Now shirtless, hung over, and with sweat pouring off him as he dug more deeply, the kid probably felt horrid. Good.

"How much farther?" Hector leaned on the shovel and panted.

"You're getting closer."

"Hey, Preacher."

Adam looked up from his notes and waved. "How're you doing, Coach?"

Gabe Borden strolled up the steps. "I hear our boys did a little drinking last night." Gabe looked across the lawn at Hector, who waved. Gabe didn't return the greeting.

"Hector says Bobby didn't, but, yeah, Hector did. That's why he's digging that hole."

Gabe nodded. "Good punishment. Now I need to do a little of my own. I'm going to suspend him and the other guys who participated for the first game of the season and threaten a lot more. I have a list from an unnamed source."

"Fine with me."

"I'm going to put the fear of God in him." Then he stopped watching Hector and faced Adam. "Sorry about that. Guess that fear-of-God thing is your job."

"Hey, I appreciate the extra voice. Sometimes you have to get their attention, make them listen."

"Double team."

The two men nodded to each other in perfect agreement, then folded their arms and watched Hector dig.

A few minutes later, Bree walked across the lawn. After greeting the two men and Janey, she shouted at Hector, "I heard what you did last night, you idiot."

Hector, covered with sweat and probably aching in every joint of his body as well as both eyes and his head, put down the shovel and squinted. He didn't say a word. From Bree's posture, tone, and words, he must have figured nothing he said would make a bit of difference and that Bree probably wasn't even close to finished with him.

"You got drunk and the preacher had to come get you?" She shook her head. "I can't believe you were so stupid." She took a step closer and leaned toward him, just in case he couldn't hear her shouts.

Adam bet he wished he'd taken a few more aspirin.

"Why did you do that?" Bree demanded. "Does the coach know?" She looked up at the porch. "Coach, do you know what this idiot did last night?"

Gabe nodded. "I plan to talk to him after he finishes digging that hole."

"I can talk now, Coach." Hector dropped the shovel.

"No, you keep digging. Preacher and I'll tell you when you're done."

"I shouldn't talk to you ever again," Bree said. "I thought you were smarter."

"Okay. I did something dumb. I'm sorry. I apologized to Pops and I'm apologizing to you, and pretty soon, I'm going to apologize to Coach and he's going to get really mad at me. On top of that, I still have to dig this hole."

"Serves you right." Bree turned and strode away.

"Want to go to homecoming with me?" Hector asked.

"That kid has a terrible sense of timing," Coach mumbled.

"What?" She turned back to face him. "You go out and get drunk with the guys, you get in trouble, and I'm yelling at you and the coach is going to suspend you and the preacher has you digging a big hole. Isn't that enough for one day? How could you ask me to go to the dance with you when all this stuff is going on?"

Hector shrugged and picked up the shovel. "Okay. If you don't want to go."

"I didn't say I wouldn't go with you." Bree stalked toward him and glared. "Are you serious?" she demanded. "After what you did? I have my reputation to think of."

"I'm not proud of what I did." Hector glanced at the men on the porch then back to Bree. "I'm sorry I disappointed you. I disappointed myself, too." He cleared his throat. "Of course I'm serious about homecoming. Wouldn't ask you if I wasn't." He started to dig again. "Want to go? Pops and I are figuring things out like cars and flowers."

She considered his words. "Okay, then. Yes, I'll go with you, but no drinking."

"Okay." He pulled out a shovel load of dirt and tossed it in the growing heap. "I'll call you later."

As Bree walked off, Hector glanced at Adam with a victorious smile before he went back to shoveling.

"Don't you think that's pretty big for a base for a basketball hoop?" Gabe asked.

"Could be, but he can always fill it in. It'll be the strongest post in town. Come inside and cool down. I'll have him dig for another half hour and tell him to stop."

As he entered the room Adam used for everything except cooking and sleeping, Gabe stopped at the family pictures on the bookcase. "Who's this?" he asked casually and pointed.

"My sister."

"Guess she got the good looks in the family."

"Thanks." Adam looked at Hannah, laughing with their parents, looking carefree and very young. The backdrop was the giant Ferris wheel in London. "She doesn't look like that anymore."

"When was this taken?" Gabe turned toward Adam with a frown.

"Three years ago."

"She's changed?"

"When I saw her a year ago, she'd changed. She's a doctor. Travels around Africa caring for people in refugee camps." Adam shook his head. "She says she loves it, that she's doing God's work, but it wears on her. I worry but she doesn't listen."

As he moved toward the kitchen, Adam saw Gabe take the photo from the bookcase and study it.

❦

Hector and Adam made the trip to Cogansville Federal Prison in a car borrowed from Winnie. They didn't talk much. Even when Adam made an occasional comment to show his support, Hector answered in a short but polite sentence, then returned to his thoughts.

As they approached the town, Hector said, "Someday you're going to have to get a better car. You can't keep borrowing them."

"I know, but people don't seem to mind."

Hector nodded. "Nice bunch of people in Butternut Creek."

On the return trip, Hector said, "My father's doing okay. He wants to come back home when his sentence is up, but I don't know if that's best for him. You know, same old crowd."

"How would you feel about his being in town?"

"By the time he gets out, I'm going to be old enough he wouldn't bother me. But Janey, I worry about her." He glanced at Adam. "She'll be in high school. Tough to be in high school when your father's been in prison. The kids don't let you forget it. And he could bother her, make her remember what life was like when the three of us lived together and his druggie friends slept there."

"Hector, we'll work on this together. If your father comes back to Butternut Creek, you and I and Janey will face that together. Until then, we'll go visit him as often as you need to."

"Thanks," Hector mumbled, then turned away and stared out the window for a few minutes. Then he asked, "Pops, did you ever drink?"

"Yeah, I had a couple of beers in high school and college, even got drunk a few times, but that's it. I stopped drinking anything when I started seminary."

"You did? I mean, you got drunk and you stopped drinking." Hector shook his head. "I've never known anyone who stopped drinking."

"I figured a minister shouldn't drink. Not because of morality but because of example." He searched his brain for the Bible verse he wanted to toss in here. "I can't remember this exactly, but Paul wrote that just because I can do something that doesn't hurt me, my example could lead another astray. There are some recovering alcoholics in the congregation."

"Really? Who?"

"Can't tell you. Confidential, you know. But suppose they see me drink a beer and that would have them start drinking again? Or a teenager saw me with a beer and started to drink. What kind of an example would I be?"

"That's a little far-fetched, Pops."

"Yeah, I guess it is, but I don't need a beer that much."

"Could put a little weight on you." A flicker of a smile appeared on Hector's face. "You're still too skinny."

"Yeah, so will chocolate. I'll stick to cake and donuts and Ouida's muffins."

Chapter Twelve

Adam looked forward to seeing Gussie. Of course he did. Her presence always brightened his day.

But at this moment, it didn't. Actually, he'd begun to wonder about him and Gussie a few days back when he'd asked her to meet him for dinner instead of coffee and she'd turned him down. And there had been a special musical program at the old theater on the square where Mac would be playing in an ensemble, but Gussie said she couldn't attend that, either.

Yesterday he'd paid particular attention to Willow and Sam in church. They really loved each other, showed it in everything they did. Not that they made out on the pew or acted in any way inappropriate, but they held hands. Sam looked at her with such love. When they stood for the hymns, they sort of tilted toward each other, as if gravity, or another force, pulled them together. That was what he wanted.

And Gussie jumped when he touched her.

Suck it up, Adam lectured himself. He and Gussie had only been together a few weeks. There was time. He'd told her he wouldn't push. Patience.

But were they together? Really? They weren't even dating. For an hour every week, if she didn't have something else to do, they chatted over coffee and pie. The only variety came in which kind of pie they ordered. Frustrated as he felt, knowing he'd expected a little more than emailing two or three times a week or the occasional coffee in Marble Falls, he wasn't ready to give it up.

He didn't believe she was stringing him along. It was that "broken" thing. If he could get through that, find out what the problem was, maybe they could fix it. If not, at some time he might think of giving up.

But having faith and hope didn't mean he didn't notice the deeper problems that surfaced every time they met. He couldn't get through to her. She was always lovely and charming, but she'd completely closed off the part of her life that haunted her, displaying only the glorious and glossy exterior. Oh, he bet he knew more than most people about her. She'd talked, briefly, about her problem, but almost immediately she erected that barrier again.

So why did she even bother to drive to Marble Falls to meet him? And why did she continue to answer his emails in a breezy, friendly way that didn't give him any insight into who Gussie Milton was?

For this reason, once they were seated in a booth inside, each with a cup of coffee in front of them, he said, "Gussie, I want to see you more. I want to take you on a date, go out for dinner, head into Austin for a play, spend more time together."

Her smile disappeared quickly when he said those words. "But . . . but we are dating," she said.

"No, Gussie, we are not," he stated firmly. He hated that flutter of fear in her expression but had to finish. "We meet for coffee and discuss church, that's what we do. Today we're going to discuss a tubing trip for the youth."

"I told you . . ." She stopped and swallowed hard. "I asked you to be patient."

"Gussie, I'm not pushing. Okay, I am, but I need to understand. I want to date you, I want to see you more often, to get to know you better. I'd like to know what's happening, to share whatever hurt you so much."

"I can't talk about it. Not here."

"Okay." He reached out and took her hand. She didn't pull away. "Can we talk about whatever *it* is soon?"

"I'll email you the details."

He blinked. "Email?"

"I can't talk about it."

"Can we discuss whatever this is in person, after you send the email?"

"You may not want to, once you know."

"Can we get together when I know what happened?"

Surprisingly, she put her other hand over his before she pulled both away. All the glow that was Gussie had disappeared. She looked at him from somber eyes in a serious face. "It's not only my opinion.

You know I'm broken, too. You recognize that. You just said you wonder why I can't give you more. Maybe we need to decide—either now or after you read my email—if we want to see each other more."

"Can I heat up your coffee?" A waitress reached between them to fill their cups. "Everything all right here?"

Everything was obviously not all right but both he and Gussie said, "Fine," and smiled at the waitress as she topped off their cups.

"This isn't the right place or time," she said after the waitress took off.

He'd lost this round.

❦

"Someday I'm going to shoot your father," Gussie's mother said from the kitchen.

Having just walked in from the disastrous meeting with Adam, Gussie would've preferred time alone. However, with her father's life at stake, she probably should talk her mother down. She placed her purse on the sofa and went into the kitchen to stand next to her mom, who was looking out the back window at the yard.

"He has no sense, none at all."

Gussie's father pruned bushes behind the house.

"It's hot this afternoon and he's not well." Her mother turned around to glare at Gussie as if the whole thing were her fault. "He still has that cough although he tries to hide it, and he's no spring chicken. He says he's over the pneumonia."

Gussie put her hand on her mother's shoulder. "Mom, he's seventy-four years old. You've been married over fifty years. He's not going to change. We both know that."

"Of course I do. That's why I'm so frustrated. And I'm not about to change, either, you know. I'll always fuss at him." She closed the curtain as if not seeing her husband would allow her to stop worrying about him. "Oh, enough about your father. Tell me about your young man. Did you have a nice afternoon?"

"Very nice," she lied. No reason to upset her mother even more. "He's not really my young man."

Her mother considered the statement. "You said he was. Has that changed? Are you having second thoughts?" She took a deep breath before asking, "Gussie, does he know what happened to you? Have you told him?"

"Oh, that took place so long ago—"

"Gussie," she interrupted. "Does he know what happened to you?"

"Mom, don't bug me about this. It's my life."

"Yes, dear, I know, but . . ."

Because her mother didn't seem likely to let the subject go and she didn't want to upset her, Gussie forced a smile. "I'm fine, really. I'm going to go out and help Dad," she said as she turned and left the kitchen.

That evening, Gussie sat in front of her computer and studied the screen. The problem with writing about personal matters with a word processor was that she didn't have the sensual pleasure of wadding up a bad draft and throwing it on the floor.

She began to type until she had an email that covered three screens. Too much information. She clicked it into MAIL WAITING TO BE SENT and started over until she had the few words that explained what had happened. If he didn't turn away from her—and she truly believed Adam wouldn't—he could ask her more. Maybe she would answer.

She placed that one in her TO BE SENT folder because she needed to consider, to ponder, to decide her course.

❧

Monday evening, Adam and Hector had played a hard game of one-on-one at the new hoop, the inaugural game. After that, about fifteen players—male and female—chose sides and played until nearly ten o'clock.

"Gets really dark back here," Bobby said.

True. The lights had been placed in the parking lot to provide security, not luminosity.

When they could no longer see the ball and Bobby had hit Hector in the back with a fast, hard pass, the game disbanded and the players wandered off. After a shower, Adam sat in front of his computer. Would he find a message from Gussie? He had no idea what to expect, what she would say, but he hoped.

Nothing there.

Because the email didn't arrive until late Tuesday evening and he'd been too busy to check earlier, Adam didn't find it until noon on Wednesday on his office computer. He'd waited impatiently but now that he had it, he didn't want to open it.

The subject glared at him from the email queue: "Hello." Innocuous and non-threatening. He kept staring at it.

Maggie had left by then so he had complete solitude. Probably no one would interrupt unless one of the retired men showed up. They often stopped in because they had plenty of time. No one figured a minister did anything from Monday through Saturday, so they felt they should keep him company for hours. He always stopped whatever he was doing to talk because he considered those minutes to be ministry. Usually, he attempted to run them off after twenty or thirty minutes so he could get some work done.

Well aware he was allowing his thoughts to wander because he did not want to open that email, his finger hovered over the OPEN button. Would he find a way to be with Gussie after he read this? Would she permit him to see her again? He believed that as soon as he clicked that button, their lives would change. Maybe it had been better to ignore the barrier and accept what Gussie had to give.

Coward. She'd been brave enough to write him. He should have enough courage to read it.

He opened the email.

"I was raped when I was eighteen by my boyfriend."

That was all.

Oh, Lord. He closed his eyes and dropped his head. "God, please grant Gussie your healing love and bless me with understanding," he prayed.

He read the few words again. How should he answer? He had so little to go on. Finally he wrote, "I'm sorry that happened. May I come to Austin or Roundville to see you?"

That evening, he had the reply. "No, let's meet in Marble Falls for coffee Monday. As usual."

So he sent flowers, yellow and orange roses.

The next day, he sent more.

On the third day, he found an email from Gussie with the subject "STOP!" He opened it to read, "Thank you. I appreciate the flowers but save your money for something you really need."

As if he didn't really need Gussie.

❧

Adam couldn't get used to how early school started in Texas. It was the first Friday of September and the kids had been back in school for two weeks, football would start shortly, and life had settled into a steady flow.

Yes, life had become fairly peaceful, leaving him plenty of time to worry about Gussie until Jesse and Ralph came into his office, Ralph carrying a large tool satchel and Jesse a small carton.

"Hear you don't have an intercom in here," Jesse said. "You know Ralph used to work for the phone company." He nodded toward Ralph, who looked like a lineman in his white shirt, gray slacks, and heavy boots. "I'm only the gofer." Jesse wore his usual jeans, plaid shirt, and cowboy boots. "But I can do a lot of stuff. We're going to install one."

Oh, please, Lord, no. Adam had heard tales about the havoc retired men could wreak on church wiring. At a lunch meeting with the ministerial alliance, Mattie described the time she couldn't use the computer without turning on the light in the bathroom. With that, all the other ministers had chimed in with horror stories. Adam bet he'd have one to tell in a few days.

He should have more faith. "I didn't realize you worked for the phone company, Ralph," Adam said. "When was that?"

"One summer when I was in high school."

Fifty-some years ago, Adam figured.

"But things haven't changed all that much," Ralph said confidently. "And we've got instructions on the box." He held it up. "Thought we'd put a line through to the fellowship hall, too." He pointed in that direction. "Keep you from having to go down there to talk to people."

Ralph made it sound as if that area was hundreds of yards away and filled every hour with a whirl of activity and thousands of people who needed to be accessed. Adam wished it were, but at this time, AA met there twice a week, the vets' group on Wednesday, and yoga at noon on Monday.

But why object? If they wanted to set up an intercom, fine. Adam didn't want to turn anyone away, and he bet their wives would be happy for them to be out of the house and useful.

Besides, what could go wrong? Surely with wireless technology, installing an intercom was a simple matter of plugging it in.

Without waiting for his approval, the two men put their burdens down and began opening the box. Even going after the carton with scissors, a knife, and a saw, they couldn't get it open. That should have been a clue.

As Adam watched the men from the door between offices, Maggie stood beside him and whispered, "You aren't going to let them do this, are you? You do know that they'll mess up the phone system, right?"

"Have faith. How hard can this be? I probably could do this." He patted Maggie's shoulder before she huffed off. "Guys, I'm going to make some visits while you're working to get out of your way."

But they didn't hear him. They were celebrating the defeat of the cardboard box too loudly to notice.

After dropping by the nursing home, stopping to chat with Ouida, and grabbing a sandwich at home, Adam headed back to the office to check in with Jesse and Ralph. When he walked into the reception office and flicked the light switch, nothing happened.

From the silence, he realized the men had left. In the light from the door and the windows, he could see wires—telephone or electrical or both, he couldn't tell—dangling from the ceiling. He picked up the phone. No dial tone.

The light switch in his office didn't work, either. Taking care not to fall over or bump into anything, Adam navigated to the window, opened the blinds, and looked around. On the corner of his desk sat a little box with two buttons on it. One of the buttons bore the label MAGGIE; the other, FELLOWSHIP HALL. To test the system, he pressed the one for the front office. Nothing. Didn't seem to be hooked up yet. Even if it was, they'd turned the electricity off. He glanced at the dark, dead screen of his monitor. After checking that the machine was turned on, he flipped the control of the power strip off then back on.

He glanced overhead at the dangling wires. They didn't look live. No electrical charges zapped out the ends, but he wasn't going to touch them to find out. He felt pretty sure Ralph and Jesse had cut off the electricity here before they began their work. With that thought, Adam picked up the flashlight he kept in his desk, went into the hall, and opened the fuse box to shine the light inside. Yes, two circuits had been shut off.

Nothing would work.

On top of that, the heat smothered him, felt hotter than mid-July when the air conditioner struggled to cool the offices. He reached up and couldn't feel any air circulating from the vent over his desk. The ceiling fan didn't move.

Adam glanced down at his computer for the time. Of course, it didn't appear on the dark screen or on the electric clock plugged into the wall. He looked at his wrist: one thirty. The men had probably knocked off for lunch. He'd work at home, get out of their way until they finished.

❧

When Adam arrived the next morning, the electricity was still off. The wires still dangled from the ceiling. Of course, with the electricity off, the offices had no phone, no computers, and no air-conditioning.

"Might want to move your things to the fellowship hall," Maggie said. "That's what the ministers usually do after Ralph has messed with the wiring." Even in the dim light, Adam could make out her expression. It said, *I told you so.*

He flipped out his cell and dialed Ralph.

"Oh, Preacher," his wife Annabella said. "He's up in Waco. You know, he was in the army. Has his physical today at the VA."

"Do you know when he'll be home?"

"Oh, not until eight or nine at the earliest. He likes to shop, get a nice meal before heading back."

"What about tomorrow? He left some wires hanging and the electricity's off."

"Oh, dear. We're headed out in the morning to visit our kids up in Corsicana. He said they ran into some problems with that installation in the church and he needs to pick up a few parts. He'll probably finish up next week."

"Would you mention I called and ask if he would stop by as soon as possible? We do have church Sunday."

"Oh, I'm sure he left the electricity on in the sanctuary."

"Great." Realizing the sarcasm that came from his frustration probably wasn't the right tone, he added, "I'd really appreciate his calling me ASAP."

"Of course."

After Annabella hung up, Adam called Jesse. "Hey, Jesse," he said before he realized the answering machine had picked up. "Please give me a call on my cell as soon as possible."

About all he could do. He headed to the fellowship hall.

Unfortunately, wires hung from the ceiling and the lights didn't go on there, either.

Maggie stood in the door, barely hiding her smile. "How hard could installing an intercom system be?"

"I should call an electrician."

"Not a good idea. You'd hurt their feelings."

"But look at this mess. We won't be able to use the fellowship hall, either." He paced and mulled his options. Few came to mind.

"Shove everyone outside after church to keep them away from the wires," Maggie suggested. "Have the ladies come up with refreshments. Make it like an outside reception, a special occasion."

He headed down to the diner to talk to Miss Birdie. After he explained the situation, she said, "Sure, Preacher. We can take care of that."

Then she laughed, a sound Adam had heard only a handful of times. It always startled him with the pure delight it expressed.

"I know you can't stop them from making repairs to the church, but the past minister limited Jesse and Ralph to maintenance that didn't require the opening of walls or ceilings. He made another rule. They had to make all repairs on Monday so normalcy could be restored by Sunday." She cackled. "Guess you've learned your lesson."

*

"How was your weekend?" Gussie smiled at him, completely comfortable as if she'd never written him that email, as if he didn't know about the rape.

Denial? Or did she feel as if telling him closed the discussion? Had she dealt with this problem from her past and it no longer haunted her? No, if she had she never would have leaped away from his touch nor told him she was broken. His best guess was not only denial but *I don't want to talk about this* as well.

He hadn't expected that response but should have. Gussie was always happy and smiling, always up except for the few minutes she'd allowed him past her facade. No, not a facade. Gussie truly was upbeat, most of the time, but he'd caught a glimpse of that other part of her. Now she'd made it off limits again. Okay, he'd accept that. For now.

*

Gussie rubbed the handle of the coffee cup before she glanced up at Adam, who also rubbed the handle of his coffee cup. For the first time ever, conversation between the two lapsed once they'd discussed Ralph's and Jesse's repairs and her parents' health.

"I'm going to order a piece of pie," she said.

Scintillating, that's what she and her conversational gambits were.

"What kind?" Adam asked.

Poor man. He couldn't think of what to say, and she felt sure he wouldn't bring up the topic of her email. She certainly didn't want to. Even writing it had been painful. Sending the short message had taken every bit of courage she possessed.

"I like the rhubarb but I'm going to be adventurous and try lemon meringue."

"Aah," he said. "Risky. I'll try apple."

They placed their orders and, once the waitress walked off, stared at each other.

"How's Hector?"

They discussed the Firestones for a few minutes.

What else could they talk about? She'd thought she and Adam could discuss nearly everything but that one topic, the unspeakable, hung between them like a scrim in a theater. They could both see it but both refused to acknowledge it, pretended it didn't exist even as it separated them.

She'd been very clear about her privacy. She knew if they wanted to move on, to speak about what she always called "the event," she'd have to bring it up. The waitress set their pieces of pie in front of them. She took another gulp of coffee and fed herself several forkfuls she couldn't even taste.

Adam took a few bites then stopped and watched the ice cream melt down the slice and puddle on his plate. "I'm not very hungry," he said.

Okay. If Adam not eating his pie didn't signal his mood, nothing would.

"What did you think . . ." She stopped because the words stuck in her throat. After a quick drink of water and an internal repetition of the Serenity Prayer, Gussie said, "What did you think about my email?"

"I appreciate that you shared that with me." He smiled gently, then picked up his fork and took another bite of the now soggy pie.

Was that it? Had he returned to his dessert because she'd relieved him of the necessity of bringing up the subject of her email or because he didn't want to discuss it anymore?

When would she stop trying to figure people out? A bite of pie could simply be a bite of pie.

Sometimes her brain kept going and working as she attempted to figure life out. Even with that, she couldn't make sense of the situation between Adam and her, couldn't seem to figure out what to do next. Like him, she kept cutting off little parts of the pie, chewing and swallowing. She concentrated very hard on the fork as if she feared jabbing herself in the eye instead of putting it in her mouth.

"Gussie, if you want to discuss what happened or need anything from me, tell me," he said. "I'm willing. I care about you."

With several bites of that delicious pie left, she put down her fork, pulled together every particle of her courage, and said, "I'd been dating Lennie for about a month. We met in freshman composition and I trusted him."

She glanced at Adam. "I'd never been drunk before. And I've never been drunk since."

He put down his fork and listened.

"I thought, *What kind of college student has never even had a drink of anything?* Isn't that the college experience? Drinking and carousing and experimenting?"

"Gussie, you don't have to tell me this, not now, not here, if you're uncomfortable."

"If I don't tell you now, I may not have the nerve another time." She took in a deep breath. "Lennie said he'd take care of me, make sure I didn't drink too much or get in trouble. I believed him. We went to a fraternity party and I drank a couple of glasses of something fruity they were serving. Illegal because I was eighteen, but no one cared. It was good. I couldn't even taste the alcohol but it packed a punch." She reached out and grabbed his hand, holding on so tightly her fingers hurt.

She didn't like talking about this, not a bit. But as she turned to scan the other patrons of the restaurant, she realized this could be a good place to talk about the event. Here, as emotion burbled inside her, she couldn't allow herself to lose control surrounded by all these people.

"The alcohol hit me hard. I don't know why. Could be because I'm not a drinker or I drank it too fast or that fruit juice tasted so sweet—anyway, I got woozy and sick. I could barely stand up and had to lean against something—a wall or a chair—to walk." She blinked tears back. "I'm so ashamed."

He squeezed her hand. "You can stop now. You don't have to say more."

"Yes, I do." The words poured. "Lennie took me back to his apartment. He said I could sleep it off there. I didn't want to go back to the dorm in that condition. When I woke up—I don't know how much later—he was on top of me." She pulled her hand back, picked up her glass and drained it. "I never reported him. At first, I wanted to forget everything, then, as time went on . . . well, too much time had passed. The police would wonder why I hadn't reported it and Lennie had witnesses I'd had too much to drink. I couldn't handle that. I wanted to forget, pretend it never happened." She glanced at him with wide eyes. "I still do."

She stood quickly, nearly knocking the table over. "I have to go now," she said and tossed a bill on the table.

Before she fled, she noticed Adam's pale face and his eyes filled with an emotion she couldn't interpret at the moment. Feeling like the stupidest of idiots for opening up *here*, she forced herself not to flee from the restaurant but stopped at the door. A mistake because Adam caught up with her before she could leave.

Okay, what now, Miss I'll-tell-the-story-my-way? Hadn't she learned this wasn't about someone else at another time? "The event" was that *she*, Gussie Milton, had been raped by a man she'd trusted, a man she'd thought she could fall in love with.

She heard Adam tell the waitress the money was on the table, then he held the door for her.

Once outside, he took her hand. "Gussie." He stopped speaking as if he didn't have any more idea what to do next than she did. They could not stand in the middle of Marble Falls only a few yards from the heavy traffic on Highway 281 with cars and trucks whizzing past them. "I'm sorry."

"Not your fault." Gussie fumbled through her purse looking for her keys. "Don't worry. I'm fine."

"Oh, sure, I'm going to let you drive home now."

When had she given him permission to tell her what she could and couldn't do? Well, back when she'd told him about "the event." And probably when she'd run out of the restaurant and now, when she was standing in the parking lot quivering.

"I know I can't." She closed her purse and looked at him for a few seconds before she leaned against him. How odd that she'd do that, but how great that he stood there, warm and trustworthy. "I know, but I've always run home for comfort." *And to hide*, she added to herself. She didn't say the words aloud because she'd already given up more of herself to Adam than she had to anyone other than her parents.

"We need to find a place that's more private," he said.

From the movement of his body, she could tell he was looking around for inspiration, but she didn't want to lift her head or step away from him.

"I won't leave you to face this alone." He handed her a Kleenex. He'd learned to carry a pocketful, one of his ministerial tools and necessities.

"Thanks," she said. "I'm not crying." But she was, she realized when she felt her cheeks, and she was having trouble breathing. Odd when she felt like a huge burden had been lifted from her by sharing. "It may not look like it but I feel better than I have for years." She stepped back. "Let's take a walk."

❧

Gussie had leaned against him for comfort and support. In the restaurant, she'd put her hand on his while she told him what had happened to her. A much-abridged story, he guessed, but nonetheless a step forward.

They didn't speak as they walked down to a park overlooking the lake. "Gussie, I'm sorry that happened to you."

"Thank you, Adam. For listening and not turning away."

He wanted to question her, find out more. But not now. They found a bench looking over the lake and sat down. She even touched his hand again. Yes, he'd like more but, for now, having Gussie next to him felt like more than enough.

Someday they'd have to talk about what happened next, after the rape, but not now. He didn't believe she could take it. Instead of speaking, they watched the water. Together.

Chapter Thirteen

Adam had a spring in his step. A stupid phrase he'd never thought he'd use, a saying that went back generations. He also had a song in his heart and smile on his face. He walked like the conqueror of the world and wished he could tell Miss Birdie that he thought the Widows' matchmaking efforts could stop, be called completed and successful.

He didn't, of course. In the first place, Miss Birdie would act obnoxious in her victory. Secondly, he didn't want to talk about him and Gussie possibly becoming an "us" because what had seemed like a bridge crossed now felt like only a minor change. He'd hoped the confession signaled that she was falling or had fallen or perhaps anticipated falling in love with him. Now it seemed more like a tiny step, that maybe the idea of falling in love no longer nauseated her.

And, third, there were those other old expressions his grandmother had repeated: "Many a slip 'twixt the tongue and the lip" and "Don't count your chickens." Et cetera.

Two or three times a day, he and Gussie emailed or texted. They set up a date for Friday, the format to be decided later. Once she'd called to say she was headed toward San Saba and would he meet her for lunch in Butternut Creek? The sight of them together had made Miss Birdie glow as she bustled around them, filling nearly full glasses of tea and forcing dessert on them. After that, they'd wandered around the courthouse, sat for a while on a bench in the square, and chatted. One of his best afternoons ever.

Life hadn't changed much in Butternut Creek. Ouida continued to improve. He'd officiated at the wedding of Winnie and the general, Sam's father. They'd gone off somewhere for a honeymoon.

Wires no longer dangled from ceilings all over the church. Some of the men—not Jesse and Ralph, who'd admitted defeat—had coiled them up and capped them off, then turned the power back on. He and Maggie still had to shout at each other, but they had phones and lights as well as large holes in the ceilings of the offices and the fellowship hall.

Through the window, Adam could see the new basketball hoop in the parking lot. Great idea. Used at night and weekends, and no doubt would be a busy place this coming summer. As the coach had decreed, Hector dribbled everywhere except the church. He'd decided that wouldn't be respectful—but he dribbled the ball right up to the front door. After several accidents, Adam had banished it from the parsonage as well.

He'd emailed stories about Butternut Creek to his sister as he did every Friday. In one he told another story about Chewy and a backpack, finishing it with, "He's become one of the church's best evangelistic tools." She seldom answered, but she needed his support. He hoped the funny stories cheered her up. He couldn't imagine anything more different from his life here and hers over there. How did she do it?

His parents wrote they'd visited Paris. The Chunnel had become a shortcut to Europe for them. They loved Europe and planned to send him a ticket so he could visit soon.

Life was good. Today he was going to wallow in being happy.

He began by looking at a computer file of church members he needed to call and chose one he hadn't seen in church.

"Hello, Mrs. Gibson," he said. "This is Adam Jordan, minister at the Christian Church."

Silence.

"How are you doing this morning?"

"Fine." Her voice sounded begrudging, as if she hated to give out even this small bit of information.

"I'm sorry I haven't gotten in touch with you sooner. The chair of the elders tells me you're a member of the church but haven't been able to attend for a while."

"That's right." Another pause followed. "What's your name again?"

"Adam. Adam Jordan, I don't believe I've met you."

"Reverend Jordan, nice of you to call." Her quiet voice quivered. "The problem is that it's hard for me to make it on Sunday morning. I have a lot of trouble with my joints—arthritis, you know—and I don't get moving until about noon. Then a migraine hits and puts me in bed, in the dark."

"Sounds as if you have a lot of physical problems. I'm sorry to hear that."

"Thank you. On top of that . . . well, you don't want to hear an old lady complaining about her aches and pains."

How to answer that? "If you want to talk about them, please tell me."

For another few minutes, she gave what his uncle Bob, a physician, had called "an organ recital," describing the appalling condition of her heart and her liver and various other ailments he didn't catch. He stopped taking notes after several repetitions of the phrase, "None of the doctors thought I'd live."

"You know, our elders take communion to people who can't make it to church. Could they drop by this Sunday? Would that be convenient?"

Again silence. Had they been disconnected? No, there was no dial tone. He glanced at the phone to see that the *in use* button glowed red. "Mrs. Gibson?" he asked.

"I am not," she said testily, obviously insulted, "I am *not* a shut-in. I shop for myself. I play Bunco with my friends. I drive. I go to the beauty parlor. I am not a shut-in and don't need the elders to bring me anything or for you to visit."

With that, she disconnected. He knew for sure when the dial tone beeped from the speaker. Adam turned the phone off and laughed.

Although too weak to go to church, it seemed Mrs. Gibson could do anything else she wanted.

An imp inside him wanted to turn her name over to the elders, but that would only cause those leaders trouble. Instead he wrote, "Call next year. Don't treat as shut-in," on Mrs. Gibson's card and filed it.

❦

Birdie listened to the sounds of Carlos the Cat coming from the bathroom: *Whap! Whap! Whap!*

Mac had put Ping-Pong balls in the tub and the silly animal loved to bat them around. Mac said they'd given him new life. Instead of sleeping twenty-three hours a day, now Carlos slept twenty-two hours and fifty minutes and played in the bathtub for a few minutes several times a day.

She hated it when the cat wanted to continue chasing those balls and Birdie wanted to settle down for a nice soak. Whose joints were more important? The breadwinner's or those of a skinny, elderly cat?

Didn't Birdie work to put food in his bowl? Nevertheless, she never bothered him.

Oh, my, had she gotten soft. Allowing a cat to inconvenience her because the girls adored him and he scratched people who tried to move him.

She stood up from Bree's bed where she'd been contemplating a far more difficult problem.

Fashion or style or just plain pornography?

School had been in session for almost a month. Still hot here in Texas, would be through part of October. Wasn't the heat that bothered Birdie. It was the clothing, those doggone tiny tops the girls liked to wear. Said it was too hot to wear regular T-shirts. So why was the district spending taxpayer money for air-conditioning if the girls had to wear those bits of nothing to stay cool?

Not that Birdie accepted that excuse. She'd been young once.

Bree told her grandmother that everyone—well, all the girls— wore tops with straps so narrow their bra straps showed. Just plain slutty, Birdie told her granddaughters that, but she couldn't make any headway. School dress code allowed it. The other girls wore it. Some even tried to get by with sheer tops, but the principal gave those girls a hoodie to wear or sent them home.

Didn't Bree understand what happened when a girl wore clothes like that? Elmer had allowed Martha Patricia to get away with anything. He spoiled her terribly and look what had happened. After Elmer died, Martha Patricia had left town with that no-good father of both her girls and it had all started when Elmer allowed her to wear tight shorts.

Mercedes had passed on a story about a woman who dressed like the daughter to show her how terrible she looked. Said the woman had put on a tank top without a bra and that had gotten the message over to her daughter.

Might as well try it, but she refused to leave off underwear.

After opening Bree's drawer and taking out a shirt with what she'd called spaghetti straps during her youth centuries ago, she shook it out. Then she took her blouse off and slipped the shirt on over her head. It settled across her shoulders and hung down to her hips, huge on her. The straps of her old-lady bra showed white under the coral top. She studied her image for nearly a minute, aghast at what and who stared back at her. She couldn't carry this off. She'd feel mortified to show anyone else, even her own granddaughters, her desiccated torso, ropy arms, and saggy neck, much less the thick straps of her bra. She looked like the scrawny old woman she was.

When had she gotten so old? She still felt like that girl who planned to start college to be an English teacher. Then she and Elmer had fallen in love at the prom, and her life had changed because Elmer had to stay in town to take over his father's carpentry business. Years later, she ended up here, looking at her elderly self in the mirror.

Not that she'd change anything, except what happened with Martha Patricia, but she would have slowed down those years. They'd flown by much too fast.

Yes, here she stood, looking like a skinny old lady and wishing she had a few of those pretty curves Blossom had. She couldn't allow anyone to see her like this. She'd have to think of some other way to teach the lesson.

Bree was a good girl. Everyone said that, but everyone wasn't thinking about the effects of hormones on a teenager's ability to reason or resist temptation. Could be one soft, lovely evening with the moon hitting the right angle, romantic music on the radio, and a sweetly scented breeze calling out thoughts of love and lust, two young people could get carried away. Goodness knows, it had happened to enough people.

Birdie guessed she'd have to trust Bree. She sure as anything wouldn't leave the bedroom in this outfit.

❧

Adam had bought a new tie, dark blue with a gold pattern. Didn't go with his suit, but he'd borrowed Hector's prom-and-homecoming slacks. A little short but they fit well otherwise. With dark socks, no one would notice.

At last, he and Gussie were going out with Willow and Sam. Adam had issued a stern "no-joking" order to Sam and could only hope the former marine would behave. If not, Willow would put the kibosh on her husband. She handled him effortlessly. Sam was so much in love with his wife, he'd do whatever she said.

They'd take Willow's car into Roundville, because none of them trusted Adam's car enough to make it both ways, despite the fact that Adam made the trip weekly. Willow and Sam would drop him off at the Miltons', and Adam and Gussie would go to Austin and back in her car.

After greeting Mr. and Mrs. Milton—Yvonne and Henry—he escorted Gussie to the car and reached for her keys.

"Oh," she said. "Are you driving?"

He nodded, hand still out.

"Don't you trust my driving?"

"It's not that." He didn't understand this odd streak of machismo he hadn't realized he had. But he couldn't seem to tamp it down. He needed to drive. The thought of not doing so, sitting in the passenger seat while Gussie drove, made him anxious.

"Are you afraid I'll get lost? Or have an accident?"

"I can't explain it. I'm sorry." He took the keys from her hand. "I have to drive."

"Men," she groaned.

"Besides, if you drove, I wouldn't be able to open your car door." He performed that. "And help you in."

"Delicate flower that I am." She laughed as she allowed him to assist her.

Sam had made reservations at a nice place on Red River for a celebration. Sam would finish his class work and student teaching in December and had a teaching job at the middle school starting in January.

"At least I no longer have to live off my rich wife," Sam said after they'd settled at the table. "But, you know, I like being a kept man." He glanced at his wife and grinned before he turned back to Adam. "Let me give you some advice. Marry a woman who makes more money than you and can keep you in style."

Across from Adam, Willow laughed. "Oh, yes, we live in such style."

Next to him, Adam could feel Gussie tense.

"Sam and I live in the house Sam's aunt left him," Willow explained. "It's a little small but it's free."

"And we're together," Sam said.

To change the subject because the waves of adoration between Sam and Willow had become stifling, Adam asked Gussie, "What looks good to you?" as she perused the menu.

Maybe this double date hadn't been the best idea in the world. He could almost see little hearts floating between Sam and Willow and cherubs strumming harps over their heads.

And yet, he thought as he glanced at Gussie, as nauseating as it was to see such affection at close quarters, wouldn't it be nice to take part in it? To care for someone that much and show it? Through a touch? A kiss? Or a besotted glance? Because the Petersons did nothing unacceptable. They were deeply in love and showed it.

Yes, as obnoxious as he found the display between Willow and Sam, he probably felt that way because he envied them.

"Congratulations on the job," Gussie said to Sam after they'd ordered.

"We have more news," Sam said. "We're pregnant." He smiled so broadly, the corners of his lips nearly reached mid-cheek.

"How wonderful," Gussie said.

"When?" Adam reached across to take Willow's hand.

"March. You're the first people we've told, except for family."

"Boy or girl?" Gussie asked.

"We don't care. The general is hoping for a granddaughter." Sam put his arm around the back of Willow's chair. "Winnie's just excited to have another grandchild. She never expected to have any."

"Don't let him fool you. He really wants a girl." Willow gestured toward her husband. "He has big plans to spoil his little princess."

"We're going to have to find a bigger house, because there's no way we can fit another person in."

After dinner, they strolled toward one of Gussie's favorite music venues, Sam and Willow in front. Sam held Willow's hand and, again, Adam noticed how they listed toward each other, drawn together.

He wanted that.

❦

"Girls, get over here and pick up your shoes," George shouted out the back door.

Carol and Gretchen dashed in from the yard. Each grabbed her own sandals and said, in union, "Sorry, Daddy."

They hugged his legs before heading upstairs without a whimper or a complaint or a put-upon sigh, no sign of rolling eyes.

A miracle. Ouida'd witnessed a true miracle.

She wouldn't have believed this months ago. Nor would she have believed what the house looked like. The living room was neat and fairly clean but under the coffee table were some books. A few toys lurked in a corner. Crayons spread across the small table he'd brought downstairs for the girls. A little clutter, enough so that the old George would have been overwhelmed. Now he didn't even blanch when he spotted a dust bunny, which he'd always considered to be a seed of destruction and plague.

"Do you need anything?" he asked. Her husband had dressed for work in his usual well-tailored suit, silk tie, and gleaming shoes.

He looked the same—well, maybe a little harried—and sounded the same—except his voice held a note of exasperation occasionally, perfectly natural for the father of two—but he acted differently. No longer the passive man who barely lived with the rest of the family, he'd taken hold, seemed in charge.

"Help me to my feet," she said. Feeling like a Weeble—she both wobbled and occasionally fell over—she grasped his hand and struggled to stand. After a few months, she now spent most of the day out of bed, often in George's seldom-used recliner with her bootless leg elevated. She took care of herself, fixed lunch, started dinner, went to the bathroom, all that as long as she kept the cane close to lean on when she had to stand. This week, they planned to move the bed back upstairs, and she could take a bath again.

"Got to get on the road." George glanced at his wrist. Unfortunately his expensive watch had been a casualty of a conflict over chocolate versus white milk a week earlier. He looked at the wall clock, which was a little askew. After the first fifty attempts to straighten it, he'd given up and now merely tilted his head to read it. "I'll be back by six with dinner."

That evening at six o'clock exactly—of course—George pulled into the driveway.

Dinner. Ouida pushed herself to her feet, then clutched her stomach. It had been bouncing around all day. She couldn't be pregnant, could she? No, she'd had morning sickness with the others and this wasn't morning. She'd thought making love on a bed in the middle of the living room when the girls might wake up seemed risky. George found that element of danger exciting—he was not always staid.

Carol and Gretchen ran downstairs and dashed to the window to wait for their father.

"I've got dinner," he shouted as he came in.

"What did you get?" Carol jumped up and down in excitement.

"Fried artichoke hearts with furry gravy," he said.

When the girls broke into laughter, George beamed.

But the mere thought of fried artichokes with furry gravy added to the odor of what he'd really brought home and hit her hard. Her insides clenched and burned. Must be the flu that Bree had mentioned, the one that had hit all her friends. Ouida struggled to keep her insides truly inside her.

"Hi, sweetheart," George said after he put the bag on the kitchen table and came back to stand in front of Ouida. "How are you doing? You look a little pale."

At exactly that moment and before she could even turn her head or put her hand in front of her mouth or shove him away, she lost the battle.

She vomited.

Even worse, she'd thrown up on George. When she finished heaving and spewing, she opened her eyes. Still standing in front of her, he looked down. She followed his gaze.

The eruption had hit only the bottom few inches of his beautifully tailored slacks, but his shoes—oh, dear, his beloved shoes, his adored oxfords with the lovingly cared-for, formerly brilliantly shining leather—were covered with her afternoon snack. How devastating for him.

"I'm sorry," she whispered. When he didn't answer, she lifted her eyes to his face.

Stunned, that's how he looked. He'd changed a great deal, he'd become the George she'd fallen in love with and married, but even that much freer George wasn't the kind of man who appreciated being thrown up on.

Was there anyone who did? Mothers got used to it but didn't look forward to such an occurrence. She didn't know what to say, how to soothe him, so she watched him, stricken with guilt and humiliation.

At first George drew himself up very straight. His stiff neck seemed to elongate as he stared down at the wreckage of his shoes.

"I'm so sorry. I know how much you love those shoes."

Behind him, she could see the girls clutching each other's hands and, eyes wide, watching their parents, studying the mess covering their father's feet.

He lifted his eyes to her face, his expression and body relaxed. "Gretchen, get your mother a pan from the kitchen, then bring a couple of towels. Carol, get her a wet cloth and a glass of water."

Then he looked at her gently. "I'm sorry you're sick." After inspecting her hand, he took it in his. "It must be terrible to have gone through so much and, now that you're getting better, to have this happen." He took a towel from Gretchen and tossed it over the stuff on the floor. He took the rag Carol handed him and wiped Ouida's face gently. "Rinse your mouth out." He handed her the water. "Then let's get you cleaned up and in bed."

At that moment, Ouida fell in love with George even more deeply because she knew, really knew, how much he loved her. He loved her more than his dignity, his sense of smell, and those formerly gorgeous Ferragamo shoes.

❦

"How are you doing?" George greeted Adam at the front door Wednesday evening as the preacher entered the living room to see Ouida on the sofa, with a cup of coffee on the end table at her side. She wore a bright aqua top, her shiny curls bristled around her head, and she glowed.

"You're looking well." Adam settled on a chair across from her, then glanced from Ouida to her husband. They both glowed.

"Yes, well, yes," Ouida stammered. "Adam, we've worked matters out between us, and we have some news for you."

"Oh?"

"First, I'm going to hire a manager for the firm." George sat and took his wife's hand. "A manager who'll take care of the day-to-day details and give me more time to spend with the family."

"It will mean less income but we're fine," Ouida said.

"Or maybe not. Could be more help will lead to expansion," George explained. "But I don't care, as long as I can spend more time with the girls and . . . and the new one."

"The new one?"

"Yes, Preacher, that's the second bit of news. We're expecting. I'm due in seven months."

"Isn't that wonderful," Adam said sincerely.

"Not on George's schedule at all. Earlier than he'd planned."

"But I'm really happy about it." George gazed at her with deep adoration.

This looked like a George whom Adam hadn't known existed, a completely different and much more approachable George, a George in love with his wife and not ashamed to show it.

Ouida was pregnant, Adam thought as he walked back to the parsonage. It seemed almost like calving season around here. A terrible, stupid, misanthropic thought, Adam realized as soon as it hit him, but envy had overwhelmed his good humor and usual love for others.

After all his years of being a bachelor, he suddenly discovered he wanted a family just like everyone else, his friends, his neighbors. But he'd fallen in love with a woman who didn't act as if their relationship would end up in a family. She seldom allowed him to touch her, and only when she initiated it. In fact, they were more like buddies, he and Gussie. Buddies who went to movies together or met for coffee.

He wanted more, much more.

If he broke up with Gussie, he didn't have many choices of other women to bear his children.

Whoa, had he really considered breaking up with Gussie?

Yes, they'd been "together" for nearly two months, and she still refused any physical intimacy other than holding hands now and then and an occasional kiss. Last week, he'd put his arm around her shoulders and she'd allowed it for a few seconds before she subtly twisted away. He'd gotten the message.

What was wrong with him? Why had he allowed such a platonic relationship? Why had he settled?

Oh, not that he wanted to jump into bed with her. No, that was a lie. He did, but he knew it would be too soon for her and against his belief in commitment and marriage. Plus as a minister, he'd accepted that people held him to a higher moral standard. But could they start with a little cuddling and three or four kisses at a time?

They were going to meet for coffee again Monday. Of course: coffee. He'd allowed them to get into this rut where Gussie felt comfortable and he felt frustrated: coffee in Marble Falls and once in a while a movie or a date where they drove separate cars. She seemed perfectly content with this. He wasn't.

He wanted more.

Was he expecting too much too soon from a woman who'd been raped? They should discuss that, talk about the physical relationship. Would there ever be a physical relationship?

Not that he wanted to push her. He just needed to know.

He'd bring it all up Monday. Could be she wanted more, too, and was too shy to take action. He doubted that. *Gussie* and *shy* were antonyms. If her body language when they'd spent the evening with Willow and Sam had told him anything, it was that she felt comfortable with the present arrangement but the idea of anything else—well, she alternated between fear and lack of interest.

For the first time, Adam didn't look forward to seeing Gussie.

That afternoon, Adam and Gussie met at the coffee shop but decided to walk around the east side of the lake in the autumn sunshine. They chatted about their day, about the health of Gussie's parents, about church and life.

But when Adam reached to take Gussie's hand, she jumped.

Not the reaction he was hoping for. Before he could think about them, the words he'd thought all day rushed from his mouth. "I want more."

Gussie took a step back before she turned to face him. "You want more?"

"From you."

"I'm very happy with how things are," she said tersely. "Why change it? This works. And you promised not to push me."

"Gussie," he said. He paused, hoping her expression and body language would change from wary to calm and happy. When it didn't, Adam reached out to take her hand again, but she pulled it away. "That's what's wrong. Wanting to hold your hand isn't pushing. Wanting our relationship to grow isn't pushy."

"Feels that way."

"No, it's natural. It's natural for a man to want to kiss a woman he's seeing. It's also usual for her to kiss him with a modicum of enthusiasm."

"We've kissed."

He nodded. "A dozen times, when you've allowed it. I wasn't really allowed to participate as . . . umm, vigorously as I'd liked, and I felt you weren't into it."

"Whose lips were they? I was there."

He stopped himself from answering. Arguing wouldn't work, wouldn't build their relationship, but he had no idea how to explain this to her. She looked like a frightened creature, trapped. Not at all what he'd considered when he'd thought this scene through, but he should have. How could he get through to her without upsetting her?

Dear Lord, he prayed. *Please give me wisdom and courage and the right words.*

"Gussie, I don't want to argue. I'm stating a fact. Our relationship has stalled. I want more. I want to see you more often. I want to treat you like the woman I'm dating, not like my dear friend or my sister."

"Oh, so you kiss your sister on the mouth?"

He wanted to tell her that there wasn't much difference between how he and Gussie kissed and how he kissed his sister except for the part of their faces where the kisses landed. He didn't. She couldn't handle that now, and that depressed him greatly.

"What do you expect? What do you want from me?" she asked in a grim voice, as if he'd pushed her toward the guillotine.

"I want . . . I want what a man wants from a woman, when two people are in a . . ."

"I know what a man wants." She shook as she spat the words out. "I know exactly what a man wants."

"Gussie," he said patiently and clearly, "I'm not Lennie."

She took another step back.

"And I'm not attacking you."

"Feels like it."

How could he reach her? Not by doing anything that seemed threatening.

"I want a future with you, to see you more. I want to be with you more often. I care about you, and not the way a man feels toward his sister. I want to show you that. I want more."

For a moment he felt like Oliver Twist holding out his empty bowl.

"I don't have any more." She folded her arms in front of her and pulled her shoulders forward, nearly huddling.

He studied her and felt guilty. For a moment, he considered stopping, accepting what she could give. But that wasn't good, not for either of them.

To build her trust, he worded his next comment carefully. Calming words, not confrontation. "I don't agree. You have so much love and caring and faith inside you. I only ask that you share them with me, with a man who cares for you deeply."

Trapped. Gussie felt trapped. She'd never thought Adam, a man who said he cared about her, would give her an ultimatum. Not that he'd threatened anything, but she knew what he meant, what would come next. This was exactly how her previous attempts to date had ended up, only far more quickly.

This time felt worse because she'd hoped things would turn out differently. She'd prayed that Adam would be content with how she wanted to continue. Adam was a better man than the other guys. Those failures should have warned her that she hadn't healed yet, but denial ran deep.

She'd hoped Adam would stick with her while she worked her life out. But, if she hadn't done that in thirteen years, how could she ever have believed it would happen now?

"You said you wouldn't push," she repeated. Oh, stupid to say that because Adam wasn't a demanding man. Adam had been more patient than she had any right to expect. She didn't want to lose him. She'd miss the joy of picking up an email from him or meeting him for coffee, looking forward to that.

She didn't want to give up the hope that Adam could fix her.

But that evening with Willow and Sam? She never wanted to do something like that again, couldn't repeat that experience, because those hours had underlined the difference between how each couple defined *relationship*. Caring for each other deeply, displaying that affection . . . well, she couldn't do that. Not ever.

"I'm happy with how things are," she stated. "I believe our relationship has deepened and will continue to grow." She sounded like an announcer on an infomercial for a dating service. No, even worse, she sounded like a complete idiot, a frightened fool.

As her eyes caressed Adam's face, she realized that his strong, square chin didn't just make him better looking. Now it jutted out stubbornly. This was not a happy man. He was serious.

He wanted more.

"Maybe," he said slowly. "I know I'm pushing it here, but I need to know. Maybe sometime we could talk about . . . oh, I don't know, sex?"

She blinked. "How crude."

"I'm not asking for anything now. But I need to know where this is going. I've thought about marriage, but, if we do get married, I'd want a marriage in every way. Does that possibility exist in the future?"

She didn't meet his eyes.

"It's natural." He gestured at Gussie, then toward himself. "How do you think we got here? Our parents did have sex at least once or twice. I'd like to know if the idea of having a physical relationship when we get married is at all realistic."

"I don't want to even think about that."

"I know you don't, but I do. It's not a bad thing. I care for you and want more between us."

"I told you I had problems. I warned you," she stated defensively. Her normal way of reacting when pushed: Blame the other person. Really immature. She needed to learn better coping skills. She needed to listen to Adam and respond like a normal person. She was thirty-one, the rape had happened thirteen years earlier. A normal person shouldn't still be so broken she couldn't respond to a man she believed she could love, so broken she couldn't communicate with him naturally, so broken she shrank from intimacy of any kind.

"Gussie," he said, his voice soft with concern and caring. "I want to fall in love with you, but you keep me at arm's length." When she began to speak, he held up his hand. "You told me about the date rape and your distrust of men. Thank you for sharing that. But I'm not the guy who hurt you. I'm a man with normal expectations and hopes. I want to make a life with you, share a bed with you. You can trust me. After the months we've been together, you know you can trust me."

Yes, she knew that. Adam was the best man she'd ever met.

"My parents," she said. "They're getting old, not in the best health. My father hasn't been out of the hospital for so long. They supported me when I fell apart. I owe them."

"Do you owe yourself anything? Do you plan to start having a life of your own at any time? I'd like to be part of it, but I won't always be around, Gussie."

The thought of not having her parents around and Adam's having moved on tore at her, but the words that spilled from her lips weren't the ones she should say. "You're not expecting me to choose between you and my parents, are you? Because I can tell you . . ."

"Gussie." He took her hand. This time she let him. She didn't know why. But after a few seconds, his touch made her feel such tremendous longing she had to pull her hand away. He let it go.

The hope that he'd keep her hand in his and persuade her to marry him someday warred inside her brain with the idea that she couldn't do that. She just could not. Not that she could explain it, but the idea of turning her life and happiness and body over to a man, even to Adam, scared her. She might could work this out if Adam stood next to her and held her hand and forced her to face her life.

But he didn't. No, he treated her as an adult, like a thirty-one-year-old woman who should be able to make decisions herself.

Instead of doing what she wanted, even knowing Adam would never hurt her, she couldn't speak. As always, she'd chosen to passively allow her life to flow past and not to leap into it.

"Have you even thought about marriage? With me?" he asked.

"You're really going for the jugular here," she said with an awkward laugh that even she knew didn't express mirth.

"Have you?" He kept his eyes on her face.

"Umm." What a stupid thing to say. Not even a word, just a sound, but her brain seemed unable to come up with anything else. "Umm," she repeated.

He watched her for a few more seconds. "That tells me what I need to know. Let me know when you're ready for more, if you ever are." He watched her for a few more seconds. "I'm going back to get my car. Do you want to come with me?"

"Adam, please. Be patient," she whispered.

On those words, he turned away.

She swallowed hard and watched Adam walk back along the path to the sidewalk and up the street. When she lost sight of him, she knew he'd get into his ugly old car and drive off.

This didn't count as a good-bye. Impossible that their involvement with the youth of the area wouldn't throw them together. They'd see each other again, at the tubing party and other events. Maybe she should give up working with the churches and the kids to avoid ever seeing him.

No, she couldn't. Not that.

So she sat on a bench and didn't move, didn't think for five or ten more minutes.

After that, she stood and headed toward her car. Once inside, she turned the ignition, listened to the soft purr of her engine. For a moment she thought of Adam driving back to Butternut Creek in his old clunker and broke out in tears.

❦

If he could have, Adam would have wept, but he knew that wasn't macho nor particularly appropriate. He'd broken up with Gussie. It had been his decision and that gave him no right to hurt.

Not that they'd had anything to break up. Meeting for coffee, a couple of movies, and one dinner didn't exactly signify a deep, enduring passion on her part. Besides, he'd set all of them up. Gussie hadn't taken an active part or showed much interest in their being together.

But she had shared something with him she hadn't, he felt sure, shared with many others. He could understand where she was, could appreciate the knowledge she'd trusted him that much, but he couldn't fall in love alone.

To hell with deep enduring passion. They could have their love—Sam and Willow and the Kowalskis and their new babies and happy families, he thought bitterly as he pulled into the drive.

Why had he turned on his friends? He'd become a curmudgeon, a grumpy nearly twenty-seven-year-old grouch who envied people who loved each other because he didn't have that. As a minister, as a person, as a Christian, he shouldn't feel like this. No matter how frustrated and alone he felt, he couldn't stop caring about others.

"Most loving God," he whispered. "Please help me to stop feeling sorry for myself and to appreciate the lives and joys of others. Amen." He spent several minutes in meditation and hoped that would handle his negative feelings.

The question that haunted him, the one he feared even in quiet contemplation, was how he should handle the Widows. They had high expectations. They'd grilled him about meeting with Gussie. If they didn't see him making progress on the marriage front, they'd be after him, and right now he couldn't handle that covey of matchmakers. He most especially could not handle the head matchmaker.

Which meant he wouldn't say a word. Let them figure it out. He got out of the car and headed toward the porch.

"Excuse me," said an attractive blond woman who stood by the porch of the parsonage. "My son lost his backpack and someone said you might have it."

Darn Chewy.

"I'm Adam Jordan, minister at the Christian Church."

"Diane Fuller." She shook his hand.

"I'm afraid my dog gets out sometimes and brings things home." He waved toward the porch. "We try to find who they belong to, but those two had no identification."

"The red one." She ascended the steps to the porch, knelt, and unzipped it. "Yes." She nodded as she took out a notebook. "This is Paul's." Then she smiled.

A nice smile.

"It's hard being a single mother," she said. "I'm divorced," she added with a toss of her hair. "Keeping up on Paul's possessions isn't easy."

The woman was interested in him, flirting. Amazing. She wore nice slacks, a white shirt, and black heels. All in all, Diane Fuller looked like a nice person, a pretty woman, but he felt nothing for her. Had the weeks of frustration with Gussie leached all the interest and optimism from him?

No, he didn't think so. Maybe he was just a little tired now.

He could only hope Miss Birdie didn't find out about this woman, ever.

"I'm sure it is." He paused before he asked, "Do you and your son have a church home?"

❦

By the time she reached Roundville, Gussie had stopped crying. After pulling into the driveway, she flipped open a compact and glanced at herself in the mirror. Her eyes weren't too red, but she'd better fluff a little powder on her nose.

There. No one would guess how she felt.

As soon as Gussie entered the living room, her mother asked, "What's wrong, dear?"

How did she always know? Well, today Gussie must look wrung out and red-eyed.

"Nothing, Mom. I'm a little tired."

If Gussie had thought she could go around the living room and into the hallway without saying more, she was wrong. After all these years, she should know her mother wouldn't allow that.

"Come, sit down and talk to me."

Her mother's soft, sweet tone covered a determination Gussie could admire and fear but never ignore. If she did, her mother would follow her all over the house. Into the yard. Once she'd even stood behind Gussie's car when her daughter had attempted to leave without answering all of her questions.

She sighed and entered the living room for a debriefing. Might as well get it over with. She sat in the chair across from her mother. "Where's Dad?"

"He's taking a nap again. Can't seem to get his strength back." She knitted a few more stitches before she asked, "How's Adam?"

"He's fine." Gussie counted to five—quickly—before she stood and attempted to escape. "I'm going to look in on Dad."

"No, no." Her mother waved Gussie back into the chair. "I did that just before you got here. He was sleeping." She waited until Gussie sat. "Is everything okay between you two?"

Gussie closed her eyes and attempted to come up with an answer that would satisfy her mother, not that any existed.

"Oh, dear, he's not your young man any longer. I had such hopes for the two of you."

"No, Mother, he's not my young man."

"What happened?"

"Nothing." Gussie kept an eye on her mother, attempting to read her expression. "We weren't moving forward so we decided not to see each other again."

"Aah. Very civilized and mature."

Gussie nodded.

Her mother nodded. "Well, why don't you go look in on your father. Dinner's in the oven. I'll dish it out when he wakes up."

Gussie knew better than to think she'd fooled her mother about anything. Fortunately, she was too sweet to pry.

❧

Gussie hadn't looked forward to the tubing on the Guadalupe River. It was late September and the water held a little chill, but they got a cut rate that fit the budget. Even worse than the cold water, she'd see Adam.

Mature and civilized, she repeated to herself. Mentally, that worked, at least until the first time she spotted him. She repeated the mantra, but the words did not calm her, not a bit.

He should not be allowed to wear a sleeveless T-shirt and swim trunks. Oh, the trunks were the long, floppy kind and the shirt certainly didn't display a gratuitous amount of his body, but he still looked good. She had to make an effort not to hyperventilate. But what hurt most was what was inside the man. He was a good person who cared about her.

She had only herself to blame for being too much of a coward to accept what Adam had offered. She should talk to him, greet him, tell him how good it was to see him. Instead, she shouted, "Hey, Adam," waved, and kicked away in the other direction.

Gutless, spineless coward.

❧

The sun beat down on the tubers, hundreds of them from all over Central Texas mingling with their group of three dozen. A great day to be on the river, and possibly the last Saturday warm enough. Adam glanced at Janey, who floated along a few feet from him, drinking a root beer and humming.

Farther away, he heard Gussie's laugh float across the water. Six or seven of the youths twirled her tube around in circles.

He really loved her laugh.

"Hey, guys, you're making me dizzy. Stop!" she shouted.

With a grin which quickly changed to a frown when he realized this was as close as he'd get to her again, he watched for another minute. She waved. He waved back.

"Hey, Janey." Mac floated up next to them. "Having fun?" At Janey's nod, Mac continued, "Gussie's great, isn't she, Adam?"

He hoped she couldn't read his expression through his dark glasses, the zinc oxide on his nose, and the shadow of his University of Louisville cap.

"Yeah. Great," he agreed. He turned his head to search for Hector and found him kicking his tube beside Bree. That romance seemed to be chugging right along. As usual, Bobby flirted with several girls.

Adam hoped Mac would float away during the time he scrutinized the crowd, identifying and mentally counting the number of young people he'd brought from Butternut Creek.

"You can't ignore me," Mac said from a few feet away.

"Yes, I can." Adam grabbed Janey's tube and kicked hard. "We're going to float around and see how everyone's doing." Could he escape from Mac? Probably not.

After he'd maneuvered the two tubes across half the river, he could hear Mac behind him.

"Don't forget. I'm a runner. Strong legs," she shouted. "Slow down. I need to ask you something and you don't want me to shout it across the water."

With that threat, he paddled back toward the pillar's granddaughter, pulling Janey along with him. Genes ran true. She'd never give up.

"Why aren't you and Gussie floating down the river together?"

she asked once they were within two feet of each other. "Making goo-goo eyes?"

"In answer to the second question, I've never made goo-goo eyes at anyone in my entire life." He ignored the first point. Make Mac ask again.

"Why aren't you and Gussie together?"

The kid never gave up. A true MacDowell.

"We adults have to watch all of you from different places, to keep you safe." To show how seriously he accepted that responsibility, he paddled his tube around to scan the group. "I'd hate to get home and have to explain to your grandmother why only Bree made it back to Butternut Creek."

He could feel Mac's eyes on the back of his head but didn't want to actually face her. He bet she could have read his expression even if he covered it with an iron mask.

"The water's pretty low. Hope no one gets stuck under the bridge," he stated.

"You're not going to answer," she stated right back.

He kept his hold on Janey's tube and kicked away with legs that had played basketball for years. She'd never catch up.

"I'm going to tell Grandma," she threatened as he retreated.

"Go ahead," he said. Might as well get it over with. Miss Birdie and the Widows should know they'd failed and would have to start all over again. He could only hope that humiliation would make them stop looking for a wife for him.

Oh, sure. As if the Widows didn't enjoy humiliation, especially that of their minister.

❦

A few hours later, the flotilla had nearly arrived at the dock where they'd get out of the river, give up their tubes, and get in a bus to shuttle back to the departure point.

Gussie gave a deep sigh of relief. She'd survived. They'd get back to the cars and vans and head out and she wouldn't have to see Adam for months. Surely by that time, she wouldn't lust after him.

Except, of course, everyone—except Gussie and, she imagined, Adam—wanted to gather at the barbecue place on the frontage road for a last meal together, as if they hadn't spent nearly four hours in a river together. She couldn't get out of it without making a fuss, because tradition demanded that meal.

Fortunately, Adam and a bunch of kids had found a booth on the far side of the restaurant and Gussie had shoved her bunch toward the other side, where she sat with her back to him.

Once they'd settled, Gussie discovered that Mac had joined their group. No surprise. The kids pretty much intermingled.

Between ordering and the arrival of their meals, Mac leaned toward Gussie. "Have you heard," the junior matchmaker said, "about the new single woman in town who Grandma wants to fix up with Pastor Adam?"

"How interesting," Gussie said.

"Blond, professional woman. Smart, pretty."

"None of my business."

It wasn't, Gussie reiterated once she arrived back in Roundville and dropped the kids off at their homes. It had been a week since Adam had demanded more from her than she could give. Now he'd moved on.

No, Mac had said the Widows had found a new match for him. Not his fault. The Widows never gave up. Indefatigable in their efforts, unrelenting in their actions, unflagging in devotion to their cause, and inexorable. The Widows would find Adam a mate if they had to import her from Maine. It wouldn't be Gussie.

She felt implausibly sad. Why should she feel sad when she'd turned down what he'd offered? Of course, she still had her parents and the church and her business. They'd made her happy for years. Why wasn't that enough?

Maybe because she hadn't been happy all those years? Merely content or comfortable or only okay but not really happy?

Click went her brain as that idea slipped into place. She'd been treading water all these years. Yes, she'd accomplished stuff. A university diploma and a successful business. But she hadn't moved on. Stuck in the same place for thirteen years and fooling herself into believing she'd achieved her goals and dreams.

Chapter Fourteen

Mac tells me you and Gussie Milton are no longer . . ." Miss Birdie paused to search for the word. "An item," she finished.

Adam wondered why it had taken so long for the Widows to descend on him. He figured they'd have ambushed him after church last week or the previous day. He guessed Mac hadn't squealed on him until the end of the week. Yesterday the pillar had glared at him when she filed out of the sanctuary but hadn't said a word. Probably had needed a powwow.

He could only be thankful he'd had all this time to prepare.

"Come in, ladies." He stood and waved toward the four chairs in front of his desk. He'd warned Maggie when she got in that they'd show up. He'd known they wouldn't arrive until after ten with the work schedules of Mercedes and Miss Birdie, but he knew they'd come.

Once they'd settled in their usual places, Adam sat down and asked, "How are you doing today? Busy at the diner, Miss Birdie?"

"Pfutt," she said, a sound he hadn't discovered the exact meaning for. "Don't change the subject."

"I didn't realize we'd chosen a subject of the conversation yet," he said with a pleasant smile.

"You and Gussie Milton."

"Now, now, Bird." Mercedes patted her friend's arm. "We can certainly take time for pleasantries."

"Good morning, Pastor," Blossom said, then sat forward in the chair and leaned toward him with a sweet sympathetic expression. "How are you doing?"

Darn, he could stand Miss Birdie's pushiness but Blossom's sympathy about killed him.

"Fine, thank you." He turned toward Winnie. "How are you and the general?"

"Don't try to change the subject," Miss Birdie said. "You know when you mention the general, she'll talk about him forever. Crazy about the man. Hardly thinks about anything else. Maudlin."

"I don't know if that's the word you want," Mercedes said. She stopped speaking when Miss Birdie glared at her and substituted, "Yes, Pastor, Mac mentioned that you and Gussie were no longer seeing each other."

"We have never seen a great deal of each other," he said. "She and I met for coffee or for a movie but there was no great romance."

"You two went to Austin with Sam and Willow," Winnie said.

"Yes, a very nice evening spent with friends."

After that statement, he folded his hands and watched them calmly. Miss Birdie blanched. Winnie narrowed her eyes and scrutinized him. Mercedes tilted her head as if wondering what to do next. Blossom, as usual, didn't seem quite sure what had happened.

"With friends?" Blossom asked him, then turned toward the pillar. "Weren't they supposed to be more than friends? Didn't we hope they'd get married?"

"Yes, we did," Miss Birdie snapped. "I for one am very disappointed."

"I am, too," Blossom agreed.

The remaining Widows didn't seem to have anything to add but nodded in enthusiastic agreement.

Still Adam sat at the desk, hands folded and mouth closed, until the cluster of disappointed Widows stood, nodded, and left.

For a moment he felt flush with victory. The Widows had come but they hadn't conquered him. He'd learned to handle them and felt strong and certain. For a moment.

Then he felt a sense of loss. Conquering the Widows didn't give him nearly the elation he'd always thought it would. In fact, victory felt a little flat. Playing with them was more fun. Having them attempt to find his wife, well, when the choice had been Gussie, he'd really rooted for them.

Besides, he had no idea what they might do next, and he didn't feel nearly as confident about facing the unknown.

❧

"What do we do next?" Mercedes asked as they stood in the parking lot.

"A disappointing development," Winnie said.

"Very disappointing," Blossom agreed.

"We're going to have to start all over." Birdie sighed. "And I don't know how." She shook her head. "I thought they were perfect for each other."

"Perfect." Blossom shook her head in time with Birdie.

"Maybe Gussie doesn't want to get married," Mercedes added. "She's over thirty and still single. Could be she wasn't as perfect as we'd hoped. Could have baggage."

"Could be her parents," Blossom said. "I cared for my in-laws for years."

The four considered that.

"Did anyone see that blond woman with her son in church Sunday?" Winnie broke in on the contemplation. "Let's check on her. I can get her name from Maggie if the woman signed the friendship register. I'll visit her and see what I can find out, welcome her to the community and ask her to come back to church."

Bossiest woman Birdie had ever met, but a good plan nonetheless. They all agreed and put Winnie in charge of that investigation before they left.

❦

"Reverend Jordan, this is Mariah Wilson calling from the elementary school. I'm the counselor here."

What had happened? "Is Janey all right?" he asked.

"Oh, yes, although we do have a concern."

He waited.

"Her teacher has noted that Janey struggles with her work although she seems like a bright little girl."

"I've noticed that."

"I wanted to make sure everything was okay at home."

"Yes, Janey seems to be settling in well, but it is an adjustment. I'll talk to her," he said.

The kids' schedule made life and discussions difficult. Janey always arrived home by four and started homework at the kitchen table. They ate late, after Hector got home from practice, then she took everything up to her room to work at her desk. She had no time to watch even thirty minutes of a television show. When the season started, they'd go to all Hector's games together, but for the most part Janey studied.

After dinner, as they cleaned up the dishes, Adam said, "I need to talk to you guys."

"Pops, I've got a big American history test tomorrow and I'm on KP tonight."

"I know." He'd listed all their tests on a calendar in the kitchen. "But this is important. Sit down. I'll take care of the dishes when we're through."

Once they'd cleared and wiped the table, they sat down.

"Janey, I received a call from Mrs. Wilson at your school today." He paused to consider how to phrase this without upsetting her. "How are your studies going?"

"Okay." She dropped her eyes.

"Are you having any difficulties?"

When she didn't answer, Hector took over. "Janey, you've always had to work really hard in school. I've noticed you study all the time but your grades still aren't good."

Tears rolled down Janey's cheeks. "I try."

Adam handed her a Kleenex. "You aren't in trouble. We know you're smart. We know how hard you work."

"B-b-but, no matter how hard I try." She stopped and wiped her eyes. "No matter how I try, I can't do as well as my friends. I don't know why. I feel stupid."

"Janey." Adam took her hand. "You aren't stupid. Your brother and I know that."

"But Amy and Cassandra always get perfect spelling papers and their tests are put on the bulletin board. Mine never are."

Adam had seen her spelling tests, the letters uneven and red marks all over.

She looked at both men. "I don't want to be different. I don't want to have special classes in a special room."

Hector said, "Janey, you're smart. I know that." He pointed back at Adam. "Pops knows that. But you spend so much time studying, hours longer than I do. Do you like to spend every minute studying?"

"No-o-o." Her voice quivered. "I'm tired of studying all the time."

Adam watched the Firestones and felt guilty. He should have noticed this. He should have gone to the school about Janey's grades and her efforts.

"Hey." Adam knelt next to her, balancing on one knee, to look into her eyes. "It's going to be okay, really. We'll talk to your teacher and the counselor and see how we can help you. Hector and I and all the people at church will make sure you're fine." He put his hand on her shoulder. "We love you and want the best for you. Do you understand that?"

Janey nodded, then slid out of the chair and onto Adam's knee. She put her arms around his neck and leaned against him. She felt warm and trusting. A wave of emotion and gratitude nearly over-whelmed him.

"I'm sorry I didn't notice earlier. I don't know much about little girls."

Janey hugged him more tightly, and Hector put his hand on Adam's shoulder.

"Most loving God," Adam prayed. "Thank you for the Firestone children. They have blessed my life so richly."

"Hey, Pops, stop or you're going to make me cry, and players don't cry."

As she walked home from the diner, Birdie glanced at the sky. Getting cloudy. Forecast said rain, not good weather for homecoming. She got to the front of her house and stared at it. She'd have to paint it soon but where would the money come from? Maybe she could hire Hector. And the Adirondack chairs, the ones Elmer had made so they could sit on the porch and wave to their neighbors, needed a coat of stain.

After Elmer passed when the girls were young, Birdie'd spent a lot of time out here, praying for strength to get through the next day. With the girls' activities, she didn't have time now.

Two chairs. No one to sit in Elmer's and she never sat in the other. Maybe she should give one away. Could be she should find someone to sit in the other.

Should she encourage Farley a little?

Ptsh. She was too old for romance.

But a little companionship, that would be nice.

In Kentucky, the rain usually pattered down. Sometimes it pelted but usually it pattered gently for hours or days or, in February, weeks.

Texas rain also pattered and pelted, but many times it came down in one huge mass. At times, it seemed as if the clouds gave up on sending the drops down one by one and, as if worn out, they dropped the whole cloudful of water at once. It looked and felt as if a pail had been turned over on the Hill Country, over land too hard and dry to absorb it all.

Not that this fit any scientific explanation of rain, but it worked for Adam.

"Surely they aren't going to play in this weather, are they?" Adam asked Miss Birdie. The high school football game—the homecoming game followed by the dance—was scheduled for that night. He'd ducked into the diner when the storm started and decided to stay for lunch.

"Not if there's lightning in the area, but this doesn't look like a thunderstorm." She placed his order in front of him: a chicken salad sandwich and Coke. Then she surrounded that with a basket of more fries than he could consume in a week, a huge dish of fried apples, and a piece of cherry pie with two dips of ice cream.

"Now that you're putting on some weight, we can't let you get skinny again," she explained. Then she stood back. "A little rain never hurt anyone. The players wear special cleats and such."

"But the band doesn't march in this weather, does it?" He took a bite of the sandwich.

She stared back at him as if he were speaking classical Greek. "Why wouldn't they?" she asked, her tone scathing.

He finished chewing. "Because the field will be muddy?"

"So?" She put her fists on her hips. "We aren't some namby-pamby Kentuckians. We're Texans. What would have happened at the Alamo if Jim Bowie had decided the weather was too cold or rough or rainy to defend liberty?"

Adam thought he remembered that the siege of the Alamo hadn't been about defending liberty but stealing land, but he didn't respond. Nor did he mention that Jim Bowie had a lot of Mexicans shooting at him and had little choice whereas the students didn't really *have* to march down a slippery field. The pillar probably thought they, as Texans, did have to.

"And the area band contest is next week. Our kids placed in the top group in the region and will move on to state if they do well. They need the practice." She turned and strode away, still angry, Adam thought, that he'd questioned the fortitude of Texas youth.

If anyone was more fanatic than a football coach, it was the band director and the grandmother of one of the band members.

"And," she proclaimed from halfway across the restaurant. "If you want fields of bluebonnets in the spring, you'd better welcome rain in the fall and winter."

With that, the other diners turned to glare at him, which made Adam feel as if the whole town would blame him for a drought and the death of wildflowers should the rain stop.

That evening, he watched the players sliding and falling on the field. Adam settled in to watch a game of mud ball, glad he'd worn a sweatshirt and jacket under the waterproof poncho. "Are you all right?" he asked Janey. She had demanded to come because Bobby played on defense.

She nodded.

"Tell me if you get cold." Before they'd left, Hector had bundled his sister in several layers, then turned to Adam and said, "Pops, I'll be home from the dance late. Don't wait up for me. Makes me feel like a kid to have to check in."

"I don't wait up because I don't trust you," Adam said. "I wait up because I want to make sure you're home. Can't sleep if I don't know that."

"Aah, that's nice." With a grin, Hector had loped off to watch Bree play volleyball.

At halftime, the band slipped all over the field, tripping on the ruts dug out during the first half, but they kept playing the program. That impressed Adam. He had no idea how one controlled a trombone or tuba while falling down, but the musicians did with only a few missed notes.

The members of the dance team, wearing their cowgirl outfits, finished the performance covered with splattered mud but with huge smiles.

Despite the slips and falls and pitchy notes, the crowd cheered every second of the performance. These kids belonged to Butternut Creek. As the students marched off the field, everyone on the home side of the stadium stood and pulled their arms from their plastic coverings to clap and cheer proudly.

That night, to keep Hector from feeling like a kid, Adam pretended to be asleep when he came home.

Didn't fool Hector. He came into the bedroom and sat on the side of the bed to scratch Chewy's ears. "Had a good time. Pop, you can go to sleep now. I'm home."

❦

As the fall grew closer to winter, leaves changed, at least the little bit they changed in Texas. Most of the green leaves stayed the same. Some of them turned a bright red, but the rest looked as if they'd rusted.

With basketball practice starting, Hector and Adam didn't get much time to play ball together, but a lot of kids in the neighborhood used the hoop in the parking lot. Adam joined occasionally and considered those contests good for the relationship of the church with its neighbors.

He and Janey rode the family-of-the-team buses to Hector's out-of-town games in Bandera and even as far as Dripping Springs. Hector's play had improved so much, Adam knew he could no longer challenge him. Not that he'd confess that to the kid. Bobby, a feisty and intelligent point guard, attracted scouts as well. The team looked great, well coached and intense.

"We're going to have a great year," Adam emailed his sister, attaching a picture of Hector going up for a rebound that had been in the newspaper.

The next day, Hannah wrote back, "What's the matter?"

He sent an email about another win, the coach, and Hector's improvement playing point forward.

"I don't care about the coach."

Adam reread those words. Hannah had never been a fan of athletes, but she sounded angry and mean. Probably under a lot of stress. He wished he could help her.

He read on. "I don't really care about basketball unless you're playing. I do care about Hector and hope to meet him and Janey someday, but what's wrong with you?"

He wrote back, "Leave me alone."

She answered, "Okay, now I'm really worried. What's wrong?"

He solved her persistence by not answering. Nothing she could do from Kenya.

Wrong. Hannah wrote their mother, who emailed, "Your sister tells me there's something wrong. What?"

He couldn't ignore his mother. Well, he could, but it was useless. She could challenge the Widows for the title of most relentless. However, she also knew when to shut up, a skill the Widows and his sister should learn.

"I don't want to talk about it," he wrote back and copied it to his sister. "Leave me alone."

Both did.

❦

"I don't think that new blond woman is going to work," Winnie said. "She's not minister's wife material. Entirely too worldly and here for only six months while her bank opens a branch down on Highway 29."

"Only six months?" Birdie asked. "The preacher can't work that fast."

"Where does that leave us?" Blossom asked. "Where can we find another single woman?"

"We should send out a message to the churches in the area, see if they have any single women who might be interested in a minister,"

Winnie suggested. "Send it to the president of their women's group and ask for suggestions."

"Winnie, will you be in charge of that?" Birdie asked, to regain control. Then she looked at each woman. "What ideas do you have to help us find a wife for the preacher?"

"We tried Reverend Patillo, but that didn't work out."

"Oh? The Presbyterian minister?" Blossom asked. "What happened?"

"Nothing." Birdie snorted. "Absolutely nothing."

"That was the problem," Mercedes added.

"Then Bird recognized that if Pastor Adam and Reverend Patillo got married, the children might all attend the Presbyterian Church with their mother. Might could live in the manse instead of the parsonage."

"Oh, dear, no." Blossom gasped. "That would ruin everything. We need their children at the Christian Church."

"Exactly," Birdie said. "So we have to come up with something to keep those children in our church."

Each took another sip of coffee. "I could check with my neighbors about their daughters or nieces," Blossom volunteered.

"Most important, we have to find him a wife everyone will like and will make the preacher happy," Winnie said.

"My sister in Abilene has a daughter." Immediately after Blossom said the words, she shut her mouth firmly and puckered her lips as if maybe, if she just sat silently, everyone would forget what she'd said.

"Well?" Birdie asked.

"I forgot, she's a nun. But they would share a common interest in theology and churches."

"Don't need a celibate woman for the preacher," Birdie said. Good thing Blossom had other good attributes like having a very good cook and knowing just how to entertain, because nothing she said ever contributed to the discussion.

"I'm concerned." Mercedes looked around the group. "I don't see anyone better for Pastor Adam than Gussie Milton. I really don't."

The others murmured agreement.

"I think Gussie's the one. We should do everything we can to bring them back together," Mercedes said. "That has to be our goal."

After a moment of silence, Blossom suggested, "We could invite them for dinner at my house."

"Might not be a bad idea," Birdie said as she nodded at Mercedes.

❧

As soon as Adam hung up, he leaned back in his chair and stared out the window.

What do the Widows have in mind?

When Blossom called to invite him to a little get-together at her home, suspicion filled him. It had the fingerprints of the matchmakers all over it.

And yet it could be nothing more than a thoughtful invitation from Blossom, a dinner party for him and a few others. She hadn't specified who else would join them, and he was too polite to ask. The words *Are the other Widows going to be there?* had trembled on his lips, but he'd swallowed them.

He had to warn Gussie. He didn't want her to be embarrassed and he couldn't face her again, not with the Widows clucking around and matchmaking. Of course, if they hadn't invited Gussie, the email would seem strange. But if they had, she'd appreciate the warning.

Maybe they'd invited another woman, in which case he'd have to go and act polite. Maybe they'd dug up a woman who fit him. Maybe they hadn't. Regardless, he couldn't turn down an invitation from a church member no matter how suspicious it sounded. He looked forward to getting to know Blossom and eating the wonderful dinner he knew her cook would prepare.

Just in case the invitation came from the Widows' usual motive, he wrote a quick email to Gussie and sent it. Later that evening, he received a message from her.

"Thanks for the heads-up. The invitation was on my computer when I got home. I declined. They never give up, do they?"

No, they didn't, but now he could look forward to a great meal and chagrined Widows.

Chapter Fifteen

Gussie couldn't sleep. Every night, she tossed and turned and found herself staring at the ceiling at three o'clock, knowing she'd have to get up in a few hours. In an effort to gain a little rest, she breathed in and out, deeply, and recited the Lord's Prayer. After thirty minutes, she felt closer to the Lord but even farther from sleep.

After a few days during which she dozed during slow periods at work, Gussie set a pattern to soothe her to sleep. It started with a long, hot bath, after which her skin was so wrinkled she felt like a shar-pei puppy. After that, she listened to relaxation CDs. She followed all the instructions, but no matter how long she stayed in the tub or how far she descended on the fantasy elevator or how warm and relaxed she felt lying in the imaginary sunshine of the flower-covered meadow, she could not make the final descent into deep, restful slumber.

On the advice of friends, she drank warm milk, chamomile tea— not on the same evening—put a lavender sachet under her pillow, and ate a graham cracker. None worked. She refused to try feng shui because she could not believe having the bottoms of her feet face the door would help in the least.

Finally, she dug through the drawer where she tossed stuff and pulled out a little machine that played various soothing sounds. She'd never found sounds of the forest relaxing because the birds tweeted so loudly. Her father had ruined sounds of the sea, telling her he could hear calls for help from far away. The sound of rain made her have to get up and go to the bathroom, hardly conducive to deep sleep, and thunderstorms woke her up. She chose the soothing babbling stream. After replacing the batteries, she placed it on her bedside table, turned it on, relaxed in bed, closing her eyes and, again, breathing deeply and rhythmically.

Five minutes later, she'd fallen into a deep slumber.

When she woke up in the morning two hours later, she realized she spent far too much time preparing herself for a few hours of sleep. She needed to do something different. She needed help, and she really needed sleep.

❦

If there was anyone Gussie did not want to see that afternoon, it was Clare.

Actually, she had a list of people she would prefer not to see. It included many citizens of Butternut Creek, but Clare's name appeared at the top.

And yet Clare's huge black SUV sat in the parking lot of her studio. She was just too tired to have this conversation and yearned to drive off without stopping at the studio, but she couldn't. She had a disk filled with photos she had to download and print. Besides, she hadn't seen her best friend in such a long time.

Several times Gussie had emailed Clare that, although she and Adam had split, she was fine. Clare knew her too well to believe it. Then, in her most recent email, Gussie had foolishly mentioned the invitation from the Widows for their matchmaking dinner and Adam's warning. When she confessed she'd turned down the invitation, Clare had called her immediately. Gussie'd allowed the machine to pick up. But Clare would never give up, even if she had to show up in person towing all three children with her. When she heard honking behind her and realized she held up a line of traffic, Gussie turned into the lot and parked. Once inside, she saw Clare holding her youngest, Ashley. She knew she couldn't hold her friend at arm's length. She could not resist mother and baby. Clare had pulled out every weapon she had. How unfair.

Gussie hardened her heart—one last effort to escape Clare's loving insistence. Then Ashley gurgled.

Darn it!

"Okay," Gussie said, giving in. "Let me have the baby. Come into my office and we can talk. I don't have any more appointments today." She waved to Justine behind the reception desk. "Go on home. I'll close up."

Once they'd each grabbed a bottle of water from the fridge, Gussie and Clare settled in the two comfortable chairs and Gussie cuddled Ashley. Clare didn't bother with how long it had been and how good it was to see her, or with giving an update on her other two kids. No, she got straight to the point, as usual.

"Gus, do you love Adam?"

Gussie looked down at Ashley, who was waving her little fists in her honorary aunt's face and making baby noises.

"Gus." Clare's voice sharpened. "You know I am genetically incapable of staying out of the lives of people I love. You know I won't go away."

The two sat in silence for nearly a minute before Clare said, "But I will leave you alone. Because I love you so much, I will fight my instinct to pry into your personal life. All you have to do is tell me to leave."

"Yes, I think I love Adam," Gussie mumbled.

"Does he love you?"

"I don't know." Gussie shrugged. "He said he wanted to. I think that meant maybe he does."

"He's a minister," Clare said. "Don't you think he usually tells the truth?"

"Probably."

"Okay, let's try this again." Clare slid her chair over the laminate flooring closer to her friend. "Do you think Adam loves you?"

Gussie swallowed hard. "Yes."

"Why aren't you together?"

"You make it sound so simple. Sometimes love isn't enough."

"Gus, don't intellectualize. Talk to me."

She looked at Clare's expression of love and concern. "I don't know. I'd really thought I was okay, that I'd gotten over the rape and gotten back my life, until I met Adam. I was functioning, at least." She would've held a hand up to keep Clare from interrupting but both were full of baby. Instead she glared. "Yes, you mentioned, often, that you saw signs, like the guys I'd date for a month and break up with, but I didn't realize that.

"I don't think things will work out with Adam. I can't be with him right now the way he wants, and it's not fair for me to ask him to wait when I don't know if . . ."

Clare watched sympathetically.

"But still, I know I need to do something. I just don't know what yet. When I've worked things out—or even if I haven't—I'll get in touch with you. I promise."

Clare stood and moved toward Gussie to lean down and hug her. "I love you. And you know, no matter what happens with Adam, you need to do this for you."

"I know. I'm lucky to have you as a friend. Most of the time."

"And don't you forget that."

❦

"Nothing has worked." Birdie felt like crying. Never had she faced such a failure. She glanced around at the Widows gathered at the diner to discuss the crisis.

"It was a setback, but we haven't tried that much." Winnie spoke up—as usual. "We had that dinner without Gussie, but what else could we have done?"

"I don't know what to do next," Mercedes said. "We can't give up. If we do, we'll lose one of our core tenets."

"We could wait until another single woman moves into the area," Blossom suggested.

"Not likely." Winnie shook her head disconsolately. "The economy and the attractions of Austin draw young people to the big city."

"But wasn't the dinner party nice?" Blossom asked. "Even if only the preacher and the three of you showed up. I had a nice time."

No use explaining to the woman that the purpose hadn't been to chat with the preacher.

"Mac and Bree tell me that Gussie is set on taking care of her parents," Birdie explained. "Seems she's very devoted to them."

"Do you think maybe she won't or can't commit to the preacher because of them?" Winnie asked.

"My, my," Blossom said. "That does make sense."

"What do we do about it?" Mercedes asked. "Other than taking dinner down to Roundville and dragging the preacher along, I don't see a solution."

"Tea," Blossom said.

The other three turned to stare at her.

"We could take tea to them." She batted her eyes. "To Gussie's parents and talk to them about the situation. A polite chat over tea."

Who'd've believed it? Blossom had come up with another good idea.

"You're right," Mercedes said. "Surely they'd be interested in what's going on."

Winnie pulled her ever-present notebook and pen from her bag. "All right, let's brainstorm."

Within ten minutes, the Widows had a plan and a purpose and renewed dedication. Gussie Milton and the preacher would get married if the Widows had to follow them down the aisle with pitchforks.

❦

"Pops, you know the Widows aren't going to give up on you," Hector said as he cleared the table. "Bree told me that."

Great.

"Not going to give up on you and Gussie," he clarified, though Adam knew what he'd meant. "Bree says they thought about that blond lady but didn't think she was right for you."

Good news.

"As far as we can tell, whatever they have planned will take place sometime soon, maybe this week."

"They have *plans*?" Oh, please, no. Their ideas always meant inexorable determination on their part and deep humiliation on his. "What do they have in mind?"

"Don't know. Miss Birdie didn't tell her. Bree could tell *something* was going on because the Widows have been so secretive and she heard your name mentioned when her grandmother took a phone call." Hector rinsed a place off. "Your name and Gussie's."

Adam felt as frustrated as if he were on the deck of the *Titanic*, watching the ship approach the icebergs while he shouted, "Danger ahead!" Nothing he could do would stop or delay the impending and inevitable catastrophe.

The situation required constant vigilance. He could almost feel the ice floe forming around him, but he had no idea where the flood of destruction would come from.

He waited for the tide to submerge him.

Lots of water images and none of them worked together. He didn't care. He was a scared man, not a poet.

Despite his certainty the Widows would act soon, he heard nothing. Two days, then a week. Nothing happened. The Widows didn't converge on him. He heard nothing from Gussie. Good news that she didn't have anything to report on the Widows. Bad news that he didn't hear anything from Gussie about herself.

Still, he waited fearfully.

And hopefully.

❦

On Friday, the Widows met at the church to go to Roundville. They'd use Blossom's big, luxurious car that made them feel like they were riding in a softly upholstered cocoon.

"But you're not driving," Birdie told Blossom when they all arrived in the parking lot. "When you carried me home from the diner the other day, I thought you were going to kill me." She reached for the keys as she explained to Mercedes and Winnie. "I swan, she drives so fast and talks the entire way and fiddles with the radio and the air-conditioning, weaving all over the road. Thought we were going to run over every dog and cat on the way. Old Jacob Russell was pushing his walker across the street and nearly had a stroke. Poor man was shuffling as fast as he could."

Without a murmur of protest, Blossom handed the keys over and they all piled in, Mercedes in the passenger seat with Winnie.

Winnie got her notebook out and flipped it open. "Let's make sure we've checked everything off." For the next hour, the Widows chatted about the plan.

When the car arrived in Roundville, Mercedes said, "Slow down, Bird. I know how to get there."

"Don't show off. I do, too. We used to come here all the time when Gussie's mother was in charge of women's programs for the district."

The two argued about which road to take and which direction to turn until, somehow, they arrived at the Miltons' home. All four got out. Blossom took the keys to her car, popped the trunk, took out several huge tote bags, and they all marched up the walk.

Before they could ring the bell, the door flew open.

"My, my, my." Yvonne smiled at the women in front of her. "Birdie MacDowell and Mercedes Rivera, how wonderful to see you. It's been years."

"Hello, Yvonne," Mercedes said. "These are our friends from Butternut Creek, Winnie Jenkins and Blossom Brown, also members of the Christian Church."

"I'm Yvonne Milton. Please, come in." She stepped aside and motioned the four inside. "What's the occasion?"

"Oh, we were just in the neighborhood and thought we'd drop by," Birdie explained.

Yvonne studied their expressions closely. Roundville, ten miles from the main highway on a winding two-lane road, wasn't a place one visited on a whim. Too polite to point that out, Yvonne led them into the living room, where Henry read the newspaper in his recliner.

"Don't get up," Birdie commanded.

Because Henry knew her well and understood equally as well the futility of disobeying her, he relaxed back in the chair.

"Sit down, please." Yvonne motioned toward the love seats and took a chair. The six sat quietly and nodded toward one another for nearly a minute because—how could the Widows not have considered this?—after all their meticulous planning, they'd forgotten one thing. They hadn't decided who would open the conversation and what the chosen Widow would say.

Birdie glanced around. Not one of the Widows looked as if she would say anything. It was up to Birdie. Mercedes and Blossom were too gracious to push ahead and Winnie—well, that woman might say the wrong thing. In a tough situation, the leader had to take over.

"Your daughter won't marry our preacher because she has to stay here and take care of you." There. The problem was out in the open.

"What?" Yvonne sat up straight and glared at Birdie.

Henry lowered the footrest on his chair, stood, and strode toward Birdie. Standing only inches away, he demanded, "What gives you the right to say that? Yvonne and I would never come between our daughter and happiness."

"Birdie MacDowell," Yvonne said. The words coming from her mouth sounded as if they had brilliant vocal flames surrounding them. "You've gone too far this time."

Birdie blinked. She'd never seen either Milton angry.

"What Birdie means to say," Winnie began.

The Miltons turned toward Winnie as one and glared.

"Who are you?" Yvonne asked in a tone that successfully shut the bossy woman up.

"I'm sorry," Winnie whispered.

Henry simply glowered at the assembled Widows.

"You need to allow your daughter to make her choice, to get married if she wants to. Our minister . . ." Birdie stopped speaking and actually cowered. Never before had she cowered, but the look on Henry's face frightened her. For a moment she considered that, perhaps, she hadn't used the most judicious words. No, she'd spoken the truth. The Miltons had overreacted.

"You don't think we love our daughter?" Henry thundered.

"Now, now, now." Blossom spoke in a gentle, calm voice and held up her hand. She stood and approached Henry with more courage than Birdie could have mustered. "I think we have a slight misunderstanding."

"Misunderstanding?" Henry exploded. "That woman—" He pointed at Birdie, his hand shaking. "That woman told us we have kept our daughter from happiness."

"I don't believe she meant it exactly like that."

Yes, Birdie had, but she hadn't expected Henry's reaction. Not that she shouldn't have. If anyone had said that to her about Bree or Mac, she'd deck 'em. Birdie sat back, vanquished and annoyed because she had to allow Blossom Brown to rescue her, their mission, and the happiness of the preacher.

"Why don't we go into the kitchen, just the three of us?" Blossom pointed to herself then the Miltons and spoke in a sugary sweet voice that made Birdie want to stomp her feet.

Instead she mumbled "Hrmph" to herself.

Blossom continued, "My cook makes the most delicious coffee cake. I brought one to share with you." She turned toward Yvonne. "Cook uses real butter and fresh eggs and has little, tiny chips of walnuts and apples with a streusel topping." She took Yvonne's arm. "I know you'll like it."

Slowly and amiably, Blossom urged the two out of the living room and into the kitchen.

"And tea," Birdie heard the newest Widow say. "Cook makes the most wonderful tea. I brought a carafe of that. Or, if you prefer, she packed mocha cappuccino in a thermos. Now, I'm sure you have lovely china, but I brought my mother's favorite along."

Birdie let out the breath she'd been holding and whispered a prayer of gratitude for help coming from unexpected sources. Neither Winnie nor Mercedes said a word. Both looked a little shell-shocked.

The three Widows sat quietly in the living room. They could make out rustling sounds in the kitchen, the clink of china, and bits of conversations, a word here and another there, but nothing more. At least they didn't hear Henry shouting. Absence of loud voices probably signaled a suspension of hostilities.

"You should have known better than to let me talk first," Birdie whispered after about ten minutes.

"We didn't know you'd make such a terrible mess of it," Mercedes said.

"We should've," Winnie added.

"Yes." Birdie sighed. "You should have. I'm sorry."

The three Widows didn't move for nearly half an hour, sitting in silence with their backs straight and hands folded in their laps. During the entire time, all Birdie could think about was that she had destroyed their mission. Their most important effort at matchmaking had failed because of her. A bitter defeat due to her incompetence.

The sound of movement and laughter came from the kitchen. Blossom returned to the living room with a happy Yvonne and a smiling Henry.

"So good to meet you." Blossom grinned at both Miltons.

"Please drop by anytime." Henry took her hand and shook it. "I'll carry your bags out."

"And make sure you send me that recipe," Yvonne said. She hugged Blossom.

Within minutes, the Widows were back in the car. Actually, Birdie realized, three Widows and one Matchmaker.

"What happened in the kitchen?" Birdie asked, humbled and greatly chagrined for her part in what could have been a failed maneuver.

"We had tea and coffee cake and chatted."

"And?" Winnie prompted.

"And we worked things out. Yvonne is going to talk to Gussie, try to see how much of what we guessed is true. She'll handle it. We can relax. She did swear us all to an oath of secrecy. We are not to mention this to anyone. They want to deal with this themselves."

"Besides, we don't want the preacher to know we meddled," Mercedes said.

All four nodded.

"Thank you, Blossom," Birdie said, so filled with relief she could have hugged the woman if they weren't in the car. Not that she actually would, even when they got back to town. Although she had to push the words out, Birdie again said, "Thank you."

Anyone who thought having to acknowledge the success of another person in carrying out her mission didn't mortify her didn't know Birdie MacDowell very well. Her failure and the need to thank Blossom Brown humiliated her.

❦

"Dear," her mother greeted Gussie as she arrived home from work. "Your father and I need to have a little chat with you."

Uh-oh. The words *need to have a little chat* constituted the highest level of the early warning signal. *Want to talk to you* meant a serious problem but at a lower level—say, roaches in the kitchen or weevils in the flour. *Need to have a little chat* meant a severe hazard, a red-level threat, a national emergency, perhaps enemy attack or a constitutional crisis.

Or an egregious transgression on Gussie's part.

"Let's sit here in the living room," Mom said. "To be comfortable."

Oh, sure, Gussie would be comfortable for this "little chat."

Her mother wore a lacy white shirt with her cameo, another sure sign of an impending emergency and the possible arrival of Arma-

geddon. For a merely important talk, she wore her pink T-shirt with
the rabbit on the front.

Gussie glanced at her father who attempted to look uninvolved,
sinking back in his recliner with his newspaper in front of him. This
was the equivalent of a high-pitched warning signal screaming, *Leave
me alone. I'm not part of this.*

"Let me go upstairs . . . ," Gussie said before her mother shoved
her toward a chair.

Her mother recognized the words Gussie used when she attempted to escape a crisis.

When she didn't sit, her mother took Gussie's elbow and escorted
her to the chair.

Thoroughly warned that she would *not* like the coming "chat" but
acknowledging she couldn't get out of it, Gussie sat.

Loving God, save me, Gussie prayed silently.

For the first time Gussie could remember, her mother had a difficult time beginning what she called "the chat" and Gussie called
"the grilling." Mom sat, crossed her legs, and swung her right foot
left and right. She played with the cameo, rubbing a thumb over the
silhouette of a rose and fiddling with the clasp.

"Gussie," she said at last, her voice serious. "We had visitors today. From Butternut Creek."

"Not Adam." *Oh, please, let it be Adam. Please, do* not *let it be Adam.*
When she realized how hopeless and hopeful her voice must have
sounded—hard to accomplish that with only two words—Gussie
cleared her throat and asked in a neutral voice, "Adam?"

"No, Birdie MacDowell, Mercedes Rivera, and two other women.
I believe you know them?"

"The Widows?" Darn. This was serious. Again, hope and despair
filled her.

"I'd forgotten that's what they call themselves." Mom nodded.
"Yes, the Widows."

Gussie attempted to wait out her mother, force her to bring up
the subject. She should know better. After all these years, she could
never beat her mother at the waiting game.

After a long silence, Gussie asked, "Why shouldn't they stop by?
Aren't you and Miss Birdie and Mercedes old friends?"

"Why do you think they stopped by?"

Gussie shrugged. As useless a reaction as attempting to stop Sha-
quille O'Neal when he drove for the basket.

"To talk about Adam?" Gussie asked, then paused, hating to add
the rest. "And me? Not, of course, that there is an 'Adam and me.'"

Her mother leaned toward Gussie and shot her the glare of death. "They tell me," she said, "the reason you and their nice minister broke up is because of us, your father and me, because you feel as if you must take care of us for the rest of our lives and have put your happiness on hold." She leaned back and crossed her arms. "Is that true?"

"Oh, no." Gussie shook her head. "No." Again, her mother said nothing. "Well, only a little bit. You know how much I love you. If you hadn't supported me after . . ." She couldn't finish the sentence.

"After what?" her father said, breaking into the conversation.

He'd been so quiet, she'd nearly forgotten he sat only five feet from her. She swiveled to look at him, "You know," she said.

"But you can't say it." He tilted his head and studied her face. "Maybe if you could, you'd do better, maybe start healing."

"I've healed," she squeaked, which pretty much gave her feelings away. She *thought* she'd healed until she met Adam. If healed meant she wanted to live normally and fall in love, well, she'd missed the mark by miles.

"You were saying that if we hadn't supported you after Lennie hurt you so badly, you would have fallen apart?" Mom leaned forward, this time her eyes filled with compassion.

"Yes."

"And, because of that, you have to take care of us forever?"

"When Dad went in the hospital, I realized how . . . how . . ."

"Old and frail and sickly we've gotten?" Dad asked. "I resent that."

"No, I . . ."

"What I really resent—" He tossed the paper on the floor, a sure sign of agitation. "What I do resent is that you didn't talk to us about this, you shut us out. We didn't realize a problem existed until these . . . these Widows dropped in and told us."

"We should have spotted that, Henry. Gussie hasn't been herself recently."

"She seemed happy," her father said. "She looked great until a few weeks back. We know she does that, covers up her feelings." He paused. "You're right. We should've realized she acted happy on the surface so we wouldn't worry."

"Yes, underneath she wasn't happy," Mom said.

"Hello," Gussie said. "I'm right here. You shouldn't talk about me while I'm sitting right here."

"Dear, I'm sorry. Would you prefer to leave the room so we can talk about you more comfortably?"

"No. Talk *to* me."

"All right. We should have noticed you haven't been happy since you and your young man broke up."

Did her mother not realize that, if they'd broken up, Adam no longer could be considered "her young man"?

"We want to know if that's our fault and what we should do." Dad lowered the recliner footrest, stood, and moved to sit in a chair next to Gussie. He took her hand. "I can even quote the Bible here: 'A man leaves his father and his mother and cleaves to his wife.'" He held his other hand up when Gussie began to protest. "Think we can read that as a woman leaves her parents as well. That's what people do, they start a new family. They become one flesh, Gussie, exactly as your mother and I did."

"If you want that for yourself, we do, too," her mother said.

"If you don't, we still don't want you to give up your life to stay with your aging, decaying parents. Maybe you'd like to move to Austin, be closer to work. Most important, we don't want to be used as an excuse for you not to find the life you want. We don't want you to hide behind us because you're afraid."

Was she afraid? Well, yes, of course, for many reasons. Her parents were aging. Their health concerned her greatly.

And Adam. She thought about him, wondered about her feelings, about trusting, but the-cleaving-and-becoming-one-flesh part scared the living daylights out of her.

"What would you do if I didn't live here?"

"We lived a long time on our own, dear. We survived before you were born, while you were a child, and after you went off to college."

"I hear the Baptist retirement center may have openings," her father said. "We could buy one of those little houses. We have lots of friends there, and they all say it's a good life."

Oh, so they did have choices. Shame spread through her that she'd considered herself their only future. Humbled, she asked, "Would you like that?"

"A house takes a lot of upkeep," her father said.

"Since the dog died last year, we haven't needed a yard," Mom added.

"What we're saying, dear, is that you don't have to—in fact, you shouldn't—give up your life for us. We have other options. We want you to find happiness."

Gussie smiled. What a mess she'd made of things. "I'm sorry. I should have talked to you. I shouldn't have assumed I'm indispensable."

"Of course you're indispensable, but not in the way you think.

You're our daughter. We love you, but you aren't our nurse or care-giver or keeper. You're our beloved daughter." Dad squeezed her hand. "What do we need to do? What do you need to do? Do you love this Adam?"

She looked from her mother to her father while she considered the question. "Yes, Dad, I think I do, but I'm frightened." Her voice broke on the last word.

Her mother stood and took Gussie's other hand. "As much as I hate to admit this, we should thank those Widows for dropping by. Now we can start to work on your future." Her mother paused. "Oh, and we asked them not to mention this visit to Adam or anyone in Butternut Creek."

"They agreed?" Didn't sound at all like the Widows.

"Yes, we came to a meeting of the minds on many subjects," Mom said.

"Thanks, Mom and Dad." Gussie stood, pulled both parents to their feet for a group hug. "I'm going upstairs. I need to think." This time, her mother allowed her to leave. Once in her bedroom, she settled at the computer and opened her mail. The usual: spam and a couple of notes from friends, including two from Clare. Adam hadn't written her for weeks. Not that she blamed him.

What now? Should she write him and explain? Maybe pray for guidance? Ask him to pray for her?

No, not yet. She knew what she had to do—what she and God needed to do together. She needed to get straight, come to peace with her past in a way that didn't mean celibacy or require her to toss up roadblocks between her and what she wanted, really wanted: to be with Adam. She wouldn't get in touch with him until she knew she could give all of herself. She could only hope he still wanted her.

Chapter Sixteen

Hello, Gussie." With a nod. Fran Finster, Gussie's counselor, welcomed her into her study. It was a calm room with light blue walls, windows looking out over Zilker Park, curtains of soft blue flowers on a white background, and enough clutter strewn around to look cozy but not sloppy. If this weren't Texas, she'd probably have a fire crackling in the fireplace. "Sit down."

Fran didn't fit the friendly setting. She wore her dark hair in an angular cut that reached her shoulders in the front. With a green shirt, she wore black slacks and what Gussie guessed were comfortable if incredibly ugly shoes.

"How are you doing?" Fran asked, her voice clipped but also filled with concern.

Nice touch, Gussie thought, that note of concern in her voice. Gussie knew the real Fran had the heart of a shark. She dug deep and never forgot a single word Gussie had uttered.

"Not so great if I'm back here." Gussie settled in a cushioned chair that faced Fran's desk and leaned back. "I need the tough lady who'll put me back together."

"I can help, but you have to do your part this time: to promise to work hard, stay with me, face what you have to, and not run away." Fran settled in a chair across from Gussie. "You left too early last time."

"I really believed I was okay, functioning well. The studio has become successful."

"And your parents?"

"Getting older but still fairly healthy for people in their seventies."

"If everything is going so well, why are you here?"

Gussie struggled for words, then took a deep breath and made herself speak before she could hide behind her usual dodge of logic. "I ran into something I hadn't expected. A man."

"You ran into a man? In your car?"

Aah, she'd forgotten Fran's play-dumb act. Not that she actually was dumb. Though her tactics differed, she was just as determined as Gussie's mother. Fran truly was *she who could not be ignored*. But this time Gussie wanted to explain, as hard as it was.

"I met a man I'm very attracted to." Gussie shrugged. "I didn't expect that. I should have realized that *not* expecting to find a man attractive meant I wasn't cured, but I didn't. As long as life remained on an even keel, I fooled myself into believing I was handling things very well."

"And this man has made you to look at yourself?"

Gussie nodded.

"Good for him! What's his name?"

"Adam Jordan." Okay, that was the easy part. She knew Fran's questions would become intrusive little by little, but that was good, really. Intrusive meant the counselor would search for the core of the problem. "We met at—"

"Before we go into that," Fran said, "I want you to tell me about your rape."

She stiffened. "I don't want to talk about the rape. I want to talk about Adam and our relationship."

"Oh, I see. You want to discuss your relationship with Adam," Fran stated. "Then explain why you are here. You could discuss that with Adam or a girlfriend or your mother."

Fran watched her expectantly.

Gussie had nothing. If she talked to her parents, they'd look sad and sympathetic, and she couldn't handle that. Clare would listen but not in silence, and Adam . . . she couldn't discuss anything with Adam until she knew how she felt. Fran was right. Gussie leaned forward, head down and eyes closed, and began the story of the rape, the one Fran had forced her to repeat over and over.

When she finished, tears rolled down her cheeks and pain ate her up inside. Until the rape, she'd hadn't realized mental pain could also become physical anguish.

"There," Gussie said. "Are you satisfied?"

"Tell me again."

"Fran, we've done this before, over and over."

"Have you told that story to anyone since our last appointment?"

"Yes. To Adam."

"How did he react?"

"Fine. He was very sympathetic."

"And you? How did you do?"

Gussie didn't want to answer that. She closed her eyes and shut herself up inside.

"You still cry and you still hurt, Gussie. I haven't seen you for three years," Fran said. "We have to start from the beginning and build from there again. This time, you have to thoroughly confront that experience, your pain and trauma, but here, in a safe place."

"I don't want to."

"You know what I always say, Gussie. The wound is where the healing starts. Doesn't do a bit of good to approach the trauma any other way, to tiptoe around what hurts. As you relive the pain, the healing will begin."

Gussie opened her eyes and forced herself to speak. "I was eighteen and in my second semester of college . . ."

After she finished the second telling, Fran said, "I'll need to work with you intensively for at least eight to ten weeks. I also want you to come to the rape survivors group every Tuesday evening."

"But most of them have been really raped. In dark alleys or in their homes by men they didn't know. Compared with them, I wasn't really raped."

"Gussie, if you did not give your consent, you were raped. You have to deal with it that way, not as something you asked for because you were drunk or because you were in a vulnerable situation. You were violated. That is the definition of rape."

"But I knew Lennie wouldn't kill me. I wasn't that frightened of fighting him off, not like women who are assaulted in an alley."

"No, but a man you trusted and cared about sexually assaulted you. Until you accept that, you won't mend. Until you get angry— furious, overwhelmed by rage—about that violation and Lennie's part in it, you won't get better. You're too detached from what really happened. You have to feel."

Gussie sighed, then took her calendar out and wrote in dates.

"I have another question. Why, Gussie? Why now? You know this thing with Adam still might not work out as you hope."

"I know, but I have to try. I have to face up to how lonely and broken I am. I want to be a normal person. I want to fall in love. I want to love a man even if it's too late for me and Adam." She nodded. "Yes, I'm ready, and I'll do it your way."

Even though December had arrived, Adam didn't consider it winter. Here winter consisted of a few weeks at the end of January when the weather got cold enough for people to stop wearing flip-flops.

Life went on. The church had sponsored a Halloween party in the fellowship hall. Janey had sung a solo in the community celebration of Veterans Day.

He and Janey continued to go to every one of Hector's games. With each, Hector improved. The team hadn't yet lost a game. Letters from colleges arrived daily and had piled up as schools showed interest in Hector.

During all these weeks, Adam had heard nothing from Gussie. He'd decided not to make contact himself, not to push her. He'd recover. A year ago, he hadn't even realized a Gussie Milton existed. Surely he could move on.

The Widows remained oddly quiet—not that he complained, but it confused him. Could be they'd run out of options. He'd heard the blond woman had started to keep company with a man in San Saba.

A minister in Austin had invited him to join a group of friends for a picnic in Zilker Park and introduced Adam to a ministerial student. They'd had fun at the outing and Adam knew she wanted him to call her, but the idea of having a long drive to see her—well, he'd done that and didn't want to again.

"Okay, it's time for you to come out of that funk," Mattie said at breakfast. They sat at what Miss Birdie referred to as "their table," where she always placed them so she could keep an eye—and an ear—on them.

"What funk?"

"Everyone knows Gussie Milton dumped you for her parents."

"She didn't . . ." He cleared his throat. No way he'd talk to anyone about what happened with Gussie, even to protect his masculine image and ego. "I'm not in a funk. It was mutual."

"Oh, yeah? Mac showed me a picture of Gussie Milton. She's way hotter than you are, out of your class."

One of the problems with a small town—that everyone-knows-everyone's-business thing.

"Thanks," he said. "Have I ever told you how much I appreciate your friendship and support?"

"No, but you can."

Uh-oh. This tone of voice sounded exactly like the one she'd used when she made him go to the wedding with her. He dug into his pancakes.

"Some friends in Austin are having a Christmas party. I need a date."

That's exactly what he'd guessed. He took another bite.

"I need a date," she repeated. "And you're it."

He chewed and took another bite because he didn't want to respond. After he finished chewing, Mattie still hadn't spoken. He wiped his mouth, took a drink of juice, and said, "I don't want to go. Didn't I make it clear the wedding was a onetime deal?"

"If I go alone, I'll feel like such a loser."

"You aren't. You've just hit a dry spell. It isn't as if single men are running all over Butternut Creek."

"I know."

"You have to come to grips with the situation. You and your fiancé aren't going to get together again."

"Don't want to."

"I'm not going with you. You have to accept the fact that you're not dating and don't let it bother you. Let go."

"Yeah, and how's that letting-go working for you?" When he didn't answer, she said, "I know. I tell myself that, but it's hard to move on."

Didn't he know that.

"Do you know how many men would even ask a woman minister out? With the handful of men in a fifty-mile radius, you are about it."

When he didn't answer, she went on. "Men are afraid of women ministers, afraid we'll have no interest in kissing, like we're nuns."

"Mattie, I don't need to hear this."

"And none of them would even consider marrying a minister. That's not the life a man wants. They're afraid they'd have to act pious and give up beer and bring a casserole to a church dinner. Adam, I want to get married. I want children."

He blinked because he wanted to ask *With me?* but felt fairly certain he'd never get those words out.

"But don't worry." She buttered her toast before she said, "You'd probably be more trouble than it's worth."

❧

When Hector pulled into a parking space in front of the dentist's office and turned off the ignition, the vehicle gave its usual five or six gasps and several huffs before the engine stopped.

This time, Hector didn't sigh. He merely shook his head and got out of the heaving vehicle. Throwing the keys to Adam, Hector said, "You can drive it back. I'm embarrassed to be seen in it."

"You're going to walk back?"

"No, I'll go with you, but I might hide in the backseat with a blanket over me."

❦

"I'm trying a new recipe." Ouida placed a covered plate on Adam's desk. "Chocolate chip muffins."

Chocolate chip muffins, a combination of two of his favorite things. Why hadn't he heard of these before? He lifted the napkin and studied the beautifully rounded morsels.

"These look wonderful." He picked one up and asked, "What's the occasion?" before he pulled the paper off and took a bite.

"George said chocolate is not for breakfast." She dropped into a chair. "He says it's a special treat, like a dessert or a snack, but not breakfast." She smiled. "George has some pretty strict beliefs, but he's trying to relax, trying to be more accepting." She waved toward the plate. "These should help. I'm serving them for breakfast tomorrow." She frowned. "Or maybe they are too rich. George may be right. What do you think?"

Busy with savoring the deliciousness of the muffin, he couldn't respond immediately. At last he swallowed the thick richness, ignored the question because he didn't want to be involved in a discussion about the nutritional value of chocolate chip muffins, and said, "Things between you and George going well?"

"Oh, yes, Preacher. Thank you. Without your advice, I'd never had the courage to change. Without you, I'd still be ironing George's shorts and starching those dresser scarves and feeling dissatisfied."

Because he'd taken another bite—stupid knowing he'd need to respond to Ouida, but he couldn't resist the lure of chocolate chip muffins—he attempted to mumble, *I didn't do anything*, but couldn't with his mouth so full. Instead he shrugged and attempted to look both wise and caring, difficult while chewing.

"You didn't tell me *what* to do, I know that, but you encouraged me, listened to me while I worked things out for myself. Thank you."

He nodded as wisely as a man with a mouthful of muffin can. "We've started work on my studio in the attic, decided to install a skylight up there. George figures it will increase the value of the house, and I'm happy to have more light."

He nodded again. What he really needed was a cup of coffee or a glass of water because, as tasty as the muffin was, the density nearly defeated him.

"I have to warn you." She smiled at him.

He thought about smiling back at her but felt chocolate probably covered his teeth. Instead, he raised his eyebrow as if asking a question.

"We're coming to the Christmas Eve service, the whole family." She laughed. "I didn't want you to keel over in shock. Carol is excited about the candles and Gretchen loves being in church." She shook her head, the action a nice counterpoint to his nods. "They want to come so George and I have to. They like church and I have to admit attending hasn't hurt them." She stood, waved, and turned toward the door.

By the time Adam finally swallowed, she'd disappeared.

He was glad the girls liked church, glad it hadn't hurt them, and delighted George and Ouida would attend Christmas Eve. Everyone he loved would be gathered in the sanctuary that night.

Well, almost everyone.

"Hello, Preacher."

Adam looked up to see a professorial-looking man who squinted at him through thick glasses.

"I'm Martin Hanford, the organist for Sunday."

"Hello, Mr. Hanford. Good to meet you." Adam stood. "What can I do for you?"

"Yes, well, I'd like to practice on your organ. I've played here a few times, before you arrived. Your organ has a recorder in it. I'd like to record the music for Sunday. At the right time in the service, I just mash the PLAY button." The organist showed how he'd do that. "Boom, the music starts and plays with no mistakes."

Makes you wonder why we need an organist, Adam thought but didn't say. He did say, "Sounds fine. Let me show you . . ."

"No, no. I've been in the sanctuary before and your secretary gave me a bulletin so I know what to play. But I would like to know if there's anything special you'd like for Sunday because it *is* the first Sunday in Advent."

"Can't think of anything."

With that, Mr. Hanford strode off and Adam returned to work on his sermon.

❧

Not nearly as easy as it had sounded, Adam reflected. At the beginning of the service that Sunday, Mr. Hanford played—at least the organ did—a lovely prelude. With that nearly completed, the organist glanced at Adam, who waited in the narthex. Before Adam could give the signal for him to play the opening hymn, it began.

Startled at the rapid change, the congregation leaped to their feet and Adam hurried down the aisle after Nick, who served as acolyte. Because the acolyte's candle hadn't been lit yet, Nick arrived in the chancel area with no way to light the other candles.

Still, the opening hymn boomed out from the organ. Nick look at Adam, confusion in his eyes. "What do I do," he whispered.

Willow ran forward from the narthex with a book of matches. She struck one, lit Nick's candle, and hurried away. As soon as the candles were finally lit, the second hymn emerged from the organ while Adam was still making his way to the pulpit.

The organist cursed as he madly pressed buttons and attempted to turn the recording off. He looked up, aghast that his words had echoed through the sanctuary. "I'm sorry. I'll rewind."

As Adam made announcements, he could hear a few notes coming from the organ as Mr. Hanford attempted to find the correct place. When they stopped, Adam believed the problem to be solved.

Not so fast.

When he asked the congregation to rise for the second hymn, instead of the notes of "Come, Thou Long Expected Jesus," the prelude began. The congregation stood motionless, then smiled, then titters began when the organist again muttered, "Damn." This time, he didn't apologize, just glared at the organ as if it were possessed.

He mashed a few buttons on the recorder again, harder. By the time the correct hymn began, Adam felt sure no one could sing because only he and the pillar could keep a straight face. However, Miss Birdie, with Hector and Bree doubled up next to her and nearly hysterical by this time, didn't look as if she could keep it up much longer. For that reason, Adam began the hymn in his shaky tenor. Fortunately, Janey recovered when she heard his pitiful voice and began to sing. Her clear voice filled the sanctuary and returned the congregation to a worshipful air.

At least, until what sounded like small explosions sounded from the inside of the organ.

All eyes turned again to Mr. Hanford, tie loosened, suit coat off, and sweat pouring down his face as he glared at the organ. He pressed the buttons again but nothing happened.

"Shh—" Mr. Hanford started.

"Shucks," Adam shouted over him. Now what? "Shucks, folks, let's not sing the next hymn. Let's go straight to the scripture."

While the worship leader began the Gospel text, Adam walked to the organ and asked sympathetically, "Problems?"

Sadly, Mr. Hanford didn't recognize the concern in Adam's voice.

He said, "Okay, if you're so smart, play it yourself," then grabbed his jacket and stalked off.

Another organist down. Another sermon shortened. Another congregation that arrived early at the Subway.

As folks filed out, Hector said, "Pops, don't ever get a regular organist. The subs really make the service fun."

Lord, how Adam wished he could share this with Gussie.

The ladies of the church and the few men they could force to help them had decorated the parsonage for Christmas weeks earlier. As usual—well, at least like last year—the house smelled and looked wonderful and felt even more like home. Electric candles stood at each window, ready for Adam to turn on at sunset. Pine boughs wound around the staircase and decorated the fireplace. Mistletoe hung over the doors, and red ribbons and plaid bows filled any empty spaces.

Adam leaned back in the sofa, took the beauty in, and sighed with contentment. He'd just read a card from the Smiths, who'd stayed in the parsonage a year earlier. Deanne and Missy were fine. They sent love and gratitude and a huge box of homemade goodies.

"Pops, we need to buy a tree from the Letterman's Club," Hector said, interrupting his moment of peace and joy to snatch a cookie. "It's our big fund-raiser of the year and we all have to bring people to the lot."

"We have a tree." Adam pointed at the beautiful fir, huge and full, its branches laden with ornaments and other baubles the ladies had donated. It nestled in the corner of the living room with splendor.

"I was thinkin' we could move it into the front hall, by the curve in the staircase."

"It would look good there," Adam agreed.

"Then we'll put the new tree in the corner." Hector pointed. "I've got the rope in the car to tie the tree up there to bring home, and Miss Birdie gave me some ornaments."

Adam knew he wouldn't get out of this. Hector—and, therefore, Adam—had to support athletics. With a sigh because he'd hoped to spend the evening on the couch watching a college football game, Adam stood.

"Pops, what time is it?" Hector asked once they were in the car. "They close at five."

"It's three twenty."

"How do you know that? The dashboard clock says four twelve."

"Subtract an hour and add eight minutes," Adam explained.

Hector sighed deeply. Adam knew he wanted to say, *Why don't you get a new car? One on which most of the stuff works.* But Hector also knew that ministers of small-town churches didn't make a big salary.

❧

The selection of trees wasn't great.

"They've been picked over a little, Pops."

Because of the disappointment in Hector's voice, Adam boomed, "Nonsense. I'm sure we'll find a great tree," with much more confidence than he felt.

The best one turned out to be four feet tall, spindly and crooked, and uglier than any tree Adam had ever seen, but the expense supported a good cause. He pulled out his wallet and handed one of the parents who ran the lot a twenty. The man kept his hand out.

"Ten more," he said.

Adam wanted to tell the man, *You've got to be kidding,* but he didn't. That statement would embarrass Hector. Instead he asked, "Throw in a stand?"

After he paid, Adam picked up the stand and tree, which weighed less than a middle-size cat, and carried them toward the car. As he did, needles showered off.

"I'll help you carry that." Hector took a few steps toward Adam and his burden.

"I can handle it." Instead of tying it to the top of the car, Adam squished the fragile tree into the trunk because, after all, very little could make it look worse. He tossed the stand inside, tied the trunk shut with the tree hanging a bit out the side, and walked around the car.

Once home, as they moved the thing inside the parsonage, it shed needles down the hall and into the corner of the television room.

"Janey," Adam shouted up the staircase. "Want to help us trim the tree?"

He could hear her hop down the stairs and skip into the room. The fact that she now hopped and skipped and sang delighted him.

Then she stopped short and looked at the tree, her eyes moving slowly from the top, down to the trunk. It didn't take long.

"What's that?"

"It's our Christmas tree," Hector said with obviously artificial enthusiasm.

"I like the one in the hall better," she said.

"Wait until we get this set up and decorated and have all the presents underneath," Adam said. "You won't recognize it."

First problem: The stand was too big. Hector held the tree and Adam twisted the screws but when Hector let go, the tree tipped out of the stand and fell onto the floor, leaving half of its remaining needles there in a pile.

"I'll clean it up." Janey ran into the kitchen, came back with a broom and dustpan, and started sweeping at the front door.

"Duct tape," Adam said. "Get some from the tool chest."

When Hector came back with the silver roll, they put the tree back up and Adam attached it to the stand. It took nearly four feet of tape, but, at last, the stand grasped the trunk firmly.

"It's crooked," Janey said from her observation post on the sofa.

Unfortunately, when Hector let go of the tree, it fell over again, taking the tightly attached stand with it.

"It's never going to balance, Pops." Hector lifted the tree. "Center of gravity's on the front and right."

Adam walked from one side of the tree to the other as Hector held it. "I'll be right back." He ran to the kitchen, grabbed the tool chest, pulled a roll of string out, and came back. "We'll have to attach the tree to the wall to keep it from falling."

"What?" Hector shook his head.

"Hold the tree. I'll fix it." With that, Adam twisted several eye-bolt screws into the frames of the window behind the tree, then cut the string in four-foot lengths, threaded each piece through the eye in the screw head, and tied it to the tree, attempting to center it.

Hard to center a tree with two thirty-degree curves.

"Hector, let go now." Adam stood back. The tree didn't fall over, but the string showed white against the dark wood of the window frame.

"That should do it," he said.

"I like the one in the hall better," Janey said.

Although he had to agree, Adam said, "Let's get the ornaments on and that Christmas tree skirt around the bottom. That should hide the duct tape. You won't recognize it when we're finished."

They got busy decorating, but, sadly, when they finished they could still recognize the tree. Only ten ornaments found a secure home on the fragile, twisted, and nearly naked branches. No amount of tinsel or shiny balls could hide the fact that this was the same skinny tree they carried in, tied up, and taped in place.

"It's really pretty," Janey said, probably in an effort to make the two men feel better.

Adam and Hector took a few steps back and studied it before all three started to laugh.

"Pops, we can never let anyone else see this tree."

Maybe they could find a big bag to cover it, but Adam didn't think one would fit—not with all those strings holding the thing up.

"It's going to be bald by Christmas." Hector choked the words out and they all started to laugh again.

Chewy wandered in to investigate all the noise. He glanced at Janey, then at Hector and Adam, then discovered the tree. He moved into attack position. His usual attack position consisted of lying on the floor with his tummy up for any thief to scratch.

But not this time. When he caught sight of the thing in the corner, he turned into a ferocious guard dog, primed to protect his home and loved ones. The hair on his back bristled, he leaned forward ready for action, his big bottom up in the air, then began to bark at the scrawny, nearly bare intruder. Although they finally got him quieted this time, every time he walked through this room, the barking and the challenge began anew.

❧

Running late as usual, Gussie pulled into the parking lot of the grocery store about four fifteen. She'd promised Kathy Grant at the Ministerial Alliance of Austin that she'd help for their holiday food drive. She parked, leaped from the car, and ran inside to the manager's office.

"Here are your flyers," he said. "There are boxes at each exit for shoppers to place their donations. You're here to remind them to do that."

Gussie took the stack of paper and found a place to stand next to the shopping carts. Not many people here yet, sort of a lull. The few shoppers who came through accepted the papers and glanced at them as they moved farther into the store.

At nearly five, the crowd hit. Hordes of women dashed through the door and inside. They converged on the line of buggies, each grabbed one, and advanced into the grocery area as if a race had started and the first to pick up dinner won.

Every time Gussie held out an information sheet, the woman either glared at her or ignored her. Not one took the piece of paper. Gussie could nearly feel a breeze from their quick rejection as they rushed past.

Perhaps she should be a little more assertive. Gussie stood in the middle of the aisle the women scooted through and blocked them from the carts.

A particularly large and determined group entered the store and nearly stampeded over her. She tried to stand her ground, but ultimately had to jump aside before she was knocked off balance as they jerked the carts free and whipped them around.

Standing in their way was not the way to go.

Recognizing failure, she tried another tactic. Looking and attempting to sound angelic, she reached out a hand and said, "Help a person in need have a happy holiday."

The shopper didn't look, didn't listen, didn't even seem to realize she existed.

After this happened several more times, the checker closest to her said, "That's how they are on Friday afternoons. After work, these women have to pick up dinner, get home, put it on the table, then drive or send the kids off to their activities. This is the rudest time of the week. They're unpleasant to us, too."

Slight solace.

She glanced at the nearly empty collection box. Maybe she should just grab a cart and fill it herself. But first, she'd try once more.

As a harried woman moved past her, Gussie attempted to hand her a flyer. The woman ignored her and kept pushing her cart.

That was when Gussie lost it. "What's the matter," she shouted. "Don't you care about hungry kids?"

Didn't faze the woman. She probably didn't hear her words, but Gussie was horrified by her own behavior.

"I can't believe I said that." Glancing at her hands, she realized they shook. She was supposed to be a Christian. She had shouted at a perfectly innocent stranger. Worse, she was going to do it again, verbally attack the next person who ran past her. She was suddenly, inexplicably furious. She'd never lost control like this and had no idea how to leash it. She had to get out, away from everyone.

She dropped the flyers in a checkout lane and nearly ran out of the store with the anger still burning through her and no idea what to do with it. Gussie Milton didn't lose her temper this way, never. She forgave trespasses. She handled life evenly. Yet this fury filled her, so thick and caustic she could almost taste it. She ran to her car. The rage grew stronger and hotter until it finally overwhelmed her. In the middle of the packed parking lot, she dropped her purse and began to pound on the hood of her car.

"Damn you, Lennie Brewer. Damn you!" She kept pounding, bruising her fists but not caring. "Damn you."

Oh, yes, it hurt but it also felt wonderful, invigorating, even liberating. Emotion flowed out and she felt powerful and in control even though it seemed obvious she was not. "I hate you for what you did to me," she screamed.

She had no idea how long she yelled and pounded and felt that power. Fortunately, because the motto of the city was "Keep Austin Weird," no one paid much attention to her. If she'd been bleeding or on fire or unconscious, they would have helped, but no one would interfere with a good hissy fit.

Then, as the anger slowly dissipated, every bit of strength flowed out with it. She became so weak she nearly fell down. Leaning on the side of the car, she grabbed the door handle and, with great effort, pulled it open and slid inside

"I'm fine." She waved a good Samaritan away. "Thank you."

As soon as she closed the door and found herself in near privacy from the shoppers who raced around the lot, she burst into deep, gulping sobs that felt as if they were torn from inside her. Pain and agony—as physical as it was mental—filled her. She clutched her stomach and rested her forehead on the steering wheel.

She bawled and blubbered and wept and howled. Lifting her head, she allowed herself to beat on the steering wheel, each blow accompanied by a mental picture of what Lennie had done to her. With each wail and every punch, she felt better.

When she finally allowed herself to slump, she realized there was no way she could drive herself home. She felt completely wrung out. Her parents didn't drive in Austin anymore, and she couldn't let them see her like this. They'd be devastated.

She fumbled in her purse for her cell and hit a number on speed dial. When he answered, she said, "Adam, I need you. Can you come pick me up in the parking lot of the grocery store near my studio?"

Chapter Seventeen

Gussie sounded terrible. Her voice quivered and she hadn't said anything more after that one question, only clicked the phone off. Was she sick? Had she had an accident? What had happened?

Fortunately, he'd been in Austin to make hospital calls and to get a few supplies for the Christmas Eve service. Even through the terrible Austin traffic he drove like an idiot and arrived in fifteen minutes. He parked next to Gussie's car.

But he didn't see her. No one sat in the car waiting for him. Where was she? He jumped out of his car and ran to hers to look in the window on the passenger side. She lay across the backseat, quiet, her eyes closed.

Was she unconscious? Had she fainted?

"Gussie," he shouted and pounded on the window. He tried the door and found it open. As he scooted in, he lifted her head to his lap.

She snored.

Not unconscious. Asleep. When he shook her gently, she blinked, then stretched.

"Adam?" She smiled, a true Gussie smile. "I'm so glad to see you." She struggled to sit up.

"What happened? Why did you call? Are you all right?"

"I needed you," she said simply.

Before he could react to those words, she burst into tears and threw herself against him. He had no choice but to put his arms around her and hold her while she cried, exactly what he wanted to do.

Oh, he knew this didn't fix everything, but it was a beginning. He worried about her hysterical sobs and rubbed her back and whispered soothing promises, words of comfort. He'd do that for however long it took for her to pull herself together.

Within a few minutes, she stopped crying, wiped her tears with a couple of napkins from Wendy's, and became quiet, her head still against his shoulder. Had she fallen asleep again?

No, she sat up and leaned away from him. "Guess you'd like an explanation."

He nodded. "Considering the fact that last time I saw you, you waved merrily at me while tubing down the river, and today you called me sobbing, yes, I would."

"Okay." With one more swipe at her cheeks and nose, Gussie closed her eyes to gather herself. "First, do you know that the Widows visited my parents in October while I was at work?"

"What?" Oh, Lord. "When? What happened? How did the Widows keep this secret? They never can."

"My parents negotiated a non-disclosure pact. They didn't want anyone to know about this until I decided what to do."

After that, Gussie filled him in on that afternoon, ending with, "I don't know what they said because Blossom had a private chat with them. Somehow she got them to believe I'm using them as a shield to hide from life." She paused and nibbled her lip before she forced out the words. "And love."

He watched her, still confused. "Then what?"

"When I got home, my parents called me in for a little chat, to explain that I was not to hide behind them. Not a comfortable moment but necessary and very helpful. I realized I needed help, that I can't heal myself. I went back into counseling. I'm ready to change." She took his hand. "I have a reason to change."

"What's that reason?" He wasn't about to act on the profound hope she meant him.

"You're going to make me spell this out, aren't you?"

He nodded. "I have to know. I don't want to misread anything."

"You are the reason." She paused before adding, "And I am the reason. I want to explore what's between us." She paused and seemed to struggle to express her thoughts. "I want more. I want what you want. I want to be with you and I want to be healthy."

He should say something but couldn't think of the right words. As a minister, he should be able to come up with something.

With that hesitation, she looked down at her hands. "I care about you deeply," she murmured. "I probably am in love with you, but you know how pathetically wishy-washy I can be."

"That's one of the things I like about you." He laced his fingers through hers.

Then she lifted her eyes to gaze into his. "I want to think about marriage." She swallowed hard. "And I have thought about sharing your bed."

He pulled her close to him and held her. She didn't tug away, she didn't push him, she didn't scream. Not screaming always felt like a good first step.

"I love you, too," he murmured into her beautiful hair. Then he lowered his lips and kissed her on the lips. A lovely sweet kiss, which became a promise.

After a pleasant interlude, he realized they were, after all, in the grocery store parking lot and fully visible to the growing throng of shoppers. He stopped kissing her, content to have his arm around her, her head against his shoulder.

Then she burst into laughter, that wonderful, joyful sound. He pulled back to look at her.

"I'm sorry. I know I'm irreverent. When I used to think about finding the man I wanted to spend the rest of my life with, I pictured myself singing and dancing and laughing and incredibly happy." She shook her head. "But look at me. I'm a mess. I've been crying. My eyes are red and swollen."

"Not part of your dream?"

"No, but you are." She snuggled against his chest again. "And I'm happy."

"Why today?" he asked after nearly a minute. "What made you decide to call me today?"

She told him about the scene in the store, which made him laugh. She joined in when she realized how funny it was.

"And then the anger flowed out, really for the first time since Lennie raped me." She spoke calmly and with quiet confidence, not glossing over the attack or blaming herself.

"Healing," he said.

"I know I'm not completely okay."

"None of us are."

"I'll still need counseling for a while and will always have an underlying resentment, but I have to accept it as part of my life. That event shaped and influenced who I am. Now I feel ready to move past it. Finally."

"Have you forgiven Lennie?"

"I don't know." She paused. "No, that's not right. I may someday but I haven't yet. Facing what he did to me is a small step." She struggled to explain. "I think there may be some acts that cannot be forgiven and that rape is one of them. I won't hold a grudge or let the memory of him control my life anymore. I'd never seek revenge. But forgive him? I don't think he deserves that."

He could quote scripture and even Shakespeare about forgiveness, but this wasn't the time. She was too raw. Maybe in the future she'd forgive him. Was she right that there were some sins the victim shouldn't be forced to forgive?

She picked up his wrist and glanced at his watch. "It's nearly seven! My parents will worry."

"Call them. Tell them you and I are having dinner and you'll be home later."

❧

"Guess who called me this morning?" It was three days before Christmas, and Blossom wore a grin of such deep satisfaction and secrecy, it made Birdie want to slap her silly. Not that she would, but her palm did itch. She looked at the other Widows around their usual table in the diner to gauge their reactions.

"Don't play games with us," Winnie warned.

Blossom, so pleased with herself, only smiled, an expression that said, *I know something you don't know.*

"Come on, tell us," Mercedes said, falling right into Blossom's trap.

"Yvonne Milton called me."

"Yvonne Milton called *you*?" Birdie couldn't believe it.

Blossom nodded. "Yes, we've kept in touch often since our visit to Roundville."

"Really?" Mercedes asked. "What did she say?"

Blossom preened for a few seconds before glancing at Birdie's frown. "She said that the preacher and Gussie had dinner together Friday, *and* yesterday he came to Roundville for supper."

"Oh," the others breathed in unison.

"And the Miltons—all three of them—are coming to the Christmas Eve service."

"Sounds like this is getting serious," Mercedes said.

Suddenly peace filled Birdie and she didn't care who took the honors for making the match. This would count as the highest achievement of the Widows' career. She would shower gratitude on Blossom.

"Well done." Birdie laughed.

"Yes, well done," Mercedes echoed.

"In no time, they'll be engaged, then married, then producing little Jordans." Birdie drew herself up in pride. "And now, ladies," she said with a confident nod, "we have a wedding to plan."

❧

Unfortunately, attempting to shield the small spindly tree from the friends who trooped through the parsonage became impossible. People streamed in with Christmas goodies and with small gifts for the kids they wanted to place under the tree. As they arrived, Janey led everyone back to the pitiful specimen of flora to leave the offerings.

By Christmas Eve, gifts were piled high around the little tree with the listing star on the top. Before they left for the eight o'clock church service, the two children stood in front of it, holding hands.

Hector shook his head. "Pops, I don't know what we did to deserve this."

"Don't worry about that. Accept love with a generous heart."

Janey took Adam's hand, held on to it tightly, and began to sing, "'Silent night, holy night . . .'"

A perfect moment. Adam could feel himself becoming a warm blob inside as joy and gratitude flooded him. Add to this the anticipation of celebrating Christmas Eve with Gussie and her parents, of all of them sharing cookies and opening presents together, and he felt incredibly blessed.

"'. . . Sleep in heavenly peace,'" Janey finished.

For a moment, the three stood in front of the tree and drank in the moment of being a family.

Then the church bells began to ring. Almost eight. "Let's go." Adam let go of Janey's hand and dashed out toward church. Without time to grab his robe, he entered the chancel as the last bell rang and stood before the worshippers gathered there to read the words from Luke that always filled him with awe: "To you is born this day in the city of David a Savior, who is Christ the Lord."

In the darkness of the sanctuary, the only sources of light came from the Christ candle on the communion table and a reading light on the lectern. Janey had volunteered to lead the congregation in the first stanzas of favorite carols interspersed with readings of the familiar Christmas stories from Luke and Matthew.

At the end of the service, Adam read from John: "Jesus spoke to them, saying, 'I am the light of the world; he who follows me will not walk in darkness, but will have the light of life.'" Then the congregation stood and began to file forward to take a candle from Adam and light it. Adam watched each pass: Bree and Mac with Hector and

Bobby, followed by Miss Birdie, Mercedes, and Blossom; Sam and
Willow, their boys each unusually solemn, the general and Winnie;
Jesse and Howard and all the elders. Close to the end were Ouida
and Carol with George holding a sleeping Gretchen.

All these people gathered here had become not only his congregation but his family; Butternut Creek, his home.

As he glanced to welcome the last few approaching the table, he
smiled at the Miltons. Yvonne and Henry picked up their candles
and said, "Blessings, Adam."

Gussie reached forward and took a candle from him. She whispered, "Merry Christmas," lit the candle, and moved past him to join
the chain stretching around the sanctuary.

Then Adam lit his candle and joined the circle, watching each
of the beloved faces glowing more brightly than the flames in front
of them.

"'Joy to the world,'" Janey began, and the congregation joined.

Next to him, Gussie's strong voice took up the tune. When he
looked down, she took his hand.

He leaned toward her, filled with the promise of her touch and
her presence and her love.

When the congregation completed that verse, Adam repeated.
"'Rejoice! For to us this day is born a Savior, Christ the Lord.'"

The organist began to play "Gloria in Excelsis Deo" as the worshippers extinguished the candles and moved out of the sanctuary,
into the beauty that was Butternut Creek. The sound of their murmured greetings mingled with the scent of pine as everyone headed
home.

Ahead of them, Hector chatted with the Miltons and Janey
skipped toward the parsonage.

And, as Adam followed, Gussie walked beside him.